The Essential
Pauline E. Hopkins

The Essential Pauline E. Hopkins

Pauline E. Hopkins

MINT EDITIONS

The Essential Pauline E. Hopkins contains work that was first published between 1900–1903.

This edition published by Mint Editions 2021.

ISBN 9781513282916 | E-ISBN 9781513287935

Published by Mint Editions®

 MINT
EDITIONS
minteditionbooks.com

Publishing Director: Jennifer Newens
Design & Production: Rachel Lopez Metzger
Project Manager: Micaela Clark
Typesetting: Westchester Publishing Services

Contents

WINONA: A TALE OF NEGRO LIFE

Of One Blood or, The Hidden Self

Introduction

For the writer of color, the issue of identity and Otherness has continued to influence, and in some ways predetermine, the limit of opportunity in their written work. There is a conflict of representative politics that asks the writer of color not only to be a cultural informant but also to present their inherent Otherness in a way that fits white-dominated society's master narrative. In addition, their choice of craft, which relies on the assumption that their work must be—at all times—a statement of their oppression as a people, is therefore not "universal." This makes it seemingly impossible for a writer of color to produce a work that is both credited for its merit and acknowledged by the strength of its craft.

In truth, writers of color are not always representatives of their cultures, nor do they want to be; however, as they cannot remove their color—and by extension their gender or sexual orientation—from a narrative, these writers exist in a complex doubleness of wanting to showcase this Otherness while simultaneously not wanting to be denied because of it.

One could argue that the publishing industry—critics, readers, and white writers—tend to believe that writers of color are only capable of writing works that are autobiographical in nature or that highlight a sense of struggle, and that the vast land of imagination and creativity is exclusively for white writers and readers*. This collected volume of the work of Pauline Elizabeth Hopkins exists to dispute that notion and to also highlight an extraordinarily talented voice in the African American literary canon.

In her lifetime, Hopkins produced three major works of fiction and one short story that spanned romance, mystery, and science fiction genres, making her a pioneer for modern Black speculative fiction. In spite of racism and other social injustices, Hopkins made her *Black* voice known, choosing not to write the narrative that was expected of Black authors at the time and instead writing the narratives that *she* wanted to read. In doing so, Hopkins became a part of the tradition of reimagining self-actualization and agency through the conventions of genre.

Sage Bailey
Berkeley, CA 2021

---

* Lee, Lisa. "Report from the Field: Racial Invisibility and Erasure in the Writing Workshop."

CONTENDING FORCES

I

A Retrospect of the Past

We wait beneath the furnace-blast
The pangs of transformation;
Not painlessly doth God recast
And mould anew the nation.
Hot burns the fire
Where wrongs expire;
Nor spares the hand
That from the land Uproots the ancient evil.

—J. G. Whittier

In the early part of the year 1800 the agitation of the inhabitants of Great Britain over the increasing horrors of the slave trade carried on in the West Indian possessions of the Empire was about reaching a climax. Every day the terrible things done to slaves were becoming public talk, until the best English humanitarians, searching for light upon the subject, became sick at heart over the discoveries that they made and were led to declare the principle: "The air of England is too pure for any slave to breathe."

To go back a little way in the romantic history of the emancipation of the slaves in the islands will not take much time, and will, I hope, be as instructive as interesting. Tales of the abuses of the slaves, with all the sickening details, had reached the Quaker community as early as 1783, and that tender-hearted people looked about themselves to see what steps they could take to ameliorate the condition of the Negroes in the West Indies, and to discourage the continuation of the trade along the African coast.

Thomas Clarkson, a student at Cambridge, was drawn into writing a prize essay on the subject, and became so interested that he allied himself with the Quakers and investigated the subject for himself, thereby confirming his own belief, "that Providence had never made that to be wise that was immoral; and that the slave trade was as impolitic as it was unjust."

After strenuous efforts by Mr. Pitt and Mr. Fox, Parliament became interested and instituted an inquiry into the abuses of the slave trade. Finally, Mr. Wilberforce was drawn into the controversy, and for sixteen years waged an incessant warfare against the planters, meeting with defeat in his plans for ten consecutive years; but finally, in 1807, he was successful, and the slave trade was abolished.

These assailants of the slave trade had promised not to try to abolish slavery; but in a short time they learned that the trade was still carried on in ships sailing under the protection of false flags. Tales of the cruelties practiced upon the helpless chattels were continually reaching the ears of the British public, some of them such as to sicken the most cold-hearted and indifferent. For instance: causing a child to whip his mother until the blood ran; if a slave looked his master in the face, his limbs were broken; women in the first stages of their accouchement, upon refusing to work, were placed in the treadmill, where terrible things happened, too dreadful to relate.

Through the efforts of Granville Sharpe, the chairman of the London committee, Lord Stanley, minister of the colonies, introduced into the House of Commons his bill for emancipation.

Lord Stanley's bill proposed *gradual* emancipation, and was the best thing those men of wisdom could devise. Earnestly devoted to their task, they sought to wipe from the fair escutcheon of the Empire the awful blot which was upon it. By the adoption of the bill Great Britain not only liberated a people from the cruelties of their masters, but at the same time took an important step forward in the onward march of progress, which the most enlightened nations are unconsciously forced to make by the great law of advancement; "for the civility of no race can be perfect whilst another race is degraded."

In this bill of gradual emancipation certain conditions were proposed. All slaves were entitled to be known as apprenticed laborers, and to acquire thereby all the rights and privileges of freemen. "These conditions were that praedial should owe three-fourths of the profits of their labors to their masters for six years, and the non-praedial for four years. The other fourth of the apprentice's time was to be his own, which he might sell to his master or to other persons; and at the end of the term of years fixed, he should be free."

In the winter of 1790, when these important changes in the life of the Negro in the West Indies were pending, many planters were following the course of events with great anxiety. Many feared that in the end their slaves would be taken from them without recompense, and thereby render them and their families destitute. Among these planters was the family of Charles Montfort, of the island of Bermuda.

Bermuda's fifteen square miles of area lays six hundred miles from the nearest American coast. Delightful is this land, formed from coral reefs, flat and fertile, which to the eye appears as but a pin point upon the ocean's broad bosom, one of "a thousand islands in a tropic sea."

Once Bermuda was second only to Virginia in its importance as a British colony; once it held the carrying trade of the New World; once was known as the "Gibraltar of the Atlantic," although its history has been that of a simple and peaceful people. Its importance to the mother country as a military and naval station has drawn the paternal bonds of interest closer as the years have flown by. Indeed, Great Britain has been kind to the colonists of this favored island from its infancy, sheltering and shielding them so carefully that the iron hand of the master has never shown beneath the velvet glove. So Bermuda has always been intensely British,—intensely loyal. Today, at the beginning of the new century, Bermuda presents itself, outside of its importance as a military station for a great power, as a vast sanatorium for the benefit of invalids. *A* temperate climate, limpid rivers, the balmy fragrance and freshness of the air, no winter, nature changing only in the tints of its foliage,—have contributed to its renown as a health giving region; and thus Shakespeare's magic island of Prospero and Miranda has become, indeed, to the traveler:

The spot of earth uncurst,
To show how all things were created first.

Mr. Montfort was the owner of about seven hundred slaves. He was well known as an exporter of tobacco, sugar, coffee, onions and other products so easily grown in that salubrious climate, from which he received large returns. He was neither a cruel man, nor an avaricious one; but like all men in commercial life, or traders doing business in their own productions, he lost sight of the individual right or wrong of the matter, or we might say with more truth, that he perverted right to be what was conducive to his own interests, and felt that by owning slaves he did no man a wrong, since it was the common practice of those all about him, and he had been accustomed to this peculiar institution all his life.

Indeed, slavery never reached its lowest depths in this beautiful island; but a desire for England's honor and greatness had become a passion with the inhabitants, and restrained the planters from committing the ferocious acts of brutality so commonly practiced by the Spaniards. In many cases African blood had become diluted from amalgamation with the higher race, and many of these "colored" people became rich planters or business men (themselves owning slaves) through the favors heaped upon them by their white parents. This being the case, there might even have been a strain of African blood polluting the fair stream of Montfort's vitality, or even his wife's, which fact would not have caused him one instant's uneasiness. Moreover, he was a good master, and felt that while he housed his slaves well, fed them with the best of food suited to their occupations and the climate, and did not cruelly beat them, they fared better with him than they would have with another, perhaps, or even if they held property themselves.

The speeches of Mr. Pitt, Mr. Burke and others, together with the general trend of public sentiment as expressed through the medium of the British press, had now begun to make an impression upon some of the more humane of the planters on this island, and among them was Mr. Montfort. Uneasiness now took the place of his former security; thought would obtrude itself upon him, and in the quiet hours of the night this man fought out the battle which conscience waged within him, and right prevailed to the extent of his deciding that he would free his slaves, but in his own way. He determined to leave Bermuda, and after settling in some other land, he would gradually free his slaves without impoverishing himself; bestow on each one a piece of land, and finally, with easy conscience, he would retire to England, and there lead the happy life of an English gentleman of fortune.

With this end in view, being a man of affairs and well acquainted with the whole of the American continent, he naturally turned his eyes towards the United States, where the institution flourished, and the people had not yet actually awakened to the folly and wickedness exemplified in the enslavement of their fellow-beings. For reasons which were never known, he finally made choice of Newbern, N. C., for a home.

Sunday was and is the high holiday in all tropical climes. On that day the slave forgot his bonds. It was noon; the early service of the Church of England was ended. The clergyman of the parish had accompanied Charles Montfort home. Mrs. Montfort was visiting friends, so the two gentlemen dined alone. The clergyman was rather glad that he had the opportunity of seeing Mr. Montfort alone, and had used all his powers of persuasion to turn him from his proposed exodus. It was of no avail, as the good man soon found; and with a sigh, he finally took his hat and prepared to leave. Both stood outside the house upon the broad walk beneath the shade of the fragrant cedars and the fruitful tamarind trees. The silence of deep feeling was between these two men. The clergyman could only remember the reverence he had always received, and the loving service given him by this family. Montfort thought with pain of the holy ministrations of this silver-haired man, who had pronounced the solemn words that bound him to his gentle wife, had baptized his children, and (tenderest act of all) had buried the little daughter whose grave was yonder, beneath the flowering trees in the churchyard. Yes, it was sad to part and leave all these tender ties of friendship behind.

"The bishop will come himself, Charles, to persuade you that this is a dangerous step you are about to take," finally the good man said, breaking the silence.

"Why dangerous? Is it any more so for me than for those who left England to build a home here in the wilderness?"

"Different, very different. The mother hand was still over them, even in these wilds. Out there," and he pointed in the direction of the bay, "they tell me that for all their boasted freedom, the liberty of England is not found, and human life is held cheaply in the eyes of men who are mere outlaws. Ah! but the bishop," he continued with a sigh, "he can tell you; he has seen; he is not a weak old man like me. He will talk you out of this plan of separation from all your friends."

Again silence fell upon them. In the direction of the square a crowd of slaves were enjoying the time of idleness. Men were dancing with men, and women with women, to the strange monotonous music of drums without tune, relics of the tom-tom in the wild African life which haunted them in dreamland. Still, there was pleasure for even a cultivated musical ear in the peculiar variation of the rhythm. The scanty raiment of gay-colored cotton stuffs set off the varied complexions,—yellow, bronze, white,—the flashing eyes, the gleaming teeth, and gave infinite variety to the scene. Over there, waterfalls fell in the sunlight in silvery waves; parti-colored butterflies of vivid coloring, and hummingbirds flashed through the air with electrical radiance; gay parrakeets swung and chattered from the branches of the trees.

"Where, my son," said the clergyman, indicating the landscape with a wave of his hand, "will you find a scene more beautiful than this? How can you leave it and those who love you and yours?"

"Beautiful, indeed; and I will confess that it grows dearer as the time for my departure draws near," answered Montfort. "I will walk with you," he continued, as the clergyman turned in the direction of the road. As they passed through the wide entrance gates a Negro woman was weeding her little garden; her pickaninny was astride her back, spurring his mother as a rider his horse. The woman and the child looked up and smiled at the master and his guest, and the woman put the child on the ground and stood upright to bob a queer little courtesy. They walked along in silence until they reached the plaza.

"My son, will you not be persuaded?"

"Father, I have made up my mind firmly, after due consideration. I believe it is for the best."

They paused a moment at the square; then the holy man said solemnly, as he raised his hand in benediction: "If it then be for the best, which God grant it may be, I pray the good Father of us all to keep you in safety and in perfect peace." He turned and disappeared in the crowd.

Charles Montfort was immediately surrounded by his friends, who greeted him joyously, for he was a genial man and had endeared himself greatly to his neighbors.

"Still determined to leave us, Charles?" inquired one.

"Yes, for the good of myself and family. How can we submit tamely to the loss of our patrimonies without an effort to reimburse ourselves when a friendly land invites us to share its hospitality?

"There is truth in your argument for all who, like you, Charles, have a large venture in slaves. Thank heaven I am so poor that a change of laws will not affect me," said one.

"Where a man's treasure is, there also is his heart. It is nature. Almost you persuade me, Charles, to do likewise," remarked another.

"As I have told you, I will retain my patrimony and free my slaves, too, by this venture in the United States under a more liberal government than ours."

"Ah! Charles," remarked another listener, "you forget the real difference between our government and that of the United States. And then the social laws are so different. You will never be able to accustom yourself to the habits of a republic. Do you not remember the planters from Georgia and Carolina who fought for good King George, and were stanch Royalists? They retired to the Bahamas when our cause was lost in the American colonies. My brother has just returned from a trip there. He tells strange tales of their surprise at many things we do here. I fear it is but a cold welcome you will receive from men of their class."

"Certainly," replied Montfort, "I shall try to be a good subject or citizen of whatever country I may be compelled to reside in for a long or short time."

"But surely you will not expose your wife to the inconveniencies of life in that country," said another.

"She has had her choice, but prefers hardships with me to life without me," proudly returned Montfort.

"A willful man must have his way," murmured one who had not yet spoken, "and I will give you three months to stay in the land of savages before you will be returning to us bag and baggage."

"Well," laughed Montford, "we shall see." Twilight had fallen now, and Montfort bared his head to the refreshing sea breeze which fluttered every leaf. When he bade his friends good night, finally, and started on his homeward walk, the arguments of the good clergyman and of his friends were present in his harassed mind, and he wondered if he were doing wrong not to be prevailed upon to yield to the opinions of others. Once he almost determined that he would give it all up and remain in this land of love and beauty. To collect his scattered thoughts and calm his mind he turned toward the bay, and stood upon the beach, still allowing the breeze to play about his heated temples. Never before had he appreciated his home so much as now, when he contrasted it with the comparative barrenness of the new spot he had chosen. The water was alive with marine creatures; the sea aflame. The air was full of light-giving insects, incessantly moving, which illumined the darkness and gave life to every inanimate object. Over all the moon and stars were set in the cloudless deep-blue sky of coming night. Alas! his good angel fled with the darkness, and morning found him more determined than ever to go on with his project.

When it became generally known in Bermuda that Charles Montfort had decided to leave the place of his birth and establish himself in a foreign land, many friends gathered about him and advised him to reconsider his determination. Montfort laughingly invited them to join him in his new venture, and then earnestly pointed out to them the dangers which threatened their fortunes. He painted his plans in glowing colors, and ended by promising them that in less than twenty-five years he would land in England, a retired planter, his former slaves free and happy, and he himself rich and honored.

Having an immense amount of property to transport, it happened that Mr. Montfort was compelled to make two trips to Newbern before he removed his family to their new home; but after much energetic work and many difficulties, the little family looked through blinding tears at the receding shores of what had been a happy home. A week later a noble ship stood off the shores of North Carolina. On the deck was Charles Montfort; his wife hung upon his arm; beside the devoted couple were Charles, Jr., named for his father, and Jesse, the young darling of his mother's heart. Silently they gazed upon the fair scene before them, each longing for the land so recently left behind them, though no word of regret was spoken.

II

THE DAYS "BEFORE THE WAR"

O Freedom! Thou art not as poets dream,
A fair young girl with light and delicate limbs,

Thy birthright was not given by human hands:
Thou wert twinborn with man.

T he shores of Pamlico Sound presented a motley crowd of slaves, overseers, owners of vessels, and a phantasmagoric landscape very charming to eyes unaccustomed to such scenes. It was near the noon siesta. In the harbor lay three or four vessels ready to be loaded with their freight of rice, tobacco or cotton. The sun poured its level rays straight down upon the heads of all. A band of slaves sang in a musical monotone, and kept time to the music of their song as they unloaded a barge that had just arrived:

> *Turn dat han' spike roun' an' roun',*
> *Hol' hard, honey; hol' hard, honey.*
> *Brack man tote de buckra's load,*
> *Hol' hard, honey; hol' hard, honey*
>
> *Neber 'fo' seed a nigger like you,*
> *Hol' hard, honey; hol' hard, honey.*
> *Allers tinkin' 'bout yer ol' brack Sue,*
> *Hol' hard, honey; hol' hard, honey.*
>
> *Ef I was an alligater what'd I do?*
> *Hol' hard, honey; hol' hard, honey.*
> *Run 'way wid ol' brack Sue,*
> *Hol' hard, honey; hol hard, honey.*
>
> *Massa ketch yer, what'd he do?*
> *Hi, hi, honey; hi, hi, honey.*
> *Cut yer back an' ol' brack Sue's,*
> *He, he, honey; he, he, honey.*

> *I cuss massa 'hin' de fence,*
> *Hol' hard, honey; hol' hard, honey.*
> *Massa don' hyar make no differyence,*
> *Hol' hard, honey; hol' hard, honey.*
>
> *Turn dat han' spike roun' an' roun',*
> *Hol' hard, honey; hol' hard, honey.*
> *Brack man tote de buckra's load,*
> *Hol' hard, honey; hol' hard, honey.*

As the refrain died away the bell for the noon rest sounded faintly in the distance, gradually drawing nearer, and again their rich and plaintive voices blended together in sweet cadences as they finished placing the heavy load to the satisfaction of their drivers:

> *Hark, dat merry, purty bell go*
> *Jing-a-lingle, jing-a-lingle, jingle bell,*
> *Jing-a-lingle, jing-a-lingle, jing-a-lingle bell,*
> *Jingle bell, jingle bell.*

Even so sang the children of Israel in their captivity, as they sat by the rivers of Babylon awaiting deliverance.

Just now a ship, which had some time since appeared as a dark spot on the horizon, turned her majestic prow and steered for the entrance to the sound. Immediately the pilot boat in the harbor put out to her. Everyone on the shore became eagerly intent upon the strange ship, and they watched the pilot climb aboard with all the interest which usually attends the slightest cause for excitement in a small community.

The ship came on very slowly, for there was little wind, under topsail, jib and foresail, the British flag at the peak and the American flag at the fore. The people on shore could see the captain standing by the pilot, the anchor ready to be dropped, and the bowsprit shrouds loose. But now their interest was divided with a new arrival. A man on horseback rode down to the shaky wooden platform which served as a landing place for passengers; behind him, at a respectful distance, rode a white-haired Mulatto. The man leaped from his horse and threw his reins to the slave, signaled a couple of Negroes in a boat, jumped into it as they, obedient to his sign, pulled alongside the wharf, and was rowed

PAULINE E. HOPKINS

swiftly out to the advancing ship, which was now making considerable headway toward the shore.

Among the idlers on the wharf was one whom everyone addressed as Bill. He was large, or rather burly, carried a rawhide in his hand, and from his air of authority toward them, was evidently the overseer of the gang of slaves who were loading the tobacco barge. From out the crowd a man who had been sitting idly on a bale of cotton moved toward him.

"Holloa, Bill," he said, addressing the owner of the rawhide.

"Howdy, Hank"; returned Bill, surveying the other curiously, "whar in time did you drap from?"

Hank did not reply directly. He shifted the tobacco quid in his mouth from one cheek to the other, then with a nod of the head toward the approaching vessel, asked: "Whar's she from?"

"Hain't been in town lately, I reckon, or you'd know all about the 'Island Queen' from Bermudy. Planter named Montfort on her. He's movin' his niggers here to Caroliny; gittin' too hot fer him back thar," replied Bill, with a backward jerk of his thumb in the supposed direction of Bermuda. "How's things up yer way?"

"Fair, fair to middlin', Bill; thar's been some talk 'bout a risin' among the niggers, and so we jes tuk a few o'them an' strun 'em up fer a eggsample to the res'. I tell you, Bill, we jes don't spec' to hav' no foolin' 'bout this yer question of who's on top as regards a gentleman's owning his niggers, an' whomsoeveder goes ter foolin' with that ar pertickler pint o' discusshun is gwine ter be made a eggsample of, even ef it's a white man. Didn'hyar nuthin' 'bout a circus up our way, did yer?"

Bill scratched his chin and shook his head in the negative.

"Wall, 'twas this here way: Jed Powers, you 'member Dan Powers' Jed, don' yer? Dan thet was tarred an' feathered fer selling good likely whiskey ter niggers? Bill nodded in the affirmative. "Jed Powers wuz seed walkin' with Jimison's wench Violy. Be blowed ef he wasn't gittin' ready ter cut an'run ter Canidy with her!"

"Don'b'lieve yer, durned ef I do," said Bill.

"Fact! Be durned ef it ain't jes so."

"Wall! of all the onnat'rall cusses!"

"But his wurst offense, in gineral, wuz thet he wuz meanin'fer to marry her!" Hank paused in his narrative to allow a full appreciation of his statement to be impressed upon Bill's mind.

"Wus an' wus!" groaned the latter. What is we comin' to, by thunder! I allays took Jed to be a decen' sort o' cuss, too. What's the committee doin' 'bout it?"

"Wall, we sot out to stop thet fun, anyhow. We got him after a hot chase, an' we put him in jail; an' las' week we guv him his trial. Jedge sentenced him to fifty lashes an' hangin' by the neck untell he wuz dead. But somehow or nuther folks is gittin' squeamish. Jedge don' durst to hang him; he'll jes guv him the fifty lashes an' a talkin' to on the immoralty o' his acts an' ways. Jedge tol him he wuz young an' had a chance to 'pent from the desolate ways o' his youth, of which his wurst failin' wuz a-wantin' to marry niggers, leastwise he'd end in hell, shure. Jedge tol' him everythin' 'cordin' ter law an' jestice. We wuz calkerlatin' ter have a celebrashun to which all the leading citizens o'this county would 'a' been bid, but, o' course, not havin' the hangin' sort o' took the ginger out o' the whole business."

"I hain't a doubt o' yer horsepertality in case o' the event, Hank; we's allays got along mighty comf'table tergether," replied Bill, nodding an emphatic approval of all that Hank had said. The whole speech had been liberally punctuated with copious floods of tobacco juice, which formed a small river between the two men.

"Best thing I know of down our way," said Bill, after they had taken another good look at the ship, "the best thing I know of was a raffle over ter Jellison's auction-rooms. A raffle's a great thing fer pickin up bargains in niggers an' horses. This pertickler one was fer a bay horse, a new light buggy an' harness, an' a Mulatto gal Sal. The whole thing wuz wurth fifteen hundred dollars, an' we had fifteen hundred chances at a dollar a head. Highest throw took first choice; lowest, the remainder. Winners to pay twenty dollars each fer refreshments."

"Leetle bit selfish o' you, Bill, ter keep all thet to yerself," said Hank, giving Bill a reproachful glance.

"Mabby so, mabby so. But you won't lose nuthin', Hank, ef I can help yer in the footur. 'Pears like some one wuz a-tellin' me," he continued reflectively, "thet yer wuz a-wurkin' fer the county 'bout thet time fer board an' clo's."

"Be durned ef I wuzn't," replied Hank with great candor. "Shot at a free nigger an' killed Brady's dog Pete. Ef it'd been the nigger I'd happened ter kill, hit would 'a' been all right; but bein' 'twas a bluded hound thet had tred hundreds o' runaways, it wuz anuther question; an' not havin' the muney ter pay a fine, an' Brady bein' purty mad, why in I went fer a munth."

"Wall, as I was a-sayin', ter perceed, by a lucky chance it wuz my fust choice, an' I choose the gal. I knowed she wuz a fust-class breeder an' my muney wuz shure fer a hundred per cent on her."

"I swear ter gosh, but yer right, Bill; mate her with the right sort an' you's got yer own muney.

Both men now turned their attention to the advancing ship.

"I see ol' Pollock's got 'em in tow," remarked Hank reflectively, after a moment's silence. "Ans Pollock's as crafty as can be. No 'fense meant, yer know; seems he's yer boss still; mean cuss ef he's rich's a jedge"; he continued, "s'pose they've got a heap o' money, too."

"Can't say as to thet," replied Bill, "but they bought Pollock's ol' place, an' it looks as though money might be plenty the way everything has been fixed up fer the missis."

The noon hours were now over, and a great deal of confusion reigned, caused by the arrival of a ship in port with so rich a man as Mr. Montfort aboard. The two friends became separated in the ensuing bustle which attended the landing of the party. During the preceding conversation a carriage and teams for transporting the baggage and slaves had drawn up alongside the shore; and as Mr. Montfort stepped on the rickety wharf and assisted his wife to do the same, a murmur of involuntary admiration ran through the motley crowd of rough white men and ignorant slaves.

Grace Montfort was a dream of beauty even among beautiful women. Tall and slender; her form was willowy, although perfectly molded. Her complexion was creamy in its whiteness, of the tint of the camellia; her hair, a rich golden brown, fell in rippling masses far below the waist line; brown eyes, large and soft as those seen in the fawn; heavy black eyebrows marking a high white forehead, and features as clearly cut as a cameo, completed a most lovely type of Southern beauty.

The two children followed their mother closely. They were sturdy boys, who resembled her in the beauty of their features; and in Jesse, the baby, a still greater resemblance could be traced, because the hair had been allowed to remain in long, soft curls. So they came ashore to their new home, obsequiously waited upon by Mr. Pollock, and lovingly attended by their numerous slaves. In an instant the family was seated in the waiting vehicle; and before the spectators could fully realize the beauty and elegance of the newcomers, they were whirled away, and the carriage was lost in a cloud of dust.

Hank Davis and Bill Sampson met once more before they left the wharf. "Ef they hain't got an overseer, I'm goin' to 'ply fer the job"; said Hank, "never seed sich a booty in my life."

Bill Sampson scratched his head meditatively: "Strikes me, Hank, thet thet ar female's got a black streak in her somewhar."

Hank stared at Bill a moment, as though he thought he had suddenly lost his senses; then he burst into a loud guffaw. "You git out, Bill Sampson."

Wall, maybe," said Bill, "maybe so. Thar's too much cream color in the face and too little blud seen under the skin fer a genooine white 'ooman. You can't tell nothin' 'bout these Britishers; they're allers squeamish 'bout thar nigger brats; yas, sah, very squeamish. I've hern tell that they think nuthin of ejcatin' thar black brats, and freein' 'em, an' makin' 'em rich."

"You go to the devil"; returned Hank, as he moved away, "you're wus' nan ol' nigger, allers seein' a possum up a tree; an' 'taint no possum 'tall,—nuthin' but er skunk."

Apologists tell us as an excuse for the barbarous practice of slavery, that it was a godlike institution for the spread of the gospel of the meek and lowly carpenter's son, and that the African savage brought to these shores in chains was a most favored being.

Such may be the thoughts of the careless and superficial mind; but when we survey the flotsam and jetsam left from the wreck of the Civil War, we can deceive ourselves no longer; we must confess that the natural laws which govern individuals and communities never relax in their operation. The fruit of slavery was poisonous and bitter; let us rejoice that it no longer exists.

III

"Coming Events Cast Their Shadows Before"

In sooth I know not why I am so sad:
It wearies me; you say it wearies you;
But how I caught it, found it, or came by it,
What stuff 'tis made of, whereof it is born,
I am to learn;
And such a wantwit sadness makes of me
That I have much ado to know myself

—*Merchant of Venice*

The old Pollock homestead was an exquisite spot. The house was a long, low, rambling structure, consisting of many large, airy rooms inside, and ornamented without by piazzas supported by huge pillars. Immense trees shaded the driveway and embowered the stately white mansion. Gay parterres of flowers ornamented the rolling lawn, which divided the great house from the Negro quarters which were picturesquely visible at a convenient distance from it.

Within the house Mr. Montfort had gathered all the treasures which could possibly add to the comfort and pleasure of his lovely wife. Beautiful rugs covered the floors, fine paintings adorned the walls, gleaming statuary flashed upon one from dd nooks and corners. In the library music had found a home in the most comfortable corner of the room. On a table one might find a volume of Goethe in the original; on the grand piano the score of a then-popular opera; while a magnificent harp, standing near, hinted of musical talents highly cultivated.

Business had prospered with Montfort; his crops flourished; but a nameless trouble seemed to be halting upon the threshold of the home he loved, and to threaten those whom he cherished so fondly.

The first year of residence in Newbern had been very pleasant for the Montforts. Society, such as it was, opened its arms to the family and voted the highly cultured wife and cherub children great additions. The house was a favorite resort for all the young people of the neighborhood. Mrs. Montfort had been educated in England, and had brought with her to the provincial families with whom she now associated all the refinements of the Old World. Having great wealth for the times, she had always been indulged in every whim by the doting bachelor uncle who had made her his heiress, but who had died soon after her marriage to Charles Montfort. As Grace Montfort, she found again the love her uncle had delighted to lavish upon his adopted child.

Possessed of a bright, joyous nature, she liked nothing better than to gather about her the young men and women of the neighborhood and make life pleasant for them; and they in turn learned from her customs and refinements which otherwise might never have come their way. Everyone voted her the dearest and most beautiful woman they had ever known, and all would have gone merry as a marriage-bell, *but* (if it were not for the *buts* and *ifs* of this life, what a pleasant place the world would be) into this paradise of good feelings and admiration came Anson Pollock with his bitter envy and his unlawful love, and finally with his determination to possess the lovely Grace Montfort at all hazards.

Gradually the friendly relations of the neighbors turned to coldness and reserve. It was whispered about that Montfort was about to free his slaves. This in itself was a dangerous doctrine at that time in that part of the world, and a man suspected of entertaining ideas of freedom for slaves must either change his tactics or his residence, or else forfeit life and property. Then again, Bill Sampson's words to Hank Davis had somehow found a voice, and the suspicion of Negro blood in the veins of Mrs. Montfort was a deathblow to a proud spirit and social aspirations. These two serious charges had spread abroad like wildfire.

It was a hot morning, a very hot morning in early summer. There had been no rain for some time. Mrs. Montfort lay in a hammock outside the breakfast-room windows. Lucy, her maid, was mending lace and children's garments a short distance away.

Lucy was Mrs. Montfort's foster sister; both were born on the same day. Their relations had always been those of inseparable friends rather than of mistress and slave.

"No rain today, Lucy. I never used to mind the heat at home (this with a sigh). How fair it must be over the blue waters of the bay; I can almost "smell the cedars outside the entrance gates."

"Yas, Miss Grace" (to Lucy her mistress was always "Miss Grace"), "I do feel sort o' squeamish myself sometimes when I tink of the gals all dancin' Sundays in the square; but reckon we'll git used ter these people here arter a-while; leastwise, I hope so."

Mrs. Montfort did not reply, and her maid noticed, as she glanced anxiously at her mistress, that a frown was on her face. Lucy sighed.

"Miss Grace" had been noted once for her sunny, cheerful temper. Now all was changed.

Beyond the rolling lawn fields of cotton could be seen, the leaves twisting in the heat and the steady glare of the sun. Zigzag fences separated the cotton from fields of corn; away in the distance dim aisles of pine trees stretched their dark arms towards the heavens, their dark foliage suggestive of cool shadows and quiet glades. The road wound in and out among the pines, through a woodland, and terminated in the highway just visible from the piazza. Inside the long, open windows little Jesse played at building houses with the bags of golden eagles that his father kept in a drawer of his escritoire.

"Grace, Grace, Lucy," called the child, "my houses won't stay up; come in and help me."

Just then a group appeared coming around a corner of an outbuilding. Two men walked beside a pony, astride whose back sat Master Charles. As they approached the house the gentlemen swept off their wide-brimmed hats in a gallant salute to Mrs. Montfort, which she returned by rising from her recumbent position and dropping a low courtesy. The gentlemen were Mr. Montfort and Mr. Pollock. Jesse, hearing the pony's feet, came out the window and ran down the piazza steps to his father, who, as Charles sprang to the ground, lifted the excited child to the pony's back. Mrs. Montfort watched the approach of the little procession with a pleased smile. She made a fair picture in her elaborately embroidered white morning robe, her beautiful hair arranged in drooping curls at the sides of her head, as was the fashion of the time.

See me, Mama Grace," cried Jesse, as he clapped his little hands, and dug the heels of his tiny-slippered feet into the pony's side, in imitation of his father on horseback. As Montfort watched him, the picture of his last Sunday in Bermuda arose before him: the little Negro child astride his mother's back, spurring her like a rider his horse; and in his ears rang the pleasant voice of his silver-haired pastor. At the piazza steps he called a servant to take away the pony, and turned to enter the house, followed by Mr. Pollock, with Jesse in his arms and Charles by his side. Jesse kept up an incessant chatter. They passed through the breakfast-room, where Montfort placed the child upon the floor.

"Charles, help me build my houses!" he cried, attracted to his late employment at sight of the golden eagles. "See, papa, all my houses tumble down. Charles' houses don't fall down, but mine always do. Come and help me, Charles."

"You are not patient enough, my son," replied the father, smiling down upon his petulance. "You must be patient and persevere, and after awhile you will be able to make your houses stand. Isn't that right, Mr. Pollock?"

Pollock stood a little apart, gazing in amazement at the scene before him. *Golden eagles given to a child to play with* was a little beyond him. He made no direct reply to Mr. Montfort's remark, and if the latter had been an observant man, he might have been a bit puzzled at the expression on his face. But Charles Montfort was ingenuousness itself, seeing in no man an enemy. Anson Pollock was his opposite; his ruling passion was covetousness. His eyes were fairly dazzled by the sight of the gold so carelessly strewing the floor. It positively took away his breath.

"Come, Pollock, we will talk over those matters in my study," said Montfort presently. "My son," he added, as he paused at the doorway, "be careful not to lose your ducats. They are your portion to pay your college bills when you cross the ocean to finish your education."

"Going to send him abroad to study?" carelessly inquired Pollock.

"Oh, yes; America's all right for me, but bonny England for my boys."

Anson Pollock, whom Charles Montfort had chosen for his friend, was a man of dashing appearance. He carried his years jauntily, and had a good opinion of himself where women were concerned. He was made much of by the ladies in the vicinity because of his wealth. It mattered not that his wife had died mysteriously. Rumor said his ill treatment and infidelity had driven her to suicide; it had even been whispered that he had not hesitated to whip her by proxy through his overseer, Bill Sampson, in the same way he did his slaves; but rumor is a lying jade. Nevertheless, his fair speech, auburn curls and deep-blue eyes, so falsely smiling, won his way, and Mr. Pollock was the popular ladies' man of two counties.

He had showered Mrs. Montfort with assiduous attention since her arrival three years before, but he soon found that he made no headway. Once he dared to tell her of his passion—that from the first moment he saw her aboard the "Island Queen" he had been maddened by her beauty.

"Why do you tell me this?" she cried, in angry amazement at his daring. "Am I so careless of my husband's honor that his friends feel at liberty to insult me?"

"Granted that I overstep the bounds of friendship in speaking thus to you, but it is from no lack of respect; rather the deed of one who risks all upon one throw of the dice. Have mercy, I pray you, and grant me your friendship—your love."

Then Grace Montfort said, while her eyes blazed with wrath: "Mr. Pollock, we are strangers here, my husband and I. He trusts you, and I have no wish to disturb that trust; but if you ever address such words to me again, I shall let Mr. Montfort know the kind of man you are. I promise you that he will know how to deal with you." This conversation had taken place one night at a grand fête, where Grace had been the belle of the assembly; they were in the conservatory at the time. Anson Pollock was not accustomed to having his advances received in this way by any woman whom he elected to honor with his admiration. As the indignant woman swept back to the ballroom, he stood and watched her with an evil look, which meant no good. After that they met as usual, but Pollock had never ventured to speak to her again of love. Outwardly he was the same suave, genial gentleman, but within his breast was a living fire of hatred. The two men became faster friends than ever. Mrs. Montfort was pleased to have it so; they had so few friends in this alien land; she felt so lonely, so helpless. She dreaded making enemies. It was but the lull before the storm.

When the study door had closed behind the two men, Mr. Montfort dropped his pleasant, careless manner and faced Mr. Pollock with an anxious face.

"Pollock," he began abruptly, "I'm worried."

"What about?" asked Pollock, turning from the window, where he seemed to be viewing the landscape.

"Have you heard the rumors about my wife being of African descent?" Montfort asked, coming very close to Pollock, as though afraid the very air would hear him. "There are threats, too, against my life because of my desire to free my slaves."

"Nonsense!" exclaimed Pollock. "I have heard the rumors about Mrs. Montfort, but that is nothing—nothing but the malice of some malicious, jealous woman. As for the threats against your life, how can you think of such things a second time. You are among the most chivalrous people on the face of the earth, who will protect you in your home."

Montfort stood a moment before his friend, gazing at him earnestly; then he said: "Pollock, if anything happens to me, I want you to promise me to help my wife and babies to get back to Bermuda."

"Why, what can happen, man; you are nervous without a cause."

"In that safe," continued Montfort, not heeding the interruption, "you will find money and deeds; promise me that you will save them for my family."

"I promise; but it is all nonsense." "I shall hold you to your promise," replied Montfort solemnly.

The committee on public safety generally met once a month. They had a chairman, but no one knew his identity save a chosen few of the committee. Indeed very little was known positively, as to the identity of any of the members; certainly no one would ever have suspected the elegant Anson Pollock of being connected with such an organization.

On this particular evening—Bill Sampson lounged by the Jefferson house on the lookout for some of his friends. Anson Pollock sat on the broad steps, evidently on the watch for some one, too. "Hi, Bill!" he called, as the latter came in sight.

"Holloa! want me?" returned Bill; and at a nod from his employer, he followed him through the entrance to a small back room, generally used for the meetings of the committee.

"Anything new for the committee tonight?" asked Pollock, as he lounged over the back of a chair. Bill took a seat on the edge of the table and began cutting circles in the air with his rawhide. Bill Sampson was a character in his way. One could not imagine Newbern without Bill, and no one could possibly imagine Bill without his rawhide.

"Wall, mabby, mabby; depends on what you call wurk. Somebody," with a sly glance at Pollock from beneath his bushy eyebrows, "somebody's been circlatin' a r'port about a fren' o' yourn."

"Well," replied Pollock sharply.

"Looks like we'd treed a 'possum, sho."

"Well."

"Somebody says how's Montfort's slaves is wurkin' fur part pay; leastways, every mother's son o' them'll be free inside o' five years."

"Anything else?"

"We kin' o' thought that'd do fer a spell. He's done nuff in that ar to convict him an' buy his halter. Thet'll do fer one pint."

"But that don't cover the case. What luck have you had in spreading the other report?"

"Wall," said Bill, as he shot a copious draught of tobacco juice over the sanded floor, "mos' the fellers think it a pity 'bout Mis' Montfort. Blamed nice 'ooman. She's been mighty good to Jeff Peterson's fam'ly, an' Jeff he feels mighty uncomf'table 'bout hurtin' on her, durned ef he don'."

"You and Jeff want to do your duty," replied Pollock. "No matter about sentiment. Influence is great with certain people, and if niggers are tolerated in any way, it will end in weakening the law, and then good-by to our institutions."

"Course, course; we 'tend ter do our duty; yas, sir, our whol duty; but it beats all nater 'bout Mis' Montfort. I knowed she wuz mixed the minute I seed her, but 'ain't nuff to 'tract 'tention." He paused a moment, and then said with a sigh: "Well, Cap'n, what's yer orders?"

Pollock saw that the man's sympathy was more than half enlisted on the woman's side, and with arch diplomacy changed his tactics. He handed Bill a cigar, saying, "We may as well make ourselves comfortable"; and before the latter had fairly begun to enjoy the fragrant weed, had called for whiskey and was pressing him to help himself. Under its stimulating influence Bill soon lost what slight scruples he had felt, and was as eager for the downfall of the unfortunate family as his patron.

"Well, Bill," continued Pollock, "the first thing to be done is to put Montfort out of the way; then it will be plain sailing. The next question is: Who will do that job?"

"Reckon I know jes' the man—a man o'the right sperrit, who'll be glad to serve his country fer a reasun'ble consideration. An' thet remin's me, how much o' the property is to be resarved fer you?"

"The boys may have what they can get of it; I don't care for any part of the spoils; all I want is the mother and the children."

"Jes' so; wall, now, seein's I understan' the case jes' as you want it, I'll lay low, set the boys on; you keep shady an' stan' ready the minute the mine's fired. I ain't got a cuss agin Montfort myself, but the institootion must be respected. Sure thar's plenty o' whiskey an' stuff in the cellur? 'Twould look kin' o' mean in Montfort not to have a full cellur. It's a big job, an' the boys'll be thirsty." With this, the two worthies arose from their seats and sauntered through the door and up to the bar.

A day or two after the foregoing, Hank Davis, true to his word, formally applied to Mr. Montfort for the position of overseer on his plantation.

"What made you think that I wanted an overseer?" asked Montfort, as he pushed his hat off his face a little farther and eyed the petitioner critically, mentally vowing that he would never place even a horse in the power of such an ill-favored, beastly looking fellow.

"Wall, most Southern gentlemen don't keer ter have a nigger overseer. It spiles 'em; they gives themselves airs, an' git sot up in thar idees. Thought mabby you, bein' a stranger, mightn't know our ways. You see, it's jes' hyar, we have certain rules in this commoonity that we all mus' 'bide by ef we want t'void trouble." As Hank ventured this last remark in a cautious manner, he scraped the gravel of the walk with one foot while he slyly noted the reception of his venture by an upward cast of his eye.

Charles Montfort looked at him a moment with a slumbering wrath before he asked with dangerous coolness: "What do I understand by what you have just said, Mr. Davis? Do you mean to insinuate that a man cannot do as he will with his own property?"

"Wall, no; not eggsactly; but it's jes' hyar, to speak plainly as 'tween fren's," replied Hank, as he shifted his tobacco to the other side of his mouth, "the plain fac' is: I want the job of drivin' yer niggers, an' you'll want me to keep the commoonity fren'ly to yer now it's got out thet yer a-gwine ter set the gang free byme by."

Charles Montfort possessed one characteristic of the West Indian to a marked degree, and that was a bad temper under just provocation. Without more ado he seized the offending Hank by the collar, and with his riding whip, which he carried in his hand, he administered a sound flogging to the offender. As he released him, he said: "When you leave my grounds, don't you ever set your foot inside the gates again, or it will be the worse for you."

Hank said nothing as he raised himself from the ground where the irate man had thrown him, but as he turned to leave the place he looked at Mr. Montfort; and even in his wrath at the insolence of such a mongrel cur, as he mentally styled Davis, Charles Montfort felt a shudder of real physical fear pass over him for a moment. Surprised at himself, he turned to enter the house, dismissing the whole incident as a piece of impudence which he had done well to chastise.

Taking it all in all, Mr. Montfort was not feeling very happy on this June morning, as he sat upon the piazza thinking over the late encounter. An hour passed swiftly away; still the master of the house continued his meditations; but now he had changed his seat for a thoughtful promenade up and down the broad piazza. Finally he said softly to himself: "Yes, that is just what I will do; I'll send Gracie and the little fellows home for awhile on a visit, and there they shall stay until I know just what the trouble is here about the slaves, and certain insinuations concerning my family are cleared up." When a man makes up his mind that he has solved a difficult problem that has worried him, he generally has an air of relief which is the more pathetic, that in nine cases out of ten he does not believe that his remedy will prove effective, although he fancies that he so believes.

When Hank Davis left Mr. Montfort he moved slowly down the sun-baked road, nursing his wrath and swearing vengeance. Nothing but the life of the man who had inflicted such an insult upon him could wipe it out. He had received the same treatment that he had given hundreds of his associates, until his name and presence had become a terror in the county where he resided. Hitherto he had given his orders and they had been obeyed; but here was a man, a comparative stranger, for whom he considered that he had been willing to do a great kindness, for a consideration, and not only had he met with a refusal of his request but at the same time had received personal violence of a character that was most galling to the spirit of any free-born Southern man—an ordinary cowhiding, such as he would mete out to his slave. As he thought more and more about the matter he grew more, and more filled with a desire for vengeance, not the ordinary kind, but something extraordinary. As he gradually turned over in his mind schemes for the undoing of the Montforts, he was accosted by the voice of Bill Sampson, calling to him from across the fields. Bill was overseeing the harvesting of a great field of cotton, and the voices of the slaves could be heard droning out their weird and plaintive notes, as they sought by song movement to lighten the monotony of their heavy tasks and bring solace to their sad hearts. Some, in their simple ignorance, may not have known why they were sad, but, like the captive bird, their hearts longed for that which was ever the birthright of man—property in himself. Crushed out of sight for many years, the seed of desire for all those things which make a man, and sweeten toil, was struggling ever toward the light of civilization denied to these poor, ignorant, enslaved souls.

Hank sat down on a log by the wayside and beckoned Bill over to him. The latter came slowly across the field and seated himself astride one end of the log.

"Howdy, Hank"; "Howdy, Bill," passed in greeting between the two cronies.

"'Pears like to me, Hank, yer a-lookin' pale," remarked Bill, as he trailed his whip backward and forward in the dust.

Hank could stand it no longer; and with a terrible imprecation, he unfolded to his friend his tale of woe and insult. Bill listened with eager curiosity, and a satisfied, knowing look might have been seen to settle about the corners of his eyes and mouth.

"Wall, wall," said he, "these ar' great times when a d—West Ingy half-white nigger can raise his hand agin a white man. Be yer hurt much, Hank?"

"Some in my body, but more in my feelin's."

"What ar' we a-comin'to? I tell you, Hank, it is 'bout time sumthin' was done."

"That's all well enough to talk," replied Hank, "but what kin a man do agin the money thet thet feller's got to back him up? I cayn't see a handle on him."

"Wall," replied Bill, "I *kin.*"

"You *kin*!" exclaimed Hank, while a slow smile of derision covered his face; "wall, I'd jes? like to know how."

"Yer kin laugh, Hank Davis, but it's a fac'. 'Taint goin' to be no hard job, nuther, to git all thet money, all them purty trinkets and fine furniture, and the seven hundred niggers in our pockets *ef*"—(and here he paused as though to give emphasis to his words) "*ef* we wurks the thing right."

"Damn it all, man, why don't yer let out?" demanded Hank, as he rose excitedly from his seat on the log. "I'm the man to help on anythin' agin thet man, an' yer knows it. No need of yer bein' so infernal aggravatin' 'bout tellin' me."

Bill laughed at his companion's excitement. "Easy thar, easy, Hank. This ar' a mighty titlish job, but we kin wurk it—we kin wurk it. Fust place, yer see Montfort's brought them slaves o'hisn hyar and don't tend to keep 'em only 'bout ten years, and then every one o' them will have bought hisself, accordin' to the laws thet ar' governin' them over to the West Indies. Now, yer know ther's a bad eggsample to set befo' the niggers roun' this town. Eny way, we's goin' to think so," drawled Bill, with an expressive wink at his friend. "It's a law of the United States that ef eny man is caught creatin' dissatisfacshun among the slaves he desarves death, and death he gits. Now, this ar Montfort has been causin' trouble fer us by his eggsample. Every nigger roun' hyar knows all 'bout his 'rangements fer givin' his slaves thar freedom, and I tell yer, Hank, its causin' dissatisfacshun 'mong all our slaves. An' then the money, honey, the money! sech sights of it all done up in little shammy-skin bags, an' thet boy Jesse settin' on the floor amoosin' hisself buildin' houses with them gold eagles!"

Hank listened to his companion's words with open mouth. As the latter finished he said, with a look of admiration: "Wall, I'll be d–d! Now, look a-hyar, Bill Sampson, yer needn't tell me thet all thet yer have just unfolded to me is yer own idees, 'cause yer could no more hev got them thoughts through yer thick head than I could. Some one's been fixin' yer up. Out with it now, an' tell me the whole thing. Ef we's goin' inter this business, we's got to be square on the deal with our fren's. Who's the bottom o'this thing?"

Bill produced a plug of tobacco, offered his friend a chew and took one himself. "What I'm tellin' yer, Hank, is 'tween fren's," said he, chewing and crossing his legs.

"Jes' so," replied Hank.

"I wuz tellin' yer the 'riginater o' this plan, or I wuz about to." Bill paused to spit out some of his tobacco juice on the ground, so that it would not overflow the tank, so to speak, and run out of each corner of his mouth. "Beats all nater, Hank, how a man'll git dead set onter a piece o' caliker."

"Meanin' by that, Bill, that Ans Pollock's got set on some gal."

"Fact!" said Bill, with a wink.

"Who's?" asked Hank.

"It mote be Mis' Montfort herself, Hank."

"Sho, you don' say, re'lly," said Hank, with a wicked look. "Don'blame him, blamed ef I do. But thet's all the good it'll do him."

Bill cut the air into imaginary circles with his whip, and without taking any notice of his friend, continued: "As I was sayin', Ans Pollock, he says ter me, Bill, thet's a dooced purty 'ooman o' Montfort's,' an' I tol' him what I thought 'bout her havin' black blud in her somewhar. 'Mabby,' says he, 'mabby.' An' then he says, kin' o' generous like, 'I'd take the 'ooman an' the two brats, an' the boys might hev the slaves, an' the money, an' the fixin's in the house.' I tol' him I knew the boys 'd stan' by him in enything he might do to rid a peaceful neighborhood of sech a disturbin' critter as Montfort. I tol' him I thought yer would be 'bout the very match to light on Montfort, so he wouldn't give us eny more trouble. An' so we've been waitin' fer the business ter 'velop itself good an' ripe, an' I jes' think this 'tack o' Montfort's on yer will 'bout do the business fer the whole o' them."

"Bill," said Hank Davis, as he held out his hand to his friend, "we's allers been pardners, an' I reckon we allers will be."

IV

The Tragedy

Thus man devotes his brother, and destroys him;
And worse than all, and most to be deplored
Chains him, and tasks him and exacts his sweat
With stripes that Mercy, with a bleeding heart,
Weeps when she sees inflicted on a beast.

—Cowper

Kismet," says the Oriental, when unaccountable evils beset his path; "It is fate," says the Anglo-Saxon, under like circumstances: but fate is the will of Providence after all. Nature avenges herself upon us for every law violated in the mad rush for wealth or position or personal comfort where the rights of others of the human family are not respected. If Charles Montfort had been contented to accept the rulings of the English Parliament, and had allowed his human property to come under the new laws just made for its government, although poorer in the end, he would have spared himself and family all the horrors which were to follow his selfish flight to save that property.

The sun rose clear and resplendent a few mornings later. On this particular morning Nature outdid herself. There was a blending together of all the sweet forces—odorous air, golden sunshine, musical sounds from bird and from bush; it was pure happiness to feel the lifeblood leaping in one's veins; to feel the marvelous joy of living.

Eight o'clock was the usual breakfast hour for the Montforts. The family had just assembled at the table; Aunt Cindy had brought in the great silver coffee urn and placed it beside Mrs. Montfort. Mr. Montfort had settled himself in his chair with a weekly paper, for in this rural neighborhood a newspaper once in a week was a great luxury, when his attention was caught by the sound of hoofbeats of several horses on the road. Mrs. Montfort, with usual Southern hospitality, looked over her well-appointed board to make sure that all was in order for dispensing those creature comforts so dear to the entertainer and the entertained.

The hoofbeats drew nearer and paused on the graveled walk. Montfort hastened to the door, while Mrs. Montfort turned toward the entrance of the breakfast-room with a pleasant smile of welcome on her lips. She heard a number of voices speaking together in an excited jumble, then a shot, followed by a heavy fall. Little Jesse ran from his station by his mother's side through one of the long windows opening upon the piazza. She heard his scream of "papa, papa!" and then again the jumble of excited voices. With little Charles clinging to her skirts she stumbled blindly to the entrance and faced the crowd of angry men, headed by Anson Pollock. Hank Davis had done his work well, and Charles Montfort lay dead with a bullet in his brain, sped by an unseen hand. Mrs. Montfort's arms were grasped by rude hands, and she was forcibly drawn out upon the veranda, where in the sunlight of the beautiful morning she saw the body of her husband lying face downward. She was dimly conscious of hearing the cries of frightened slaves mingled with the screams of her children. Through it all she realized but two things that the lifeless object lying there so still was the body of her husband, and that the sensual face of Anson Pollock, whom she had grown to loathe and fear, was gloating over her agony, devilish in its triumph. Then she lost consciousness.

As she lay upon the green sward, oblivious to thought and feeling, supported by her weeping maid, who had been ordered to care for her mistress by Mr. Pollock, Hank Davis came and stood for a moment looking down upon the unconscious woman. Suddenly an evil smile lighted up his countenance. He looked around, but saw nothing of Anson Pollock, who had disappeared within the house, searching for money and papers in the safe. Now was his time. This woman's husband had flogged him—he would have a sweet revenge. Those lily-like limbs, the tender flesh that had never known aught but the touch of love, should *feel the lash as he had*.

He called to Bill Sampson to help lift her; and despite the prayers and tears of the poor slave girl who followed her beloved mistress until Sampson knocked her senseless with the butt end of his rawhide, they bore the hapless lady to the whipping post. She revived as they reached the spot; and when she realized the fate in store for her, the sweet woman's strong soul failed her. She uttered a wild cry of agony as the rough hand of Hank Davis was laid upon her to tear her garments from her shrinking shoulders.

"Charles, my husband, save me!" she cried, and fell fainting upon the ground. There was none to answer the heartrending appeal. He who would have shed his heart's best blood for her, lay cold in death. She was soon restored to consciousness, for Hank's savage instinct for revenge would only be appeased by the victim's full realization of her sufferings.

She was bound to the whipping post as the victim to the stake, and lashed with rawhides alternately by the two strong, savage men. Hank Davis drew first blood by reason of his wrongs at Mr. Montfort's hands. With all his mighty strength he brought the lash down upon the frail and shrinking form. O God! was there none to rescue her! The air whistled as the snaky leather thong curled and writhed in its rapid, vengeful descent. A shriek from the victim—a spurt of blood that spattered the torturer—a long, raw gash across a tender, white back. Hank gazed at the cut with critical satisfaction, as he compared its depth with the skin and blood that encased the long, tapering lash. It was now Bill's turn.

"I'll go you one better," he said, as he sighted the distance and exact place to make his mark with mathematical precision, at the same time shifting his tobacco from the right to the left cheek. Again the rawhide whistled through the air, falling across the other cut squarely in the center. Another shriek, a stifled sob, a long-drawn quivering sigh— then the deep stillness of unconsciousness. Again and again was the outrage repeated. Fainting fit followed fainting fit. The blood stood in a pool about her feet.

When Hank Davis had satiated his vengeful thirst he cut the ropes which bound her, and she sank upon the ground again—unconscious bleeding, friendless, alone. Lucy had hidden in the smokehouse with the two children, that they might not witness their mother's agony.

Meantime, the committee on public safety, instigated by Anson Pollock to put down an imaginary insurrection (having no existence but in his own mind, and supposed to have originated with the slaves of Charles Montfort) and to legalize the looting of the house, took possession of the mansion. Soon the crowd had stripped it of its furniture and all the articles of value. The house itself was fired, and Grace Montfort again became conscious of her misery in time to see the dead body of her husband flung amid the burning rafters of his dwelling. Two and two the slaves were handcuffed together to be driven to the market place. Mrs. Montfort, secured to her maid, was placed in a wagon with her two children; and so the miserable woman was driven away from her outraged home.

In those old days, if accused of aiding slaves in a revolt, a white man stood no more chance than a Negro accused of the same crime. He forfeited life and property. This power of the law Anson Pollock had invoked; and to add to the devilishness of the plot, had used Bill Sampson's suggestion of black blood in Mrs. Montfort, to further his scheme for possessing the beautiful woman. So the two children and their mother fell to the lot of Anson Pollock as his portion of the spoils. Shortly after these events Grace Montfort disappeared and was never seen again. The waters of Pamlico Sound tell of sweet oblivion for the brokenhearted found within their soft embrace.

After the loss of their mother the two lads clung very closely to each other. So many changes had come to them, such desperate, bloody scenes had dazed their brains and terrified them, that even the loss of their mother seemed but in keeping with the rest. Bewilderment at so much sorrow, the numbness of black despair was ever with them.

Pollock's rage was terrible when he learned that Mrs. Montfort had destroyed herself. He grew morose and unsociable, so that his society was no longer sought in the county. He seemed to have a superstitious fear of the children, and for a long time would not tolerate them in his presence. It was common talk among the slaves that Mrs. Montfort "walked," weeping and wringing her hands, night after night about the plantation.

But wonder could go no farther when Pollock elected to take Lucy in the place he had designed for Mrs. Montfort. God's mysteries are past man's understanding; and thus the poor black girl became his instrument to temper the wind to the shorn lambs. Night after night she stole away to the little attic under the eaves laden with dainties to tempt the appetite of the children. For hours she would sit hushing Jesse's sobs upon her ample breast, and speaking words of comfort in her poor, blind way to Charles.

When a year had dragged its slow length past, a stranger in the town stopped Bill Sampson on the street one day and asked him if he knew where he could hire a likely boy to go with him into the woods for a few days and help arrange specimens of the quartz in that locality. He was looking up the minerals in that section for speculators, he said. Bill promised to get him a boy, and asked Pollock's permission for Charles to go with the man.

"I don't care what you do with him, only keep him away from me. I'll sell him south soon," said Pollock.

So it happened that Charles went every day for a month with the mineralogist. The lad's appearance, education and refinement puzzled the man for a time, until he learned the tragic story.

"Charles," said he, a few weeks later, "I am about to leave this part of the country. I don't want to leave you here. Do you think Mr. Pollock could be induced to part with you?"

"O sir!" cried Charles, throwing himself at the gentleman's feet, "for the love of God buy me and my little brother. If you will only take us to Bermuda, some one there will pay you back. My father had money there; we have friends there. O sir, for the love of God!"

The man looked at the weeping boy as through a mist. He had a tender heart.

"I will tell you something, Charles," said he kindly, as he raised the lad and drew him to a seat beside him on the grass, with his arm tenderly enfolding the child. "I am an Englishman, but it will not do to have that fact known here, for then I would be powerless to help you. Anson Pollock would never sell you to me if he knew that fact. I have been trying to buy you and Jesse, but Pollock wants to keep the boy for a valet. He intends to sell you south; you are too old to forget, and he fears you. Now I propose to buy you; and as soon as possible I shall take you to Bermuda, collect the proofs there concerning your family, and then go to England, invoke the power of the home government, and demand Jesse's freedom and indemnity from the United States government for all the outrages perpetrated against your family. Can you keep this secret, and will you try and be patient until I can accomplish my purpose?"

"I will do anything you say," replied the boy humbly, "but I hate to leave Jesse. O mama, mama, my beautiful mama!" and with a burst of grief he cast himself upon the velvet turf.

The mineralogist lost no time in completing the purchase of Charles, and in a few days they left the town. Then little Jesse, the petted darling of a luxurious home, found himself alone in the power of Anson Pollock. He must wait upon him obsequiously by day, and be ready to answer his call at any hour of the night. Under his enemy's eye by day and night, hopeless, utterly alone upon the wide waste of waters which represented his life. Oh, how black, boundless, trackless, was the unknown future to this unfortunate child! Once, after his brother was sold, he resisted his master—rebelled with all his puny strength. He was severely flogged. That night he slept in the lonely cabin kept as a sort

PAULINE E. HOPKINS

of prison for refractory slaves. Not a sigh disturbed the silence of the night as he lay in pain, gazing up at the stars which shone so peacefully through the dilapidated roof. He thought himself delirious, or was it indeed possible that God had taken compassion on his loneliness and allowed the comfort and help of communion with the dead! He saw his murdered father and mother.

Hand in hand they passed and repassed over the gaping holes in the roof of the hut. His father's noble, loving face smiled upon him; his mother's curls moved in the faint breeze, while her loving glance seemed to say: "Courage, courage, we are ever near you."

"Father, Grace, speak to me!" he shrieked in agony.

Then he seemed to feel their actual presence, tangible though viewless, beside him in the hut. Calmness came to him, and a change grand to see in that slight frame. Unconsciously he asked the question: "How long must I endure before I join you in heaven?"

It seemed to him that he was answered: "Many days, and even years; but fear not, we will never leave thee."

After that night Jesse's childhood appeared to slip from him, and he became a man in thought. He studied his master, and matched low cunning with lofty determination. He rebelled no more, was silent, not provoking Anson Pollock's wrath. The time seemed long and dreary waiting for the freedom he had resolved to have; still he was patient. Sometimes at night, when rolled in his blanket on the hard floor, he would weep over the painful past. Then he would feel the touch of a tiny hand upon his eyelids. It was his mother's hand; he knew it to be so. Then he would lose himself in sweet dreams and awaken in the morning refreshed and comforted. So the years rolled on until he was sixteen. Meantime, nothing was heard from Charles and his supposed friend. Jesse had made up his mind that Charles was either dead or else lost to him forever.

Jesse was now a man in stature, though still slender, with the saine haughty bearing and distinguished appearance that had marked his father. Anson Pollock, upon whom age and the memory of dreadful crimes were making fearful inroads, began to look up to the boy and lean upon him for aid in his various plans for making money. He had spoken to him of making him the overseer, in place of Bill Sampson, and had even hinted at his taking a mate. Then Jesse knew that his probation was nearly over. That spring Pollock, as was the common practice among planters, made out passes for Jesse and sent him to

New York in charge of a vessel filled with produce, and charged to bring back necessary merchandise for use on the plantation. Pollock thought the boy still too young to venture to leave him. Indeed Jesse had no such idea when he started on his trip to the North. When the vessel reached New York, Jesse performed all the necessary duties—disposed of the produce, and reloaded the ship for its homeward voyage. The night before they were to sail he sat on the wharf watching the crews of other vessels making ready for departure. His mind was engrossed with thoughts of Charles. He feared some evil had befallen him.

"At any rate," he said to himself, "I shall never see him again. And must I remain in servitude? Can I do nothing to help myself, since all hope is gone in that direction?" Just then a group of men paused in front of him. They did not know he was a slave.

"Will you give passage to two on board your vessel? You are bound for Newbern in the morning, aren't you? We'll pay you what you charge," said one of the group respectfully.

"Speak to the cap'n," called out a man standing near; "that's nuthin' but a nigger you're talkin' to."

"Well," said the one who had first addressed him, "you're a likely boy, anyhow; who do you belong to?"

Jesse arose from his seat, white with passion, and said to the man: "I am no man's property; I belong to Jesus Christ!" The question had answered itself. When the vessel sailed the next morning, Jesse was far on his road to Boston.

Traveling then was done by stage, and was a slow process; but about a week later he stood beside the stone wall that enclosed the historic Boston Common, and as he watched the cows chewing their peaceful cuds and inhaled deep draughts of freedom's air, he vowed to die rather than return to Anson Pollock.

He found work in Boston. It mattered not that it was menial work; he was happy. But fate or Providence was not done with him yet.

One day he received word that Anson Pollock was on his way to Boston in search of him. Again he made a hurried journey. This time to Exeter, N. H. In his character of a fugitive slave, the lad had from the first cast his lot with the colored people of the community, and when he left Boston he was directed to see Mr. Whitfield, a negro in Exeter, who could and would help the fugitive.

Late one afternoon, just before tea time, a comely black woman stood in her long, lowraftered kitchen preparing supper before the open fireplace. There was every indication of plenty in the homely furnishings. As the woman passed rapidly from the cupboard to the table she would touch with her foot the rockers of the little red cradle which stood in the center of the floor. The baby in it was crying in a fretful way. "Oh, hush, Lizzie," said the mother; "don't be so cross. There came a low rap at the open door, and in answer to her "Come in," Jesse stepped into the room.

"Is Mr. Whitfield in?" he asked, as he doffed his hat respectfully. "No," was the reply, "but I expect him every minute. Sit down, won't you? He'll soon be in to his supper, I guess."

Mrs. Whitfield thought him a white man, come on business with her husband. "A handsome lad," she thought. Jesse seated himself; and then as the child continued to cry, said: "Shall I rock the cradle for you, ma'am? The child seems fretful."

Fifteen years later Jesse married Elizabeth Whitfield, the baby he had rocked to sleep the first night of his arrival in Exeter. By her he had a large family.

Thus he was absorbed into that unfortunate race, of whom it is said that a man had better be born dead than to come into the world as part and parcel of it.

V

Ma Smith's Lodging-House

Let not Ambition mock their useful toil,
Their homely joys, and destiny obscure;
Nor Grandeur hear with a disdainful smile
The short and simple annals of the poor.

—GRAY

T hank heaven that is done," said Dora, as she sat down wearily in her mother's large rocker in the cosy kitchen. She had been upstairs the best portion of the day preparing a room for an expected lodger. There had been windows to wash, paint to clean, a carpet to tack down, curtains to hang and furniture to place in position—in short, the thousand and one things to do that are essential to the comfort of the lodger and the good reputation of the house.

"Are you very tired, daughter?" queried her mother, as she glanced with loving pride at the graceful figure before her, at the smooth bands of dark brown hair, now a little ruffled and disordered, and at the delicate brown face, now somewhat puckered and out of sorts from weariness.

"Well, not very tired, mummy dear; only this continual scrub and dig is not always the cheerful work we would like to think it. Still I don't care as long as the house pays."

The mother sighed as she asked: "Did you give her the front or back square?"

"Oh, I gave her the front square after all. She's too beautiful for that dreary back room. I know that it is not business to let a good-paying room go under our usual price, but she's a 'steady'; she has the best of references. Father Andrew gives her the best of characters, and so I'll chance getting my money back out of the next cross-grained old bachelor who comes along. See how mercenary I am getting to be since I undertook to direct the fortunes of a lodging-house"; and with a gay laugh the daughter jumped from her seat, every trace of fatigue gone, and grasping her mother about the waist, whirled her around the room to the accompaniment of a sweet, shrill whistle of the latest popular waltz. In the midst of the frolic there came a loud ring of the doorbell, and placing her panting and protesting mother in the rocker just vacated, she vanished; and soon her voice was heard above, as she directed the placing of the luggage of the expected lodger.

The Smith family consisted of the mother, daughter and son. A few years before the opening of our story the father had died, leaving a delicate wife, a young daughter, and a son just ready to enter college; also a house in a respectable part of the South End of Boston, Mass., with a heavy mortgage upon it. Like many colored men living in large cities, his life had been a continual struggle with poverty and hard work, combined with a desire for advancement for his children, and a clean, self-respecting citizenship for himself. Smith was a free-born Southern Negro—a Virginian. His father had bought himself, and married a free Woman. After the birth of Henry his mother died; and when his father married again, his aunts brought him to the city of New Bedford, where he had imbibed, along with copious draughts of salt air, an unwavering desire for all the blessings of liberty, and strong notions that a man must depend upon himself in great measure and carve out his own fortune to the best of his ability with such tools as God had furnished him.

Henry Smith's early manhood was spent upon the sea; and when he at last settled in Boston, he could converse about foreign ports and countries with the ease and familiarity of personal knowledge. Possessed of very little education, yet he concealed the fact admirably under a naturally intelligent manner. Soon after he ceased to follow the sea he married a handsome Mulattress from New Hampshire, and with her help saved a small sum of money enough to make the first payment on a home; then began the struggle of their lives. The masses of the Negro race find for employment only the most laborious work at the scantiest remuneration. A man, though a skilled mechanic, has the door of the shop closed in his face here among the descendants of the liberty-loving Puritans. The foreign element who come to the shores of America soon learn that there is a class which is called its inferior, and will not work in this or that business if "niggers" are hired; and the master or owner, being neither able nor willing to secure enough of the despised class to fill the places of the white laborers, acquiesces in the general demand, and the poor Negro finds himself banned in almost every kind of employment. Henry Smith had his ambitions; but like all of his meek race, he would not or at least had no desire to contend with the force of prejudice, and quietly took up his little business of repairing old clothes in the same patient spirit of the Jew "old clo'" vender or pawnbroker.

Two children were born to this worthy couple—William Jesse Montfort and Dora Grace Montfort. When Willie was seventeen and Dora twelve their father sickened and died. Thenceforth the burden of the support of the little family fell upon the mother. Willie was preparing to enter college, but he cheerfully gave up his plans and secured a place as bellboy in one of the fashionable hostelries with which Boston abounds; and soon by his attention to business, his gentlemanly manners, and intelligent understanding of all that was required of him, made himself invaluable to his employers. Twenty dollars a month with board and "tips" was a very respectable showing for a lad of seventeen, and Willie felt himself repaid when he saw the great help and comfort his small earnings gave to his dear mother. Dora was kept at her studies until she was graduated from the high school. Meantime Mrs. Smith, or "Ma" Smith, as she was called by all the young people of her acquaintance, increased their income by letting furnished rooms.

The mother and daughter shared the same sleeping-room, and will declared himself in favor of an attic chamber as being the least desirable for renting purposes. There he established himself in a very comfortable nest, furnished after the fashion dear to all young fellows' hearts, with everything "handy." The only occasions upon which will and Dora were known to quarrel were the weekly cleaning days, when the latter would insist on "tidying up Will's room." Then shoes were moved from the mantel and the blacking brushes from the top of the dressing-case; collars, cuffs and ties were placed in their proper receptacles, and garments hung in the clothespress. Then Will would scold a good deal because he "couldn't find things," but by the next morning he would have them "handy" again. Many lodgers were obtained through Will's acquaintance with young men at the hotel where he worked, and very soon the mother was able to see that the debt upon the home which she hoped to leave her children, was slowly but surely disappearing. Deep in her heart was the cherished hope that when the mortgage was paid Willie would be free to choose a profession; but they never mentioned among themselves the hope which was cherished in each breast.

As the years rolled slowly by the children saw that their mother could not do as much as formerly; and so by degrees, after Dora had finished school, the burden of the care of the house fell upon her strong young shoulders, and 1896 found her taking full charge, and proving herself to be a woman of ability and the best of managers, husbanding their small income to the best advantage.

With about every avenue for business closed against them, it is surprising that so many families of color manage to live as well as they do and to educate their children and give them a few of the refinements of living,—such as cultivating a musical talent, gratifying a penchant for languages, or for carving, or for any of the arts of a higher civilization, so common among the whites, but supposed to be beyond the reach of a race just released from a degrading bondage. Whatever grace or accomplishment may be the order of the hour, it is copied or practiced among some portion of the colored population. We may well ask ourselves how this is done. Among the white Americans who perform domestic or personal service, how rare it is to meet the brilliant genius of a Frederick Douglass; but with this people it is a common occurrence to find a genius in a profession, trade, or invention, evolved from the rude nurturing received at the hands of a poor father and mother engaged in the lowliest of service, who see not the nobility of their sacrifices in the delight afforded them in watching the unfolding of the bud of promise in their offspring. From the bosom of the earth we take the diamond; pearls from the depth of the sea; from the lowliest walks of life we cull the hope of a future life beyond the perplexing questions of this present existence. Why should we wonder or question, then, when we see the steady advance of a race overriding the barriers set by prejudice and injustice? Man has said that from lack of means and social caste the Negro shall remain in a position of serfdom all his days, but the mighty working of cause and effect, the mighty unexpected results of the law of evolution, seem to point to a different solution of the Negro question than any worked out by the most fertile brain of the highly cultured Caucasian. Then again, we do not allow for the infusion of white blood, which became pretty generally distributed in the inferior black race during the existence of slavery. Some of this blood, too, was the best in the country. Combinations of plants, or trees, or of any productive living thing, sometimes generate rare specimens of the plant or tree; why not, then, of the genus homo? Surely the Negro race must be productive of some valuable specimens, if only from the infusion which amalgamation with a superior race must eventually bring. This is a mighty question. Today, with all the heated discussions of tariff reform, the parity of gold and silver, the hoarding of giant sums of money by trusts and combinations, still the Negro question will not "down"; it is the most important, the mightiest in the land, and is quietly assuming greater proportions as it forges its way to the front to take its place shortly as the gravest question in the councils of the nation.

When Dora returned to the kitchen her mother had about finished the preparations for supper. The short winter afternoon had dropped into early twilight. Every alternate night was Will Smith's early night home from the hotel, and the little family always managed to have an inviting tea and to pass a cheerful evening together. Lately another person had attached himself to the Smiths; a fellow-waiter with Will had finally worked himself into the profession of law, and having established himself in business in a down-town office, had put his admiration for Dora into words, and it was understood that in due course of time they would marry.

Dora lighted the lamps, drew the curtains, and looked about the cosy kitchen with a satisfaction which might well be pardoned, for even in palatial homes a more inviting nest could not be found. The table was carefully spread with a nicely ironed cloth of spotless white, red-bordered napkins lay at each plate, a good quality of plated silverware mingled with the plain, inexpensive white ware in which the meal was to be served. Ma Smith, in her neat calico dress and long white apron, busied herself in making the tea and coffee and seeing that the delicate muffins were browned to just the right turn, while Dora busied herself in putting the finishing touches to a house dress for her mother.

"Well, Dora," said her mother, as she bustled about the room, "does the young woman seem pleased with your arrangements? I am sure she ought to after all the labor you spent on that room."

"She says she is greatly pleased with everything. Say, ma, she's got a typewriter, and she says she picks up a good living at home with it. Talk about your beauties! my, but she's the prettiest creature I ever saw! expect all the men in this house will be crazy over her."

"Yes, dear," replied her mother with a quiet laugh; "you don't want John making eyes at her, do you?"

Dora laughed as she said: "I'd just drop John P. Langley if I thought he admired any woman more than he did me. But really, ma, you won't be able to keep from loving her; she has the sweetest and saddest face I ever saw. I have read of the woman with a story written on her face, but I never believed it anything but a fairy tale. You'll believe me when you see her and talk with her."

PAULINE E. HOPKINS

"There are the boys," said her mother, as the sound of voices reached their ears, together with the closing of the front door and great stamping of feet to brush away the snow. The next moment the door opened, and two young men entered the cheerful room, and with jest and laugh bade the two women good evening.

Will Smith was tall and finely formed, with features almost perfectly chiseled, and a complexion the color of an almond shell. His hair was black and curly, with just a tinge of crispness to denote the existence of Negro blood. His eyes were dark and piercing as an eagle's. Ladies of high position followed his tall form with admiring glances as he moved about his duties at the hotel, and wondered that so much manly beauty should be wasted upon an inferior race.

John Langley, his companion, was shorter in stature and very fair in complexion. His hair was dark and had no indication of Negro blood in its waves; his features were of the Caucasian cut. He possessed a gentle refinement of manner, apt to take well with the opposite sex; but to a reader of character, the strong manhood and honesty of purpose which existed in Will Smith were lacking in John Langley. He was a North Carolinian—a descendant of slaves and Southern "crackers." We might call this a bad mixture—the combination of the worst features of a dominant race with an enslaved race; and in some measure John Langley would bear out the unfavorable supposition upon close acquaintance. Many of his young friends did not care for him because he developed a revengeful trait of character. He liked his ease, and enjoyed indulging himself in every luxury that his modest means would allow. He had, moreover, a carefully concealed strain of sensuality in his nature, which as yet had never been aroused to an overindulgence in illegitimate and questionable pleasures; and with it all he had a mercenary streak, which made love of money his great passion. He possessed great political acumen and was strong in debate, which attracted a certain class of politicians around him. These attributes, combined with the practice of his profession, might eventually make or mar his fortunes in the untried future that stretched before him.

Seated at the pleasant tea table, the gay laugh and jolly joke went round, and even Ma Smith forgot her years and contributed her share of mirth to the general good time.

"Talking about funny things happening," said Ma Smith, "your grandfather, Will, was a comical genius. You know that I have told you there were fourteen in our family—all girls, and very near each other in age. When your aunts, Fanny and Lottie, began to receive company there was a great time to keep it from father for awhile. Mother was heart and hand with the girls and wanted to see them have a pleasant time, but father did not like it. Your grandfather worked hard and at night was very tired, so the dear old man would go to bed soon after his supper and pipe. Then was the girls' time. A fire was made in the parlor, which was at the front of the house, a good distance away from father's room, and by the time the young man arrived to make his call the old gentleman was generally sound asleep. One night, however, things did not work so well. In those days we had large open fireplaces; stoves did not come in until I was about five years old. I can see that low-ceiled parlor now with its brick hearth and brass andirons holding the glowing logs, the flames crackling and shooting upward, the firelight dancing and shining on the little cupboard doors on each side of the chimney. There was a rag carpet on the floor— your grandmother made her own carpets from rags; and our floors were covered with large handmade rag mats, for no housekeeper was counted much who did not have a large supply of such things. There were china figures on the mantel, and vases filled with golden-rod gathered the summer before. The furniture was mahogany, polished until you could see your face in any part of it. There was a red cloth on the table which stood between the two windows, and in the center of it was a large astral lamp trimmed about the edges with long crystal pendants, which we children called diamonds. We thought nothing could be more elegant than that lamp. It was a wedding present to your grandmother."

"Did you have kerosene in those days, ma?" asked Dora.

"Lord bless you, no; we burned whale oil or sperm oil in that lamp. Poor people used candles. Your grandmother used to save her fat and clarify it and mix it with beeswax to harden it, and we made our candles every week as regularly as we did the family cooking. Sometimes there was danger of the supply of oil giving out in the stores, and then oil cost a great deal of money; that never lasted long, however, and in a few weeks some New Bedford whaler would be in port with a large cargo of whale oil, and then there would be a big supply selling cheap."

"I don't see how you got along without stoves and things," observed Dora; "baking day must have been a terror."

"We had tin kitchens and Dutch ovens. We never had any trouble."

"What's a tin kitchen?" asked John.

"It's an oven made of tin, for roasting meat. It stood on four legs about a foot from the floor, and had a place for a charcoal fire at the back, and a chimney to carry off the smoke. The front fastened by a hasp to the back and could be let down to put the food on the little grate inside. It was a very convenient arrangement, and I wish I had one this minute. A Dutch oven was very much like our iron kettles which we use for boiling; there was a grate inside to hold the food."

"It must have been a great nuisance keeping house under such circumstances."

"Well, what became of the young man that particular evening, ma?" chimed in Will.

"This night father was restless and did not retire with his usual promptness, and we had only just got him out of the way when the expected caller arrived. However, everything went on very well, and you may be sure that there was much peeping and giggling on the part of the half-grown sisters who were denied the great privilege of the parlor and company as yet. Your grandmother sat in the kitchen knitting and trying to keep the younger children in order, when to her consternation the door opened and in walked father. 'Elizabeth,' said he, 'I hear a man's voice in the parlor. What's the trouble?' Poor mother tried to explain, and murmured something about a gentleman calling on Fanny. 'A man,' roared father, 'calling on my daughter!' and the first thing we knew, he seized the bucket of water from the kitchen dresser—we had wells in those days, and a bucket of water always stood on the dresser—and started for the parlor and flung the door open. Without speaking to the astonished occupants of the room, he stalked to the fireplace and deliberately poured the water upon the blazing wood; then he turned to the caller and said: "Young man, if you have a home, go to it; this is no half-way house for the accommodation of young squirts. 'Fanny,' he said, turning to your aunt, 'you go to bed, and don't let this thing occur again.' The young man left as quickly as possible, and poor Fanny retired to her room greatly mortified."

"That's good discipline for girls," said John with a laugh. "If we had more fathers after that stamp, we fellows would get better wives."

"And we girls better husbands," chimed in Dora. "Still, I pity poor Aunt Fanny."

"The fellow wasn't much or he'd have stuck, and not been driven off that way. I'd have made the old gentleman like me in spite of himself if I had meant business," said Will. "Oh, by the by, did your new lodger come, Dora?"

"Yes; and, Will, I never met anyone so beautiful in all my life. You'll be fascinated when you meet her."

"That's you all over, Dora; all your swans generally turn out geese. I'll bet you a new pair of Easter gloves that she's a rank old maid with false teeth, bald head, hair on her upper lip"—

"All right, Will Smith, all right. Just wait until you see her! I'll wager a new pair of embroidered silk suspenders that you're over head and ears in love with her long before that time."

"I'll hold the stakes," cried John.

They rose from the table now, and John said, with a tender glance at Dora: "I thought some one would enjoy seeing the 'Old Homestead.' It's at the Boston Theatre tonight; don't you want to go, Dora?" Dora's eyes sparkled as he held the two tickets before her.

"Get your things on, Dora; you've just time to reach the theatre before the curtain rises," said her brother.

In a little while the house was quiet, and the mother and son settled down to the enjoyment of a quiet evening together.

VI

Ma Smith's Lodging-House—*Concluded*

The gray day darkened into night,
Made hoary with the swarm
And whirl-dance of the blinding story,
As zigzag wavering to and fro,
Crossed and recrossed the winged snow.

—Whitter

February drew slowly to a close. Boston had lain for the past three or four days in the grasp of the snow king. At No. 500 D Street each tenant seemed content to keep within the bounds of his or her small domain, literally "frozed up," as Mrs. Ophelia Davis expressed it.

No one had seen much of the new lodger. She passed in and out each morning with a package of work in her hand; and all day long, from nine in the morning until late at night sometimes, the click of the typewriter could be heard coming from the "first front-square," which interpreted meant the front room on the second floor. Dora had been very neighborly and had called on Miss Clark frequently. There was a great fascination for her about the quiet, self-possessed woman. She did not, as a rule, care much for girl friendships, holding that a close intimacy between two of the same sex was more than likely to end disastrously for one or the other. But Sappho Clark seemed to fill a long-felt want in her life, and she had from the first a perfect trust in the beautiful girl.

Mrs. Smith had furnished her rooms substantially and well, but there had been no attempt at decoration. The first time Dora entered the room after Sappho had settled herself in it, she was struck at the alteration in its appearance. The iron bedstead and the washing utensils were completely hidden by drapery curtains of dark-blue denim, beautifully embroidered in white floss; a cover of the same material was thrown over the small table between the windows; plain white muslin draperies hid the unsightly but serviceable yellow shades at the windows; her desk and typewriter occupied the center of the room, and a couch had been improvised from two packing-cases and a spring, covered with denim and piled high with cushions; two good steel engravings completed a very inviting interior.

"How pretty you have made it," observed Dora, looking curiously around the room.

Sappho came and stood beside her, and the two girls smiled at each other in a glow of mutual interest, and became fast friends at once.

"I always carry these things with me in my travels, and I find that I can make myself very comfortable in a short time with their help."

"I wish you would show me how to do this embroidery," said Dora, as she lifted the edge of the denim curtain before the toilet stand and critically examined it. "This is beautifully done. Where did you learn?"

"I will teach you with pleasure," replied Sappho; but Dora noticed that she did not tell her where she had learned.

"Do you like your work—is it hard?" asked Dora, as she idly wandered from one object to another in the pretty room, pausing beside the desk to glance admiringly at a pile of neatly written sheets, just taken from the machine.

"Oh, I like the work very well. Sometimes the dictator is obtuse, or long-winded, or thinks that the writer ought to do his thinking for him as well as the corrections; then it is not pleasant work. But, generally speaking, I prefer it to most anything that I know of. Do sit down," she continued, pushing a chair toward Dora.

"This man receiveth sinners," read Dora from a pamphlet on the desk, as she turned to accept the offered chair. "I see that is your illuminated text for the day. Are you a Christian?" Then she saw an ivory crucifix sus pended at the left side of the desk, and stopped in some confusion.

Sappho dropped the dress she was mending, and for a moment her eyes took on the far-away look of one in deep thought. Finally she said: "I saw you glance at the crucifix. I am not a Catholic, but I have received many benefits and kindnesses at their hands. Your question is a hard one to answer. I am afraid I am not a Christian, as we of our race understand the expression; but I try to do the best I can."

> 'And he who does the best he can
> Need never fear the church's ban
> Nor hell's damnation.
> God recks not how man counts his beads,
> For righteousness is not in creeds

> *Nor solemn faces;*
> *But rather lies in Christian deed*
> *And Christian graces';*

quoted Dora softly. "For my part, I am sick of loud professions and constant hypocrisy. My religion is short, and to the point—feed the starving thief and make him an honest man; cover your friend's faults with the mantle of charity and keep her in the path of virtue."

"Then you are not one of those who think that a woman should be condemned to eternal banishment for the sake of one misstep?"

"Not I, indeed; I have always felt a great curiosity to know the reason why each individual woman loses character and standing in the eyes of the world. I believe that we would hang our heads in shame at having the temerity to judge a fallen sister, could we but know the circumstances attending many such cases. And, after all we may do or say," continued the girl softly, "the best of us, who have lived the purest lives on earth that mortal can conceive, find at last that our only hope lies in the words of that text—'This man receiveth sinners.'"

"You are a dear little preacher," said Sappho gently, as she looked at Dora from two wet eyes; "and if our race ever amounts to anything in this world, it will be because such women as you are raised up to save us."

Dora laughed and said, as she rose from her seat: "I think I am forgetting my errand." And making an elaborate bow, she continued: "If it please your royal highness, I present to you the compliments of the occupants of No. 500 D Street, with the request that you will honor us on Sunday evening, at half after seven, in the parlor of the worthy landlady of said house, where an informal reception will be held to further the better acquaintance of Miss Sappho Clark with her fellow-occupants of said house. Music during the evening. Refreshments at nine sharp; after which, you are all expected to retire to your rooms like virtuous citizens."

"I herewith most gratefully accept your kind invitation," replied Sappho, with a deep courtesy.

"Ta, ta, then, until Sunday night. I sha'n't see you before that. I shall be lost for the remainder of the week 'getting ready for comypany'"; and Dora, with a gay laugh, ran lightly down the stairs.

Mrs. Smith, after many trials, found that her house contained respectable though unlettered people, who possessed kindly hearts and honesty of purpose in a greater degree than one generally finds in a lodging-house. Her great desire, then, was to make them as happy together as possible, and to this end she had Dora institute musical evenings or reception nights, that her tenants might have a better opportunity of becoming acquainted with each other. She argued, logically enough, that those who were inclined to stray from right paths would be influenced either in favor of upright conduct or else shamed into an acceptance of the right. It soon became noised about that very pleasant times were enjoyed in that house; and that a sick lodger had been nursed back to health, instead of being hustled into the hospital ambulance at the first sign of sickness. It was also whispered that to enjoy these privileges one must be "pretty nice," or as some expressed it: "You've got to be high-toned to get in there." The result, however, justified Mrs. Smith's judgment, and rooms were always hard to get at No. 500 D Street.

Saturday was a busy day for Dora and her mother. At these little gatherings Mrs. Smith always gave her guests plenty of good homemade cake, sandwiches, hot chocolate, and on very special occasions, ice cream or sherbet. Sunday night there was to be ice cream in honor of the new lodger. "Good things to eat," said Ma Smith, as she industriously beat eggs, sugar and butter together in a large yellow bowl, "good things to eat make a man respect himself and look up in the world. You can't feel that you are nobody all the time if once in a while you eat the same quality of food that a millionaire does."

Dora lighted the lamps all over the house on Sunday night as soon as it fell dark. In the parlor there was a handsome piano lamp, which was only used on special occasions; it was lighted, and threw a soft, warm glow over the neat woolen carpet, the modest furniture and few ornaments. In a corner stood Dora's piano, given her on her sixteenth birthday by her brother. Very soon after seven o'clock the guests began to drop in; and as Dora and her mother were busy still over a few last preparations, Will and John volunteered to act as the reception committee.

The first comers were the two occupants of the basement rooms,— those which would have answered for the dining-room and kitchen of a moderately well-to-do family living in this class of house. Mrs. Ophelia Davis and Mrs. Sarah Ann White were friends of long standing. They were both born in far-away Louisiana, had been raised on neighboring plantations, and together had sought the blessings of liberty in the North at the close of the war. Mrs. Davis had always been a first-class cook, while Mrs. White tempted fortune as a second-girl. As their ideas of life and living enlarged, and they saw the possibilities of enjoying some comfort in a home, they began to think of establishing themselves where they could realize this blessing, and finally hit upon the idea of going into partnership in a laundry. After looking about them for a suitable situation for such a project, their choice finally fell upon Mrs. Smith's house, because of her known respectability, and because they could there come in contact with brighter intellects than their own; for, strange to say, it is a very hopeless case when a colored man or woman does not respect intelligence and good position.

"Yas, Sis'r Smith," said Mrs. Ophelia Davis the day she and Sarah Ann White went to engage the rooms; "yas'm, I'm tired o'livin' in white folkses' kitchens. Yas'm, thar's lots o' talk 'bout servant gals not bein' as good as enybody else, specially cooks. Yas'm, I kin git my five dollars a week with enyone; but ef you puts on a decent dress to go to church with a Sunday afternoon, the mistis is a wonderin' how you kin 'ford sech style and you nuthin' but a cook in her kitchen. Yas'm, I've got a silk dress, two of 'em, an'a lace shawl an' a gold watch and chain. People wants ter know how'd I git 'em. I come by 'em hones', I did. Yas'm, when my ol' mistis left her great big house an' all that good stuff—silver an' things-a-layin' thar fer enyone to pick up thet had sense 'nough to know a good thing an'git it ahead of enybody else, I jes' said to myself: "'Phelia, chile, now's yer time!' Yas'm, I feathered my nes', I jes' did. Sarah Ann, you 'member that time, honey, an' how skeered we was fer fear some o' them Union sojers would ketch us. You stuffed yerself with greenbacks, but, honey, I took clo's, too."

"Bless Gawd, Sis'r 'Phelia," replied her friend, with a chuckle and a great shaking of her fat sides; "bless Gawd, I disremember how much I did took in that ar pile; but Lord love yer, honey, I'se got some o' that money yet."

The two women engaged the rooms and prospered in their enterprise. The clothes under their deft fingers seemed to gain an added prettiness. They became the style; and no young bride on the Back Bay felt that she was complete unless "The First-class New Orleans Laundry" placed the finishing polish on the dainty lingerie of her wedding finery.

Tonight Mrs. Davis wore the famous black silk dress and gold watch and chain of ante bellum days, and Mrs. White was gay in, a bright blue silk skirt and rose-colored silk shirtwaist. She said that she did not believe in any of your gloomy colors; for her part, she'd be dead soon enough and have a long time enough to stay "moulderin' inter clay, without buryin' herself befo' it was time." The next arrival was the young student preacher from the "first square-back." He was due at a prayer meeting; but when the time came for him to go there, he peeped over the banister and caught sight of Dora flitting back and forth in the entries, and then a whiff of Ma Smith's famous white cake was borne temptingly to his nostrils and banished the last scruple. He satisfied his conscience by hugging to his breast the idea that his presence was necessary to give the festivities the religious air which was needed for Sunday evening. In his Prince Albert coat and high white stock and tie he entered the parlor early, so that proper decorum might be maintained. Two dressmakers from the "second-front and back" now appeared and were made very welcome by the family; and then Sappho entered.

Her dress was plain black, with white chiffon at the neck and wrists, and on her breast a large bunch of "Jack" roses was fastened. With modest self-possession she moved to Mrs. Smith's side, and soon found herself being presented to the occupants of the parlor. For a moment or two there was an unbroken hush in the room. Tall and fair, with hair of a golden cast, aquiline nose, rosebud mouth, soft brown eyes veiled by long, dark lashes which swept her cheek, just now covered with a delicate rose flush, she burst upon them—a combination of "queen rose and lily in one."

"Lord," said Ophelia Davis to her friend Sarah Ann, "I haven't see enything look like thet chile since I lef' home."

"That's the truth, 'Phelia," replied Sarah Ann; "that's somethin' God made, honey; thar ain't nothin' like thet growed outside o' Loosyannie."

"Miss Clark," said Mrs. Davis, during a lull in the conversation, "I presume you're from Loosyannie?"

"My mother was born in New Orleans," replied the girl.

"I knowed it," cried Mrs. White, as she triumphantly glanced around the room. "Ol' New Orleans blood will tell on itself any. where. These col-blooded Yankees can't raise nuthin' that looks like thet chile; no, 'ndeed!"

Two or three of the young friends of the family who lived in the neighborhood had now arrived, and the conversation became very animated. Then it was announced that a literary and musical programme had been provided. Dora played an opening piece, which was a medley of Moody and Sankey hymns; Will sang "Palm Branches" in a musical baritone voice; John contributed a poem, and two young friends gave the duet from "Il Trovatore." After a little persuasion Sappho rendered the "Chariot Race" from "Ben Hur" in true dramatic style, and breathing so much of the stage that the Rev. Tommy James, the young theologian, felt that possibly he might have made a mistake in going into such hilarious company on the Sabbath.

"Now," said Mrs. Ophelia Davis, "I'm goin' to sing 'Suwanee River.' None o' yer high falutin' things can tech that song." Dora accompanied her, and soon the air was filled with Mrs. Davis' ambitious attempts to imitate an operatic artist singing that good oldtime song. With much wheezing and puffing—for the singer was neither slender nor young—and many would-be fascinating jumps and groans, presumed to be trills and runs, she finished, to the relief of the company. Her friend, Mrs. White, looked at her with great approval, and immediately informed them that 'Phelia made a great impression the Sunday before at Tremont Temple.

"The whole congregation was to sing 'Where's My Wandering Boy.'—'Phelia had no paper to see the words,—not as thet made eny matter, 'cause 'Phelia can't read nohow,—an' the gentleman next us on the other side, he gave 'Phelia a paper thet *he* had. The man wanted ter be perlite. Well, 'Phelia was thet flattered thet she jes' let herself go, an' thet man never sung another note, he was so '*sprised*. After the second verse 'Phelia saw the distraction she was makin', an' she says to me, says she: 'How's thet, Sarah *Ann*?' an' I says to her: '*That's out o' sight, Phelia*!' "You jes' ought ter seen them white folks look! they was paralyzed! Why, you could hear 'Phelia *clean* above the orgin!"

Meantime the young people in the room had gathered in a little knot, and were discussing many questions of the day and their effect upon the colored people. During a pause in the music the last remark made by John Langley was distinctly heard: "Yes, I must admit that our people are improving in their dress, in their looks and in their manners."

"What's that, John Langley?" asked Mrs. Davis, as she leaned forward to catch the words of the speaker; "colored people improvin' in ther manners? I should think they was! Don't yer fool yerself 'bout thet, now, will yer? The other night Sarah Ann and me was goin' down to Beacon Street to 'liver some goods, an' the car was crowded with people, an' thar was a pile o' young colored folks on it from the West End. Some o' them was a-standin' up in thet car, an' every onct in a while I noticed thet a passenger'd squirm as ef suthin' had hit him. Finally I got so mad

I jes' couldn't see along with sech antics from them critters a-disgracin' theirselves and the whole o' the res' o the colored population, an' I jes' elbowed myself into thet crowd o'young jades—what's thet (as Will murmured something under his breath), was they gals? yas, they was; young *jades,* every one o' them! Now what do yer think they was a-doin'?" she asked, as she swept her gaze over the company.

"Not being a mind-reader, I wouldn't dare to say," replied John Langley, with a grin of delight.

"*They was a–trampin' onto the feet of every white man an' woman in thet car to show the white folks how free they was*! I jes' took my ambriller an' knocked it into two or three o them thet I knowed, an' tol' 'em I'd tell ther mothers. Improvin' in the manners! should think they was!"

At this moment refreshments were served, and the attention of the company was turned to the wants of the inner man.

Dora had placed a pretty little tea table at one side of the room, and Sappho had promised to pour the tea and chocolate. At a sign from Mrs. Smith she took her place, and soon the steaming beverage was cheering the hearts of the guests. The young men vied with each other in serving her. The tea table became the center of attraction, in fact, for the whole room. Even the divinity student was drawn into the magic circle, and divided his attention between Sappho and Mrs. Ophelia Davis, for whom he seemed to have a very tender regard.

The girl was naturally buoyant and bright, and the influence of the pleasant company in which she found herself seemed to inspire her, and yet no man would have overstepped the bounds of propriety with her in his manner. The pleasant word and jest were free from all coquetry: John was dumb before so much beauty and wit. Will was so blinded by her charms that he was scarcely conscious of what he was doing; but not a word or movement of hers was lost to him.

Dora watched the tea table smilingly. She loved to see her friends enjoy themselves. It never occurred to her to be jealous of the attention given Sappho by her brother and John Langley.

Presently there were many pleasant compliments passed on the enjoyable evening which had so quickly flown, and each gentleman proposed a toast, which was drunk in a cup of hot chocolate; and as the clock struck ten, they all joined hands and united in singing "Auld Lang Syne" and "Praise God, from whom All Blessings Flow." The evening was over; the lights were out; but up in John's attic chamber the two young men smoked a social cigar before separating for the night.

PAULINE E. HOPKINS

They were silent for some time, and then Will said: "Miss Clark is a very beautiful woman; don't you think so, John?"

"Well," replied John, "beauty is not the word to describe her. She's a stunner, and no mistake,"

John went to bed; but Will sat by the fire a longer time than usual, thinking thoughts which had never before troubled his young manhood; and, unconsciously, one face—the face of Sappho Clark—formed the background of his thoughts.

VII

Friendship

What is so great as friendship? The only reward of virtue is virtue:
the only way to have a friend is to be one.

—Emerson

After that evening the two girls were much together. Sappho's beauty appealed strongly to Dora's artistic nature; but hidden beneath the classic outlines of the face, the graceful symmetry of the form, and the dainty coloring of the skin, Dora's shrewd common sense and womanly intuition discovered a character of sterling worth—bold, strong and ennobling; while into Sappho's lonely self-suppressed life the energetic little Yankee girl swept like a healthful, strengthening breeze. Care was forgotten; there was new joy in living. It was the Southern girl's first experience of Northern life. True, the seductive skies of her nativity had a potent hold upon her affections, but truth demanded her to recognize the superiority of the vigorous activity in the life all about her. The Negro, while held in contempt by many, yet reflected the spirit of his surroundings in his upright carriage, his fearlessness in advancing his opinions, his self-reliance, his anxiety to obtain paying employment that would give to his family some few of the advantages enjoyed by the more favored classes of citizens, his love of liberty, which in its intensity recalled the memory of New England men who had counted all worldly gain as nothing if demanding the sacrifice of even one of the great principles of freedom. It was a new view of the possibilities and probabilities which the future might open to her people. Long she struggled with thoughts which represented to her but vaguely a life beyond anything of which she had ever dreamed.

Sappho generally carried her work home in the morning, but ten o'clock would find her seated at her desk and ready to begin her task anew. Some days she was unoccupied; but this did not happen very frequently. These free days were the gala days of her existence, when under Dora's guidance she explored various points of interest, and learned from observation the great plan of life as practiced in an intelligent, liberty-loving community. Here in the free air of New England's freest city, Sappho drank great draughts of freedom's subtle elixir. Dora was interested and amused in watching the changes on the mirror-like face of her friend whenever her attention was arrested by a new phenomenon. It was strange to see this girl, resembling nothing so much as a lily in its beautiful purity, shrink from entering a place of public resort for fear of insult. It was difficult to convince her that she might enter a restaurant frequented by educated whites and meet with nothing but the greatest courtesy; that she might take part in the glorious service at fashionable Trinity and be received with punctilious politeness. To this woman, denied association with the vast sources of information, which are heirlooms to the lowliest inhabitant of Boston, the noble piles, which represented the halls of learning, and the massive grandeur of the library, free to all, seemed to invite her to a full participation in their intellectual joys. She had seen nothing like them. Statuary, paintings, sculptures,—all appealed to her beauty-loving nature. The hidden springs of spirituality were satisfied and at rest, claiming kinship with the great minds of the past, whose never-dying works breathed perennial life in the atmosphere of the quiet halls.

Now was the beginning of the storm season in New England, and on stormy days the two girls would sit before the fire in Sappho's room and talk of the many things dear to women, while they embroidered or stitched. So they sat one cold, snowy day. The storm had started the afternoon before and had raged with unceasing fury all night,—snow and rain which the increasing cold quickly turned into cutting sleet. Morning had brought relief from the high winds, and the temperature had moderated somewhat; but the snow still fell steadily, drifting into huge piles, which made the streets impassable. It was the first great storm Sappho had seen. It was impossible for her to leave home, so she begged Dora to pass the day with her and play "company," like the children. Dora was nothing loathe; and as soon as her morning duties were finished, she told her mother that she was going visiting and would not be at home until tea time. By eleven o'clock they had locked the door of Sappho's room to keep out all intruders, had mended the fire until the little stove gave out a delicious warmth, and had drawn the window curtains close to keep out stray currents of air. Sappho's couch was drawn close beside the stove, while Dora's small person was most cosily bestowed in her favorite rocking-chair.

It was a very convenient stove that Sappho had in her room. The ornamental top could be turned back on its movable hinge, and there was a flat stove cover ready to hold any vessel and heat its contents to just the right temperature. Sappho was prouder of that stove than a daughter of Fortune would have been of the most expensive silver chafing-dish. very near lunch time, so the top was turned back, and the little copper teakettle was beginning to sing its welcome song. Dora had placed a small, round table between the couch and the rocker. A service for two was set out in dainty china dishes, cream and sugar looking doubly tempting as it gleamed and glistened in the delicate ware. One plate was piled with thinly cut slices of bread and butter, another held slices of pink ham.

Sappho lay back among her cushions, lazily stretching her little slippered feet toward the warm stove, where the fire burned so cheerily and glowed so invitingly as it shone through the isinglass door. She folded her arms above her head and turned an admiring gaze on the brown face of her friend, who swayed gently back and forth in her rocking-chair, her feet on a hassock, and a scarlet afghan wrapped about her knees. Dora was telling Sappho all about her engagement to John Langley and their plans for the future.

"I think you will be happy, Dora, if you love him. All things are possible if love is the foundation stone," said Sappho, after a slight pause, as she nestled among her pillows. Dora was sitting bolt upright with the usual business-like look upon her face.

"I like him well enough to marry him, but I don't believe there's enough sentiment in me to make love a great passion, such as we read of in books. Do you believe marriage is the beautiful state it is painted by writers?"

"Why, yes," laughed Sappho; "I wouldn't believe anything else for your sake, my little brownie."

"No joking, Sappho; this is dead earnest. Don't you ever expect to marry, and don't you speculate about the pros and cons and the maybes and perhaps of the situation?" asked Dora, as she filled the cups with steaming cocoa and passed one to her friend.

"Dora, you little gourmand, what have you got in the refrigerator?" A box ingeniously nailed to the window seat outside, and filled with shelves, and having a substantial door, was the ice-box, or refrigerator, where Sappho kept materials handy for a quick lunch. Dora closed the window and returned quickly to her seat, placing a glass dish on the table as she did so. "It's only part of a cream pie that ma had left last night. I thought it would help out nicely with our lunch."

"What, again!" said Sappho significantly. That's the fourth time this week, and here it is but Friday. You'll be as fat as a seal, and then John P. won't want you at any price. Take warning, and depart from the error of your ways before it is too late."

Dora laughed guiltily and said, as she drew a box from her apron pocket: "Well, here are John's chocolate bonbons that he brought last night. I suppose you won't want me to touch *them*, for fear of getting fat."

Sappho shook her head in mock despair.

"And your teeth, your beautiful white teeth, where will they be shortly if you persist in eating a pound of bonbons every day? Think of your fate, Dora, and pause in your reckless career forty inches about the waist and only scraggy snags to show me when you grin!"

"Thank heaven I'll never come to that while there's a dentist in the city of Boston! I'll eat all the bonbons I want in spite of you, Sappho, and if you don't hurry I'll eat your slice of cream pie, too." At this dire threat there ensued a scramble for the pie, mingled with peals of merry laughter, until all rosy and sparkling, Sappho emerged from the fray with the dish containing her share of the dainty held high in the air.

Presently lunch was over, and they resumed their old positions, prepared to "take comfort."

"You haven't answered my question yet, Sappho."

"To tell you the truth, I had forgotten your remark, Dora; what was it?"

"I suspect that is a bit of a fib to keep me from teasing you about getting married. What I want to know is: Do you ever mean to marry, or are you going to pine in single blessedness on my hands and be a bachelor-maid to the end?"

"Well," replied Sappho, with a comical twist to her face, "in the words of Unc' Gulliver, 'I mote, an' then agin I moten't.'"

"What troubles me is having a man bothering around. Now I tell John P. that I'm busy, or something like that, and I'm rid of him; but after you marry a man, he's on your hands for good and all. I'm wondering if my love could stand the test."

"That's queer talk for an engaged girl, with a fine, handsome fellow to court her. Why, Dora, 'I'm s'prised at yer!'" laughed Sappho gaily.

"I'm not ashamed of John P.'s appearance in company; he looks all right; but when one is terribly in love one is supposed to want the dear object always near; but matches,—love matches,—my child, turn out so badly that a girl hesitates to 'git jined to eny man fer betterer or worserer,' as Dr. Peters says. Then I get tired of a man so soon! (This with a doleful sigh.) I dread to think of being tied to John for good and all; I know I'll be sick of him inside of a week. I do despair of ever being like other girls."

Sappho laughed outright at the woe-begone countenance before her.

"It is generally the other way: the men get tired of us first. A woman loves one man, and is true to him through all eternity."

"That's just what makes me feel so *unsexed,* so to speak; I like John's looks. He's the style among all the girls in our set. I like to know that I can claim him before them all. It's fun to see 'em fluttering around him, kindly trying 10 put my nose out of joint. I must say that I feel real *comfortable* to spoil sport by walking off with him just when they think they've got things running as they wish. Yes, it's real *comfortable* to know that they're all as jealous as can be. But for all that, I know I'll get tired of him."

"Let us hope not, if you have really made up your mind to marry him. Dora, sometimes I am afraid that you mean what you say. I notice that you call him "John P.: What's the P for?"

"Pollock—John Pollock Langley. His grandfather was his father's master, and Pollock was his name," sang Dora, as she rocked gently to and fro. "Now, there's Arthur Lewis," she continued; "he's jolly fun. He isn't a fascinator, or anything of that sort; he's just good."

"Who is he?" asked Sappho, with languid interest.

"Properly speaking, he's Dr. Arthur Lewis. We were children together, although he is five years older than I. He's a fine scholar and a great business man. He has a large industrial school in Louisiana. He's gone up in the world, I tell you, since we made mud pies on the back doorsteps; but I never think of him except as old Arthur, who used to drag me to school on his sled."

There was a gleam of fun in Sappho's eyes, as she said demurely: "You seem to know all about him. Was he ever a lover of yours?"

"Lover! no, indeed!" Dora flushed vividly under her brown skin. "The idea of Arthur as my lover is too absurd."

"Excuse me, dear, for my mistake," said Sappho mischievously. "I didn't know but that he might be the mysterious link which would join love, marriage and the necessary man in a harmonious whole."

"Well," said Dora, after a slight pause, blushing furiously, "I don't say he wouldn't like the rôle. You'll see him soon; he's coming to Boston on business in a few weeks. Oh, we've had rare times together." She sighed and smiled, lost for the moment in pleasant memories. Sappho smiled, too, in sympathy with her mood.

"Ah, yes; I think I understand. Poor John!"

"John's all right. Don't shed any tears over him," said Dora testily. They sat awhile in silence, listening to the sound of the whirling frozen flakes wind-driven against the window panes. It was scarce three o'clock, but darkness was beginning to envelop the city, and it was already a pleasant twilight in the room.

"Tell me about Dr. Lewis and his work, Dora," said Sappho presently. "Do you know, he interests me exceedingly."

"I don't really understand Arthur's hobbies, but I believe that he is supposed to be doing a great work in the Black Belt. His argument is, as I understand it, that industrial education and the exclusion of politics will cure all our race troubles."

"I doubt it," returned Sappho quickly, with an impatient toss of the head. "That reasoning might be practically illustrated with benefit to us for a few years in the South, but to my mind would not effect a permanent cure for race troubles if we are willing to admit that human nature is the same in us as in others. The time will come when our men will grow away from the trammels of narrow prejudice, and desire the same treatment that is accorded to other men. Why, one can but see that any degree of education and development will not fail of such a result."

"I am willing to confess that the subject is a little deep for me," replied Dora. "I'm not the least bit of a politician, and I generally accept whatever the men tell me as right; but I know that there is something very wrong in our lives, and nothing seems to remedy the evils under which the colored man labors."

"But you can see, can't you, that if our men are deprived of the franchise, we become aliens in the very land of our birth?"

"Arthur says that would be better for us; the great loss of life would cease, and we should be at peace with the whites."

"Ah, how can he argue so falsely! I have lived beneath the system of oppression in the South. If we lose the franchise, at the same time we shall lose the respect of all other citizens. Temporizing will not benefit us; rather, it will leave us branded as cowards, not worthy a freeman's respect—an alien people, 'without a country and without a home.'"

Dora gazed at her friend with admiration, and wished that she had a kodak, so that she might catch just the expression that lighted her eyes and glowed in a bright color upon her cheeks.

"I predict some fun when you and Arthur meet. I'll just start you both out some night, and you'll be spitting at each other like two cats inside of five minutes. Arthur thinks that women should be seen and not heard, whère politics is under discussion."

"Insufferable prig!" exclaimed Sappho, with snapping eyes.

"Oh, no, he isn't; Arthur's all right. But you see he is living South; his work is there, and he must keep in with the whites of the section where his work lies, or all he has accomplished will go for naught, and perhaps his life might be forfeited, too."

"I see. The mess of pottage and the birthright."

"Bless you! not so bad as that; but money makes the mare go," returned Dora, with a wink at her friend, and a shrewd business look on her bright little Yankee face. "I say to you, as Arthur says to me when I tell him what I think of his system: 'If you want honey, you must have money.' I don't know anything about politics, as I said before, but my opinion won't cost you anything: when we can say that lots of our men are as rich as Jews, there'll be no question about the franchise, and my idea is that Arthur'll be one of the Jews."

"Oh!" exclaimed Sappho disgustedly, as she resumed her lounging position.

"Sappho, how did you come to take up stenography? I should have thought you would have preferred teaching."

"I had to live, my dear; I could not teach school, because my education does not include a college course. I could not do housework, because my constitution is naturally weak."

It was noticeable in these confidential chats that Sappho never spoke of her early life. Dora had confided to her friend every event of importance that had occurred in her young life; and, in harmless gossip, had related the history of all the friends who visited the house intimately; but all this had begot no like unburdening to eager ears of the early history of her friend. Wonderful to relate, however, Dora did not resent this reserve, which she could see was studied. It spoke well for the sincerity of the love that had taken root in her heart for Sappho, that it subdued her inquisitiveness, and she gladly accepted her friendship without asking troublesome questions.

"How did you finally succeed in getting work? I have always heard that it was very difficult for colored girls to find employment in offices where your class of work is required."

"And so it is, my dear. I sometimes think that if I lose the work I am on, I shall not try for another position. I shall never forget the day I started out to find work: the first place that I visited was all right until the man found I was colored; then he said that his wife wanted a nurse girl, and he had no doubt she would be glad to hire me, for I looked good-tempered. At the second place where I ventured to intrude the proprietor said: 'Yes; we want a stenographer, but we've no work for your kind.' However, that was preferable to the insulting familiarity which some men assumed. It was dreadful! I don't like to think about it. Father Andrew induced the man for whom I am working to employ me. I do not interfere with the other help, because I take my work home; many of the other clerks have never seen me, and so the proprietor runs no risk of being bothered with complaints from them. He treats me very well, too."

"I have heard many girls tell much the same tale about other lines of business," said Dora. "It makes me content to do the work of this house, and not complain."

"You ought to thank God every day for such a refuge as you have in your home."

"I cannot understand people. Here in the North we are allowed every privilege. There seems to be no prejudice until we seek-employment; then every door is closed against us. Can you explain this?"

"No, I cannot; to my way of thinking the whole thing is a Chinese puzzle."

"Bless my soul! Just look at that clock!" exclaimed Dora, as she scrambled to her feet and began gathering up her scattered property. "Five o'clock, and tea to get. Sappho, you've been lazy enough for one day. Come down stairs and help me get tea. The boys will be here in no time, as hungry as bears."

Piloted by Dora, Sappho became well acquainted with ancient landmarks of peculiar interest to the colored people. They visited the home for aged women on M Street, and read and sang to the occupants. They visited St. Monica's Hospital, and carried clothes, flowers, and a little money saved from the cost of contemplated Easter finery. They scattered brightness along with charitable acts wherever a case of want was brought to their attention.

Dora had accepted the position of organist for a prominent colored church in the city. There was a small salary attached to the place, which she was glad to receive. Sappho usually went with her to choir rehearsals, and sitting in the shadows, well hidden from view, would think over the romantic history of the fine old edifice. The building, so the story ran, was the place of worship of a rich, white Baptist congregation in the years preceding the emancipation. Negroes were allowed in the galleries only. Believing this color-bar to be a stigma on the house of God, a few of the members protested, but finding their warnings unheeded, withdrew from the church, and finally found a Sabbath home in an old building long used as a theatre. These people prospered, and grew rich and powerful; colored people were always welcome in the congregation. The society in the old church, left to itself, had at last been glad to sell the building to its present occupants. Thus the despised people, who were not allowed a seat outside of the galleries, now owned and occupied the scene of their former humiliation. It was a solemn and wonderful dispensation of Providence, and filled the girl's heart with strong emotion.

During these evenings, when she waited for the close of the rehearsals, she became acquainted with many odd specimens of the race: men of brain and thought, but of unique expression and filled with quaint humor. One of these characters was known as Dr. Abraham Peters, Doctor Peters was a well-read man, greatly interested in scientific research, but who had lacked the opportunity to obtain information in his youth. He had been a slave when a boy, a few years before the Civil War. Now he was the church janitor, and to eke out his scanty income kept a little bootblack stand just around the corner from the church, and knowing something of medicine and nursing the sick, had advertised himself as a magnetic physician. He displayed much skill in practice, and had acquired something of a local reputation. Doctor Peters and Sappho were good friends, and he brought out all his store of knowledge, proudly displaying it for her approval.

"You see, Miss Sappho, I've knocked 'bout the worl' some consid'ble," he said one night, in his soft Southern tones and quaint Northernized dialect, as they sat in the cosy vestry waiting for the close of the rehearsal. "Ben po'rer than eny chuch mouse. But I've saved somethin', an' I know the worl'. Perhaps you's int'rest'd 'nuff in an ole man to want to hear how I come to 'vertis myself as a magnifyin' doctor, an' where I picked it up, eh?"

"Yes," replied Sappho, "I certainly am interested in your story."

"Well, while they're caterwaulin' on that Easter anthem in ten flats, I reckon I'll have time to tell you all 'bout it. Fust I knowed 'bout magnetics was brought to my 'tention down home. Some people said I had the evil eye, an' some said it was only a *strong* eye, but be that homsomever, it was a bad eye, an' a terror ter watermilyun thieves when it was my watch on the chickun houses. *Magnifyin'* an' *hoodooin'* is 'bout the same thing down thar, tho' sense the 'srender mos' all ol'-time doin's is done 'way. 'Bout the time I realized that I had this power I had 'sperinced ruligeon, an' had been jestified an' concentrated, so that I got the blessin'. Them days, too, I was a-sottin' out to court my Susie (that's my wife), an' all the young fellers 'roun' the county was a-sprucin' up to her jes' like crows 'roun' carr'on. Sunday was the day I had mos' on my mind, 'cause they'd ride up an' hitch thar mules in a line all along the ole man's fence (you see he had right smart prop'ty, an' I spec' that had a mighty drawin' infloonce on some of them shif'less fellers who hadn't nuff skonsh to start thar own mule team up a hill), an' thar they'd sot like so many buzzards, waitin' fer a chance to sly Susie off to chuch under my nose. I had ter wurk lively, I tell you; Susie was kin' o' skittish an' res'less, an' it was fus' come, fus' sarved, with her, bein' she had her choice. Well, jes' at the time I got the blessin' I got the insurance that Susie was gwine ter have me. All the fellers was satisfied but Possum Tooit. Possum an' me was boys together, an' we'd both run each other purty hard strivin' to come through fust at the mourner's bench as well as to git the gal. Possum was beat when he found I had a full hand and had swept the pot."

"Oomhoo!" laughed Brother Jones, who was an interested listener to Doctor Peters' story. "Oomhoo, Brother Peters; done guv yerself 'way. What you know 'bout 'full hands an' pots?'"

"Who give himself 'way, Brother Jones? Ever hear me say Ise better'n enybody else in this chuch? I'm er man, sah, I'm er man! Ise done truspassed on the flesh-pots of Egypt as much as eny other man. Don't yer 'oomhoo' me, Brother Jones, no sah!"

"Tech a sore place, Brother Peters, tech a sore place," laughed the brother as he walked away, his shoulders shaking like great mounds of jelly. It was some minutes before Doctor Peters could recover his equilibrium and go on with his tale.

"Possum Tooit was so mad an' disapinted that he finally challenged me to fight a jewel. I wasn't in no state of mind to be killed by any of his hoodoo tricks, Possum bein' an export at puttin' spells an' sech like on enybody fer from twenty-five cents up to five dollars; neither did I want Susie to think I was 'fraid of Possum Tooit. So thar I was 'tween a hawk an'a buzzard. Well, I accepted the challenge, an' bein' the defendant in the matter, of course, I had the choice of weapons, an' I choose rifles. We kep' mighty secret 'bout the 'rangements, an' met at moonrise on a field jes' back of the graveyard. The seconds measured off ten spaces after we'd shooken hands, an' we each stepped to our places. Tho' it was a solemn 'casion, I wasn't skeered, but Possum was a rollin' up the whites of his eyes, an' you could hear his teeth chatter worse than dried corn shuks. Ike Watkins was head second, an' he stood 'tween us, holdin' his red bandanna in his han' waitin' to say the word. 'Gemplemen, is you ready?' he says. "Let her go, Ike,' says I. * Take aim,' says he, an' I pinted the rifle at Possum, an' callin' up all the power in me I threw it along the body of the gun plumb 'tween Possum's eyes jes' above the bridge of his nose. An' that was a fair target, 'cause the bridge of Possum's nose was a miracle fer size. Possum gave a yell when he felt the strength of that eye, that would a split yer year-pan in two. An' in two seconds he was in the worst alpaca fit you ever seen. The seconds acknowlcdged me the victor by a reckless invention of Providence, they bein' aware that the adversary wasn't hit by nary bullet, the rities bein' loaded with salt fer fear of mischief. Possuim owned up like a man that I was more powerful than him, because of the sufernatral strength in my bad eye."

"Well, I kep'on prayin' fer mo' faith until I got the power in my hands, an' by lavin'em on a sick pusson I could 'lectrocute 'em instantly; an'thar bad feelin's would disappear. People got the notion I could pray a pusson right out the grave, an' my fame spread abroad until I began charging fer my services, explainin' to my patients that the dead might be raised, but not fer nuthin', after which I seed a fallin' off in my poperlarity. Business bein' purty brief jes' then, I took Susie an' moved up Norf, an' went ter cookin' on a steamboat. I've done mos' everythin' in this worl', honey, as I tol' you, to git an hones' livin' without stealin' it. An' I dunno," added the old man reflectively, as he stroked the gray, stubby fringe on his chin, "I dunno as I'm eny too good of I got pushed real hard to help myself out; humans is humans, an' I've seen many a well-'tentioned feller settin' in the caboose when times was hard, an' the mule mortgaged for full value to three men at once to buy meal an' bread, an' hog an' hominy, an' terbaccer. But mos' in ginerally, I've got along without silin' my hands with other people's prop'ty. Well, honey, they gave me fifteen dollars a munf an' found, fer bein' head cook, an' I paid ten dollars a munf house rent out of that. Things was purty brief, purty brief. Times was more an' more spurious, an' it was work yer wits, Abraham Peters, to git a livin'. I jes' didn't know whicher way to turn."

"One day I got a telegraph at the other end of the route that the baby was dead an' no money to pay the undertaker, an' the ole 'ooman sick in the bed from worryin'. The Lord jes' seemed to pour his blessin' down on us in a house full o' chillun. After Susie'd had twenty I used to pray the Lord to stop blessin' us that way, 'cause he could see fer himself that too many blessins was a gittin' to be a nuisance. I cooked the dinner myself that day, bein' the other cook was ashore, an' you believe me, I sung an' I prayed an' I wrastled fer help in that ole steamboat kitchen down behin' my bigges' brass biler where I was kivered from pryin' eyes. All of a suddint I felt the power, an' the Lord spoke to me an' he said: 'Git up, Abraham Peters, an' go out an' hoodoo the fust man you meet.' Bless yo, chile, I riz up in a hurry an' started out, not knowin' no more than nuthin' what was meant by that. Fust man I saw when I got on deck was the cap'n; I went up to him, an' I smiled. I must have been a purty picture with my face all grease an' tears. I says, not thinkin' what wurds I was goin' ter utter: 'Mornin', Cap'n; how's yer corporosity seem to segashiate?' Cap'n he roared; you could a heard him holler up to Boston. He slapped me on the back, an' says he: 'Abe Peters, that's the gol darndest thing I ever heard.' With that he hauled out a five-dollar bill an' gave me, an' walked off laughin' fit to kill hisself. By night I had twenty dollars in my pocket, an' everybody on the boat was a callin' me 'corporosity segashiate.' I've used that hoodoo ever since, an' I ain't found nary white gempleman can seem to git 'way from it without showing the color of his money."

"One of the owners of the boat took a great liking to me, an' he says to me one day, says he: 'Abe, how'd you like to wurk ashore so you could be nearer your family an' git better pay?' 'Like it?' says I. 'If you don't want to pulverize me, don' make me no sech an offer.' He laughed a bit, an' then he says: 'I've got a big buildin' up Washington Street, an' I want a trusty man to keep it clean an' look after the tenants. I'll give you ten dollars a week.'"

"I took off my cap, an' I truly bowed down to that man, an' I says: 'The Lord's been a wurkin' on yer heart, 'Mr. Pierson.' Maybe he has,' says he; 'anyholli you can pack up an' go ashore next trip: pour place'll be waitin' fer yer.' Fust thing I knowed I was a bossin' a big job of janitorin. Mos' of the people in the buildin' was Christian Science. After they'd got a little bit acquainted with me they found out the power I had in my hands fer lavin' on. 'Twant long before I was a pickin'up right smart nussin' nights. Don't suppose you know much 'bout this Science business, do you?" Sappho confessed her ignorance.

"Christian Science is a faith-cure; that is, it's usin' yer brains an trainin' 'em to know that there's nuthin' 'tall the matter with you ef you only think there ain't. They argify that all sickness is a mistake, 'cause it's 'maginary: I don't b'lieve that, though, cause I had the rheumatism while I was there, an' the doctors started in to cure me by prayin' an' wurkin' on my body through my spirit, an' it warn't no more good than muthin' 'tall. I've got as much faith as eny livin' man, but rheumatism is one o them things that'll convince you agin' your will; it will draw speech out of a deef mute an make a blind man see, when them pains is a grindin' inter your bones an' jints worse than a saw cuttin' thro' knots in a cord wood stick. I'm free to say that curin' my mind didn't have no effect on my pain, an' I jes' kep' on seein' blue blazes an' swearin' like mad. I'll 'low that faith can move mountains, faith, as *lectle* as a mustard seed, an' that's mighty small. Ef you b'lieve you'll get what you wants an' asks fer, that's faith. That's good; that's all right. Trouble is we *don't b'lieve it 'cordin' to scripter*. We git mad when our prayers ain't answered, not thinkin' it's 'cause we ain't got horse sense nuff to use *discretion* in puttin' our faith on subjects that is approvin' to the Lord, an' will fit in with his own idees 'bout runnin' the business of the universe. An' that's where faithcure is weak, 'cause it's comin' in 'junction with God. Faith-cure won't operate on any man where it was *pre*ordinated that a *pre*tickler man was to die with a *pre*tickler complaint. No'm, we ain't up to comin' in 'junction with the Lord's business. There's a number of grand diversions to Christian Science. There's hypnism an' pessimism an' a number of other isms, but they all bear the same way—a sort of applostic healin' of sickness. The doctors kept after me 'bout my gifts of healin', an' very kindly showed me wherein I could make an hones' dollar, an' business bein' business I finally determined to adop' magnifyin' as a perfeshun. I've been in the business nigh upon ten years now, an' I've picked up as good a livin' as any colored gempleman who has wurked a sight harder an' had to take piles o' unregenerate sass from his boss."

That night they walked home together after the rehearsal: the four young people—Dora and John, Sappho and Will. Some one of the choir boy's walking ahead of them was singing in a sweet, high tenor voice the refrain of an old love song: "Couldst thou but know how much I love thee." It suited Will's mood, and voiced his dream exquisitely.

Across the heavens the Northern Lights streamed in radiance. Meteors bright and shooting stars added to the beauty of the night. The moon, at its full, shed the light of day about them. The wind whispered amidst the leafless branches of the huge old trees on the Common and Public Garden as they passed them on their homeward way. Once Will took her hand in his; she let it stay a moment while she made an incoherent little speech about clouds and trees. Will said nothing. It was not time yet, he told himself. He would wait a little longer.

VIII

The Sewing-Circle

Where village statesmen talked with looks profound,
Imagination fondly stoops to race
The parlor splendors of that festive place.

Yes! Let the rich deride, the proud disdain,
These simple blessings of the lowly train;
To me more dear,
One native charm than all the gloss of art.

—Goldsmith

Ma Smith was a member of the church referred to in the last chapter, the most prominent one of color in New England. It was situated in the heart of the West End, and was a very valuable piece of property. Every winter this church gave many entertainments to aid in paying off the mortgage, which at this time amounted to about eight thousand dollars. Mrs. Smith, as the chairman of the board of stewardesses, was inaugurating a fair—one that should eclipse anything of a similar nature ever attempted by the colored people, and numerous sewing-circles were being held among the members all over the city. Parlor entertainments where an admission fee of ten cents was collected from every patron, were also greatly in vogue, and the money thus obtained was put into a fund to defray the expense of purchasing eatables and decorations, and paying for the printing of tickets, circulars, etc., for the fair. The strongest forces of the colored people in the vicinity were to combine and lend their aid in making a supreme effort to clear this magnificent property.

Boston contains a number of well-to-do families of color whose tax-bills show a most comfortable return each year to the city treasury. Strange as it may seem, these well-to-do people, in goodly numbers, distribute themselves and their children among the various Episcopal churches with which the city abounds, the government of which holds out the welcome hand to the brother in black, who is drawn to unite his fortunes with the members of this particular denomination. It may be true that the beautiful ritual of the church is responsible in some measure for this. Colored people are nothing if not beauty-lovers, and for such a people the grandeur of the service has great attractions. But in justice to this church one must acknowledge that it has been instrumental in doing much toward helping this race to help itself, along the lines of brotherly interest.

These people were well represented within the precincts of Mrs. Smith's pretty parlor one afternoon, all desirous of lending their aid to help along the great project.

As we have said, Mrs. Smith occupied the back parlor of the house as her chamber, and within this room the matrons had assembled to take charge of the cutting out of different garments; and here, too, the sewing machine was placed ready for use. In the parlor proper all the young ladies were seated ready to perform any service which might be required of them in the way of putting garments together.

By two o'clock all the members of the sewing-circle were in their places. The parlor was crowded. Mrs. Willis, the brilliant widow of a bright Negro politician, had charge of the girls, and after the sewing had been given out the first business of the meeting was to go over events of interest to the Negro race which had transpired during the week throughout the country. These facts had been previously tabulated upon a blackboard which was placed upon an easel, and occupied a conspicuous position in the room. Each one was supposed to contribute anything of interest that she had read or heard in that time for the benefit of all. After these points had been gone over, Mrs. Willis gave a talk upon some topic of interest. At six o'clock tea was to be served in the kitchen, the company taking refreshment in squads of five. At eight o'clock all unfinished work would be folded and packed away in the convenient little Boston bag, to be finished at home, and the male friends of the various ladies were expected to put in an appearance. Music and recitations were to be enjoyed for two hours, ice cream and cake being sold for the benefit of the cause.

Mrs. Willis was a good example of a class of women of color that came into existence at the close of the Civil War. She was not a *rara avis*, but one of many possibilities which the future will develop from among the colored women of New England. Every city, or town from Maine to New York has its Mrs. Willis. Keen in her analysis of human nature, most people realized, after a short acquaintance, in which they ran the gamut of emotions from strong attraction to repulsion, that she had sifted them thoroughly, while they had gained nothing in return. Shrewd in business matters, many a subtle business man had been worsted by her apparent womanly weakness and charming simplicity. With little money, she yet contrived to live in quiet elegance, even-including the little journeys from place to place, so adroitly managed as to increase her influence at home and her fame abroad. Well-read and thoroughly conversant with all current topics, she impressed one as having been liberally educated and polished by travel, whereas a high-school course more than covered all her opportunities.

Even today it is erroneously believed that all racial development among colored people has taken place since emancipation. It is impossible of belief for some, that little circles of educated men and women of color have existed since the Revolutionary War. Some of these people were born free, some have lost the memory of servitude in the dim past; a greater number by far were recruited from the energetic slaves of the South, who toiled when they should have slept, for the money that purchased their freedom, or else they boldly took the rights which man denied. Mrs. Willis was one from among these classes. The history of her descent could not be traced, but somewhere, somehow, a strain of white blood had filtered through the African stream. At sixty odd she was vigorous, well-preserved, broad and comfortable in appearance, with an aureole of white hair crowning a pleasant face.

She had loved her husband with a love ambitious for his advancement. His foot on the stairs mounting to the two-room tenement which constituted their home in the early years of married life, had sent a thrill to her very heart as she sat sewing baby clothes for the always expected addition to the family. But twenty years make a difference in all our lives. It brought many changes to the colored people of New England—social and business changes. Politics had become the open sesame for the ambitious Negro. A seat in the Legislature then was not a dream to this man, urged by the loving woman behind him. Other offices of trust were quickly offered him when his worth became known. He grasped his opportunity; grew richer, more polished, less social, and the family broadened out and overflowed from old familiar "West End" environments across the River Charles into the aristocratic suburbs of Cambridge. Death comes to us all.

Money, the sinews of living and social standing, she did not possess upon her husband's death. Therefore she was forced to begin a weary pilgrimage a hunt for the means to help her breast the social tide. The best opening, she decided after looking carefully about her, was in the great cause of the evolution of true womanhood in the work of the "Woman Question" as embodied in marriage and suffrage. She could talk dashingly on many themes, for which she had received much applause in by-gone days, when in private life she had held forth in the drawing-room of some Back Bay philanthropist who sought to use her talents as an attraction for a worthy charitable object, the discovery of a rare species of versatility in the Negro character being a sure drawing-card. It was her boast that she had made the fortunes of her family and settled her children well in life. The advancement of the colored woman should be the new problem in the woman question that should float her upon its tide into the prosperity she desired. And she succeeded well in her plans: conceived in selfishness, they yet bore glorious fruit in the formation of clubs of colored women banded together for charity, for study, for every reason under God's glorious heavens that can better the condition of mankind.

Trivialities are not to be despised. Inborn love implanted in a woman's heart for a luxurious, esthetic home life, running on well-oiled wheels amid flowers, sunshine, books and priceless pamphlets, easy chairs and French gowns, may be the means of developing a Paderewski or freeing a race from servitude. It was amusing to watch the way in which she governed societies and held her position. In her hands committees were as wax, and loud murmurings against the tyranny of her rule died down to judicious whispers. If a vote went contrary to her desires, it was in her absence. Thus she became the pivot about which all the social and intellectual life of the colored people of her section revolved. No one had yet been found with the temerity to contest her position, which, like a title of nobility, bade fair to descend to her children. It was thought that she might be eclipsed by the younger and more brilliant women students on the strength of their alma mater, but she still held her own by sheer force of will-power and indomitable pluck.

The subject of the talk at this meeting was: "The place which the virtuous woman occupies in upbuilding a race." After a few explanatory remarks, Mrs. Willis said:

"I am particularly anxious that you should think upon this matter seriously, because of its intrinsic value to all of us as race women. I am not less anxious because you represent the coming factors of our race. Shortly, you must fill the positions now occupied by your mothers, and it will rest with you and your children to refute the charges brought against us as to our moral irresponsibility, and the tow moral standard maintained by us in comparison with other races."

"Did I understand you to say that the Negro woman in her native state is truly a virtuous woman?" asked Sappho, who had been very silent during the bustle attending the opening of the meeting.

"Travelers tell us that the native African woman is impregnable in her virtue," replied Mrs. Willis.

"So we have sacrificed that attribute in order to acquire civilization," chimed in Dora.

"No, not 'sacrificed,' but pushed one side by the force of circumstances. Let us thank God that it is an essential attribute peculiar to us a racial characteristic which is slumbering but not lost," replied Mrs. Willis. "But let us not forget the definition of virtue—'Strength to do the right thing under all temptations.' Our ideas of virtue are too narrow. We confine them to that conduct which is ruled by our animal passions alone. It goes deeper than that—general excellence in every duty of life is what we may call virtue."

"Do you think, then, that Negro women will be held responsible for all the lack of virtue that is being laid to their charge today? I mean, do you think that God will hold us responsible for the *illegitimacy* with which our race has been obliged, as it were, to flood the world?" asked Sappho.

"I believe that we shall not be held responsible for wrongs which we have—*unconsciously* committed, or which we have committed under *compulsion*. We are virtuous or non-virtuous only when we have a *choice* under temptation. We cannot by any means apply the word to a little child who has never been exposed to temptation, nor to the Supreme Being 'who cannot be tempted with evil.' So with the African brought to these shores against his will—the state of morality which implies willpower on his part does not exist, therefore he is not a responsible being. The sin and its punishment lies with the person *consciously* false to his *knowledge* of right. From this we deduce the truism that 'the civility of no race is perfect whilst another race is degraded.'"

"I shall never forget my feelings," chimed in Anna Stevens, a school teacher of a very studious temperament, "at certain remarks made by the Rev. John Thomas at one of his noonday lectures in the Temple. He was speaking on 'Different Races,' and had in his vigorous style been sweeping his audience with him at a high elevation of thought which was dazzling to the faculties, and almost impossible to follow in some points. Suddenly he touched upon the Negro, and with impressive gesture and lowered voice thanked God that the mulatto race was dying out, because it was a mongrel mixture which combined the worst elements of two races. Lo, the poor mulatto! despised by the blacks of his own race, scorned by the whites! Let him go out and hang himself!"

In her indignation Anna forgot the scissors, and bit her thread off viciously with her little white teeth.

Mrs. Willis smiled as she said calmly: "My dear Anna, I would not worry about the fate of the mulatto, for the fate of the mulatto will be the fate of the entire race. Did you never think that today the black race on this continent has developed into a race of mulattoes?"

"Why, Mrs. Willis!" came in a chorus of voices.

"Yes," continued Mrs. Willis, still smiling. "It is an incontrovertible truth that there is no such thing as an unmixed black on the American continent. Just bear in mind that we cannot tell by a person's complexion whether he be dark or light in blood, for by the working of the natural laws the white father and black mother produce the mulatto offspring: the black father and white mother the mulatto offspring also, while the *black father* and *quadroon* mother produce the black child, which to the eye alone is a child of unmixed black blood. I will venture to say that out of a hundred apparently pure black men not one will be able to trace an unmixed flow of African blood since landing upon these shores! What an unhappy example of the frailty of all human intellects, when such a man and scholar as Doctor Thomas could so far allow his prejudices to dominate his better judgment as to add one straw to the burden which is popularly supposed to rest upon the unhappy mulattoes of a despised race," finished the lady, with a dangerous flash of her large dark eyes.

"Mrs. Willis," said Dora, with a scornful little laugh, "I am not unhappy, and I am a mulatto. I just enjoy my life, and I don't want to die before my time comes, either. There are lots of good things left on earth to be enjoyed even by mulattoes, and I want my share."

"Yes, my dear; and I hope you may all live and take comfort in the proper joys of your lives. While we are all content to accept life, and enjoy it along the lines which God has laid down for us as individuals as well as a race, we shall be happy and get the best out of life. Now, let me close this talk by asking you to remember one maxim written of your race by a good man: 'Happiness and social position are not to be gained by pushing.' Let the world, by its need of us along certain lines, and our intrinsic fitness for these lines, push us into the niche which God has prepared for us. So shall our lives be beautified and our race raised in the civilization of the future as we grow away from all these prejudices which have been the instruments of our advancement according to the intention of an All-seeing Omnipotence, from the beginning. Never mind our poverty, ignorance, and the slights and injuries which we bear at the hands of a higher race. With the thought ever before us of what the Master suffered to raise all humanity to its present degree of prosperity and intelligence, let us cultivate, while we go about our daily tasks, no matter how inferior they may seem to us, beauty of the soul and mind, which being transmitted to our children by the law of heredity, shall improve the race by eliminating *immorality* from our midst and raising *morality* and virtue to their true place. Thirty-five years of liberty have made us a new people. The marks of servitude and oppression are dropping slowly from us; let us hasten the transformation of the body by the nobility of the soul."

> For of the soul the body form doth take,
> For soul is form and doth the body make,

quoted Dora.

"Yes," said Mrs. Willis with a smile, "that is the idea exactly, and well expressed. Now I hope that through the coming week you will think of what we have talked about this afternoon, for it is of the very first importance to all people, but particularly so to young folks."

Sappho, who had been thoughtfully embroidering pansies on white linen, now leaned back in her chair for a moment and said: "Mrs. Willis, there is one thing which puzzles me how are we to overcome the nature which is given us? I mean how can we eliminate passion from our lives, and emerge into the purity which marked the life of Christ? So many of us desire purity and think to have found it, but in a moment of passion, or under the pressure of circumstances which we cannot control, we commit some horrid sin, and the taint of it sticks and will not leave us, and we grow to loathe ourselves."

"Passion, my dear Miss Clark, is a state in which the will lies dormant, and all other desires become subservient to one. Enthusiasm for any one object or duty may become a passion. I believe that in some degree passion may be beneficial, but we must guard ourselves against a sinful growth of any appetite. All work of whatever character, as I look at it, needs a certain amount of absorbing interest to become successful, and it is here that the Christian life gains its greatest glory in teaching us how to keep ourselves from abusing any of our human attributes. We are not held responsible for compulsory sin, only for the sin that is pleasant to our thoughts and palatable to our appetites. All desires and hopes with which we are endowed are good in the sight of God, only it is left for us to discover their right uses. Do I cover your ground?"

"Yes and no," replied Sappho; "but perhaps at some future time you will be good enough to talk with me personally upon this subject."

"Dear child, sit here by me. It is a blessing to look at you. Beauty like yours is inspiring. You seem to be troubled; what is it? If I can comfort or strengthen, it is all I ask." She pressed the girl's hand in hers and drew her into a secluded corner. For a moment the flood-gates of suppressed feeling flew open in the girl's heart, and she longed to lean her head on that motherly breast and unburden her sorrows there.

"Mrs. Willis, I am troubled greatly," she said at length.

"I am *so* sorry; tell me, my love, what it is all about."

Just as the barriers of Sappho's reserve seemed about to be swept away, there followed, almost instantly, a wave of repulsion toward this woman and her effusiveness, so forced and insincere. Sappho was very impressionable, and yielded readily to the influence which fell like a cold shadow between them. She drew back as from an abyss suddenly beheld stretching before her.

"On second thoughts, I think I ought to correct my remarks. It is not really *trouble*, but more a desire to confirm me in my own ideas."

"Well, if you feel you are right, dear girl, stand for the uplifting of the race and womanhood. Do not shrink from duty."

"It was simply a thought raised by your remarks on morality. I once knew a woman who had sinned. No one in the community in which she lived knew it but herself. She married a man who would have despised her had he known her story; but as it is, she is looked upon as a pattern of virtue for all women."

"And then what?" asked Mrs. Willis, with a searching glance at the fair face beside her.

"Ought she not to have told her husband before marriage? Was it not her duty to have thrown herself upon his clemency?"

"I think not," replied Mrs. Willis dryly. "See here, my dear, I am a practical woman of the world, and I think your young woman builded wiser than she knew. I am of the opinion that most men are like the lower animals in many things—they don't always know what is for their best good. If the husband had been left to himself, he probably would not have married the one woman in the world best fitted to be his wife. I think in her case she did her duty."

"Ah, that word 'duty.' What is our duty?" queried the girl, with a sad droop to the sensitive mouth. It is so hard to know our duty. We are told that all hidden things shall be revealed. Must repented and atoned-for sin rise at last to be our curse?"

"Here is a point, dear girl. God does not look upon the constitution of sin as we do. His judgment is not ours; ours is finite, his infinite. *Your* duty is not to be morbid, thinking these thoughts that have puzzled older heads than yours. *Your* duty is, also, to be happy and bright for the good of those about you. Just blossom like the flowers, have faith and *trust.*" At this point the entrance of the men made an interruption, and Mrs. Willis disappeared in a crowd of other matrons. Sappho was impressed in spite of herself, by the woman's words. She sat buried in deep thought.

There was evidently more in this woman than appeared upon the surface. With all the centuries of civilization and culture that have come to this grand old world, no man has yet been found able to trace the windings of God's inscrutable ways. There are men and women whose seeming uselessness fit perfectly into the warp and woof of Destiny's web. All things work together for good.

Supper being over, the elderly people began to leave. It was understood that after nine o'clock the night belonged to the young people. A committee had been formed from among them to plan for their enjoyment, and they consulted with Ma Smith, in the kitchen, as to the best plan of procedure.

"The case is this," said the chairman, who was also the church chorister: "Ma Smith has bought four gallons of ice cream, to be sold for the benefit of this fair. It's *got* to go, and it rests with us to devise ways and means of getting rid of it."

"Get up a dance," suggested Sam Washington, a young fellow who was the life of all social functions.

"Dance!" exclaimed Ma Smith, "not in this house."

The choir-master surreptitiously kicked Sam on the shins, as he said soothingly: "Under the circumstances I see no other way, as we've *got* to sell the cream, and there's no harm in dancing, anyway."

"You ain't going to object to our dancing, are you, Ma? It's all old fogyism about dancing being a sin," chimed in Sam.

PAULINE E. HOPKINS

"Oh, but my son, I've been a church member over thirty years, a consistent Christian, and I never was up before the board for behavior unbecoming a professor. Think of the disgrace on me if the church took it up," she expostulated tearfully.

"Look here, Ma, the deacons and ministers are all fooling you. It's the style for church members to go to the theatre and the circus, to balls and everything you can mention. Why, I've seen our own pastor up to see the Black Crook, and laughing like all possessed at the sights. Fact!"

"Why, Samuel!" said Ma Smith, "how can you stand there and tell me such awful stories?"

"Not a bit of a story," declared the brazenfaced Sam, "it's as true as gospel. I'll find out what seat the minister gets next June when the circus comes into town, and I'll get a seat for you right behind him. If you've never been to the circus, Ma, and to see the seven-headed lady and the dancing mokes, you ought to go as soon as possible. Think of the fun you're missing."

"Oh!" groaned the good woman in holy horror, "how you do go on."

"But that ain't nothing to the ice cream," continued Sam, "and them girls in there have got to be warmed up, or the cream will be left, and there won't be a thing doing when the committee calls for the money."

"That's so," replied Ma Smith, beginning to weaken in her opposition.

"Well, mother," said Will, who had been an amused listener to the dialogue, "we'll have the dance, and it shall be *my* dance for *my* company. No one shall trouble you; you will have nothing to do with it."

"Well, if you say so, Willie, it's all right," replied his mother with a fond smile; "you are master in this house."

In the meantime the furniture in the parlors had been moved out by other members of the committee, and in one corner a set of whist players were enjoying themselves at ten cents a head for a thirty-minute game, which ended at the stroke of a small silver bell, their places being taken by others.

Already it was getting very warm in the crowded rooms. The doors leading into the entry had been thrown open, and couples were finding seats in convenient nooks waiting for dancing to begin. The girls were thinking of ice cream. Rev. Tommy James gravitated toward Mrs. Davis's corner. She had not gone out with the other matrons.

"I enjoy a real good time as much as anybody, children," she said; "and when it comes to dancing, you can't lose your Aunt Hannah."

The Reverend Tommy was always at his ease with Mrs. Davis. She led him along paths which caused him no embarrassment.

He knew that she looked up to him because of his education and his clerical dignity. On his side, he admired her rugged common-sense, which put him at his ease, and banished the last atom of his "ladylike" bashfulness. Early in the winter he had been brought to realize the nature of his feeling for Mrs. Davis, by seeing Brother Silas Hamm, recently left a widower, and having ten children, making a decided stampede in the widow's direction. Reverend Tommy was grieved. To be sure, she was old enough to be his mother, but she had many good points to be considered. She was a good worker, experienced in married life and ways of making a man comfortable. Then her savings must be considered. When Tommy reached this last point he always felt sure that she was the most desirable woman in the world for a young minister. He felt hopeful tonight, because he had seen Brother Hamm and his bride in church the Sunday before. Mrs. Davis opened the conversation by speaking of the bride and groom.

"Hamm and his bride looked mighty comfut'ble in chuch Sunday, didn't they?"

"*He* did. I'm glad he's settled again. It is not good for man to be alone."

"'Deed I'm glad, too."

"*You*—well, well, I'm real glad to hear *you* say it."

"What for?" asked the widow coyly, looking down and playing with her fan.

"I—I didn't know how you and Brother Hamni stood."

"Stood! Well, I never."

"I thought Brother Hamm had been trying to get you," whispered Tommy, sitting closer and putting his arm across the back of her chair.

"Law suz, Mr. Jeems, how nervous you does make me. Do take yer arm away, everybody'll be a-lookin' at yer, honey. I'm 'sprised at yer thinkin' I'd look at Hamm an' all them chillun. Massy knows what the 'ooman he's got's gwine to do with 'em." But she looked so mild and smiling that Tommy went into the seventh heaven of delight, and so lost his head that when he heard the call "Another couple wanted here!" he took Mrs. Davis on his arm and stood up on the floor, forgetful of the fact that he was within a few months of his ordination. A goodnatured matron not connected with the church had volunteered to supply the lack of an orchestra. Waltzing was soon in full blast, and the demand on the ice-cream cans was filling Ma Smith's heart with joy, tempered with inward stings of conscience and fear of the Steward's Board. Dora was dancing assiduously and eating ice cream at John's expense, he meantime saying that if she kept on she would turn into a frozen dainty, to say nothing of a frost in his pocketbook. Dora declared that it was for the good of the cause, and he'd "just got to stand it." She was wildly happy because of the tender familiarity between her brother and her friend. *A* long-stemmed rose that Will wore in his button-hole had been transferred to Sappho's corsage. Dora smiled as she caught the half-puzzled, half-wondering expression on her mother's face.

It was approaching twelve o'clock when it was proposed to wind up the festivities with the good old "Virginy" reel. Sam Washington was the caller, and did his work with the fancy touch peculiar to a poetic Southern temperament. He was shrewd and good-natured, and a bit of a wag. He knew all the secret sighings of the ladies and their attendant swains. A lively girl whom everyone called "Jinny," remarked to Sam, referring to the fact that Sam was on probation: "Your class-leader won't recommend you to the Board for membership after tonight."

"Now, Jinny," replied Sam, stopping in his business of arranging couples, "don't make yourself obnoxious bringing up unpleasant subjects. I'll take my medicine like a man when the time comes; but I'd bust, sho, if I didn't git loose tonight. I'm in good company, too," he grinned, nodding toward Reverend Tommy and Mrs. Davis, who were just taking their places on the floor. "If this is good for Tommy, it is good enough for me."

All reserve was broken down the instant the familiar strains of the Virginia reel were heard. The dance was soon in full swing—an up-and-down, dead-in-earnest seeking for a good time, and a determination to have it if it was to be got. It was a vehement rhythmic thump, thump, thumpity thump, with a great stamping of the feet and cutting of the pigeon wing. Sam had provided himself with the lively Jinny for a partner, and was cutting grotesque juba figures in the pauses of the music, to the delight of the company. His partner, in wild vivacity, fairly vied with him in his efforts at doing the hoedown and the heel-and-toe. Not to be out. done, the Rev. Tommy James and Mrs. Davis scored great hits in cutting pigeon wings and in reviving forgotten beauties of the "walk'round." Tommy "allowed" he hadn't enjoyed himself so much since he came up North.

"Yes," said Sam, "this beats the cake-walk all holler. Now then, one more turn and we're done. Forward on the head; balance yer partner;

swing the next gent; swing that lady. Now swing yer rose, yer pretty rose, yer yaller rose of Texas. All promen*ade*."

Everybody declared it had been a wonderful evening. "Thank the Lord it's over," said Ma Smith to Mrs. Sarah Ann White, who was helping her in the kitchen.

"Well," said the latter, pausing in her work with her arms akimbo, "sech sights as I've seen tonight I never would have believed. 'Phelia Davis, what ought ter be a mother in Jerusalem, kickin' up her heels in your parlor like a colt in a corn-field; and that Tommy Jeems, no more fittin' fer a minister than a suckin' babe, a-traipsin' after her like a bald-headed rooster."

IX

"Love Took Up the Harp of Life"

Love took up the glass of Time, and turn'd it in his glowing hands;
Every moment, lightly shaken, ran itself in golden sands.
Love took up the harp of Life, and smote on all the
chords with might.

—Tennyson

Will Smith sat the next evening in his room trying to engage his mind and chain his wandering thoughts upon an important prize thesis. As a brilliant philosophical student destined to shine in the future in the world of science, he had been requested to become a competitor for the prize. Ever and anon his attention wavered, and finally he threw his books and papers to one side with a sigh, and rising to his feet paced the floor impatiently. Two soft eyes looked into his; the low music of a gentle voice seemed all about him.

"Pshaw!" he exclaimed impatiently, "I have laughed at others only to become more of a drivelling idiot than any of the men I have ridiculed. I never thought mere beauty in a woman could move me so." The smile induced by pleasant thoughts lingered on his face as he threw himself upon his couch and tried to bring order out of the chaos of his thoughts.

Smith's hopes were all for a finishing course at college, and then a course in philosophy at some good German university. Philosophy was a mania with him. In vain had bishops and clergymen of all denominations warned him that his mania might become a passion, which would draw him from a right conception of the Word, and dull his appreciation of the beauties of Revelation. Will contended that religion and the natural laws were not antagonistic, and that being convinced and thoroughly grounded in his faith, he but discovered fresh evidence of infinite perfection in the doctrine of his Master when he sought to expand his faculties and illuminate his mind by seeking a clearer perception of the interesting relation which weak humanity bears to the glorious mysteries of life and the grandeurs of creation.

He laughed at the idea of Latin and Greek being above the caliber of the Negro and likely to unfit him for the business of bread-getting in the peculiar position in life to which the Negro, as maintained by some, was destined from the beginning. With him Latin and Greek represented but tools which he used to unlock the storehouse of knowledge. The development of his race was a matter of first importance to his mind. The only way to bring the best faculties of the Negro to their full fruition, he contended, was by the careful education of the moral faculties along the lines of the natural laws. No Negro college, he argued, ought to bestow a diploma upon man or woman who had not been thoroughly grounded in the rudiments of moral and natural philosophy, physiology, and political economy.

At twenty-five Smith found himself about to realize his hopes. He was fitted to enter Harvard University and graduate after a short course there. His articles in local magazines had attracted the favorable notice of scientific men, and one wealthy gentleman had offered him a course at Heidelberg after graduation. Emerson's words on character were an apt description of the strong personality of this man: "A reserved force which acted directly by its presence, and without (apparent) means."

His sister's friends possessed no attraction for him; he treated them as little girls, looking down upon them from the superior height of his twenty-five years with a gentle condescension, tempered always by the natural chivalry of generous nature toward the weak and helpless. He was a favorite with women, old and young, in spite of his careless, half-haughty ways. Many a sigh was wafted after his handsome, unconscious self, as a pretty maiden who had fancied that *she* had at length conquered the unconquerable, saw her chains fall from him as lightly as a cobweb is brushed away. What had come to him now at the glance of a soft, fawn-like eye, the touch of a hand, a caressing smile, the sound of a sweet voice? Sappho had been with them two months, but Will felt that he must have known her for years. Suddenly he passed from youth to manhood, and realized man's destiny. He had assisted his mother and sister with happy pride, but now the desire to shield, to protect, to love one being supremely above all others, rose and surged within him with a mighty strength.

Although love had come to Smith like a flood sweeping all barriers before it, yet the very strength of his desire for her love but served to restrain decided action. He approached the desired end slowly and carefully, not to defeat his own plans. He was well aware that Sappho's nature was a rare one, dwelling much upon lonely heights, the home of extraordinary moral sensitiveness and high intellectual development. Again he saw her advancing toward him in the mazes of the dance: her hand lay in his; her soft hair brushed his face; her sweet breath came to him from smiling rose-leaf lips, and intoxicated his senses.

"The starlike beauty of immortal eyes," fringed by long, curling lashes, flashed at him from the four corners of his dingy room. What tender thrills of sympathetic feeling had seemed to enfold his senses as he gazed into their limpid depths—what beauty and strength lurked in the mobile, sweetly smiling mouth! The delicately moulded chin on which the God of Love had left his impress, might have served as the model for a sculptor. She and no other should be his wife—God willing.

Propinquity is responsible for many matches. It was pleasant for Sappho, when she returned mornings from delivering her work, to find her fire burning briskly and the room well warmed. It was a comfort to her not to have the ugly problem of ashes, wood and coal to solve. Not that she was too proud, or that she thought housework of any kind beneath her; but what woman does not feel it a relief to find the machinery of the home running smoothly without her aid. She thought nothing about ways and means, taking it for granted that there was nothing unusual in finding things pleasant, and she congratulated herself on being so fortunate in having "heat" included in Ma Smith's modest charges for lodging. Upon her return one morning, as she mounted the stairs to her room she saw from the light reflected that her door was open. Someone, within the room was singing in a fine baritone voice a verse of an old song:

> Of all the days that are in a week,
> I dearly love but one day.
> That is the day that comes between Saturday and Monday.
> For then I dress all in my best
> And roam with my dear Sally;
> She's the darling of my heart
> And she lives in our alley.

She pushed the door open and entered. Her cheeks were glowing from her walk in the bracing morning air, but her face assumed a serious, questioning look as she discovered Will just finishing up his self-imposed morning task. He gave an extra flourish to the brushes to cover his confusion and annoyance, and kept right on polishing off the little heater with his dubious-looking black cloths well filled with stove polish.

"Well!" she exclaimed.

"Good morning," returned Will, with a businesslike flourish of nis cloth, as, having finished the stove, he proceeded to touch up the bright piece of zinc under it. "How will she take it?" he asked himself. "Well!" she repeated.

"Quite well, thank you," said Will, this time with a quizzical grin on his face.

"I had no idea *you* were the fireman, Mr. Smith."

"No? In the words of Doctor Peters, 'I do mos' anythin' in the wurl, honey, to git an hones' livin' without stealin' it.'"

Will had donned one of his mother's ample kitchen aprons for the protection of his clothing. The bib was pinned well up in front across the broad expanse of shirt bosom; the ample folds of the apron-skirt enveloped his limbs to his ankles; the long strings, crossed in the back, met in front in a huge bow-knot. There was a streak of smut across one eye, and the side of his nose was polished to perfection. The picture was too much for Sappho, and peal after peal of laughter shook her slight frame.

"Oh, Mr. Smith," she said, when she could find breath, "you do look *so* funny!"

"'Twas ever thus from childhood's hour,'" quoted Will, marching up to the mirror to survey his beauty spots; "I do look rather fetching," he continued, with a confidential smile at his laughing companion.

"Do you do this every day?" asked Sapp! suddenly sobering down.

"Do what every day?" "Why, make my fire?"

"It's not your fire any more than anyone else's fire."

"I'm very sorry."

"Sorry! sorry about what? It isn't a crime, is it, for a man to make a fire for his women folks?"

"But I'm not your 'women folks.'"

"Look here," said Will in an aggrieved tone, balancing a hod of ashes in one hand and a pile of stove brushes in the other, "are we going to quarrel?"

"There is no reason why we should if we agree," said Sappho, smiling gravely. "That means that we shan't quarrel if I agree to whatever you are going to propose. What is it you want to say?" he asked, becoming grave in his turn. "Is it that I have behaved unmanly in visiting your room in your absence? Why cavil about a little thing of that sort? I do this for you as I would for Dora."

"Oh, if you look at it that way"—she began, a trifle confused by his apparent unconsciousness.

"How else ought I to look at it?"

"How horrid you are."

"Horrid! I don't see what I've said that is so very dreadful."

"You speak so well so cross."

"I speak like a man talking to a silly girl."

"Now you are rude again; calling me names."

"Children must be kept in their places," he said banteringly.

"You're making fun of me." "Of course I am. What do you expect?"

"But you mustn't make my fire again."

"I am sorry you found it out; I didn't intend you to know it."

"I can't pay for having the work done, and it is not proper for you to do it; there is no reason why you should do such work for me."

"Suppose we play you are my other sister; that will make it all right, won't it?

"No," came firmly from Sappho's lips; "no more fires."

"See here, I've hit it! Play I'm your father." "Ridiculous!"

"What, neither brother nor father? How'd it do to imagine that you're my mother? You can't find fault with that, surely."

"How silly you are."

"No likee me for sonny?" queried Will, with a sad shake of his head.

"If you don't leave this room instantly, William Smith, I'll call your mother," replied Sappho, laughing in spite of herself.

"The best play, though, would be sweethearts," he continued, as though she had not spoken.

"Sweethearts!"

"Yes, sweethearts; and I believe I could win the game, too, in spite of your reserve."

"You must be very sure of your power, young man. You need a lesson in diffidence." He held her gaze for a moment, and there was so much earnestness in the persistent dark eyes that she blushed furiously. He turned and abruptly left the room. No more was said about the fire, but will continued to perform common everyday duties for her the same as for his sister. She did her part, too. Many an evening he found her helping Dora, darning socks or replacing lost buttons. Will's manner had changed toward her from that day; from easy familiarity it changed to a mixture of timid reserve and marked deference. Sappho noticed it, but somehow she liked it better. It spoke to her silently of tender, sacred thoughts. Tonight he thought of the scene just pictured, as he sat there in his room. She and none other should be his wife—God willing.

In another part of the house Ma Smith sat before the fire in her chamber and meditated on many things. The knitting with which the busy hands were always engaged when at leisure, dropped in her lap, and lay there unheeded. She thought of the incident of Sappho and the rose of the night before, and the merry, teasing look that had flashed out at her for one instant from Dora's laughing eyes. Could it be possible that she was about to lose her son? Dora's engagement to John Langley had been a source of great satisfaction to her; the old-fashioned notion was still strong within her that it was the right destiny for girls to marry, and that the only cause for a mother to grieve in the idea of marriage for her daughter was the awful chance of that daughter's remaining single. The girl's life should be lost in that of the wife and mother. Such an end to maidenhood was a happy achievement for the girl and a glory to her family. But with her boy it was different. He was her first-born, and memory was busy tonight with the past.

Her Will with a wife! herself a grandmother! To renew at this age the joys which had been hers when first he lay within her arms soft morsel of humanity, with sweet brown face and melting black eyes that mirrored themselves within the citadel of her heart. Ma Smith had known much sorrow in her life. She could tell you of hard times when it seemed that the combined efforts of her husband and herself would not avail to keep the wolf from the door. She knew what it was to bake and brew, to mend and make over, to minister to the needs of childhood with increasing maternal cares near at hand. With all this, the offered work which added a few dollars to their little store was always gladly accepted. But she would tell you also that she would not have given one hour of those days, with all their privations, for the happiness that she enjoyed when in the privacy of a humble home she counted her "precious jewels"—an honest husband and two beautiful children. "Yes," she was wont to say, "we had a hard time, and sometimes the waters of affliction seemed about to sweep us from our foothold, but somehow just when everything was darkest we could see the light of prosperity

PAULINE E. HOPKINS

shining through the clouds, and we would take courage, bless the Lord, and keep on struggling."

Tonight she lived those struggles over again, and tried to imagine what it would be to have another share the love and reverence of the idolized son. At first it seemed that she could not endure the thought; but then she remembered how happy she had been in her married life, and prayed the Lord to deliver her from selfish desires. Who was she to stand in the way of her son's happiness—a son whom she loved? Sappho Clark was beautiful; she believed her to be a girl of exemplary conduct. Sappho was always deferential to her, giving to the elder woman the gentle deference which, coming from youth, is so dear to those advanced in years. So with a heart overflowing with love, and filled with kind and tender thoughts, it was no mystery where the pretty old face had caught its added charm of heavenly brightness. So Dora found her when she returned from spending the evening with some young friends.

"Why, mummy dear, I declare you are growing younger and handsomer every day. We girls must look to our laurels if you keep on growing so pretty."

"Well, my love, I have been thinking of your father tonight, and how happy we were when you and Will were wee tots."

Dora knew well what had set her mother thinking. She appreciated her feelings. She knew that her mother had always felt that no woman could be good enough for Will's wife. She felt instinctively that her mother had faced the difficulty alone that evening and conquered it, effacing herself and her desires for the happiness of her son. With her usual impulsiveness Dora threw herself on her knees beside her mother's chair, and drawing her face down to her, kissed the wrinkled brow and smoothed the soft white hair.

"Mummy, dear," she said, "you have made up your mind to give him up to Sappho if things turn out that way?"

"Yes, my dear," replied her mother, with her hand upon the dark braids beside her. "I will not say that it was not a struggle, but mothers know, if they stop to think, that they must lose their babies sometime. Your father and I made a home for ourselves, so I must look forward to the time when you young birds will want to build a nest away from me. But what is the matter with you, Dora? you look worried. Is anything wrong?"

"Oh, no," replied the girl, as she rose from her knees by her mother's side and began putting her things away and preparing for the night.

"Isn't it strange what a queer old world this is? If you are happy I am not, or vice versa. It does seem that one thing or another is always happening to vex a body. And the worst of it is that it may happen that we are impatient and unhappy about things that are trivial. I don't feel sweet-tempered tonight, and really, I can't tell why."

Ma Smith glanced at her daughter sharply but said nothing, as Dora thrust her bare feet into bedroom slippers and proceeded to undo the thick masses of curling brown hair, and brush and arrange it for the night. The mother knew that her daughter would unburden her mind presently, and so she waited patiently. It was not like Dora to be petulant and have moods. She was a happy, healthy, active girl, with a kindly disposition.

"Ma," said Dora after a silence, "why is it that Southern colored people seem to be so prejudiced against the Northern colored people? I always fancied that we were all in the same boat, and that mere accidental locality was not to be considered."

"That is true, my dear; but it must be that you imagine the prejudice to exist that you mention; surely we have outgrown such ideas, as a race, by this time."

Dora shook her head obstinately. "I fancied that the Wilsons slighted me tonight, and that they would have been better pleased if John had chosen a Southern girl."

"You are over-sensitive, Dora."

Dora did not reply, and after a moment's silence continued: "John said that he had not met a decent-looking woman who was Northern-born, and that when he did see a pretty colored girl on the street he knew without asking that she was a Southerner."

"That was rather thoughtless in John, but I don't think he meant to hurt your feelings, daughter."

"I cannot imagine what has got into him lately; he's not like himself. Oh, I do wish I was handsome like Sappho Clark! All the men are wild over her."

"Well, my dear, you don't harbor hard feelings against Sappho on that account, do you? That would not be like you, Dora, and would grieve me very much."

"Sappho is the best and dearest girl on earth, and I only hope that Will may be so lucky as to marry her. And, mummy; I hope Will will speak to her right off, so as to get the matter straightened out; there won't be a blessed man left to us girls if she remains single long."

Her mother smiled. "Daughter, I want to say just a word to you about our conversation: Don't allow jealousy to lurk in your heart; don't brood over unkind words; cast them from you. And I would have you remember, also, that sectional prejudice has always been fostered by the Southern whites among the Negroes to stifle natural feelings of brotherly love among us. Dissension means disunion. Carry these thoughts always in your mind, and act accordingly. Do not allow yourself to be made unhappy."

Meanwhile on the floor above them Sappho turned restlessly on her pillow, thinking of a noble head and bright dark eyes. She knew that Will Smith loved her. What woman does not feel the subtle intertwining of a kindred spirit linked to her own by the decree of Destiny, long years, perhaps, before either restless soul has entered upon its earthly pilgrimage. She was not happy in her knowledge. Under cover of the friendly darkness she gave up the long struggle for self-control, and indulged in the grief that she knew was hers for all eternity. Oh, for death, the solitude of the grave and self-forgetfulness.

"What have I done, what have I done to suffer thus? To give up all joy, and have only misery for all my life. I love this man; I know it now! I want his love, his care, his protection. I want him through life and beyond the grave, we two as one—my husband. Oh, my God, help me, help me!" Heavy sobs shook her frame. Broken exclamations fell from her lips. "I cannot! It must not be! So good, so noble! Oh, the happiness of home and love! must I be shut from them forever?"

Far into the night the agony of sobs continued. At last with a murmured prayer for help she fell asleep.

X

The Fair

"Boisterous jest and humor unrefined,
That leave, though rough, no painful sting behind;
Warm social joys surround the Negro's cot.

No ennui clouds, no coming cares annoy,
Nor wants nor sorrows check the Negro's joy."

The days went on apace at No. 500 D Street, but a spirit of restlessness seemed to pervade the atmosphere; expectancy was on tiptoe. Everyone was absorbed in preparations for the fair. Such a time had not been known for years among the colored people. Every available individual was pressed into the service.

Naturally many factions had arisen, and a fierce but friendly rivalry divided the different societies within the church. Some of these were none too cordial to the outsiders who had joined them, and whom they dubbed in derision "the colored 400."

"I'd jes' like to know," said Sister Mary Jane Robinson, with a hand on each hip, "I'd jes' like to know who asked the '400' fer eny o' thar help? I've been a member hyar fer more'n thurty years, and this chuch has lived without 'em." This was one morning directly after service, while the good sisters were waiting for class to begin. As the fair was the all-absorbing topic at present, conversation naturally ended in going over all the interesting details connected with it.

"Lor', Sis' Robberson, what mortal diffurunce does it make as long as the chuch gits the money? The mo' helpers we has the easier it makes it fer we-uns," replied Sister Scott, as she endeavored to pour oil on the troubled waters. Sister Robinson was a veritable firebrand; she spoke first and thought afterwards.

"Thar's that Mrs. Willis with her High Chuch' notions," continued Sister Robinson. "Sister Smith has made her presidunt of the fine arts and fancy work department. Warn't eny o'the members o' this chuch good enough, an' they didn't know enough, did they, to 'tend to that bisiness! Thar's that pianner an' that silver set an' that ar gold watch an' chain that's goin' to be voted fer. Ef that stuff don't be lef' right hyar in this chuch thar's gwine ter be trouble. An'as fer that dimon' pin that's to go to the one who sells the most admission tickets—well, now, ef the hard wurkin' sisters o'this chuch what swets over the washtub earnin' an' hones' livin' don't desarve it, then what's the matter? yas, I wants ter know what's the matter?" Here the irate woman sawed the air with hand and arm as she laid down the law on the back of the nearest settee. By this time a group of sisters attracted by her loud tones had gathered around, anxious to learn what the trouble could be.

"Well, honey," said one meek-looking woman, "don't le's borry trouble. The way the committee has fixed the bisness I cayn't see how thar can be eny monkeyin' with the votin' or sellin' o' the tickets. I do declar', my dear, I think the right ones will git the prizes."

"I'm a-doin' my level best," said another sister with hands hard and horny with toil, "I'm a-doin' my level best to git that dimon' pin fer my Mandy. I've got William Vanderbilt and Charles Sumner Astor Gould and the twins all out sellin' tickets 'mong my white people. An' I tell you, sisters, you's all goin' to have a hard time to git 'way with yer Aunt Hanner Jackson this time."

The family surname was Jackson, but Mrs. Jackson liked to name her children for all the celebrities that she heard of, and sometimes it made a bewildering combination when one found that William Vanderbilt was represented by a sprightly little Negro boy with crispy hair and beadlike black eyes.

"That silver service is jes' my size," here chimed in another sister, "an' it's goin' hard with anyone what tries to git it 'way from me; I'm sellin' tickets to beat the ban. I've done picked out a sideboard fer it down to Osgood's. I can git it fer a dollar down an'a dollar a week, an' expec' to have it ef it takes me all the summer an' winter ter pay fer it."

"Talkin' 'bout the prizes, ain't yer?" spoke up another sister who had just joined the group, "thet gold watch an' chain is jes' what Jim Anderson wants. 'Jim,' I says to him, 'thar's yer chance fer a good easy way ter git yer a watch.' He's jes' raisin' heaven an' earth a-gittin' votes fer hisself."

"Hope you all won't be disapinted," here Sister Robinson broke in again, "but ef yer listens to me you'll watch them high-toned colored folks you all's been gittin' ter help yer. They never come 'roun' people that they don't hold on a 'quality with theirselves 'thout it means suthin' These ejecated folks is allers lookin' to make suthin'. Most o' them's too lazy to wurk. They wouldn't tech a flatiron or a washtub with a ten-foot pole, an' they'd ruther live on dried codfish fer a month than to do their own scrubbing. Ef eny o'them whitefolksey colored ladies gits them prizes, I'm goin' fer to take out my letter, an' put my wurk into some chuch what will presheate it; you hyar me!"

"Now sisters," chimed in the meek one again, "none o' yer ain't said a word 'bout tryin' to git one o' the prizes fer yer pastor. I do think that's a leetle bit selfish in us. S'pose we give him the pianny."

"Hump!" grunted Sister Robinson," when I jined this chuch I jined the meetin'-house an' not the minister! I reckon he kin jes' look out fer hisself; 'sides he's got a orgin an' don't need a pianny. He gits his cellery, don't he?" she queried, as she glared at the group about her. Taking their silence for consent she continued in a firm voice: "He's too much everythin' to everybody, an' that wife o' hisn is too white fer me. I used ter be takin' fresh eggs an' ham an' chickuns out to that house all the time, but resuntly I'se been reasunin' with myself, an' I camed to the conclusion that I won't do it no mo'. Can't tell what *is* the matter with these colored men; a good wholesome-lookin' colored woman with kinkey hair don't stan' no livin' chance ter git a decen'-lookin' man fer a husban', an' I fer one am a-settin' my face agin them men."

"Purty much so, purty much so!" came from various ones in the group.

"Lord knows, Sis' Robberson," said Sister Scott, "may be you *is* right; an' ef thar's eny monkeyin' goin' on we's all goin' ter s'port yer in whatever yer thinks is the bes' course."

"All right," replied Sister Robinson, considerably mollified by this concession. "I'll jes' take good care thet none o' *us* gits imposed on. Phelia Davis an' Sarah Ann White has got charge o' the 'fectionery table an' the salads, but ef I don' knock 'em silly with roast pig, corn dodgers an' biled cabbage, then I'm a sinner!" Sister Robinson walked away, followed by a number of admiring satellites. Sister Scott and Sister Jackson were left alone.

"Good Lawd!" said Sister Scott to Sister Jackson, "Good Lawd! 'Mandy Jackson, did you hear Mary Jane Robberson talk? Thar ain't nuthin' the matter with her, only she's 'fraid thet somebody's gwine ter hol' the moneydraw fastened agin her. I tell yer them '400' folks she's runnin' 'll keep a close watch on her an' how much money she takes in at the 'old Southern dinner-table,' you hyar me!"

"An' I fer one am glad of it," replied Sister Jackson. Mary Jane Robberson thinks she owns this chuch an' everyone in it sence

Mr. Jacobs lef' John Robberson thet five hundred dollars, an' they bo't thet house out o' town."

"Bless yer soul, honey, thet's jes' so. I never see what a little posterity makes some people have a swell head. I tell yer, honey, we'd better all o' us keep our eye on the money-draw.

"When folks gits to buyin' houses-um, chile, watch 'em!"

On Monday evening the fair opened. At five o'clock in the morning all the women who could get there made their appearance at the church, where the janitor was waiting to receive them. The first floor of the building contained a large lecture-room, three class-rooms, the pastor's study, a dining-room and a kitchen. Each chairman of a committee had a certain space assigned to her by Ma Smith; then that committee took charge and proceeded to beautify the spot and arrange their wares for inspection. Ice cream, oysters, salads and temperance drinks were to be served in a fairy-like grotto formed by grouping evergreen trees together. Among the trees small tables were to be set, making a charming solitude à deux. Electricity, cunningly concealed in rose-colored shades, was to furnish the lighting. Pretty girl-waiters, in white dresses and fancy caps, completed a fascinating picture. This section was under the immediate direction of Mrs. Ophelia Davis and Mrs. Sarah Ann White.

"You hear me, Sarah Ann," said Ophelia Davis to her friend, "you hear me, that Mary Jane Robberson means trouble. She's down on the aristocracy; she don't 'tend to give the minister a show over them prizes, an' you an' me's got to keep a whip han' over her somehow. The minister's goin' to git a new suit o'clo's out o' this, an' you an'me's gwine to have thet pianny! Lord knows whether there'll be one brick o'this chuch lef' on another when this fair is done, but she ain't gwine ter walk on me, you hyar me. I'm a-studyin' fer her, an'ef she runs up agin me thar'll be trouble."

Meanwhile Mrs. Robinson and her coterie stood around and looked at the unique ideas for a fair which had been developed, and wondered how it was that the "400" people and their followers always had such a happy knack of getting everything just right. Her committee had intended to have nothing but a plain dining-room, but after seeing the gorgeous display made by Mrs. Davis and Mrs. White, a hurried meeting was called to consult about ways and means of defeating the enemy. All the other women stopped their work, too, and came to admire the effects gained by the introduction of the lights and the tête-à-tête tables.

"A very happy thought," said Mrs. Willis, as she glanced approvingly about her. "Where did you get the idea?"

"I got it up to Mis' Mason's when Molly Mason was married."

"That's where you lived so long, wasn't it, Mrs. Davis?" asked one of the girls, as she paused a moment in her work of arranging festoons of evergreens, and stood back to note the effect.

"I lived there an' nowhere else the first fifteen years I was up North," replied Mrs. Davis proudly.

"Were they very wealthy? Do you ever see them nowadays?" asked Mrs. Willis.

"Mis' Mason was wurth her millions, an' Molly was her only chile," replied Mrs. Davis, now fairly launched on her favorite subject. "The Mason wedding" had passed into a proverb among the young people who were acquainted with Mrs. Davis. "You see, when Molly was married, Mis' Mason took it into her head to have a caterer from Boston do the work of feeding the guests. She was livin'in Worcester then. Even the servants were invited to the weddin'. She had a house that matched her money, you may jes' reckon, and the whole o her lawn was used fer feeding an' fer dancin'. There were two acres o' lan' nuthin' but lawn, an' all among the trees you could see little tables set out an' plenty o'lanterns, although in the dancin' pavilion they jes' connected a gas-pipe with the main one, an' had the place lit with gas jes' as ef you was in the house."

"You ought to ask them to contribute to the fair, and help you out with your table," remarked Mrs. Willis,

Mrs. Davis cocked her head on one side and said, with a knowing wink at Mrs. Willis: "Now, ain't yer talkin', honey, an' mebe I ain't writ to her an' tol' her all 'bout Mary Jane Robberson! Jes' yer hol' on, chile, tell yer sees me paralyze her."

"Did you go to the wedding, Mrs. Davis?" asked Sappho, who, being something of a stranger, did not know all the little points about the wedding.

"*Who, me*?" exclaimed Mrs. Davis; "yes'm, I jes' *did*! Lor', chile, but Mis' Mason's a lady borned; she don't know how to be like some o' yer Northern people. Sho! these ladies up here are so 'fraid thet the black 'll rub off. Down South the big white folks has nussed so meny black mammies thet they don' know nuthin' else fer their chillun. It don' matter how black you is ef yer willin' to keep in the mud. Up here it's diffurunt; you can do all right and live all right, but don't put yer han' on a white man or woman, or they 'll have a fit fer fear the black 'll rub off."

"I suppose you went to the wedding dressed to kill," said one of the girls.

"Lor', chile, I had to have a new light silk fer *that*, I tell yer. An' sech a time as I had when I went to git me a pair o' paten' leather shoes. Clorindy, gal," she called to a young woman who was placing trees in position, "what kin' o' way do you call that to put them trees? You ain't got a bit o' eye fer bein' an artis', your ferpendicler is all crooked. Bring me a cheer thar, some one o' you gals, and let me fix thet tree right." Having straightened out the matter of the trees, she returned panting and puffing to the refreshment bar. "As I was sayin', the man said he didn't hev a shoe in the shop thet would fit me. I tol' him I knowed better; he jes' said thet 'cause I was a colored 'ooman. Then he went to the show-window and took out a pair, an' tol' me to set down an' he'd try 'em on me an' see ef they'd do, an' ef they would I might have 'em, an'he'd git another pair thet 'd do fer signs jes' as well as them. I tol' him I didn't care a bit ef they was signs; why didn't he trot 'em out when I asked him fer 'em fust? 'Well,' he says, 'they's number 'levens, an' I didn't want ter *insult* yer.' '*Insult nuthin'*,' says I, 'as long as I can git 'em on.' They fitted me all right, only they kin' o' cramped me across my bunyon. I always has a hard time with that dratted bunyon o'mine. I managed to wear 'em, though I'm free to say thet i never felt as though I got my muney out o' the plagy things. As I was sayin', I was cook, an' the second girl was colored, too; we jes' hired an open barush to drive to the chuch in—I b'lieve in doin' things right—an' I tell you the white folks was dumb when we druve up that night to the chuch do' an' stepped out o'the kerrige onto the strip o' carpet under the yawnin', fer all the worl' jes' like quality. We got 'long all right tell we struck the entry, then Sally kin' o' hung back when she saw a big usher lookin' fer all the worl' like a picter-book, standin' ther an' tellin' us to wait our turn to be seated in the fambly pew. Yes, 'ndeed! Bless yer soul, Mis' Mason had done put us into one o' the fambly pews! I'm used to them sort o' things myself, but yer see, Sally she's kin' o' low-down corn-shucker, not used to nothin' 'tall, an' I kep' my eye onto her; I could see it inter her face thet she intended to give me the slip an' bolt an' hide herself. 'Oh, Mis' Davis,' says she, 'has we got to walk all the way up thet aisle with one o' them white gemplemen?' 'Yes, Sally, we has, an' it won't kill us nuther to be like live gentry fer onct in our lives.' Jes' then one o' them made fer me, an' I only had time to whisper: 'Brace up, Sally, an' be a 'ooman,' when

I foun' myself walkin' up the aisle on thet white man's arm, as big as Cuffy, an'a-sweatin' to beat the ban'.'"

"What became of Sally?" asked Sappho.

"Bless yer soul, Miss Sappho, when she sawed me go she jes' broke an' run down them steps plum inter the street, an' made tracks fer the house all dressed as she was in white shefong, an' when I got back thar she was a-standin' up in the middle o' the kitchen floor grinnin' like a Chessy cat. 'Mis' Davis,' says she, 'Mis' Davis, I wouldn't a-walked up thet chuch aisle with thet white gempleman fer a thousan' dollars, 'deed'n I wouldn't.' I was so mad with thet fool gal thet I jes' itched ter spank her well. How we to 'vance eny ef we don't 'brace our 'tunities, I'd like ter know?"

All the committees worked willingly, and soon every one of the departments had been provided with appropriate enclosures like quaint pictures set in exquisite frames. The bare walls disappeared, and the whole place burst into beauty bewildering enough to draw the money from the pockets of the spectators who would come with the evening to help a worthy charity. Mrs. Robinson, with her "old-fashioned busy bees," as they called themselves, had hurriedly decorated the dining-room with American flags and Christian Endeavor banners. The long, white-covered tables looked very inviting, and the motherly women in black dresses, white aprons and bandanna handkerchiefs tied into fantastic head-coverings, added another charm which their soft Southern accent completed. Late in the afternoon the tired workers examined the results of their labors with much satisfaction.

PAULINE E. HOPKINS

XI

The Fair—*Concluded*

"In feasts maturing busy hands appear,
And jest and laugh assail the ready ear."

On Monday evening at 7 p.m. the doors of the fair were opened. In the center of the hall the prize piano was advantageously placed; and Dora, as the organist of the church, displayed its merits in a few well-chosen numbers. There were selections given also by a banjo, guitar and mandolin club of local reputation. Cozily ensconced behind a bower of tropical plants and flowers they discoursed popular selections in a manner which displayed most favorably the really fine musical ability which each one of them possessed. In another corner of the hall, under a tent which represented an Indian lodge, was a great and mysterious attraction: Madam Frances, spiritualistic soothsayer and marvellous mind-reader, had offered her services to the committee, and would send out bulletins, at so much a letter, on subjects supposed to be unknown to all the world but the persons themselves. The young people were in a futter over this particular feature, the men no less so than the women. Who could tell what might happen through her agency? Long delayed questions might be asked; unknown feelings might be revealed to anxious hearts. One might buy a lucky charm and present it to his inamorata, and by contact with it her coldness should vanish. Henry might receive a letter whose sweet perfume should banish the thoughts of Susan and turn his wandering heart to its first allegiance. Oh, happy race! which even now, when life is but a bare existence, though torn by howling mobs and scourged by fire, finds pleasure in the simple pastimes of innocence.

Superstition is supposed to be part of the Negro's heritage. They have brought much of it from their native Africa. "It gives color, picturesqueness—light and shade we may say to the darkness of life and complexion which so far has marked the Negro for its own. Claiming kinship with the Egyptians and other black races of the Eastern continent, the Negro is thought to possess wonderful powers of necromancy. Races are like families. The East Indian shows remarkable ability to awaken the superstitious fears of a community in his native country; so with the Egyptian; so with the Negro. But transplant them on a foreign shore and much of their supposed power vanishes. So with the Negro. We hear much of spells and charms being put upon unpleasant neighbors; wonderful stories of lizards being taken from the leg or arm of an enemy, placed there by the arts of the voodoo doctor and cured by the same gifted party. But if we notice, these wonderful and terrorizing acts were never perpetrated against the inhuman master or mistress of the isolated plantation, never upon enemies wearing a white skin, but always upon the humble associate and brother in bondage. Be these things true or false, the Negro no longer holds the distinction of being the only race that believes in the pretensions of those who claim to be able to look into the future with mesmerized sight favored by hidden powers, that have a knowledge of coming events. In these days of palmistry, phrenology, card-reading, mind-reading, lucky pigs, rabbit's feet worn on the watch-chain for luck, and four-leaved clover encased in crystal and silver for the same reason, who shall say that the Negro has not lost his monopoly of one great racial characteristic?

Madam Frances was supposed to be skilled in the occult arts which were once the glory of the freshly imported African. Wonderful tales were told of her ability to foretell the future. Her services were of great value to the managers of the fair, for her fame had been rumored abroad, through the members of the church, and it was popularly reported that some of the richest people in the city would visit the fair, if for nothing but to test the ability of this woman. And as one gazed upon her he might be pardoned for thinking that within that dark house, moulded upon symmetrical lines, and appearing as though cut from purest ebony, albeit somewhat thin and spare, as became one past the meridian of life and now upon the road leading downward into the shadows of the last valley through which we must pass on our outward journey toward the spheres of celestial light, dwelt a rare mind. How did she look?

"I knew a princess; she was old,
Crisp—haired, flat featured, with a look
Such as no dainty pen of gold
Would write of in a fairy book.

> *Her face was like the Sphinx's face, to me,*
> *Touched with vast patience, desert grace,*
> *And lonesome, brooding mystery.*
>
> *Nothing of the loveliness*
> *This strange, sad princess seemed to lack;*
> *Majestic with her calm distress*
> *She was, and beautiful, though Black."*

A quaint conceit which gave great pleasure to the children, big and little, was the pretty great-nephew of the seeress who, dressed in costume, represented Mercury and carried messages to the fortunate ones remembered by the mystic powers of Futurity. Alphonse was a beautiful boy about eight years old, with golden curls and dark blue eyes that looked out on life, from beneath their sweeping lashes with a glance all too melancholy for one of his tender years. There are children who seem to have been born with the shadows of life heavy upon them. So it was with little Alphonse. He passed from groups of merry young people and pleasant elders who, attracted by the beauty of the weird child, sought to beguile him with soft caress and loving touch; he would stand quietly waiting until the speaker had finished his question, would answer carefully, and suffer the caresses as though accepting them as a part of his duty, and would return to the tent and his aunt, evincing no desire for the frolic and fun which belongs to the golden days of childhood. Many influential whites were present in order to display their philanthropic interest in the welfare of the colored people. They gazed with surprise upon the child, and could not be convinced when told that he was a Negro, and identified by ties of blood with the blackest men and women in the crowded company. In a distant corner Sappho sat keeping a strict account of the moneys received. Occasionally she would leave her seat and mingle with the crowd. Gowned in a pure white china silk with a bunch of her favorite Jacks in her corsage, she moved "a daughter of the gods divinely fair." And many a thought came into the heart of one learned doctor as he gazed on the child and the beautiful girl, and then upon faces ebony-hued but bright and sparkling with the light of freedom and intelligence. In that moment a cloud passed from before his mental vision, and he beheld in all its hideousness the cankering sore which is eating into the heart of republican principles and stamping the lie upon the Constitution. Expediency and right must go hand in hand. There is no room for compromise.

Sappho was tired, and one of the young girls in her Bible class, noticing the weariness of her attitude, insisted upon assuming the duties of cashier for an hour. She gladly availed herself of the girl's offer, and turned with a sigh of relief to find a secluded seat where she could watch unobserved the passing of the gay throng. As she turned a hand was laid gently on her arm, and Will Smith's gay voice sounded in her ear: "Whither away, fair lady?"

Sappho smiled back into the debonair face as she replied: "Just to the fairy grotto to rest a while."

"I will accompany thee, fair queen," hummed Will, as he drew her hand within his arm and moved slowly through the crowd toward the refreshment room. No more was said until they reached the spot; then Will seated her at one of the most secluded tables, placing himself upon the opposite side.

"Lord love yer, Sarah Ann, jes' see that couple!" said Mrs. Davis to Mrs. White. "Ef that ain't a match then no matter! See him look at her! I'se goin' to wait on them myself; an' Sarah Ann, you keep these young squirts busy in some other corner; there ain't nobody goin' ter spile sport ef I can help it."

Mrs. Davis bustled over to the young people and literally beamed upon them. "Good evening; now Mr. Smith, what be you an' Miss Sappho goin' to have? You see I've jes' camed over to wait on yer myself."

"Good evening, Mrs. Davis; you are looking as bright and charming as a rose.

"How are the refreshments going?

"Charmin'!" responded Mrs. Davis, secretly delighted at the compliment. "Ain't you 'shamed to talk like that to an ol' 'ooman? You young fellers gits worse every day. Jes' see Miss Sappho lafin' at you! Well, thank God, we's doin' well tonight, took in a pile o' money so fur. Mary Jane Robberson thinks she's goin' to down me in this here refreshment room, but jes' you wait 'tel Friday night!"

"What about Friday night?" asked Sappho.

"Nuthin', only I've got a big s'prise waitin' fer Mary Jane Robberson."

"Friday will be a mighty unlucky day for Sister Robinson, eh?" laughed Will.

"Thar won't be a thing doin' fer her, honey, you'll see. I'se gwine ter paralize her!"

"I'll bet my money on you every time, Mrs. Davis," laughed Will. "I have every confidence in your business sagacity. I feel sorry for Sister Robinson."

"She'll need yer sorrow," replied Mrs. Davis. Mary Jane Robberson's jealous, an' when people gits jealous they can't do the bes' thing in the bes' place. I ain't jealous o' nobody, an' I'se jes' settin' back here watchin' her kill hersef, as cool as a sittin' hen. I had a letter from Mis' Mason, an' she says as how she's goin' ter stan' by me. You know what that means, don' yer, honey? Oysters, coffee, ice cream and cake fer two," she murmured, repeating Will's order. "My head's level, thar ain't a thing the matter with it," she finished, as she turned to execute the order.

A silence fell between the two as they sat within the shadow of the trees, content to be with each other. Will was happy to have the privilege of feasting his eyes upon the lovely face opposite him, which dimpled and blushed in such a charming manner beneath his glance. Never before had she seemed to abandon herself so completely to the influence of his passion; but tonight she laid aside her coldness and seemed ready to accept the homage which he was longing to lay at her feet. The girl felt it.

"Why," she asked herself, "why should I always walk in the shadow of a crime for which I am in no way to blame? Why deny myself all the pleasures of a home and love with such a man as he who will offer me the noblest heritage of woman?"

The more she thought the stronger became her resolve not to fight against fate, but to accept the goods the gods provided without question. She would rise above maddening fears, penance for involuntary wrongs, the sackcloth and ashes of her life, and be as other women, who loved and were beloved. So she smiled on Will bewitchingly; sallies of wit and fun flashed from her pretty lips in a way which was as fascinating as bewildering. Will knew her to be well educated, but had never supposed that she possessed the exquisite art of repartee. Tonight he caught glimpses of an ideal woman and wife, and the glimpse intoxicated him. Now Love was kind.

They had very nearly finished their lunch when the room was invaded by Dora, followed by Doctor Lewis, who had arrived from New Orleans the last of the previous week.

"Oh, here you are, Sappho, I've been looking for you everywhere. Have you had one of Madam Frances's predictions? She is creating a sensation."

"No," replied Sappho, "I have not. Have you one? Is it good?"

"Yes, I have one. For my part I think it's rubbish. Just listen," and she read from a slip of paper in her hand:

> *All that glistens is not gold;*
> *Often have you heard this told.*
> *Despise the false; welcome the true,*
> *So shall you receive your due.*

"Now whatever in the world does she mean by all that?"

"Where's John?" asked her brother rather abruptly; "has he had a message, too?"

"Yes; and he's so mad that he won't give anyone a decent word," replied his sister. I'm sure," she continued, "if I felt as hateful as John Langley has acted tonight, I'd stay at home."

"Do you remember how his message read?" asked her brother.

"Yes," said Dora, "it was something like this: 'He who expects gain shall lose. Be faithful to the object of your choice, or merit the fate reserved for fickleness and deceit.'"

"Can't blame him for feeling wrathy over such a fortune as that, can you, Lewis?" asked Will, turning to his sister's companion.

"Gad, no!" replied the doctor. "If he would only prove unfaithful to the object of his choice' how happy some other fellow might be."

Dora looked at her companion with scorn on her countenance. "I just think I hate you sometimes, Arthur Lewis!" she exclaimed, as she turned to leave the room.

"Oh, I say, Dora, do have something before you go," urged the unlucky fellow, as he followed his angry companion toward the door.

"No, I won't have anything. I do believe you just love to see John Langley quarrel with me, but it won't do you a bit of good, Arthur Lewis, not a bit."

As they vanished from sight Will turned to Sappho and said: "Dora and John worry me, Miss Clark; I fear that there is trouble ahead for my little sister if she marries him, and I could find it in my heart to wish that her choice had fallen on Lewis. He is a thoroughly good and capable man, and loves the girl devotedly."

"Let us hope that all things may turn out for the best," replied Sappho.

"I don't know why I should worry you with this, Miss Clark," said Will, as he turned toward her with a light in his eyes which a man gives to but one woman in the world. "Miss Clark—Sappho—"

"Ah, here you are." This time it was John Langley who had broken in upon the lovers. He came up to them smiling, polished, bland. Sappho wondered why she had never noticed how very disagreeable John Langley's smile was. She shuddered a bit as he drew nearer to them. Behind him walked the little Mercury, and in his hand he held a white missive just drawn from the small black velvet bag which hung at his side.

"Mercury wanted to find you, Miss Clark, and as I had a message for you from your mother, Will, I ventured to interrupt your earnest conversation. I hope I don't intrude. He bowed with easy grace to Sappho and bade her good evening, at the same time taking the chair which will vacated as he rose to go to his mother.

"Thank you, John. No, you do not intrude. Miss Clark, I shall see you again shortly, I hope. I would very much like to finish our conversation."

Sappho bowed and he turned away. She followed the retreating figure with her eyes; John watched her jealously, and the child stood and watched them both. Finally with a sigh she opened the note, but before reading it turned to murmur a gentle apology to Langley.

"Oh, never mind me," he returned pleasantly; "if you get such a mongrel mixture as the one sent to me, I shan't envy you the pleasure you'll get out of it."

"It wasn't pleasant, I remember. Dora told us about it."

"Pleasant! A regular death's head at a feast, I call it. Do read yours, Miss Clark, and see if you haven't something better."

"Let me see: The mysterious stars bespeak for you better luck than you have already had. Harassed and perplexed by fickle Fortune, love shall find a way.

"Bravo!" cried John. But how could it be otherwise? If the same blood which inaugurated the Trojan wars, of which fair Helen was the object, still runs in the veins of the gods of love and fortune, they could not resist the influence of so much youth and beauty as we are blessed with here tonight."

"And what shall I say in reply to so gallant a speech, Mr. Langley? To my way of thinking, such words should be uttered to one alone. You must have forgotten Dora." Sappho turned to the waiting child and drew him into her lap.

"Because a man is engaged to one girl does that spoil all the pleasure which lies in meeting others? One woman can never tie my wandering fancy; my heart is large enough to appreciate the charms of the fair sex wherever discovered. Dora don't like it, I know, but she'll get used to it after we are married," he said, recklessly.

Sappho kissed the child on her lap, and placing the postage for her letter in his hand, told him to run away. "Truly, Mr. Langley, you appear in a new light. Why do you tell your thoughts to me, who am Dora's friend? I do not wish to hear them."

There was a mocking smile on his face as he turned to her from watching the child. "A pretty boy that. His is beauty of a rare kind. Do you know, I fancy that he resembles you."

"Really, Mr. Langley, you grow very strange in your conversation. I shall have to beg you to excuse me," and with a haughty little bow she left the place:

John watched her departure with a slight smile on his face. "Oh, beauty is the wine of life, fair woman, for me," he hummed beneath his moustache. The smile was still on his face as he ordered a cup of coffee and proceeded to drink it leisurely.

The fair had been very popular, and most successful from a business point of view. The week was now drawing to a close. The community was on the qui vive over the rivalry between Mrs. Robinson and Mrs. Davis. Racy developments were looked for on the closing night. Every woman had ranged herself on one side or the other, and not a few of the men had been led by their vigorous wives to declare themselves for a chosen leader.

Friday night was to end the sale of votes on the prizes. Saturday was to be devoted to counting up the votes, so that at nine o'clock that night the successful winners could be announced. The pastor was asked to allow the fair to run another week, but he declined emphatically, saying that so many controversies had grown out of it that another week would seriously deplete his membership and bring disaster upon the cause of religion. So that idea was abandoned. Wednesday Mrs. Robinson was ahead on the piano but behind on the dining-room receipts. Thursday night Mrs. Davis was ahead on the piano but behind on the receipts in the refreshment room. So luck flauctuated until the rivals found themselves neck and neck, so to speak, at eight o'clock on Friday night. Anyone who had watched Mrs. Robinson would have noticed that her face wore a satisfied smirk which told that she anticipated an easy victory, and the knowing ones of her satellites told each other that "Sis' Robberson was all right."

Mrs. Davis viewed the action of her rival with stolid countenance, from which the envoys of the other side, who stood about trying to catch a word to repeat to their champion, could gain no comfort. To her trusted henchmen she whispered: "Jes' you watch me keep 'em guessin' I'm a-goin' to show 'em, shortly, that the 'race am not to the swif'er nor the battle to the stron'er, but to her what enjureth untel the end.'"

As half-past seven approached various savory smells could be traced to the "old Southern dining-room," but above all the enticing scents which were ever introduced to aggravate the palate of the lover of good living, the knowing ones could trace the odor of a rare and tempting dainty—the opossum! Yes, Mrs. Robinson had conspired with her Southern friends and received a tempting animal direct from the "Old Dominion," and on this eventful night she stood in the middle of the dining-room triumphantly directing the placing of the dish upon the main table, which was carefully arranged with covers laid for twenty-five persons. The ordinary patrons of the room were turned from the door, and even the pastor was not allowed to enter, being told that the dining-room had been engaged for an hour by a private party. At eight o'clock a message was brought to her by a lad stationed at the outside entrance to the vestry, and Mrs. Robinson immediately hurried to the door to receive a sleigh-load of young white ladies and gentlemen who had come from among the wealthy people of the city, for whom Mrs. Robinson was a faithful servant, to help her triumph over her enemies. With head thrown back and held very high, and satisfaction beaming from her countenance, the good sister marched in at the head of the company like a successful warrior on his return from victory. The assembled company made way, gazing with awe upon so many representatives of wealth and influence. Then they were lost within the sacred precincts of the dining-room, into which Mrs. Robinson ushered them. The pastor was sent for presently, and attended by the most prominent trustee on the Board, he waited upon the guests who had so honored his flock. During the interview which ensued the door was closed to the gaze of the inquisitive crowd, but after half an hour the good man came forth with the guests and proceeded to show them the points of interest in the fair. A few minutes before nine they took their departure, seemingly well pleased with what they had seen.

"Well, Sis' Davis," said one of the brothers when the door closed upon the visitors and the company felt at liberty to enjoy itself after its own fashion, "well, sister, that ruther gits ahead of you. Sis' Robberson's got you dead sure this time."

He laughed with a good-natured chuckle which was meant to be very aggravating.

"Beats who? *me*?" snorted Mrs. Davis, as she turned upon the questioner with a stony stare. "White folks don't scare Ophelia Davis. I'se seed 'em befo' in my life, an' I've eat at the table wif 'em, that's mo'. Didn't hev to hev the do' sheton me to keep me out the dining-room 'cause they was feered the black'd rub off. I think too much o' my white people to trot 'em up here to this one-cen' 'fair."

"No use, Sis' Davis, we's got yer," laughed another member who had just come up. "Robberson's smart.

"Smart!" cried the irate woman, now thoroughly angry. "You-alls havin' yer hallelujah meetin' too soon. Don' holler 'tell yer knows what yer hollerin' 'bout. I ain't beat tell nine o'clock sharp, when the polls is closed."

"Five minutes is all you's got, anyhow. Can't change much in five minutes," laughed another.

Just at this moment a messenger boy made his way from the door and was conducted to the judges' seat. He handed them an envelope which upon being opened was seen to contain two bits of paper.

"Please step this way, Mrs. Davis, and make your mark for value received," called out one of the judges.

Mrs. Davis was escorted to the table by a curious crowd, anxious to know the meaning of this latest sensation. The judge stood up after she had signed, and said: "Ladies and gentlemen, knowing the interest that you take in all that relates to the two ladies who are rival candidates for the piano, and also for the ten dollars for the largest amount taken at a refreshment table, I beg leave to state that one hundred and fifty dollars have been contributed by Mrs. Mason and Mrs. Molly Mason Farnham, to be used for buying votes in the favor of Mrs. Davis in the contest for the piano, and to swell the receipts at her refreshment tables.

As I hold my watch in my hand it is now one minute of the closing hour of the polls. Any more votes?" He paused and looked around. "No more? then I have the honor of informing you that the polls are closed. No more tickets can be bought, and I may as well say right here that Sister Davis will have the most votes; she'll stand at least five hundred ahead. Now I propose that we give that we give three cheers for Sister Davis."

And they were given with a will, led by the pastor, who stood upon a chair and swung his bandanna handkerchief wildly in the air.

Mrs. Davis was greatly excited. "Sis' Robberson's got me, has she? Beat, am I? How 'bout it, honeys, how 'bout it?"

Sister Mary Jane Robinson was carried home sick in a herdic.

The next night brought a great crowd to see the distribution of the prizes. The fun waxed warmer and warmer as each name was called. When young 'Mandy Jackson was called to receive the diamond pin, her twin brothers turned handsprings in the aisle, and yelled out: "Hi, 'Mandy, yer a peach! We-uns did the bisness fer yer, yer bet."

Sister Susanna Johnson received the muchcoveted silver set, and thought with pride of the handsome sideboard, and made up her mind then and there to give the Stewardess Board such a tea as they had not had for many a day, before another week rolled over her head.

Jim Anderson walked up to the judges' stand feeling very bashful and with a fearful grin on his face, when his name was called for the gold watch and chain.

"Wet it, Jim! wet it!" cried one of his friends.

"Set 'em up, ol' man!" roared another, as Jim returned to his seat. "Don't be 'shamed; do the right thing by the boys."

Jim Anderson was angry. He was a trustee, and was looked up to by all the young members as an exemplary Christian. Jim made up his mind not to stand it, and he paused on the way to his seat and offered to take the speaker and "set him up" by standing him on his head if he'd only come out where he could get at him, "makin' a fool o' him right out in chuch."

This stopped the fun in that direction, for Jim was a beef-lugger at the "big" market, and they had a wholesome regard for his muscle.

But when Mrs. Davis was called for the piano and the ten dollars, the excitement broke out with renewed vigor: "Speech! speech!" resounded from all over the hall.

"You must say a word to your friends, sister," said the pastor. Then she stood up.

"Friends, I'm much obbligated to yer fer makin' all this noise over me, but bein' a lonesome ol' 'ooman, an' with no ejkation, I cayn't make no speech. I'll jes' say thar's nuthin' mean 'bout me. I don' feel good 'cause some o'us is took sick 'long o'all this. Now, pastor, I want yer to take this ten dollars over to Sis' Robberson an' tell her we's quits, an' I fergive her fer all her mean feelin's to me. Will you do it?"

The pastor promised, and for a while pandemonium reigned. And after that the pastor could not forbear saying a few words about how good it was "to dwell together in brotherly love." Sister Sarah Ann White said "the brothers had nuthin' to do with it, it was Ophelia Davis an' nobody else."

Mrs. Davis, true to her word, had not forgotten the pastor; and all the women, mindful of the feeling engendered by Mrs. Robinson against him, had secretly gone about among the "400," and money enough had been contributed to buy him a fine new Sunday suit, made up in the latest clerical fashion. After all the prizes had been presented, the women formed in a body, and headed by Ma Smith, marched up to the judges' seats and presented him with the result of their good feelings. So everybody was made happy.

It was estimated that the proceeds of the fair exceeded the eight thousand dollars hoped for, and no church had more sincere cause to rejoice on the next Easter Sunday than the body of people comprising the church on X Street, who on that memorable day consecrated anew to God their house of worship free from all encumbrances.

XII

A COLORED POLITICIAN

O, that estates, degrees and offices
Were not derived corruptly, and that clear honor
Were purchased by the merit of the wearer!
How many then should cover that stand bare!
How many be commanded that command!

—MERCHANT OF VENICE

John Langley occupied an office in the business portion of the city among the most reliable lawyers in the profession. He held that association with success would in the end bring the desired quality to any one.

He had never been moved by a generous heart-impulse in his whole life. Actual need found no pity dwelling in his breast. The comfortable home which the thrift of Smith had founded and the industry of the family had fostered to prosperity, influenced his devotion to Dora to an extent which if realized by her would have led to his instant dismissal by that impetuous young lady. According to his way of thinking, the wife ought to contribute as much to the expenses of the household, by having a comfortable nest-egg before marriage, as the husband. He listened to the romantic story of the Montfort family with eagerness, and while regarding it as a fanciful creation of the mind, yet he felt that he must look it up and be very sure that a dollar could not be gained from it, before he marked it in his mind as valueless. He meditated on the subject constantly, but with the shrewdness characteristic of his nature, carefully concealed his thoughts from every one. He had no idea where he should begin to unravel this great mystery of family connections lost within the fog-banks of life in London, but he intended to try.

Langley's nature was the natural product of such an institution as slavery. Natural instinct for good had been perverted by a mixture of "cracker" blood of the lowest type on his father's side with whatever God-saving quality that might have been loaned the Negro by pitying nature. This blood, while it gave him the pleasant features of the

Caucasian race, vitiated his moral nature and left it stranded high and dry on the shore of blind ignorance, and there he seemed content to dwell, supinely self-satisfied with the narrow boundary of the horizon of his mental vision.

He remembered little of his parentage, but what had most impressed him was that somewhere in the dim past a woman, presumably his mother, had boasted that through her he was a direct descendant of the North Carolina Pollocks. So he clung to the name, and called himself John Pollock Langley. Neither the Smiths nor he connected his name in any way with the Montfort story; it was a mere coincidence.

If taken in his first state, fresh from the woods and streams of his nativity, the Negro be subjected to the saving influences of the Christian home where freedom and happiness, education and morality abound, the Anglo-Saxon would lose the main arguments which he uses against the black brother; rather would he bow humbly in recognition of the ebony-hued miniature of God. Subject the Anglo-Saxon to the whip and scourge, grind the iron heel of oppression in his face until all resemblance to the human family is lost in the degradation of the brute, take from wives and mothers the sacredness and protection of home in the time before birth, when moral and intellectual development are most dependent upon pre-natal influences for the advancement of generations to come; join to all this the uncontrolled bestial passions of humanity, and what have you? classic features and a godlike mind? No! rather the lineaments of hideous despair, fearful and hopeless as the angel forms that fell from heaven to the black gulf of impenetrable hell.

Up from the South there came one morning early in March the report of another lynching. The skies were heavy with gray, storm-laden clouds, not darker nor more threatening than the dire and bloody news the daylight ushered in. For a month or two peace had seemingly reigned in southern latitudes, but it was the slumbering of passion, not its subsidence. At table, in the cars, at the office, in the workshop, men read with sick hearts the description of another illegal act of distorted justice, wherein the sufferings of the poor wretches were depicted only too truthfully for the peace of the community:

> Jim Jones, a burly black Negro accused of the crime of rape against the person of a beautiful white woman, was taken from his home by a number of our leading citizens, and after being identified by his victim, was carried into the woods, where, before

an immense concourse of people, he was bound to a tree, pieces of his flesh were stripped from his body, his eyes were gouged out, his ears cut off, his nose split open, and his legs broken at the knees. After this the young woman stepped forward and poured oil upon the wretch, and the wood being piled about him, she applied the torch to light the fire which was to consume the black monster. Leaving some of the party to watch the funereal pile, a posse went into the city and brought to the scene of vengeance Sam Smith, Bill Sykes and Manuel Jackson, who were accused of hiding the guilty wretch from the justice of the populace. These three men were hanged to the nearest trees in full sight of the burning wretch, who made the day hideous with his cries of agony. We think the Negroes of this section have been taught a salutary lesson.

—Torchlight

The American Colored League was made up of leading colored men all over New England. These men were in communication with the colored people in every section of the country, for there is no community of colored people so remote that a branch of the great National League of American Colored Men cannot be found within easy reach of all. To the Boston branch of this society the people of all sections of the country look for aid and comfort, not because of any acknowledged superiority of its members, but solely on account of the advantages which they are supposed to enjoy under the beneficent rulings of the grand old Commonwealth of Massachusetts. We do not claim for Massachusetts, in her policy toward the Negroes within her gates, freedom from prejudice or error. There is prejudice enough, heaven knows, prejudice which is fed every day by fresh arrivals from the South and by intermarriage between Southern women and the sons of Massachusetts. But Massachusetts is noted for being willing to see fair play: she hears the complaints of the Negro, and listens with attention to the accusations of the Southern whites, weighs the one against the other, and, naturally enough, the scales tip in favor of the white brother. From one class the Negro suffers in the state and is contemptuously flouted; from another he receives the hearty word of encouragement, backed by the all-powerful dollar which goes to feed such universities as Hampton, Tuskegee, and the like.

News of the latest horrible event had just reached the officers of the American Colored League. A call had been issued through the church and press for a public indignation meeting at the church on X Street, and John, as one of the executive committee of the League, was turning over in his mind ways and means of making it a success. With pencil in hand and paper before him he sat thinking. Outside, the sound of the typewriter clicking away for dear life came to his ears, mingled with the whistle of the office boy as he shuffled in and out, attending to his morning chores. John hired a white office boy and a white stenographer, not because he would not have liked to patronize his own people, but because he thought that it would be pleasanter for his patrons to meet their own race when business compelled them to visit him, and because he wished everyone to realize that *he*, at least, had no prejudice in his heart toward anyone. This was what he told the committee from the League when they waited on him and asked him to give the office work to two worthy representatives of their race, and pointed out to him that it was his duty so to do as a leading man of influence among them. Some of the committee were unkind enough to say that they believed that Langley was as prejudiced toward black people as any Anglo-Saxon; but as he denied it most emphatically, there was nothing more to be said about the matter, though many colored men voted him a "sneak" in private, and had a watchful eye on all his movements.

Usually John had no difficulty in fixing his attention on the humdrum routine of the office, but today his thoughts wandered. Sappho Clark had touched a vein in his nature which was a revelation to himself. Sensuality was prominent in the phrenological development of his head, although no one of his associates would have called him a libertine. Nevertheless, there it lurked ready to assert itself when conditions were ripe to call it into action. Sappho represented the necessary conditions. Her beauty intoxicated him; her friendlessness did not appeal to his manliness, because, as we have intimated, *that* was an unknown quality in the makeup of this man. Her coldness urged him on; and Jealousy, the argus-eyed attendant of Love, and its counterfeit—Infatuation—warned him that Will's love was returned, and made him impatient to force upon her an acceptance of his own devotion, at whatever cost. He did not contemplate marriage, because he intended to marry Dora for mercenary reasons. But to his mind that was no obstacle to the consummation and lifelong duration of an illicit love. He had detected in Sappho's personality a coldness more in accordance with the disposition of women of the North than with that of one born beneath the smiling skies of the languorous

Southland. Where, with such a face and complexion, had she imbibed a moral character so strong and self-reliant as her conduct had shown her to possess? Not by inheritance, if he read the signs aright. Then, he argued, if she had acquired that stately, cold, dispassionate bearing by force of habit only, the time would surely come when unexpectedly the true nature would reassert itself. Ah, he could wait! Meantime he could watch for opportunities to coax the unwilling bird within the net.

"Gentleman to see you, sir," announced the office boy, laying a card on the table before him. Langley glanced at the card and then said: "Show the gentleman in, and remember I'm 'engaged' to anyone who calls while he is here." As the boy left the room he thought to himself: "I wonder what brings the Hon. Herbert Clapp here today. Something uncommon, I warrant."

Langley arose to receive his visitor with an easy grace which was a distinguishing point in his personality. Men would tell you privately keen, far-sighted politicians—that they believed Langley to be "tricky," but that he had such a pleasant way with him that you would give in to him when you knew, within your own mind, that he would "do" you out of a case in court or a hundred dollars with the suavity of a Lord Chesterfield; or as one politician expressed it: "He has such a d oily way with him that a man forgets to 'fire' him until it is too late." He received his guest with empressement, bade him good-morning in a cordial voice, seated him in the easiest chair which the cozy office contained, and, before his hat had fairly reached a resting-place, had produced a box of fine cigars, and made him comfortable.

"Deuced pleasant office you have here, Langley," remarked the visitor as he lit a fragrant Havana and proceeded to enjoy himself man-fashion.

"Oh, it isn't bad," replied Langley, "though if my practice allowed it I would be glad to take more commodious quarters." John had helped himself to a cigar, and was now contemplating the ceiling through rings of curling smoke. Apparently he watched a belated fly trail its body slowly over the white space, but really his mind was alert and watchful to find a clue as to the nature of the business which had caused this man to call upon him. Mr. Clapp had visited him twice before since he had been in business, and each time his call had brought substantial profit, in a political way, to his little bank account.

"Horrible thing, this latest case of lynching," Mr. Clapp remarked after an interval of silent enjoyment.

"Yes," replied John, "pretty bad. Isn't it most time for the Administration to take it up? You can't expect us to stand this sort of thing always, and not strike back."

"What'd you gain by doing that?" questioned Mr. Clapp.

"I'll tell you," replied John, looking earnestly at his visitor, "there are thirty-five thousand of us in this state alone. We can be organized, if the work is done by the right ones and in the right way. We can help start a new party, if nothing more."

"That won't do any good, John, we can down you. Colored people won't stick together; and then where'd you be?"

"We'd stick all right if once we got started," returned John doggedly.

"No you wouldn't; you're so confoundedly jealous of honors. Each one of you wants all there is for himself, and you never know when to get off, individually. We white men know this, and it is easy to upset your plans."

"I know that there is a great deal of truth in what you say, but that won't always be the case with us; we are growing away from it more and more every day; and with the missionary work that the League is doing, we expect to fight you one of these days, and knock the party clear over the ropes.

"You'll never do it!" declared Mr. Clapp.

"Time will tell You don't expect to succeed in keeping us out of employment, shoved in a corner to starve and to be burnt alive, without getting square sometime, do you? There would be some satisfaction in throwing you fellows out and putting others in, if a new party is the outcome of the issue, and seeing some of you, who have your pockets filled with the salaries which the Government has heaped upon you, shoved out of a job and your vast schemes for growing richer, at the expense of the lives of just such poor unfortunates as the Negroes you are allowing the South to burn in order to keep in power, blown to the devil. We can at least do that much."

"I didn't expect such talk from you, Langley," said Mr. Clapp, his lips tightening in a tense line about the mouth.

"I suppose not. I've always been pliable, like the rest of the race. Things are changing."

"The dollar will fetch you every time, John."

"Not this time, anyhow," was the dogged reply.

"Pshaw! You people are standing in your own light."

"Yes, I think we are. Been doing the same old thing for the last thirty-five years.

"What do you mean?" demanded Mr. Clapp, growing white with suppressed passion. "Is that a reflection?"

"Don't lose your temper, Colonel; the man who gets mad always gets the worst of it," replied John blandly. "I want to ask you a question: Did you ever hear of such a thing as a man being robbed and murdered in the house of his friends?" He looked Mr. Clapp squarely in the eye. The latter shifted uneasily in his seat. "That's what's been done to my people."

"Well, you can't complain; you've had all you're worth."

"Had all we're worth! Yes, you give us a bootblack stand in the corridor of the State House, and think we are placated."

"You can't expect anything more until you have earned it. Besides, you're incompetent to fill any higher position. I have had a number of your best men tried in clerical positions, and you always fail to compete favorably with an ordinary white clerk. You can't ask the people to pay for ignorant incompetents."

"Ha, ha, ha!" laughed John, as he lay back in his chair and winked at the Colonel, "that's a good one! What do you think I've been doing since I've been in the law business in this city? Why, the greenest ward-heeler knows that neither a white nor black man is competent to fill an office if the heads of the department where he is employed wish to get rid of him. The civil service is a good thing, but even that can't save a man from becoming incompetent when his resignation is desired by any one in authority. That's no argument at all. And as for our earning our rights didn't earn them at Wagner and Fort Fisher and at Fort Pillow; we haven't held the casting vote, and floated you from poverty into affluence."

"But the South, man!" exclaimed the Colonel, pounding the table before him with his fists until the dust sprang from the covers of the volumes lying there," the South has rights as well as you. They are white men, man; you can't expect us to leave them out. All sections must be satisfied, and if you love your country as you should, you will be willing to sacrifice a little for the good of the whole. It won't hurt you; you can't miss luxuries and positions that you have never been used to!" The Colonel was shouting at the top of his lungs. John sat calmly waiting for the storm to subside.

"Then what I have heard so often is true, that the South is in the saddle."

"Eh?" said the Colonel, subsiding limply into his chair and wiping his heated face on his handkerchief. "Well, I might as well own it; to you; I know it will go no farther. It is so in great measure, Langley. That is the reason we want your people to go slow. This is a great country. Each man is for the good of his own section. Can't blame 'em, can you?"

"No; and neither can you blame us for trying to get the best we can for the good of our race. You'll find we mean to do it."

"You mean to do it—yes, but the white man rules in this country every time, John, because he's born for the business, and it's just as well for you to keep the few friends you've got, and not drive them away because you're sore over your disappointments. You know nothing about business, you've no capital, no money, and we've got you every time."

"Threats do not frighten me, Colonel; nearly nineteen hundred years ago Christ sat at supper with his friends, and one of them, with a kiss still warm on his lips, betrayed him to crucifixion. What have we to expect from our friends?"

"Now, look here, Langley, don't say hard things, and don't get mad. I will admit every word that you say. It is all true, d—it!" he exclaimed as he arose to his feet and began walking up and down the floor with rapid strides. "I imagine I should feel even worse than you do if I were one of your race, but you see things are as they are, and why not make the best of a bad matter? Your people can't help themselves. If you rose in the South and appealed to arms you would soon be exterminated; for of course the South is our brother, and in an uprising of that sort, the National arms would necessarily be directed against the 'rioters,' as they would be termed. Individually, I might feel the justice of your cause; others might feel with me; but expediency would make me fight against you. And that brings me to my errand here today. It is the duty of every one of us to wait for justice, and not to countenance excitement and bloodshed. I assure you upon my honor as a man, that if the colored people are only patient for a while longer, this thing will be settled amicably. We have great plans for pacifying the South, and if we have the help of every good citizen we shall sooner be able to bring about a season of peace and prosperity, not only to the colored people, but to the whole country."

"Talk's cheap. I've heard that old gag so many times that it's grown stale."

"But we intend to do the square thing this time."

"It ain't in you to do the square thing by us. It is as natural for you to cheat us and maltreat us as it is for boys to pull out the wings and legs of flies. You say now you've got no power to stop lynching. If you haven't the power before election, where will you get it after the votes are in? No, sir; it's votes you want, and after you get them, and all the subsidies, corporations, and trusts are riding easily on the front seat of the coach for another year, you won't know us; and robbing and killing the black man can go right on."

"You talk like a fool, John Langley. You're jeopardizing the best chance you ever had since Lincoln issued the Emancipation Proclamation."

"That's all right. Promises are like pie-crust, made to be broken. You may be the best we can do, and the best is d—— poor. Colonel, you just make up your mind to one thing: we're coming high this time. It's going to cost you something; yes, sir, right smart."

"I tell you, Langley, we have a hard fight to give your people even the little that they do get. It's your duty to listen to reason in this matter. What do you want, anyhow?"

"We want our men given something beside boot-blacking in the employment of the state. We want our girls given a chance as clerks; that's what we want. Anything unreasonable in that?"

"No; that isn't unreasonable, but d——it all, man, other employees would 'kick."

"Let 'em 'kick.' Turn 'em out and get others; the civil service lists are always full." John faced the angry man with grim determination on every feature. He thought to himself: "The Colonel wants something done, and he might as well know that it's going to take a good thing to get me on his side."

"All right! I see what's the matter with you; you want to fight!" exclaimed the angry Colonel. "All right! be pig-headed; don't listen to reason; plunge the country into a race war in spite of all we've done for you, especially for your leaders; and when your race is exterminated, put the blame where it belongs. I wash my hands of the whole business!"

"Oh," replied John, with a conciliatory air, "I don't want to see bloodshed any more than you do, and I am just as ready to accept amicable terms for my race as you are to offer them. I only want to convince you that we can do something if conditions are right."

"You're all right, John, my boy," returned Clapp, as he slapped Langley on the back, apparently very ready to grasp the olive-branch of peace; "you stick to the party and the party 'll stick to you. We don't want to quarrel, do we?"

"No, that won't pay," said John.

Each man now resumed the seat which he had vacated under the excitement of the moment, helped himself to another cigar, and again contemplated the ceiling through rings of smoke. John noticed that the fly had made the circuit of the ceiling, and was moving toward him from the opposite side of the room. After a moment's silence the Colonel said:

"Your folks are going to have a meeting about this last atrocious affair, aren't they?"

"Yes; I was just looking over the list of speakers as you came in."

"I suppose they're pretty mad?

Yes; pretty hot."

"By the way, Langley, your name is up for the place of City Solicitor, to fill the vacancy made by the death of Calvin. I suppose you'll accept it if you pull it off?"

This was the first that John had heard about any such place being offered to him, but he took it as a matter of course, and his eyes sparkled as he replied: "That would suit me to a T."

"That settles it, then; it's a go. Now I tell you what you do," he continued between the puffs of fragrant smoke; "you hold that meeting down among your people to a calm level. Don't let your fire-eaters like Judge Watson raise the devil of a row, and throw dirt on the party. You keep that end down and I'll work the papers." "Just so," replied John.

"How's the city election going down your way, anyhow?" asked the Colonel, after a few more explicit directions to Langley concerning the work he would have him do.

"Pretty fair. Some of the voters want to take their own heads, but they can be managed."

"Well, here's an order on the committee for money waiting to be used in your district in an emergency. Draw when you need it." Then he arose from his chair to take his leave. Mighty good cigars you keep, John."

"Help yourself, Colonel, help yourself." The Hon. Herbert Clapp graciously took a half-dozen and stored them away in a capacious coat pocket. After a few more commonplace remarks Langley accompanied his visitor to the door, they shook hands, and the interview was ended.

XIII

The American Colored League

Shall tongues be mute when deeds are wrought
Which well might shame extremest hell?
Shall Pity's bosom cease to swell?
Shall Honor bleed?—shall Truth succumb?
Shall pen and press and soul be dumb?

No;—by each spot of haunted ground
Where Freedom weeps her children's fall,—
By Plymouth's rock and Bunker's mound,
By Griswold's stained and shattered wall,
By Warren's ghost, by Langdon's shade,
By all the memories of our dead!

By their enlarging souls, which burst
The bands and fetters round them set,
By the free Pilgrim spirit nursed
Within our inmost bosoms, yet,
By all above, around, below
Be ours the indignant answer,—No!

—Whittier

When Judge Watson, the president of the League, reached his office on that eventful March morning, he found his desk deluged with telegrams from all over the country. From the South the cry was: "Can nothing be done?" "Where is Massachusetts? Has our old friend been turned against us at last?" "For God's sake help us!" "How long, O Lord, how long!" "Let the voice of the League be heard from every city, town and village in the Union. Speak, and let our voices be heard!"

Such were the messages that compelled the hoary-haired veteran of a hundred anti-slavery meetings to crush back the sobs which arose in his throat as he, too, reiterated the cry of an afflicted people: "How long, O Lord, how long!" That day the executive committee of the League met and asked themselves what could be done. "Nothing," was the final decision after debating the question, "but to agitate." This plan they proceeded to put into execution. Notices were sent all over New England of a gigantic public meeting to be held at the church on X Street, on the Tuesday evening following. The press, with one or two exceptions, sided either openly or secretly against the Negroes, North and South. "Ah, ah!" they cried, "see how the Negro abuses the great privileges which we have bestowed upon him." In view of this fact, the League decided that a conservative white man should be asked to address the meeting, along with men imbued with the old abolition spirit, and in this way each side could have a chance to represent the subject as seen from its point of view. "Let us, once and for all, look at the question dispassionately; if the fault be ours, let us acknowledge it like men, and seek to amend it; if it belongs to others, may God help them to do right."

The excitement among the colored people was intense: prayers were held in all the churches the Sunday preceding. Telegrams were received from the branches of the League all over the state that delegates would represent them. The meeting would be a great expression of public opinion.

Dr. Arthur Lewis was head of a large educational institution in the South devoted to the welfare of the Negroes. Every year he visited the city, and assisted by a quartette of singers, who were also members of the school, collected large sums of money from the best class of philanthropic citizens, who gave to the Negro not only because they believed he was wronged, but also because they believed that in great measure his elevation would remove the stigma under which the Southern white labored. For the loyal white man there would be no greater joy in life than to see his poetic dream of superiority to all other governments realized in the "land of the free and the home of the brave." He knows that this can never be while the Negro question keeps up the line of demarkation which marks the division of the North from the South. True and loyal son of his country, he would sacrifice any race, any principle, to bring about this much-desired consummation; so he contributes his money to build up manufacturing interests at the South to his own material disadvantage in the North: to develop uncultivated land there, and to educate the Negro with the hope that in the general advance the latter question may be buried from public notice, if not obliterated. Delusive hope that grasps at shadows!

That momentous Tuesday evening rolled quickly round. The committee asked that the meeting should open at half-past seven, on account of the time needed by the speakers, and long before the hour appointed the large edifice was filled to overflowing. And what a crowd! They came from towns remote, from the farm, from domestic service in the homes of wealth and from among the lowly ones who earn a scanty living with scrubbing-brush and pail. Doctor, lawyer, politician, mechanic every class sent its representative there to help protest against the wrongs of down-trodden manhood.

The platform was heavily draped in Ameri. can flags supplemented by wide bands of mourning. Pictures of the anti-slavery apostles peered out at the audience from the folds of the national colors. Speakers and representative citizens were seated upon the platform, and visiting delegates occupied seats in close proximity. The choir had volunteered its services, and, after a prayer by the pastor, rendered Mrs. Julia Ward Howe's "Battle Hymn of the Republic" in masterly style. In listening to the martial strains the pulse of the vast concourse of people was strained with excitement and expectation. The stillness was intense as the gray-haired president of the League and chairman of the meeting arose in his seat and passing to the desk, rapped for order.

"Fellow-citizens and men and women of my race: The occasion for this meeting is one of great solemnity. Forty years ago, when as a young man I sat at the feet of Sumner, Phillips, Garrison, Pillsbury, Charles Lenox Remond, Nell, Robert Morris, Fred Douglas and all the mighty host of anti-slavery fathers, we thought that with the abolishment of slavery the black man's destiny would be accomplished, and fixed beyond a peradventure. Today a condition of affairs confronts us that they never foresaw: the systematic destruction of the Negro by every device which the fury of enlightened malevolence can invent. In whatever direction we turn, the clouds hang dark and threatening. This new birth of the black race is a mighty agony. God help us in our struggle for liberty and manhood! Agitation and eternal vigilance in the formation of public opinion were the weapons which broke the power of the slaveholder and gave us emancipation. I recommend these methods to you today, knowing their value in the past.

> "'Up then act! Thy courage wake!
> Combat intrigue, injustice, tyranny,
> And in thine efforts God will be with thee.'"

He then called upon the Hon. Herbert Clapp, as a representative of the party and of the sentiment of the best white people of the country, to address the meeting.

The political contingent gave him a hearty welcome as he moved with stately tread to the front of the platform. He said:

"The topic to be discussed is a very serious one, and I feel deeply how incompetent I am to deal with it, how incompetent most of us are to attempt the solution of the question before us. As a white man looking upon the South as my brother, and desiring to see the welfare of that section secured along with the rights of the brother in black, I feel the responsibility which rests upon me tonight to be fair and just, impartial to both sides in what I may say. I ask you tonight as rational people to look at this question from both points of view; to be calm and logical; to be willing, as just men of intelligence and judgment, to see and acknowledge wrong wherever you find it among your own people, and to be willing to consult as to the best method of procedure to rectify mistakes which if corrected may lead to an amicable adjustment of all difficulties in the South. As a friend of both sides, I ask you to do this."

"I am not here to apologize for the South; she has her ills and her sins. What section has not? Let us thank God that sectionalism is dead."

"Now, then, let us try to appreciate the relations of the Negro at the South. All history shows that two races, approaching in any degree equality in numbers, cannot live together unless intermarriage takes place or the one is dependent and in some sense subject to the other. Miscegenation by law will never take place in the South. No matter how much we people of the North may differ with our brothers of the South, this point will always remain fixed. Miscegenation, then, being out of the question, nothing remains for the Negro but to be dominated by the white man there. I hold that the Negro in American civilization is a problem of a vast deal more import than we are inclined to believe. The problem is national, not sectional. The sin of slavery was the sin of the nation, and that sin stands before us today full of menace, full of peril to the whole people. The Southern brother claims, and with some justice I think you will allow, that under the influence of scalawags and carpet-baggers, mostly composed of unprincipled Northern white men, the Negro has opposed, politically, everything that he thinks the white man wants. Upon this subject Prof. H. M. Brown, a Negro and member of the faculty of Hampton Institute, says: 'The greatest enemy to the Negro and the greatest obstacle to his progress is the politician, and the Negro politician is the worst of all.'"

"You cannot deny that the well-behaved Negro has the respect of the community in which he lives at the South. Witness the death of a highly respected Negro in Georgia a short time ago. He never dabbled in politics, and his death was deplored by white and black alike. In thirty years forty per cent of the illiteracy at the South among the colored people has disappeared, due no doubt to environment and emulation of the whites. All kinds of employment, trades, professions, etc., are open to the Negro at the South, and you know that counts for a great deal. Here at the North the pressure is so great from the white laborer that we are forced, to some extent, to bar against the colored brother. I am ashamed to say it; but let us state the case truthfully, if at all.

"To come to the case in hand, I wish it to be distinctly understood that I am absolutely opposed to mob law. But there is an unwritten law, not peculiar to any section, which demands the quickest execution, in the quickest way, of the fiend who robs a virtuous woman of her honor to gratify his hellish diabolism. Human nature is the same throughout the civilized world. If in return for all the benefits conferred upon the Negro at the South, which I have enumerated previously, they give us the heinous crime of rape, what shall we say? Where find excuses for such ingratitude? Surely as men we must have sympathy for the pure and virtuous woman who carries with her a living shame, in a living death, in a life all too long for its miseries, if it lasts but for a day."

As he finished and returned to his seat, a sigh like a broken moan seemed to come from the very heart of the multitude, but not a movement broke the stillness. The Hon. Herbert Clapp felt that his part of the exercises was a failure. After à pause, the chairman introduced Doctor Lewis as a leading representative of the race whom they would, doubtless, be glad to hear express his views upon the momentous question under consideration. He was received with liberal applause, and said:

"I agree with our friend the Hon. Herbert Clapp in about all that he has said in relation to the grievous matter before us. think that he has stated the case as impartially as it is possible so to do. The moment there is a lynching in the South, it is made the pretext for many press comments and public meetings among ourselves, and a general agitation of the question in the wrong way. The result is that you people at the North get a wrong idea of the matter. The published accounts of your meetings here do us at the South, who are working along the best lines that we know of for the elevation of the race, an injury, and often retard us greatly in the accomplishment of our designs. Take the Black Belt, and within its circumference you will find the densest ignorance, as well as bright intelligence of no ordinary quality. Among those people you will find the vicious ones who would rather drink, carouse, and fight than do a day's work to keep themselves from the penitentiary. Such men can be bought, bribed, worked upon for the furtherance of any plan or scheme that may suggest itself to the wily brain of the unscrupulous politician. These men are dangerous to the peace of the community, and it is such men who commit the deeds of violence with which the country is horrified at short intervals. If we cannot reach these men individually, we hope to reach their children. Thus we have planned that with the aid of our universities we shall at length root out evil and ignorance, and in the future give our race a clean, pure citizenship. As our friend has stated—politics is the bane of the Negro's existence. Those of us who eschew that subject, let matters of government take care of themselves, while we look out for our own individual or collective advancement, find no difficulty in living at the South in peace and harmony with our neighbors. If we are patient, docile, harmless, we may expect to see that prosperity for which we long, in the years to come, if not for ourselves then for our children. I am an optimist in regard to the future. I have great hopes of the better class of Southern people themselves."

"Let us remember that the South was more conquered than persuaded. The Confederates did not surrender their convictions with their swords. Immediately after the war Henry W. Grady would have been looked upon as a monstrosity. It was a severe blow to the South when the slave gained his liberty. As the South gains wealth and resources I think that the problem will grow less difficult. It is the idea of the Negro holding political preferment that is so hard for the North and South to swallow. But if we give them time and do not hurry them, they will grow gradually accustomed to the new era. Convince the South that we do not want social equality, neither do we wish to rule. We want nothing but our God-given rights as men."

"I believe in the humanizing influence of the dollar judiciously expended for educational advantages, 'holding it better and wiser to tend the weeds in the garden than to water the exotic in the window.' We should strive to obtain the education of the industrial school, seeking there our level, content to abide there, leaving to the white man the superiority of brain and intellect which hundreds of years have developed."

He ceased speaking and sat down amid murmurs of applause, mingled with disapprobation. Some among the audience began to grow restless. Was this what they came to hear-an apology, almost an eulogy upon the course pursued by the South toward the Negro? Other speakers—white and colored—followed; then the chairman introduced our friend John Langley. He came to the front of the platform with his usual graceful bearing. He was well known among the people, especially the younger contingent, and was received with liberal applause.

"My friends," he said, "I shall not detain you with any lengthy remarks upon the situation, because there are speakers to follow me. I am glad of the opportunity to say what I think about lynch law: It is a terrible thing to contemplate. The crime which provokes it is still more terrible, to my thinking. I utter no eulogy upon the position of the South toward the Negro, neither do I harbor undue resentment for the grievous wrongs which I feel they have, in some measure, heaped upon I am willing to leave the punishment of criminals, the suppression of mob violence, with the national government, being convinced that in good time the government so trusted will acquit itself with equity toward my race. You have listened to the speeches made by our friend, the Hon. Herbert Clapp, and our brother, Dr. Arthur Lewis, upon whose word we can implicitly rely, because he works, lives, and moves among the very happenings of which we know nothing save by reading. It is discretion to act coolly, calmly and deliberately; to look at all sides of a question before we jump at conclusions. I can see nothing to be gained, if, as we have been advised, we took up arms in defense of our rights of citizenship. Extermination would speedily follow. Let us not invite destruction. But we have opportunities of advancement. Let us seize them. Let us await the issue of events with patience, trusting in the fealty of our party leaders, putting faith in their sagacity to push our claims and redress whatever grievances we may have, at a seasonable time. We thoroughly understand the attitude of the whites. Let us not offend the class upon whom we depend for employment and assistance in times of emergencies. By so doing, if we cannot have amity we can have peace."

XIV

Luke Sawyer Speaks to the League

My ear is pained,
My soul is sick with every day's report
Of wrong and outrage with which earth is filled.
There is not flesh in man's obdurate heart;
It does not feel for man: the natural bond
Of brotherhood is severed as the flax
That falls asunder at the touch of fire.
He finds his fellow guilty of a skin
Not colored like his own; and, having power
To enforce the wrong for such a worthy cause,
Dooms and devotes him as a lawful prey.

—Cowper

Scarcely had the speaker taken his seat amid suppressed murmurs of discontent, when a tall, gaunt man of very black complexion arose in his seat among the delegates, and in a sonorous bass voice uttered the solemn protest of Patrick Henry, so famous in history: "Gentlemen may cry 'Peace! peace!' but there is no peace!"

In an instant confusion reigned. Women fluttered their handkerchiefs, and above waves of applause and cheers could be heard cries of "Hear, hear!" "Platform! platform!" The chairman rapped for order, and when he could make himself heard, asked the delegate to come to the platform; another speaker was waiting, but the audience would be glad to hear anything he might have to say. As he passed up the aisle and mounted the steps of the rostrum, the people saw a man of majestic frame, rugged physique and immense muscular development. His face was kindly, but withal bore the marks of superior intelligence, shrewdness and great strength of character. He might have been a Cromwell, a Robespierre, a Lincoln. Men of his physiological development—when white—mould humanity, and leave their own characteristics engraved upon the pages of the history of their times.

"Friends," said he, when he stood before them, "I come from

Williamstown, in the western part of this state, to be a delegate at this meeting. Here are my credentials to show that I am in good standing in the League where I belong. (He handed his papers to the chairman.) I want to impress that fact upon the minds of this assembly, because I am going to tell you some awful facts before I get through." He paused, and with his handkerchief wiped the tears and perspiration from his face. "Friends, I am thirty years old and look fifty. I want to tell you why this is so. I want to tell you what brought me here. I want to tell the gentlemen who have spoken here tonight that conservatism, lack of brotherly affiliation, lack of energy for the right and the power of the almighty dollar which deadens men's hearts to the sufferings of their brothers, and makes them feel that if only they can rise to the top of the ladder may God help the hindmost man, are the forces which are ruining the Negro in this country. It is killing him off by thousands, destroying his self-respect, and degrading him to the level of the brute. These are the contending forces that are dooming this race to despair!"

"My name is Lycurgus Sawyer; Luke they call me for short. When I was about ten years old my father kept a large store in a little town in the state of Louisany. I had two brothers and a sister. My mother was a fine woman, somewhat better educated than my father. Through her influence he went into this business of trading, and soon had the largest business and as much money as any man in the county. Father didn't care to meddle with politics, for, with the natural shrewdness of many of us, he saw that that might be made an excuse for his destruction. When I was about ten years old, then, a white man in the village, seeing the headway my father was making in accumulating property, opened a store on the same street. Father said nothing, but his customers still continued to trade with him, and it seemed that the other man would be compelled to give up. About this time father received threatening letters ordering him to move, and saying that in case he did not do as ordered he would lose his life. Mother was frightened, and advised father to get out of the place, but he, anxious to save some part of his hard earnings, waited to sell his stock and houses before seeking a home elsewhere. One night a posse of men came to our house and began smoking us out. You don't know anything about that up here, do you? Well, you'll get there if things keep on as they're going. My father had arms. He raised the window of his sleeping-room and fired into the mob of cowardly hounds. Thoroughly enraged, they broke open the doors back and front, seized my father and hung him to the nearest tree, whipped my mother and sister, and otherwise abused them so that they died next day. My brothers were twins, still so small that they were but babes. The mob took them by the heels and dashed their brains out against the walls of the house! Then they burned the house. I saw all this, and frenzied with horror, half-dead with fright, crept into the woods to die. I was found there by a colored planter named Beaubean, who lived in the next township. He pitied me and took me home. That, gentlemen, was my first experience of lynching. Do you think it is possible to preach 'peace' to a man like me?"

The house was filled with the cries and groans of the audience. Sobs shook the women, while the men drank in the words of the speaker with darkening brows and hands which involuntarily clinched themselves in sympathy with his words.

"But that is not the only story I can tell. Here's another. I will tell it to you, and you can digest it at your leisure."

"Monsieur Beaubean was an educated man, descended from a very wealthy family. His father had been his owner. When the father died he left to his son, born of a black mother, an equal share of the estate along with his legitimate heirs. They made no objections, so he got it."

"Monsieur Beaubean had married a quadroon woman of great beauty—Louisany abounds in handsome women of color; they had two children, a boy and a girl. She was three years old when I went to live with them. I remained in the family twelve years. I learned many things there; along with the trade of blacksmithing I learned to esteem myself as a man."

"I cannot describe to you the beauty and loveliness of that child. As a boy I worshipped her, and as a man I loved her; not with the hope of ever having a return of the feeling she had aroused in me, but as a faithful dog that would lay down his life for those who shelter and care for him, so I felt to Beaubean's family, and especially to that child. When Mabelle, as we called her, was old enough, she was sent to the Colored Sisters' School in the city of New Orleans. It was my pleasant duty to drive her into the city each day and go for her at night."

"Monsieur Beaubean had a half-brother—a white man—who was very wealthy and stood very high in politics. In fact, he was in the State Senate. He was very warm in his expressions of friendship for the family, and especially so in his assumption of relationship. I noticed that he seemed extremely fond of Mabelle. One day, after she had passed her fourteenth birthday, she had a holiday from school, and went with

PAULINE E. HOPKINS

some schoolfellows to visit a companion who lived in the city. They returned at night without her, saying that she went into a store with Monsieur Beaubean's brother, and they had not seen her since."

"Can you imagine what a night was passed by that family? No, you cannot, unless you have been through the same experience. The father went in one direction and I in another. All night long we searched the city streets; nothing could be heard of her. Finally we went to police headquarters and secured the services of a detective. After three weeks of incessant searching we found her a prisoner in a house of the vilest character in the lowest portion of the city of New Orleans—a poor, ruined, halfcrazed creature in whom it was almost impossible to trace a resemblance to the beautiful pet of our household. These arms bore her forth from that vile den and restored her to a brokenhearted parent. I think that I must have gone mad. If I had had the man there then that committed the crime (he raised one gaunt arm above his head, and standing in that attitude seemed the embodiment of vengeance) I would have taken him by the throat and shaken him (he hissed the words through clinched teeth), shaken him as a dog would a rat until he was dead! DEAD! DEAD! We took her home, but I believe that her father was a madman from the time he placed his eyes upon her until he was murdered. And who do you think had done this foul crime? Why, the father's half-brother, uncle of the victim!

"Crazed with grief, Monsieur Beaubean faced his brother and accused him of his crime. 'Well,' said he, 'whatever damage I have done I am willing to pay for. But your child is no better than her mother or her grandmnother. What does a woman of mixed blood, or any Negress, for that matter, know of virtue? It is my belief that they were a direct creation by God to be the pleasant companions of men of my race. Now, I am willing to give you a thousand dollars and call it square.' He handed Monsieur Beaubean a roll of bills as he spoke. Beaubean seized them and hurled them into the villain's face with these words: 'I leave you to carry my case into the Federal courts and appeal for justice.' Unhappy man! That night his house was mobbed. The crowd surrounded the building after firing it, and as an inmate would show his head at a window in the struggle to escape from the burning building, someone would pick him off. So it went all that night. I seized Mabelle and wrapped her in a blanket. Watching my chance I stole from the house after the fire was well under way, and miraculously reached a place of safety. I took Mabelle to the colored convent at New Orleans, and left her there in the care of the sisters. There she died when her child was born!"

As the speaker stood silently contemplating his weeping, grief-convulsed audience, a woman was borne from the auditorium in a fainting condition. John Langley from his seat on the platform leaned over and asked an usher who the lady was. "Miss Sappho Clark," was his reply.

Amid universal silence, the silence which comes from feeling too deep for outward expression, the speaker concluded: "A tax too heavy placed on tea and things like that, made the American Colonies go to go to war with Great Britain to get their liberty. I ask you what you think the American Colonies would have done if they had suffered as we have suffered and are still suffering?"

"Mr. Chairman, gentlemen call for peace, and I reply: 'Peace if possible; justice at any rate.' Where is there peace for men like me? When the grave has closed over me and my memories, I shall have peace.

"Under such conditions as I have described, contentment, amity—call it by what name you will—is impossible; justice alone remains to us."

XV

Will Smith's Defense of His Race

Thank God for the token!
Thank God that one man as a free
Man has spoken!

—Whittier

S omeone at this moment began to sing that grand old hymn, ever new and consoling:

"Jesus, Lover of my soul,
Let me to thy bosom fly,
While the nearer waters roll,
While the tempest still is nigh."

When quiet once more reigned, amid intense silence the chairman arose and introduced Mr. William Smith as the last speaker of the evening. Tremendous applause greeted him, for he was known to be an able and eloquent debater.

"Friends," he said, "I shall not attempt a lengthy and discursive argument; I shall simply try to answer some of the arguments which have been advanced by other speakers. I have no doubt that they have spoken their honest convictions. Now let us look at the other side of the question.

"We know that the Negro question is the most important issue in the affairs of the American Republic today. We are told that there are but two ways of solving the vexed question of the equality of the two races: miscegenation by law, which can *never* take place, or complete domination by the white race—meaning by that *comparative servitude.*"

"Miscegenation, either *lawful or unlawful, we do not want.* The Negro dwells less on such a social cataclysm than any other race among us. Social equality does not exist; no man is forced to receive another within the environments of intimate social life. 'Social position is not to be gained by pushing.' That much for miscegenation. The question now stands: Which race shall dominate within certain parallels of latitude south of Mason and Dixon's line? The Negro, if given his full political rights, would carry the balance of power every time. This power the South has sworn that he shall never exercise. All sorts of arguments are brought forward to prove the inferiority of intellect, hopeless depravity, and God knows what not, to uphold the white man in his wanton cruelty toward the American Ishmael.

"We are told that we can receive education only along certain elementary lines, and in the next breath we are taunted with not producing a genius in science or art. A Southern white man will tell you that of all politicians the Negro is the vilest, ignoring the fact that for corrupt politics no race ever can or ever will excel the venality of a certain class of whites. Let us, for the sake of illustration, glance at the position of the Irish element in politics. They come to this country poor, unlettered, despised. Fifty years ago Pat was as little welcome at the North as the Negro at the South. What has changed the status of his citizenship? Politics. The Irishman dominates politics at the North, and there is no gift within the power of the government that does not feel his influence. I remember a story I heard once of an Irishman just landed at Castle Garden. A friend met him, and as they walked up the street said to him: 'Well, Pat, you are just in time to vote for the city government election.' 'Begorra,' replied Pat, 'an' is it a guvimint they have here? Sure, thin, I'll vote agin it.'"

"The Irish vote, then, is massed at certain strategic points in the North, and its power is feared and respected. The result has been a rapid and dazzling advance all along the avenues of education and wealth in this country for that incisive race. To the Negro alone politics shall bring no fruit."

"To the defense of slavery in the past, and the inhuman treatment of the Negro in the present, the South has consecrated her best energies. Literature, politics, theology, history have been ransacked and perverted to prove the hopeless inferiority of the Negro and the design of God that he should serve by right of color and physique. She has convinced no one but herself. Bitterer than double-distilled gall was the Federal success which brought Negro emancipation, domination and supremacy."

"Disfranchisement is what is wanted by the South. Disfranchise the Negro and the South will be content. He, as the weaker race, can soon be crowded out."

"Many solutions of the question of Negro domination have been advanced; among them the deportation of the Negro to Africa has been most warmly advocated by public men all over the country. They argue that in this way the prophecy of the Bible will soonest be fulfilled; that 'Ethiopia shall stretch forth her hand and princes shall come out of Egypt.'"

"The late Henry Grady told us 'that in the wise and humane administration, in the lifting the slave to heights of which he had not dreamed in his savage home, and giving him a happiness he has not yet found in freedom our fathers (Southern men) left their sons a saving and excellent heritage (slavery).' Another man, also a Southerner, has told us: 'In education and industrial progress this race has accomplished more than it could have achieved in centuries in different environment, without the aid of the whites. The Negro has needed the example as well as the aid of the white man. In sections where the colored population is massed and removed from contact with the whites, the Negro has retrograded. Segregate the colored population and you take away the object-lesson.' Here, then, is the testimony of two intellectual white men as to the dependence of the Negro upon his proximity to the whites for a continuance of what advancement he has made since the abolishment of slavery. Is such a race as this fit at the present time to carry enlightenment into a savage and barbarous country? Can the blind lead the blind? Would not the Negro gradually fall into the same habits of ignorance and savagery from which the white slave-trader so humanely rescued him when he transported him into the blissful lap of American slavery? The Negro cannot be deported."

"It is being argued that the Negro is receiving education beyond his needs or his capacity. In short, that a Negro highly educated is a Negro spoiled. I agree with the gentleman on the other side that education alone will not produce a good citizen. But, of those who would curtail his endeavors to reach the highest that may be opened to him, I would ask: Of what use has education been to you in the upbuilding of the social and political structure which you designate the United States of America? What are the uses of education anyhow?"

"To those who know the constitution of the brain as the organ of the moral and intellectual powers of man, education is of the highest importance in the formation of the character of the individual, the race, the government, the social life of any community under heaven. The objects presented to the mind by education stimulate in the same manner that the physical elements of nature do the nerves and muscles—they afford the faculties scope for action. Education is knowledge of nature in all its departments. The moment the mind discovers its own constitution and discerns the importance of the natural laws, the great advantage of moral and intellectual cultivation as a means of invigorating the brain and mental faculties, and of directing the conduct in obedience to the laws of God and man, is apparent. It is important that the Negro should not be hampered in his search after knowledge if we would eliminate from his nature any tendency toward vice that he may be thought to possess, and which has been largely increased by what he has imbibed from the example and the close, IMMORAL ASSOCIATION which often existed between the master and the slave. From my own observation I should say that in this country today the science of man's whole nature—animal, moral and intellectual—was never more required to guide him than at present, when he seems to wield a giant's power, and in the application of it to display the selfish ignorance of an overgrown child."

"We come now to the crime of rape, with which the Negro is accused. For the sake of argument, we will allow that in one case out of a hundred the Negro is guilty of the crime with which he is charged; in the other ninety-nine cases the white man gratifies his lust, either of passion or vengeance. None of us will ever forget the tales told us tonight by Luke Sawyer; the wanton passions he revealed and which it has taken centuries of white civilization to develop, disclosing a dire hell to which the common crime of the untutored Negro is as white as alabaster. And it is from such men as these that the appeal comes for protection for woman's virtue! Do such examples as these render the Negro gentle and pacific? No; he sees himself traveling for years the barren Sahara of poverty, imprisonment, broken hopes and violated home ties; the ignorant, half-savage, irresponsible human animal who forms the rank and file of a race so recently emancipated from servitude, sees only revenge before his short-sighted vision."

"Rape is the outgrowth of a fiendish animus of the whites toward the blacks and of the blacks toward the whites. The Southern white is unable to view the feared domination of the blacks with the dispassionate reasoning of the unprejudiced mind. He exaggerates the nearness of that possibility, which is not desired by the blacks, and, like the physician sick of a mortal disease, is unable to prescribe for himself, and cannot realize that the simple remedy, gently applied, will lift him from his couch of pain. Lynch law prevails as the only sure cure for the ills of the South."

"'Lynchings are justifiable on two grounds,' says a thoughtful writer: 'First, if they are consonant with the moral dignity and well-being of the people; and secondly, if they stop, and are the only sure means of stopping, the crime they avenge.' Lynching does not stop crime; it is but a subterfuge for killing men. It is a good excuse, to use a rough expression, to go a-gunning for niggers.'"

"Lynching was instituted to crush the manhood of the enfranchised black. Rape is the crime which appeals most strongly to the heart of the home life. Merciful God! Irony of ironies! The men who created the mulatto race, who recruit its ranks year after year by the very means which they invoked lynch law to suppress, bewailing the sorrows of violated womanhood!"

"No; it is not rape. If the Negro votes, he is shot; if he marries a white woman, he is shot; if he accumulates property, he is shot or lynched he is a pariah whom the National Government cannot defend. But if he defends himself and his home, then is heard the tread of marching feet as the Federal troops move south ward to quell a 'race riot.'"

"The South declares that she is no worse than the North, and that the North would do the same under like provocation. Perhaps so, if the offender were a Negro. Take the case of Christie Warden and Frank Almy, which occurred in New Hampshire only a few years ago. Where could a more atrocious crime be perpetrated? The refinement of intellectual pursuits, the elegancies of social intercourse, were the attributes which went to make up the personnel of the most brutal murderer that ever disgraced the history of crime. Centuries of culture and civilization were combined in his make-up. The community where the girl lived and was respected and beloved did not lynch the brute. The white heat of passion led men to lay aside all pursuits for days in order to hunt the criminal from his hiding-place. New Hampshire justice gave him counsel and every means to defend himself from the penalty of his horrid crime. *That was in the North*!"

"Human nature is the same in everything. The characteristic traits of the master will be found in his dog. Black, devilish, brutal as they may picture the Negro to be, he but reflects the nature of his environments. He is the Hyde who torments the Dr. Jekyll of the white man's refined civilization!"

"My friends, it is going to take time to straighten out this problem; it will only be done by the formation of public opinion. Brute force will not accomplish anything. We must agitate. As the anti-slavery apostles went everywhere, preaching the word fifty years before emancipation, *so* must we do today. Appeal for the justice of our cause to every civilized nation under the heavens. Lift our. selves upward and forward in this great march of life until Ethiopia shall indeed stretch forth her hand, and princes shall come out of Egypt."

When he had finished there was not a dry eye in that vast audience. Every heart followed the words of the pastor as with broken utterance he invoked the divine blessing upon the meeting just ended. Slowly they dispersed to their homes, filled with thoughts that burn but cannot be spoken.

The papers said next day that a very interesting meeting occurred the night before at the church on X Street.

XVI

John Langley Consults Madam Frances

MACBETH. Tell, me, thou unknown power,—
FIRST WITCH. He knows thy thought:
　　Hear his speech but say though nought.
MACBETH. Whate'er thou art, for thy good caution thanks;
　　But one word more,—
FIRST WITCH. He will not be commanded: here's another,
　　More potent than the first.

　　　　　　—MACBETH

M any things troubled John Langley. The fact that Dora and he seemed to have lost the close relationship which had distinguished the first period of their engagement, and that she now studiously avoided him and accepted with alacrity all the attention which her childhood's lover so ardently showered upon her, did not disturb him so much as the utter indifference of Sappho Clark. How to bend her to his will was the thought which absorbed his waking hours and haunted him even in sleep. She should not escape him; on that he was determined.

This morning as he walked down town to his office he turned over various plans in his mind, and finally determined to go that very day and consult Madam Frances, who had been voted such a tremendous success at the fair which had just closed. John believed that the seeress could help him, and he was not so polished and refined as to hesitate to use such means to accomplish an end.

When he reached the office he noticed that an invitation to a dinner given that very evening by the Canterbury Club lay upon the desk; in his absorption in other things he had forgotten the dinner. He pushed his work at the Court House to a quick finish and retraced his steps to the office, and telling the boy that he would not return before three o'clock, hurried toward the quarter of the city in which the fortune-teller lived.

J. Street is in the very heart of what is called the "Negro quarter" of the West End; it is also popularly known among colored people as "the

Hill." Here Madam Frances lived in a small ten-foot wooden building which she hired.

"The Hill" has been the scene of many stirring incidents in the peculiar history of the colored people. On the J. Street side the old St. Paul's Baptist Church is situated. This historic old building was the first church the colored people owned in Massachusetts. There were five brothers—black men—bearing the name of Paul, who were educated in England in the reign of George III. One of them—Thomas—determined to return to England and beg for funds to build a colored church in America. He was well received and his mission was successful. Twenty years ago an old Negress—a centenarian—was living who had herself picked up bricks in the streets of Boston in the early morning, and carried them to the spot where the building was being erected. She did this because although too poor to give money toward furthering the enterprise, she felt that she must contribute in some way to the erection of this first colored house of worship in this part of the country. This same woman remembered seeing Thomas Paul bring into the church a large bandanna handkerchief filled with the English gold he had begged abroad, the first Sunday the building was used for worship.

St. Paul's Church became the sacred edifice where the desire for freedom was fostered in the heart of the Negro. There such men as Garrison and Phillips defied the vengeance of howling mobs that thirsted for the lives of the Negro champions.

O glorious times! who can think of them without a quicker heart-throb and a wildly fluttering pulse? O honored men! O happy dead, gone to receive the reward promised to all who do the work of the Master!

As we read of the deeds of such men the question will obtrude itself: Is it the foreordained destiny of some to achieve greatness? and if not foreordained, would these same great ones remain inert and impotent like the mediocre majority? Many of us strive to do what we can, but our efforts do not seem to amount to much. In the present emergency which confronts us as a race, no leader has yet pressed forward to take command, as in those glorious old days; no Sumner to receive upon his precious body the stripes intended for the poor, downtrodden black man.

> *"God rest us all—we know not what we are!*
> *What nature wills, not what we wish, are we."*

PAULINE E. HOPKINS

Let us press forward and take courage and do the little that we can, leaving the rest to God. The hand of the Divine Architect will fit each life into its own niche, to form an intricate whole of preconceived beauty.

Near the head of G. and P. Streets stands the well-known Twelfth Baptist Church, a split from St. Paul's, and world renowned under its beloved pastor and founder, Leonard Grimes. Just across the way, on P. Street, was the home of the venerable and honored Lewis Hayden. The history of Massachusetts is forever linked with that of the Anti-slavery Movement, and the Anti-slavery Movement is entwined about the familiar street-corners of the old West End.

John reached the house and rang the bell of the quaint abode. A colored girl, who was evidently a servant, answered the ring, and told him that Madam Frances was now at lunch, and would not be at liberty until an hour later. However, he might come in and wait, if he wished, and she would ask the Madam to see him before her usual time. On second thoughts, she did sometimes see people before her hours. (This was after John had discreetly slipped a small piece of silver into her hand.) She waited on him up the narrow stairway and seated him in a small back room adjoining the audience room.

John took a seat a little behind the door, thereby being completely sheltered from observation. Indeed, a person passing the door on entering or leaving the building would not be likely to see him, and would declare the room empty; but from his seat he commanded a full view of the passageway.

He had looked the bare and sparsely furnished room over and settled back in his chair for a tedious period of waiting when the door of the next room opened and his attention was attracted by the sound of a voice which he thought he knew: "That money will do what you wish for the boy, Aunt Sally, and"—then the door was closed. John started to his feet in great excitement. Surely he knew that voice! Again the door must have swung open, for he caught the words of the conversation distinctly: "There is no need for him to know—let him continue to think"—he heard no more. Again the door closed. It must have been fully five minutes that he stood intently listening, but nothing more rewarded him. Suddenly the door opened and shut and then he heard the quick, light footfall of a woman and the frou-frou of silken skirts, together with a delicate perfume that he recognized. He drew back as far as possible behind the shelter of the door, and then as he judged from the sound that she was upon the stairs, he ventured from his hiding place, and finding the entry clear, peered over the banisters just in time to catch a full view of the beautiful face of Sappho Clark. As she passed out she had dropped her handkerchief; John picked it up; there in the corner were her initials: "S. C."

He returned to his seat in the bare little room, holding the delicately scented piece of cambric in his hand with the feeling of a man who is on the verge of discovering something of importance to himself. He was confused and uncertain in his thoughts, but when he could command himself sufficiently to reason, he felt that it was very foolish in him to wonder at Sappho's presence there; all girls were eager to consult those who could unveil for them anything pertaining to the future. How silly for him to make a mystery of a common happening; still he was restless, disquieted; vague suspicions assailed his mind.

Madam Frances's niece! What could be her motive in hiding her relationship to the old fortune-teller? That she had one he was confidant. The child, too! She appeared never to have seen him before the fair. They had acted in concert. Madam Frances and the boy seemed not to know Sappho, and by their manner denied all previous knowledge of her. Here was something to unravel. But he was used to solving mysteries; it was his business. He would constitute himself a committee of investigation, he told himself; he owed it to the community, to himself, to the Smith family, who were so fond of her. So he planned that the sin of another poor human soul, a vague fraud against no one in particular but society in general, doing wrong to no one, should be suddenly stripped of its coverings. He mused here alone, buried in deep thought, forgetful of the hour and his surroundings. Uncanny shadows were filling the corners of the bare little room when an idea came to him which fairly made him shiver. He could feel the blood recede from his face under the excitement of the moment and grow cold in his veins. "Heaven above!" he whispered, "it cannot be possible that what I suspect is true that child—his resemblance to her— this woman the child's great-aunt and also Sappho's aunt—the secrecy!"

As he sat there engrossed in speculation the maid who had answered his ring came into the room to tell him that the Madam would see him. He still held the handkerchief in his hand, and said as he held it toward the girl: "The lady who just went out dropped it. I think she called Madam Frances 'Aunt Sally.'"

"Oh, yes," replied the girl, as she took it from him. "I will give it to Madam. Miss Clark comes here a great deal. She is Madam Frances's niece."

John's thoughts were in a whirl as he followed the girl to the door of the room Sappho had just quitted. Why had he never heard of this relationship before? He was quite certain that the Smiths knew nothing of it, or he would have heard it spoken of about the house or at the fair. There was a mystery, then, about her. Just at this point he awoke to a realization of the fact that he was within a darkened room. It took a moment for his eyes to become accustomed to the semi-twilight of the apartment, and then he seated himself in a chair beside a small table which the girl pointed out to him before she left the room, and which was evidently intended for visitors.

"How do you do?" said a voice, and turning in the direction from whence it came he beheld the wrinkled, black face, and gaudily turbaned head of Madam Frances. As he returned her greeting another voice said:

"How d'y do? Lord love ye, how d'y do?"

Then he saw that a large green parrot was perched on the back of the chair in which Madam Frances was seated. On the table beside him was a silver dish holding two large sea-green stones, in the depths of which one could easily trace the outlines of white coral islands, birds, beasts and reptiles. In one corner of the room was a large screen covered with unbleached cotton. The table beside Madam Frances held a curious instrument which resembled a ship's compass, and on its surface the signs of the zodiac came and went at the will of the seeress. Many curious things were in this darkened room, and no matter how much one might wish to disbelieve the power of this woman to foretell the future, he could not fail to be impressed with the surroundings. And, after all, our surroundings influence our lives and characters as much as fate, destiny or any supernatural agency.

Madam Frances held out her hand for her fee, and as he laid a silver dollar across her palm, she said:

"She will escape you, and you will lose the other one, too. Better stop now, and keep the one you hold."

"Keep the one you hold, fool, fool, fool!" screamed the parrot's shrill voice.

"You come to me for advice about certain property that you would like to get. There is money all about you, piles of it. You will meet one soon who will tell you something of importance concerning a large sum of money. You say you did not come here to find that out. But it is here, and the dial does not lie."

She pointed to the face of the compass-like instrument before her. John felt very uncomfortable as the old woman peered at him from eyes which, while they seemed almost sightless, yet impressed one as being able to pierce the secrets of the soul.

"There are three things you wish to ask about," she continued. "Look on the screen and behold the answer to a question."

John looked toward the screen and saw what appeared to be dim shadows forming there, which gradually took on the shape of a banquet table, and seated around it was a company of men, among whom he recognized himself and his friends William Smith and Doctor Lewis.

"When you are at that table, in the company of those men, you shall have the answer to one of the questions you would ask me. Look again," she said, and John saw to his amazement that the cloth of which the screen was made had resumed its color, and another shadowy outline was beginning to form. As he gazed in wonder the outlines took shape before his astonished eyes, and he saw the altar of a church. Before a priest a man and woman knelt in bridal dress. The man placed a ring upon the woman's finger. As the picture faded the faces of the couple were turned toward him for one moment, and he recognized Sappho Clark and Will Smith.

"Look again," said the voice of the seeress. He did so, and saw before him a noble ship; on her deck stood a man and a woman. The picture faded before he could distinguish the features of either party. "These are all I am permitted to show you now," said Madam Frances. "These pictures contain the answers to your questions."

"Do I understand them to mean that I shall be defeated in my plans? that I shall not enjoy a part of the wealth which you see about me?"

"You will be defeated, and you will not enjoy the wealth that is about you; unless"—she paused, shook her head, mumbled some unintelligible jargon, as if conversing with the unseen, again shook her head.

"If not a sharer of the wealth you see, what will my fate be, and in what line shall I prosper? Surely you can tell me something about my success in life."

"Enough has been shown to you. Why persist? But look again, if you will not be advised."

Again he looked at the screen, and saw dark outlines resolve themselves into shapes. He saw what appeared to be a field of ice and snow, vast and unbroken—terrible in its dreary isolation. It faded, and he turned to the fortuneteller in desperation:

"What has such a scene to do with me?"

"Remorse, remorse! who can tell the end of life?" mumbled the crone, as if in self-communion. At length she seemed to come to herself, and said in clear accents:"If you would let an old woman advise you, I should say choose the right path, no matter what the cost. But men are foolish always, foolish always for a pretty face."

She touched a bell on the table beside her, and the boy Alphonse came from behind the curtain and gravely motioned the visitor to follow him out.

"For a pretty face," croaked the parrot, rousing himself from a nap as John left the room. As he descended the stairs the words of the parrot followed him:

"Fools, fools; all men are fools for a pretty face!"

John cursed his own folly in seeking the fortune-teller's aid as he went slowly back to his office, puzzling over the things he had seen and heard. He was a well-read man, and tried to account for these strange things. He knew from reading, the mediumistic powers of all created things; he knew something of the wonderful agencies of electricity and magnetism. The appliances in the room had suggested magnetism as the medium; "yet," he argued, "the same phenomena might have been produced by the power of hypnotism." He knew enough of the latter to practice it in a way for the amusement of his young friends, but had thought himself impervious to its influence. But with all his reasoning he could not convince himself that there was not an intelligence—invisible and intangible—that had presented to him those soul-disturbing manifestations.

XVII

The Canterbury Club Dinner

Ill fares the land to hastening ills a prey,
Where wealth accumulates and men decay.

—Goldsmith

The Canterbury Club of Boston, which held its annual dinner on this particular evening, was composed of the flower of Boston's literary savans. At the rooms of the club men deep in scientific research touched elbows with the advanced theological scholar and the political economist. Side by side with the vital questions of the hour in the world of progress—wireless telegraphy, the philosophy of trusts, the rise and fall of monarchies, the restoration of Greek art, the philosophy of lynching was beginning to engage the attention of two hemispheres, and information was eagerly sought from every reliable source.

Now it happened that the remarkable ability of Smith in dealing with the acknowledged difficulties of the question had been spoken of to some of the members by the Hon. Herbert Clapp, the president of the club. It had already entertained Doctor Lewis, on account of his great work as an educator among his people, and John Langley because he was an important factor in his line, doing the work necessary to the life of any organization interested in active politics with which men of a delicate moral susceptibility could not be approached. It was voted to invite young Smith to this dinner as a fresh and interesting specimen of the Negro. Many fat contributions found their way annually into the treasury of the African School of Industrial and Agricultural Development, which was under the able management of Doctor Lewis, through the influence of this club. He had accomplished great things; had made himself the center of this terrible human tragedy in the heart of the Black Belt, where the college was situated; but the deadly antagonism of the South made even his iron-hearted stoicism bow to its tyrannical decrees, insomuch that he had been forced to compromise, and the educational advantages allowed the pupils had been curtailed to suit the views of those who placed a low estimate on the ability of the Negro, in spite of the many bright examples of superior intellectual endowments which exist among them. Such ideas as Doctor Lewis set forth in his many brilliant speeches in behalf of his people were logical, and showed a mind capable of grasping the needs of the moment an infinity of powerful thought under a tyrannous self-suppression.

"One man's meat is another man's poison." The colored people north of Mason and Dixon's line are conspicuous for their advancement along all the lines which are distinctive features in the formation of the polished exterior of the good citizen of such a republic as ours. Among the best circles of this community are found the highest types of intellectual, moral, religious and social improvement. What becomes of such a class as this when hampered by rules and laws made to fit the needs of the Black Belt? laws of life and living which cannot be forced, and ought not to be forced, upon the large class of colored citizens who embody within themselves the highest development of American citizenship? We believe that the spirit of fair play is not yet dead in our beloved country. We believe that there still exists beneath the seething cauldron of prejudice with which the South would deluge the advance of the Negro, brave hearts that will answer the cry of distress with patriotic alacrity, and these same brave hearts will demand for every black face, North and South, the fullest opportunity to develop whatever is best within him.

The young men had planned to go together. Their entrance created a diversion; the English member of Parliament who was the guest of honor was much surprised, although too well-bred to show it. Certainly they were fine specimens of the genus homo, whose physique demanded more than a passing glance of admiration. Curious thoughts came to Mr. Withington, the English guest; certain truths which, if applicable to England, seemed doubly so to this country, so new and untried, as it were, in the changes and subtle uncertainties of government and revolutions:

> "And a proud yeomanry, its country's pride
> When once destroyed can never be supplied."

Will the Republic learn the value of the black children of her adoption when it is too late?

The presence of these young Negroes was generally received as a pleasant innovation among that company. There was a senator from

Alabama present among the invited guests, and for a moment he felt his color rise and all the peculiar feelings of his section protest and clamor to make themselves heard when he found that he must perforce be brought into social contact with the despised ex-slave representatives. But he remembered, in time to save himself from ridicule, that he was in Massachusetts. "What matter?" was his inward thought, "some day we shall change all this."

The first course was about over before Will had a chance to look about him. He did not feel at all overpowered by the grandeur displayed. The great room with its high walls and ceiling of magnificently carved mahogany, the massive brass chandeliers, composed of hundreds of tiny electric lights which threw their sparkling rays upon the exquisitely appointed table, with the priceless ware in which the meal was served, the heavy scent of roses which perfumed the air, the silent waiters gliding in and out among the guests,—all seemed the fantastic creation of a dream.

His neighbor happened to be Mr. Withington; his vis-a-vis, a noted editor; farther down the table he recognized a foreign secretary of legation; and so on. Conversation soon became general; flashes of wit, satire, and discussions of rare value to the student—a sumptuous feast of good things. Above the click of glasses he caught snatches of conversation:

"You may search through science and find no evidence of the presence of God in the universe," declared the sharp, decisive voice of a free-thinker, who was plunged in the midst of an argument with a noted theologian of the Episcopal faith. Will listened intently for the answer. It came instantly:

"How could it be otherwise? God has a subjective existence to man; therefore man must get outside of himself to know God; in fact, man must die to attain God."

"Ah, there you go, with your mythological argument! You cover the clear statement of a fact with a veil of mysticism."

"Very true; but what is the soul, mentality, existence itself, but a living mysticism?" replied the clergyman.

The whole room had become interested by this time, and watched the play of cultured thought and keen argument with great relish.

"It is only when the subjective part of man exists as a distinct entity, then, that you think the presence of God is made clear to him?"

"Yes," replied the clergyman; "for the final end of man is the beginning of spirituality, or the true knowledge of God."

"Ah, but if we let reason speak, we find the flaws in your theory, and your ground becomes untenable. I look forward to the day which coming years shall usher in, when all the discoveries which are being made each year, and the general diffusion of scientific knowledge, shall revolutionize thought, and place God and man on an entirely different plane from that which they now occupy.

"And what is this reason or thought which you feel will do so much? It is but a loan from the Almighty, whose existence you affect to doubt. Man has no title to the property until he has permission to hold it eternally."

"And then?"

"He must have satisfied the Almighty that he is worthy."

Presently Will plunged into the conversation, impelled thereto by a certain philosophical reference with which he was familiar, and which he had studied with great interest.

"What do you think of reason and religion, Mr. Smith?" asked the free-thinker, impressed with the intelligence of his comments. "Are you one with the rest of your race in believing all this talk of spirituality?"

"I believe that reason and religion must act together to discover the perfect power and glory of God," replied Will modestly. (All eyes were for the moment bent upon him.) "There is perfect harmony between them; and it is our own shortsightedness which causes us to doubt."

"Do you not believe that by seeking knowledge, and dedicating life to the welfare of mankind and obedience to God in our several vocations, our best faculties will be gratified? wealth, fame, health, and all other good things will flow in a stream, and our delight remain permanent?" asked Doctor Lewis at this stage of the argument.

"Not necessarily obedience to God," replied the free-thinker. "Certain causes bring certain effects, without reference to a presiding deity."

"That's it!" said the Southerner, sotto voce, to his next neighbor. "Negroes are all alike with regard to religion; ignorant, thieving, dirty and lazy, but withal crammed full of religious enthusiasm. You should know them as I do—shouting, screaming, frothing at the mouth with the outpourings of the 'spirit,' and as soon as they are outside of the church door, robbing hen-roosts and watermelon patches. Bah!"

Low as his words were spoken, they caught the ear of Will. His flashing black eyes were turned upon the speaker as he said with a courtly bow:

"Granted that all you say is true, still the Negro does not sin against ages of accumulated knowledge of right and wrong. It is not absolute incapacity in the Negro either, but mere want of information, arising from lack of intelligent exercise of the perceptive faculties. These faults you speak of are but the remnants of an old irresponsible life. The majority of our race has turned aside forever from the old beaten paths of slavery into the undiscovered realms of free thought and free action. Some of the race may abuse the newly acquired liberty by petty pilfering or an overflow of religious enthusiasm, but the Negro has changed, whether you realize it or not; *times.* have will changed, and the Negro with them."

There was a murmur of applause as he finished speaking.

"Well," returned the Southerner, "we will grant that some of you are making progress, but you cannot claim that as a race you are capable of becoming such examples of manhood as you and your friends. To most of you the mystery of government will always remain a mystery; and the hope of assimilating many things which are second nature to the white man, will never become a reality to your race."

"I believe that the same rules which govern all races will be applicable to mine," returned Will. "If men are rude and foolish, down they must go. When at last in any race a new principle appears, an idea, *that* conserves it. Ideas only save races. If the black man is feeble and impotent, unimportant to the existing races—not on a parity with the best races, the black man must serve and be exterminated. But, if he carries within his bosom the element of a new and coming civilization, he will survive and play his part."

"Hear, hear!" cried the foreign secretary of legation, applauding vigorously, delighted at the strong, combative style in which the brave young fellow met the ancient enemy of his race. "No race is hopelessly lost to the world of progress that produces such manly specimens within fifty years of emancipation."

"England is troubled over the fact that the two races do not mix, and to all appearances never will," now joined in Mr. Withington. "There seems to be no common ground between them; they cannot live together harmoniously. Can you, gentlemen, explain this to me? I should like to carry back with me, when I return, a clear realization of the facts in the case as viewed by each party to the question. That is part of my mission in this country."

"It is true," said Doctor Lewis, "that our condition is alarming to a degree. Over ten thousand graves made since the war by mob violence,

PAULINE E. HOPKINS

are dotting the South, and of these ninety per cent are the graves of black men."

"You do not get these facts abroad because newspaper reports are doctored by local Southern writers who participate in the lynchings. Free speech and public discussions are not allowed. In the South you must think and speak as the mob dictates," here chimed in John Langley.

"But surely you have constitutional equity before the law? you can gain redress from the Federal government?"

"Constitutional equity is a political fiction," laughed Will.

"Reconstruction is a failure, then?" asked Mr. Withington.

"Reconstruction is not a failure, although the whole South will tell you so, and the North is being persuaded to so believe; the Negro was the living force which rent asunder the old methods of the slave-holding states and brought them out into the healthful light of decent, God-fearing living. But they are trying to take all the credit for the good we may have done them, from us. The lines are drawn more sharply than before the emancipation. Constitutional amendments are dead letters; the ballot-box is nil," replied Will.

"All of which goes to show that race is stronger than law," broke in the Southerner.

"Rather that barbarism is superior to civilization."

"What about the crime of rape?" asked Mr. Withington.

"In nine cases out of ten," replied Lewis, "you will find that the Negro is guiltless of this awful crime. It is brought forward to alienate the sympathy of all decent men from us. It is a crime that strikes the home ties, and as such is the most deadly weapon that has yet been used against us. We invite investigation in this direction, and you will then find that it is not a characteristic of the black man, although *it* is of the white man of the South."

"You cannot prove your assertions!" exclaimed the Southerner, white with passion.

"I can."

"Name a case."

"John Thomas of Georgia."

"He was guilty, and deserved his fate. You, gentlemen, must have heard the story of the atrocities committed by that man. The woman's husband was brutally murdered and she was assaulted. We made the fate of the black devil a terrible example for the rest of his kind in Georgia."

"Do you not know that that story has been proven false all through? It was this way, gentlemen: After the man Thomas was lynched, the colored people were convinced of his innocence. A sum of money was raised by subscription to hire the services of a reputable detective to investigate the matter. He visited the scene of the alleged crime, and it was found that Thomas worked for Cragen on his farm. Thomas heard that his mother was sick, and wished to visit her; having no money, he applied to Cragen for his pay. This enraged the latter, and he drew his revolver to shoot the Negro. Quick as a flash Thomas seized an axe which happened to be lying near, and struck Cragen, killing him instantly. He then fled to the woods. Mrs. Cragen says that Thomas did not assault her; she never saw him."

"And for defending himself they lynched him?" said Mr. Withington, with a look on his face which expressed incredulous astonishment, combined with disgust.

"Yes; that was the detective's report, given under oath. What the man suffered at the hands of the lynchers could only be equalled by the sufferings of the martyrs of Nero's time. If every case of Negro lynching could be investigated, we should discover fearful discrepancies between the story of the mob and the real truth."

"That does not prove that white men are ravishers," said the Southerner, returning to the charge.

"Oh," replied Will, with a significant shrug of the shoulders, "take the representatives of my race who are with you tonight. How did we get our complexions, soft curls and regular features? Our ancestors were black, flat-featured, and had many other racial marks. Your race does not intermarry with Negroes, does it? That being the case, the answer is self-evident."

"Do you not think, then, that under the circumstances the Government ought to assist the Negro to leave the country?" asked Mr. Withington.

"Never!" cried Will, with glowing countenance, "Never! Here where we have been so outrageously maligned, let us refute the charge like men!"

"That sounds well," said the Southerner with a sneer, "but how will you do it?"

"By using the methods of the South," replied Will quickly; "create sentiment for the race and against its detractors."

"And if you get nothing else out of it, the agitators will do a good business and fill their pockets with money."

"Agitation will do much," said Will calmly, unruffled by the other's display of anger. "It gave us freedom; it will give us manhood. The peace, dignity and honor of this nation rises or falls with the Negro. Frederic Douglas once said: 'Ultimately this nation will be composite. There is a strong demand—a growing demand for a government capable of protecting all its citizens—rich and poor, white and black—alike.' The causes for such a government still exist. It remains to be seen if the prophecy will be fulfilled."

One of the founders of the American Academy at Rome was present, and conversation now turned upon the development of American talent in art. The political aspect of Great Britain in South Africa and the complications likely to arise therefrom was another interesting topic, but under it all the sentiment expressed and the words spoken by the representatives of an humble race that night lingered in the heart of each scholar and thinker who had heard them.

Will had a pressing engagement, and was obliged to excuse himself to the president of the club. He withdrew as quietly as possible. Those nearest him shook him warmly by the hand, and told him that they hoped to hear from him again, and soon, on the same interesting topic.

Mr. Withington now attached himself to John Langley for the remainder of the evening, seeming well pleased to find himself in such company. As they bade each other good-night at the close of the festivities he said to John, as he placed his card in his hand:

"I leave tomorrow for Canada, on business connected with the Home Office. I may never return to this country, but I want you to believe that I am deeply interested in the welfare of your people. Write to me whatever comes up of importance to the race, and I will do what I can to make sentiment in my own country for you, and as far as money will go, you shall have the benefit of the help it will give."

John bade him good-by, and even his conservative heart was warmed by contact with so good a man. After he had reached his room he took the card from his pocket, and before putting it in a place of safety read the address:

CHARLES MONTFORT-WITHINGTON, M. P.
BLANKSHIRE,
ENGLAND.

For a long time he sat there staring at the card in his hand. Where had he heard that name before? "Charles Montfort!" Why, it was the family name of Mrs. Smith! Instantly the words of Madam Frances came to his mind, and a great light seemed to illumine his thoughts: "When you are at that table in the company of those men, you shall have the answer to one of the questions you would ask me."

How often he had listened to the story told by Ma Smith with an incredulous smile. It had seemed to him the idle boasting of a mind entering its dotage. Charles Montfort!—and from England! Heavens! if there should be truth in this fairy tale!

XVIII

What Easter Sunday Brought

'Twas Easter Sunday. The full-blossomed trees
Filled all the air with fragrance and with joy.

—Longfellow

The days passed very quietly at No. 500 D Street. The excitement occasioned by the fair, and the extraordinary agitation which had attended the meeting of the American Colored League, had somewhat abated. Softer thoughts and feelings had taken possession of the public mind, for it was very near to the celebration of Easter. The two girls, Dora and Sappho, felt restrained in their intercourse because, although by tacit consent nothing was said of John's treacherous conduct toward Dora, each knew that the other had discovered it. Dora felt aggrieved and ill-treated; and who could blame her? Doctor Lewis was drawn into the trouble through his attachment to Dora. He pitied her injured feelings; he knew that if she were free and he offered her his love, it would be accepted, and he was not too proud to have done this if it had been an honorable act. He knew that it would not be an honorable act to ask her to break her promise to Langley at this stage of the drama, but within his heart hope grew stronger each day. He saw that John was hopelessly infatuated with Sappho; he saw Dora knew this and resented the wrong done herself, although as yet she could hardly put her thoughts into words. Daydreams began to break in upon the dull monotony of his methodical existence; he watched the signs of growing discontent with all a lover's impatience to grasp the happiness which he felt would, after a time, be his. He was willing to work, to wait, to serve, if only he might claim her love at last. Oh, the nobleness of a good man's love! If women would but prize it, how many more happy homes we should see, and how much brighter the world and life would be. Toward Langley he was savage; and then, too, he was puzzled.

One night they were all invited to attend a reception given at the house of a friend. He was with Dora and John. Dora addressed a remark to John, and receiving no answer, turned to look in his face for the reason. His gaze was fixed upon Sappho, who was surrounded by every eligible man in the house. And such a look! love—hatred—tenderness—the gamut of passion was disclosed by the look bent upon the. unconscious girl before them. Dora shuddered as if a chill had struck her, and turning to Lewis held a cold and trembling little hand appealingly toward him. He took it gladly into his firm and loving clasp, and tenderly asked her if she would like to go home. She grasped the offer instantly with evident relief. She left John's side to seek the ladies' dressing-room for her wraps; he, absorbed in thoughts of Sappho, did not miss her presence. Lewis sent word to Will that he was taking Dora home because she was feeling very tired. He apologized to the hostess, engineered all the delicate details of social life with neatness and dispatch, and met the harassed girl at the foot of the staircase, ready to lead her home without arousing disagreeable comment.

"What does the beggar mean?" he asked himself more than once that night. "He does not seem inclined to give Dora up, and yet he is completely gone 'over the other one." But, like a prudent man, he said nothing; he kept his own counsel and watched.

Since the meeting at which Sappho had fainted, the girl had grown more silent and depressed. People said: "Yes, she is beautiful, but so cold and silent."

She and Will had scarcely spoken since the night of the fair, but each felt and knew that it would be but a short time before the story of their love must be settled for good and all. So the days crept by and brought the crisis of these lives, so strangely interwoven.

Easter Sunday fell early in April that year. The city had donned its gayest attire to welcome the return of the celebration of Christ's triumphal resurrection. The morning service was ended. The exultant organ peals, the glorious strains of hymns of victory poured forth by highly trained voices in hundreds of augmented church choirs all over the city, still seemed to vibrate upon the listening air even after the churches had given up their crowds of worshippers. Sappho had been to the mission church of St. Augustine, on P. Street, at the West End. Here the good Fathers of the Mission of St. John had reared a church, and elected to bend their efforts particularly to the salvation and upraising of the poorest of God's children. This church, with its beautiful silver chimes, given by a wealthy Boston woman in commemoration of the life and services of the lamented Bishop

Brooks, is destined to stand for ages as a memorial of the deeds of philanthropy which have always been a distinguishing feature of the true spirit of Massachusetts.

The sound of the bells lingered with her like a benediction. For the first time in weeks a tranquil mind was hers. The spirit of the day was upon her in full measure; to her the risen Christ was a reality, and his triumph over sin and death was to her bruised spirit a promise and a blessing. Stepping lightly along she gained the Public Garden and crossed the rustic bridge, skirting the lake as she walked toward the Arlington-street entrance. Many admiring glances followed the graceful figure, clad in its fresh, jaunty, tailor-made suit of gray. The strong wind kissed the pure face and gently lifted the clustering curls from the white brow, where Cupid lurked in every curve and delicate thread of gold. The Garden was very beautiful this year; it had blossomed with more than its usual luxuriance for the annual festival. Beds of crocuses, gaudy tulips and hyacinths dotted the landscape side by side with the modest violet and exquisite pansy. God's smile was everywhere. April's sun and showers had blessed the earth, and

> *"Cold Nature, by his amorous kiss*
> *Stung sweetly, stirred his limbs and felt*
> *A thrill of immemorial bliss."*

Someone sat upon a garden seat awaiting her coming. Far down the mall he espied the solitary figure. 'Twas she herself! As he gazed upon the advancing figure of the girl he loved he felt his heart swell within him, and tender thrills of joy filled his soul, too full for utterance. He noticed that she wore a bunch of violets today, instead of her favorite Jacks. They were more in keeping with the sentiment of the day. There they rested in a splendid cluster upon her breast—modest and beautifully fragrant. "As sweet as a violet herself," he thought, as he murmured to himself:

> *"The breeze runs riot with thy charms,*
> *O faint, delicious, springtime violet!"*

As a man Will Smith was not ashamed of the passion which consumed him. An honor. able love has its own subtle charm. Now was his opportunity! The almost deserted paths were secure from intrusion.

She was not indifferent to him; today should end suspense. He would have her answer.

Sappho caught sight of him directly she entered the path. She hesitated—turned then stood still, as if conscious of his resolution. He saw her hesitation, and read her thoughts by virtue of that harmony which is love's perfection. He arose and stood before her, hat in hand. His apparent coolness and self-possession did what he intended it should: restored her calmness; and when she placed her hand in his and responded to his cheery greeting, she was herself again.

"Do not hurry away," he said, as she turned as if to resume her walk. "Let us sit a moment and enjoy this charming view of beautiful Boston."

She stood a moment gazing at the fair prospect spread out before them.

"How peaceful, beautiful and calm the landscape seems. If earth be so fair, what must be the beauty of heaven?" she said, after a slight pause.

"Indeed, yes," replied Will, as he glanced at the fair face beside him with something like awe. For a moment he felt that he stood in the presence of a saint; earthly passion seemed out of place.

After a moment's silence she seated herself, mechanically protesting that she had promised Dora to help her with her Sunday-school class at half-past one.

"Never mind," said Will, "it is real Sunday. school work for you to look after me a bit. I'm sure I need Bible lessons." At this they both laughed, and then Sappho asked:

"Where ought the lesson to be?"

She saw instantly by the change in his expression that she had given him his opening, and immediately lost the self-possession she had just gained.

"'And Jacob loved Rachel; and said, I will serve thee seven years for thy younger daughter,'" quoted Will softly, as he looked at the gentle face and downcast eyes beside him. Sappho said nothing, but gazed intently at the landscape with unseeing eyes, as she nervously clasped and unclasped her delicately gloved hands. Suddenly she felt one small hand drawn within a strong, warm clasp.

"There are shadows on your face; why are they there? You think all kinds of sad thoughts. Tell them to me, Sappho."

"Nay," she said at length, "why should I? they are not clear even to myself. You would not understand my vagaries. Why should you be bothered with them?"

"Because, Sappho, my beautiful one, my darling, I love you—surely you know it—I have loved you from the first moment that I saw you. Be my wife, my blessing."

She did not answer; her face had grown very white. "Have I frightened you? Do not think me cruel, Sappho; you do not know how much I love you."

She was still silent, but another look satisfied him that she was not angry. The gloved hand stopped fluttering, and lay quietly within his clasp.

"You do not think me presumptuous? You are not angry? Tell me that you love me."

"Wait one moment," she said; and then he saw that she was trembling violently.

"Don't you care for me a little?" he asked anxiously, "or have I been living in a fool's paradise the past two months?"

"I do care for you," she whispered, in a voice so low that only a lover could have heard it.

"Ah!" he cried impetuously; "then I will never let you go!"

"Ah, Will, I wonder if it is right for me to love you, or to allow you to love me?"

"Most decidedly it is right. Why do you doubt?"

"You have known me such a short time," she protested.

"I know that you are the dearest girl in all the world to me," he replied, holding her hand still more tightly clasped. "You are mine now, and nothing shall part us. I shall always remember this day as the happiest of my life. You do not know how dearly I love you."

"I shall know if you persist in telling me so often," she said, smiling at his impetuosity.

"Heaven bless you, Sappho, my dearest. I shall never tire of ringing the changes on love."

"Why should you care so much for me?" she asked wistfully. "I have no family—no friends—no money—"

"I have family enough for both of us," he returned quickly. "My mother loves you, my sister adores you; what more is there to be desired?"

"But there are things which you ought to know—things connected with the past—"

"I do not care for the past," he broke in; "all I ask is that you love me above all other men, as I adore you above all other women."

She was carried away by the vehemence of his wooing. All obstacles seemed, indeed, but trifles before this all-absorbing, passionate, eager warmth of youth's first love. Poor soul! poor starved and storm-beaten heart! Something of life that was dead leaped again into existence and loosened the icy hand that had for years locked up the fountain of youthful joy. She felt drawn out of herself as she looked into the eyes of love and met the luminous light which transfigured the face of her lover.

> *"Ask me no more; thy fate and mine are sealed:*
> *I strove against the stream and all in vain;*
> *Let the great river take me in the main:*
> *No more, dear love, for at a touch I yield;*
> *As me no more."*

Silently she turned to him and placed the other hand within his clasp, and burst into a tempest of weeping.

"Sappho!" he cried, in a transport of delight, as he tried to dry her tears; "my darling, my wife!"

O happy Easter Day!

They sat there a long time in heart communion, reviewing the history of their short acquaintance, and the wonderful thing that had happened to them. They planned that Sappho should stay with Will's mother while he went abroad, and then when his course was finished they would be married immediately upon his return. They would keep their sweet secret a little while. They could not share this hallowed day with others. It was consecrated and holy to them because of its dear association with the hidden stream of their united lives.

John Langley was returning from an errand down town, and attracted by the beauty of the morning, determined to cross the Garden on his way to the South End. Suddenly, beneath the trees he espied the lovers. He paused a moment. They were so much absorbed in each other that they had not seen him. He turned aside into a path which ran very near to them on one side, and paused beneath the shadow of some friendly trees where he was secure from observation and could watch their movements unseen.

The happy light on Will's expressive countenance did not escape him; he noted, too, the shy happiness and deep, tender love which shone in Sappho's eyes. His heart was on fire with hot, jealous rage, and he resolved that their marriage should never take place. He was not sure of Sappho's past, but he would try a bold maneuver and trust to luck. He would accuse her as though certain of the facts. If that did

PAULINE E. HOPKINS

not work, he would try some other game. He who had laughed at love without money, found himself even contemplating the sacrifice of one for the other, if dishonest means should not succeed in winning her. He watched them for a time, and then, judging by their movements that they were about to leave the spot, turned reluctantly away, planning ways and means of bringing his schemes to a successful issue.

Sappho had been taking her meals with the family lately, but tonight she excused herself from dinner on the plea of a headache. Will had gone back to the hotel.

"Headache must be a great cosmetic," said Dora slyly. She had seen that Will and Sappho returned from morning church together and from certain signs had drawn her own conclusions about how matters stood between them. "I never remember seeing you look better or more beautiful than you do tonight." Sappho laughed joyously as she ran lightly up the stairs to her room. Tomorrow they would know her secret.

She glanced at her mirror as she passed it. Where was the usually pale, sad face that it reflected? They called her cold and proud. What would the world say if it could see that brilliant, vivid, flashing beauty that the mirror gave back to her astonished gaze? Truly love was a wonderful cosmetic. She sank into the inviting willow rocker, and for a while gave herself up to the happiness which was so intense as to be almost painful. There was no thought of evil mingled with the joy that wrapped her round about. No forebodings assailed her; the intoxication of the moment was complete. She was lost in dreamland as she sat there thinking of her lover. Will had said to her: "I am not a man to hold love lightly; it is no jest with me. My love is the one woman in the whole world to me above all others. shall love you living and dying, and be true to you in life and death." The words rang in her ears like sweetest music.

There were extra services at all the colored churches that night, because owing to the fact that most of the worshippers were employed as domestic servants, evening was the only time convenient for their employers to spare their services. She heard the outer door close upon one after another until the house settled down to the perfect quiet of solitude.

She then arose from her seat and proceeded to change her street attire for a pale blue cashmere house dress with delicate ecru lace at the throat and wrists. She hummed strains of the Gloria heard that morning in church as she stood before the glass and took the pins from her hair. The shining coil of burnished gold fell almost to her feet. So she stood with the brushes poised in air as the door opened softly and John Langley came quickly into her room. Thus they stood for a brief second of time: she colorless with amazement and fear; he overwhelmed with the exquisiteness of the picture before him. The brushes falling from her hands broke the silence. Anger flamed in her eyes.

"I did not hear you knock, Mr. Langley; what can I do for you?"

His face was pale, his eyes wavering and bloodshot; his whole expression indicated a terrible determination. The almost insulting coldness of her tone exasperated him.

"I did not knock," he replied, as he stepped into the room. "You do not offer me a seat," he sneered, as he sat down on the couch.

"This is hardly the time or place for parlor civilities," she replied significantly. "Do you not know that the house is empty?"

"I do; and as I wish to speak with you privately, and as this is my only chance, I will not let it slip me," said John.

"Really! I cannot understand what private business you can have with me," returned Sappho haughtily; "but if it be so, pray state the nature of it as quickly as possible."

"I will," he replied. He paused a moment, as if collecting his forces. "You and Will seem to have come to an understanding, judging by what I saw on the Public Garden this morning," he said finally.

Sappho flushed warmly as she replied: "And in what way does that concern you?"

The girl looked so beautiful and spirited that he longed to crush her with the weight of his surmises.

"Will Smith is a very proud man as well as a very just man. His pride of family is his besetting sin. Do you think that it will be for his best interest to marry you?" he asked significantly

"And why should it not be?" questioned the girl haughtily, although a hand of ice seemed closing about her heart.

"*You* can best answer that question," was the guarded reply.

"Mr. Langley, your intrusion into my private apartment is unpardonable; your innuendoes are still more so. If you have anything to say, please say it; if not, let us close this remarkable interview." She moved toward the door as if to open it. In an instant he seized her arm and stopped her.

"Do not be rash. It is better for you to listen to me and not arouse my enmity. *I have seen Luke Sawyer, and I know your secret* Mabelle Beaubean!"

The attack was so sudden she did not think of defending herself. He had never in his life seen emotion so terrible depicted upon the human countenance as her face presented at that moment. She shrank from him with shivering dread, beating the air with both hands, as though in her agony she warded off the approach of some gruesome apparition.

"Not that name—not that name!" she gasped, as she turned her beautiful, ghastly face from side to side, as though seeking air. She seemed about to faint. Then she sank upon the floor and literally groveled there, her face hidden by the long hair which enveloped her like a veil.

John was nonplussed at the perfect success of his plot; he was exultant. The terror of the girl was awful to behold. Surely he had her now. She must turn to him for help.

"Sappho," he said in feigned pity, "I feel for you. God knows I am sorry for this, and that I should have been the one to bring it upon you. But think of your story, and its effect upon Will if he should learn it after marriage!"

"I was a victim! an innocent child!" moaned the figure on the floor.

"I know," said John, "but girls of fourteen are frequently wives in our Southern climes, where women mature early. A man as supercilious as Will in his pride of Northern birth would take no excuse, and would never forgive."

"Ah! what can I do?" cried the unhappy woman, as she rose to her feet and began to pace the floor. "Have I not suffered enough?" Now was the time for which he had waited and planned.

"Sappho, do not think that I forget how abominable I must appear to you. I know what you will say that I betray my friend, and worse than that, the girl who holds my promise; but my excuse is that my passion is stronger than honor, stronger than reason. There are men in the world who would not forsake you, and who would always befriend you. Give up Will, and trust yourself to me. I am making money in my profession. I can and will do well by you. Your story need never be known."

"Doubtless you mean it in kindness," replied the girl wearily, "and I thank you, but I can never marry anyone but Will."

"Marriage!" exclaimed John, "who spoke of marriage? Ambitious men do not marry women with stories like yours!"

At last the murder was out—his meaning clear!

For one moment Sappho was speechless with disgust.

"Infamous villain!" she said at length, "you abuse my forlorn condition. Leave me! Never till this moment have I realized the depths of my degradation!"

"I go at your command," said John. "I give you one week to think over what I have said. At the end of that time."

"Go! go! will you go?" interrupted Sappho, pointing to the door with queenly dignity.

With a low bow John Langley passed out and closed the door behind him.

Sappho turned the key in the lock and sank upon the couch overcome with the horror of her situation. Nervous spasms shook her frame as she mentally measured the abyss of social ostracism and disgrace which confronted her. A thunderbolt from a clear sky had shattered her hopes and dashed the cup of happiness from her lips. Heartrending sobs of anguish mingled with passionate appeals to heaven for mercy, tore her frame as she contemplated this sudden overthrow of her dreams of a bright future. The quiet which had attended her life since she had settled in Boston was rudely interrupted, and the ruin which threatened her was the more stupendous because unlooked for in the direction from which it came.

She got up at length, and going to the dressing-table, began mechanically to collect her jewelry. She caught sight of her face in the glass. What a change from the glowing beauty of one short hour ago! She looked at the pale, drawn countenance with scorn. "Men call me beautiful," she murmured bitterly; "what has beauty been to me but a curse?"

She heard the closing of doors and the voices of the returned church-goers. Could it be possible that she was the same happy girl whose smiling face had been given back from the mirror so radiantly a short hour ago? She heard the front door close again. It was Will's step upon the stair. He paused at her door a moment, and then passed on to the floor above. How often she had listened for that familiar tread. Her heart kept repeating: "Never again never again."

Two hours later deep silence had fallen upon the house. A form attired in black, closely veiled, and carrying a traveling bag, passed from No. 500 D Street into the night, boarded an electric car, and was swallowed up in the heart of the metropolis.

Will in his room had fallen into his first sleep when he thought he heard the sound of noiseless footsteps in the hall. He listened a moment, and then concluded that he was mistaken. Who could be moving through the house at that hour? No, he was mistaken. His thoughts were all with Sappho. He lived over again the words and scenes of the morning. He heard the clocks strike twelve, one, two; then he fell into a deep, dreamless sleep.

XIX

The Bitter Arrow

O, Breaking heart that will not break,
Oriana!
O, pale, pale face so sweet and meek,
Oriana!

—Tennyson

The next morning found the household early astir. It is a rule in hotels that a "late watch," as it is called, exempts the employee from an early appearance for duty the next morning. On these mornings Will breakfasted with his mother and sister. Since Sappho had boarded with them this humble meal had become a feast to him.

He arose very early on this eventful Monday morning and hurried down the stairs, bursting to impart his good news to the sympathetic ears of his loved ones. He entered the kitchen just as Dora was laying the cloth for breakfast.

"What in the world brings you down so early?" she asked in a surprised tone as he entered the room.

"Oh, I couldn't stay in bed this morning of all others," he said, as he kissed her lightly on the cheek; "I am too happy."

"What under the sun is the cause of so much joy, that it brings so lazy a boy out of bed an hour before his time?"

"How did you feel when you were first engaged to John? weren't you light-headed and silly?"

"Oh, I dare say I was silly enough," replied Dora with a sigh. At the mention of John a cloud seemed to settle down upon the brightness of her usually sunny face. "But what has that to do with your early rising? I don't see the analogy between the two."

"Congratulate me, Dora, Sappho has promised to marry me."

"Oh, Will! Why did I not think of that? I declare I suspected something of the sort yesterday, but other things put it out of my mind. I am so glad!" cried Dora. "Where when—how did it occur?"

"Yesterday on the Public Garden. I met her coming from church," he replied proudly. "Do you see the analogy now between your engagement and my early rising?" he added, laughing

"I should say so! How selfish of you to keep it to yourself all this time; you might have told us. Mother! mother! come quickly, I have something to tell you!" she called, moving toward the next room.

"Yes, Dora, dear," replied the voice of Ma Smith, "just a minute!"

"Oh, hurry, hurry, mummie; it won't keep."

"Yes, yes, you excitable child; what is it? Nothing wrong with your brother"—she stopped as she caught sight of his smiling face. He went up to her and took her in his strong young arms—he was an affectionate son.

"Nothing wrong, mummie dear, but your boy is very happy. Will you have Sappho for a second daughter?"

"Gladly, my son," replied his mother; and then she sank upon a chair, overcome as she comprehended the full meaning of his words.

"Why do you cry, mother dear, if the idea is not unpleasant to you?" asked Will, somewhat alarmed by her tears.

"Oh, Will, my boy, you will not let this new love cause you to forget the love of your old mother?"

"Never!" cried Will, as he pressed his lips to the sweet old face. "I would not be worthy of happiness could I be so ungrateful."

"Don't mind mother, Will; she cries on principle, because it is the proper thing for weddings and funerals. Isn't that so, mummie mine?" laughed Dora, as she wiped a suspicious moisture from her own eyes.

"But what keeps Sappho so late? she's generally down by this time," she continued, with a glance at the little Swiss clock on the mantel.

"I'm going up stairs after the laggard, and have it out with her for keeping such news to herself. I know she's bashful."

Dora sprang up the stairs with a bound, and paused outside the door to rap. Receiving no answer she rapped again, and then tried the handle of the door. It yielded to her touch, and then she noticed that the key was on the outside. She threw the door open with a vague sense of something unusual in such a proceeding. The room was empty. She paused a moment in bewilderment as she glanced about her, and then saw the bed undisturbed in its snowy smoothness. Thoroughly alarmed now, she ran to the head of the stairs and called her brother.

Wondering what could be the trouble, Will hurried from the kitchen, closely followed by his mother. Upstairs they found Dora standing in the middle of the room with a frightened face.

"I found the key on the outside, the door unlocked. She is not here; and see, the bed has not been slept in; the closet door is open; some of her clothing is gone, and all her jewelry."

Will stood beside her, gazing about the cozy nest with troubled eyes,

"When did you see her last?" he asked finally.

"At dinner yesterday; she complained of a headache, and went to her room to lie down."

"She was here at half-past eleven, when I came in, for I saw a light in her window as I came down the street."

"Well, children, there is nothing to worry about," said Mrs. Smith; "she has probably gone out and will return shortly. There can't be any great mystery about her absence."

Just then the door-bell rang.

"There she is now," said Will, as he bounded down the stairs in answer to the summons. The two women stood expectant, waiting for the sound of her voice. They heard nothing but the closing of the door and Will's steps returning. Presently he stood before them with a letter in his hand.

"It is for me," he said, in answer to their looks of inquiry. "I think it is from Sappho."

His face was ashen; his hands trembled. He turned the square package over once again—then mechanically, as in a dream, he tore the envelope open. The anxious women watched him as he ran his eyes rapidly over the written page, and then with a groan sank into a chair.

"What is it, Will? what has happened?" cried his mother and sister with one voice. Great drops of perspiration stood upon his forehead.

"O my God!" was his reply to the agonized entreaties of the two women. He threw his arms upon the desk beside him and dropped his head upon them. The letter fell upon the floor.

Mrs. Smith was a great sufferer from nervous weakness. Seeing her son's unhappiness, she began to tremble and sob hysterically. Dora was badly frightened; but knowing that she must be calm for all their sakes, said:

"Mother, calm yourself. Do you not see that Will needs help?" She closed the open door to keep out curious intruders who might possibly be about, and then she picked up the letter.

"Read it!" groaned Will; "I can never tell you."

Dora read it aloud:

PAULINE E. HOPKINS

Will:

When you receive this I shall be far away. What I am writing to you I ought to have told your family long ago. It must forever stand between us and marriage.

You remember the story told the night of the public meeting of the League by Luke Sawyer—the night I fainted? *I am the unfortunate Mabelle Beaubean!*

I did not die. The good Sisters gave out that story in order to destroy my identity. Madam Frances is my grand-aunt. The boy Alphonse is my child! O my God! how can I live and write these words?

John Langley came to my room tonight, after everyone was at church. He has found out my story, and has offered me the greatest insult that a man can give a woman. He has made me realize how much such a marriage with me would injure you. Disgrace shall never touch you or yours through me.

Forgive me for deceiving you—for loving you; it is all the wrong that I have done you.

O love my love—how can I give you up? You will never know the bitterness of the step I am taking!

SAPPHO

Mrs. Smith shuddered as she listened to the words being read. Could it be possible that this strange, unexpected confession had come from the beautiful girl they knew so well?

Dora was weeping bitterly when she finished; so was her mother. They sat there stunned into silence. Every pulse beat at fever-heat in Will's body. His nerves were strained almost beyond endurance; they were a thousand needle-points of pain. How could he bear this terrible news that had come to him! Luke Sawyer's story was written before his eyes in letters of fire. He saw with acute clairvoyant sight the beautiful child—the brutal captor—the horrid surroundings of the vile den to which he had consigned her—her struggles within the brutal grasp—all the sickening details of that horrible violation of chastity were mirrored within his brain. Time could never eradicate them. God of heaven! how could he bear to think that his beautiful Sappho—his pure girl-love, had been subjected to such brutality! And then the child! Agony of agonies! He could not suffer more and live!

There was something awe-inspiring in his great affliction to the women who loved him. Dismal silence had seized upon them all. Then a sob—dreadful to hear—broke from Will. He staggered across the room and fell on his knees by his mother's side and buried his face in the folds of her dress. It was a way he had in early childhood when anything distressed him. Then his mother comforted him as in childhood days— his head upon her tender breast—her dear wrinkled hands, as if in blessing, resting upon his grief-stricken brow.

At length Dora broke the silence.

"Oh, that poor, miserable girl! think of her sufferings—of the weight of the secret she carried with her. What a crucifixion for a proud spirit like hers! This terrible curse of slavery! shall we never lose the sting of degradation? Think of John, too! How did he find it out? what a heartless scamp he must be! I confess the whole thing is an enigma to me."

"To think she should believe us capable of feeling anything for her but sympathy! You must find her, Will, and bring her back home," said Ma Smith.

"Yes, mother; but any girl would act as she has. Think of her humiliation to be obliged to own such a story to her lover! I do not wonder that she turned a coward and fled. But Will will find her, never fear."

Will had regained something of self-control. But what a change had come to that debonair countenance! Dora's heart ached as she looked at him. He arose from his knees by his mother's side and stood a moment as if bewildered.

"I am going to hire the best detective in the city to find her. But first I will settle with John Langley," he said at last.

"Give him this!" cried Dora, snatching her engagement ring from her finger. "Tell him I hope never to see his face again."

"Poor little sister. Must you suffer, too?"

"Don't pity me, Will!" she exclaimed with flashing eyes. "I am well rid of such a man."

Will kissed them both solemnly and went out.

The two women, left alone, went softly about the pretty room folding away the scattered articles of wearing apparel, which they watered with many bitter tears, and finally closing the blinds and drawing down the curtains. She will return, they told each other, hoping against hope. We will leave things as they are. And then went out and locked the door.

PAULINE E. HOPKINS

Such incidents as we have pictured above are not uncommon in any community where slavery has cast its baleful shadow. Emancipation has done much, but time and moral training among the white men of the South are the only cures for concubinage.

We may right a wrong, but we cannot restore our victim to his primeval state of happiness. Something is lost that can never be regained. The wages of sin is death. Innocent or guilty, the laws of nature are immutable. So with shoulders bent and misshapen with heavy burdens, the Negro plods along bearing his cross—carrying *the sins of others.*

Time was no more. I stood there gazing at the approaching forms of matchless beauty advancing toward the judgment seat of God. And I asked a question: "Who are these arrayed in white?" And one of the elders answered: "These are they who come out of great tribulation!"

Fortunately it happened that it was an hour when the inmates of No. 500 D Street were busy attending to their various vocations. No one need know more of Sappho's disappearance than the family felt to tell. They made one exception to this resolve. It was about ten o'clock when Doctor Lewis called. The mother and daughter were just sitting down to the meal so sadly interrupted. In answer to questions asked in friendly solicitude because of their troubled looks, the whole miserable story came out.

"It is fortunate that I happened in," he said, when he had heard all they could tell him.

"I will go right down to Langley's office. It is useless to allow more trouble to grow out of this unhappy affair. Those men must not meet alone."

Amazed, startled, dumbfounded at this romance in real life, he hurried away toward the business portion of the city. But under his anxiety to serve his friends, who could blame him if thoughts of the broken engagement and all that it meant to him would intrude upon him? His heart kept singing: "Free to be won—free to be won."

John had risen early and left the house before any one was astir. He could not sleep. Up and down the deserted streets he paced, gazing at the silent stars and baring his head to the cold, refreshing breeze of the April morning Haunted—tormented—conscience not yet sufficiently seared to commit so mean an act without regret, would be heard. What if the girl should defy him—expose him! He cursed his own folly, her beauty, his own infatuation. Turn as he would, he could not shut out the beautiful, despairing face.

"And there rises ever a passionate cry
From underneath in the darkened land—"

There is something magical in the mystery of night and the shadows of early dawn. Then the mystery of creation and our own hidden nature seem to be revealed faintly to our dull sensibilities. The soul beholds itself all unadorned as it must stand before Almighty God. He raised his eyes to heaven and there beheld the beauty of myriad stars and undiscovered worlds bespangling the firmament. Never before had he noticed their sublimity. By the tremulous half-light of the early dawn his deed of the night before appeared despicable devilish. For a time his head dropped in shame before the accusations of his soul. There came dimly to his beclouded faculties a realization of the possibilities of a life which might have been his under opposite conditions from those in which he was born. Events of his childhood in the South came to him through the mist of years. He saw himself a half-starved beggar in the city streets, a deserted child claiming kindred with none, allowed a shelter in a poor Negro cabin for charity's sake, begging his bread from the generous passer-by. Somehow he had learned his letters. Then he became ambitious to learn more. He heard talk of a country to the north which seemed to his childish imagination a fairyland. He determined to go there; so he started on his wearisome journey at an age when the loving mother trembles to have her darling exposed to the perils of the busy streets without a strong hand to guide him through its dangers. All his capital was in his nimble baby feet. He charmed coin from the people wherever he went by his expert dancing. He could do the breakdown and many intricate shuffles in a way that delighted his audiences. When he reached the North he managed to buy a bootblack's outfit; then he worked his way into a hotel kitchen. He went on from one thing to another, always keeping the one end in view—to acquire an education.

He had prospered. He had accomplished the acquisition of knowledge at the expense of the non-development of every moral faculty. He did not realize that he was a responsible being, or that morality was obligatory upon him. With him, might was right. This man was what he was through the faults of others. If there be truth in the assertion that we create ourselves in the life we live on earth, the sphere that makes our heaven or hell within the illimitable realms of futurity, then it may be that the pitying eye of Heaven sees the struggles

PAULINE E. HOPKINS

of these irresponsible ones of earth who are monuments of man's inhumanity to man, and sends a warning, pleading voice along the dim, resounding aisles of self-communion. It is a law of the All-wise that Nemesis shall walk beside us in every wrong that we commit. For joy we pay, for sorrow, too, and also for the ill we do. We call the recoil which comes from evil-doing, retribution, which being the fruit of evil, is coexistent with it. John had given no thought to the needs of his soul in his pursuit of wealth and position. Tonight he had the feeling that he had given all for nothing; that in his blind, egotistical seeking for his own gratification he had overstepped the bounds, and that retribution would put a check upon his desires.

That night his better angel triumphed, and he resolved that he would apologize to Sappho, make up with Dora, and tell Will all his surmises about Mr. Withington. But when day light flooded the city he had resolved to let matters remain as they were. Love, honors and a competency were his for the taking, but he had risked all for what? He would soon know.

Ten o'clock found him sitting listlessly before his desk. It happened that he had no cases in court that morning. He pushed his work one side; he could not think; ever before his eyes was a vision in pale blue, with-floating golden hair and appealing eyes. His hand shook as if with the palsy as he raised his pen to dip it in the ink-well. With an oath he dashed it from him. He did not indulge in liquor as a rule, but he made up his mind to have a glass of whiskey when he went to lunch. Presently he heard the door open. He looked up at the sound, and met the eyes of the friend he had betrayed—Will Smith stood before him! John sprang to his feet. His eyes dropped before the steady regard of the other. Thus they stood a moment. At last Will broke the painful silence.

"What have I ever done to you, John, that you should treat me as you have?"

"What do you mean?" stammered John.

"Do you ask me that?"

"I do," came faintly from John's lips.

"I will reply by asking you another question. Has your love for Dora turned to hate, that you can deliberately humiliate the girl you have wished to make your wife, as you have her?"

John's courage seemed to have deserted him. He stood before Smith like the culprit that he was.

"Of what do you accuse me?" he cried at length, in desperation.

"Does not your conscience answer? If not, read that," and Will handed him Sappho's letter.

John took it, and even as his hand grasped the sheet of paper he began to turn over in his mind a way out of this dilemma. As he finished reading it his mind was made up. He returned it to Will with a shrug of his shoulders and a smile more significant than words. The ashen face of his friend should have warned him.

"I did not intend to humiliate Dora, for men do many like things which never come to the ears of the woman they call wife. Accidentally I learned Miss Clark's story. I also learned by observation that there were other stories just as piquante. You will thank me when you know all. She is beautiful. What would you have? Am I different from other men who have made like proposals to a *fille de joie?*"

Scarcely had the words passed his lips when Will was upon him.

"You miserable, lying hound!" he shouted, beside himself with rage and grief. He grasped John by the throat. Again the door opened, and Doctor Lewis ran toward the struggling figures.

"Will! John! are you both mad? Do you want to create a public scandal?" He succeeded in separating them, and then threw him. self between them. So they stood panting and glaring at each other like angry beasts.

"Take me out of this, then!" cried Will, "or I won't answer for myself! Here is your ring!" He took the ring Dora had given him, and threw it at Langley "I will give you until tonight to get your luggage out of my house. If you are there tomorrow morning, I will shoot you like the cur you are."

Doctor Lewis drew him from the room. The door closed. Thus they who had been friends for years parted.

John stood there alone in his silent office, looking out on the dreary vista of brick walls and the network of wires, in awful solitude with his thoughts of the past and his blank future. The sun of prosperity had set on him forever—he felt it—knew it. His own hand had wrought this ruin to himself. said his heart and conscience.

XX

MOTHER-LOVE

What is it to die?
To leave all disappointment, care and sorrow,
To leave all falsehood, treachery and unkindness,
All ignominy, suffering and despair,
And be at rest forever! O dull heart,
Be of good cheer! When thou shalt cease to beat,
Then shalt thou cease to suffer and complain!

—LONGFELLOW

Meantime Sappho had descended from the car at the corner of Arlington and Boylston Streets on that eventful Easter night; she entered the Garden, and impelled by an uncontrollable impulse, walked again through the paths where a few hours before she had known so much happiness. She knew no fear; the darkness concealed her. Again she sat upon the seat where she had passed the brightest moments of her life. A neighboring clock struck one.

It was then the first hour of a new day—the dawn for her of fresh misery. A cold, sharp wind struck her with chilling force; she shivered, but still sat there buried in hopeless despair. Fearful indeed is the plan of existence which rules our mortality. Innocent or guilty, our deeds done in the flesh pursue us with relentless vigor unto the end of life. Sometimes the rough winds of adversity are tempered to the shorn lamb who is not responsible for acts which are forced upon him; God in infinite wisdom and justice remits the severity of our sufferings; but the tracings still remain upon the sands of life—we bind up the wounds—they heal, but the scars remain.

Sappho possessed a brilliant mind and resolute character. If she had been a religious devotee she would have been as devout and as fervid as a disciple of old. If a sinner, the queen of them all. She had strength of will enough for a dozen women, which, if ever started on the wrong road, would be difficult to redirect into the paths of right. She had suffered much in meekness, but now dumb rage awoke her passions.

For a time the spirit of revenge held full sway in the outraged heart. Revenge was all she craved; she shivered at the dark thoughts which came to her. "Revenge" whispered the swaying branches of the trees above her head—"revenge" seemed whispered in the chilling winds about her—revenge upon her seducer and upon the man who had dashed the cup of happiness from her lips and most wantonly insulted her in her weakness. Then came the blessed relief of tears—like a flood—they relieved the overcharged brain and saved her reason. She fancied, as she sat there trying to account for the evil that pursued her, that Conscience spoke in condemnation of her neglect of her child. She had felt nothing for the poor waif but repugnance. Her delicate nervous organization was naturally tinged with superstition, and she felt that God had sat in judgment on her willingness to forget her child. "Dost thou question the providences of God? Know that my ways are not the ways of men. A tender soul will be demanded at thy hands in the vast eternity. Who art thou, to question the ways of Infinity? Jesus Christ came into the world under the law. Who art thou, to question the wisdom of the Most High? Lo, there is the field—the life of a child—work for a bounteous harvest." At length she rose from that seat resolved that come what would she would claim the child and do her duty as his mother in love and training. She would devote her life to him. They would nevermore be separated.

She met no one in her lonely walk through the now-deserted city streets. She was so benumbed by the shock she had received that she would hardly have noticed any insult that might have been directed to her. At length she reached the door of Madam Frances's house. All was dark. No light, no welcome. So was her life made dark and desolate by the curse of slavery. She rang the bell twice with a strong hand; presently she saw the faint gleam from a lamp through the sidelights, and then her aunt's familiar voice asked: "Who is there?"

"It is I, Sappho; open the door, Aunt Sally."

She heard the click of the key as it turned in the lock, and in another moment she stood within the entry facing her aunt's curious, frightened face. In another moment she dropped her weary frame in a chair in the reception room. Sappho told her aunt the whole story. The elder woman was nonplussed and startled; she had not counted that anyone would be able to identify her niece with poor, unfortunate Mabelle Beaubean. They sat there for a long time going over the situation, and consulting about what was best to be done. Sappho told her aunt that she was determined to take the boy with her in future. Madam Frances said nothing, for she saw that her niece was determined.

"I must leave Boston; that is clear," said Sappho.

"Certainly, that will be best for a while," replied her aunt. "But you must remember that it is always darkest just before the dawn."

"I shall return to New Orleans and lose myself in that city. I shall get work there, and my case will not be noticed, because it is not uncommon. In time I shall forget."

"As soon as you are settled there I will join you with the boy. I will continue to tell fortunes, and we shall live very happily, no doubt. I shall not be here long; my sands are almost run, but I should like to see you safe and happy before I go. But remember what I say to you now, Sappho child: in doing your duty, happiness will come to you, the greater and more abiding for the trouble which has preceded it."

"Perhaps so," replied Sappho; "but, Aunt Sally, I shall take the boy with me tomorrow when I leave for the South. I will never part with him again on earth."

"Well, my dear child, I see no necessity for you to become a martyr in order to do your duty. However, do as you think best. Now go and try to get a little rest."

"Here is one of my mother's diamond rings; take it, Aunt Sally, and sell it for me. I have no money."

The old woman took the ring, and Sappho went into the small side-room where Alphonse slept. She undressed and lay down beside the boy, but not to sleep. She gazed on the innocent face with mingled feelings of sorrow and regret as she thought of the lonely, loveless life of the child. She had been so wicked to put him from her. It was her duty to guide and care for him. She would do her duty without shrinking. Her head ached and her eyes burned and were hot and dry; they refused to close. So the moments flew by as she tormented herself with fancies of Will's horror of her when he should learn her story on the morrow, and remembrances of John Langley's coarse insults, which even now made her cheeks burn with shame. She wept bitter tears over her cherished love dream. But under it all there was a feeling of relief now that she had made up her mind to a future which the child should share. Her shipwrecked life seemed about to find peace. There was a new light in her eyes as she gazed on the sleeping child. Impulsively she folded him in her arms, and Alphonse awoke. The awakening of childhood is beautiful. She gazed with new-found ecstacy at the rosy face, the dimpled limbs, and thought that he was hers. Her feeling of degradation had made her ashamed of the joys of motherhood, of pride of possession in her child. But all that feeling was swept away. Alphonse looked at her first in wonder and then in alarm. Again she kissed him passionately—the frail little child, whose delicate frame seemed cut from alabaster. She had only this tender creature to cling to in all the world; the only plank between her and desperation.

"I am your mother, Alphonse," she said in answer to his looks of inquiry.

"My mamma is gone away to heaven," replied the child solemnly, as he watched her earnestly with great dark eyes of wonder.

"No, dear, I am your mamma, come back to keep you with me always. Won't you love your poor unhappy mamma?"

The child put up one slender hand and smoothed her cheek.

"You're the pretty lady I saw at the fair. I didn't know you were my mamma."

"Mamma couldn't claim you then, darling, but now she's going to take you away, and you will always live with her. Won't you like that?"

The boy nodded his sleepy little head, put up his dewy red mouth and pressed a sweet, wet kiss on her face, then he nestled confidingly in her arms and fell fast asleep again. She held him closely folded against her throbbing heart, and something holy passed from the sweet contact of the soft, warm body into the cold chilliness of her broken heart. The mother-love chased out all the anguish that she had felt over his birth. She wondered how she had lived without him—how she could have remained separated from him. In this new and holy love that had taken possession of her soul was the compensation for all she had suffered. She could not see it then, but in the long intervals of time it would be revealed to her understanding. Now she felt that her losses could not be paid, but in the years which followed she learned to value the strong, chastening influence of her present sorrow, and the force of character it developed, fitting her perfectly for the place she was to occupy in carrying comfort and hope to the women of her race.

The next evening Sappho left Boston. As the train rolled out from the station on its south ward journey her heart sank; tears were in her eyes; she felt that now, indeed, all links were severed between her and Will. She had borne up bravely, and now she told herself that she must not give way. She clasped the tender fingers of the boy closer still. He was her anchor. The lady passengers on the train regarded her curiously, she was too beautiful for pity; the men with equal curiosity, but compassion for her youth and beauty mingled with it. When she reached Washington fatigue began to tell upon her—fatigue and hopeless misery. She longed for the journey's end. Mentally and physically she was overtaxed, and but for the child she would have broken down.

She did not mind anything now. As she moved farther south the brutality of the conductor who ordered her out of the comfortable day-coach into the dirt and discomfort of the "Jim crow" car, with the remark that "white niggers couldn't impose on him; he reckoned he knew 'em," failed to arouse her.

The Sisters of the Holy Family always have representatives at the various railroad stations in New Orleans. These Sisters not only solicit alms, but look out for friendless or unfortunate colored women. As Sappho stepped from the train, holding the child by one hand and her baggage check in the other, a Sister, impelled by something in the white, worn face, stepped up to her and spoke a kindly word of interest. Sappho looked at her and tried to answer, as she placed the check and her purse in the Sister's hand. The nun put out her arms just in time to receive Sappho's form as she was sinking insensible upon the platform, her strength at last succumbing to the terrible strain upon mind and body. The nun obtained a carriage and took the two travelers to the convent the child to the orphanage, the mother to the hospital. So once again Sappho found a refuge in the convent in her time of dire necessity. No one recognized her, for a complete change had been made in the Sisterhood.

A long spell of low fever ensued, but to Sappho in her weakness the rest and comfort that came to her harassed mind was like sun and shade in a grassy glade of perfect peace. The nuns were greatly interested in her, and concluded that she was as good as pretty,

"She is like the angels in the picture of the Crucifixion, so sweet and sad. She has more tears in her heart than in her eyes."

"She is not of our faith," said another, "but we will do our best for her, as the Mother says: *le bon Dieu* knows best."

It was evening in New Orleans. The streets, the great arteries of a crowded metropolis, were lighted by the glare of myriad gas-lamps, thus dispelling the darkness like artificial suns. The roll of vehicles blended with the other sounds, the hum of millions rising in a confused roar above the housetops and mingling with the clouds of evening.

In a small, bare room Sappho lay, at the end of a long corridor. The rays from a lamp outside the room came faintly in, dispelling the semi-darkness. The light from the soft Southern moon gleamed faintly through the windows, making the room like the cloisters of heavenly mansions. To that quiet haven of rest the turmoil and bustle of life did not reach. There the dying, the sick, the convalescent lay undisturbed by the hurrying march of humanity.

She had just sent Alphonse away. Every day he had been allowed to go to her since she had been getting better. It was a rare sight to see the two together—the lovely girl who held the child in such a passionate embrace, and the delight of the child in his "beautiful mamma."

No questions had been asked her concerning her life or history, but she felt it her duty to make a confidante of the Mother Superior. Tonight she had sent for her, and presently the Mother glided in, with her noiseless step and gentle, assuring manner. The holy woman sat there a long time in silence after listening to Sappho's story. Such confidences were not new to her. At length she placed a toil-worn brown hand upon the girl's head with a murmured "Benedicite."

"What shall I do, Mother?" asked the girl, as she reverently kissed the gentle hand.

"Ah, we must think and pray. You do not wish to become a Sister?"

"No; I must accept the desire of God in the child. I will take a mother's place and do my duty."

"It is hard for one so young and beautiful to resist the world and its temptations," replied the Mother regretfully; "but we will help you, and the convent will be a home for you always."

Sappho thanked her tearfully.

"My child, I will think over all you have said; I will pray to be shown what it is best to do. Now, go to sleep; rest, and pray to the Holy Mother of Sorrow, and Christ will comfort you.

She glided noiselessly from the room. Sappho, already comforted by her benign influence, fell asleep.

A month later Sappho had very nearly recovered from the effects of her illness. She moved—a quiet and subdued figure—about the convent corridors, helping in every way. She had written to her aunt, and received an answer saying that she would soon be in the city. The old fortune-teller returned to her home only in time, however, to die at the convent. So Sappho found herself doubly alone in the world.

One day soon after the death of her aunt the Mother Superior sent for her to come to her in her private room—the parlor of the convent.

PAULINE E. HOPKINS

"My child," she said, "I have been thinking much about you, and I have tried to benefit you. Are you still determined to pass as the boy's mother?

"Yes, Mother, I am."

"Well, then, you must be Madame Clark."

"No," replied Sappho hastily; "no more deception."

"I am glad to see that you are ready to bear all things in meekness for His sake. But you are not called upon to make too many sacrifices. God sees your heart and will reward you in his own good time. I have a place for you that I think will just suit you. Monsieur Louis of Opelausas is in want of a governess for his two granddaughters. He is a man of color, and has lost all of his family but these two children. He is an old man with a competency, and he will pay you well for your services. Alphonse can stay with us; you can pay a stipulated sum for his board and be able to see him every week. What do you think of it, my daughter?"

"I will do as you advise, Mother; you are only too kind. When shall I go?"

"Monsieur Louis will be here tomorrow to see you. If everything is satisfactory, you can go next week."

The morrow came, and with it Monsieur Louis. He was a tall, aristocratic-looking man of dignified bearing, though one soon perceived that age had bent his once firm shoulders. His hair, now entirely white, added to his venerable appearance. His face was gentle and kindly, and immediately won Sappho's heart. He, in his turn, was much impressed by her youth and beauty. He thought of the days of his own youth, when such a face as hers would have robbed him of his sleep. He thought, too, of the wife and daughter who had been taken from him, leaving his life but a succession of lonely days. "Let the past die," he murmured impatiently to himself; "I feel this beautiful girl-widow will bring peace and joy to my poor motherless girls."

In another week Sappho had accepted the liberal terms Monsieur Louis offered her, had taken a tearful farewell of Alphonse and the Sisters, and was ensconced in her new home.

The house was pleasant; it stood in its own grounds; an old-fashioned, typical Southern residence, with wide gardens and a carriage drive winding around a smoothly cut lawn. The interior was well furnished, comfortable, and every want abundantly supplied. She combined the duties of housekeeping with those of teaching, and soon became the moving spirit of the home, warmly loved by her little charges, and enthusiastically admired by the servants. It was a happy, restful life; it suited her. Its retirement, its quiet interior, recalled her childhood's happy home. Monsieur Louis, although much older, reminded her of her father, and attracted her by his gentleness. Traveling in a desert, as it were, she had come suddenly and unexpectedly upon an oasis of grass, cool shadows and running streams. Here, indeed, was peace. Had her lot been always cast in these pleasant, peaceful shades, how different her life might have been. But the iron of suffering had seared her heart. Her life now bade fair to be tranquil and monotonous enough. Why could she not be happy? she asked herself. She tried not to allow herself to think upon the past; but when night came she lay awake hungering for the sight of face, the touch of a hand, the glance of an eye. Sometimes the craving grew almost too powerful to be resisted, and once she started to dress, resolved to return to Boston, find Will, and trust all to his love. But she remembered. "His scorn I could not bear. I should die at his feet." She told herself that life was done and nothing remained but patience. So she sat dumb and submissive beneath her martyrdom.

Monsieur Louis was puzzled by the beautiful girl-widow, but he asked no inconvenient questions. He was content to accept the goods which the gods had provided him in the person of his governess, deeming himself very fortunate to have a woman of her refinement to take charge of the education of his granddaughters. He did not believe her to be a widow. He had strange thoughts when he looked at the pretty child Alphonse, who came so frequently to the house to visit his mother. The child was always made welcome for his own sake as well as for his mother's. He shook his head and sighed as he watched the two together. Such cases were only too common in the South. Like a wise man he accepted the inevitable, and tried to do the best with it that he could. "Let me bring as much good as possible out of evil," was his thought in self-communion. So he smiled on the two forlorn ones; encouraged the mother and respected her secret. One year glided slowly by; another followed. Sappho had grown accustomed to her new duties and resigned to her life.

Monsieur Louis's great hobby was his rosegarden. There he worked, assisted by the children. Alphonse spent a great part of his time with his mother, sharing the instruction of the two girls. No one would have recognized in the gay lad the quiet, melancholy child of three years before. Sappho would often sit on a garden seat watching the three children. For a time she would forget her troubles in the joy of gazing

PAULINE E. HOPKINS

upon the animated, happy face of her child. Yes, there lay consolation for all her sufferings. Alphonse was expanding like a flower beneath the influence of his mother's love and devotion. He was her consolation.

Late one afternoon she sat on the terrace, a book in her lap, her thoughts far away. Alphonse brought her a bunch of roses. The child looked at her earnestly a moment, and then said:

"Mamma, why are you always so sad when you sit on the terrace alone?"

"I am not sad, Alphonse," she replied, kissing him on his forehead.

"Oh, yes, you are. When I am a big man I shall find the tall, handsome gentleman who gave you flowers at the fair."

"Why, Alphonse!"

"Have I said anything wrong, mamma?" he asked anxiously.

"Not wrong, my child, but mamma prefers that you never speak of the past to anyone."

"I will do just as you say, Mamma Sappho!" he cried, impetuously throwing his arms about her neck in a bearlike hug.

Somewhat startled by the child's precociousness, she sat there after he left her, watching the red sun slowly dropping out of sight in the west. The peaceful stillness of approaching darkness rested on the landscape. She heard a step and turned to perceive Monsieur Louis, who seated himself beside her on the rustic settee.

"We shall have a thunder shower before morning; see how heavy the clouds are hanging."

"I have been watching them," replied Sappho.

"Miss Clark, how long have you been with us?" he asked abruptly.

"A few months more than two years. Why, Monsieur Louis?"

"You have been happy?" he asked, ignoring her question.

"Happier than I can say."

"Do not let what I am about to say distress you; but I want you to make me your confidant and tell me all your sad story, not from idle curiosity, but because I have grown to love you and the boy."

"Oh, monsieur!" was all Sappho could say.

Then he spoke again. She had only a confused idea of his words, but his meaning was clearly written in her heart.

"My child," he said gravely, taking her hand, "I am an old man, experienced in the ways of the world. I have seen and understood more of your story than I have seemed to. My heart yearns for you and the child. I am old and selfish, perhaps, but I offer you a home for yourself and the boy, an honorable name, and ample means to protect you when I am gone. In short, will you consent to marry an old man and make his few remaining years peaceful? Take time to reflect," he said, as she started to interrupt him; "and my child, while you reflect, think of me. You have grown about my heartstrings. I could not rest in my grave if I left you alone and friendless."

About Sappho's heart there was a strange feeling of suffocation, a feeling such as a martyr might have experienced at the stake.

"I cannot answer now," she said at length; "this is a strange idea to me."

"Take time," he replied; "but weigh my proposition well. There is plenty here; there is no one in the wide world to mar your peace, only an old man and two little girls. You shall be happy and honored."

"I will give you my answer in a week," she said, as she arose trembling from her seat.

"It is two weeks to Easter. Let me know your answer then." And turning, he left her as abruptly as he had come.

XXI

After Many Days

"The Lord blessed the latter end of Job more than his beginning."

The days dragged their weary length along. May passed; June and its roses faded into the languid heat of July. Still no trace was found of Sappho. Madam Frances had gone from the little house on J. Street, and she, together with the child, had vanished and left no trace. There had been a nine-days' wonder over the departure of Miss Clark, but outside of the few who were in the secret, no one knew the facts.

Will had received his degree from Harvard and was now looking forward to going abroad. But the eager zest and joy of pursuit and accomplishment were gone; duty alone remained.

It was rumored that John Langley had attached himself to the family of a well-to-do colored man of prominence in the city, and that he was very busily engaged in ingratiating himself into the good graces of the daughter of the house. People gossiped and speculated as to the cause of the broken engagement between him and Dora Smith, but from lack of information this sensation died out also.

Three months after Dora had broken with Langley the situation between her and Doctor Lewis was unchanged. The intimacy of early childhood was resumed, but she was shy and reserved beyond a certain point. Finally Doctor Lewis had been obliged to return to his charge in the South, but before he went he had obtained a promise from Dora to enter into correspondence with him. He had not dared to express the real interest and meaning which lay behind his request. The poor girl felt humiliated; her womanhood shamed; although to her surprise the happiness of life which had seemed quenched behind this flood of sorrow that had overtaken her was beginning to shine upon her again as buoyant youth regained its wonted sway. She respected Doctor Lewis, and appreciated the value of the position he had made for himself, but she did not intend to enter into another engagement immediately; she had almost determined to remain single for life until she heard of Langley's conduct. After that came the fear that he might think that she regretted the past. No; she could not remain single; she would marry one whose manliness she could respect, if she did not love him. Love was another thing, with which, she told herself, she was done.

Dora possessed the rare talent of being an interesting correspondent; indeed, her literary talents would have been valuable if cultivated. Doctor Lewis soon found this out. She gave him fascinating glimpses of the possibilities of an inner nature which perfect love and trust might develop. These short views thrilled his being with the hope of winning so rare a prize for his life companion. He pursued her unceasingly. Flowers of rare beauty and fragrance, fruit and books, found their way to her home each week. John had been rather an indifferent lover; but who could resist the impetuous onslaught of a generous nature that truly loved?

Now, when the heat of July had brought with it his annual vacation, he had returned to the North. Upon their first meeting he said to her:

"Dora, I will take no denial. No; do not speak. I know what you would say. I am willing to wait for love, because I feel sure that it will come in time."

And she, nothing loth, yielded to the stronger nature with a feeling of peace and contentment to which she had long been a stranger. So October was set for the wedding; and as the days passed, Dora felt that this time she had made no mistake.

It was toward the end of July Ma Smith sat in her pretty parlor talking with Mrs. Ophelia Davis. Mrs. Davis had just heard the news of Dora's prospective marriage to Doctor Lewis.

"I'm jes' as glad as I can be. Dear, dear; it don't seem possible that so many things have happened to change the prospectus since last winter when we sat in this very room having such a good time, an' Miss Clark had jes' ben interduced, an' was so hansum, an' sech a way with her an' so forth. You know, I thought your Will was goin' to git completely smashed on her. It's funny how mistook a body can git 'bout fellers and gals. You think they're goin' crazy over each other when all of a suddint—Lordy! they've up an' married some po' plain critter that you never thought they'd give a second look to. They'd heve made a hansum couple, too. Jes' borned fer each other. Then there's the smashup 'twixt Dora and Langley. Mercy knows, I don't blame her. I allers thought he had a downish sort o' look. Drat them sickly, peeky lookin: men! *Me! no ma'm!* I wouldn't look at one o. them! No ma'm! Dear, dear! it do seem strange. But that wasn't what I wanted to say tickler to you."

PAULINE E. HOPKINS

She smoothed down her long white apron as she murmured to herself: "'Phelia, whar is you?" She was evidently embarrassed. After thinking a moment she continued:

"Now, 'bout this house. What are you goin' to do with it?"

"We haven't concluded yet what we will do with it. I'm going South with Dora until Will finishes at Heidelberg; then, after he has settled upon his future field of work, I am to live with him."

"Exactly so. Then I s'pose you'll be willin' to rent the house ef you git a good tenant?"

"Yes; I suppose so."

"Now, Sis'Smith, I want to ask you ef you've eny ejections to my takin' it?"

"Certainly no objections; but isn't it a great responsibility for a woman alone in the world?" asked Mrs. Smith, greatly surprised.

Mrs. Davis smoothed the folds of her ample white apron nervously—coughed—stammered—blushed.

"Well, truth is, Sis' Smith, you know people make changes in this life; fac' truth, indeed, ma'm, we's always changin', an' I'm thinkin' o' changin' to double harness fer a while."

"I want to know!" exclaimed Ma Smith, now properly astonished and interested. "And who is the happy man?"

Mrs. Davis wiped the perspiration from her face with the back of her hand as she replied with a nervous laugh:

"Oh, you know him well! It's Mr. Jeemes."

"What! Mr. James! why, he's nothing but a boy!" exclaimed Ma Smith.

"Course I know he's young, but I'm not so old myself."

"Why, how old are you, Sister Davis?"

"I don't know that I mind tellin' you, 'cause you're safe. I'm all of thirty-five. Ginerally speakin', I never tell nobody my exac' age, 'cause it's none o' thar bisiness."

"*Thirty-five years!* Impossible! Why, it's thirty-five years *since* the war. You were a widow at that time, weren't you?"

"That's my age, anyhow," was the sullen answer.

"But, Sister Davis, you must be fifty years old at the very least," said Ma Smith, persisting that she was right in her calculations,

"Fifty nuthin'!" replied Mrs. Davis, somewhat offended at Mrs. Smith's pertinacity. "I'm thirty-five years old, an' I reckon thet I'm the one what knows best when I was borned."

"I'm sure I hope you will be happy with Mr. James," Ma Smith hastened to reply, seeing that Mrs. Davis was really offended.

"Is he going to leave college?" she continued, retiring with graceful discretion from the contest.

"No; he's goin' to graduate. The society he's been preaching fer Sundays is goin' to give him their church, and I'll keep the laundry a-goin' an' rent rooms."

"I'm sure I'll be very glad to let you have the house. I don't know anyone I'd rather let it to."

"Then that's settled," said Mrs. Davis, with a sigh of relief. "I thought you'd say that. Now, you see, all yer ol' lodgers can keep their rooms, an' it will seem jes' like home to them. Mr. Jeemes is that fond o' me tell Sarah Ann calls me an ol' fool, an' says all he wants is my money, and a right smert 'ooman to work fer him. I telled Sarah Ann, 'go git a man fer yourself an' quit bein' jealous.' She says to me, 'I will, an' it won't be a boy jes' turned twentyone.' Sarah Ann an' me'll have to part after I'm married, she's that jealous." Mrs. Davis had regained all her good humor, and was very complacent over Ma Smith's evident interest in her story.

"Now that would be a pity, after you've been together so long," remarked the latter.

"She's got to drop sayin' ticklish things to me. A 'ooman's got a right to git married, ain't she?" Mrs. Davis was now fairly started on a congenial subject, and her words flowed in a torrent.

"Mr. Jeemes says he knows the Lord sent me fer to be a helpmeet to him, an' I dassay he's right. Sarah Ann says my money's the helpmeet' he's after, an' somebody to cook good vittals to suit his pellet. But I know better; he's a godly man ef he ain't much to look at."

"How did you happen to take a fancy to each other?"

"Lord, he's sech a good critter! The first I noticed was the night you had that swaree here last winter. Some o' the men got to talkin' 'bout 'ooman bein' the weaker vessel, an' subjugatin' theirself to be led by men an' not go prespirin' after work an' sech likes which belongs to men. Mr. Jeemes he held to it thet 'ooman's all right to ejecate herself even to be a minister, fer no man could be suferior to 'ooman, 'cause she was his *rib*. An' ever sence that I kin' o' thought what a shame it was fer a man to be minus one o' his ribs all along o' 'ooman, untell I made up my mind thet ef Jeemes wanted me he *could have back his lost rib*. All this spring he's been a-ridin' me on his bike down in the kitchen every

PAULINE E. HOPKINS

day after we got through washin' an' had cleaned up, so I could go ridin' with him in the Fens an' all out o' town this summer. After I'd learnt, one day he came in with a beautiful bike an' saddle. The nex' day we was ter ride ter the Park. I hed on my new pale blue bicycle suit with a pink shirtwaist an'a white sailer hat an' tancolored shoes an' gloves. I tell you I looked some! Mr. Jeemes had on a black suit with a gray linen duster, an' he did look extinguished in his beaver hat an' that white choker an' tie o'hisn which I must say I do admire. We got along purty well. Everybody was a-lookin'an' a-gappin' at us. Sarah Ann says it was 'cause we looked like a couple o'jay birds stuffed."

"We got along all right untell we was a-comin' down a hill. Mr. Jeemes was a-coastin', an' the tail o' that linen duster o'hisn was a-sailin' out behin' like a flag floppin'in an east wind. The fust thing I knowed he was a-stickin' fast head fust into a pile o' sand where they was makin' mortar to build a cellar, an' me on top o' him! Wasn't it a mercy thet we wasn't stuck in the mortar? Jeemes is purty black, but he was a white man when he got out o'thet san' heap. As fer me, I tore my gloves, los' my hat, an' busted a new pair o' corsets right off me. Besides thet, I nearly swallered my upper teeth, an' I lost my bangs. They picked me up an' carried me into a house they was a-buildin', an' give me a chance to fix myself up a bit. But I 'clar to you them corsets was no good never after thet; an' it cost me ten dollars to fix thet upper set o' teeth so I could wear 'em agin; I never have seen them bangs sence."

"We was thet done up that Jeemes sent fer a kerridge to bring us home; an' fifty dollars won't excuse the damages to them bikes. Comin' home an' settin' so close together, beside the trouble we'd had makin' us feel kin' o' tender o' each other, Jeemes put his arm 'roun' me—an' I don' see how ever in time he did it, bein' the corsets warn't no good, an'me 'bou: as small as a bag o' taters—he put his arm 'roun' me, he did, an' he says, says he: 'Le's git married, 'Phelia!' I was thet stonished an' set back you could heve knocked me down with a feather, an' was thet weak from bein'overcamed by my feelin' thet all I remember was thet I fell on his neck like the patrihawks did in the Bible where they tell 'bout Abraham, Isaac an' Jacob, Shem, Ham, Meshack an' 'Bednego you 'member how the minister tol' us all 'bout that in the Skripter lesson las' Sunday night, don't you? I ain't got no 'bility fer readin', but I's got a mem'ry, thank Gawd. As I was a-sayin', I jes' fell onto his neck, an' I says to him: 'Mr. Jeemes, ef *you* *want yer rib, I'm her.*' Thet's the way it camed 'bout, an' we's yoin' ter be married purty soon, 'though Sarah Ann says I'm a mortalized ol' ijit, an'a insane mannyack, an' Jeemes knows what he's a-fishin' fer. She's insultin', mos' insultin'."

Mrs. Smith sympathized with her, and after more talk about the rent of the building and other matters dear to the heart of the housewife, they separated.

For a long time Ma Smith sat there in the quiet, shaded room, buried in deep thought. She made a charming picture. White was her favorite color for summer wear, with a tiny crimson cashmere shawl thrown about her shoulders, to keep off the chill which comes so naturally to old age. She had been a handsome woman, and still retained traces of former beauty. Thick bands of snowy hair, falling in natural waves, were coiled closely at the back of a well-shaped head. Her clear olive complexion contrasted pleasantly with eyes large, soft, and black, heavy black eyebrows and long curling lashes. An aquiline nose, thin lips and delicately shaped ears gave her a very pleasing countenance.

As she sat there her whole life passed in review. She thought of her children, and how much she had to be thankful for in them. But more than all, the story told her so often by her father of his early life and that of his father and mother, was fresh within her mind as she sat there dreaming. Months afterward she looked back upon that day, and remembered with wonder her own tranquility.

"The surpreme hours unnoted come."

She heard the door-bell ring, but it did not disturb her reverie. There was a knock at the door of the room where she was sitting. Then the door opened, and Mrs. Davis ushered in a tall, elegant white man of distinguished address, and about her own age. Mrs. Davis closed the door behind him and vanished.

"Mrs. Smith, I presume?" he said in a pleasant voice as he advanced toward her. It was a voice of rare carrying power—deep, rich, musical, and had moved the House of Commons to enthusiasm on more than one memorable occasion in the politics of Great Britain.

"Yes," she replied, rising from her seat.

"I called to see Mr. William Smith, and I dislike to be disappointed. Will he be at home He handed her his card as he finished speaking, and she read the inscription:

Charles Montfort-Withington,
Blankshire,
England.

"Pray be seated, Mr. Withington," she said, as she placed a chair for her visitor. "I am William's mother; he will be in very soon."

Mr. Withington thanked her, and having seated himself, glided easily into conversation; at the same time his keen eye noted his surroundings. Nothing in the quiet, unpretentious, shaded room escaped him. The large glass bowl of flowers—sweet peas and nasturtiums predominating—filled the room with fragrance; there were three or four water-color paintings set in simple frames—pictures of rural scenes. The few choice pieces of china and bric-a-brac which adorned the mantel, the open piano, the general good taste, even elegance of the apartment, appealed strongly to the artistic sense of the cultured gentleman who had been reared in the luxury of ample wealth. Mrs. Smith herself was a revelation to him. By what art of necromancy had such a distinguished woman been evolved from among the brutalized aftermath of slavery?

"I had the pleasure of meeting your son and conversing with him at the annual dinner of the Canterbury Club in February last. I was much impressed with his views on the condition of the Negroes in this country. Being interested in every phase of racial development which bears upon the science of political economy, I felt that after my Canadian business was settled I would try and meet him again. I intended to write and ask him to meet me at the Vendome, but on second thoughts I concluded to try and see him in his own home."

"He will feel greatly flattered at your kind remembrance," Mrs. Smith replied.

"Are you aware, madam, that your son possesses rare intellectual gifts?" he continued, after a slight pause. "I must confess to a feeling of curiosity to learn how such characters are nourished among a people like yours."

Mrs. Smith looked at him thoughtfully a moment, and then said:

"Sir, it would afford me great pleasure to give you a sketch of his life so far, if you would care to listen."

"It is what I desire most to hear."

The great man listened to her humble story with marked attention, as she related the history of early struggles which her husband and she had braved for the maintenance and education of their children. It was a story common enough among Negroes ambitious to avail themselves of the privileges which were now open to them—a story of faithful fathers bearing insult and injury to keep the meanly paid employment; of mothers "spending weary days and nights over the washtub and ironing-board in order to get money to educate their children." It seemed marvelous to the listener. As she closed, he said impressively:

"Your story is a revelation to me, madam. Are there many histories like yours among your people? In what a different light you would appear as a race, if the statements made by your detractors could be stripped of calumny and deception. Believe me, you have my heartfelt sympathy, and I shall do all that I can to promote kindly feelings in England for our unfortunate black brother in America. And it is against such spirits of nobility and self-sacrifice that many would close the entrance door to the higher education of the century! Blind and foolish prejudice! Monstrous injustice!" He paused a moment to collect himself and overcome his indignation.

"Madam, how is it that you maintain so excellent an address and manner? and from whom, may I ask, without being considered impertinent, did you inherit your superior intelligence?"

"Ah, sir; that is a sad story connected with the lives of those long since passed away."

"But you seem perfectly happy."

"Yes; but it is the happiness chastened by wrongs endured and grief subdued." She paused as though forgetful of her visitor, and then resumed in a low tone:

"Yes; there are strangely tangled threads in the lives of many colored families—I use the word 'colored' because these stories occur mostly among those of mixed blood. But few have a stranger or more romantic history than my father's,—Will's grandfather; I never speak of it for fear of ridicule. I was attracted by the name of Montfort on your card. It is uncommon; I was a Montfort before marriage."

Mr. Withington uttered an exclamation which was unheeded by the woman before him, who was lost in the clouds of the past. His face wore an expression of intense interest.

Presently she continued:

"It is a homely subject to introduce to one familiar with the sorrows of the wealthy and prosperous alone; but it teaches that misfortune is the common lot of all mankind."

"I await your story with anxiety." And truly it seemed so, for Mr. Withington had left his seat and was pacing slowly up and down the room. Mrs. Smith began her tale like one who describes a vision passing before her eyes. She told it in almost the exact words of the story which we have given as the first part of this narrative. In the midst of the recital Will entered the room from another door, and paused in astonishment at the scene before him. Mr. Withington shook hands with him noiselessly, and signed him to keep silence and not disturb the speaker. His own emotion was intense; tears trembled in his eyes; his bosom heaved; his countenance was pale and distressed. When she had finished he said:

"And have you no proofs of this story—no letters?"

"Alas, nothing! Poor father destroyed all in a fit of despondency when his brother's letters ceased to come. Then he lost his little property, and after that he removed to Boston. I believe my father died of a broken heart. God did not intend that his wrongs should be righted." As she finished, the tears weru streaming from her eyes.

Mr. Withington ceased his nervous promenade, and taking both her hands in his, replied solemnly:

"Not so, dear cousin, for such I believe you to be; never doubt God's goodness or justice. I believe that I hold the key to solve this riddle! I believe that I am your relative, descended directly from your father's brother; your grandfather's brother," he said, turning to Will, who stood an amazed spectator of this extraordinary scene,

"Impossible!" exclaimed mother and son with one breath.

"Nothing is impossible with God. How often have I heard *my* father tell very much the same tale I have just listened to. *Let me assure you that the letters of Jesse Montfort to his brother Charles are still in existence!* They are preserved as a sacred legacy, together with a sworn statement of the main facts as we know them, in this remarkable case. Your uncle Charles married his rescuer's daughter, and as is the custom among old English families where the name would become extinct upon the marriage of the only child—a daughter—he assumed the name of Withington in conjunction with his own. The United States Government was sued by Withington, Sr., and he recovered 1, one hundred thousand dollars damages for Charles, but no trace of Jesse could be found The money is held for him or his heirs by the Government. I can furnish you the necessary proof upon my return to England. Tell me not that the time of miracles has departed! Is not this a direct intervention of the hand of

Providence that we, so widely separated, should at last become known to each other?"

He paused, overcome by emotion. Mrs. Smith wept quietly. Broken words of praise to God—of joy—of sorrow for the dead—of hope for the future—passed her lips from time to time. Ah! who can paint such a scene? Finally Mr. Withington embraced them both—his kinswoman and Will, his kinsman.

"Be assured that I shall bend every effort to prove this story, and spare no money to establish you in your rights."

Then, unable longer to control his feelings, telling Will to join him in an hour at his hotel, he hastily left them.

Alone together the mother and son fell upon their knees to give thanks to God for his unspeakable goodness.

When Mr. Withington had thought over the story which had come to him so strangely, he was profoundly impressed with the inscrutable ways of God. How wonderful was the knowledge that he had been led by devious paths to find these humble relatives. By accident alone had it been accomplished. "No, not by accident," he told himself, "but by the direct intervention of All-wise Justice." So noble was the nature of this man that he never once thought of the possible ridicule that might come to him through his new kinspeople. He thought only of the tie of blood. When it was placed before him in this light by Will, his reply was characteristic of the man:

"At home it will not be noticed; the opinion of narrow-minded, prejudiced people *here* does not matter."

Mr. Withington now spent long days with the Smiths. There was much to learn of the past history of each family. These were days of happiness to the newly found relatives days fraught with wise lessons to himself. He was the best of friends with Dora; indeed, he was a man who inspired confidence and love. Very soon he was the recipient of the story of all her recent trials with John, and poor Will's unhappy love episode. He approved Dora's choice in Doctor Lewis, and had the latter's promise to take her across to Europe at the earliest opportunity. For Will he had a strong man's sympathy, and encouraged him to hope that all might yet be well. So potent was his hopefulness that will brightened perceptibly and became more like his old ambitious self, to the great delight of his mother and sister.

He in his turn told them the story of Charles Montfort: How his benefactor had returned to America in the hope of finding and rescuing

Jesse, after establishing the boys' claim to the estate of their murdered father. He found that the child had disappeared, leaving no trace behind him. How Charles had rejoiced over the later discovery of his brother, and how he had grieved over the final estrangement. Then on the eve of his departure for America to personally search Jesse out, he was stricken with paralysis, and remained a helpless invalid until his death. Meantime the business of establishing the identity of the Smiths was going forward as swiftly as possible.

Mr. Withington communicated with his family lawyer, who came from England, bringing with him certain valuable papers bearing upon the case, engaged a leading firm of American lawyers to act in conjunction with the English lawyer, interviewed the authorities at Washington, and secured the services of one of the best detectives in the country to ferret out evidence to prove Jesse's identity. Money flowed from his lavish hand, and all the legal machinery that was essential to prompt action was soon set in motion. One day Mr. Withington received a letter from the detective asking him to go to Bermuda and see an important witness. He started immediately upon receiving it, accompanied by Will Smith and his lawyer. A letter from Will to his mother after they had reached the island was filled with fresh surprises. What follows is an extract:

> We have come across a wonderful coincidence. In hunting for evidence in Bermuda, the detective heard of an old woman a centenarian who was formerly a slave in North Carolina. We found her living with her daughter and granddaughter (both old women; the granddaughter is sixty); all of them were once slaves. The old woman's mind is clouded on all subjects but one—the Montfort murder! She was an eye-witness of the atrocious crime. She lived for years as the mistress of Anson Pollock, and knew that he tracked Jesse to Boston, where he lost all trace of him. The day we visited her it was pathetic to hear her grieve over the children; one would have thought them still helpless little ones. My dear mother, this woman is but another evidence of the all-powerful hand of the Almighty—this poor, decrepit, half-blind centenarian is *Lucy, Grace Montfort's fostersister and maid!*
>
> The granddaughter is married, and her husband and children are here. When the Civil War ended they

determined to settle in Bermuda, and here they have lived ever since in a cottage which is almost a but, supporting themselves by selling sugar-cane in small sticks—the same as our candy-shops sell sticks of candy to the children—and other products of their garden, in the market-place. Prepare yourself for another surprise.

The youngest woman had a child while in slavery, by Anson Pollock, Jr., a grandnephew of old Anson Pollock, whom we all have so much reason to remember. The poor woman seems much distressed over this boy, who, it appears, was taken from her when he was but six months old, and sold with many others to a man who farmed Negro babies for the market. She asked me if I had ever in my distant home met a young man called John Pollock Langley. *He is her son!* I gave her an evasive answer, and told her I would inquire about such a person, and let her know the result. I shall write John these facts. He can use his own pleasure then about claiming his relatives. How fortunate the estrangement which resulted in breaking the engagement between John and Dora. I never could have tolerated the idea of a descendant of the Montforts being united in the close relation of marriage with one of the villainous and unscrupulous Pollocks. Let us thank God for another mercy. Mr. Withington feels as I do. He has invested some money in a small annuity for our humble friends,—enough to keep them from want. The nobility of this man is something remarkable. We sail from here for home by the next steamer, so we shall be in time for the wedding.

Your loving son,
WILL

P. S.—I reopen this letter to tell you of the death of Lucy; old age the cause. After she learned that I was Jesse's grandson, and heard the story of his life, with the renewed intelligence often vouchsafed to those just upon the border of the happy land, her prayer was: let Thy servant depart in peace." How soon her prayer was answered.

WILL

PAULINE E. HOPKINS

In the last beautiful days of October Dora became the wife of Doctor Lewis, and went with him to his far-off Southern home to assist him in the upbuilding of their race.

And what a wedding it was! The skies were fair and bright. The romantic story of the Smith family had become noised about, and as it was a church wedding the sacred edifice was crowded to suffocation. Doctor Lewis was well and favorably known, and that was of additional interest to the spectators. The small girls who formed Dora's class in Sunday-school, dressed in white, preceded the pretty bride, strewing flowers in her path. Then the bride followed on the arm of her brother, Doctor Lewis meeting them at the altar, where he had been accompanied by the ushers. Dora would have no bridesmaids. Gowned in the simplest white muslin frock she stood and solemnly plighted her vows to the man of her choice.

They were a striking couple: she serious, he so grave and steadfast. So it should be, taking up a new life, with its endless need of forbearance, trust, and mutual affection. Each knew that with one all was not yet given with the abandonment of perfect love. Each felt, too, the deep waters that surrounded Will the shadow of a tragedy that lay about his life. What wonder that an unusual solemnity enfolded this couple as they took their vows upon them. But it was a solemnity that quiets, soothes and strengthens.

As the bride came down the aisle on her husband's arm at the conclusion of the ceremony, she caught for one instant the full gaze of John Langley. She never forgot that look; so full of despair and unhappiness. She said nothing about it to husband or brother, but it haunted her for many an hour.

Well, well, it was over, and they passed out to the carriage, and thence to the house.

There was a great reception after the ceremony; but just before Dora left her room to take her place with the receiving party, a package was placed in her hand. She opened it, and found it a jewel-box containing a heavy gold bracelet set with pearls, which outlined a delicate vine of pansies traced about the golden band. No note or card was attached— nothing but her name and the date of the marriage. Dora locked it away with her many gifts, amid painful thoughts; she knew instinctively that John was the giver. A week later the happy couple left Boston, accompanied by Mrs. Smith, followed by the heartfelt good wishes of all who knew them, for their future prosperity. So with fair skies and favorable winds they entered upon the untried sea of matrimony.

The case of Smith *vs.* the United States did not come to a public trial; it was heard privately before a court composed of the judges of the Supreme Court of the United States. The English heirs had received their portion years before; the Government only awaited the production of the necessary proofs to establish the identity of Mrs. Smith beyond a peradventure. Detectives went over the ground carefully. The records of real estate transfers, chattels, etc., were all found intact among the files of the courthouse at Newberne, North Carolina. Jesse was traced from the time he fled from Anson Pollock until he settled in Exeter, New Hampshire, and married Elizabeth Whitfield.

By this woman he raised a family of twelve children, five of whom, including Mrs. Smith, were born in Exeter. Up to the time of her birth he had prospered, and had accumulated a good property, but in an evil hour he went upon the bond of his employer, who, failing to meet his liabilities, involved Montfort in his ruin. Unmanned by recurring misfortunes, Jesse Montfort removed to Boston, and never again seemed to have the ambition to try to retrieve his losses. Born in an evil hour, under an unlucky planet, this man's life was but a path of sorrow to the grave, which he welcomed as a refuge from all vicissitudes.

As Mr. Withington had said, the letters in his possession from Jesse to Charles Montfort, yellow and time-stained, completed a perfect chain of evidence. The sum of one hundred and fifty thousand dollars was awarded to Mrs. Smith as the last representative of the heirs of Jesse Montfort. Justice was appeased.

The case was a nine-days' wonder; startled society and all the world—a life drama whose power touched the deep wells of human feeling.

XXII

"So He Bringeth Them Into Their Desired Haven"

All is ended now, the hope and the fear and the sorrow;
All the aching of heart, the restless, unsatisfied longing,
All the dull, deep pain, and constant anguish of patience!

Even as rivulets twain, from distant and separate sources,
Seeing each other afar, as they leap from the rocks, and pursing
Each one its devious path, but drawing nearer and nearer,
Rush together at last, at their trysting-place in the forest;
So these lives
Rushed together at last, and one was lost in the other.

—LONGFELLOW

Three years rolled slowly away and were numbered with the past. Will Smith had finished his course at Heidelberg, and for nine months had traveled in foreign capitals. He was much changed. Honors were thick upon him; *honores mutant mores.* His bearing was that of a man accustomed to the respectful attention of his equals, sure of himself, his position, his attainments—a wealthy cosmopolitan. He had been a handsome young fellow; he added now to mere good looks, grace, ease, elegance, and an imposing, well-developed intellectuality which marked him as a thinker and an originator. His eyes alone were unchanged, and had the same kindly expression, although there lurked within their hazel depths a sadness which in repose became absolute mournfulness.

The ambition of his life was the establishment of a school which should embrace every known department of science, where the Negro youth of ability and genius could enter without money and without price. This was his pet scheme for the future. No wife or child would ever be his, he told himself; but he would be a father to the youth of his race. Thus he mused and planned until one day there came a letter from his sister saying that his mother's health was very much broken, and that she longed for the presence of her boy. Will packed up, and April found him in the United States once more, at the home of his sister in New Orleans.

Thoughts of Sappho were seldom far from him; he thought of her as one gone to the land of delight—purified by her sufferings here. The first night that he passed on board ship he had dreamed of her. He dreamed that he stood in a grand cathedral, and listened to strains of delicious melody chanted by an invisible choir. *Christe eleison, Kyrie eleison*, floated to his ears, and the glad strains of the Gloria. Presently upon the altar before him appeared a vision of the Virgin and Child, but the face of the mother was Sappho's, the child by her side was the little Alphonse. He tried to reach her in vain. She smiled and beckoned him on as she receded at his approach; then he awoke. His dream haunted him. He interpreted it as a promise that they should be united in heaven. The meeting with his mother and sister and the renewal of old ties somewhat deadened painful memories, until reawakened when he heard them call his sister's beautiful child "Sappho."

The home to which Doctor Lewis had taken his bride was very beautiful. One passed from the highway down a long avenue framed by majestic palms, and so upon the college campus which was surrounded by dormitories built of substantial brick. Doctor Lewis's house was a fine brick cottage, plentifully supplied with porches and piazzas. Its framework was a succession of terraces planted with gorgeous beds of flowers indigenous to the Southern clime. The long French windows stood open to catch the soft breezes of April. This house and the numerous dormitories, museums, the chapel, and buildings which held lecture-rooms and class-rooms, were all built by the pupils of the school. The students made the brick which entered into the composition of the various buildings; the carpenter shop, carriage and blacksmith shops afforded fine facilities for imparting practical knowledge of these useful industries.

Beyond the college grounds—to the right extended the market gardens, which not only supplied the school with vegetables, but also added a goodly sum to the college fund. There, too, were the grazing pastures for horses and cows. The dairy was a long, low, shedlike brick building, beautifully clean and sweet; its brick floors were spotless, the walls adorned with shining utensils for setting milk for cream, and for churning this same cream into butter. Hundreds of hens and chickens roved in small family bands about the immense poultry yards; from all

PAULINE E. HOPKINS

of which came some revenue to help defray the expenses of this human hive of industry. "Many institutions do not spend one cent for domestic labor during the whole school term. The time usually given to football and other games in white colleges is utilized by the colored student in useful toil." Doctor Lewis's school was of this class. The tuition, board, lodging, laundry work and incidentals were not over twelve dollars per month. "People with such a love for knowledge that they are willing to toil for it, may be relied on to use that knowledge properly."

Will threw himself into the work of visiting Doctor Lewis's pupils and the neighboring schools with eagerness. He acquainted himself thoroughly for future reference, with the curriculum of academical life as conducted along the lines pertaining to Negro education. After gaining a clear insight into it all, he said to Doctor Lewis:

"I hold that a man to gain true self-respect and independence must not be hampered in any way by prejudice. I would remove my school far from such influences."

"Where would your choice fall for the establishment of such a paradise?" asked Doctor Lewis with a smile.

There are places enough in the world. One could easily find such an environment abroad. There across the water, associated on equal terms with men of the highest culture, the Negro shall give physical utterance to the splendid possibilities which are within him."

"Chimerical and quixotic," returned Doctor Lewis with a shake of the head. "It can't be done."

"I shall try it, nevertheless, and leave the results I hope for to the leveling hand of Time."

If ever a doubt of Dora's happiness had troubled Will's thoughts, it was dispelled now that he saw her a contented young matron, her own individuality swallowed up in love for her husband and child. She had apparently forgotten that any other love had ever disturbed the peaceful current of her life. She was pained, however, to find, in their first private interview, that Will still clung to a hopeless memory, as it seemed to her.

"You say that you never expect to see her again, that you think her dead. Why not, then, seek to solace yourself for her loss by marrying some good girl who will make you happy?"

"Sappho is the kind of woman to occupy a man's thoughts. Beside her all others are uninteresting and tame."

"I know it, Will; but it would please me, and mother would die happy if she knew that you were at peace in your mind."

"Do not talk of it!" he cried impatiently; "I cannot please you in that way. I shall never marry."

After that Dora said no more, but tried to make his visit pleasant in every possible way. Will wished to establish a home with his mother in the North, but she was feeble, and he did not care to separate her from Dora. So he drifted with the tide, waiting for circumstances to direct his wandering feet.

"Have you visited the Sisters of the Holy Family yet?" asked Dora on Good Friday morning as they sat at breakfast.

"No," replied Will. "Arthur has promised to accompany me there, but something always intervenes."

"Don't miss it on Sunday morning. The Easter service is divine."

The convent of the Holy Family was founded in 1842 by three good women, in the very heart of the stronghold of slavery, and under the most depressing influences. There is but one other mother-house and novitiate for colored women in the United States, and that is in the city of Baltimore. The service held in the chapel by the Sisterhood of the Holy Family on Easter morning is famous throughout the South. Easter is Easter the world over, and the earth seems to take on an added beauty in honor of the day. But Easter in New Orleans is something to dream of, and defies description.

Will's thoughts were solemn ones, and mingled with pain, for was not this the anniversary of his greatest joy and his most bitter sorrow. He walked toward the chapel through silent streets filled with earnest worshippers on the way to early Mass. It was a familiar sight to Will, who had passed so many months in Catholic countries. Morn was breaking in the east; the air was filled with the faint sounds of returning life; the sweet odor of the magnolia, mingled with a thousand other subtle perfumes, intoxicated the senses. The sun had not yet risen as he glided quietly into the church and took a seat in a secluded corner, to watch the entry of the congregation.

Until Easter morning the pictures of Christ, Mary and Joseph were veiled, but now the statues had emerged from their concealment in indication of the spiritual change in us which was wrought by the coming forth of Christ from the tomb. Tapers glowed and flowers bloomed everywhere. The Sisters stood with their dark faces uplifted in the full light which fell from the stained glass windows, making a picture long to be remembered. The stillness, the coolness, the swiftly moving, silent figures, the slanting rays of sunlight growing higher and higher, seemed to calm the troubled spirit of the man, and to impress his very soul with the greatness and glory of pure religious devotion. Involuntarily his thoughts were wafted upward in solemn supplication to the Father of all good.

He saw the entrance of the convent boarders, the orphan girls, the orphan boys and the novices, still in an exalted state of religious enthusiasm. All in the crowded edifice were on their knees now, listening to the intonations of the gold-robed priest. The sun burst forth in full glory and poured its rays in dazzling hues through the rose-stained windows. Simultaneously, the choir of female voices filled the air with the heavenly strains of the *Kyrie eleison*, gliding swiftly into the grandeur of the *Gloria in Excelsis*. It filled every corner of the building, stole into the heart and overflowed into space. Then the whole congregation, led by the Sisters, moved toward the Holy Communion—backward and then toward the right. As the children passed him Will started to his feet and almost cried out, for there before his eyes was the figure of little Alphonse, clad in the regulation garb of the Orphanage! He restrained himself by a mighty effort, and fell back in his seat overcome. Tumultuous thoughts overwhelmed him. The mother must be near! Could it be possible that she lived? and if she lived, was she indeed dead to him in her refuge behind convent walls? He heard no more of the service, but waited impatiently for the end. It came at last.

It was some time before he could reach the street on account of the dense crowd, but finally he found himself upon the sidewalk, and asked a passer-by to direct him to the Orphanage. The stranger politely piloted him to the door of the house on St. Peter Street. He rang the bell, and sent his card to the Mother Superior by a novice in the regulation black dress and white bonnet. She bade him enter, and left him in a bare room overlooking a paved court, where groups of children could be seen at play. He stood there with his back to the door, buried in deep thought and filled with misgivings. Suddenly a door opened behind him and a voice said: "I will bring him back tomorrow, Sister."

Surely he knew that voice! He turned, and there before his blinded vision stood the realization of his dream, holding the boy by the hand! One swift glance showed him that she was in street attire; that she was not a member of the Order. She saw and recognized him at the same instant. With a mighty cry of joy and thanksgiving he clasped her in his arms.

"O, that 'twere possible,
After long grief and pain,
To find the arms of my true love
Round me once again!"

Sappho was welcomed right royally by Doctor Lewis, Dora and her mother, as one risen from the dead; tears, smiles, kisses greeted her. It seemed that they would never be able to control their emotion. Then she told them of her flight to New Orleans with the child, of the death of the old fortune-teller, and her own employment as a governess in the family of the wealthy colored planter in Opelausus, and the placing of the boy with the Sisters. She in her turn listened with wonder to the fairylike tale of the wealth that had come to her lover's family.

Late that afternoon she sat once again in close heart communion with her lover. Each had much to tell.

Seated beside her on the sofa, Will folded her closely to his heart again with one deep, heavy sob which attested the man's suppressed anguish.

"Oh," he said, at last, "it has been like a hideous nightmare since I read that letter which you sent me. I can scarcely believe in the blessed reality that I hold you safe in my arms once more."

She put back the clustering curls from his brow, noting with pain the many white hairs which threaded those raven locks. She laid her cheek against his as she said:

"I know only too well all you have gone through."

"Why did you leave me, Sappho? Had you no confidence in my love for you? How meanly you must have judged me if you thought me capable of holding you responsible for the monstrous wrong committed against you."

"Ah, Will; I had suffered so much at the hands of selfish men! Can you wonder that I mistrusted you, and felt that you would only despise me when you knew all?"

Then he told her of his interview with John Langley, holding back nothing but the insulting insinuations.

"But, dearest, the detectives were at the convent; they even interviewed Luke Sawyer. Poor fellow, he was completely overcome when he found that you were alive, and he dropped his work and devoted months to tracing your whereabouts in this very city. How you have managed to hide yourself, and Dora living right here in New Orleans with you, is the mystery."

"Yes; but it is an easy matter to become lost in a great city like this. You must remember that I kept away from every familiar spot; even the Sisters in the convent had been changed, so that there was no one to remember me, the former Mother Superior having died. When I was strong enough to go about, you had ceased searching for me."

"And all this secrecy was for what?" asked Will reproachfully

"I thought it was for the best."

"I loved you, Sappho; could you not trust that love?"

"Ah, Will, forgive me for all the suffering I have caused you."

Will laid his cheek to hers. "What is there I would not forgive, if anything there were to forgive, for the sweet comfort of holding you once again to my desolate heart."

Then she wept a few delicious tears within the shelter of his arms, and he told her of his plans for her and the boy. They would go abroad; but first they would seek out Luke Sawyer and reward him for his faithfulness; every one who had ever been kind to her or the boy should be rewarded.

That evening Will accompanied Sappho home. Alphonse was left with Dora. Monsieur Louis was astonished to see a handsome stranger assisting Sappho from the carriage. Her joyous face told its own story, and the kind old man knew instinctively that she had found her lover and he had lost the joy of his old age. Will was delighted with all he saw and heard in the peaceful, happy home, the refuge of his love. In the soft twilight of the fragrant terrace Sappho told Monsieur Louis her story, her hand tightly clasped in Will's. "Ah!" cried Monsieur Louis, "I thought it; I thought it!" Then Will supplemented it with the romantic history of his family, and his life since Sappho's flight. The old gentleman listened entranced. "It is indeed a fairy tale of love and chivalry such as we read of only in books," he said at last with a long-drawn breath. Then he told them many interesting tales of slave life and its complications as he had known them. It was nearly midnight when Will left, promising to return the next day and complete arrangements for a wedding which was to take place immediately. Monsieur Louis insisted that he should furnish the wedding dress and breakfast, and be allowed to give the bride away. So a second Easter Day closed on happy love—a love sanctified and purified by suffering.

John Langley, soon after Dora's marriage and the acquisition of fortune to the Smith family, suddenly gave up his business, and started off with the first daring adventurers who were allured from home by the dazzling promise of immense fortunes to be dug out of the earth in the new Eldorado—the Klondike gold-fields.

John was unhappy. He was willing to admit that he had viewed things in a false light, and consequently had made a mess of his own happiness. He still retained an ardent enthusiasm for his profession, but he needed a change. He would divert his mind from his recent disappointments by travel in strange lands, and after he had acquired a large fortune he would settle down to the practice of law and do good among his fellows as a sort of atonement for his early mistakes. He placed his business in the hands of his partner, first making a will, in which he bequeathed to his mother's family in Bermuda the savings he would leave in the bank, in case he did not return.

"I only make this will for form's sake," said he to his partner, as he gave it into the latter's keeping. "I'll be back here inside of two years and dazzle you with my wealth."

He joined a party made up of hardy Eastern men, and they started on their journey with bright anticipations of a golden future. After many adventures and much suffering they reached the goal, only to find gaunt famine awaiting them with gruesome countenance. Day by day the cold increased; day by day the stock of provisions dwindled. Each morning they counted up the dead. One morning it was five; the next, fifteen. Ten only remained alive out of a party of thirty, and these so weak as to be unable to remove the bodies from the common cabin. John learned to pray then: "May the Lord, in His infinite mercy, come to our rescue."

One morning seven more bodies lay close together in the bunks. It was plain then that a few hours would end the sufferings of the remainder. The last spark of fire had gone out. Two biscuits and a quart of water was all the sustenance left. Delirium seized upon all but John. He felt sick at heart. He prayed "God's will be done!" All that night a heavy gale blew, and before morning two more poor souls went out into space. John was then alone, the last survivor of thirty gallant men. He dragged his body outside the door and away from the charnel-house. "Let me die under the open sky, with the moon and stars for company." He told himself that the old fortune-teller had been right in her prediction: the field of ice and snow which had been shown to him stretched before him in dreary, unbroken silence. Overhead unknown constellations looked down upon his misery; the moon, cold, large, and spectral, poured an intense yet dreary light upon the scene.

He recalled the deep wisdom of lessons he had recently learned—the philosophy of life and death, assurance of the soul's individuality, and the worthlessness of this earthly clay tenement. He thought of his newly found mother, whom he had been ashamed to acknowledge. His sight failed, his limbs lost their feeling, his heart was nearly pulseless—it was death. "O God! receive my soul. Dear, dear mother"—The child of sunny climes folded himself more closely in his blankets for the last time, and slept to wake no more on earth. So the dawn of Easter Sunday found him. That undisciplined soul went forth to wander in celestial spheres, there to continue the salutary lessons begun on earth, under the guidance of God's angels, who minister to the needs of the immortal soul.

Not many months after a merry party might have been seen upon the deck of a Cunarder bound for Europe. It consisted of Doctor Lewis, Dora, little Sappho, Ma Smith, Will, Sappho-now Will's wife-and little Alphonse. They were all going to make the long-promised visit to Mr. Withington.

Sappho was happy in contemplating the life of promise which was before her. Will was the noblest of men. Alphonse was to him as his own child. United by love, chastened by sorrow and self-sacrifice, he and she planned to work together to bring joy to hearts crushed by despair.

They stood upon the deck that night long after the others had retired to their staterooms, watching the receding shores with hearts filled with emotion too deep for words.

> *"My wife, my life. O, we will walk this world*
> *Yoked in all exercise of noble end,*
> *And so through those dark gates across the wild*
> *That no man knows*
>
> *Lay thy sweet hands in mine and trust to me."*

TALMA GORDON

The Canterbury Club of Boston was holding its regular monthly meeting at the palatial Beacon-street residence of Dr. William Thornton, expert medical practitioner and specialist. All the members were present, because some rare opinions were to be aired by men of profound thought on a question of vital importance to the life of the Republic, and because the club celebrated its anniversary in a home usually closed to society. The Doctor's winters, since his marriage, were passed at his summer home near his celebrated sanatorium. This winter found him in town with his wife and two boys. We had heard much of the beauty of the former, who was entirely unknown to social life, and about whose life and marriage we felt sure a romantic interest attached. The Doctor himself was too bright a luminary of the professional world to remain long hidden without creating comment. We had accepted the invitation to dine with alacrity, knowing that we should be welcomed to a banquet that would feast both eye and palate; but we had not been favored by even a glimpse of the hostess. The subject for discussion was: "Expansion; Its Effect upon the Future Development of the Anglo-Saxon throughout the World."

Dinner was over, but we still sat about the social board discussing the question of the hour. The Hon. Herbert Clapp, eminent jurist and politician, had painted in glowing colors the advantages to be gained by the increase of wealth and the exalted position which expansion would give the United States in the councils of the great governments of the world. In smoothly flowing sentences marshalled in rhetorical order, with compact ideas, and incisive argument, he drew an effective picture with all the persuasive eloquence of the trained orator.

Joseph Whitman, the theologian of world-wide fame, accepted the arguments of Mr. Clapp, but subordinated all to the great opportunity which expansion would give to the religious enthusiast. None could doubt the sincerity of this man, who looked once into the idealized face on which heaven had set the seal of consecration.

Various opinions were advanced by the twenty-five men present, but the host said nothing; he glanced from one to another with a look of amusement in his shrewd gray-blue eyes. "Wonderful eyes," said his patients who came under their magic spell. "A wonderful man and a wonderful mind," agreed his contemporaries, as they heard in amazement of some great cure of chronic or malignant disease which approached the supernatural.

"What do you think of this question, Doctor?" finally asked the president, turning to the silent host.

"Your arguments are good; they would convince almost anyone."

"But not Doctor Thornton," laughed the theologian.

"I acquiesce whichever way the result turns. Still, I like to view both sides of a question. We have considered but one tonight. Did you ever think that in spite of our prejudices against amalgamation, some of our descendants, indeed many of them, will inevitably intermarry among those far-off tribes of dark-skinned peoples, if they become a part of this great Union?"

"Among the lower classes that may occur, but not to any great extent," remarked a college president.

"My experience teaches me that it will occur among all classes, and to an appalling extent," replied the Doctor.

"You don't believe in intermarriage with other races?"

"Yes, most emphatically, when they possess decent moral development and physical perfection, for then we develop a superior being in the progeny born of the intermarriage. But if we are not ready to receive and assimilate the new material which will be brought to mingle with our pure Anglo-Saxon stream, we should call a halt in our expansion policy."

"I must confess, Doctor, that in the idea of amalgamation you present a new thought to my mind. Will you not favor us with a few of your main points?" asked the president of the club, breaking the silence which followed the Doctor's remarks.

"Yes, Doctor, give us your theories on the subject. We may not agree with you, but we are all open to conviction."

The Doctor removed the half-consumed cigar from his lips, drank what remained in his glass of the choice Burgundy, and leaning back in his chair contemplated the earnest faces before him.

We may make laws, but laws are but straws in the hands of Omnipotence.

> "There's a divinity that shapes our ends, Rough-hew
> them how we will."

And no man may combat fate. Given a man, propinquity, opportunity fascinating femininity, and there you are. Black, white, green, yellow—nothing will prevent intermarriage. Position, wealth, family, friends—all sink into insignificance before the God-implanted instinct that made

Adam, awakening from a deep sleep and finding the woman beside him, accept Eve as bone of his bone; he cared not nor questioned whence she came. So it is with the sons of Adam ever since, through the law of heredity which makes us all one common family. And so it will be with us in our re-formation of this old Republic. Perhaps I can make my meaning clearer by illustration, and with your permission I will tell you a story which came under my observation as a practitioner.

Doubtless all of you heard of the terrible tragedy which occurred at Gordonville, Mass., some years ago, when Capt. Jonathan Gordon, his wife and little son were murdered. I suppose that I am the only man on this side the Atlantic, outside of the police, who can tell you the true story of that crime I knew Captain Gordon well; it was through his persuasions that I bought a place in Gordonville and settled down to spending my summers in that charming rural neighborhood. I had rendered the Captain what he was pleased to call valuable medical help, and I became his family physician. Captain Gordon was a retired sea captain, formerly engaged in the East India trade. All his ancestors had been such; but when the bottom fell out of that business he established the Gordonville Mills with his first wife's money, and settled down as a moneymaking manufacturer of cotton cloth. The Gordons were old New England Puritans who had come over in the "Mayflower"; they had owned Gordon Hall for more than a hundred years. It was a baronial-like pile of granite with towers, standing on a hill which commanded a superb view of Massachusetts Bay and the surrounding country. I imagine the Gordon star was under a cloud about the time Captain Jonathan married his first wife, Miss Isabel Franklin of Boston, who brought to him the money which mended the broken fortunes of the Gordon house, and restored this old Puritan stock to its rightful position. In the person of Captain Gordon the austerity of manner and indomitable will-power that he had inherited were combined with a temper that brooked no contradiction.

The first wife died at the birth of her third child, leaving him two daughters, Jeannette and Talma. Very soon after her death the Captain married again. I have heard it rumored that the Gordon girls did not get on very well with their stepmother. She was a woman with no fortune of her own, and envied the large portion left by the first Mrs. Gordon to her daughters.

Jeannette was tall, dark, and stern like her father; Talma was like her dead mother, and possessed of great talent, so great that her father sent her to the American Academy at Rome, to develop the gift. It was the hottest of July days when her friends were bidden to an afternoon party on the lawn and a dance in the evening, to welcome Talma Gordon among them again. I watched her as she moved about among her guests, a fairy like blonde in floating white draperies, her face a study in delicate changing tints, like the heart of a flower, sparkling in smiles about the mouth to end in merry laughter in the clear blue eyes. There were all the subtle allurements of birth, wealth and culture about the exquisite creature:

> "Smiling, frowning evermore, Thou art perfect in love-lore,
> Eve varying Madeline,"

quoted a celebrated writer as he stood apart with me, gazing upon the scene before us. He sighed as he looked at the girl.

"Doctor, there is genius and passion in her face. Sometime our little friend will do wonderful things. But is it desirable to be singled out for special blessings by the gods? Genius always carries with it intense capacity for suffering: 'Whom the gods love die young.'"

"Ah," I replied, "do not name death and Talma Gordon together. Cease your dismal croakings; such talk is rank heresy."

The dazzling daylight dropped slowly into summer twilight. The merriment continued; more guests arrived; the great dancing pagoda built for the occasion was lighted by myriads of Japanese lanterns. The strains from the band grew sweeter and sweeter, and "all went merry as a marriage bell." It was a rare treat to have this party at Gordon Hall, for Captain Jonathan was not given to hospitality. We broke up shortly before midnight, with expressions of delight from all the guests.

I was a bachelor then, without ties. Captain Gordon insisted upon my having a bed at the Hall. I did not fall asleep readily; there seemed to be something in the air that forbade it. I was still awake when a distant clock struck the second hour of the morning. Suddenly the heavens were lighted by a sheet of ghastly light; a terrific midsummer thunderstorm was breaking over the sleeping town. A lurid flash lit up all the landscape, painting the trees in grotesque shapes against the murky sky, and defining clearly the sullen blackness of the waters of the bay breaking in grandeur against the rocky coast. I had arisen and put back the draperies from the windows, to have an unobstructed view of the grand scene. A low muttering coming nearer and nearer, a terrific roar, and then a tremendous downpour. The storm had burst.

Now the uncanny howling of a dog mingled with the rattling volleys of thunder. I heard the opening and closing of doors; the servants were about looking after things. It was impossible to sleep. The lightning was more vivid. There was a blinding flash of a greenish-white tinge mingled with the crash of falling timbers. Then before my startled gaze arose columns of red flames reflected against the sky. "Heaven help us!" I cried; "it is the left tower; it has been struck and is on fire!"

I hurried on my clothes and stepped into the corridor; the girls were there before me. Jeannette came up to me instantly with anxious face. "Oh, Doctor Thornton, what shall we do? papa and mamma and little Johnny are in the old left tower. It is on fire. I have knocked and knocked, but get no answer."

"Don't be alarmed," said I soothingly. "Jenkins, ring the alarm bell," I continued, turning to the butler who was standing near; "the rest follow me. We will force the entrance to the Captain's room."

Instantly, it seemed to me, the bell boomed out upon the now silent air, for the storm had died down as quickly as it arose; and as our little procession paused before the entrance to the old left tower, we could distinguish the sound of the fire engines already on their way from the village. The door resisted all our efforts; there seemed to be a barrier against it which nothing could move. The flames were gaining headway. Still the same deathly silence within the rooms.

"Oh, will they never get h ere?" cried Talma, ringing her hands in terror. Jeannette said nothing, but her face was ashen. The servants were huddled together in a panic-stricken group. I can never tell you what a relief it was when we heard the first sound of the firemen's voices, saw their quick movements, and heard the ringing of the axes with which they cut away every obstacle to our entrance to the rooms. The neighbors who had just enjoyed the hospitality of the house were now gathered around offering all the assistance in their power. In less than fifteen minutes the fire was out, and the men began to bear the unconscious inmates from the ruins. They carried them to the pagoda so lately the scene of mirth and pleasure, and I took up my station there, ready to assume my professional duties. The Captain was nearest me; and as I stooped to make the necessary examination I reeled away from the ghastly sight which confronted me—*gentlemen, across the Captain's throat was a deep gash that severed the jugular win*!

The Doctor paused, and the hand with which he refilled his glass trembled violently.

"What is it, Doctor?" cried the men, gathering about me.

"Take the women away; this is murder!"

"Murder!" cried Jeannette, as she fell against the side of the pagoda. "Murder!" screamed Talma, staring at me as if unable to grasp my meaning.

I continued my examination of the bodies, and found that the same thing had happened to Mrs. Gordon and to little Johnny.

The police were notified; and when the sun rose over the dripping town he found them in charge of Gordon Hall, the servants standing in excited knots talking over the crime, the friends of the family confounded, and the two girls trying to comfort each other and realize the terrible misfortune that had overtaken them.

Nothing in the rooms of the left tower seemed to have been disturbed. The door of communication between the rooms of the husband and wife was open, as they had arranged it for the night. Little Johnny's crib was placed beside his mother's bed. In it he was found as though never awakened by the storm. It was quite evident that the assassin was no common ruffian. The chief gave strict orders for a watch to be kept on all strangers or suspicious characters who were seen in the neighborhood. He made inquiries among the servants, seeing each one separately, but there was nothing gained from them. No one had heard anything suspicious; all had been awakened by the storm. The chief was puzzled. Here was a triple crime for which no motive could be assigned.

"What do you think of it?" I asked him, as we stood together on the lawn.

"It is my opinion that the deed was committed by one of the higher classes, which makes the mystery more difficult to solve. I tell you, Doctor, there are mysteries that never come to light, and this, I think, is one of them."

While we were talking Jenkins, the butler, an old and trusted servant, came up to the chief and saluted respectfully. "Want to speak with me, Jenkins?" he asked. The man nodded, and they walked away together.

The story of the inquest was short, but appalling. It was shown that Talma had been allowed to go abroad to study because she and Mrs. Gordon did not get on well together. From the testimony of Jenkins it seemed that Talma and her father had quarrelled bitterly about her lover, a young artist whom she had met at Rome, who was unknown to fame, and very poor. There had been terrible things said by each, and threats even had passed, all of which now rose up in judgment against the unhappy girl. The examination of the family solicitor revealed the fact that Captain Gordon intended to leave his daughters only a small annuity, the bulk of the fortune going to his son Jonathan, junior. This was a monstrous injustice, as everyone felt. In vain Talma protested her innocence. Someone must have done it. No one would be benefited so much by these deaths as she and her sister. Moreover, the will, together with other papers, was nowhere to be found. Not the slightest clue bearing upon the disturbing elements in this family, if any there were, was to be found. As the only surviving relatives, Jeannette and Talma became joint heirs to an immense fortune, which only for the bloody tragedy just enacted would, in all probability, have passed them by. Here was the motive. The case was very black against Talma. The foreman stood up. The silence was intense: We "find that Capt. Jonathan Gordon, Mary E. Gordon and Jonathan Gordon, junior, all deceased, came to their deaths by means of a knife or other sharp instrument in the hands of Talma Gordon." The girl was like one stricken with death. The flower-like mouth was drawn and pinched; the great sapphireblue eyes were black with passionate anguish, terror and despair. She was placed in jail to await her trial at the fall session of the criminal court. The excitement in the hitherto quiet town rose to fever heat. Many points in the evidence seemed incomplete to thinking men. The weapon could not be found, nor could it be divined what had become of it. No reason could be given for the murder except the quarrel between Talma and her father and the ill will which existed between the girl and her stepmother.

When the trial was called Jeannette sat beside Talma in the prisoner's dock; both were arrayed in deepest mourning. Talma was pale and careworn, but seemed uplifted, spiritualized, as it were. Upon Jeannette the full realization of her sister's peril seemed to weigh heavily. She had changed much too: hollow cheeks, tottering steps, eyes blazing with fever, all suggestive of rapid and premature decay. From far-off Italy Edward Turner, growing famous in the art world, came to stand beside his girl-love in this hour of anguish.

The trial was a memorable one. No additional evidence had been collected to strengthen the prosecution; when the attorney-general rose to open the case against Talma he knew, as everyone else did, that he could not convict solely on the evidence adduced. What was given did not always bear upon the case, and brought out strange stories of Captain Jonathan's methods. Tales were told of sailors who had sworn to take his life, in revenge for injuries inflicted upon them by his hand. One or two clues were followed, but without avail. The judge summed up the evidence impartially, giving the prisoner the benefit of the doubt. The points in hand furnished valuable collateral evidence, but were not direct proof. Although the moral presumption was against the prisoner, legal evidence was lacking to actually convict. The jury found the prisoner "Not Guilty," owing to the fact that the evidence was entirely circumstantial. The verdict was received in painful silence; then a murmur of discontent ran through the great crowd.

"She must have done it," said one; "who else has been benefited by the horrible deed?"

"A poor woman would not have fared so well at the hands of the jury, nor a homely one either, for that matter," said another.

The great Gordon trial was ended; innocent or guilty, Talma Gordon could not be tried again. She was free; but her liberty, with blasted prospects and fair fame gone forever, was valueless to her. She seemed to have but one object in her mind: to find the murderer or murderers of her parents and half-brother. By her direction the shrewdest of detectives were employed and money flowed like water, but to no purpose; the Gordon tragedy remained a mystery. I had consented to act as one of the trustees of the immense Gordon estates and business interests, and by my advice the Misses Gordon went abroad. A year later I received a letter from Edward Turner, saying that Jeannette Gordon had died suddenly at Rome, and that Talma, after refusing all his entreaties for an early marriage, had disappeared, leaving no clue as to her whereabouts. I could give the poor fellow no comfort, although I had been duly notified of the death of Jeannette by Talma, in a letter telling me where to forward her remittances, and at the same time requesting me to keep her present residence secret, especially from Edward.

I had established a sanitarium for the cure of chronic diseases at Gordonville, and absorbed in the cares of my profession I gave little thought to the Gordons. I seemed fated to be involved in mysteries.

A man claiming to be an Englishman, and fresh from the California gold fields, engaged board and professional service at my retreat. I found him suffering in the grasp of the tuberclefiend—the last stages. He called himself Simon Cameron. Seldom have I seen so fascinating

PAULINE E. HOPKINS

and wicked a face. The lines of the mouth were cruel, the eyes cold and sharp, the smile mocking and evil. He had money in plenty but seemed to have no friends, for he had received no letters and had had no visitors in the time he had been with us. He was an enigma to me; and his nationality puzzled me, for of course I did not believe his story of being English. The peaceful influence of the house seemed to sooth him in a measure, and make his last steps to the mysterious valley as easy as possible. For a time he improved, and would sit or walk about the grounds and sing sweet songs for the pleasure of the other inmates. Strange to say, his malady only affected his voice at times. He sang quaint songs in a silvery tenor of great purity and sweetness that was delicious to the listening ear:

> *"A wet sheet and a flowing sea,*
> *A wind that follows fast,*
> *And fills the white and rustling sail*
> *And bends the gallant mast;*
> *And bends the gallant mast, my boys;*
> *While like the eagle free,*
> *Away the good ship flies, and leaves*
> *Old England on the lea."*

There are few singers on the lyric stage who could surpass Simon Cameron.

One night, a few weeks after Cameron's arrival, I sat in my office making up my accounts when the door opened and closed; I glanced up, expecting to see a servant. A lady advanced toward me. She threw back her veil, and then I saw that Talma Gordon, or her ghost, stood before me. After the first excitement of our meeting was over, she told me she had come direct from Paris, to place herself in my care. I had studied her attentively during the first moments of our meeting, and I felt that she was right; unless something unforeseen happened to arouse her from the stupor into which she seemed to have fallen, the last Gordon was doomed to an early death. The next day I told her I had cabled Edward Turner to come to her.

"It will do no good; I cannot marry him," was her only comment.

"Have you no feeling of pity for that faithful fellow?"

I asked her sternly, provoked by her seeming indifference. I shall never forget the varied emotions depicted on her speaking face. Fully revealed to my gaze was the sight of a human soul tortured beyond the point of endurance; suffering all things, enduring all things, in the silent agony of despair.

In a few days Edward arrived, and Talma consented to see him and explain her refusal to keep her promise to him. You must be present, Doctor; it is due your long, tried friendship to know that I have not been fickle, but have acted from the best and strongest motives.

I shall never forget that day. It was directly after lunch that we met in the library. I was greatly excited, expecting I knew not what. Edward was agitated, too. Talma was the only calm one. She handed me what seemed to be a letter, with the request that I would read it. Even now I think I can repeat every word of the document, so indelibly are the words engraved upon my mind:

> MY DARLING SISTER TALMA: When you read these lines I shall be no more, for I shall not live to see your life blasted by the same knowledge that has blighted mine.

> One evening, about a year before your expected return from Rome, I climbed into a hammock in one corner of the veranda outside the breakfast-room windows, intending to spend the twilight hours in lazy comfort, for it was very hot, enervating August weather. I fell asleep. I was awakened by voices. Because of the heat the rooms had been left in semi-darkness. As I lay there, lazily enjoying the beauty of the perfect summer night, my wandering thoughts were arrested by words spoken by our father to Mrs. Gordon, for they were the occupants of the breakfast-room.

> "Never fear, Mary; Johnny shall have it all—money, houses, land and business."

> "But if you do go first, Jonathan, what will happen if the girls contest the will? People will think that they ought to have the money as it appears to be theirs by law. I never could survive the terrible disgrace of the story."

> "Don't borrow trouble; all you would need to do would be to show them papers I have drawn up, and they would be glad to take their annuity and say nothing. After all, I do not think it is so bad. Jeannette can teach; Talma can paint; six hundred dollars a year is quite enough for them."

> I had been somewhat mystified by the conversation until now. This last remark solved the riddle. What could he mean? teach, paint, six

hundred a year! With my usual impetuosity I sprang from my resting-place, and in a moment stood in the room confronting my father, and asking what he meant. I could see plainly that both were disconcerted by my unexpected appearance.

"Ah, wretched girl! you have been listening. But what could I expect of your mother's daughter?"

At these words I felt the indignant blood rush to my head in a torrent. So it had been all my life. Before you could remember, Talma, I had felt my little heart swell with anger at the disparaging hints and slurs concerning our mother. Now was my time. I determined that tonight I would know why she was looked upon as an outcast, and her children subjected to every humiliation. So I replied to my father in bitter anger:

"I was not listening; I fell asleep in the hammock. What do you mean by a paltry six hundred a year each to Talma and to me? 'My mother's daughter' demands an explanation from you, sir, of the meaning of the monstrous injustice that you have always practised toward my sister and me."

"Speak more respectfully to your father, Jeannette," broke in Mrs. Gordon.

"How is it, madam, that you look for respect from one whom you have delighted to torment ever since you came into this most unhappy family?"

"Hush, both of you," said Captain Gordon, who seemed to have recovered from the dismay into which my sudden appearance and passionate words had plunged him. "I think I may as well tell you as to wait. Since you know so much, you may as well know the whole miserable story." He motioned me to a seat. I could see that he was deeply agitated. I seated myself in a chair he pointed out, in wonder and expectation,—expectation of I knew not what. I trembled. This was a supreme moment in my life; I felt it. The air was heavy with the intense stillness that had settled over us as the common sounds of day gave place to the early quiet of the rural evening. I could see Mrs. Gordon's face as she sat within the radius of the lighted hallway. There was a smile of triumph upon it. I clinched my hands and bit my lips until the blood came, in the effort to keep from screaming. What was I about to hear? At last he spoke:

"I was disappointed at your birth, and also at the birth of Talma. I wanted a male heir. When I knew that I should again be a father I was torn by hope and fear, but I comforted myself with the thought that luck would be with me in the birth of the third child. When the doctor brought me word that a son was born to the house of Gordon, I was wild with delight, and did not notice his disturbed countenance. In the midst of my joy he said to me:

"Captain Gordon, there is something strange about this birth. I want you to see this child."

Quelling my exultation I followed him to the nursery, and there, lying in the cradle, I saw a child dark as a mulatto, with the characteristic features of the Negro! I was stunned. Gradually it dawned upon me that there was something radically wrong. I turned to the doctor for an explanation.

"There is but one explanation, Captain Gordon; there is Negro blood in this child."

"There is no Negro blood in my veins," I said proudly. Then I paused—*the mother*!—I glanced at the doctor. He was watching me intently. The same thought was in his mind. I must have lived a thousand years in that cursed five seconds that I stood there confronting the physician and trying to think. "Come," said I to him, "let us end this suspense." Without thinking of consequences, I hurried away to your mother and accused her of infidelity to her marriage vows. I raved like a madman. Your mother fell into convulsions; her life was despaired of. I sent for Mr. and Mrs. Franklin, and then I learned the truth. They were childless. One year while on a Southern tour, they befriended an octoroon girl who had been abandoned by her white lover. Her child was a beautiful girl baby. They, being Northern born, thought little of caste distinction because the child showed no trace of Negro blood. They determined to adopt it. They went abroad, secretly sending back word to their friends at a proper time, of the birth of a little daughter. No one doubted the truth of the statement. They made Isabel their heiress, and all went well until the birth of your brother. Your mother and the unfortunate babe died. This is the story which, if known, would bring dire disgrace upon the Gordon family.

To appease my righteous wrath, Mr. Franklin left a codicil to his will by which all the property is left at my disposal save a small annuity to you and your sister.

I sat there after he had finished his story, stunned by what I had heard. I understood, now, Mrs. Gordon's half contemptuous toleration and lack of consideration for us both. As I rose from my seat to leave the room I said to Captain Gordon:

"Still, in spite of all, sir, I am a Gordon, legally born. I will not tamely give up my birthright."

I left that room a broken-hearted girl, filled with a desire for revenge upon this man, my father, who by his manner disowned us without a regret. Not once in that remarkable interview did he speak of our mother as his wife; he quietly repudiated her and us with all the cold cruelty of relentless caste prejudice. I heard the treatment of your lover's proposal; I knew why Captain Gordon's consent to your marriage was withheld.

The night of the reception and dance was the chance for which I had waited, planned and watched. I crept from my window into the ivy-vines, and so down, down, until I stood upon the window-sill of Captain Gordon's room in the old left tower. How did I do it, you ask? I do not know. The house was silent after the revel; the darkness of the gathering storm favored me, too. The lawyer was there that day. The will was signed and put safely away among my father's papers. I was determined to have the will and the other documents bearing upon the case, and I would have revenge, too, for the cruelties we had suffered. With the old East Indian dagger firmly grasped I entered the room and found—that my revenge had been forestalled! The horror of the discovery I made that night restored me to reason and a realization of the crime I meditated. Scarce knowing what I did, I sought and found the papers, and crept back to my room as I had come. Do you wonder that my disease is past medical aid?

I looked at Edward as I finished. He sat, his face covered with his hands. Finally he looked up with a glance of haggard despair: "God! Doctor, but this is too much. I could stand the stigma of murder, but add to that the pollution of Negro blood! No man is brave enough to face such a situation."

"It is as I thought it would be," said Talma sadly, while the tears poured over her white face. "I do not blame you, Edward."

He rose from his chair, rung my hand in a convulsive clasp, turned to Talma and bowed profoundly, with his eyes fixed upon the floor, hesitated, turned, paused, bowed again and abruptly left the room. So those two who had been lovers, parted. I turned to Talma, expecting her to give way. She smiled a pitiful smile, and said: "You see, Doctor, I knew best."

From that on she failed rapidly. I was restless. If only I could rouse her to an interest in life, she might live to old age. So rich, so young, so beautiful, so talented, so pure; I grew savage thinking of the injustice of the world. I had not reckoned on the power that never sleeps. Something was about to happen.

On visiting Cameron next morning I found him approaching the end. He had been sinking for a week very rapidly. As I sat by the bedside holding his emaciated hand, he fixed his bright, wicked eyes on me, and asked: "How long have I got to live?"

"Candidly, but a few hours."

"Thank you; well, I want death; I am not afraid to die. Doctor, Cameron is not my name."

"I never supposed it was."

"No? You are sharper than I thought. I heard all your talk yesterday with Talma Gordon. Curse the whole race!"

He clasped his bony fingers around my arm and gasped: "*I murdered the Gordons!*"

Had I the pen of a Dumas I could not paint Cameron as he told his story. It is a question with me whether this wheeling planet, home of the suffering, doubting, dying, may not hold worse agonies on its smiling surface than those of the conventional hell. I sent for Talma and a lawyer. We gave him stimulants, and then with broken intervals of coughing and prostration we got the story of the Gordon murder. I give it to you in a few words:

"I am an East Indian, but my name does not matter, Cameron is as good as any. There is many a soul crying in heaven and hell for vengeance on Jonathan Gordon. Gold was his idol; and many a good man walked the plank, and many a gallant ship was stripped of her treasure, to satisfy his lust for gold. His blackest crime was the murder of my father, who was his friend, and had sailed with him for many a year as mate. One night these two went ashore together to bury their treasure. My father never returned from that expedition. His body was afterward found with a bullet through the heart on the shore where the vessel stopped that night. It was the custom then among pirates for the captain to kill the men who helped bury their treasure. Captain Gordon was no better than a pirate. An East Indian never forgets, and I swore by my mother's deathbed to hunt Captain Gordon down until I had avenged my father's murder. I had the plans of the Gordon estate, and fixed on the night of the reception in honor of Talma as the time for my vengeance. There is a secret entrance from the shore to the chambers where Captain Gordon slept; no one knew of it save the Captain and trusted members of his crew. My mother gave me the plans, and entrance and escape were easy."

"So the great mystery was solved. In a few hours Cameron was no more. We placed the confession in the hands of the police, and there the matter ended."

"But what became of Talma Gordon?" questioned the president. "Did she die?"

"Gentlemen," said the Doctor, rising to his feet and sweeping the faces of the company with his eagle gaze, "gentlemen, if you will follow me to the drawing-room, I shall have much pleasure in introducing you to my wife—*nee* Talma Gordon."

HAGAR'S DAUGHTER: A STORY OF
SOUTHERN CASTE PREJUDICE

I

In the fall of 1860 a stranger visiting the United States would have thought that nothing short of a miracle could preserve the union of states so proudly proclaimed by the signers of the Declaration of Independence, and so gloriously maintained by the gallant Washington.

The nomination of Abraham Lincoln for the presidency by the Republican party was inevitable. The pro-slavery Democracy was drunk with rage at the prospect of losing control of the situation, which, up to that time, had needed scarcely an effort to bind in riveted chains impenetrable alike to the power of man or the frowns of the Godhead; they had inaugurated a system of mob-law and terrorism against all sympathizers with the despised party. The columns of partisan newspapers teemed each day in the year with descriptions of disgraceful scenes enacted North and South by pro-slavery men, due more to the long-accustomed subserviency of Northern people to the slaveholders than to a real, personal hatred of the Negro.

The free negroes North and South, and those slaves with the hearts of freemen who had boldly taken the liberty denied by man, felt the general spirit of unrest and uncertainty which was spreading over the country to such an alarming extent. The subdued tone of the liberal portion of the press, the humiliating offers of compromise from Northern political leaders, and the numerous cases of surrendering fugitive slaves to their former masters, sent a thrill of mortal fear into the very heart of many a household where peace and comfort had reigned for many years. The fugitive slave had perhaps won the heart of some Northern free woman; they had married, prospered, and were happy. Now came the haunting dread of a stealthy tread, an ominous knock, a muffled cry at midnight, and the sunlight of the new day would smile upon a broken-hearted woman with baby hands clinging to her skirts, and children's voices asking in vain for their father lost to them forever. The Negro felt that there was no safety for him beneath the Stars and Stripes, and, so feeling, sacrificed his home and personal effects and fled to Canada.

The Southerners were in earnest, and would listen to no proposals in favor of their continuance in the Union under existing conditions; namely, Lincoln and the Republican party. The vast wealth of the South made them feel that they were independent of the world. Cotton was not merely king; it was God. Moral considerations were nothing.

Drunk with power and dazzled with prosperity, monopolizing cotton and raising it to the influence of a veritable fetich, the authors of the Rebellion did not admit a doubt of the success of their attack on the Federal government. They dreamed of perpetuating slavery, though all history shows the decline of the system as industry, commerce, and knowledge advance. The slaveholders proposed nothing less than to reverse the currents of humanity, and to make barbarism flourish in the bosom of civilization.

The South argued that the principle of right would have no influence over starving operatives; and England and France, as well as the Eastern States of the Union, would stand aghast, and yield to the master stroke which should deprive them of the material of their labor. Millions of the laboring class were dependent upon it in all the great centers of civilization; it was only necessary to wave this sceptre over the nations and all of them would acknowledge the power which wielded it. But, alas! the supreme error of this anticipation was in omitting from the calculation the power of principle. Right still had authority in the councils of nations. Factories might be closed, men and woman out of employment, but truth and justice still commanded respect among men. The pro-slavery men in the North encouraged the rebels before the breaking out of the war. They promised the South that civil war should reign in every free state in case of an uprising of the Southern oligarchy, and that men should not be permitted to go South to put down their brothers in rebellion.

Weak as were the Southern people in point of numbers and political power, compared with those of the North, yet they easily persuaded themselves that they could successfully cope in arms with a Northern foe, whom they affected to despise for his cowardly and mercenary disposition. They indulged the belief, in proud confidence, that their great political prestige would continue to serve them among party associates at the North, and that the counsels of the adversary would be distracted and his power weakened by the effects of dissension.

When the Republican banner bearing the names of Abraham Lincoln for President and Hannibal Hamlin for Vice-President flung its folds to the breeze in 1860, there was a panic of apprehension at such bold manoeuvering; mob-law reigned in Boston, Utica and New York City, which witnessed the greatest destruction of property in the endeavor to put down the growing public desire to abolish slavery. Elijah Lovejoy's innocent blood spoke in trumpet tones to the reformer from his quiet grave by the rolling river. William Lloyd Garrison's outraged manhood brought the blush of shame to the cheek of the honest American who loved his country's honor better than any individual institution. The memory of Charles Sumner's brutal beating by Preston Brooks stamped the mad passions of the hour indelibly upon history's page. Debate in the Senate became fiery and dangerous as the crisis approached in the absorbing question of the perpetuation of slavery.

At the South laws were enacted abridging the freedom of speech and press; it was difficult for Northerners to travel in slave states. Rev. Charles T. Torrey was sentenced to the Maryland penitentiary for aiding slaves to escape; Jonathan Walker had been branded with a red-hot iron for the same offense. In the midst of the tumult came the "Dred Scott Decision," and the smouldering fire broke forth with renewed vigor. Each side waited impatiently for the result of the balloting.

In November the Rubicon was passed, and Abraham Lincoln was duly elected President contrary to the wishes and in defiance of the will of the haughty South. There was much talk of a conspiracy to prevent by fraud or violence a declaration of the result of the election by the Vice-President before the two Houses, as provided by law. As the eventful day drew near patriotic hearts were sick with fear or filled with forebodings. Would the certificates fail to appear; would they be wrested by violence from the hands ordered to bear them across the rotunda from the Senate Chamber to the hall of the House, or would they be suppressed by the only official who could open them, John C. Breckenridge of Kentucky, himself a candidate and in full sympathy with the rebellion.

A breathless silence, painfully intense, reigned in the crowded chamber as the Vice-President arose to declare the result of the election. Six feet in height, lofty in carriage, youthful, dashing, he stood before them pale and nervous. The galleries were packed with hostile conspirators. It was the supreme moment in the life of the Republic. With unfaltering utterance his voice broke the oppressive stillness:

"I therefore declare Abraham Lincoln duly elected President of the United States for the term of four years from the fourth of March next."

It was the signal for secession, and the South let loose the dogs of war.

II

During the week preceding the memorable 20th of December, 1860, the streets of Charleston, S.C., were filled with excited citizens who had come from all parts of the South to participate in the preparations for seceding from the Union. The hotels were full; every available space was occupied in the homes of private citizens. Bands paraded the streets heading processions of excited politicians who came as delegates from every section south of Mason and Dixon's line; there was shouting and singing by the populace, liberally mingled with barrelhead orations from excited orators with more zeal than worth; there were cheers for the South and oaths for the government at Washington.

Scattered through the crowd traders could be seen journeying to the far South with gangs of slaves chained together like helpless animals destined for the slaughter-house. These slaves were hurriedly sent off by their master in obedience to orders from headquarters, which called for the removal of all human property from the immediate scene of the invasion so soon to come. The traders paused in their hurried journey to participate in the festivities which ushered in the birth of the glorious Confederate States of America. Words cannot describe the scene.

> "The wingèd heralds by command
> Of sovereign power, with awful ceremony
> And trumpet sound, proclaimed
> A solemn council forthwith to be held
> At Pandæmonium, the high capital
> Of Satan and his peers."

Among the traders the most conspicuous was a noted man from St. Louis, by the name of Walker. He was the terror of the whole Southwest among the Negro population, bond and free; for it often happened that free persons were kidnapped and sold to the far South. Uncouth, ill-bred, hardhearted, illiterate, Walker had started in St. Louis as a dray-driver, and now found himself a rich man. He was a repulsive-looking person, tall, lean and lank, with high cheekbones and face pitted with the small-pox, gray eyes, with red eyebrows and sandy whiskers.

Walker, upon his arrival in Charleston, took up his quarters with his gang of human cattle in a two-story flat building, surrounded by a stone wall some twelve feet high, the top of which was covered with bits of glass, so that there could be no passage over it without great personal injury. The rooms in this building resembled prison cells, and in the office were to be seen iron collars, hobbles, handcuffs, thumbscrews, cowhides, chains, gags and yokes.

Walker's servant Pompey had charge of fitting the stock for the market-place. Pompey had been so long under the instructions of the heartless speculator that he appeared perfectly indifferent to the heart-rending scenes which daily confronted him.

On this particular morning, Walker brought in a number of customers to view his stock; among them a noted divine, who was considered deeply religious. The slaves were congregated in a back yard enclosed by the high wall before referred to. There were swings and benches, which made the place very much like a New England schoolyard.

Among themselves the Negroes talked. There was one woman who had been separated from her husband, and another woman whose looks expressed the anguish of her heart. There was old "Uncle Jeems," with his whiskers off, his face clean shaven, and all his gray hairs plucked out, ready to be sold for ten years younger than he was. There was Tobias, a gentleman's body servant educated at Paris, in medicine, along with his late master, sold to the speculator because of his intelligence and the temptation which the confusion of the times offered for him to attempt an escape from bondage.

"O, my God!" cried one woman, "send dy angel down once mo' ter tell me dat you's gwine ter keep yer word, Massa Lord."

"O Lord, we's been a-watchin' an' a-prayin', but de 'liverer done fergit us!" cried another, as she rocked her body violently back and forth.

It was now ten o' clock, and the daily examination of the stock began with the entrance of Walker and several customers.

"What are you wiping your eyes for?" inquired a fat, red-faced man, with a white hat set on one side of his head and a cigar in his mouth, of the woman seated on a bench.

"'Cause I left my mon behin'."

"Oh, if I buy you, I'll furnish you with a better man than you left. I've got lots of young bucks on my farm," replied the man.

"I don't want anudder mon, an' I tell you, massa, I nebber will hab anudder mon."

"What's your name?" asked a man in a straw hat, of a Negro standing with arms folded across his breast and leaning against the wall.

"Aaron, sar."

"How old are you?"

"Twenty-five."

"Where were you raised?"

"In Virginny, sar."

"How many men have owned you?"

"Fo."

"Do you enjoy good health?"

"Yas, sar."

"Whipped much?"

"No, sar. I s'pose I didn't desarve it, sar."

"I must see your back, so as to know how much you've been whipped, before I conclude a bargain."

"Cum, unharness yoseff, ole boy. Don't you hear the gemman say he wants to zammin yer?" said Pompey.

The speculator, meanwhile, was showing particular attention to the most noted and influential physician of Charleston. The doctor picked out a man and a woman as articles that he desired for his plantation, and Walker proceeded to examine them.

"Well, my boy, speak up and tell the doctor what's your name."

"Sam, sar, is my name."

"How old are you?"

"Ef I live ter see next corn plantin' I'll be twenty-seven, or thirty, or thirty-five, I dunno which."

"Ha, ha ha! Well, doctor, this is a green boy. Are you sound?"

"Yas, sar; I spec' I is."

"Open your mouth, and let me see your teeth. I allers judge a nigger's age by his teeth, same as I do a hoss. Good appetite?"

"Yas, sar."

"Get out on that plank and dance. I want to see how supple you are."

"I don't like to dance, massa; I'se got religion."

"Got religion, have you? So much the better. I like to deal in the gospel, doctor. He'll suit you. Now, my gal, what's your name?"

"I is Big Jane, sar."

"How old are you?"

"Don' know, sar; but I was born at sweet pertater time."

"Well, do you know who made you?"

"I hev heard who it was in de Bible, but I done fergit de gemman's name."

"Well, doctor, this is the greenest lot of niggers I've had for some time, but you may have Sam for a thousand dollars and Jane for nine hundred. They are worth all I ask for them."

"Well, Walter, I reckon I'll take them," replied the doctor.

"I'll put the handcuffs on 'em, and then you can pay me."

"Why," remarked the doctor, "there comes Reverend Pinchen."

"It is Mr. Pinchen as I live; jest the very man I want to see." As the reverend gentleman entered the enclosure, the trader grasped his hand, saying: "Why, how do you do, Mr. Pinchen? Come down to Charleston to the Convention, I s'pose? Glorious time, sir, glorious; but it will be gloriouser when the new government has spread our institootions all over the conquered North. Gloriouser and gloriouser. Any camp-meetin's, revivals, death-bed scenes, or other things in your line going on down here? How's religion prospering now, Mr. Pinchen? I always like to hear about religion."

"Well, Mr. Walker, the Lord's work is in good condition everywhere now. Mr. Walker, I've been in the gospel ministry these thirteen years, and I know that the heart of man is full of sin and desperately wicked. Religion is a good thing to live by, and we'll want it when we die. And a man in your business of buying and selling slaves needs religion more than anybody else, for it makes you treat your people well. Now there's Mr. Haskins—he's a slave-trader like yourself. Well, I converted him. Before he got religion he was one of the worst men to his niggers I ever saw; his heart was as hard as a stone. But religion has made his heart as soft as a piece of cotton. Before I converted him he would sell husbands from their wives and delight in doing it; but now he won't sell a man from his wife if he can get anyone to buy them together. I tell you, sir, religion has done a wonderful work for him."

"I know, Mr. Pinchen, that I ought to have religion, and that I am a great sinner; and whenever I get with good, pious people, like you and the doctor, I feel desperate wicked. I know that I would be happier with religion, and the first spare time I have I'm going to get it. I'll go to a protracted meeting, and won't stop till I get religion."

Walker then invited the gentlemen to his office, and Pompey was dispatched to purchase wine and other refreshments for the guests.

Within the magnificent hall of the St. Charles Hotel a far different scene was enacted in the afternoon. The leading Southern politicians were gathered there to discuss the election of Lincoln, the "sectional" candidate, and to give due weight and emphasis to the future acts of the new government. There was exaltation in every movement of the delegates, and they were surrounded by the glitter of a rich and powerful assemblage in a high state of suppressed excitement, albeit this meeting was but preliminary to the decisive acts of the following week.

The vast hall, always used for dancing, was filled with tables which spread their snow-white wings to receive the glittering mass of glass, plate and flowers. The spacious galleries were crowded to suffocation by beautiful Southern belles in festive attire. Palms and fragrant shrubs were everywhere; garlands of flowers decorated the walls and fell, mingled with the new flag—the stars and bars—gracefully above the seat of the chairman. In the gallery opposite the speaker's desk a band was stationed; Negro servants in liveries of white linen hurried noiselessly to and fro. The delegates filed in to their places at table to the crashing strains of "Dixie"; someone raised the new flag aloft and waved it furiously; the whole assembly rose *en masse* and cheered vociferously, and the ladies waved their handkerchiefs. Mirth and hilarity reigned. The first attention of the diners was given to the good things before them. After cigars were served the music stopped, and the business of the day began in earnest.

There was the chairman, Hon. Robert Toombs of Georgia; there was John C. Breckenridge of Kentucky, Stephen A. Douglas, Alexander H. Stevens, and Jefferson Davis.

"Silence!" was the cry, as Hon. Robert Toombs, the chairman, arose.

"*Fellow Delegates and Fellow Citizens:* I find myself in a most remarkable situation, and I feel that every Southern gentleman sympathizes with me. Here am I, chairman of a meeting of the most loyal, high-spirited and patriotic body of men and their guests and friends, that ever assembled to discuss the rights of humanity and Christian progress, and yet unable to propose a single toast with which we have been wont to sanction such a meeting as this. With grief that consumes my soul, I am compelled to bury in the silence of mortification, contempt and detestation the name of the government at Washington.

"I can only counsel you, friends, to listen to no vain babbling, to no treacherous jargon about overt acts; they have already been committed. Defend yourselves; the enemy is at your door; wait not to meet him at the hearthstone,—meet him at the door-sill, and rive him from the temple of liberty, or pull down its pillars and involve him in a common ruin. Never permit this federal government to pass into the traitorous hands of the black Republican party.

"My language may appear strong; but it is mild when we consider the attempt being made to wrest from us the exclusive power of making laws for our own community. The repose of our homes, the honor of our color, and the prosperity of the South demand that we resist innovation.

"I rejoice to see around me fellow-laborers worthy to lead in the glorious cause of resisting oppression, and defending our ancient privileges which have been set by an Almighty hand. We denounce once and for all the practices proposed by crazy enthusiasts, seconded by designing knaves, and destined to be executed by demons in human form. We shall conquer in this pending struggle; we will subdue the North, and call the roll of our slaves beneath the very shadow of Bunker Hill. 'It is a consummation devoutly to be wished.'

"And now, I call upon all true patriots in token of their faith, to drink deep of one deserving their fealty,—the guardian and savior of the South, Jefferson Davis."

Vociferous cheers broke forth and shook the building. The crowd surrounding the hotel took it up, and the name "Davis!" "Davis!" was repeated again and again. He arose in his seat and bowed profoundly; the band played "See the Conquering Hero Comes"; a lady in the gallery back of him skilfully dropped a crown of laurel upon his head. The crowd went mad; they tore the decorations from the walls and pelted their laurel-crowned hero until he would gladly have had them cease; but such is fame. When the cheers had somewhat subsided, Mr. Davis said:

"I must acknowledge, my fellow-citizens, the truth of the remarks just made by our illustrious friend, Senator Toombs. I was never more satisfied with regard to the future history of our country than I am at present. I believe in state rights, slavery, and the Confederacy that we are about to inaugurate.

"The principle of slavery is in itself right, and does not depend upon difference of complexion. Make the laboring man the slave of *one* man, instead of the slave of society, and he would be far better off. Slavery, black or white, is necessary. Nature has made the weak in mind or body for slaves.

"In five days your delegates from all the loyal Southern States will meet here in convention. I feel the necessity that every eye be fixed upon the course which will be adopted by this assembly of patriots. You know our plans. South Carolina will lead the march of the gallant band who will give us the liberty we crave. We are all united in will and views, and therefore powerful. I see before me in my colleagues men to whom the tranquility of our government may be safely confided—men devoted and zealous in their interest—senators and representatives who have managed everything for our aid and comfort. Few of the vessels of the navy are available at home; the army is scattered on the Western frontier, while all the trained officers of the army are with us. Within our limits we have control of the entire government property—mints, custom-houses, post-offices, dock-yards, revenue-cutters, arsenals and forts. The national finances have been levied upon to fill our treasury by our faithful Southern members of the late cabinet. Yes, friends, all is ready; every preparation is made for a brief and successful fight for that supremacy in the government of this nation which is our birthright. (Tremendous applause.)

"By the election just thrust upon us by the Republican party the Constitution is violated; and were we not strong to sustain our rights, we should soon find ourselves driven to prison at the point of the bayonet (cries of 'Never, never!'), ousted from the council of state, oblivion everywhere, and nothing remaining but ourselves to represent Truth and Justice. We believe that our ideas are the desires of the majority of the people, and the people represent the supreme and sovereign power of Right! (Hear! hear! cheers.) For Abraham Lincoln (hisses) nothing is inviolate, nothing sacred; he menaces, in his election, our ancient ideas and privileges. The danger grows greater. Let us arise in our strength and meet it more than half way. Are you ready, men?"

"We are ready!" came in a roar like unto the waters of the mighty Niagara. "What shall we do?"

"No half measures; let it be a deed of grandeur!"

"It shall be done!" came in another mighty chorus.

"In such a crisis there must be no vacuum. There must be a well-established government before the people. You, citizens, shall take up arms; we will solicit foreign re-enforcements; we will rise up before this rail-splitting ignoramus a terrible power; we will overwhelm this miserable apology for a gentleman and a statesman as a terrible revolutionary power. Do you accept my proposition?"

PAULINE E. HOPKINS

"Yes, yes!" came as a unanimous shout from the soul of the vast assembly.

"Our Northern friends make a great talk about free society. We sicken of the name. What is it but a conglomeration of greasy mechanics, filthy operatives, small-fisted farmers, and moonstruck Abolitionists? All the Northern States, and particularly the New England States, are devoid of society fitted for well-bred gentlemen. The prevailing class one meets with is that of mechanics struggling to be genteel, and farmers who do their own drudgery, and yet who are hardly fit for association with a gentleman's slave.

We have settled this matter in the minds of the people of the South by long years of practice and observation; and I believe that when our principles shall have been triumphantly established over the entire country—North, South, West—a long age of peace and prosperity will ensue for the entire country. Under our jurisdiction wise laws shall be passed for the benefit of the supreme and subordinate interests of our communities. And when we have settled all these vexed questions I see a season of calm and fruitful prosperity, in which our children's children may enjoy their lives without a thought of fear or apprehension of change."

Then the band played; there was more cheering and waving of handkerchiefs, in the midst of which John C. Breckenridge arose and gracefully proposed the health of the first President of the Confederate States of America. It was drunk by every man, standing. Other speakers followed, and the most intemperate sentiments were voiced by the zealots in the great cause. The vast crowd went wild with enthusiasm.

St. Clair Enson, one of the most trusted delegates, and the slave-trader Walker sat side by side at the table, and in the excitement of the moment all the prejudices of the Maryland aristocrat toward the vile dealer in human flesh were forgotten.

The convention had now passed the bounds of all calmness. Many of the men stood on chairs, gesticulating wildly, each trying to be heard above his neighbor. In vain the Chair rapped for order. Pandemonium reigned. At one end of the long table two men were locked in deadly embrace, each struggling to enforce his views upon the other by brute strength.

One man had swept the dishes aside, and was standing upon the table, demanding clamorously to be heard, and above all the band still crashed its brazen notes of triumph in the familiar strains of "Dixie."

A Negro boy handed a letter to Mr. Enson. He turned it over in his hand, curiously examining the postmark.

"When did this come, Cato?"

"More'n a munf, massa," was the reply.

Mr. Enson tore open the envelope and glanced over its contents with a frowning face.

"Bad news?" ventured Walker, with unusual familiarity.

"The worst possible for me. My brother is married, and announces the birth of a daughter."

"Well, daughters are born every day. I don't see how that can hurt you."

"It happens in this case, however, that this particular daughter will inherit the Enson fortune," returned Enson with a short laugh.

Walker gave a long, low whistle. "Who was your brother's wife? Any money?"

"Clark Sargeant's daughter. Money enough on both sides; but the trouble is, it will never be mine." Another sharp, bitter laugh.

"Sargeant, Sargeant," said Walker, musingly. "'Pears to me I've had business with a gentleman of the same name years ago, in St. Louis. However, it can't be the same one, 'cause this man hadn't any children. Leastways, I never heard on eny."

"Perhaps it is the same man. Clark Sargeant was from St. Louis; moved to Baltimore when the little girl was five years old. Mr. and Mrs. Sargeant are dead."

"Same man, same man. Um, um," saidWalker, scratching the flesh beneath his sandy whiskers meditatively, as he gazed at the ceiling. "Both dead, eh? Come to think of it, I moight be mistaken about the little gal. Has she got black hair and eyes and a cream-colored skin, and has she growed up to be a all-fired pesky fine woman?"

"Can't say," replied Enson, with a yawn as he rose to his feet. "I've never had the pleasure of meeting my sister-in-law."

"When you going up to Baltimore?" asked Walker.

"Next week, on 'The Planter.'"

"Think I'll take a trip up with you. You don't mind my calling with you on your brother's family, do you, Mr. Enson? I would admire to introduce myself to Clark Sargeant's little gal. She moight not remember me at first, but I reckon I could bring back recollections of me to her mind, ef it's jes' the same to you, Mr. Enson."

"O, be hanged to you. Go where you please. Go to the devil," replied Enson, as he swung down the hall and elbowed his way out.

"No need of goin' to the devil when he's right side of you, Mr. Enson," muttered Walker, as he watched the young man out of sight. "You d—d aristocrats carry things with a high hand; I'll be glad to take a reef in your sails, and I'll do it, too, or my name's not Walker."

III

S t. Clair Enson was the second son of an aristocratic Maryland family. He had a fiery temper that knew no bounds when once aroused. Motherless from infancy, and born at a period in the life of his parents when no more children were expected, he grew up wild and self-willed. As his character developed it became evident that an unsavory future was before him. There was no malicious mischief in which he was not found, and older heads predicted that he would end on the gallows. Sensual, cruel to ferocity, he was a terror to the God-fearing community where he lived. With women he was successful from earliest youth, being possessed of the diabolical beauty of Satan himself. There was great rejoicing in the quiet village near which Enson Hall was situated when it was known that the young scapegrace had gone to college.

The atmosphere of college life suited him well, and he was soon the leader of the fastest set there. He was the instigator of innumerable broils, insulted his teachers, and finally fought a duel, killing his man instantly. According to the code of honor of the time, this was not murder; but expulsion from the halls of learning followed for St. Clair, and much to his surprise and chagrin, his father, who had always indulged and excused his acts as the thoughtlessness of youth's high spirits, was thoroughly enraged.

There was a curious scene between them, and no one ever knew just what passed, but it was ended by his father's saying:

"You have disgraced the name of Enson, and now you dare make a joke to me of your wickedness. Let me not see your face in this house again. Henceforth, until you have redeemed yourself by an honest man's career, I have but one son, your brother Ellis."

"As you please, sir," replied St. Clair nonchalantly, as he placed the check his father handed him in his pocket, bowed, and passed from the room.

That was the last heard of him for five years, when at his father's death he went home to attend the funeral.

By the terms of the will St. Clair received a small annuity, to be enlarged at the discretion of his brother, and in event of the latter's death without issue, the estate was to revert to St. Clair's heirs "if any there be who are an honor to the name of Enson," was the wording of the will. In the event of St. Clair's continuing in disgrace and "having no honorable and lawful issue," the property was to revert to a distant branch of cousins, "for I have no mind that debauchery and crime shall find a home at Enson Hall."

After this St. Clair seemingly dropped his wildest habits, but was still noted on all the river routes of the South as a reckless and daring gambler.

His man Isaac was as much of a character as himself, and many a game they worked together on the inexperienced, and many a time but for Isaac, St. Clair would have fared ill at the hands of his victims. Isaac was given to his young master at the age of ten years. The only saving grace about the scion of aristocracy appeared in his treatment of Isaac. Master and slave were devoted to each other.

As a last resource young Enson had gone in for politics, and the luck that had recently deserted him at cards and dice, favored him here. The unsettled state of the country and the threatening war-clouds were a boon to the tired child of chance, which he hailed as harbingers of better times for recreant Southern sons. He would gain fame and fortune in the service of the new government.

All through the dramatic action of the next week when history made so fast in the United States, when the South Carolina convention declared that "the union then subsisting between herself and other states of America, was dissolved" and her example followed by Mississippi, Florida, Alabama, Georgia, Louisiana, Texas, Virginia, Arkansas, North Carolina and Tennessee, all through that time when politics reached the boiling point, St. Clair, although in the thickest of the controversy, busy making himself indispensable to the officials of the new government, was thinking of the heiress of Enson Hall. He was bitter over his loss, and ready to blame anyone but himself.

In his opinion, Ellis was humdrum; he was mild and peaceful in his disposition, because his blood was too sluggish and his natural characteristics too womanish for the life of a gentleman. Then, too, Ellis, was old, fifteen years his senior, and he was twenty-five.

St. Clair shared the universal opinion of his world (and to him the world did not exist north of Mason and Dixon's line), that a reckless career of gambling, wine and women was the only true course of development for a typical Southern gentleman. As he thought of the infant heiress his face grew black with a frown of rage that for the time completely spoiled the beauty women raved over. His man Isaac, furtively watching him from the corner of his eye, said to himself:

"I know dat dar's gwine to be a rippit; Marse St. Clair never look dat a way widout de debbil himself am broked loose." In which view of the case Isaac was about right.

St. Clair made up his mind to go home and see this fair woman who had come to blast his hopes and steal his patrimony for her children. Perhaps as she was young, and presumably susceptible, something might be done. He was handsome—Ah, well! and he laughed a wicked laugh at his reflection in the mirror; he would trust to luck to help him out. He ordered Isaac to pack up.

"Good Lawd, Marse St. Clair! I thought you'd done settled here fer good. How comes we go right off?"

"We're going home, Isaac, to see the new mistress Enson and my niece. Haven't I told you that your master, Ellis was married, and had a daughter?"

"Bress my soul! no sar!" replied Isaac, dropping the clothes he held upon the floor. His master left the room.

"Now de Lawd help de mistress an' de little baby. I love my master, but he's a borned debbil. He's jes' gwine home to tare up brass, dat's de whole collusion ob de mystery."

St. Clair Enson took passage on board "The Planter," which was ready to start upon its last trip up Chesapeake Bay before going into the service of the Confederate government. At that time this historic vessel was a side-wheel steamer storing about fourteen hundred bales of cotton as freight, but having accommodations for a moderate number of passengers. No one of the proud supporters of the new government dreamed of her ultimate fate. The position of the South was defined, and given to the world with a loud flourish of trumpets. By their reasoning, a few short months would make them masters of the entire country. Wedded to their idols, they knew not the force of the "dire arms" which Omnipotence would wield upon the side of Right. One of the most daring and heroic adventures of the Civil War was successfully accomplished by a party of Negroes, Robert Small commanding, when the rebel gunboat "The Planter" ran by the forts and batteries of Charleston Harbor, and reaching the flagship "Wabash" was duly received into the service of the United States government.

St. Clair Enson went on board the steamer with mixed feelings of triumph and chagrin—triumph because of the place he had made for himself in the councils of the new government and the adulation meted out to him by the public; chagrin because of his brother's new family ties and his own consequent poverty.

For a while he wandered aimlessly about, resisting all the tempting invitations extended by his numerous admirers in the sporting and political world to "have something" at the glittering bar. But his pockets were empty—they always were—and he finally allowed himself to be cajolled to join in a quiet game in the hope of replenishing his purse, where he saw the chances were all in his favor.

The saloon was alight with music and gaiety; the jolly company of travelers and the gaudy furniture were reflected many times over in the gilded mirrors that caught the rays of a large chandelier depending from the center of the ceiling. To the eye and ear merriment held high carnival; some strolled about, many sought the refreshment bar, but a greater number—men and even women—took part in the play or bet lightly on the players, sotto voce, for pastime. The clink and gleam of gold was there as it passed from hand to hand. Six men at a table played baccarat; farther on, a party of very young people—both sexes—played loo for small stakes. There were quartets of whist players, too; but the most popular game was poker, for high stakes made by reckless and inveterate gamblers.

St. Clair and his party found an empty table, and Isaac, obedient to a sign from his master, brought him the box containing implements for a game of poker. All the men were inveterate gamblers, but Enson was an expert. Gradually the on-lookers gathered about that one particular table. Not a word was said; the men gripped their cards and held their breaths, with now and then an oath to punctuate a loss more severe than usual.

The slaver-trader Walker sauntered up to the place where St. Clair sat, and stood behind him.

"What's the stakes?" he asked of his next neighbor. The man addressed smiled significantly: "Not a bagatelle to begin with; they've raised them three times."

"Whew!" with a whistle. "And who is winning?"

"Oh, Enson, of course."

"Why 'of course?'" asked Walker with a wicked smile on his ugly face.

"He always wins."

"I reckon not now," returned Walker, as he pointed to the play just made.

"He's dealing above board and square, and luck's agin him."

It was true. From this time on Enson played again and again, and lost. The other players left their seats and stood near watching the famous gambler make his play. Finally, with a muttered curse, he staggered up from his chair and started to leave the table with desperate eyes and reeling gate. But he stopped as if struck by a sudden inspiration, and resumed his seat.

"What will he do now?" was the unspoken thought of the crowd.

"Isaac, come here," called out Enson. "I will see you and five hundred better," he continued, addressing his opponent, as the boy approached, and at a signal from him climbed upon the table. The crowd watched the strange scene in breathless silence.

"What price do you set on the boy?" asked the winner, whose name was Johnson, taking a large roll of bills from his pocket.

"He will bring eighteen hundred dollars any day in the New Orleans market."

"I reckon he ain't noways vicious?" asked Johnson, looking in the Negro's smiling face.

"I've never seen him angry."

"I'll give you fifteen hundred for him."

"Eighteen," returned Enson, with an ominous tightening about the mouth.

"Well, I'll tell you what I'll do, the very best; I'll make it sixteen hundred, no more, no less. That's fair. Is it a bargain?"

Enson nodded assent. The crowd heaved a sigh of relief.

"Then you bet the whole of this boy, do you?" continued Johnson.

"Yes."

"I call you, then," said Johnson.

"I've got three queens," replied Enson.

"Not enough," said the other.

"Then if you beat three queens, you beat me."

"I have four jacks, and the boy is mine." The crowd heaved another sigh as one man.

"Hold on! Not so fast!" shouted Enson. "You don't take him till you *show* me that you beat three queens." Johnson threw his five cards upon the table, and four of them were jacks! "Sure," said Johnson, as he looked at Enson and then at the crowd.

"Sure!" came in a hoarse murmur from many throats. For a moment all things whirled and danced before Enson's eyes as he realized what he had lost. The lights from the chandelier shot out sparkles from piles of golden coin, the table heaved, faces were indistinct. He seemed to hear his father's voice again in stern condemnation, as he had heard it for the last time on earth. His face was white and set. He was a man ready for desperate needs. It seemed an hour to him, that short second. Then he turned to the winner:

"Mr. Johnson, I quit you."

Isaac was standing upon the table with the money at his feet. As he stepped down, Johnson said:

"You will not forget that you belong to me."

"No, sir."

"Be up in time to brush my clothes and clean my boots; do you hear?"

"Yas, sir," responded Isaac, with a good-natured smile and a long side-glance at Enson, in which one might have seen the lurking deviltry of a spirit kindred to his master's. Enson turned to leave the saloon, saying:

"I claim the right of redeeming that boy, Mr. Johnson. My father gave him to me when I was a lad. I promised never to part with him."

"Most certainly, sir; the boy shall be yours whenever you hand me over a cool sixteen hundred," returned Johnson. As Enson moved away, chewing the bitter curd of disappointment, Walker strolled up to him.

"That's a bad bargain Johnson's got in your man, Mr. Enson."

"How? Explain yourself."

"If he finds him after tomorrow morning, it's my belief it won't be the fault of Isaac's legs."

"Do you mean to say, sir, that I would connive at robbing a gentleman in fair play?"

"Oh, no; it won't be your fault," replied Walker with a familiar slap on Enson's back, that made the latter wince; "but he's a cute darkey that you can sell in good faith to a man, but he won't stay with him. Bet you the nigger'll be in Baltimore time you are."

"I'll take you. Make your bet."

Walker shook his head. "No, don't you do it. Luck's agin you, an' I won't rob you. That nigger'll lose you, sure."

Enson made no reply, but stood gazing moodily out upon the dark waters of the Atlantic, through which the steamer swiftly ploughed her way. Finally Walker continued:

"Why don't you try another game? Keep it up; luck may change. I'll lend you."

Enson waved his hand impatiently and said: "No; no more tonight. I have not a cent in the world until I eat humble pie and beg money from my brother."

"Tough!"

"Thank you. I do not want your sympathy."

"My help, then. Perhaps I can help you. Enson smiled derisively at the endless black waves and the moonless sky.

"No man can do that. I have made my bed hard and must abide the issue."

"Oh, rot! Be a man, and keep on fighting 'em. You'll be all right presently. Never say die."

"Perhaps you have a plan to compass the impossible," returned Enson with a sneer.

"I should say so. I've been thinking a good deal about your brother's marriage, and my old friends, the Sargeants. What would it be worth to you now to find a way to break off this marriage?"

"Break it off! Why man, that can't be done. What are you driving at?"

"Easy there, now. I said 'break if off,' and I meant 'break it off.' They used to tell me when I was a boy that two heads was better'n one ef one was a sheep's head. Same case here. Job's worth ten thou. I can see three thou right in sight, that would make your bill about seven thou." Walker settled his hat at the back of his head, thrust his hands deep in his hip pockets, and gazed out over the dark waters with a glance from his ferret-like gray eyes that seemed to pierce the blackness.

"I don't understand you, Walker; explain yourself."

"I understand myself, and that's enough. All you've got to do is to put your I O U to a paper calling for seven thousand dollars conditional on my rendering you valuable service in a financial matter. Savey?"

"I'd do anything that would break this cursed luck I'm having. Can you do anything? What do you mean, anyhow, Walker?"

"Never mind what I mean. You meet me at Enson Hall. Wait for me if you get there first. Be ready to sign the paper, and I'll show you as neat a job as was ever put up by any man on earth. That's all." Walker turned as he finished speaking and walked away. St. Clair looked after him, uncertain what to think of his strange words and actions.

IV

The morning sun poured its golden light upon the picturesque old house standing in its own grounds in one of the suburban towns adjacent to Baltimore—the Baltimore of 1858 or 1860.

The old house seemed to command one to render homage to its beauty and stateliness. It was a sturdy brick building flanked with offices and having outbuildings touching the very edge of the deep, mysterious woods where the trees waved their beckoning arms in every soft breeze that came to revel in their rich foliage. This was Enson Hall. The Hall was reached through a long dim stretch of these woods— locusts and beeches—from ten to twelve acres in extent; its mellow, red-brick walls framed by a background of beechtrees reminded one of English residences with their immense extent of private grounds. In the rear of the mansion was the garden, with its huge conservatories gay with shrubs and flowers. Piazzas and porticoes promised delightful retreats for sultry weather. The interior of the house was in the style that came in after the Revolution. An immense hall with outer door standing invitingly open gave greeting to the guest. The stairs wound from the lower floor to the rooms above. The grand stairway was richly embellished with carving, and overhead a graceful arch added much to the impressive beauty which met the stranger's first view. The rooms, spacious and designed for entertaining largely, had panelled wainscotting and carved chimney-pieces.

Ellis Enson, the master of the Hall, was a well-made man, verging on forty. "Born with a silver spoon in his mouth," for the vast estate and all invested money was absolutely at his disposal, he was the envy of the men of his class and the despair of the ladies. He was extremely good-looking, slight, elegant, with wavy dark hair, and an air of distinction. Since his father's death he had lived at the Hall, surrounded by his slaves in lonely meditation, fancy free. This handsome recluse had earned the reputation of being morose, so little had he mixed with society, so cold had been his politeness to the fair sex. His farms, his lonely rides, his favorite books, had sufficed for him. He was a good manager, and what was more wonderful, considering his Southern temperament, a thorough man of business. His crops, his poultry, his dairy products, were of the very first quality. Sure it was that his plantation was a paying investment. Meanwhile the great house, with all its beautiful rooms and fine furniture, remained closed to the public, and was the despair of managing mammas with many daughters to provide with eligible husbands. Enson was second to none as a "catch," but he was utterly indifferent to women.

Just about this time when to quarry the master of Enson Hall seemed a hopeless task, Hagar Sargeant came home from a four years' sojourn at the North in a young ladies' seminary.

The Sargeant estate was the one next adjoining Enson Hall; not so large and imposing, but a valuable patrimony that had descended in a long line of Sargeants and was well preserved. For many years before Hagar's birth the estate had been rented because of financial misfortunes, and they had lived in St. Louis, where Mr. Sargeant had engaged in trade so successfully that when Hagar was six years old they were enabled to return to their ancestral home and resume a life of luxurious leisure. Since that time Mr. Sargeant had died. On a trip to St. Louis, where he had gone to settle his business affairs, he contracted cholera, then ravaging many large cities of the Southwest, and had finally succumbed to the scourge. Hagar, their only child, then became her mother's sole joy and inspiration. Determined to cultivate her daughter's rare intellectual gifts, she had sent her North to school when every throb of her heart demanded her presence at home. She had developed into a beautiful girl, the admiration and delight of the neighborhood to which she returned, almost a stranger after her long absence.

A golden May morning poured its light through the open window of the Sargeant breakfast-room. A pleasanter room could scarcely be found, though the furniture was not of latest fashion, and the carpet slightly faded. There was a bay window that opened on the terrace, below which was a garden; there was a table in the recess spread with dainty china and silver, and the remains of breakfast; honeysuckles played hide-and-seek at the open window. Aunt Henny, a coal-black Negress of kindly face, brought in the little brass-bound oaken tub filled with hot water and soap, and the linen towels. Hagar stood at the window contemplating the scene before her. It was her duty to wash the heirlooms of colonial china and silver. From their bath they were dried only by her dainty fingers, and carefully replaced in the corner cupboard. Not for the world would she have dropped one of these treasures. Her care for them, and the placing of every one in its proper niche, was wonderful to behold. Not the royal jewels of Victoria were ever more carefully guarded than these family heirlooms.

This morning Hagar was filled with a delicious excitement, caused by she knew not what. The china and silver were an anxiety unusual to her. She felt a physical exhilaration, inspired, no doubt, by the delicious weather. She always lamented at this season of the year the lost privileges of the house of Sargeant, when their right of way led directly from the house to the shining waters of the bay. There was a path that led to the water still, but it was across the land of their neighbor Enson. Sometimes Hagar would trespass; would cross the parklike stretch of pasture, bordered by the woodland through which it ran, and sit on the edge of the remnant of a wharf, by which ran a small, rapid river, an arm of Chesapeake Bay, chafing among wet stones and leaping gaily over rocky barriers. There she would dream of life before the Revolution, and in these dreams participate in the joys of the colonial dames. She longed to mix and mingle with the gay world; she had a feeling that her own talents, if developed, would end in something far different from the calm routine, the housekeeping and churchgoing which stretched before her. Sometimes softer thoughts possessed her, and she speculated about love and lovers. This peaceful life was too tranquil and uneventful. Oh, for a break in the humdrum recurral of the same events day after day.

She had never met Ellis Enson. He was away a great part of the time before she left home for school, and since she had returned. If she remembered him at all, it was with the thought of a girl just past her eighteenth birthday for a man forty.

This morning Hagar washed the silver with the sleeves of her morning robe turned up to the shoulder, giving a view of rosy, dimpled. arms. "A fairer vision was never seen," thought the man who paused a moment at the open window to gaze again upon the pretty, homelike scene. As Hagar turned from replacing the last of the china, she was startled out of her usual gay indifference at the sight of a handsome pair of dark eyes regarding her intently from the open window. A quick wonder flashed in the eyes that met hers; the color deepened in his face as he saw he was observed. The girl's beauty startled him so, that for a moment he lost the self-control that convention dictates. Then he bared his head in courteous acknowledgement of youth and beauty, with an apology for his seeming intrusion.

"I beg pardon," Enson said in his soft, musical tones; "is Mrs. Sargeant at home? I did not know she had company."

"I am not company; I am Hagar. Yes, mamma is at home; if you will come in, I will take you to her."

He turned and entered the hall door and followed her through the dark, cool hall to the small morning-room, where Mrs. Sargeant spent her mornings in semi-invalid fashion. Then a proper introduction followed, and Ellis Enson and Hagar Sargeant were duly acquainted.

At forty Enson still retained his faith in womanhood, although he had been so persistently pursued by all the women of the vicinity. He believed there were women in the world capable of loving a man for himself alone without a thought of worldly advantage, only he had not been fortunate enough to meet them.

He had a very poor opinion of himself. Adulation had not made him vain. His face indicated strong passions and much pride; but it was pride of caste, not self. There was great tenderness of the eye and lip, and signs of a sensitive nature that could not bear disgrace or downfall that might touch his ancient name. After he left the Sargeant home Hagar's face haunted him; the pure creamy skin, the curved crimson lips ready to smile,—lips sweet and firm,—the broad, low brow, and great, lustrous, long-lashed eyes of brilliant black—soft as velvet, and full of light with the earnest, cloudless gaze of childhood; and there was heart and soul and mind in this countenance of a mere girl. Such beauty as this was a perpetual delight to feast the eyes and charm the senses—aye, to witch a man's heart from him; for here there was not only the glory of form and tints, but more besides,—heart that could throb, soul that could aspire, mind that could think. She was not shy and self-conscious as young girls so often are; she seemed quite at her ease, as one who has no thought of self. He was conscious of his own enthralment. He knew that he had set his feet in the perilous path of love at a late day, but knowing this, he none the less went forward to his fate.

After that the young girl and the man met frequently. She did not realize when the time came that she had grown to look for his coming. There were walks and drives and accidental meetings in the woods. The sun was brighter and the songs of the birds sweeter that summer than ever before.

Ellis fell to day-dreaming, and the dreams were tinged with gold, bringing a flush to his face and a thrill to his heart. Still he would have denied, if accused, that this was love at first sight—bah! That was a well-exploded theory. And yet if it was not love that had suddenly come into his being for this slender, dark-eyed girl, what was it? A change had come into Ellis Enson's life. The greatest changes, too, are always unexpected.

It was a sultry day; there was absolutely no chance to catch a refreshing breeze within four walls. It was one of the rare occasions when Mrs. Sargeant felt obliged to make a business call alone. From the fields came the sound of voices singing: the voices of slaves. Aunt Henny's good-natured laugh occasionally broke the stillness.

"Now I shall have a nice quiet afternoon," thought Hagar, as she left the house for the shadow of the trees. Under the strong, straight branches of a beech she tied three old shawls, hammock-like, one under another, for strength and safety. It was not very far from the ground. If it should come down, she might be bruised slightly, but not killed. She crawled cautiously into her nest; she had let down the long braids of her hair, and as she lolled back in her retreat, they fell over the sides of the hammock and swept the top of the long, soft grass. Lying there, with nothing in sight but the leafy branches of the trees high above her head, through which gleams of the deep blue sky came softly, she felt as if she had left the world, and was floating, Ariel-like, in midair.

After an hour of tranquility, footsteps were audible on the soft grass. There was a momentary pause, then someone came to a standstill beside her fairy couch.

"Back so soon, mamma? I wish you could come up here with me; it is just heavenly."

"Then I suppose you must be one of the heavenly inhabitants, an angel, but I never can pay compliments as I ought," said a voice.

"Mr. Enson!" Hagar was conscious of a distinct quickening of heart-action and a rush of crimson to her cheeks; with a pretty, hurried movement she rose to a sitting position in her hammock; "I really am ashamed of myself. I thought you were mamma."

"Yes," he answered, smiling at her dainty confusion.

"Mr. Enson," she said again, this time gravely, "politeness demands that I receive you properly, but decency forbids I should do it unless you will kindly turn your back to me while I step to earth once more."

The man was inwardly shaking with laughter at the grave importance with which she viewed the business in hand, but not for worlds would he have had her conscious of his mirth.

"I can help you out all right," he said.

"No, I am too heavy. I think I will stay here until you go."

"Oh—but—say now, Miss Hagar, that is hard to drive me away when I have just come; and such an afternoon, too, hot enough to kill a darkey. Do let me help you down."

"No; I can get out myself if I must. Please turn your back."

Thus entreated, he turned his back and commenced an exhaustive study of the landscape. Hagar arose; the hammock turned up, and Ellis was just in time to receive her in his arms as she fell.

"Hagar—my darling—you are not hurt?" he asks anxiously, still holding her in a close embrace.

"No; of course not. It is so good of you to be by to care for me so nicely," she said in some confusion.

"Hagar—my darling," he said again, with a desperate resolve to let her know the state of his feelings, "will you marry me?" She trembled as his lips pressed passionate kisses on hers. The veil was drawn away. She understood—this was the realization of the dreams that had come to her dimly all the tender springtime. Never in all her young life had she felt so happy, so strangely happy. A soft flush mounted to cheek and brow under his caresses.

"I don't understand," murmured the girl, trembling with excitement.

"My darling, I think I have said it more plainly that most men do. Hagar, I think you must know it; I have made no secret of my love for you. Have you not understood me all the days of the spring and summer?"

"Are you quite sure that you love me? You are so old and wise, and I so ignorant to be the wife of so grand a man as you."

She glanced up fleetingly, and flushed more deeply under the look she met. He folded her closer still in his arms. His next words were whispered:

"My love! lift your eyes to mine, and say you love me."

Hagar had not dreamed that such passion as this existed in the world. It seemed to take the breath of her inner life and leave her powerless, with no separate existence, no distinct mental utterance.

Gently Ellis drew back the bright head against him, and bent over the sweet lips that half sought his kiss; and so for one long moment he knew a lifetime of happiness. Then he released her.

"Heaven helping me, you shall be so loved and shielded that sorrow shall never touch you. You shall never repent trusting your young life to me. May I speak to your mother tonight?"

"Yes," she whispered.

And so they were betrothed. Ellis felt and meant all that he said under the stress of the emotion of the moment; but who calculates the effect of time and cruel circumstance? Mrs. Sargeant was more than pleased at the turn of events. Soon Ellis was taking the bulk of the business of managing her estates upon his own strong shoulders. These two seemed favored children of the gods all that long, happy summer. She was his, and he was hers.

The days glided by like a dream, and soon brought the early fall which was fixed for the wedding festivities. All was sunshine. The wedding day was set for October. On the morning of the day before, Hagar entered her mother's room as was her usual custom, to give her a loving morning greeting, and found nothing but the cold, unresponsive body, from which the spirit had fled. Then followed days that were a nightmare to Hagar, but under Ellis' protecting care the storm of grief spent itself and settled into quiet sadness. There was no one at the Sargeant home but the bereaved girl and her servants. At the end of a month Ellis put the case plainly before her, and she yielded to his persuasions to have the marriage solemnized at once, so that he might assume his place as her rightful protector. A month later than the time originally set there was a quiet wedding, very different from the gay celebration originally planned by a loving mother, and the young mistress took her place in the stately rooms of Enson Hall. When a twelve-month had passed there was a little queen born—the heiress of the hall. Ellis' happiness was complete.

V

It was past the breakfast hour in the Hall kitchen, but Marthy still lingered. It was cold outside; snow had fallen the night before; the clouds were dull and threatening. The raw northern blasts cut like bits of ice; the change was very sudden from the pleasant coolness of autumn. The kitchen was an inviting place; the blaze shot up gleefully from between the logs, played hide-and-seek in dark corners and sported merrily across the faces of the pickaninnies sprawling on the floor and constantly under Aunt Henny's feet.

Aunt Henny now reigned supreme in the culinary department of the Hall. Her head was held a little higher, if possible, in honor of the new dignity that had come to the family from the union of the houses of Enson and Sargeant.

"'Twarn't my 'sires fer a weddin' so close to a fun'ral, but Lor', chile, dars a diffurunce in doin' things, an' it 'pears dis weddin's comin' out all right. Dem two is a sight fer sore eyes, an' as fer de baby"—Aunt Henny rolled up her eyes in silent ecstasy.

"Look hyar, mammy," said Marthy, Mrs. Enson's maid and Aunt Henny's daughter, "why don' you see Unc' Demus? He'd guv you a charm fer Miss Hagar to wear; she needn't know nuthin' 'bout it."

"Sho, honey, wha' you take me fo'? I done went down to Demus soon as dat weddin' wus brung up."

"Wha' he say, mammy?"

"Let me 'lone now tell I tells you." Aunt Henny was singeing pin-feathers from a pile of birds on the floor in front of the fire. She dropped her task to give emphasis to her words. "I carried him Miss Hagar's pocket-hankercher and he guv me a bag made outen de skin ob a rattlesnake, an' he put in it a rabbit's foot an' er sarpint's toof, an' er squorerpin's tail wid a leetle dust outen de graveyard an' he sewed up de bag. Den he tied all dat up in de hankercher an' tell me solemn: 'Long as yer mistis keep dis 'bout her, trouble'll neber stay so long dat joy won't conquer him in de end." So, honey, I done put dat charm in Missee Hagar draw 'long wid her tickler fixins an' I wants yer, Marthy, to take keer ob it," she concluded, with a grave shake of her turbanned head. Marthy was duly impressed, and stood looking at her mother with awe in every feature of her little brown face.

"'Deed an' I will, mammy."

"My young Miss will be all right ef dat St. Clair Enson keeps 'way from hyar," continued the woman reflectively.

"Who's St. Clar Enson?" asked Marthy.

"Nemmin' 'bout him. Sometime I'll tell you when you gits older. All you got ter do now is ter take mighty good keer o' your mistis and de baby," replied her mother, with a knowing wag of her head. "Fling anudder chunk on dat fire!" she called to one of the boys playing on the floor. "Gittin' mighty cole fer dis time ob year, de a'r small pow'rful lack mo' snow."

A shadow fell across the doorsill shutting out the light for a moment, that came through the half-open doorway. Marthy gave a shriek that ended in a giggle as a young Negro, tall, black, smiling, sauntered into the kitchen; it was Isaac. Aunt Henny threw her arms high above her head in unbounded astonishment.

"En de name ob de Lawd! Isaac! What's gwine ter happen ter dis fambly now, Ike, dat you's come sneakin' home?"

Isaac grinned. "Isn't you pow'rful glad ter see me, Aunt Henny? I is ter see you an' Marthy. Marfy's a mighty likely lookin' gal, I 'low." He gave a sly roll of his eye in the direction where the girl stood regarding the athletic young Negro with undisguised admiration.

"Non o' dat," sputtered Aunt Henny. "Don' you go tryin' ter fool wid dat gal, you lim' ob de debbil. Take yo'sef right off! What yer doin' hyar, enyhow? Dis ain't no place for you."

"My marse tell'd me ter come," replied Isaac, not at all ruffled by his reception. "I ain't gwine ter go right off; ain't tell'd none o' de folks howdy yit."

"*Your marse tell'd you ter come!* What fer he tell'd yer to come?" stormed Aunt Henny, with a derisive snort. "Dat's what I want ter know. *My* marse'll have somethin' ter say I reckon, ef *yer* marse *did* tell'd yer ter come. An' I b'lieve you's a liar, 'deed I do. I don' b'lieve yer marser knows whar you is at, dis blessid minnit."

Isaac chuckled. "I'se come home ter see de new mistis an' de leetle baby; I cert'n'y hope dey is well. Marse St. Clar'll be hyar hisself bimeby."

Aunt Henny stood a moment silently regarding the boy. Fear, amazement and curiosity were blended in her honest face. Plainly, she was puzzled. "De debbil turn' sain'," she muttered to herself, with a long look at the unconscious Isaac, who sat toasting his cold bare toes before the roaring fire. "Dis house got mo' peace in it, an' Marse Ellis happier den he been sence his mar, ol' Missee Enson, died; but," and she shook her turbanned head ominously, "'tain't fer long. I ain't fergit nuffin'; I isn't lived nex' dis Enson Hall so many years fer nuffin."

"I'se walk'd a long way slippin' officers"—began Isaac.

"Um!" grunted Aunt Henny, with the look of alarm still in her eyes, "officers! dat's what's de matter."

"Dey'll hab ter see Marse St. Clar, tain't me. He sol' me. I runned 'way. I come home, dat's all. Kain't I hab suthin' to eat?"

"Ef 'tain't one it's t'odder. Befo' God, I 'lieve you an' yo' marse bof onhuman. Been sol'! runned 'way! hump!" again grunted Aunt Henny.

Meanwhile Marthy had made coffee and baked a corncake in the hot ashes. Isaac sniffed the aroma of the fragrant coffee hungrily. There was chicken and rice, too, he noticed as she placed food on the end of a table and motioned him to help himself. Isaac needed no pressing, and in a moment was eating ravenously.

"Tell you de troof, Aunt Henny," he said at last, as he waited for a fourth help, "Marse St. Clar git hard up de oder night in a little play comin' up de bay, an' he sell me to a gempleman fer sixteen hundred dollars. But, Lor', dat don' hol' Isaac, chile, while he's got legs."

"Dat's jes' what I thought. No use yer lyin' ter me, Isaac, yer Aunt Henny *was born wif a veil.* I knows a heap o' things by seein' 'em fo' dey happens. I don' tell all I sees, but I keeps up a steddyin' 'bout it."

"Dar's no mon can keep me, I don't keer how much Marse St. Clar sells me; he's my onlies' marser," continued Isaac, as he kept on devouring food a little more slowly than at first.

"Lawd sakes, honey; you's de mos' pow'rfulles' eater I'se seed fer many a day. Don' reckon you's had a good meal sence yer was home five years ago. Dog my cats ef I don' hope Marse Ellis will jes' make yer trot."

"He kin sen' me back, but I isn't gwine stay wid 'em," replied Isaac, with his mouth full of food.

"You cain't he'p yo'se'f."

"I kin walk," persisted Isaac doggedly.

"Put you in de caboose an' give yer hundred lashes," Aunt Henny called back, as she waddled out of the kitchen to find her master.

"Don' keer fer dat, nudder."

Isaac improved the time between the going and coming of Aunt Henny by making fierce love to Marthy, who was willing to meet him more than half way.

The breakfast-room was redolent with the scent of flowers, freshly cut from the greenhouses; the waxed floor gleamed like polished glass beneath the fur rugs scattered over it, and the table, with its service for two, was drawn in front of the cheerful fire that crackled and sparkled in the open fireplace. All the luxuries that wealth could give were gathered about the young matron. It was a happy household; the hurry and rush of warlike preparations had not reached its members, and the sting of slavery, with its demoralizing brutality, was unknown on these plantations so recently joined. Happiness was everywhere, from the master in his carriage to the slave singing in the fields at his humble task. Breakfast was over, and as Ellis glanced over the top of his morning paper at his wife and baby, he felt a thrill of intense pride and love.

As compared with her girlhood, Hagar's married life had been one round of excitement. Washington and many other large cities had been visited on their brief honeymoon. They were royally entertained by all the friends and relatives of both families, and the beautiful bride had been the belle of every assembly. Ellis was wrapped up in her; intimate acquaintance but deepened his love. Her nature was pure, spiritual, and open as the day. Gowned in spotless white, her slender form lost in a large armchair, she sat opposite him, dandling the baby in her arms. She looked across at him and smiled.

"Well, pet," he smiled back at her, "going to ride?"

She shook her head and set every little curl in motion.

"I won't go out today, it is so cold; we are so comfortable here before the fire, baby and I."

"What a lazy little woman it is," he laughed, rising from his seat and going over to stand behind her chair, stroke the bright hair, and clasp mother and child in his arms. Hagar rested her head against him, and held the infant at arm's length for his admiration.

"Isn't she a darling? See, Ellis, she knows you," as the child cooed and laughed and gurgled at them both, in a vain effort to clinch something in her little red fists.

"This little beggar has spoiled our honeymoon with a vengeance," he replied with a laugh. "I cannot realize that it is indeed over, and we have settled down to the humdrum life of old married folk."

"Can anything ever spoil that and its memories?" she asked, with a sweet upward look into his face. "Indeed, I often wonder if I am too happy; is it right for any human being to be so favored in life as I have been."

"Gather your roses while you may, there will be dark clouds enough in life, heaven knows. No gloomy thoughts, Mignon; let us be happy in the present." He kissed the lips raised so temptingly for his caress, and then one for the child. He thought humbly of his own career beside the spotless creature he had won for life. While not given to excesses, yet there were things in the past that he regretted. Since the birth of their child, the days had been full of emotion for these two people, who were, perhaps, endowed with over-sensitive natures given to making too much of the commonplace happenings of life. Now, as he watched the head of the child resting against the mother's breast, he ran the gamut of human feelings in his sensations. Love and thanksgiving for these unspeakable gifts of God—his wife and child—swept the inmost recesses of his heart.

"Please, Marse Ellis!" cried Aunt Henny's voice from the doorway, "please, sah, Marse St. Clar's Isaac done jes' dis minnit come home. What's I gwine ter do wid him?"

"What, Henny!" Ellis cried in astonishment; "St. Clair's Isaac? Where's his master?"

"Dunno Marse Ellis, but dar's allers truble, sho, when dat lim' o' Satan turns up; 'deed dar is."

Ellis left the room hurriedly, followed by Aunt Henny. Hagar sat there, fondling the child, a perfect picture of sweet womanhood. She had matured wonderfully in the few months of married life; her girlish manner had dropped from her like a garment. Eve's perfect daughter, she accomplished her destiny in sweet content. Presently the door opened, and her husband stood beside her chair again; his face wore a troubled look.

"What is it?" she asked, with a sweeping upward glance that noted every change of his countenance.

"St. Clair's Isaac."

"Well, and is he so serious a matter that you must look so grave?"

"My dear, the slaves all look upon him as a bird of evil omen; for myself, I look upon it as mere ignorant superstition, but still I have a feeling of uneasiness. They have neither of them been at the Hall for five years. Isaac says his master is coming—that he expected to find him here. What brings them is the puzzler."

"News of your marriage, Ellis; a natural desire to see his new relative. I see nothing strange in that, dear."

"He can't feel very happy about it, according to the terms of the will; probably he has been counting on my not marrying, and now, being disappointed, comes for me to pay his debts, or perform some impossible favor."

"Why impossible?"

"St. Clair is an unsavory fellow, and his desires are not likely to appeal to a man of honor," replied Ellis, with a short, bitter laugh.

"So bad as that?" said his wife regretfully; it was the first shadow since the beginning of their honeymoon. She continued: "Promise me, Ellis, to bear with him kindly and grant him anything in reason, in memory of our happiness."

In the kitchen Aunt Henny, with little braids of hair sticking out from under turban, talked to Marthy.

"Ef Marse Ellis listen to me, he gwine ter make dat Isaac quit dese diggin's."

"Law, mammy," laughed Marthy, showing her tiny white teeth and tossing her head, "you don' want ter drive de po' boy 'way from whar he was born, does yer?" Marthy was a born coquette, and Isaac was very gallant to her.

"Dat all I gwine ter say. Nobody knows dat Marse St. Clar an' his Isaac better'n I does. I done part raise 'em bof. I reckon my ha'r'd all turn plum' white ef dem two hadn't don lef' dese parts."

"How you come to raise 'em, mammy, an' what made 'em try ter turn yo' ha'r plum' white?"

"Dev'ment, honey, pur' dev'ment! It 'pears lack 'twas only yisterday dat I was a gal wurkin' right yere in dis same ol' kitchen. Marse Sargeant he lose heap money, an' all ob dem move ter St. Louis ter 'trench an' git rich ergin; Marse Enson he want me fer ol' Miss, an' so Marse Sargeant done leave me hyar at Enson Hall. While I was hyar bof ob dem imps was born, but Marse St. Clar he good bit older dan Isaac. Many's de time he run me all ober dis plantation when he no bigger'n dat Thomus Jefferson, 'cause I wouldn't give dat Isaac fus' help from de chickuns jes' roasted fer dinner befo' de fambly done seed nary leg ob 'em. Chase me, chile, wid a pissle pinted plum' at me."

"Lordy! wha' you reckon he do ef he come back hyar now?"

"I don' reckon on nuffin but dev'ment, jes' same as he done time an' time agin when he were a boy—jes' dev'ment."

"Mammy, you say oder day when Missee Hagar git married to Marse Ellis: 'Now dat St. Clar'll stan' no chance ob gittin' de property'; what you mean by dat?"

"Didn't mean nuffin," snapped her mother, with a suspicious look at her. "G' 'long 'bout yo' bisness; you's gittin' mighty pert sence you git to be Miss Hagar's maid; you's axin' too many questions."

In a day or so the family settled down to Isaac's presence as a matter of course. Aunt Henny's predictions about the weather were verified, and the week was unpleasant. The wind blew the bare branches of the trees against the veranda posts and roared down the wide fireplaces; snowflakes were in the air. Hagar and Ellis had just come in from a canter over the country roads; she went immediately to her room to dress for dinner, but Ellis tarried a moment in the inviting room which seemed to command his admiration. The luxuries addressed themselves to his physical sense, and he was conscious of complete satisfaction in the knowledge that his wealth could procure a fitting setting for the gem he had won. Other thoughts, too, crept in, aroused by the talk of a friend where they had called on the way home. He had not thought of war, and was not interested in politics; still, if it were true that complications were arising that demanded a settlement by a trial of arms, he was ready. "Perhaps we are too happy for it to last," he muttered; "but, come what will, I have been blessed." His gaze followed Marthy's movements mechanically, as she lighted the wax candles and let fall the heavy curtains, shutting the gloom outside in the gathering darkness. He was aroused from the deep revery into which he had fallen by the sound of wheels on the carriage drive. In a moment, before he could cross the room, the door opened and St. Clair Enson entered, followed by the slave-trader, Walker.

"St. Clair! Is it possible!" he cried, striding forward to grasp his brother's hand. "Is it really you? Welcome home!" They shook hands warmly, and then Ellis threw his arm about St. Clair's shoulders, and for a moment the two men gazed in the depths of each other's eyes with emotion too deep for words. The younger man *did* feel for an instant a wave of fraternal love for this elder brother against whom he meditated (an evil) deed.

"Why, Ellis, I do believe you're glad to see me. You're ready to kill the fatted calf to feast the prodigal," St. Clair said, as they fell apart. "My friend, Mr. Walker—Walker, my brother."

"Glad to see you and welcome you to Enson Hall," said Ellis in cordial greeting, his hospitable nature overcoming his repugnance for this man of unsavory reputation.

"Thanky, thanky," said Walker, as he awkwardly accepted the armchair Ellis offered him, and drew near the blazing fire.

"Just in time for dinner; you will dine with us, Mr. Walker." Walker nodded assent.

"Well, Ellis, how's the world using you? You're married, lucky dog. Got your letter while I was at the nominating convention; it must have followed me about for more than a month. Thought I'd come up and make the acquaintance of my new sister and niece," remarked St. Clair, with careless ease.

"Yes," replied Ellis. Somehow his brother's nonchalant air and careless words jarred upon his ear. "You are always welcome to come when you like and stay as long as you please. This is your home."

"Home with a difference," replied St. Clair, as an evil smile for an instant marred his perfect features.

"He won't stand much show of gittin' eny of this prop'ty now you's got a missus, Mr. Enson," ventured Walker, with a grin. "He's been mighty anxious to meet your missus. Most fellers isn't so oneasy about a sister-in-law, but I reckon this one is different, being report says she's a high-stepper," said Walker, as he grinned at Ellis and cleared his mouth by spitting foul tobacco juice on the polished hearth. Ellis bowed coldly in acknowledgment of his words.

"Mrs. Enson will be down presently. This certainly is a joyful surprise," he said, turning to St. Clair. "Why didn't you send word, and the carriage would have met you at the station?"

"Oh, we came out all right in Walker's trap."

"I'll have it put up." Ellis rose as he spoke.

"No, no; my man will drive me back to the city shortly," Walker broke in.

"I hope you are doing well, St. Clair; where are you from now?"

"Just from Charleston, where I have made a place for myself at last Politics," he added significantly.

"Ah!"

"Great doin's down in Charleston; great doin's," Walker broke in again.

"No doubt of it; how do you think this matter will end?"

"It's goin' to be the greatest time the world ever saw, Mr. Enson. When we git a-goin' thar'll be no holdin' us. The whole South, sah, is full of sodjers, er-gittin' ready to whup the Yanks t'uther side of nex' week. That's how it's goin' to end."

"Then it will really be war?"

"The greatest one the worl' ever seen, sah, unless the Yanks git on their knees and asks our pardon, and gives up this govinment to their natral rulers. Why, man, ain't yer heard? You's a patriot, ain't you? Yer a son of the sunny South, ain't yer?"

Ellis smiled at this enthusiasm, although filled with disgust for the man.

"When one has his family to think of, there are times when he forgets the world and thinks of nothing but his home. Be that as it may, I am no recreant son of the South. I stand by her with all I possess. I can imagine nothing that would turn me a traitor to my section."

"Spoken like a man. That's the talk, eh, Enson?" he said, appealing to St. Clair, who nodded in approval.

"Do all you can, I say, for the Confederate States of America, from givin' 'em yer money down to helpin' 'em cuss."

"When the time comes I shall not be found wanting. By the way, St. Clair, your boy Isaac is here. Came on us suddenly the other day."

"Ha, ha, ha! the little black rascal. Didn't I tell you he'd do Johnson out of that money? He's the very devil, that boy."

"Like master, like man," replied St. Clair, with a shrug of his handsome shoulders.

"What is it?" asked Ellis sternly; "no cheating or swindling, is there?"

"He's a runaway. I sold him to a gentleman about a week ago," was St. Clair's careless answer.

"What is the man's name, and where is he to be found? he must be reimbursed or Isaac returned to him," said Ellis, looking sternly at his brother. "Enson Hall is no party to fraudulent dealings."

"I'm glad to hear you say that, Mr. Enson; I'm up here lookin' for a piece of property belonging to me, and said to be stopping on this very plantation."

"Impossible, sir; all our slaves have been here from childhood, or have grown old with us. You have been misinformed."

"I reckon not. As I was tellin' your brother here, it's a mighty onpleasant job I've got before me, but I must do my dooty." Walker put on a sardonic smile, and continued:

"I see, sah, that you don' understan' me. Let me explain further: Fourteen years ago I bought a slave child from a man in St. Louis, and not being able to find a ready sale for her on account of her white complexion, I lent her to a Mr. Sargeant. I understand that you have her in your employ. I've come to get her." Here the slave-trader took out his large sheepskin pocketbook, and took from it a paper which he handed to Ellis.

Ellis gazed at Walker in bewilderment; he took the paper in his hand and mechanically glanced at it. "Still your meaning is not clear to me, Mr. Walker. I tell you we have no slave of yours on this plantation,"

PAULINE E. HOPKINS

but his face had grown white, and large drops of perspiration stood on his forehead.

"Well, sah, I'll explain a leetle more. Mr. and Mrs. Sargeant lived a number of years in St. Louis; they took a female child from me to bring up—*a nigger*—and they passed her off on the commoonity here as their own, and you have *married* her. Is my meaning clear now, sah?"

"Good God!" exclaimed Ellis, as he fell back against the wainscotting, "then this paper, if it means anything, must mean my wife."

"I can't help who it means or what it means," replied Walker, "this yer's the bill of sale, an' there's an officer outside there in the cart to git me my nigger."

"This paper proves nothing. You'll take no property from this house without proper authority," replied Ellis with ominous calm. Walker lost his temper, apparently.

"I hold you in my hand, sah!" he stormed; "you are a brave man to try to face me down with stolen property."

Ellis rose slowly to his fee. Pale, teeth set, lips half parted, eyes flashing lightning—furious, terrible, superb in his wrath. His eyes were fixed on Walker, who, frightened at his desperate look, rose to his feet also, with his hand on his pistol. "You would murder me," he gasped.

Ellis laughed a strange, discordant laugh.

"There is, there must be some mistake here. My wife was the daughter of Mr. Sargeant. There is not a drop of Negro blood in her veins; I doubt, sir, if you have ever seen her. And, Mr. Walker, if you do not prove the charges you have this day insulted me by making, your life shall pay the penalty."

"Well, sah, fetch her in the room here; I reckon she'll know me. She warn't so leetle as to fergit me altogether."

Just at this moment Hagar opened the door, pausing on the threshold, a fair vision in purest white; seeing her husband's visitors, she hesitated. Ellis stepped quickly to her side and took her hand.

"My dear, are you acquainted with this gentleman? Do you remember ever seeing him before?"

She looked a moment, hesitated, and then said: "I think not."

Walker stepped to the mantel where the wax-light would fall full upon his face, and said:

"Why, Hagar, have you forgotten me? It's only about fourteen years ago that I bought you, a leetle shaver, from Rose Valley, and lent you to Mrs. Sargeant, ha, ha, ha!"

Hagar put her hand to her head in a dazed way as she heard the coarse laugh of the rough, brutal slave-trader. She looked at Ellis, put out her hand to him in a blind way, and with a heartrending shriek fell fainting to the floor.

VI

"I thought she'd remember," exclaimed Walker.

Ellis raised his wife in his arms and placed her upon a sofa. St. Clair stood watching the scene with a countenance in which curiosity and satisfaction struggled for the mastery.

"Throw a leetle water in her face, and that'll bring her to. I've seen 'em faint befo', but they allers come to."

Ellis was deathly white; he turned his flaming eyes upon the trader:

"The less you say, the better. By God! I have a mind to put a ball in you now, you infernal hound!"

"Yes, but she's mine; I want to see that she's all right," and Walker shrank away from the infuriated man.

Ellis took his wife in his arms and bore her from the room. Shortly, Aunt Henny brought them word to dine without him, their rooms were ready, and he would see Mr. Walker in the morning after he had communicated with his lawyer. The officer was dismissed, and drove back to the town. As they sat at the table enjoying the sumptuous fare and perfect appointments, St. Clair said to Walker.

"Is this thing true?"

"True as gospel. The only man who could prove the girl's birth is the one I took her from, and he's dead."

"Well, you've done me a mighty good turn, blame me if you have'nt. I shan't forget it. Here's to our future prosperity," and he touched his wineglass to his friend's.

"I don't mean you shall forget," was Walker's reply as he sat his glass down empty. "Now, siree, you hang about here for a spell and watch the movements. He'll pay me all right, but you mustn't let him snake her off or anything. Ef things look queer, jes' touch the wires and I'll be with you instanter."

On the following morning Ellis Enson's lawyer, one of the ablest men of the Maryland Bar, pronounced the bill of sale genuine, for it had been drawn up by a justice, and witnessed by men who sent their affadavits under oath.

"There is but one thing to be done, Mr. Walker," Ellis said, after listening to his lawyer's words. "What do you want? How much money will it take to satisfy you to say no more about the matter?"

"I don't bear you any malice for nothing you've said ter me; perhaps I'd do about the same as you have ef it was my case. Five thou, cash, will git her, though ef I toted her to New Orleans market, a handsome polished wench like her would bring me any gentleman's seven or eight thou, without a remark. As for the pickaninny—"

"What!" thundered Ellis, "the child, too?"

"In course," replied Walker, drawing his finger in and out his scraggy whiskers, "the child follows the condition of the mother, so I scoop the pile."

Ellis groaned aloud.

"As I was sayin'," continued Walker, "the pickaninny will cost you another thou, and cheap at that."

"I would willingly give the money twice over, even my whole fortune, if it did not prove my wife to be of Negro blood," replied Ellis, with such despair in his tones that even these men, inured to such scenes from infancy, were touched with awe.

The money was paid, and within the hour the house had resumed its wonted quiet and all was apparently as before; but the happiness of Enson Hall had fled forever.

VII

Marthy was horrified to see how her mistress arose from the couch where her husband placed her, fall on her knees beside it, and burst into wild tempestuous sobbing.

"Lor', Missee Hagar! Lor', honey! Don' cry so, don', honey!"

Hagar suddenly arose, caught her by the shoulders and turned her toward the light, minutely examining the black skin, crinkled hair, flat nose and protruding lips. So might her grandmother have looked.

"Fo' mercy sake, is you sick, Miss Hagar?" cried the girl, frightened at the strange glare in the large dark eyes. But Hagar turned away without replying. Marthy hurried down stairs.

"My soul, Mammy," she cried as she burst into the kitchen, "Miss Hagar done gone clean destructed."

Once more Hagar crouched upon the floor. She felt like writhing and screaming, only her tongue seemed paralyzed. She thought and thought with agonizing intensity. Vaguely, as in a dream, she recalled her stay in Rose Valley and the terror of her childish heart caused by the rough slave-trader. Could it be true, or was it but a hideous nightmare from which she would soon awake? Her mother a slave! She wondered that the very thought did not strike her dead. With shrinking horror she contemplated the black abyss into which the day's events had hurled her, leaving her there to grovel and suffer the tortures of the damned. Her name gone, her pride of birth shattered at one blow! Was she, indeed, a descendant of naked black savages of the horrible African jungles? Could it be that the blood of generations of these unfortunate ones flowed through her veins? Her education, beauty, refinement, what did they profit her now if—horrible thought—Ellis, her husband, repudiated her? Her heart almost ceased beating with the thought, and she crouched still lower in the dust of utter humiliation.

Then she rose and walked about the room; it was crowded with her wedding finery. She touched an article here and there with the solemnity that we give to the dead—they were relics of a time that would never return to her. She examined her features in the mirror, but even to her prejudiced eyes there was not a trace of the despised chattel. One blow with her open hand shattered its shining surface and the pieces flew about in a thousand tiny particles; she did not notice in her frenzy that the hand was torn and bleeding. Then she laughed a dreadful laugh:

first, silently; then in a whisper; then a peal that clashed through the quiet house and reached the sorrow-stricken man in the silent library. He shuddered, but did not move; he could not face her yet. Aunt Henny and Marthy stood outside the locked door and whispered to each other: "Missee Hagar done gone mad!"

She paused an instant, in her ceaseless promenade about the room, beside the dressing table where her husband's picture reposed in its nest of silk and lace; she paled and shuddered. Could she expect him to forget all his prejudices, which were also her own? Slavery—its degradation, the pining and fretting of the Negro race in bondage—had always seemed right to her. Although innocent of cruelty to them, yet their wrongs were coming home to her in a two-fold harvest. Yes, Ellis would give her up; he must; it was his duty. Only this morning she was his wife, the honored mistress of his home; tonight what? His slave, his concubine! Horrible fatality that had named her Hagar. Somewhere she had read lines that came back to her vividly now:

> *"Farewell! I go, but Egypt's mighty gods*
> *Will go with me, and my avengers be,*
> *And in whatever distant land your god,*
> *Your cruel god of Israel, is known,*
> *There, too, the wrongs that you have done this day*
> *To Hagar and your first-born,*
> *Shall waken and uncoil themselves, and hiss*
> *Like adders at the name of Abraham."*

Then she gazed once more upon the pictured face with the strained look we place upon the face of the dead before they are hidden from us forever. They brought the child to the door and begged her to open to it. She heeded it not. Let it die; it, too, was now a slave.

The night passed; it was dawn again. There were sounds of life from the house below. Some one came slowly up the stairs and paused at her door. Then Ellis's voice, sounding harsh and discordant, said:

"It is I, Hagar."

She opened the door. She nerved herself to hear what he might say. The sense of her bitter shame overpowered her, and she shrank before him, cowering as he closed the door, and stood within the room.

Twice he essayed to speak, and twice a groan issued from his white lips. How could he bear it! She stood before him with clasped hands and hanging head as became a slave before her master. How changed, too, he thought, a blight had even fallen upon her glorious beauty. He who had always upheld the institution as a God-given principle of humanity and Christianity, suddenly beheld his idol, stripped of its gilded trappings, in all its filthiness. Then in his heart he cursed slavery.

"Hagar, I have bought you of that man—Walker—he will not annoy you again."

She did not speak or raise her eyes. Ellis bit his lips until the blood ran in the effort to restrain himself for her sake.

"I have thought the matter over and much as I wish it might be otherwise, much as I would sacrifice for you, I feel it my duty as a Southern gentleman, the representative of a proud old family, to think of others beside myself and not allow my own inclinations to darken the escutcheon of a good old name. I cannot, I dare not, and the law forbids me to acknowledge as my wife a woman in whose veins courses a drop of the accursed blood of the Negro slave."

Still she stood there motionless.

Ellis was in torture. Why did she stand there like a forlorn outcast, in stony despair?

"Speak!" he cried at last, "for God sake say something or I shall die!"

Then she raised her eyes to his for one fleeting moment.

"I do not blame you. You can do nothing else."

He moved a step toward her with a smothered groan, "Dearest, dearest," he whispered, and the tone of his voice carried in it his unshaken love.

"Do not,—do not,—" broke from her white lips and with a smothered cry of agony her reserve broke down and she flung herself upon the couch face down.

Ellis went to her and knelt beside her with his arms about her. Five minutes must have passed while they communed in spirit. There was no sound but the girl's hysterical sobbing.

"I am going away," he said at length: "I cannot stay here and live. I may never return, but I shall leave you amply provided for." Then he rose to his feet and rushed from the room. She heard his footsteps echoing down the empty corridor and pause before the door of the nursery.

Ellis loved his wife devotedly, but the shame of public ostracism and condemnation seemed too much for inherited principles. An hour passed. Once more Ellis resumed his measured pacing in the library.

The clock ticked slowly on the mantel, but the beating of his heart outstripped it. He could not follow the plans he had laid out as the path of duty. His visit to the nursery had upset them; parental love, love for his innocent wife, was too strong to be easily cast aside. The ticking of the clock maddened him. It seemed the voice of doom pursuing him— condemning him as a coward—coward—coward. He could stand it no longer. Once more he mounted the stairs to his wife's room.

"Hagar, I cannot do it. We cannot alter the fact that we are bound by all the laws of God and man for better or worse. I have thought it all out, and I have planned a way."

"It is impossible," she said in quiet despair. "You cannot overcome this fearful thing that has fallen upon us. I myself think and feel as you do. It is enough; I accept my fate."

"Oh, no, no; do not say that!"

"Yes, Ellis," she repeated, her face like snow in its pallor.

"Hagar, you do not know what you are saying. You love me, and I love you as my very soul. How were we to know? How could we tell? Therefore, having committed a sin in innocence—if sin it be, and I do not so believe it, for things appear in a different light to me now—we will together live it down. Surely heaven cannot fix the seal of this crime on us forever." The supplication of his voice, his speaking eyes, shook Hagar's heart, so tired and worn with emotion. Her eyes were full of compassion as they rested on him, her lips firm and cold. "I love you, Ellis; you know that, and by that love, although I am your slave and chattel, I know that your love demands naught for your wife but honor. The force of circumstances cannot degrade you—cannot change your chivalrous nature."

"Great heavens! You misunderstand me. I have no hope, no life, apart from you, and I hold you as I cling to salvation, my love, my soul! Listen, Hagar, I have a plan." Bending over her he rapidly outlined a plan of life abroad. They would be remarried, and sail from a Northern port for Europe; there, where the shadow of this crime could not come, they would begin life anew. He had mapped it all out carefully and as she listened she was convinced—it was feasible; it could be done.

Neither of them noticed that the door was ajar; neither did they hear the light footfall that paused beside it. It was St. Clair.

"Walker was right. We must stop that game," he muttered to himself.

VIII

Two weeks had passed since Ellis left his home on the pretext of urgent business, but in reality to make necessary arrangements for an indefinite stay abroad. Ill news travels fast and it was well known all over the plantations and in the neighborhood that the terrible discovery of Hagar's origin had broken up the home life at Enson Hall. Save for St. Clair's presence, the Hall had settled back into its old bachelor state with one difference—in the mistress's suite a beautiful despairing woman sat day after day, with her infant across her knees, eating her heart out in an agony of hope and fear waiting the reprieve from a living death that Ellis's return would bring her.

Here was a woman raised as one of a superior race, refined, cultured, possessed of all the Christian virtues, who would have remained in this social sphere all her life, beloved and respected by her descendants, her blood mingling with the best blood of the country if untoward circumstances had not exposed her ancestry. But the one drop of black blood neutralized all her virtues, and she became, from the moment of exposure, an unclean thing. Can anything more unjust be imagined in a republican form of government whose excuse for existence is the upbuilding of mankind!

These were sorrowful days for the Negroes who could not bring themselves to look upon their beloved mistress as one of their race, a share in their sad destiny.

Aunt Henny spent most of her spare time praying and coaxing Hagar out of the apathy into which she had fallen.

"Bless de Lawd! I know'd dev'ment was on han' when Marse St. Cla'r done comed home," she said one morning to Marthy. "Las' time he was here ol' Marse he bus' a blud vessel in his head an' never know'd a blessed thing fer a munf, den he die. 'Fore dat he shoot a mon to de college an' beat de prefesser 'mos' to def. Dais a cuss on dat boy, sho."

"How you tink it come so, Mammy?"

"I hern tell from Aunt Di, who nussed Missee Enson. See hyar, chile, I don' no 'bout tellin' a disrespons'ble gal like you fambly secrets,—an' ef you goes to 'peatin' my words all 'roun' de plantation, I hope Marse Ellis whop yer back." Marthy rolled her eyes in terror and promised to keep her mammy's revelations as sacred as Scripture.

"You know's dat no one neber goes nigh de old summer house down dar close to de wharf at de foot ob de garden, don' you?"

Marthy nodded, and her eyes grew larger as she listened with bated breath for the ghostly story she was sure would follow.

"Jes' 'fore Marse St. Cla'r was born, ole Missee Enson was settin' in there an' a turrible thunder storm came up an' jes' raised Jeemes Henry with houses an' trees, an' tored up eberythin'. Ol' Miss so dar 'feared to move even one teeny bit her li'l' finger. While she sot dar all white an' trimbly de debbil jes' showed he face to her an' grinned."

"Sure nuff debbil, mammy?" whispered Marthy in awed accents. Her mammy nodded solemnly in reply.

"Ol' Miss jes' went onto conwulshuns an' when dey fin' her she in dead faint. Dat night Marse St. Clair was born, an' ef de debbil ain't de daddy den dat ol' rapscalion neber had a borned servant in dis sinful wurl'."

"Mammy what you tink de reason de debbil show hisse'f to old Missee Enson?"

"De trubble wid you is, Marthy, dat you is de mos' 'quis'tive gal on dis plantation; you want to know too much, but de ol' fo'ks been hyar long time say dat ol' Marse git mad one day wid Unc' Ned, an' tell oberseer 'whop him.' Unc' Ned conjure man; neber been whopped in all he life. He jes' rub hisse'f all ober wid goopher, put a snake skin 'roun' he neck, a frog in one pocket an' a dry lizard in de oder, an' den he pray to de debbil: 'Dear debbil, I ax you to stan' by me in dis' my trial hour, an' I'll neber 'sert you as long as I live. I's had de power, continer de power; make me strong in your cause, make me faithful to you, an' help me to conquer my enemies, an' I will try to deserve a seat at your right han'!'"

As Marthy listened an ashy hue overspread her face and she asked breathlessly:

"Did dey whop him?"

"Bless yer soul, gal, dat was de afternoon 'fore dey was 'gwine ter whop him in de mornin', an' dat bery night de debbil 'pear to ole Miss, an' Unc' Ned neber was whopped tell de day he died, neber."

"He must a been a power, mammy, he cert'nly must."

"But de strangest part was dis: At de bery time ole Miss seen de debbil in de summer house, de oberseer was in de barn an' he 'clar' dat ober in de east corner he saw de lightnin' play, an' while he looked he see hell wid all its torments an' de debbil dar, too, wid his cloven foot, an' a struttin' 'bout like he know'd he was boss; de oberseer was so skeered dat he run, an he run, an' he run an' he neber stop runnin' tell he git plum inter Baltymo'."

"'Spec' he know'd he 'long'd to be debbil."

"Course! An' den he sen' ol' Marse word to sen' him his clo's: 'neber lib on dat plantation agin fer twice yer money; money no 'ducemen'.'"

"Mammy, mammy," this in a whisper, "do you b'lieve Miss Hagar got nigger blud in her?"

"Course not, honey. Somebody roun' hyar done conjured her. Dat debbil, St. Cla'r, I spec. Now, Marthy, take dat big silver tray of things up dar to dat po' li'le chile, an' you keep a poundin' 'tell she ope de do,' po' li'le chile."

Marthy obediently disappeared to execute orders and Aunt Henny with a dubious shake of her head lifted up her voice in song:

> *I'm a gwine to keep a climbin' high,*
> *See de hebbenly lan';*
> *Till I meet dem er angels in a de sky,*
> *See de hebbenly lan'.*
> *Dem pooty angels I shall see,*
> *See de hebbenly lan';*
> *Why don' de debbil let-a-me be,*
> *See de hebbenly lan'.*

Day succeeded day. There was little communication between the town and Enson Hall. Inclement weather prevailed for it was now the latter part of January. The fire of curiosity still burned fiercely among the rich planters over the "Enson horror," as it was called, but up at the Hall all seemed quiet. One bitter morning St. Clair sat at breakfast the picture of luxurious ease. He felt himself master of the situation already, and had assumed all the airs of ownership. Aunt Henny felt drawn, sometimes, to "shy a plate at him," as she expressed it to herself.

The odor of roses and lilies mingled pleasantly with that of muffins and chocolate. A man came striding up the avenue. It was Dr. Gaines, the family physician, who owned a neighboring plantation.

"Where is Mr. Enson?" he asked of Isaac, who answered his clamorous call on the resounding brass knocker.

"At breakfas', massa."

"I must see him at once. I have news for him."

As the doctor entered the room, St. Clair Enson was leaning back in his chair snapping his fingers at a hound stretched on a rug at his side. The doctor was unceremonious:—

"I regret to say, that I come as the bearer of evil tidings."

"Shall I bid Isaac set another plate, doctor? No? You have taken breakfast? At this hour? You are a primitive people in this rural district, truly. You should mingle with the world as I have and become capable of enjoying the delights and privileges of civilized life. May I ask the nature of the news you bring?" The doctor was a kind old man though somewhat brusque. He averted his eyes, and answered in a low voice.

"It relates to your brother. Mr. Enson, when did Ellis leave home, and when was he expected back?"

"My brother Ellis? He left home about two weeks ago, for what reason he did not state. I do not know when to look for his return; he may drop in, unexpectedly, at any moment."

The doctor was preternaturally grave.

"And you have heard nothing from him since?"

"No, I have not."

The doctor grew graver yet.

"My dear sir, early this morning my boy Sam had occasion to cross the foot of your land, where the remains of the old wharf enter the stream, and there he stumbled upon a frightful thing—the dead body of a man!"

"Not a pleasant sight," said St. Clair as he helped himself to another hot cake.

"Evidently, the body has been there two or three days. There is an ugly wound in the head that completely disfigures the face, and an empty pistol by the side of the body tells its own pitiful tale. St. Clair Enson that dead man was—"

St. Clair shifted uneasily in his chair as he looked the speaker in the eye, then started to his feet.

"My brother?"

"Your brother!"

To Dr. Gaines's eyes the cold, pale face into which he gazed did not change, only the gaze sought the floor.

"That is strange. Was he robbed also?"

"No. A large sum of money is on the body; papers and his watch. Sam ran home to me, and I summoned help, and was among the first to reach the spot."

The hound leaped suddenly to his feet and began to howl.

"Was it murder or suicide?" asked St. Clair in a calm voice.

PAULINE E. HOPKINS

"That cannot be decided yet. Finding his valuables untouched, and his hand frozen to his pistol, seems to point to suicide; that will be determined at the inquest." Dr. Gaines turned from the window by which he was standing, and said: "The remains of your brother are being brought home."

A little procession of Negroes, with heads uncovered, advanced up the avenue, slowly, between the grand old beeches, their tread-echoing in a solemn thud upon the frozen ground. A cloth was spread decently over the mangled face. In the silence and majesty of death the master returned to his home. His unlucky life had come to a sudden close. In midnight solitude and shadowed by mystery the curtain fell on the tragedy.

St. Clair advanced with a firm step to meet the bearers; there was no sign of grief in his face. The servants crowded the hall, standing in terrified silence broken only by Aunt Henny's sobs and lamentations. St. Clair lifted the cloth that covered the dead face with a hand that did not tremble, under the curious gaze of Dr. Gaines.

"Mr. Enson," said the doctor at length, "your brother had a wife or one whom we believed his wife," he corrected at St. Clair's negative gesture. "Will you not notify her of his death? She must be suffering anxiety concerning him."

"True; I had forgotten her," muttered St. Clair with a shrug of his handsome shoulders. "Yes, doctor, you break the news to her." The doctor left the room. Presently there was a scream in a woman's voice as of one in mortal agony, an opening and closing of doors and a hurrying of feet; then silence broken only by the pitiful wail of a young child.

There was an inquest at which Walker, the speculator, corroborated the evidence of St. Clair Enson—that the deceased was laboring under great depression at the time of his leaving home, and of his avowed purpose to shoot himself as the shortest way out of his family difficulties. This testimony so clearly given produced a profound impression upon the listeners. It was hoped by many that Hagar would testify, but they were doomed to disappointment. The pistol was well-known to many friends as well as to his servants, as the one Ellis Enson always carried. The watch was the old-fashioned timepiece that his father had carried before him. The papers were legal documents made by the family lawyer and having no bearing on the case.

The jury rendered a verdict of suicide. Plainly, Ellis Enson had died by his own hand.

There was a stately funeral: St. Clair Enson buried his brother with every outward mark of wealth and pomp. The servants moved about the house with red eyes and stealthy steps while from the quarters the wind bore the sound of mournful wailing.

It was a bleak night. The new master of the Hall and the slave-trader, now his inseparable companion, sat before the fire consulting about the disposal of the slaves.

"I'm going to let them all go, Walker, and only keep a small working gang to till the ground and look after the Hall."

"Jes' so," replied Walker, as he folded a fat bundle of bills into his pocket-book and carefully replaced the same in his hip pocket.

"That's a sensible thing to do. It won't be six months from now before we'll all be fighting Yankees like mad, and then where'd your niggers be so nigh as this plantation is to Washington. Best be on the safe side is my idee. And there's the missis—" At this moment the door opened unceremoniously and Hagar came straight up to the two men, seated before the blazing fire. Her dark eyes shone like stars, her face was white as the snow that covered the fields outside, her long hair hung in a straggling mass, rough and unkept, about her shoulders and over her sombre dress. A more startled apparition could not well be imagined. An exclamation broke from the lips of both men.

"I have come without your bidding, sir, for I have something to say to you," she said, addressing St. Clair without bestowing a glance on the man Walker. She cast a wild look around the sumptuous room.

"So you take your ease while he sleeps in his coffin. You need not frown. I do not fear you. Life has no terrors to offer me now." She towered above him as he sat crouched in his chair, and she looked down upon him with a wicked glare in her eyes.

"The question I came to ask is this—St. Clair Enson, do you believe that your brother died by his own hand?"

"Most certainly," Enson constrained his white lips to answer.

"Ellis was killed, murdered—shot down like a dog! What did the pistol prove? Nothing. His pockets had not been rifled. That proves nothing. Neither his great trouble brought to him by his marriage with me—a Negro—would have driven him to self-destruction. He was murdered!"

A chill crept over her listeners. No one had ever seen the gentle Hagar Sargeant in her present character.

"Murdered?" gasped St. Clair.

"Yes," she shouted. "You are his murderer!"

He recoiled as if she had struck him a blow.

"Mad woman! You are mad I say, trouble has turned your brain!"

"It was you who drove him forth from a happy home. You who found your twin demon and brought home the story that broke his heart, ruined his life and gained for you the wealth you have always coveted. I repeat, you are his murderer!"

St. Clair cringed; then he sprang to his feet and seized her by the arm.

"This is too much for any man to stand from a nigger wench. You have sealed your own fate. Off you go, my fine madam, to the Washington market in short meter. I would have kept you near me, and made your life as easy as it has been in the past, but this settles it. Walker," he said as he turned to the speculator, "you have my permission to take this nigger and her brat whenever it pleases you." Then he released her.

Hagar eyed the man critically from head to foot.

"Selfish, devilish, cruel," she said slowly; "think not that your taunts or cruelties can harm me; I care not for them. No heart in your bosom; no blood in your veins! You are his slayer, and his blood is crying from the ground against you this very hour."

It was more than he could bear. Again he sprang from his seat and seized her arm. Walker took her by the other one and between them they dragged her toward the entrance.

"Easy, easy!" exclaimed Walker in a warning voice to St. Clair. "Don't injure the sale of your property, Enson." St. Clair dropped his hold and again returned to his seat by the fire.

"There, there, my dear, you're a leetle bit excited an' no wonder. Go to your room and rest yourself, my dear, I recommend gin. Gin with a leetle hot water, sugar and spice is very nice, very nice for hysterics, and soothing, very soothing to a gal's nerves." Walker punctuated his remarks with many a little thump and pat in her back.

With a defiant smile, Hagar paused on the threshold and said:

"It's the truth! you're his murderer, and in spite of the wealth and position you have played for and won, you have seen the last on this earth of peace or happiness." Then striking her breast, she added:

"As I have parted with the same friends! Pleasant dreams to you, St. Clair Enson, master of Enson Hall!"

IX

It will be remembered that on February 4, 1861, a provisional government was formed for the "Confederate States of America." This provisional government was soon superseded by a "permanent" one, under whose constitution Jefferson Davis, Alexander H. Stevens and other officials were to serve six years, from February 22, 1862. A Peace Congress composed of delegates from twenty states, held a session for three weeks at Washington, in February, 1862. In March, same year, a Commission also went to the Capital City to negotiate for a settlement of difficulties; but all these overtures failed. Being called to Washington as a leading delegate, with power to help settle all these great questions that were then agitating the country, St. Clair Enson and Walker decided that it would be best to close the Hall, leaving Isaac, Aunt Henny and Marthy in charge of the house, and take the rest of the hands to Washington, where so many rich and influential men would congregate from the most southern parts of the country, that they would be assured of quick sales and large profits.

On the morning of departure, the small colony of black men and women sat and stood about the familiar grounds stunned and hopeless. Here most of them were born, and here they had hoped to die and be buried. The unknown future was a gulf of despair. Ellis was a good master, kind and considerate; their sincere mourning for him was mingled with grief at their own fate.

In the midst of a motley group Hagar stood with her child clasped in her arms,—hopeless, despairing. She had felt her degradation before, but not until now had she drained the bitter cup of misery.

Ellis Enson's lawyer had questioned her about her husband's business.

"Did he give you free papers?" with a pitying glance at the fair, crushed woman.

"When he returned, he intended to take me and the child abroad after making ample settlements."

The legal gentleman sighed.

"It was a great oversight—a great mistake."

So no papers, bearing upon the case, being found, all the Sargeant fortune reverted by law to the master. Nothing could be done.

Then began the humiliating journey to Washington, herding with slaves, confined in pens like cattle, the delicately nurtured lady tasted of the torments of those accursed. Her brain grew wild; she folded her infant closer to her breast—sang, whispered, laughed and wept.

Upon reaching the private slave-pen, a number of which then disgraced the national capital, she fell into a state of melancholy from which nothing aroused her but the needs of the child.

A purchaser was soon found for the handsome slave, in a New Orleans merchant who agreed to take the child, too, for the sake of getting the mother out of the city without trouble.

At the dusk of the evening, previous to the day she was to be sent off, as the prison was being closed for the night, Hagar, with her child closely clasped in her arms, darted past the keeper and ran for her life. It was not far from the prison to the long bridge which passes from the lower part of the city, across the Potomac, to the forests of Arlington Heights. Thither the fugitive directed her flight. The keeper by this time had recovered from the confusion incident to such a daring and unexpected attempt, he rallied his assistants and started in pursuit. On and on she flew, seeming tireless in her desperate resolve. It was an hour when horses could not be easily obtained; no bloodhounds were at hand to run her down. It was a trial of speed and endurance.

The pursuers raised the hue-and-cry as they followed, gaining steadily upon the fugitive. Astonished citizens poured forth from their dwellings to learn the cause of the alarm, and learning the nature of the case fell in with the motley throng in pursuit. With the speed of a bird, having passed the avenue, she began to gain, and presently she was upon the Long Bridge. Panting, gasping, she hushed her babe, appealed to God in broken sentences, and gathered all her courage to dash across the bridge and lose herself in the friendly shelter of the woods. Oh, will she,—can she, make it! Already her heart began to beat high with hope. Courage! She had only to pass three-quarters of a mile more and all would be well, the woods would shelter her, night would cover her and save her.

Just as the pursuers passed the draw they beheld three men slowly approaching from the Virginia shore. They called to them to help arrest the runaway slave. As she drew near they formed a line across the bridge to intercept her. Now the panting woman, hard-pressed on every side, suddenly stopped.

She looked wildly and anxiously around to see if all hope were indeed gone; far below the ridge rolled the dark waters, sullen, angry, threatening. Before and behind were the voices of the profane, inhuman monsters into whose hands she must inevitably fall. Her resolution was taken. She kissed her babe, clasped it convulsively in her arms, saying:

"Alas, poor innocent, there is one gift for thee yet left for your unfortunate mother to bestow,—It is death. Better so than the fate reserved for us both."

Then she raised her tearful, imploring eyes to heaven as if seeking for mercy and compassion, and with one bound sprang over the railing of the bridge, and sank beneath the waters of the Potomac river.

X

Twenty Years Later

It was a fine afternoon in early winter in the year 1882, in the city of Washington, the beautiful capital of our great Republic. Pennsylvania Avenue was literally crammed with foot-passengers and many merry sleighing parties, intent on getting as much enjoyment as possible out of the day.

Freezing weather had been followed by a generous fall of frozen, down-like flakes. Quick to take advantage of a short-lived pleasure, vehicles of every description were flying along the avenue filled with the elite of the gay city. The stream of well-dressed pedestrians moved swiftly over the snowy pavements, for the air was too cold for prolonged lingering, watching with interest, in which envy mingled to some extent, the occupants of the handsome carriages gliding along so rapidly on polished runners. Every notable of the capital was there from the President in his double-runner to the humble clerk in a single-seated modest rig.

A sumptuous Russian sleigh drawn by two splendid black horses, with a statuesque driver in ebony handling the ribbons, attracted the attention of the crowd as it dashed down the avenue and paused near the capitol steps. Two ladies were its occupants. The elder was handsome enough to demand more than a passing glance from the most indifferent, but her young companion was a picture as she nestled in luxurious ease among the costly robes, wrapped in rich furs, from which her delicate face shone out like a star upon the curious throng. That she was a stranger to the crowd could be easily told from the questioning glances which followed the turnout.

As they passed the Treasury Department two men, both past their first youth, though one was at least twenty years older than the other, came down the steps, and paused a moment, to follow with their eyes the Russian sleigh with the beautiful girl, before mingling with the living stream that flowed from between the great stone columns and spread itself through the magnificent streets of the national capital.

"Really, Benson," remarked the elder man as they resumed their walk, "the most beautiful girl I have seen for many a day. You know everyone worth knowing; who is she?"

At this moment an elderly man of dark complexion, in stylish street costume, but with a decidedly Western air, came down the capitol steps followed by a young man. Both were warmly greeted by the occupants of the sleigh. The dark man spoke a few words to the driver, then both men entered the carriage and it dashed off rapidly.

"That is Senator Bowen, his wife and daughter. He is the new millionaire senator from California. I am not acquainted with the ladies, but after their ball I intend to become assiduous in my attentions."

"Oh! then they are the Bowens! How I wish I knew them. I predict a sensation over the young beauty. Who's the young man?"

"Cuthbert Sumner, my private secretary. Deuced fine fellow, too."

The conversation drifted away from the Bowens, and they were apparently forgotten.

"How was it at the Clarks' last night, Benson, as bad as you expected?"

"Worse if possible. It was dev'lish slow! Nothing stronger than bouillon, not a chance to buck the tiger even for one moment, not a decent looking woman in the rooms. All the women fit for pleasant company give that woman's house a wide berth. Dashed if I blame 'em. The only thing that gives the Clarks a standing is his position. I can't see how he puts up with her. If I had a sanctimonious woman like her for a wife I'd cut and run for it, dashed I wouldn't."

His companion laughed long and loud.

"No fun for you there, eh, Benson? My boy, you'll never fit into the dignified position of a father of this country, I fear. Oh, well; it's hard to teach an old dog new tricks." "Yes, but think of not being able to give your friends a decent time, because your wife has a fad on temperance and thinks it a sin to smell a claret cup or a brandy-and-soda. A man with a wife of that sort ought to leave her at home, where she could rule the roost to her heart's content. The seat of government is no place for a missionary." "Well, there's always a way to remedy such things when you know your hostess."

"Of course, of course," General Benson hastened to reply. "Our bouillon was washed down with Russian tea a la Russe. We doctored it in the coatroom."

The two men indulged in a hearty laugh.

"Well, Benson, you'll do," remarked the elder when their mirth had somewhat subsided. "For a dignified chief of a division you're a rare bird."

After a moment's silence, General Benson asked:

"Is Amelia come?"

"Yes, got here last night?"

"Good. It's a relief to be with a woman who can join a man in a social glass, have a cigar with him, or hold her own in winning or losing a game with no Sunday-school nonsense about her. It's hard work keeping up to it, Major; one needs a friend to help one out."

"When's the session end?"

"Next week, thank heaven."

"Sick of politics, too, old man?"

"No; but it's been nothing but wind. Words—words—words—"

"And mutual abuse," broke in the Major, laughing. "Exactly; with nothing accomplished. Can't seem to throw much dust in the eyes of these old fossils."

"The truth is, Benson, the South has a hard, rough road before her to even things up with the North; we've got to go slow until some of the old fire-eaters die out and a new generation comes in."

"It'll be slow enough, never you fear. At present we are in a Slough of Despond; heaven knows when we'll get out of it. My position in the Treasury brings the secret workings under my eye. I know."

"Slough!" retorted the Major; "call it a bog at once. And to think of the money we have lost for the Cause."

"And my exile abroad that my mix-up in the Lincoln assassination caused me. Do you know, Major, if it were known that I am my father's son, they'd hang me even now with little ceremony."

"Thank God they don't know it, my boy, and take courage."

"I'll get mine out of it by hook or by crook," replied Benson with a savage look. "The country owes me a fortune, and I'm bound to have it."

The two had reached the corner made historical by the time-honored political headquarters, Willard's Hotel. They paused before separating.

"By the by, Major, I'll get you cards for the Bowens' ball if you like. It would be a great chance for Amelia."

"If I like! Why, man, I'll be your everlasting debtor."

"Very well; consider it done."

"A thousand thanks." The friends parted.

General Benson entered the hotel, where he had apartments, and the Major wended his way to his home, a handsome house in a quiet side street.

XI

The Family of a Millionaire

Senator Zenas Bowen, newly elected senator from California, and many times a millionaire, occupied a mansion on 16th Street, N. W., in close proximity to the homes of many politicians who have made the city of Washington famous at home and abroad.

There were three persons in the Bowen family—the Honorable Zenas Bowen, his wife Estelle and his daughter Jewel. This was his second season in Washington. The first year he was in the House and his work there was so satisfactory to his constituents that the next season he was elected with a great flourish of trumpets to fill the seat in the Senate, made vacant by a retiring senator.

The Honorable Zenas was an example of the possibilities of individual expansion under the rule of popular government. Every characteristic of his was of the self-made pattern. In familiar conversation with intimate friends, it was his habit to fall into the use of ungrammatical phrases, and, in this, one might easily trace the rugged windings of a life of hardship among the great unwashed before success had crowned his labors and steered his bark into its present smooth harbor. He possessed a rare nature: one of those genial men whom the West is constantly sending out to enrich society. He had begun life as a mate on a Mississippi steamboat. When the Civil War broke out, he joined the Federal forces and at its close was mustered out as "Major Bowen." His wife dying about this time, he took his child, Jewel, and journeyed to California, invested his small savings in mining property in the Black Hills. His profits were fabulous; he counted his pile way up in the millions.

His appearance was peculiar. Middle height, lank and graceless. He had the hair and skin of an Indian, but his eyes were a shrewd and steely gray, wherein one saw the spirit of the man of the world, experienced in business and having that courage, when aroused, which is common to genial men of deadly disposition. Firm lips that suggested sternness gave greater character to his face, but his temper was known to be most mild. He dressed with scrupulous neatness, generally in black broadcloth. There was no denying his awkwardness; no amount of polish could make him otherwise. His relation to his family was most tender, his wife and daughter literally worshipping the noble soul that dwelt within its ungainly casket.

After Fortune had smiled on him, one day while stopping at the Bohemian, a favorite resort in 'Frisco, he was waited on by a young woman of great beauty. The Senator fell in love with her immediately and at the end of a week proposed marriage. Fortunate it was for him that Estelle Marks, as she was called, was an honorable woman who would not betray his confidence. She accepted his offer, vowing he should never have cause to regret his act. One might have thought from her eager acceptance that in it she found escape, liberty, hope.

"Yes," she said, "I will marry you."

He was dazed. He could not speak for one moment so choked was he with ecstasy at his own good fortune. He covered his eyes with his hand, and then he said in a hoarse voice: "I swear to make you happy. My own happiness seems more than I can believe."

Then she stooped suddenly and kissed his hand. He asked her where she would like to live.

"Anywhere you think best," was her reply.

He assured her that the North Pole, Egypt, Africa—all were one to him, with her and his little daughter. And so they were married.

He had never regretted the step. Estelle was a mother to the motherless child, and being a well-educated woman, versed in the usages of polite society, despite her recent position as a waitress in a hotel, soon had Jewel at a first-class school, where she could be fitted for the position that her father's wealth would give her. Nor did Estelle's good work end there. She recognized her husband's sterling worth in business and morals, and insisted upon his entering the arena of politics. Thanks to her cleverness, he made no mistakes and many hits which no one thought of tracing to his wife's rare talents. Not that Bowen was a fool; far from it. Mrs. Bowen simply fulfilled woman's mission in making her husband's career successful by the exercise of her own intuitive powers. His public speeches were marked by rugged good sense. His advice was sagacious. He soon had enthusiastic partisans and became at last a powerful leader in the politics of the Pacific Slope. All in all, Mrs. Bowen was a grand woman and Senator Bowen took great delight in trying to further her plans for a high social position for himself and the child.

Jewel Bowen's beauty was of the Saxon type, dazzling fair, with creamy roseate skin. Her hair was fair, with streaks of copper in it; her eyes, gray with thick short lashes, at times iridescent. Her nose superbly Grecian. Her lips beautifully firm, but rather serious than smiling.

Jewell was not unconscious of her attractions. She had been loved, flattered, worshipped for twenty years. She was proud with the pride of conscious worth that demanded homage as a tribute to her beauty—to herself.

Her tastes were luxuriously simple; she reveled in the dainty accessories of the toilet. To the outside world her dress was severely plain, but her dressmaker's bill attested to the cost of her elegant simplicity.

It was but a short time since Jewel had been transported from her quiet Canadian convent into the whirl of Washington life, a splendid house, more pretty dresses than she could number, a beautiful mother, albeit a step-mother, more indulgent than most mothers, fairly adoring the sweet and graceful girl so full of youth's alluring charm, and a father who was the noblest, tenderest and wisest of men. But she was a happy-hearted girl, full of the joy of youth and perfect health. She presented a bright image to the eye all through the fall, as she galloped over the surrounding country on her thoroughbred mare, followed by her groom and two or three dogs yapping at her heels.

There was perfect accord between her and her step-mother. Mrs. Bowen shared the Senator's worship of Jewel. From the moment the two had met and the child had held her little arms toward her, blinking her great gray eyes in the light that had awakened her from her slumbers, and had nestled her downy head in the new mother's neck with a sigh of content, almost instantly falling asleep again, with the words: "Oh, pitty, pitty lady!"

Estelle Bowen had kissed her passionately again and again, and from that time Jewel had been like her very own. The young step-mother trained the child carefully for five years, then very reluctantly sent her to the convent of the Sacred Heart at Montreal, where she had remained until she was eighteen. Then followed a year abroad, and her meeting with Cuthbert Sumner.

About this time events crowded upon each other in her young life. Her father's rise was rapid in the money world and, together with his political record, gave his family access to the wealthiest and most influential society of the country.

Cuthbert Sumner, her acknowledged lover, was an only child of New England ancestry favored by fortune like herself. His father, a wealthy manufacturer, was the owner of a business that had been in the Sumner family for many generations. His mother had died while he was yet a lad. It was a dull home. The son just leaving Harvard, had been expected to assume the responsibilities of his father's establishment, but having no taste for a commercial life, and being fitted by nature as well as education for a career in politics, his father reluctantly gave his consent that Cuthbert should have his wish after a few years spent in travel had acquainted him with the great world.

Mr. Sumner, senior, finding his son's desires still unchanged upon his return from abroad, used his influence and obtained for him a position in the Treasury as private secretary in General Benson's department. So young Sumner was duly launched upon the sea of politics. The world of fashion surged about him and he soon found himself a welcome guest in certain homes. He had little leisure for society, but sought it more after he attended Jewel Bowen's "coming-out" reception, a year previous to this chronicle. There he had seen a maiden in white, her arms laden with fragrant flowers, with beautiful fearless eyes which looked directly into the secret depths of his heart.

Sumner was twenty-six and this was not his first experience with women. He had been in love with the sex, more or less, since the day he left off knee-breeches. As he looked into Jewel's eyes he remembered some of his experiences with a pang of regret. He was no better, no worse than most young fellows. He had played some, flirted some, had even been gloriously hilarious once, for all of which his conscience now whipped him soundly. Jewel looked upon him with mingled feelings, in which curiosity was uppermost. In her world money was the potent factor; but in this man she saw the result of generations of culture and wealth combined.

One afternoon when they were calling, about the time of her "coming-out" party, a friend of Mrs. Bowen had mentioned him: "Such a fascinating man! and so handsome! Will you let me bring him? He's a man you must know, of course, and the sooner the better."

"We shall be very pleased," Mrs. Bowen replied; "any friend of yours is welcome."

"Thanks. That's settled then."

"He looks very different from the most of the men one meets in Washington," remarked Jewel, who was examining the pictured face that smiled at her from its ornate frame on the mantel.

"How?"

"Oh, I don't know. More manly, I suppose would explain it."

"Wait till you know him," returned the matron with a meaning smile.

"Cuthbert Sumner," Jewel repeated to herself. "Yes, they talk so much of him, all the women seem to have lost their hearts to him. I wonder if he will, after all, be worth the knowing."

That was the beginning. The end was in sight from the time they first met. It was a desperate case on both sides. None was surprised at the announcement of the engagement the previous winter. It was understood that the wedding would take place at Easter.

"The Bowens are in town." That meant a vast deal to the important section of Washington's world which constitutes "society," for the splendid mansion, closed since the daughter's brief introduction to society, it was rumored, would be added to the list of places where one could dance, dine and flirt. Festivities were to open with a ball—a marvel of splendor, for which five hundred invitations had been issued.

Senator Bowen was walking down the avenue the next afternoon, on his way home, when he was joined by General Benson, who had developed lately a passion for his society. The two men frequented the same clubs and transacted much official business together, but there had been nothing approaching intimacy between them. If the shrewd Westerner had given expression to his secret thoughts they would have run somewhat in the following vein:

"Got a hang-dog look about that off eye which tells me he's a tarnation mean cuss on occasion. He's all good looks and soft sawder. However, that don't worry me any; it's none o' my funeral."

After the two men had exchanged the usual civilities, the latest political question looming up on the horizon was discussed; finally, the conversation turned upon the coming ball.

"By the by, Senator, I wish I dared ask for cards for a friend of mine and his daughter. They have just arrived in town for the season, and know no one. He, the father, is the newly-appointed president of the Arrow-Head mines; the daughter is lovely; a fine foil for Miss Jewel. Unexceptional people, and all that."

"Certainly, General," the Senator hastened to reply, "What address?"

With profuse thanks, General Benson handed him a card, on which appeared the name:

HENRY C. MADISON.
Corcoran Building. Washington, D.C.

"I will speak to Mrs. Bowen right away."

Mrs. Bowen and Jewel were enjoying a leisure hour before dinner, in lounging chairs before the blazing grate-fire in the former's sitting-room. There was a little purr of gratification from both women as they heard a well-known step in the hall.

"Well, here you both are," was Senator Bowen's greeting as he kissed his wife and daughter and flung himself wearily into a chair.

"Tired?" asked his wife.

"Yes, some of these dumb-headed aristocrats are worse to steer into a good paying bit of business for the benefit of the government treasury, than a bucking bronco."

"How late you are, papa," here broke in Jewel from her perch on her father's knee, where she was diligently searching his pockets. It had been her custom from babyhood, and never yet had her search been unrewarded.

"I'd have been here earlier only I met General Benson and he always has so many questions to ask, especially about my little lass, that he kept me no end of time."

"Don't be wicked, papa," smiled Jewel, "because you spoil me; you think everyone must see with your eyes."

"Ah! pet; it's just wonderful how well all the old and young single fellows know me since you have grown up. But we won't listen to 'em just yet, Blossom; not even Sumner shall part us for a good bit; your pa just can't lose you for a good spell, I reckon."

"No man shall part us, dad; if he takes me, he must take the whole family," replied Jewel with a loving pat on the sallow cheek.

"We'll see, we'll see. There's another bid for an invite to your shin-dig," he continued, with a laugh, as he tossed the card given him by General Benson into his wife's lap. "It's mighty pleasant to be made much of; it's worth while getting rich just to see how money can change the complexion of things, and how cordial the whole world can be to one man if he's got the spondulix."

"My dear Zenas," said Mrs. Bowen, with a shake of her head and a comical smile on her face, "don't talk the vernacular of the gold mines here in Washington. You'll be eternally disgraced."

"Well, Mrs. Senator, I've fit the enemy, tackled grizzlies, starved, been locked up in the pens of Libby Prison, and I've come out first best every time, but this thing you call society beats me. The women make me dizzy, the men make me sick, and a mighty little of it makes me ready to quit, fairly squashed. Them's my sentiments."

A cry of delight broke from Jewel,—"O dad!" as she brought to view a package in a white paper. Mrs. Bowen left her seat to join in the frolic that ensued to gain possession of it. At last the mysterious bundle was unwrapped, the box opened and a pearl necklace brought to view of wonderful beauty and value. The senator's eyes were full of the glint and glister of love and pride as he watched the faces of his wife and daughter. After a moment he brought out another package, which he gave to his wife.

"There, Mrs. Senator, there's your diamond star you've been pining after for a month. I ordered them quite a while ago; happened to be passing Smith's and stopped in, found 'em ready and here they be. What women see in such gewgaws is a puzzler to me. I can tolerate such hankering in a young 'un, but being you're not a chicken, Mrs. Senator, and not in the market, and still good looking enough to make any man restless with no ornaments but a clean calico frock, your fancies are a conundrum to yours truly. But these women folks must be humored, I suppose."

With this the Senator plunged into his dressing-room, which adjoined his wife's sitting-room, and began the work of dressing for dinner and the theatre.

"Cuthbert coming?" he called to his daughter, who still lingered.

"Yes, papa."

"Jewel, dear, have Venus be particular with your toilet tonight; I will overlook you when she has finished."

"That the name of your new maid, Blossom?" the Senator's voice demanded. There were many grunts, groans and growls issuing from the privacy where his evening toilet was progressing because of refractory collar buttons and other unruly accessories.

"Yes, papa."

"Hump! Name enough to hang her: Venus, the goddess of love and beauty! Can she earn her salt?"

He appeared at the door now struggling into an evening vest. He employed no man, declaring that no valley de chamber should boss him around. He'd always been free and didn't propose to end his days in slavery to any slick-pated fashion-plate who didn't know the color of gold from the inside of a brass kettle.

"I don't know what I would do without her. I have been intending to speak to you for some time concerning her brother. He is a genius, and Venus has given up her hopes of becoming a school teacher among her people to earn money to help develop his talents. Can't we do something for them, papa? I have said nothing to her yet."

"Hump! You're always picking up lame animals, Blossom; from a little shaver it's been the same. If you keep it up in Washington, you'll have all the black beggars in the city ringing the area bell. However, I'll look the matter up. If the girl ain't too proud to go out as a servant to help herself along, there may be something in her."

XII

Who is She?

At eight that evening—Theatre was filled to overflowing, for Modjeska was to interpret the heart-breaking story of "Camille." Senator Bowen and his handsome wife; Jewel and Cuthbert Sumner occupied a box, and were watching intently the mimic portrayal of life. Jewel was listening earnestly to Modjeska's words; the grand rendering of the life story of a passionate, loving, erring, noble woman's heart touched her deeply. The high-bred grace, the dainty foreign accent, the naturalness of the actress, held her in thrall and she did not take her eyes from the stage. As the curtain went down on the second act she lifted her glass and slowly scanned the house. Suddenly she paused with a heart that throbbed strangely. Directly across from her sat a woman—young in years, but with a mature air of a woman of the world. "Surely," thought Jewel, "I know that face." The girl had a woman's voluptuous beauty with great dusky eyes and wonderful red-gold hair. Her dress of moss-green satin and gold fell away from snowy neck and arms on which diamonds gleamed. Just then Sumner uttered an exclamation of surprise. He had turned, almost at the same moment with Jewel, and swept a careless glance over the house, bowing to several, mostly well-known people either by profession or social standing, but had declined to see more than one fair one's invitation. Passing, as it were, a box on the left, his glance had rested on a face that instantly arrested it and caused him to exclaim. An elderly man sat with the vision of loveliness. In repose the girl's face lost some of its beauty and seemed care-worn; one felt impressed that girlhood's innocence had not remained untouched.

The lady was watching their box intently, and seeing herself discovered smiled a brilliant smile of recognition as she inclined her head in Sumner's direction holding his glance for one instant in a way that seemed to call him to her side. He bowed, then turned his head away with a feeling of confusion that annoyed him. He did not offer to go to her, however.

"Do you know her? Who is she, Cuthbert?" asked Jewel, intercepting both smile and bow.

"It is Miss Madison," he replied, lifting his glass nonchalantly. "I did not know she was in Washington. I have not seen her for three years. Looking remarkably well, is she not?"

"She is glorious! Her face somehow seems familiar to me. I must have met her. Have you seen much of her?"

"Can't say that I have. Met her at a ball at Cape May. But I found the place so dull I packed up and went home. After that I went abroad. Then I met a sweet little woman who has led me captive at her chariot wheels ever since."

Then followed some talk dear to the souls of lovers and the beauty opposite was forgotten. But throughout the next act Jewel felt her heart contract as the dusky eyes followed her movements with a restless, smouldering fire in their depths that pained her to see.

Amelia Madison watched the box opposite with hungry intensity. She was studying Jewel's face mentally saying: "There is not another woman in the house like her. She is like a strain of Mozart, a spray of lilies. My God! how he looks at her—he never looked at me like that! He respects her; he worships her—"

She sank back in breathless misery.

Aurelia Madison and Cuthbert Sumner had met one summer at Cape May. They had loved and been betrothed; had quarreled fiercely over a flirtation on her part and had separated in bitterness and pain; and yet the man was relieved way down in a corner of his heart for he had felt dimly, after the first rapture was over, that he was making a mistake, that she was not the woman to command the respect of his friends nor to bring him complete happiness. Yet after a fashion she fascinated him. Her grace, her beauty, thrilled his blood with rapture that he thought then was Love. Love came to him a later guest, and the purity and tenderness of Jewel's sweet face blotted out forever the summer splendor of Aurelia Madison's presence. Now it was all over; he knew he had never loved her, and that he was fortunate to have found it out in time.

No one knew of this episode in Aurelia Madison's life. Her father had been away on one of his periodical tours, and the girl was accountable to none but an old governess who acted as chaperone.

Since that time she had led a reckless life. Had lived at Monte Carlo two seasons, aiding her father in his games of chance, luring the gilded youth to lose their money without murmuring. Hers had been a precarious life and a dangerous one. Sometimes they were reduced to expedients. But through it all the girl held her peace, set her teeth hard, and waited for the day when she should again meet Cuthbert Sumner, trusting to the effect of her great beauty, and the fact that he had once loved her passionately, to re-establish her power over the man she worshipped. Once his wife, she told herself, she would shake off all her hideous past and become an honest matron. Honesty she viewed as a luxury for the wealthy to enjoy. Thank heaven, Cuthbert Sumner's wife could afford to be honest. They had met again, but how? All her hopes were dust.

New she saw Jewel lifted her eyes to his with devotion, love and faith in them; she saw him look down eagerly, with truest, tenderest love. The last act was on. She could bear it no longer, but rose impatiently, with rage and hatred in her heart, and attended by her father, left the house. When next Jewel stole a glance in the direction of the stranger her place was empty.

XIII

A Plot for Ten Millions

It was near nine o'clock the next morning and General Benson was still invisible. His colored valet was moving about noiselessly, making ready for his master. Breakfast was on the table in its silver covers. A bell rang; Isaac disappeared.

General Benson's renown as a great social leader rested, not only on his lavish expenditure and luxurious style of living at Willard's Hotel, where he monopolized one of the most expensive suites, but upon his mental and physical attributes as well. The ladies all voted him a charming fellow. He had a remarkably sweet and caressing voice, which added to his attractions. The many women to whom he had vowed eternal fidelity at one moment, only to abandon heartlessly the next at the rise of a new star in the firmament of beauty, sighed and wept at his defection and voted him the most perfect lover imaginable. It was hinted that one girl had committed suicide solely on his account. But still the ladies believed in his professions.

The members of the various clubs that he affected acknowledged him to be an admirable card-player, a good horseman, an expert with sword or revolver, as well as an unusually agreeable companion in a search after pleasure; generous, too, with his money. But with all his popularity and increase of fame, his fortune declined, and he found himself at the present time embarrassed for money, his capital growing smaller each month in spite of a large salary. Debts of honor must be met, and to keep a good name one's opponent must sometimes win. Then, too, he was growing old; he carried his years well, but fifty was looming perilously near.

He and his friend Major Henry Clay Madison, President of the Arrow-Head Mining Company of Colorado, newly established in the city, had a mutual interest in the great scheme that was to make the fortunes of the different shareholders, but even the generous payments he received as his share of the profits made out of verdant men of means who became easy prey because of General Benson's sweet persuasive voice and exalted position in the political world, failed to assist him out of his financial dilemma. Within a month a new scheme had entered his mind,—one that dazzled him the possibilities were so great, a scheme which if successfully handled would put millions in the pockets of a trio of unscrupulous adventurers,—Major Madison and his daughter and himself.

As the clock chimed nine, General Benson entered the room and seated himself at the breakfast table. A moment later his valet informed him that Major and Miss Madison wished to see him.

"Very well; show them in, at once."

Presently the valet ushered them in. The major we have mentioned before; he was short, stout, more than fifty, with gray hair and ferret-like eyes, close-set, and a greenish-gray of peculiar ugliness; a close observer would take exception to them immediately. He was scrupulously attired in the height of fashion. He was accompanied by the strange beauty who had attended the theatre the night before.

"Well, General, you sent for us and here we are. How are you?" was the major's greeting as he shook hands with General Benson and then flung himself into an arm-chair.

"Very well, indeed, thanks, Madison. What, is it indeed you, Aurelia?" he exclaimed on beholding the girl. "How delightful to have you with us once again!"

The lady inclined her head slightly in answer to her host's warm greeting, ignored his offered hand, and subsided onto a chair with a preoccupied air, a slight frown puckering her forehead.

"Don't mind Aurelia, General; she's mooning as usual," laughed her father.

"You are looking very fit, Major," remarked Benson, recovering from the confusion caused by Aurelia's coolness. "Have a B. and S.?"

"Don't care if I do."

Benson poured a brandy-and-soda for his guest and another for himself; passed the cigars to him and the cigarettes to Miss Madison. She took one, lit it, and drew away in a manner that showed her keen enjoyment. A smile passed over Benson's face as he covertly watched her.

"Well, Madison," the General said, after a few moments' enjoyment of the weed, "I sent for you to come here this morning on a matter of business, because I shall not be able to call on you at any time today, for I may have to go out of town at any moment on some confounded office business. It's a nuisance, I say. The office interferes too much with a man's pleasure. If my plans succeed I'll cut the whole thing."

"Indeed! I imagine we are mutually interested when you speak of 'business.' You're not ruined I take it. Do you want to borrow money of me?" said the Major with a laugh as he drew his chair a trifle closer to his friend. The lady evinced no interest in the conversation.

"On the contrary, I wish to offer you a chance to make some."

"You are extremely kind, Benson; you could not have chosen a more opportune time for your offer. Will you believe it—I was compelled to part with a diamond pin this morning," replied Madison, touching his polished shirt-front. "But what can I do for you?"

"Since we joined forces, Madison, on the strictly respectable basis, we have gained fame and influence, and but little money. It takes money to maintain our position, and plenty of it. This you know. I have studied the situation and am convinced that our only surety for providing for the future lies in a coup that shall net us millions, on which we may retire."

"Yes, but how to get it," replied Madison with a mournful shake of the head. "Work is not in our line, unsafe expedients are dangerous and not to be thought of. I do not fancy running my head into a noose. One can't do much but go straight here, and money's a scarce article."

"Be patient. You need have no apprehension that I shall suggest anything dangerous, Madison; though the time was when you were the risky one and I the one to hesitate," with a significant uplifting of the eyebrows.

"True; but time has changed my ideas. I have a hankering for respectability that amounts to a passion."

"Remain as respectable as you wish, my friend; I have a legitimate scheme that will make us masters of ten millions! No risk; nothing necessary but judicious diplomacy."

Miss Madison had evinced no interest until now, but at the words "ten millions" uttered by this man whom she knew to be practical, astute in business and no dreamer, she seemed to awaken from her lethargy. She retained her self-possession, however, and maintained her unruffled calm, remarking carelessly, even sarcastically: "May I ask the nature of the plan, General, and where my usefulness comes in?"

"I was about to explain that point, my dear; but first permit me to ask a question,—has the idea of acquiring a fortune by a wealthy marriage ever occurred to you?"

"Yes, I admit it has. But you know too well my reasons for hesitating in such a course."

Benson moved uneasily in his seat, and for a moment his eyes dropped under the steady gaze that the girl bent upon him—eyes large, dreamy, melting, dazzling the senses, but at this moment baleful. A dull flush mounted to his brow.

"See here, Aurelia, have you tried to find an opportunity?"

"Possibly," she answered coldly.

"And you met with no success?"

"Evidently not, as I am single."

"Then your efforts were misdirected."

"Do you think so?" mockingly.

"Most assuredly I do. Your attention was bestowed upon men for whom you had conceived a real liking. That is not the way to bring success in such a venture."

"It is the wrong lead for a woman like me,—an adventuress, to forget her position for one instant and allow her heart to guide her head. What fool wrote 'Poverty is no crime?' I know of none greater. It is responsible for every crime committed under the sun. It is a foul curse!"

"Why, Aurelia, girl, what has come to you this morning? You talk like a man with the blue devils after losing all night at poker," said her father.

Her answer was a shrug of her handsome shoulders as she resumed her listless attitude.

"Listen to me; I will unfold a scheme that shall remove the curse of poverty, and give you for a husband a man who will fill the bill, heart and all."

He rose, approached the mantel, and turning his back upon it, rested both elbows on the marble—a position which brought him face to face with his guests, and asked: "Are you acquainted with Cuthbert Sumner?"

"Know him by sight and reputation. Clerk in your department," replied Madison. Aurelia did not speak, but a flush came into her face, a light to her eyes. One might have felt the thrill that passed over her form.

"What do you think of him?"

"He's all right; a genial fellow, but careful not to go too far; handsome, too, by Jove. No money, though?"

"O yes," nodded Benson. "Only in the department for experience in political life. His father's very wealthy. New England manufacturer."

"Indeed!"

"He's the one I've picked for our lady here."

"But he's engaged," broke in Aurelia.

"Exactly. And that brings me to the rest of the scheme. Sumner is about to marry Bowen's daughter. By the way, Aurelia, you got the cards for the ball, did you not?" Aurelia bowed in assent.

"Jewel Bowen is the Senator's only child, and his heiress. She will receive ten millions upon her wedding day. What I propose is that Aurelia fascinate the gentleman, thus leaving the field clear for me. I have taken a decided fancy to Miss Bowen and her fortune. If I succeed there is a million for you, Madison, and another for Aurelia. Sumner, too, has pots of money, and we shall all be able to settle down into quiet respectability. What do you think of my plan?"

"By Jove, Benson," blurted out Major Madison, fairly thunder-struck at the magnificence of the vista opened before him, "what a splendid idea! How admirably you have planned things!" Benson nodded and smiled:

"All remains with Aurelia, and certainly with her magnificent beauty to help us, we need fear no failure."

"Spare me your compliments. This is probably your last chance, General. So you think I can win this Mr. Sumner from his betrothed?" she said.

"Precisely."

"That is a droll idea. Do you think—"

"I think, I repeat, that you can easily make the person referred to sufficiently in love with you to do anything you ask."

"Suppose he proves obdurate? What then? You cannot judge all men alike."

"Break the engagement, if you can do nothing more. During a fit of insanity, if it lasts but a week, an hour even, you will have ample time to accomplish my desires."

"And then?"

"I will look after mademoiselle. It will make no difference to you. Your compensation will be my affair. It is only his money that you would want."

"Oh, I see!" There was a world of sarcasm in the three words uttered by a smiling mouth. "My dear General, you are indeed a marvel! No one knows better than you how to make love to a young girl."

"You are the cleverest woman I know, Aurelia. I knew you would comprehend the situation perfectly." After a moment's reflection the girl replied: "Yes, I think I'll try it. It will probably be announced before long that the marriage is broken off. I will earn my million, never fear. I shall, doubtless, find it an agreeable task."

"And a husband, too, my girl," added her father.

"Perhaps."

"Are we to be intimate friends or simply business acquaintances?" asked the Major of General Benson.

"Business friends will be best. Let us have no appearance of collusion."

"When shall we see you again?" asked the Major as they rose to go.

"Just as soon as you have something to tell me. How fortunate that Aurelia has never been introduced to Washington society. She will take the place by storm."

Then the friends separated.

XIV

Playing with Fire

About lunch time that same morning, as Sumner was leaving the office, a note was brought to him by a servant in plain livery:

> "May we not be friends for the sake of the old days, when no other woman was dearer than I? Come to me just once."
>
> Aurelia
> New York Avenue

Sumner's brow was knit as he scanned the sheet of ivory paper in his hand, with its emblazoned monogram. He muttered an imprecation. Elise Bradford, the stenographer, glanced up from her work in surprise. Sumner was a gentleman in the office and a great favorite with all the employees; it was rare to hear an uncouth expression from the lips of this man, who honored all womanhood.

"I thought that was all over and done with," he muttered to himself. "What is the use of going through with it all again? Well, I suppose I must go once for decency's sake, but I'll take care to make short work of it. There shall be no misunderstanding."

Then softer thoughts came to him as he took from a pile of commonplace, business letters on his desk, a slim satiny envelope. It was from Jewel. He opened it and read the few lines it contained, reminding him of an appointment that he had with her for the evening.

"My little Blossom!" he said gently.

But his little Blossom did not keep him from going to see Aurelia Madison. She was less than nothing to him. He had never met her from the day he left Cape May until the night before. He never even thought of her. Yet he went to call upon her. Reluctantly and distastefully—but he went.

He was ushered into the drawing-room scented and flower-filled. A moment later Aurelia came into the room from the library. Ah, she stirred even his cold heart.

A white negligé clothed her from throat to foot, and her wonderful hair was caught in a mass low down on her neck. A deep light was in the dusky eyes that bewildered a man and weakened his energies. In an instant she came swiftly to him—the white arms were about his throat, the warm lips against his.

"My love! my love!" she murmured softly, and Cuthbert Sumner (blind and foolish) was not the kind of man to let the memory of little Blossom prevent him from holding a beautiful, yielding form closely clasped in his arms, and returning clinging kisses with interest when such a rare opportunity offered.

I question if there are many men that would.

She was playing a part in a desperate game that meant everything to her. This was her first move toward the end she had vowed to accomplish. She would be victorious; she swore it. Her rôle was not a hard one for she worshipped this man so cold and unyielding to her arts. She would have preferred the lilies of virtuous winning; debarred from that she would take the torments of a love to which she had no right. By-and-by, she said:

"Bert, do you love her very much?"

He bowed with a long look in her face.

"And Not as you loved Me!" she said passionately. "Tell me about her."

"My dear Aurelia, can a man sing the praises of one beautiful woman to another?"

"Tell me about her," she said again with the imperious gesture that Sumner remembered so well in that summer at the Cape. "I have not loved you for two long years, Bert Sumner, without learning every phase of your mind. When do you marry her?"

"At Easter," he replied proudly, disdaining further subterfuge.

"And you can sit there calmly and tell it to me—to me—," she bit her lip a moment; there was less time than she had thought.

"She is very wealthy?"

"Yes, as the world counts it, but I care not for that; if she had nothing it would be the same to me."

"I believe you. And I could see her beauty for myself; and she is good, not like me."

"She is an angel, my white angel of purity," he replied with a look of reverence on his face.

Aurelia was a gorgeous tropical flower; Jewel, a fair fragrant lily. Men have such an unfortunate weakness for tropical blooms, they cannot pass them by carelessly, even though a lily lies above their hearts.

PAULINE E. HOPKINS

Cuthbert could not ignore this splendid tropical flower; it caused his blood to flow faster, it gave new zest to living—for an hour. Jewel was his saint, his good angel; and he loved her truly with all the high love a man of the world can ever know. He trusted her for her womanly goodness and truth. And Jewel returned his love with an intensity that was her very life.

Aurelia looked at him and sighed heavily.

"May I know her?"

"I am sure, I cannot say. You may possibly meet her at some party."

"Then you do not object absolutely. I am glad, for we have invitations to Mrs. Bowen's ball. I want to go."

She looked at him keenly. "I think I have met Miss Bowen before. If I mistake not, we were at the Montreal convent at the same time. I am older than she, and left just after she entered. I remember her as a sweet cherub who resembled a pictured saint."

"Quite a coincidence," he replied with all his usual courtliness for womankind; but for all that he mentally anathematized the idiot who had sent the cards and the convent where the girls had met. He was vexed, and she felt it.

"Yes, I shall go—"

She caught her breath sharply and then fell at his feet in all her exquisite beauty.

"Can you never, NEVER love me again, Bert? My life, my soul is yours! Can you not give me a little love in return?"

He lifted her up gently.

"It is too late to ask that now, Aurelia. Try and forget that you have ever loved me. Believe me, you will be happier. No one can more bitterly regret than I the misery of our past. Let us begin anew."

She thrust him from her wildly, and bade him go if he did not wish to see her fall dead at his feet.

Cuthbert went away sadly.

He knew the full power of Aurelia Madison's siren charms. Nor was her emotion all feigned. She really felt all she had expressed. What was pride compared to the desolation that swept over her when she realized that his heart was hers no longer? Her great love obliterated even the thought of his wealth. She felt she should triumph, in spite of the coldness with which he had received her professions of love. Yes, she would be his wife, even thought it were a barren honor, since his heart was not hers.

"If his love is not for me, it shall be for no one else," she told herself, as she thought over her afternoon's work and prepared for the next move in the drama.

And so Cuthbert Sumner went back to his little Blossom, whose calm, pure face was continually before him.

XV

Renewing Old Acquaintance

The following afternoon Major Madison's carriage rolled up to the Bowen mansion on Sixteenth Street, and stopped. From it Aurelia stepped, clad richly and daintily in a becoming calling costume. She had determined to storm the citadel, as it were, and carry it by assault.

She rang the bell and asked the footman if Miss Bowen was at home.

"Yes, Miss—. What name please?"

She gave the man a card on which she had written, "Known to you as Aurelia Walker," and was shown into a morning-room to wait, Would Jewel recognize her, she wondered. Would she be pleased to meet her again?

Presently she heard the gentle frou-frou of silken skirts down the broad stairway and the next instant Jewel Bowen stood before her, holding out her hand in frankly-glad recognition—Jewel in a tea-gown that was a poem, a combination of palest rose-satin and cream lace. Surprise and pleasure mingled in her speaking face.

"The card said, 'Aurelia Walker.' Can it be possible that you are the same Aurelia whom I knew in Montreal? How delightful to meet you again."

Her greeting was most cordial, and put Aurelia instantly at her ease. After a time spent in recalling reminiscences of school life, and pleasant girlish chatter, Aurelia said:

"I must explain the change in name,—papa was embarrassed financially, and he placed me at school, calling himself Walker while he earned the money to satisfy his creditors; that saved him much annoyance, and as soon as he could satisfy their demands, we resumed our rightful name."

"Pray do not speak of it, Aurelia; such things are annoying, but cannot always be helped," replied Jewel with a smile. "Won't you come to the drawing-room and meet mamma?"

How beautiful everything was, thought the girl, as she passed up the broad marble stairs with velvet carpet in the centre, on which the foot fell noiselessly, and statues and flowers in niches and on landings, while the walls were hung with lovely frescoes that impelled one to pause and admire.

The drawing-room door was flung open, and they were in a spacious apartment with painted ceiling, and all things rich and harmonious in tone. In a moment she was standing before Mrs. Bowen, who greeted her warmly, as if truly glad to meet her daughter's school friend. No lovelier vision was ever seen than these two girls as they entered the Bowen drawing-room. Mrs. Bowen was a cultured lady and their grace and beauty gratified her taste.

She conversed freely and pleasantly with the unexpected guest, although after the first feeling of wonder and satisfaction at so much loveliness, she was surprised and puzzled at the vague feeling of distrust and dislike that personal contact with her young guest brought to her. It was intangible. She shook it off, however, the beautiful face and voice were so enchanting that she could not resist them, and felt ashamed of her distrust.

"Come and sit down by the fire and let us have a long chat before anyone else comes in. We never know how long we may be alone," said Jewel, indicating a seat near her own.

"This is very cosy and homelike," remarked Aurelia as she took the seat offered. "I have been so lonely since I came to the city."

"Poor child," remarked Mrs. Bowen in a sympathetic voice, "are you very much alone? How long since you lost your mother?"

"I cannot recall her at all, dear Mrs. Bowen," the girl answered, lifting a pair of dusky eyes, swimming in tears, for a moment to her face. "Papa is so intent on the fortunes of the mine, just at present, that he gives me very little attention. Indeed, I believe he forgets at times that he has a daughter," this last with a little sigh of martyrdom.

Mrs. Bowen melted more and more to her guest.

"Then stay and dine with us. Let me send away your carriage." She rang the bell and gave the order to the servant. "We have a few jolly people coming—not a dinner-party, you know, but just a few friends."

"I shall be delighted. How kind you are," replied Aurelia, feeling dizzy over her good luck.

"Thanks," said Jewel, pressing her hand. "Here comes tea, and with it papa."

Senator Bowen welcomed his guest with his usual Western heartiness.

"By Jove," he thought to himself, "she's a stunner! But my little girl doesn't lose a thing by contrast. What a sight for sore eyes the pair of them makes!"

Then he remarked aloud to the guest: "I know your father, my dear; I shall try and see more of him after this. My daughter's friends are my friends."

There were, beside Aurelia, four people to whom Mrs. Bowen introduced her. Two of them, the Secretary of the Treasury and his wife—she knew by sight, but Mr. Carroll West and a pretty widow, Mrs. Brewer, were total strangers. Lord Browning, the English Ambassador, and Lady Browning were shortly announced, and quickly following them came Cuthbert Sumner, completing the party.

"This is my dear friend, Aurelia Madison, Cuthbert; we were at school together. You remember that I told you at the theatre her face seemed very familiar to me."

"Delighted to meet you again, Miss Madison," he said as he bowed over her hand, suppressing a start of amazement at the sight of her. To himself he added:

"Confound the woman; what does she mean? Is she following me up? That won't help her any."

Aurelia thoroughly ingratiated herself with Lady Browning, paying her the greatest deference. Finding her ladyship much interested in religious topics and charitable projects, she affected an enthusiastic interest in them, and was rewarded by overhearing Lady Browning express herself as delighted with Miss Madison.

"Such a beautiful girl, and so intelligent to talk with."

She went down to dinner with Mr. West, who seemed much impressed with his lovely partner.

Cuthbert's attention would wander to the couple opposite him at table. West was talking to her with animation, while Aurelia smiled and sparkled, and looked irresistibly bewitching. West had but a small income for a wealthy man, and had always been incorrigible until now, but he seemed to have surrendered at last. Cuthbert watched her covertly, not at all deceived by the gaiety of her manner.

"So, the moth is still fluttering about the flame. Let her beware; I would sacrifice her without a moment's hesitation if I thought she meant Jewel harm."

He showed nothing of this outwardly, being as calm, smiling and well-bred as ever. But he was seriously annoyed by the inscrutable conduct of the woman opposite him. It was a vague feeling that he could not grasp—a shadow no larger than a man's hand.

Dinner over, the gentlemen did not linger long behind the ladies. Back in the drawing-room once more, Mrs. Bowen whispered to her husband:

"Do ask Miss Madison to play, Zenas."

"I will when I get a chance. West seems to have such a lot to say to her that it would be cruel to spoil sport."

Mrs. Bowen looked and laughed:

"I'll ask her myself then. Miss Madison, I am sure you are musical," she said to the girl, with a smile. "Will you not favor us?"

Aurelia signified her willingness and Mr. West, a minute later, had installed her at the piano, and stood by listening with delight to her playing. And she was worth listening to for she was a cultured amateur of no mean ability, and gave genuine pleasure by her performance. Mr. West was more and more infatuated each moment he spent in her society. Mrs. Bowen thanked her warmly as she rose from the instrument, followed by the plaudits of the company.

"Miss Madison," said the pretty widow, "you play beautifully."

"Do I?" gueried Aurelia, laughing, "but then I cannot sing, Jewel can, though—divinely, I hear."

"Flatterer!" said Jewel as she passed Aurelia's seat on her way to the piano, attended by Sumner.

"What is it to be?" he asked her as he turned over the contents of a folio.

"Will you choose, Cuthbert?"

A jealous pang shot through Aurelia's heart, as her ear caught the words, but she set her teeth hard.

Sumner took from the folio "Some Day," by Wellington.

"Always a favorite of mine, you know," he said.

She gave him a quick, trustful look, and smiled as she began the accompaniment.

Conversation was hushed; everyone listened while the rich, pure voice filled the room, giving the old song with the dramatic fire of a professional. There was a buzz of admiration when Jewel had finished. Cuthbert bent over with pride and delight shining in his face, and his softly-spoken "Thanks sweetheart," was heard distinctly by the woman sorely tried by jealous pain.

"Don't leave the piano; sing something else," came from all parts of the room.

PAULINE E. HOPKINS

"Very well," she said, and then gave with delicious pathos that sweet old song, "Dreaming Eyes."

The listeners were charmed. The singer rose, crossed the room and seated herself beside Aurelia. Their renewed acquaintance seemed destined to ripen into a close intimacy.

"Aurelia," the girl said as they sat there somewhat apart from the others, "Will you come with us to the—Theatre tomorrow night—we have a box?"

Surnames were dropped from that night. How did it happen? Circe alone knew. But after that these two were much together.

"Such a lovely morning, Jewel! You must come for a turn with me." or, "I shall be alone all day; do come and make the hours bright for me."

Sumner's first undefined fears gradually subsided. Time, rolling on springs of pleasure, passed swiftly bringing the night of the ball.

XVI

The Ball

The Bowen mansion was ablaze with light. Servants in livery hurried about attending the arrival of guests. Outside the house a continuous stream of carriages deposited the fortunate ones bidden to the feast.

The ball-room was a vast apartment arched, with a gallery of carved oak, in which the orchestra was seated. The rooms were filling fast, yet at no time, even when the crowd was densest, was there a pressure for room. Flowers wreathed the gallery, the national colors hung in the angles, banks of roses were everywhere. Mrs. Bowen, in white velvet, old lace and diamonds, stood near the entrance, supported by her husband, her daughter and Cuthbert Sumner. The house party was enforced by several gentlemen of political importance and their wives.

> *"Inglass of satin,*
> *And shimmer of pearls."*

Jewel Bowen stood, a flush on her cheeks, her hair falling in waving masses, pearls clasping her white throat and arms, her large gray eyes like wells of light. An only child and heiress of many millions, she would have been the bright star of fortune to the gilded youth of Washington had not Cuthbert Sumner stood first in the field; albeit, a man might be pardoned for losing his head had she possessed only her youth and beauty.

A band hidden away in the great mansion discoursed Rossini's dreamy music in a concert during the arrival of guests. Fashionable Washington greeted its world and congratulated itself on being there, discussed the host and hostess, admired the arrangements for dancing just as the dear five hundred always have done and always will do. It was evident that the Bowen ball was to be the hit of the season. The Senator was voted charmingly original, and his wife attracted as much comment and attention as the debutantes who graced the occasion.

"I hear that we are to have a new beauty introduced tonight. A girl

　　　　　　　　　　　　　　　PAULINE E. HOPKINS

who is fairly startling," remarked one man to another. The rumor was started by Mrs. Bowen saying to a number of dancing men, with a roguish smile:

"Don't fill up all your dances, for there is another beauty coming. Nobody you know, either. A stranger in the city."

"We have heard something of her charms through West, I think, Madam Bowen. You mean Miss Madison. West is fairly a drivelling idiot over her at present. I'm worried over the poor chappie."

"Tiresome man, why couldn't he allow me the pleasure of trapping society. Have either of you met her?"

"Alas, for your intended surprise, dear Mrs. Bowen, I have seen her on the boulevard once or twice," replied the one who had not yet spoken. "What a perfect pair Miss Jewel and she will make, and puzzle anyone to award the palm."

"Mrs. Bowen is certainly a charming hostess," remarked one to the other as they walked away, displaced by fresh relays of guests.

"She is really a beautiful woman, but too cold to please me," was the reply.

"She has a throat and shoulders of alabaster, a superb head and a flower-like face."

"Hear, hear! Wasting compliments on a passé elderly matron—it isn't like you, Rollins."

"A pretty woman is never passé; you fellows who are new in society have something to learn, let me tell you."

"Granted. But we don't waste ammunition on elderly females who have had their day."

"Has a woman, once a beauty, ever had her day?"

"What a queer fellow you are tonight, making flowery speeches about old folks."

"There is no denying the truth of what I said, though. It is human nature. With a woman it is her good looks—with a man his strength, which at no age will he ever admit to be materially lessened any more than a woman will allow her good looks quite gone into the past, or if they do admit a decay of their charms or strength there is still a feeling of pride in what they were once."

"Here endeth the first lesson," laughed his companion as they separated to find partners for the opening number.

Other men, older than the two recorded, remarked the nobleness and charm of the hostess.

"There is a story written on her face, if I mistake not; I would give much for the power to read it," said a famous student of psychology to a celebrated physician, as they stood together surveying the brilliant scene.

"Granted she is beautiful, but she looks a creature of snow and ice. The daughter is more to my liking."

"Yes, but you must confess that they are alike."

"Alike, yet unlike; in the daughter there is fire and life, and a little diablerie, if I mistake not."

"Ah! but the beautiful Mrs. Bowen is only step-mother to the lovely Jewel."

"Is it possible? I should have thought them of one blood. Who was madam before her marriage?"

"No one knows," was the reply, accompanied by a suggestive shrug of the shoulders. "We do not inquire too closely into one's antecedents in Washington, you know; be beautiful and rich and you will be happy here."

Meantime the room was filling fast. Directly the butler announced "General Benson," Senator Bowen moved forward a pace and shook him warmly by the hand and then presented him to his wife and daughter. A puzzled look swept over his face as he bent for an instant above Mrs. Bowen's hand. Then he stole a furtive glance at her white impassive countenance, started slightly—looked again with a quick indrawn breath. There was now a questioning look in her eyes of seeming surprise at the evident interest—a quick contraction of the straight brows, the next second the dark eyes drooped, but he felt conscious that under those long lashes they still watched him. It passed in a second of time, there was no change in the beautiful cold face of the elegant woman of the world save that one might have imagined that she grew whiter, if possible. Then he recovered himself and turned with easy self-complacency to Jewel:

"Am I too late for the first dance?" he asked in his most courtly style.

"The first is gone certainly," smiled Jewel.

"Well, never mind; the first waltz, then."

"So sorry, General, but it is promised," with an arch glance at Sumner, who was standing back of her.

"Oh! I see. You unprincipled fellow, to steal the march on the world of us who are in darkness. We must all give first place to your claim,

PAULINE E. HOPKINS

Sumner, lucky boy," he said with a genial laugh. "The fourth then? I shan't get another chance, so I must secure my luck while I can."

"With pleasure."

"And the one right after supper, dare I ask?"

"Very well," she replied again, smiling at his persistency.

The General took her card and inscribed his name against two members, and as the opening bars of the first dance sounded, and her partner came to claim her, bowed and moved away.

There was a movement near the door, and "Major Madison and Miss Madison" were announced. There was a moment's hush as they entered the ball-room, and every man present mentally uttered an exclamation of surprise and admiration. For once rumor had not lied. This woman was quite the loveliest thing they had ever seen, startling and somewhat bizarre, perhaps, but still marvellously, undeniably lovely. Her gown was a splendid creation of scarlet and gold. It was a magnificent and daring combination. Her hair was piled high and crowned with diamonds. A single row of the same precious stones encircled her slim white throat. She looked superbly, wondrously beautiful.

Truly this girl was an exquisite picture, but it bewildered one so that the eye rested on Jewel's slender, white-robed figure with pleasure, and intense relief.

Sumner was talking with Mrs. Vanderpool, the wife of a New York millionaire, as the Madisons entered, and turned at her exclamation:

"What a lovely girl! Who is she, Mr. Sumner?"

"She is the daughter of Major Madison, President of the Arrow-Head gold mines, so much talked about at present. You admire that vivid style?"

"Do introduce me, Mr. Sumner, I adore pretty girls." He was greeted by a flash from Aurelia's dark eyes, and a brilliant smile as he came up to give the desired introduction. Already she was surrounded and her ball card besieged.

"Miss Madison, Mrs. Vanderpool."

Both ladies bowed and immediately opened an animated conversation that ended in Aurelia's promising to grace Mrs. Vanderpool's german with her presence. Then Sumner gave the elder lady his arm across the room to join Mrs. Bowen. He passed Aurelia again on his way to the card-tables, in an adjoining room.

"You are going to ask me to dance, Mr. Sumner, of course?" she said to him as he paused an instant beside her chair. Her manner gave the bystanders the idea that they were old and intimate acquaintances. Her words and way jarred on Cuthbert. He took her card, and after consulting her, scribbled his name down for the after-supper dance, bowed and passed on.

He drew a deep breath of relief as he saw Jewel talking to the Russian ambassador, an old man in gorgeous dress and orders blazing on his breast.

"You are lucky, Excellency, to have a moment of Miss Bowen's time bestowed on you."

His Excellency bowed his head.

"I was just telling this lovely little lady that I must not be selfish, that I must give way for others who have a better right to her company than an old man like me."

"I have enjoyed talking with you so much," Jewel said simply.

"Thank you, my child. I see a friend of mine over in the corner. I can leave you in safe hand, now Sumner has come. By-and-by, perhaps, you will let me return and have a few more pleasant moments."

Sumner felt his vague sense of repulsion, which his encounter with Aurelia had aroused, fade, as he came in contact with the pure fascination of his betrothed. He smiled down at her tenderly. How inexpressibly sweet and lovely she was!

The band was playing a delicious waltz. Aurelia, flashing in her jewels, was flying round in the arms of West, who was her shadow. Sumner's brows met in a frown.

"How lovely Aurelia is!" cried Jewel with eager enthusiasm. "She is the most beautiful woman in the rooms."

"Bar one," said Cuthbert, smiling.

"Oh, you; you don't count. You are prejudiced," replied Jewel, laughing. "She seems to get on very well with Mr. West. I wonder—"

"Little matchmaker! I imagine West stands no chance in that quarter. He has nothing but his salary."

"Would that make a difference with her?" in a surprised, regretful tone.

"I imagine that they are not wealthy. Miss Madison, if I read her correctly, will marry for money."

The next instant his arm encircled Jewel's waist, he held her form pressed closely to his throbbing heart, and they glided away from earth to a short period of heaven.

As an intimate friend of the family, and soon to be a son of the

PAULINE E. HOPKINS

house, Cuthbert Sumner had shared the dispensing of hospitality with Senator Bowen.

"My boy," said the older man, "just fix the thing up when you see 'em laggin. I'm going into the card-room and have a game with Madison. He's an old duffer like myself. You understand all this sort of thing, but I'll be hanged if I ain't sick of it before I begin."

So Sumner had found himself pretty busy. After that waltz, however, which came just before supper, he and Jewel had a few precious moments together in the conservatory, sitting out the remainder of their dance. Then came supper, at which Sumner insisted upon being her escort. "I will not waive every enjoyment for the pleasure of others," he declared firmly.

XVII

The Spider's Web

The first dance after supper Jewel had given to General Benson.

"A short Elysium at last for me," whispered the gallant General as he passed his arm about her slight form. Jewel was a Western girl with all the independence that the term implies. She glanced up at her partner, as they whirled away, with a little amused smile slightly sarcastic; "I expected something different from you. Something at least original."

"Well, it is Elysium to find one's step perfectly duplicated."

"Oh, that is easy where one's partner is master of the art as you are. I imagine that you are one of the best dancers here."

"You are fond of dancing?" asked the General, after a silence.

"Yes; that weakness was born with me."

"In the tremendous crowd, I could not judge. But I can speak from this waltz—you dance like a fairy. Are you pleased with Washington?"

"Oh, yes; but I miss the freedom of the ranch, the wild flight at dawn over the prairie in the saddle, and many other things."

He looked at her with glowing eyes: "There we have congenial tastes. I am never so happy as when in the saddle."

The ball-room was a whirl of fair faces and dazzling toilets—the light, the heat, the perfume almost oppressive.

Knowing himself to be a fascinating conversationalist, he took advantage of a pause in the music to speak of the heat and suggest a turn in the conservatory where he knew that he could exert this power of enchantment. Jewel was nothing loth.

They stood a moment, before taking seats, at an open glass door gazing out on the gardens sered and withered and covered in places with patches of snow, but bathed in moonlight. There was something solemn in the scene, merriment seemed out of place; even soft laughter jarred on the nerves. See looked up to the heavens, where the Southern cross shone in all its brilliancy surrounded by myriads of other stars. The glorious Southern moon rode high in the sky. The flutes and viols were pouring out their maddest music.

"How glorious," Jewel said softly.

"Ay glorious indeed!"

"I mean the moon," she said.

"I mean your eyes, fair lady."

"You will persist in saying pretty things, General," she replied, turning away indifferently.

The General bit his lip in vexation. It was not to be easy work, that was plain.

There was a subdued murmur of voices and sometimes a ripple of laughter, for many couples stood, or strolled about the extensive greenhouses. They were lighted softly, from the arched dome, by silvery lamps; fountains flashed scented waters into marble basins where aquatic plants of strange beauty had found a home. Leading from the main conservatory were many arbors and grottoes, transformed for the time being by draperies of asparagus vines and roses into a charming solitude for two. The cool stillness was refreshing after the head of the ball-room.

"Really, this is well done," remarked the General, stopping to admire the effect. "None of the balls I have attended in Washington was so beautiful."

"Another compliment, General?"

"It is not flattery to speak the truth."

They seated themselves on a rustic chair for two, and the General entertained her with tales of his travels in Italy and India, and cyclone and typhoon, all very fascinating to the girl before whom life was just opening.

"Were you long out of the United States, General?"

"About ten years," he replied, looking down. "It was this way, Miss Jewel, I was a hot-blooded young fellow who could see no wrong in the decision of his section to secede from the union of states; and so, when it all ended disastrously, I gathered together what remained of my shattered fortunes, and went abroad until the pain of recollection should be somewhat dimmed. I returned almost a foreigner."

"Ah!" she said, with a gentle sigh of pity, "how dreadful that time must have been. Thank heaven, ours is a united country once more. And you are mistaken, too, in your judgment: we have no foreigners here. We have effaced the word by assimilation; so, too, we have no Southerners—we are Americans."

The General accented her remark by a courtly bow, and then he drifted into an animated description of a sail down the Mediterranean

Sea. Jewel could imagine that she inhaled the odor from boatloads of violets, brought to her senses by his wonderful descriptive powers.

At this moment their enjoyable tête-á-tête was interrupted by the sound of a woman's voice in passionate pleading.

Early in the evening Aurelia Madison had whispered to General Benson:

"If you can, take Jewel into the conservatory after supper. I shall have something interesting for her to hear."

"How are you getting on? Any progress?"

"Wait," was her answer.

After supper Sumner went to her to claim his dance. It was a duty-dance and a painful one he found it. As they floated down the long room, Aurelia gazed up at him with flushed cheeks and glittering eyes.

She had taken a great fancy to Jewel Bowen, not only because the latter was very kind to her—kinder than anyone had ever been to her in her lonely, reckless life, but because she really carried in her heart a spark of what passed for love and which would have developed but for Sumner. She could even admire Jewel's beauty without jealousy; she did not envy her her wealth although so pinched herself in money matters, and yet—strange nature of women, or of some women—for that reason she was the more determined to triumph over her as a woman, and, if she could, stab her. She had forced the friendship with that intention.

She felt instinctively that Cuthbert shrank from allowing a continuance of the intimacy between them, and she resented it. Yes, she would have her fling, her triumph; Jewel should know, beyond a doubt, that Cuthbert Sumner and his fortune was hers, belonged to her—Aurelia Madison.

Now she watched his face and resented his cold, preoccupied air.

"How quiet you are; aren't you well?"

"Never better," he replied, with an apology for his seeming indifference. After all she was a woman, and a beautiful one. Why should he try to mar her favorable reception among the élite.

"Only, I am not Jewel; is that it?"

"Pardon. Let us speak of something else. Shall I take you to have some refreshment?" he said coldly.

"Oh, let us go to the conservatory. I want air and rest," she said, slipping her hand through his arm. "I have seen nothing of you all the evening. Now you must devote a short time to me." Her air was bolder than Sumner had ever noticed before. He bowed low in acquiescence, though he would willingly have left her there.

She bit her lip and a dogged look came into her face that was not pleasant to see, and in her heart she felt that she could take the strong, handsome man and dash him senseless at her feet. She hid her feelings well, and glanced up at him with a pretty pleading look.

"Oh! Bert, I keep forgetting—of course—," then she broke suddenly, "I wish you loved her less!"

"A useless wish," said Sumner coldly. "Happen what may, Jewel must always be my first thought."

"Aye, your best and truest love," she said through her teeth.

They were in the deserted conservatory where all was coolness and shadow; Sumner walked by her side until they reached one of the grottoes, where from between the folds of the rose-curtain drapery a rustic seat held its inviting arms toward them. Aurelia dropped upon it:

"I am afraid I can't give you many minutes," he said with a cool smile. "Senator Bowen naturally expects me to assist him in looking after the guests."

The band was playing divinely and the notes came to them in waves of undulating melody. Sumner never forgot that night, and the music of the band haunted him ever after.

She sat there in sad languor that would have touched any heart but his. They talked a moment of indifferent subjects, then he arose and offered his arm with a motion that indicated a return to the ball-room. But with a low and exceedingly bitter cry she stood up.

"Must we part like this? My God! I cannot bear it! Have you no mercy, no pity?"

The tears were streaming down her cheeks, she held out her hands imploringly.

With deepest sympathy and pity he took them in his.

"Aurelia, you will forget. Believe me, dear, you will forget all this in a very little while. What good would my love do you now. It could bring you nothing but sorrow. We must forget each other. I hope—I know you will be happy yet. God be with you, dear girl." He bent down and pressed his lips to her trembling hands, feeling himself a wretch for bringing sorrow to this beautiful woman who loved him so.

But she flung her arms about him, and clung to him in desperation and the abandonment of grief, sobbing hysterically, with low, quivering moans, that cut him to the heart.

"Aurelia, do not weep so. It is torture for me to hear you."

"I hope I may die! Oh, if I only could!" she sobbed faltering and shivering, and clinging to him, and he put his arms about her and kissed her twice on the brow. Her lovely wet face was pressed close against his cheek.

A deep sigh startled him. He lifted his head. Standing in the doorway of the curtained recess, pallid as a ghost, all the graceful beauty gone from her wan face, with frightened woful eyes and despair in every feature, stood Jewel. With a loud exclamation, with rage and impatience and disgust, he shook the exquisite form from his bosom.

XVIII

It was long after midnight and the guests were leaving, when Sumner, with white, set face, sought Mrs. Bowen and asked for Jewel. She was much concerned over her daughter.

"I do not understand it," was her reply to his eager questions; "Jewel sent word by General Benson that she was not well, and had gone to her rooms. She was all right, and as gay as possible all day. I thought you would know."

Finding that he could not explain matters that night, and would accomplish nothing by waiting, Sumner left the scene of revelry, desiring to be alone. How it had all happened he could not tell. But what a sentimental fool he felt himself to be, for allowing himself to be betrayed into acting such a scene in so public a place. Still, he felt that he could blame no one but himself. Aurelia was free from any intention of scheming for how could she know of Jewel's presence at just that moment? So he argued, lulling his suspicions to rest.

At eight o'clock, while breakfasting, there came a letter from Jewel with his ring enclosed. Then, indeed, it seemed to him that life was over. With mad and bitter wrath, he cursed Aurelia Madison; then he started for Jewel's home. The servant who answered the summons was wont to have a welcoming smile for the familiar visitor. There was no expression in his well-trained face when he informed Sumner that the ladies were not at home. Night found him again at the Bowen mansion. Mrs. Bowen was coldness itself; Jewel begged to be excused.

Despair seized him. Everything, every one, was repulsive to him. Days of insane recklessness followed. A month went by in this manner— working furiously days, spending his nights in search of the excitement that is supposed to drown care. Then he grew calmer. He would seek Jewel again; he would force her trust; she should believe in him. Life was not worth living without her. For one touch of her cool hand, one glance from her calm eyes, one smile on the sweet, earnest lips, he would barter wealth and fame, and all the world had to offer—aye life itself!

They had met frequently in society during this memorable month, but Jewel passed her lover without a sign of recognition or with a slight bend of the head in acknowledgment of his reverential uncovering. General Benson was always in close attendance, and Aurelia Madison also, was often her companion.

After the usual nine days of wonderment and surmises as to the cause of the estrangement between lovers, public curiosity turned to speculating on the middle-aged general's chances with the fair heiress.

AT SEVEN O'CLOCK ONE EVENING, Cuthbert sat at his desk in his rooms lost in sombre thoughts. He had determined to devote himself to the hardest of tasks, heavy brain work, when his heart and soul were racked with agony. He was busy on a political treatise. He was considered a brilliant writer. If he could make a stir in the literary world, it would please his father, and he had no one else to think of now.

Work! Could he work? He flung out his arms over the papers on the desk before him, and bowed his head upon them.

"If I knew that the suffering was for myself alone, my Blossom, I could bear it better."

He lifted himself at last haggard and weary as with weeks of sleepless toil, resolved to devote himself to his chosen work.

"What I am I will live on to the end—Ambition my only bride." He was striving with all his young courageous heart to kill the memory of the girl he loved. It was a bitter task, and an impossible one.

Modern pessimists are fond of crying that love, as well as chivalry, has died out of our practical world. If this were true, then Sumner lived after his century, for his belief in higher and better things was intense. He had a desire to worship purity in any shape, to champion the weak, and carve a pathway to honor that was characteristic of the chivalrous days of old.

The minutes passed, half-past seven ticked away, and then eight, and he never moved. He sat with his face on his two hands, his elbows planted on the table.

"I will not think more about her," he said to himself, doggedly. "I will not—I will not."

John, his servant, a New England colored man who had known him from his youth, had put his evening clothes out in the dressing-room, and now entered the room to remind his master of an engagement to dine.

"It's time you was dressed, Mr. Cuthbert," he said in his quiet way. John was eager for his master to leave Washington and return to Massachusetts and the family home.

"'Deed," he argued to himself, "this Washington's no city for me. Give me old New England every time; it's God's own country. They's nuthin' human about the South for chocolate complected gents like me, no matter how you fix it. The pint of the argument is in the scorpion's tail. Jes' so; and this here Southern idea of colored Americans ain't good fer black nor white when you's done had a New England raisin'."

"Mr. Cuthbert's an altered man sense the night of that there Bowen ball," he told himself again and again, "if he ain't twenty years older in his looks then I'm blind in one eye and can't see out of 'tother. He'll be best off if he gets back home to the old gentleman. Dog my cats but there's something strange in this whole kickup or my name ain't John Robinson."

Sumner roused himself at last: "What's the time, John?" he was asking as the bell of the suite rang shrilly.

"If that's Mr. Badger, show him in," he said as John went out of the room.

Cuthbert stood gazing down into the fire. He heard voices outside, but he gave them no heed; there was always a good-natured controversy between his friend and his servant.

A slap on the back, and "Holloa, Sumner, old man!" made him start round and put his gloomy thoughts behind him, and greet his friends, Will Badger and Carroll West.

"Ah! How are you, Will? How are you, West? How goes it?" he said, holding out his hand in greeting to his guests.

"Thought I'd bring West with me, and after we dine at the club, take a look in at the Madisons, this is their at home night. West's agreeable," with a laugh and a meaning look in the latter's direction.

Sumner hesitated. Aurelia had written him again and again, but he had not answered her impassioned letters. She had begged him to call and let her help set matters right, but as yet, he had not been able to bring himself to comply with her request.

"Well," he replied to Will Badger after a moment, "I don't mind. Have a glass of wine while I change."

"Thanks—we don't mind," said West.

West never did mind. He was fond of a social glass, and Sumner was noted for his fine wine and excellent brand of cigars.

"Yes, we'll have a little game with the Major," he remarked, as he helped himself from the side-board. "Great fun, the Major knows a thing or two about life does the old man."

"He knows enough to win your money, I suppose, you foolish boy," replied Sumner.

"It's very little I've lost there. He always insists on returning me my money."

"Have others been as fortunate?"

"That's their own fault; the Major wins fair every time," replied West hotly.

"Oh, West, you're prejudiced in his favor," broke in Badger.

"A pretty daughter is a trump card."

"She can't help being charming and attracting men to the house," stoutly maintained West.

"Charming, but dangerous, my dear fellow."

"She's my friend. I would be more to her if it were not for my poverty. Don't malign her, Badger, I won't stand it."

"My dear boy," broke in Sumner, soothingly, "Badger and I are your friends. Don't be angry with us; we mean it for your good. Aurelia Madison is one of those women with whom mere friendship is impossible. Men must always be half her lovers and therein lies the secret of her power—of any woman's power over our sex, if she is inclined to use that power to our detriment. Oh! she's circumspect," he continued as West attempted a vehement interruption. "I believe that it is not in her to care enough for any one to kick over the advantages of respectability for his sake, but she'll sail close to the wind."

West laughed bitterly: "You speak from experience I suppose; the city is ringing with your broken engagement and its cause."

Sumner stood silent. The blow was a keen one because the wound was so recent.

"Oh, come, fellows; drop it," hastily exclaimed Badger. "What do we care for Miss Madison except as any man admires a handsome woman. She'll bowl you over, Carrie, my son; she's using you just now to suit her own purposes. You're young yet," he continued affectionately, "but when you've had two or three seasons of this sort of thing, you'll hold your own with the deepest of them."

"Yes, West," rejoined Sumner who had regained his self-possession, "there are scores of just such women in the world: I will own that once I thought Aurelia Madison divine, but," shrugging his shoulders, "I have changed my opinion, and I am not sorry to have escaped from her toils. If you enjoy her society, continue to do so, but be careful; don't let her snare you."

"You ought to do some of your preaching to old Bowen. Dogged if he ain't gone on her worse than I am; any way, it looks so; he's there every night."

"What!" exclaimed Sumner.

"Let up, West, why don't you?" said Will Badger giving him a meaning look. "It's my idea, Cuthbert, that Senator Bowen is putting money into the mine. That's what I think is the attraction. I intended to speak to you about it some days ago."

Sumner made no reply, and in a few moments the trio left the house.

Washington society, with its proneness to overlook small trespasses, was beginning to talk about the Madisons. Some declared the beautiful daughter but a bait to snare theunwary, and openly voted the Major "shady." A good deal of money changed hands in the salon of the unpretentious house on New York Avenue: it was whispered also that the mine was a gigantic swindle. As yet these reports were but floating rumors; no one had made open complaint.

Meanwhile, the evenings were gay in the drawing-room where Aurelia smiled and flirted with the greatest intellects of the great Republic. There was an excellent buffet, obsequious servants, the soft shuffle of cards, and in the billiard room room at the rear of the house, a chosen few rattled dice or gave themselves up to the fascination of rouge-et-noir.

It was past eleven when the servant opened the door of Major Madison's salon and the three friends entered. Sumner found himself in a fair-sized and well-furnished room, containing a semi-grand piano; it was the one he had entered on his formal visit. Aurelia was the only woman present. The Major came forward from a group near the fire-place to receive them.

"So pleased to see you," he said, shaking hands in his cordial fashion. "Aurelia, my dear, here is Mr. Sumner." West was already standing by the beauty's chair, and Badger had passed on to a group of men in another part of the room.

Aurelia was exquisitely dressed in her favorite colors, cream and terra-cotta, combined in a wonderful gown.

"Well, Mr. Sumner, have you honored us at last?" she queried as she laid her hand lightly in his. Then as her father moved away she said with a bitter smile:

"The fault was not mine. I would have died rather than Jewel should have heard my foolish words."

Her manner more than her words, broke down all Sumner's lingering suspicions, and he warmed perceptibly toward her. She was but a girl, impassioned, impressionable. What right had he to accuse her of perfidy. Some one came up to them and interrupted her.

Yes, she would give them music. She went to the piano and Sumner followed her. She played popular selections from the latest opera bouffe, and then a morcean in a style that satisfied the most critical taste.

Senator Bowen had just entered the house and paused for the music to cease before speaking to Miss Madison, then he went up to her passing Sumner with a cold nod. Presently Major Madison and he disappeared, and Sumner felt they had gone to the card room. He wandered about for a while seeing enough to alarm him at the ascendency Major Madison had evidently gained over the Senator. As he stood at the door of the room watching the party where Senator Bowen sat staking large sums of rouge-et-noir and losing at every turn of the wheel, he felt dejected at his own helplessness. Gaming was Senator Bowen's only vice, a legacy from the old days when as mate he played every night for weeks as the cotton steamer made her trips up and down the river highways in the ante-bellum days. Sumner determined to rescue the honest old man from the toils of these sharpers. Just then Aurelia came up to him and touched his arm.

"I wish to speak with you, Bert, come with me."

He gave her his arm and they went to the vacant library. As they passed from view one man standing back of Senator Bowen's chair watching the game said to another:

"Sumner rich?"

"Very."

"It would be a fine thing for Miss Madison to catch him in the rebound. He seems fascinated."

"Indeed it would. And why not? She is of good blood, and he does not need money."

"Ah, no! only beauty and love. She is worthy of a coronet."

The soft light of tender sympathy was on Aurelia's face. Sumner clasped both her hands in his and begged her to tell him all she knew of Jewel.

"That is why I brought you here," was her serious reply. "I mean to undo this tangled web which I have unwittingly woven."

"Is she well? does she hate me? Dare I go to her?" he asked with passionate earnestness.

Disengaging one of her hands, Aurelia laid it on his shoulder, while she answered in soothing tones:

"Jewel is quite well, Bert dear, but she is allowing General Benson to monopolize her attention; in fact, I sometimes fear that the mischief is beyond repair and that she is pledged to him. But I am sure she loves you still. Trust a woman's intuitive powers. She cannot deceive me. Whatever she has done has been in a spirit of pique which needs but your presence to overcome. We will save her if it is not too late."

"Bless you for those words," he said, "your sympathy is very sweet to me."

"Be patient, and leave it all to me; I will bring you together again."

"You have filled my mind with forbodings," he said dejectedly, "I fear it is too late."

"Not too late, Bert; leave me the hope, at least, of redeeming myself in the eyes of Jewel. I have arranged for a meeting between you on Tuesday. On that day the Senator and Mrs. Bowen go to the President's reception. Jewel has a cold and will not be able to accompany them. She expects me to spend the evening with her. I waive my engagement in your favor, Bert; see that you improve your opportunity."

Tears filled her eyes, her voice broke, she was pale with emotion. She was proud of the intense feeling she displayed, and felt that she was acting her part splendidly. For a moment Sumner was speechless, then he kissed her hand and said in a broken voice, as he turned to go:

"God bless you, Aurelia."

At four a.m., General Benson, Major Madison and Aurelia stood alone in the deserted drawing-room.

The Major waved in triumph two checks for large amounts, bearing Senator Bowen's signature.

"That's all right, Madison, but it is slow work—too slow for me. How are you getting on, Aurelia?"

She looked at him with an evil smile on her face that destroyed all its marvelous beauty: "I have told Cuthbert Sumner to call on Jewel, Tuesday evening. The Senator and his wife will be out, the girl alone. I think, General, you can do the rest, and settle the matter once for all."

"By jove, Aurelia, I will convince him of my triumph against all odds. You've earned your husband and your million."

XIX

The burst of gaiety which the ball brought into Jewel's life, made the succeeding days of gloom more depressing. Her high spirits had received a severe shock in her supposed discovery of Cuthbert's treachery, from which they rallied with difficulty.

"Don't stand there, my darling, those large windows are always draughty."

"I feel nothing of the sort, mama; don't libel this beautiful house, if you please."

"Beautiful house indeed; I shall be glad when June is come. I long for the breeze of the ranch."

"There will be more snow by tomorrow, mama."

"Of course! It seems to me that everything is out of joint. Think of snow in Washington in March!"

Jewel left the window where the light was darkening. She smiled at Mrs. Bowen and one could see how wan and delicate she looked.

"Mama, you are pessimistic today," she said kneeling beside the fire and stretching out her hands to the blaze.

Mrs. Bowen made to reply. In truth, her heart was bitter within her breast. She made an effort to appear cheerful before Jewel, not altogether successful.

The two ladies were in the favorite lounging room of the family—the small reception room. Jewel's great mass of bright hair rolled at the back of her small head, seemed too heavy a weight for it, while the hand that held the fleecy shawl about her was so shadowy as to fill one with apprehension. Yet she did not complain, only her parents noted the change in her since the night of the great ball, with feelings of uneasiness.

"My dear," said the Senator to his wife in one of their conversations about the best course in the matter, "My dear, if it were left to me, I'd shoot Sumner on sight. Out in 'Frisco his life wouldn't be worth a cuss. I've as much as I can do to keep decent and not put a ball into his miserable carcass. Think of a feller philandering after two women to once, either of them handsome enough to satisfy any reasonable man even if he is dead sot on looks in a female. Blast my eyes, Mrs. Senator, it's lucky we start for 'Frisco as soon as the session closes. I'd not answer for holding in much longer.

"Who'd have believed it possible! Sumner seems such a decent feller. Talk about deceit in women! Women ain't in it compared with these Eastern raised gents they call men!"

Then Senator Bowen retired to his club to vent his rage in pushing billiard balls about. It was during one of his fits of impotent wrath that he fell into Major Madison's toils and became an easy victim.

"Oh! my dove," murmured Mrs. Bowen to herself, as she had murmured many a time during the past few weeks; "my gentle, proud, suffering flower, how I wish I could take the pain out of your young heart and bear it for you; it is so hard to see that look on your child face, and feel that the sunshine is gone for you, and then realize that with all my love I can do nothing—nothing, nothing. A woman's life is hard, hard, from the cradle to the grave. O, God! why were we made to bear all the punishment for Adam's fall! Why are men so cruel? Why did he win her heart to throw it one side as a worthless bauble?"

Mrs. Bowen was crocheting an afghan and the needle dropped from her long white fingers and a settled look of pain crept like a veil over the beautiful proud face as she gazed into the fire.

Aurelia had been to see Jewel, had told her with many tears and sobs, of the broken engagement between herself and Cuthbert, that they still loved each other, that Sumner blamed himself for believing that he had forgotten her (Aurelia) and had engaged himself to Jewel without realizing the true state of his feelings, and now he would never marry—neither of them felt that they could know happiness without the thought of Jewel's wrongs before them. Could they not be friends still, she and Jewel? She was so lonely and miserable feeling that she had brought so much suffering on her dear friend. Mrs. Bowen heard it all but deep in her heart was a doubt of the specious pleader.

"I wish we had not been so hasty, and had given Cuthbert a chance to explain," she remarked to Jewel one day.

"There is nothing to explain," replied Jewel lifting her head proudly. "I saw and heard it all for myself. He told me he had only met Aurelia casually at the Cape, leaving almost immediately; now I find beyond a doubt, that they were actually engaged. Nothing can alter the fact that he had something to conceal and for that reason deceived me. Then, too, papa has met him at the Major's, and has heard the gossip of the clubs. It proves itself, mama; there is nothing more to be said. I—I have learnt my lesson—I shall never be so foolish again. I have to thank Mr. Sumner for teaching me worldly wisdom."

"I had thought better things of Cuthbert. I would never have believed him to be the cruel, selfish man he has proved. Well, may he have some peace before he marries Aurelia, for I suppose it will end that way. He will be punished if he marries her or I greatly mistake her nature."

Jewel knelt on, gazing into the fire. She was silent for a time, and then she said gently:

"You dislike Aurelia, mama, simply for my sake. It is not like you to be unjust."

Mrs. Bowen glanced at her sharply.

"It is not that alone, Jewel, but I believe her false. I have a presentiment that there is something wrong. O, my darling, do be careful. I think it would kill your father if anything happened to you," exclaimed Mrs. Bowen as she folded her daughter in her loving arms.

Jewel answered her tender embrace with warm kisses.

"Dear mama, the sting is taken out of all the pain when I remember that no matter what comes my own darling father and mother see no fault in their dear girl."

Ah! children who have not needed it yet, believe that the wound must be mortal that cannot be soothed by a parental balm and oil. Those dear ones have the power to restore self-respect though they may be powerless to restore happiness. Mrs. Bowen put the girl from her and left the room.

"Yes, I, too, shall be glad to return to the ranch. It will be quiet and peaceful there. I shall forget."

She shivered. "Forget," she repeated, pressing her hands to her breast, and moving to and fro in agitation, "no, no! I shall never forget—I shall remember as long as I live."

She rose to her feet and began walking the length of the room. The opening of the door aroused her, and turning with a slight frown, she saw General Benson.

The frown deepened as she saw him place a basket of lovely flowers on a table. She did not desire him to bring her gifts; but this did not cause her pain. It was the vision of a by-gone-day, when some one else was wont to come softly into the room with beautiful flowers.

Her face flushed for a moment, then became paler than ever. She gave General Benson her hand silently, he bit his lip when he saw how quickly she withdrew it.

"Sam told me I should find Mrs. Bowen here," he said courteously.

"Mama is in her room. I will ring and let her know you are here."

"Wait one moment," he pleaded. "I have brought you some flowers, Miss Jewel."

"They are very beautiful," she answered coldly; "and you are very kind, General Benson."

"Flowers suit you," he said in his soft caressing voice, that had never failed him with other women, but which was wasted on Jewel. "You should always be surrounded with them, Miss Jewel."

She did not smile. This man's admiration jarred on her. Her father liked his pleasant ways and found him a good companion to wile away the hours, but somehow she could not assume the easy familiarity of friendship with him.

She took herself to talk for her growing dislike of him. Why should she be so ungenerous to one so kind? Why should she shrink from him with a loathing she could not repress? She had never voiced her feelings but she knew that her mother felt with her toward this suave, diplomatic gentleman. She had once seem him kick the dog that followed him, cowed and faithful only through fear, and she disliked him for the cowardly act. She spoke to him about it.

"Oh, one must be in the fashion!" he replied, never dreaming of the anger and disgust beneath the girl's cold exterior. "And dogs were made to kick. People talk a lot of rubbish about the faithfulness of dogs. It's all bosh! Their devotion means dread of the whip, or a strong boot, Miss Jewel."

Jewel's disgust was so great that for the moment she lost all other feeling, every remnant of respect and liking fled. He had forgotten the incident; and though resenting the girl's coldness, he did not associate his own cruelty with it. In fact, he put it down to coquetry, and it only inflamed his admiration and strengthened his determination to make this girl his wife. He wondered if Senator and Mrs. Bowen would oppose him?

Jewel's stepmother was a woman of the world, and between General Benson and herself there was no great liking. He felt uneasy in her presence, that under her rather haughty manner a keen sight was hidden that read his motives. Senator Bowen was more to his liking. In reply to Mrs. Bowen's cautious questioning concerning General Benson, the Senator's answer was:

"The government, my dear, gives him its confidence by placing him in a responsible position. That is enough for me. Uncle Sam never employs rascals to transact his business."

Opposition or not, General Benson meant to win in the end. Aurelia might fail with Cuthbert, but he would win with Jewel. He was irritated by the delay; apart from his vanity which was injured by Jewel's indifference, it was time the engagement was announced. His creditors were unpleasantly pressing. His property in Baltimore was mortgaged up to its full value. There was nothing for it but this marriage with the California millionaire's heiress.

Heiresses were not easily found. It was only a question of time and management, and Jewel must be his wife.

"Yes, you are one of those beings for whom it seems flowers were especially created. I always think of you as a delicate lily or a white rose."

The girl's face flushed, but not with pleasure.

"Mama must see them. She will admire them," she said as she rang the bell, and sent a message to Mrs. Bowen.

General Benson bit his lip. He had intended speaking to her today, but it was not an easy thing to do. She kept him at bay.

"Have you seen Miss Madison lately?" he asked sauntering up to the fire. Jewel shook her head.

"Not this week," and the troubled look returned to her eyes.

"She is a great girl," Benson said with a laugh—he leaned against the over-mantel and stroked his moustache. "She and Sumner are going the pace. I suppose we cannot expect lovebirds to remember anything outside their paradise." Jewel shivered.

"She loves him still," he said to himself between his teeth. "Well, it is no matter; she may love him now, but I shall alter that when she is my wife."

Then with the innate cruelty of his nature he continued:

"Sumner is to be congratulated, if what I hear is true; the Madisons are a fine old Southern family, and Miss Aurelia is worthy of her race." He hid a smile behind his hand.

"It is quite refreshing in these matter-of-fact days to come upon a real genuine romance. Love, they say, is out of fashion, if so, I am afraid Sumner is a long way behind the times, for I am told he is madly in love. That I guessed the first time I saw them together. One could read his infatuation in his eyes. Miss Madison's magnificent beauty easily accounts for it. Her face is her fortune, most assuredly." Jewel drew herself away a few steps. The pain he hoped to give her was not there. She had schooled herself to bear hearing the news of the engagement at any time. He could arouse her indignation—pride; this he did successfully.

"Then it is settled. Aurelia is very beautiful," she said quietly. "She is my friend, and I think her one of the most beautiful women I have ever seen."

He smiled.

"Ah, pardon, Miss Jewel; I had forgotten while speaking that you were more than ordinarily interested. Always sweet and generous, Miss Jewel, most rarely so, for one beautiful woman seldom acknowledges another."

"Here is mama." Jewel turned to the door with a faint sigh of relief. "Will you excuse me, General Benson, I want to catch the next mail?"

General Benson did not stay much longer. He was not at his ease with Mrs. Bowen. He was furious with Jewel for retiring and leaving him with her mother. He set it down against her in his book of reckoning to be settled in a future not far-distant.

Mrs. Bowen went to Jewel after he was gone. "You have not looked at your flowers, Blossom," she said gently. Her daughter colored.

"They are very beautiful, but—"

"They give you no pleasure?"

"I do not like presents from General Benson."

"You do not like him?" queried her mother, stroking the wonderful coils of shining hair.

The girl shivered.

"No—no. I do not like him at all; he is very kind, but I cannot bring myself to like him, mama, dear."

Mrs. Bowen kissed her brow.

"Nor do I; he is a bad man and I shall find a way to stop his calling here." She paused a moment lost in deep thought. "Perhaps it is well that we do not return to Washington next fall. I am glad your father has so decided."

The small hours of the morning found Jewel still sitting before her bedroom fire. She had returned from a reception, and had dismissed her maid, telling Venus that she would manage without her.

She was thinking of words she had heard that confirmed the report that Sumner and Aurelia were engaged. She had not seen the latter for a number of days, but she felt that she might expect her at any moment to confirm the report. What is first love? Some say first love is "calf love," a silly infatuation for an insipid hero or heroine.

Others will tell you first love is the only true passion; that it comes but once to every human being; that the intense yearning for the sound of a beloved voice, the sight of an adored face, the clasp of a hand, only fills the heart once in a lifetime. The question as to whether it is the deepest love must be answered by each individual.

"The heart knoweth its own bitterness," says Holy writ. So also it knoweth its own joy. Jewel was a firm believer in the strength of first love. And now she found herself suffering the pangs of love despised, the anguish of disappointment, the humiliation of neglect. Ever before her inner sight was the merry dancing, daring, the glancing fun in those dark eyes so recently her sun. How little she had been to him that he could so soon forget.

Oh, they were beautiful eyes, she thought, with a stirring of the old rapture at her heart. What a noble face he has! high-bred, refined, and manly, too! There was not another man to compare with him; and—he belonged to another. A bitter pang smote upon her, a keen memory of the events of the past weeks. She wept over her baseless dreams, and prayed for strength to solve the problem of her life.

"How shall I meet him?" she asked herself. "How shall I be calm, conventional to Mr. and Mrs. Cuthbert Sumner?" Long she sat there pondering many things.

XX

The last of March came, but winter still lingered in the lap of spring. Jewel's couch was drawn up before the blazing fire; the parlor was snug and comfortable, just cosey enough for a semi-invalid. The room was half-panelled with oak, and the furniture was of the same material covered with bright silk and embroidered cushions.

Jewel was not well and had excused herself from attendance at the President's reception. Her mother had ensconced her in the small reception parlor promising to return early, and bidding her doze away the time until then. She was not asleep. Her eyes were open, and fixed upon the fire; they were filled with intense pain, and her hands were clenched, while now and then a shiver ran through her frame, as she turned restlessly from side to side.

She sought solitude that evening, and yet the sound of Sam's voice in the hall admitting a visitor whose tones betrayed Gen. Benson, was not distasteful to her.

He was very much at home now, and drew a low chair round between her and the fire, after bidding her good evening, took his place there, and gazed steadfastly into her face a few moments without speaking.

"Of what are you thinking?" he asked gently.

"I am thinking what a horrible thing it is that we women are always loving the wrong men—worthless, heartless men, who cannot appreciate in even a small degree the love we waste upon them."

He took one of her hands in his.

"Look at me," he said. "You are very young—you will get over this happening—this episode in the life of every young girl. Don't start. How can anyone who cares for you, help knowing that you have suffered through loving the wrong man? But time is a great healer. Now don't try to free your hand. It must belong to me some day, so why not let it rest in mine now?"

She shivered as she turned from him.

"You don't understand," she said speaking very low. "My heart is dead, or only so much alive that I can feel it ache. I can never love—never marry. I must go on living—expiating my wilful blindness in being so reckless as to love a—a villain with all my heart and soul."

The tears rolled slowly down her face.

"Won't you let me try to comfort you?" he asked.

She shook her head. "You cannot give me back the man I believed in," she replied.

Benson rose, frowning heavily.

"Can't I horsewhip him or do something to punish the scoundrel?"

"No, no!"

"You don't love him still?"

"No," she answered. "But I can never hate him. Don't let's talk about it any more," she continued wearily. "Dead loves are like dead people—talking will not bring them back."

"I will make you forget him some day," he said, kissing her hand.

"I wish you could," she replied with a sigh.

Benson felt encouraged, and determined to follow up his advantage.

"What has put you in this state?" he asked tenderly.

"Why are you not at the reception?" she laughed evasively.

"That is not answering my question?" he retorted. "Either you need a doctor or your distress of mind calls for an adviser. Shall I hold your hand, and see if I can mesmerize you into telling me all your thoughts?" he continued half-laughing. Jewel drew back in alarm. She raised herself on her arm and looked away from him into the fire.

"You have no right to question me as you know."

"Why won't you give me the right?" he asked earnestly. "Look, Jewel, I love you and trust you so much, I am ready to take you on any terms. I should be glad and proud to marry you tomorrow, and wait for time to bring me love."

"Why will you tease me?" she asked desperately. "Be my friend without asking reward, but never hope to be anything else."

The girl was sitting now on the couch that had served her for a resting place. She bowed her head; the long silken lashes lay on her cheeks.

He still held her hand; and as he gazed down upon her face, so pale and sorrowing, his pulses throbbed with greater passion.

"Jewel you are an angel! Be one to me. You have many years to live; you could not, would not pass them alone. Be merciful then to one who worships the ground you tread! I know my heart. It is yours. None other can, shall ever share it. Accept my love and me, my darling!"

He was bending over her, his breath ruffled the soft rings of her hair. His feverish earnestness moved her. She felt a great pity for him. For the time she forgot her repugnance.

"He feels as I feel," she thought.

What would she not have done for him in her compassion! Anything but what his lips pleaded for; that was impossible.

"I am so sorry—so very sorry!" she said, and the light of her eyes, even the touch of her fingers confirmed her words. "But you see I have no love to give."

"Jewel," lightly he placed his arm about her, "I give you my love; I ask but, in return, you. Let me have the right of loving you through life. I will be content; for I shall live in hope that my affection shall one day win yours. If you must think your whole first love given, let me hold the second place in your heart."

"Is second love possible?" she asked.

"Most surely. Give me that; I will be satisfied." Her lips moved; assent seemed to quiver on them, when looking up, she gazed directly into Cuthbert Sumner's eyes. He had been waited upon to the room by Sam, and had stood there looking at them without being noticed so absorbed had they been in their conversation.

With a cry Jewel staggered to her feet.

"Jewel, Jewel, hear me," cried Sumner in desperation, "I pray you, before you part us forever. Do not be rash; for God's sake, let me speak, hear me!" She waved him back as he stepped toward her.

General Benson was bewildered; his active mind comprehended instantly the peril of the moment—the frustration of his plans if he hesitated an instant—and his ready wit saved him. It was the time for decisive action. With a swift movement he placed himself at Jewel's side, took her hand in his, and thus faced Sumner.

"Mr. Sumner, this intrusion is unwarrantable. Miss Bowen is my promised wife."

Cuthbert bowed his head, and turning, rushed from the room and from the house.

C uthbert Sumner tendered his resignation to General Benson to take effect at the close of the official year, and it was accepted. "I have no feeling but friendship for you, Mr. Sumner," said the General after he had folded the document away. "I hope and trust that whatever happens we shall remember each other without enmity," he continued in his sweet voice so effective with most people. "Still, feeling that it must be unpleasant for you to serve under me, when we consider existing circumstances, without doubt what you propose is the best course."

It was ten o'clock the next day and Sumner sat at his desk looking out occasionally at the gathering storm that threatened to send March out with tumultuous blustering winds and heavy rain. The secretary and the stenographer occupied the same apartment with the chief. The ceiling of the apartment was lofty, there were elegant paintings on the walls, and the furniture was luxurious. There were rich hangings at the windows, carpets and rugs on the floor, lounges were grouped about the spacious room giving it more the appearance of a boudoir than a public office. The style of the wardrobes ranged about the walls would lead one to infer that all the conveniences for dining or longing could be easily found within its four walls. Nor would one have been mistaken in inferring such to be the case; indeed, the chief's lunch was generally served in this room in sumptuous style by his valet. It was rumored, too, that here gay spreads and bachelor parties were not unknown; happenings at which grave questions of state were sometimes decided.

A warm fire burned in the grate for there was a chill in the air that furnace heat did not entirely remove, and the large pile of blazing coals shed a glowing radiance of cheerfulness on all around.

General Benson, it was evident, though a servant of the people, was using their resources freely to gratify an extravagant taste. His was the life of a popular official floating at the ease of his own sweet will.

The only other occupant beside Cuthbert and Benson was Elise Bradford the stenographer. This woman was elegantly attired, and here again one noticed how utterly out of keeping her dress was with the work supposed to be performed by a simple government clerk. She was tall, fair and pale, with a countenance that impressed one with its resigned expression and sad dignity.

General Benson sat before his splendidly covered table where cut-glass bottles of eau de cologne gleamed, vases of fragrant flowers charmed the eye, and ornamental easels of costly style held pictures of fashionable ladies. He was looking over some papers which had just been submitted by Cuthbert. This morning he was abstracted and silent. Finally he called Sumner to him in a recess of a curtained window and said:

"Sumner, I have a favor to ask of you."

"I shall be happy to grant it if it is in my power, General."

"Thanks, I felt sure such would be your answer. I shall have to ask you and Miss Bradford to work overtime tomorrow and Sunday. This work must have our special attention. It is of such a nature that I can not confide it to an ordinary clerk. I cannot superintend to work myself because a party is to leave here on Saturday, myself among the number, for New York, on official business—two or three Senators and a Cabinet official to represent the President. We shall not return for ten days and I shall depend upon you to keep the office business in hand."

"I will do all that I can willingly," replied Sumner.

"And I think I'll go off now. The time is short until five tomorrow. I have some preparations to make. You may as well take charge at once."

Leaving Sumner he stepped to the side of Miss Bradford and engaged in a whispered conversation. Cuthbert was a discreet person and gave no heed to the couple. He was used to the manners of many high officials with their female clerks, and paid no attention to what did not concern him. He had observed that an apparent intimacy existed between his chief and Miss Bradford. If they knew that he had noticed them they gave no sign that his knowledge was an annoyance. His presence was treated with the utmost decorum.

The whispered talk kept on for some time. Finally, whatever subject had been under discussion seemed to have been satisfactorially arranged, and the chief arose from the seat he had occupied beside the lady and shook her hand warmly, with the words:

"At Easter then without fail."

"Poor Jewel," thought Cuthbert, "what will be her fate when she is the wife of this man who is but a reformed rake seeking to re-instate himself in society by a high political position and a rich marriage."

As the thought lingered in his mind, General Benson paused beside his desk. Sumner could not refrain from giving him an admiring glance nor could he wonder at the infatuation of most women for the handsome chief who stood there drawing on his gloves, his costly fur-lined coat unbuttoned and nearly sweeping the carpet giving an added charm to this handsome face, elegant figure and gracious manner.

"I have intrusted you with a delicate piece of business, Mr. Sumner." His voice was impressive. "The official relations between us have always been coordinate in character. I am confiding in you now as I would in a personal friend. You will find some additional papers to be collated in my desk," he continued drawing him behind the rich folds of the curtains back of the official desk. He gaze was fixed full in Sumner's face with such earnestness and anxiety that at once appealed to the secretary's sympathy. Sumner's face was like an open book in its candor and innocence of guile, as he replied quietly:

"You may trust me, General Benson, to respect your confidence. Personal matters have no entrance where they would interfere with obedience to my superiors."

"And, see here, Sumner, you may be detained later tomorrow night than tonight. Your work will probably keep you until sharp midnight, perhaps past. I have given the watchman notice of your being here by my orders. Here is my private entrance key and you can let yourself and Miss Bradford out without trouble. See that everything is safely closed up. You shall be handsomely compensated for your extra labor, although I know that you have no thought of the money," he added in answer to Sumner's deprecating wave of the hand. "Good-bye," and giving him his hand, the chief shook his warmly, and left the room."

They heard him descending the stairs, talking and laughing with messengers and others employed about the building, in the genial way for which he was noted among government employees.

XXII

Time and tide wait for no man; brains may throb, and hearts may ache or break, but the world rolls on just the same, for weal and woe, whether the grim skeleton that comes an unbidden guest on so many a man's hearth is shrouded in elegance or bare in all its appalling hideousness.

It was not until two P.M. of Sunday that the secretary and stenographer had time to rest as they neared the close of their labors. Sumner felt a weariness of spirit and a dull aching of the heart that was not due to overwork. Worriment had removed the fresh heartful bloom from his face, but the paleness and thinness added to its refinement and intellectuality; while the restless feverish dilation of his dark eyes rendered them singularly striking and brilliant. More than once during this wretched time he had been possessed with a longing to be back with his father in their quiet New England home.

"Yes, this shall be my last year in politics. I'll go home and take up the business for which I was born; it will please my father."

As he turned to resume his work with a sigh, he became conscious that Miss Bradford was watching him. There had been a time when he had felt a passing admiration for the good-looking stenographer, and had paid her some attention, but after he met Jewel he had never pretended to give her a second thought.

She, on her side, had not resented his dessertion but always seemed to retain a genuine regard for him which had shown itself in many neighborly acts of kindness which the close intimacy of office life often brings about between women and men. She had been rattling the keys of her typewriter at a furious rate of speed all day, and now, with a final pull of the carriage, finished her work. Then she rose with a sigh, crossed the room and flung herself down on one of the couches opposite Sumner's desk, evidently bent on conversation.

"Mr. Sumner, you look—oh, I don't know how you look, but I should say a rest would do you good."

"I shall have one when the vacation comes. I am going home and I shall not return to Washington."

"Are you going for good?" she asked in a surprised tone.

"Yes," he answered as he adjusted a pile of manuscript, and began folding up the papers scattered over his desk. "Washington holds no charm for me."

She was silent for a time and as she sat buried in deep thought she tapped the floor with one foot in restless fashion. At length she said:

"Don't think me intrusive, or that I seek to harrow your feelings, but isn't this sudden resolve the result of the misunderstanding between you and Miss Bowen?"

"I will answer you as frankly as you have asked, Miss Bradford; it is so."

There followed another pause, a silence so long that the young man thought that she had forgotten his presence. Suddenly she spoke again.

"Mr. Sumner, I like you; I trust you; why I know not, for my experience in life has not been of so pleasant a nature as to cause me to trust anyone; not a man, surely. But today I feel a desire to talk on forbidden subjects, to take someone into my confidence."

Sumner looked at her keenly as he said significantly:

"It is a safe rule, Miss Bradford, to keep one's own counsel."

"I feel impelled to tell you what I am about to disclose, by an unseen power. Do you not believe in unseen forces influencing our acts?" she asked wistfully.

"I cannot deny that I have sometimes felt the same influence of supernatural powers that you speak of, and I do firmly trust that the world of shadows and mystery to which we are all bound may be one of infinite love, infinite calm and rest."

"For those who have been upright here," while a look of pain crossed her face. "But what of those among us who have been guilty of many sins? That is the thought that haunts me tonight." She pushed her hair from her face with one hand as she looked up at him.

"Why trouble ourselves with such questions, Miss Bradford? Why not simply trust the judgment that sees not as man sees?"

She felt calmed as she looked into the true, earnest face opposite her. "Thank you," she said at last, simply. Then—

"May I tell you?"

"Whatever confidence you honor me by giving shall be sacredly respected."

"I know that. Did I not tell you that I trusted you? But you have my permission to tell Jewel Bowen as much as you think fit, for it is her due."

Sumner colored as he said:

"I am not on terms of intimacy with Miss Bowen."

"I know that, too," she replied impatiently, "but you probably will be after you hear what I have to tell you. I, too, am about to leave

Washington. When I leave the office tonight I shall never return. Easter is two weeks off, and at Easter I am to be married to General Benson."

"Married—General Benson! Impossible! You jest!" exclaimed the startled man.

"To General Benson," she repeated emphatically.

"But—Miss Bowen—"

"Will have a welcome release," she broke in. "It is a long-delayed ceremony that should have been performed five years ago. I have a son four years old, Mr. Sumner!"

Sumner could not answer her. He stared at the woman before him with unseeing eyes. He could not believe that he had heard aright.

"A son four years of age!" he repeated mechanically in shocked surprise. "This is most extraordinary! How can it be possible?" No wonder you are incredulous.

"Wait, wait!" she went on, "give me time. I will tell you all; it is your right to know. It has all been arranged so suddenly that my brain is in a whirl—I cannot think!"

She flung herself down against the cushions of the couch, and endeavored to grow calm. Sumner waited, disturbed, unhappy, heartsick, over this scene, fearing he knew not what. He watched her labored breathing, her clenched hands, and there was a long pause.

Sumner cast anxious glances over at the bowed head opposite him supported on its owner's hand. The fire blazed cheerily, and outside the wind rose, whirling the rain in great sheets against the window panes. It was a wild night.

Finally Elsie Bradford sat up pushing her hair back restlessly from her temples, and faced him white and agitated.

"All this misery that you have endured for the past month," she began slowly,—"all the sorrow, you owe to one man. He has tortured you, fooled you, deceived you—Yes, it is true; but I—God help me—I love him."

"I do not comprehend your meaning, Miss Bradford, to whom do you refer?" he asked soothingly, for there was the glitter of fever in her eyes.

"Silence!" she interrupted sternly. "I must tell you certain things for your own welfare and the welfare of the girl you love. I dare not hide them. Perhaps—who knows—it may be put down to my credit in that great future life toward which we are all journeying. In the years that are coming, when you are both happy and forgetful of this present miserable time, remember me and my misery with pity."

Sumner could only wait in pained surprise for her to continue. She pressed her hands convulsively to her heart, as she sat there white as death, and trembling all over.

"Did it ever occur to you, Cuthbert Sumner, that you are the victim of a plot?"

"You will speak in riddles, Miss Bradford. I must confess that I do not understand you."

"And yet you are a man of remarkable intelligence, and not a child in the world's ways. I cannot swear to it, but I believe that you have fallen into the net of two adventurers and a daring adventuress. Have you noticed any intimacy between General Benson and the Madisons?"

"No; they seem to be merely chance acquaintances."

"And yet, they are partners in crime, and I believe that General Benson introduced the Bowens to the Madisons."

"Great heavens! No!" cried Sumner a great light breaking in upon him at the bare possibility of such a thing being true. "Miss Bradford, are you sure?" he asked hurriedly.

"I am almost certain of the truth of what I say; you can easily ascertain if I am correct in my suspicions. I believe the intention was, your fortune for Aurelia Madison, Miss Bowen's for the General."

"But where do you get your information? Upon what are your suspicions based? Surely you have something to go upon," cried Sumner recovering from his first bewilderment.

"How can I tell you? Oh! the shame of it all will kill me," she said as she drew a long shuddering breath.

"Your distress pains me, Miss Bradford," said Cuthbert gently as he watched the wretched girl; he was moved more than he cared to show—indignant—furious over the conduct of this scoundrel in a high place. He went to one of the wardrobes and opened the door disclosing a compartment used as a wine closet. He quickly filled a glass from a costly cut-glass decanter, and carried it to the half-fainting woman urging her to drink it.

She took it eagerly from his hand and drained the glass.

"Yes, yes, I must go on. It is part of my punishment—my atonement! It is such misery, shame!" she sobbed brokenly. "I heard he was about to marry Miss Bowen. I accused him of treachery toward you in the matter. I threatened him with exposure. I told him that he must make atonement to me and the child at once. He must do it or I would speak; I would go to Miss Bowen with the whole miserable story."

"And he?" questioned Sumner gently, yet sternly, stifling his own feelings for the sake of the heart-broken woman before him, giving out strength and protection with womanly tenderness to soothe. "Tell me all, and be sure that I will speak of nothing that you desire kept secret."

"To have you understand the man known as General Benson, I must tell you a portion of my history."

"Excuse me," broke in Sumner, "you say 'known as General Benson,' is not that his true name?"

"No, it is not. And I cannot give you the true one. I have my own thoughts about it, however, When I was eighteen years of age, I came from Kentucky, where I was born, to Washington seeking employment.

I was left an orphan while an infant, and brought up by my aunt who was too poor to support me after I entered womanhood. She did the best for me that she could, however, and I started out with high hopes, telling her that I should soon be able to repay her for her kindness and care. I had heard much of the large salaries paid to government clerks, and determined to seek employment here.

Arriving in the city, I went to call upon the congressman from our district to whom I brought letters of introduction. He received me kindly, and said that he would do his best to have me appointed. After a week he sent me word to call at the Treasury Building. There he introduced me to General Benson who wanted a clerk. The General immediately engaged me, and it is needless for me to say that I was overjoyed at my good fortune. I was able to send my aunt money, and for a time I was perfectly happy. It is useless to dwell on the details—I wish to hurry over this part of my life—suffice it that in six months time I had become the chief's victim.

I am abhorrent to you, no doubt. You who have been rich all your life may despise me; but I had tasted poverty, I appreciated its effect on my future welfare, and I sickened at the thought."

She paused a moment to take breath, for she had spoken rapidly, as if eager to have done with the shameful and painful details. "Official wealth, power and opportunity were my ruin. I was led to confide in the chief by his high position; and he, like others in such places, deceived me and betrayed that confidence. He was my first lover, for I was but eighteen, and I loved him as we always love the first man who teaches us what love is. I admired his genial ways, his distinguished air, and even his success in his vices was a source of pride to me. He took advantage of my youth to mold me to his fancy, and make me like himself. Oh, I can never make you realize the depravity of our elegant chief.

For a long time he was content with my love. I was young enough and pretty enough to satisfy even him. But after a while he met Aurelia Madison, and then my agony began."

"What!" exclaimed Sumner, "do you know what you say? Aurelia Madison one of General Benson's mistresses?"

"That is not the worst thing about her," replied the woman with a bitter smile. "Will you believe me when I tell you that she is a quadroon?"

"Impossible! you rave!" almost shouted the young man.

"I would it were not true. Yes, she is a quadroon, the child of Major Madison's slave, born about the time the war broke out. That is why the two men find in her a willing tool."

"My God!" exclaimed Sumner as he wiped the perspiration from his face, "a negress! this is too horrible." Repeated shocks had unnerved him, and he felt weak and bewildered.

"Do not blame her. Fate is against her. She is helpless. The education of generations of her foreparents has entered into her blood. I should feel sorry for her if I could, but I feel only my own misery and degredation. I am selfish in my despair. Happy, prosperous people sympathize with the woes of others, but sometimes I feel like laughing at their mimic woes, my own are so much greater in comparison.

Yet Aurelia in a measure deserves our pity. The loveliness of Negro women of mixed blood is very often marvellous, and their condition deplorable. Beautiful almost beyond description, many of them educated and refined, with the best white blood of the South in their veins, they refuse to mate themselves with the ignorant of their own race. Socially, they are not recognized by the whites; they are often without money enough for but the barest necessities of life; honorably, they cannot procure sufficient means to gratify their luxurious tastes; their mothers were like themselves; their fathers they never knew; debauched whitemen are ever ready to take advantage of their destitution, and after living a short life of shame, they sink into early graves. Living, they were despised by whites and blacks alike; dead, they are mourned by none. You know yourself Mr. Sumner, that caste as found at the North is a terrible thing. It is killing the black man's hope there in every avenue; it is centered against his advancement. We in the South are flagrant in our abuse of the Negro but we do not descend to the pettiness that your section practices. We shut our eyes to many things in the South because of our near relationship to many of these despised people. But black blood is everywhere—in society and out, and in our families even; we cannot feel assured that it has not filtered into the most exclusive families. We try to stem the tide but I believe it is a hopeless task."

Sumner listened to her bound by the horrible fascination of her words. At last he said:

"But a white man may be betrayed into marrying her. I certainly came near to it myself."

"Very true; and if she had been a different woman, she would have succeeded, you would have been proud of your handsome wife because of your ignorance of her origin. As life, real life, has unfolded to my view, I have come to think that there is nothing in this prejudice but a relic of barbarism."

"Perhaps your reasoning is true; I will not attempt a denial. But I am thankful for my deliverance."

"Your feeling is natural; certainly, I do not blame you," she said, and after a slight pause resumed her narrative.

"One day the General came to me and told me that we must part. I owe you many obligations for your kindness. You have made the past few months very pleasant; of course you knew it was only for awhile, and that it must end some day. It is past now, and we will each go our way just as if we had never met. You must know that with men of the world these things are very natural and very pleasant. Here is some money;" and he thrust a well-filled purse in my hands.

My heart was filled with terror and agony. 'But you said that you loved me.' I managed to falter in a dazed way. 'Well, perhaps, for the moment. But—can't you understand these things? I will spare you as much as I can; if I am harsh you press me to it.' He spoke lightly, carelessly, to me as I stood before him crushed for all eternity—to me, who had fallen, without a thought of resistance, under the charm of his manner and beauty, that have ruined more than one woman among those who are above me in wealth and position. It is left for men to change quickly. He seemed dumb, frozen, dead to all feeling. His heart and mind were filled with the dazzling beauty of his new love—the Negress Aurelia Madison. He had nothing left for me—not even pity. Then he continued,—

'Elise, it is particularly necessary for my future plans that this affair of ours be kept secret. If you bury it in your heart, and seal your lips upon it, you shall be recompensed finally, I will never lose sight of you and the boy, but direct that a large sum shall be paid to you yearly. If not—people have died for a less offense than that.'

While he was talking I was thinking deeply and rapidly. I felt that my only chance lay in matching his cunning with diplomacy. I made up my mind to compromise the matter. He was stronger than I; I could do nothing at present. Finally I told him that I would agree to all he asked if he would allow me to retain my position in the office with him, and would provide for the boy and educate him.

This he agreed to do, and there has been a sort of armed neutrality between us ever since. I have learned much by being here. I know enough to ruin him. I planned for it and I have succeeded. He dares not go against me now, and so he has promised marriage, and I shall once more hold my head up among honest women."

Sumner felt a great wave of pity sweep over him at the thought of this delicate woman hoping to cope with the cunning deviltry of the man she had unmasked; but he could not find it in his heart to speak one discouraging word. His eyes filled with tears which were no shame to his manhood.

"Where is the child?" he asked when he could collect his scattered thoughts enough to speak.

"In Kentucky with my aunt," she replied naming a town.

"If what you tell me is true, and knowing what I do, I cannot doubt your story, General Benson is a consummate villain, a dangerous man," said Sumner as he paced the floor in excitement and wrath. "It is not possible that such things can be and go unpunished."

"You know now why I think it all a plot against you. Cannot you see for yourself?"

"Yes; I can never repay you for what you have done."

"Do not mention it. I shall be repaid if only you circumvent that woman, and all is made right between you and Miss Bowen."

It had grown very dark and Sumner lighted the gas.

"I will call a herdic and see you home," he said, "if you will come now. It is long past the dinner hour. We have been here long enough. I feel it impossible to stop here longer, the place stifles me."

"I cannot go yet," she replied, "I have papers to sort and many articles to destroy as well as to gather up. I never wish to see the place again."

"I will stay then until you are ready to go."

"No; that is not necessary, thank you. Give me the key. I will lock up and leave it with the watchman."

"Well, then, if you are not afraid," he said reluctantly. He was dazed by all he had heard and wished to be alone. When he was ready to leave, he took her hand in his and shook it warmly.

"Good-bye, my friend; you have given me renewed hope."

In after years, Cuthbert remembered her face with its varying, changing tints—hope and despair—each struggling for the mastery.

"Yes," she said softly, "I am your friend, but friendships are short—made to be severed. Still, I am sure we shall meet again. How strange it is that lives are touching thus all the time—strangers yesterday, today helping each other—let us hope so at least—touching—parting—but not forgotten—not utterly forgotten."

There was a new dignity in her manner that he had never noticed in the silent stenographer. But there was still a weary, listless tone in her voice.

He pressed her white fingers with his strong eager hand, feeling his heart throb with suppressed excitement—the joy of living once more. He lifted her cold hand and touched it with his lips.

"Good-bye, then, once more; someone said once that meant 'God bless you'; I could say no more if I knew that our parting would be eternal which it is not. I want you to know Jewel."

She looked at him steadily a moment, then her face fell; a slight tremor passed over her face; she was unaccustomed to the chivalrous treatment that men give to women whom they respect. The hand he had kissed fell to her side. As he turned to close the door of the apartment, she was still standing where he had left her, with listless hands and bent head.

XXIII

Cuthbert's mind was in a tumult as he walked down the stairs and through the corridors of the great building. His strained nerves relaxed; he felt the intense relief of a man who throws a heavy load from his shoulders.

He accepted without question the story told him by Miss Bradford and her suggestion of a vile plot by these arch-conspirators to gain possession of a fortune. The story was feasible whichever way he viewed it. "Yes, it must be so." The more the thought of it, the more he wondered at his own blindness in not solving the problem before. His eyes flashed, and he clenched his hands in anger. His mood boded ill for his enemies. Already his mind was filled with plans to disconcert the plotters.

He hailed a passing herdic and was driven to his rooms. He felt sick, giddy, his hands trembled. This unexpected revelation, while it caused him intense happiness, nearly overcame him. He longed to be alone in his rooms where he could think over what he had heard. But in the midst of his joy and his plans to see Jewel and explain this great wrong and mystery to her, came thoughts—sorrowful thoughts of the woman who had befriended him. What would be her fate? he asked himself. Surely it was but a question of time before the chief, with his method of living, would disappear beneath the maelstrom of his own unprincipled acts.

It was nine o'clock when he arrived at home thoroughly worn out. A splendid fire in the grate bade him a cordial welcome. John served him a good dinner. After making a pretense of eating, Sumner sat with his wine untasted on the table before him, smoking and staring into the fire. He sat there for hours smoking and thinking. Troubled thoughts disturbed him, shadows lingered on his face which the pleasant surroundings had not the power to dispel. He was deeply impressed by the insignificant trifles that had solved the secret of this wicked plot, in a skillful woman's hands, and more than thankful to know that through her he held the threads of the labyrinth in his own strong hands. He retired to rest worn out in mind and body. Physical and mental exhaustion brought some degree of calm, and he slept, but his slumber was fitful and broken, and he could still hear the moaning of the wind and the beating of the rain against the window panes. Mingled with these sounds were distorted dreams—bearing a shadowy relation to the scenes through which he had just passed.

In those uneasy slumbers he dreamed that he was in a deep, dark pit. Darkness blacker than the blackest night was all about him; but as he lay there, for he dreamed that he was reclining on the floor of the pit, suddenly beneath his body he felt a movement as of a monstrous body—a regular undulating movement. Then it seemed borne in upon his mind that the pit was a snake's den; the monsters— three in number—pythons of immense size to whom human victims were offered as sacrifices. He had been thrown to these sacred reptiles as their next victim. In his dream, horror and terror paralyzed both thought and action for a time. Then he realized that he must act quickly. As he looked into the dense darkness a tremulous ray of light pierced the gloom of the pit and for an instant Jewel's face smiled upon him, then disappeared. In that instant of light he discerned a ladder leading to an opening at the top of the pit, through which he must have been thrown into the horrible dungeon. As he calculated his chances of escape, he heard the dragging and sweeping of a long ponderous body in motion moving toward him. With a determined wrench he broke the spell that bound him, sprang up the ladder and reached the blessed light of day.

He awoke bathed in perspiration, shivering with horror, his heart beating with fear. He lay there a while trying to shake off the effects of his dream, but for a time it seemed impossible; it would not slip away as dreams do; it was too vivid not to leave unpleasant thoughts behind.

Finally he sprang up. It was very early but he rang for John, and took time to make a careful and refreshing toilet. By half-past eight he was ready for the excellent breakfast brought by the delighted John who had not seen his master so cheerful for many weeks.

He wrote a note and despatched it by messenger to the department saying he would be late, and to refer all matters to the assistant secretary until he came.

He wandered aimlessly about the rooms wondering how he could possibly content himself while he waited for a conventional hour to come for a call on Jewel. At length he resolved to go for a walk, and was just getting into his street garments when there was a loud ring at the outer door of the suite. John answered it. He herd a question in a man's voice:

"Is Mr. Sumner at home?"

Then as he turned from the window to answer John's call, he saw his servant's frightened face, and close behind him an officer. Sumner stood still in amazement.

"Mr. Cuthbert Sumner?" asked the officer.

"I am Mr. Sumner. What is your business with me?"

"Well, sir," said the man laboriously, "there's been a murder up at the Treasury building there. Young woman found this morning. You're wanted to be at the inquest."

"But I know nothing of this affair. Who's the woman?"

The officer pulled a paper from his pocket and held it out awkwardly toward him:

"Sorry, sir, to disturb you. Miss Bradford is the victim; you are held on suspicion being the last gent, or person, seen in her company. Charge of murder!"

"Murder!" cried the horrified man.

The officer nodded as he replied:

"Ay, sir; and bad enough it is. Prussic acid was the means, sir, given in a glass of wine. Miss Elise Bradford, clerk at the Treasury Building. Body discovered by watchman early this morning."

"Great heavens!" said Sumner reeling back, "it can't be possible that the girl is dead—murdered!"

The officer's look said plainly enough,—"you know all about it." The police are quick to make victims.

"I know nothing about it. She was all right when I left her at eight yesterday after we had finished our work. I—"

"Stop, sir," said the man. "I am bound to warn you that whatever you say will be used as evidence against you."

"Let it be so," returned Sumner haughtily. "I have nothing to hide. I am absolutely guiltless of the crime as you will find."

"Maybe so, sir," replied the man civilly. "But meanwhile you must come with me."

Sumner was calm and self-possessed.

"You are free to examine my effects," he said. "I shall be ready to go with you in five minutes."

"I cannot lose sight of you, sir."

"Certainly not."

The faithful John stood by loudly protesting against the indignities put upon his master. Sumner gave him a few directions about the rooms.

PAULINE E. HOPKINS

A herdic was called, and in five minutes the policeman and his prisoner were driven to the Police Court. The police evidence was given, and the prisoner having been remanded until after the inquest, was removed to the cells.

XXIV

Marthy Johnson knelt on the kitchen floor surrounded by heaps of fine white clothing sorting them into orderly piles. It was six o'clock on Monday morning. The gaudy little clock on the mantel, flanked by red vases elaborately gilded and filled with paper sunflowers, had just finished striking. The coffee pot was giving out jets of fragrant steam, and the pan of hot corn pone was smiling in an inviting manner from the back of the range. The square deal table between the windows held plates, mugs, knives and forks for three. The woman sang as she sorted:

> *"Oh, the milk-white hosses, milk-white hosses,*
> *Milk-white hosses over in Jerden,*
> *Milk-white hosses, milk-white hosses,*
> *I long to see that day.*
> *"Oh, hitch 'em to the chariot, hitch 'em to the chariot,*
> *Hitch 'em to the chariot over in Jerden,*
> *Hitch 'em to the chariot, hitch 'em to the chariot,*
> *I long to see that day."*

We last saw Marthy on the Enson plantation. Years have added to her weight, but other than that, hers is the same frank, fun-loving countenance, with its soft brown tint, its dazzling eyes and teeth.

Her tidy calico gown was hidden by an immense blue-and-white-checked apron, and a snowy towel tied turban-fashion hid her soft crinkly hair.

"Reckon I'd better fry that ham; it's gittin' on toward seven right smart," said Marthy with a glance at the clock. "My word, but where is mammy! I's clean worried out of my wits 'bout the child. Oliver—oh—Oliver!" she cried, opening a door which led from the kitchen to the regions above.

"What's wanting, mummy?" was wafted back in a male voice just turning into manhood.

"Your granny, Oliver; you must go hunt her child. I never knowed her to stay away all night but once befo'. You mus' git your breakfas' an' hunt her."

"Granny's all right, ma. I'm busy. Got a thesis for first recitation this morning. 'Deed I can't spare the time to go way over to the treasury from Meridian hill."

"You, Oliver, you; move yourse'f now, hyar me? Your pa's never 'roun' when he's wanted, an' your sister's slavin' herse'f like a nigger to help ejekate yer. My Lord, how worthless men folks is! You've got a *teaseus*, have you?" she continued, waxing more wroth each moment. "An' your granny that's made of you like you was a baby may be daid up thar in the treasury or moulderin' in some alley an' you hollerin' down these stairs to me that you can't go an' holp her 'cause you's got a *teaseus*. I 'spec's we's all made a fool of you a-gettin' you into college. You's jes' like yer daddy; you's the born spit of him. My word, if you don't stir them long legs o' yourn out o' this lively, I'll take you down sure's I'm yer mammy; I'll take yer down if you was as big as a house." The flood of angry words ended in a flood of tears. Her face was buried in the ample folds of her gingham apron when Oliver entered the kitchen.

He was a good-looking lad, tall and slender, a shade lighter brown than his mother, but with her pleasant, kindly face, laughing eyes and fun-loving countenance. He had a gay and fearless bearing that was the pride of Marthy's heart. She often told her mother in confidence, when Oliver was out of hearing:

"Mammy, yer gran'son's a born gin'ral; I never seen any man to 'pare with the swing dat's on him outside o' ol' Gin'ral Burnsis."

And in this opinion Aunt Henny joined.

"Now, ma, don't cry," said the boy putting his arm about his mother's neck and kissing her cheek. "I'm going right off. I'm as fond of granny as can be. Don't now go and work yourself all up. I'm going this blessed moment." Marthy cried comfortably on the shoulder of her big son and allowed him to coax her into a better frame of mind. "You are a good boy, Ollie, and I didn't mean all them hard things I jes' said, honey. Don' you go an' lay 'em up agin me, son; your ol' mammy's jes' worrited to death."

"Well, I ain't like dad, am I, ma?"

"No, bless yer heart, honey; yer ain't. You an' Venus is my comfits. Lawd, what a mis'able ol' 'ooman I'd be without you chilluns."

Marthy made Oliver sit down to his breakfast, waiting on him with a mother's fondness, piling his plate with the delicious fried ham and the smoking corn pone, and pouring his coffee with care.

"Do you know, ma," said Oliver between generous mouthfuls of bread and great gulps of coffee, as he ate with the hearty enjoyment of youth, "when I get through college, you shan't do a thing but wear a black silk dress every day and fold your hands and rock. I'm sick of seeing you in the washtub and Venus running to wait on the laides fit to break her neck. I'm going to take care of you both."

"When you 'spec' that time goin' ter come, silly chile? yer mammy 'spec' to wurk 'tell she draps inter the grave. Colored women wasn't made to take their comfit lak white ladies. They wasn't born fer nuthin' but ter wurk lak hosses or mules. Jes' seems lak we mus' wurk 'tell we draps into the grave."

"It won't be so always, ma. You'll see."

"Does you think money's jes' a growin' on bushes ready to shuck into your hand when you gits through college? Pears lak to me, Oliver, you'd better make up yer min' to hussle aroun' fer awhile. I don't want ter feel that a chile o' min's too biggotty to do anything hones' fer a livin'. Don' you turn up yer nose at washin', an' yer may jes' thank God ef you gits a 'ooman when you git jined that'll help you out in that business when college learnin' ain't payin'. An' don' spend yer extra money on silk dresses fer no 'ooman to lay roun' in. Caliker's done me all my life an' I ain't the worst 'ooman in the wurl' neither."

"Well, I'll wark fer you my own self, and I'll make money enough to keep you like a lady, college or no college."

"I wish it mote be so; but I jes' trimbles to have you talk that a-way, honey; jes' keep a still tongue and saw wood. Don't speak about your plans beforehan'. Never let anybody know what you reckon on doin' in the future 'cause the devil is always standin' 'roun' listenin' to you, an' that gen'man jes' nachally likes to put his cloven foot into a good basket of aigs an' smash 'em. 'Member what yer ma tells yer, honey."

"Now, ma, you don't believe all them old signs about hoodooing and such stuff. There isn't a thing in it, it's nothing but superstition."

"Don't talk to me 'bout yer suferstition; there is some things in this wurl that college edication won't 'splain, an' you can't argify an' condispute with 'em, neither. I've had my trials, Oliver, but tryin' to bring you an' yer sister to a realisin' sense of the sin in the wurl is hard on me, an' it lays on my mind. Now las' night I had a dream that a ghos' stood right up side 'o the bed lookin' at me. That's turrible bad luck; an' its bein' a female ghos' means that trouble is comin' to this family thro' a 'ooman. Now, this mornin' I gits up an fin' yer granny ain't been her all night. It's borne in on me that sumthin' is wrong. Where 'bouts did you drap her, honey, when you picked the clos' up las' evenin'?"

"The last place we went, ma, was to Senator Bowens. Granny went roun' to the kitchen to talk to Mis' Johnson while I went up to Venus. Granny said she was short off for breath and Mis' Johnson gave her a cup of coffee and a cutlet. Granny's fond of chicken cutlets."

"Um," replied his mother, "Mis' Johnson's a born lady cook or no cook. Chicken cutlets," she mused. "Some new Yankee fashion cookin' chicken, I reckon, bein' Mis' Johnson's from out Bos'n way. Wha's it taste like, Oliver, didn't they ask yer to have a bite with 'em"?

"Chicken cutlets are common, ma," replied Oliver, with the indifference of familiarity. "Just slap your chicken in egg and bread crumbs, drop it into hot fat and there you are."

"Do you like 'em, son?" inquired his mother, while one could see in the watery look that lurked about the corners of her mouth a determination to try chicken cutlets at the first opportunity.

"I like 'em *fine* ma."

Marthy sighed, and then returned to the original subject. "What did granny say when you lef' her?"

"She said that she'd a right smart turn of washing up and dusting that she'd left over from Saturday afternoon because the clerks were working overtime in one of the departments. I left her at the foot of the steps on the north side."

"Well, honey, I don' kno'," and Marthy shook her head dubiously. Run along to yer pa now, an' then up to the 'partment to fin' yer granny. 'Deed, God knows I hope the ol' lady's safe, but I mistrus' mighty much, I do."

"I think you're worrying for nothing, ma; I'm not a bit anxious. Sometimes has to stop late, and she might have stayed all night because she was afraid to walk home alone."

Marthy shook her head solemnly. "Wha'd she be 'fraid of a po' black 'ooman with nuthin' to steal? 'Tain't a soul gwine tech her. She ain't young an' purty makin' a 'ticemen' fer people; men isn't chasin' 'roun' street corners in Wash'nt'n after ugly ol' 'oomen's. No Oliver; fifteen year ago this blessid winter when you and your sister was tweenty tots, jes' like this yer granny stayed away, an' sot all night on top o' ninety thousan' dollars wurth o' greenbacks. The night befo' it happened I dreamt I was carried up to glory'settin' on a cloud an' playin' on a golden harp, which means suddint honors an' el'vations; nex' thing I knowed the Presidunt 'pinted mammy prominen'ly to a firmamen' persition in the 'partment at forty dollars a munf. Then I was able to sen' yer sister to school an' keep her nice in spite 'o yer daddy's racketty ways. Yer granny's holped me powful. Yer pa's money don' 'mount to a hill o' beans in my pocket, but mammy's kep' him straigh, an' ennythin'd happen the ol' lady I'd be nachally obleeged to giv' up the ghos'."

"Ef you don' fin' your granny, stop at yer pa's an' bein' as the Gin'ral's away yer pester him to try an' hunt her up. An' don' fergit to stop inter Senator Bowen's an' see yer sister. Jes' ask her ef Miss Jewel's summer wrappers is to be clar-starched or biled-starched. 'Deed, my head's clean gone runnin' after mammy this mornin'. An' ef you see the madam or Miss Jewel, make yer manners. Them white ladies is apayin' fer yer schoolin'. Git down ter bus'ness, now, hyar me, son? money talks."

As Oliver disappeared from view around the corner of the street, Marthy closed the outer door an re-entered the kitchen. Her naturally hopeful nature re-asserted itself and she took a brighter view of the situation. "I reckon I'll laugh if mammy comes in now all right. I wonder which way Ollie 'll go? Like as not he'll walk down G street an' mammy'll come on the keers. Now, I'll jes' hussle roun' an' git them clo's out o' the tub agin' they git here."

Life had been checkered for Marthy since emancipation when she had joined her lot with St. Clair Enson's Isaac, in the "holy bonds of matrimony." "Like master like man," was a true prophecy in Isaac's case, and had caused the little brown woman a world of worry.

Isaac had obtained the billet of valet to General Benson, no one knew how, for up to that time he had been a ne'er-do-well, working when the notion pleased him or when actual starvation compelled him to exert himself, at other times swearing, drinking and fighting.

It was a time of rejoicing when, upon arriving home one night, after his daily lounge about the Bay or Buzzard's Nest, looking for something to stimulate his weary system, he announced to his family that he had been "hired" by General Benson. Marthy rejoiced exceedingly although, as she told Aunt Henny,—

"What in the wurld the Gin'ral 'spects to git out o' Ike in the way o' wurk passes me."

Her mother shook her head ominously.

"De Gin'ral mus' be plum crazy. 'Twon' las'."

After three months had rolled by, the poor little brown wife began to take courage. Ike was working "stiddy" although she had not yet seen the color of his money and she was still dependent upon the washing with which a number of families supplied her, and the substantial help given by her old mother's labor at the treasury.

"Pears lak, mammy, I can see some way to raise the mor'gage."

"Fu' w'y, Marthy?"

"Ike's so stiddy."

Aunt Henny shook her head.

"Wha' you reckin de bill is, chile?" asked the old woman, removing her pipe from her mouth. Work was over and her chair and pipe in the warmest corner near the kitchen range, were comforting to the wornout frame. Aunt Henny was seventy, but save for rheumatism she had not changed since she left the Enson plantation. Sometimes she would bend her limbs, shake her head and sigh, "Dey neber be easy goin' 'gin, fuh sho', but I got a heap o' hope outen dem whilst dey ben limber, my soul; de bes' laigs I'll eber hab in dis wurl."

"We does owe on the mor'gage five hundred dollars," said Marthy in reply to her mother's question.

"My wurd, but de money grow slow; I got one hunder' dollars up stairs 'tween the feather bed an' de mattress. You make Ike fotch out de res'. Cayn't rightly feel de place is ourn till we's paid up. When I sees you an' de chillun under your own roof, I gwine ter gib up de ghos' in peace. An' Marthy, don't neber be a plum fool an let Ike wurrit you into raisin' money on de place, ef he gits inter scrapes let him git out as he gits in, widout any holp but de debbil. Ef you eber let dat mon take de bread outer yer mouf dat way, an I'm daid, I gwine ter riz up outer de grave an' hit yer; yas, I'll rawhide yer jes' as I user down on de plantation."

Marthy gasped but heaved a sigh of satisfaction over the thought of the hundred dollars.

"Well, I'se glad as glad 'bout the money, mammy. An' Ike's jes' got to pony up to the pint of that other fo' hundred dollars."

"Hump!" grunted Aunt Henny. "I don' trus' him. Dat niggah no leanin' pos' fer me. I'se gwine call on Gen'ral Benson myse'f, an' ef he de right kin' o' white gen'man, he gwine holp me in a 'spiracy ter make Ike raise dat money. Wha' you say to dat, Marthy?"

"I likes it *fine*," Marthy cried, overjoyed at what she considered a brilliant plan to subjugate the irresponsible Isaac.

Shortly after this conversation, Marthy applied to her husband for money.

"I ain't got no money fer ye, Marthy," he said in answer to her request.

"Ain't got no money, an' you been wurkin' stiddy fer munfs! What's gone come of it I'd like ter know." Isaac scratched his head in perplexity.

"I 'low to do better by yer, Marthy; you's ben a good gal to me, an' I 'low I ain't done the right thing by you in every way sence we was jined, but I'se turned over a new leaf; I ain't drawed a red cent o' my wages sence I went to wait on the Gin'ral. I jes' lef' it in his han's fer 'ves'men'. Major Madison an' Gin'ral's spec'latin' in mines. Dey owns de Arrow-Head, an' all my wages an' all de money, Gin'ral kin raise has ben put in dat gol' mine up in de Col'rady hills."

"The Lawd save us, Ike! Then we'll done lose this place,' she cried. "The mor'gage money done come due in June, an' Mis' Jenkins been mighty kind, but he's boun' to fo'close cause I hear he want money pow'ful bad to meet his needcessities. O, Lawd! what is we gwine do?" she moaned rocking herself to and fro while the tears streamed down her cheeks.

"Don' you take on, Marthy," her husband said soothingly. 'I'll git de money from de Gin-ral all right. I know I ain't been a 'sponsible man fer yer, but I'se got human feelin', ain't I? Ain't I proud o' my gal an' my boy what's in de college? Wha' you tink I'se turned over a new leaf fo' ef it warn't to see them chilluns holdin' up dar heads 'long wif de bes' ob de high-biggotty Wash'nt'n 'stockracy? Thar daddy's gwine ter make 'em rich an' when you an' me is moulderin' ter clay dem chillun's gwine ter be eatin' chickun an' a-settin' on thar own front do' steps jes' like de Presidun'."

"I don' trus' no' white man. 'Member all the money went up in the Freedman's bank, don' yer? I don' guess he'd be slow makin' a profit outen yer by keepin' yer wages. Plenty gentmen'd do it 'fore yer could bat yer eye."

"You tew ha'sh, Marthy. De Gen'ral an' de major been mighty fine ter your husban', gal. Don' you worry, dat money's safe."

"I 'spicion him jes' the same," replied his wife sullenly.

"De major do be under some repetition as a bad character, but de Gin'ral's all right. Dar's heap o' his paw in 'im," he continued in a musing voice. "Dar neber was a better man den ol' massa, an' I orter know. Law*se*, de times me an' young massa had t'gedder, bar hunts, an' gamblin' 'bouts, an' shootin' and ridin'. He goin' so fas' I skacely cud keep up tuh him. We bin like brudders. All his clo's fits me *puffick!* Our size is jes' de same as ever. En jurin' de wah I jes' picked him twice outen de inimy's han's; my sakes dem was spurious times.

PAULINE E. HOPKINS

"You, Isaac, wha' in the lan' you talkin' 'bout? Is you gone crazy? Them remarks o' yourn is suttingly cur'ous." Isaac started to his feet, and there was a guilty look on his face.

"What was I sayin', Marthy? 'Clar fo' it, my thoughts was miles 'way from hyar."

"Do hish! Ef I didn't kno' yer age, Isaac Johnson, I'd think you gone dotty. I 'clar fo' it, I hope you ain't goin' ter have sof'n o' the brain from drinkin' all Sam Smith's bad rum over to Buzzard's Nes'. I hern tell o' sech happenin's, but I pray the Lawd not to pile that trib'lation on top o' me."

After this occurrence, Aunt Henny sought General Benson's presence as the only hope of getting money out of Isaac. From this interview the old woman returned with a look of terror and consternation on her face. When questioned by Marthy as to the outcome of the interview she would say nothing of her success, only repeating the words. "I'se seed a ghos'! Lawd, my days is done."

Marthy went heavily about her work as spring approached. But for her children she would have given up the unequal struggle. Just at the darkest hour the Bowens had become interested in Venus and Oliver, and soon the little brown mother had felt a revival of hope in her breast, as she planned to make bold and go herself to Miss Jewel and ask the dear young lady to intercede with the Senator and get him to take up the hateful mortgage.

After Oliver left the house, his mother rubbed away industriously, and under her skilful fingers the delicate clothing was soon floating like snow-capped billows in tubs and boilers. When noon was signalled from the observatory upon the hill, spotless garments waved in the keen air from every line in the large drying yard at the rear of the cottage.

"'Clar fo' it, Oliver's missed his school, an' mammy ain't come yet."

Half distracted with terror and fearing the worst, Marthy sat down in the midst of her disordered kitchen and sobbed aloud.

Suddenly she heard the click of the little gate. The next moment she saw Oliver's face at the door. It needed but a glance to tell that something extraordinary had happened. He was breathless from running, his face ashen, his large eyes were distended to twice their usual size.

"O, ma, there's been a murder up to the treasury—"

"Don' tell me it's yer granny!" shrieked his mother.

"No'm; 'taint granny; it's a young lady; and Mr. Sumner that was Miss Jewel's beau is arrested, an' granny ain't been seen *nowhere* since she went into the building last night. Pa'll be home after he's been to the station to notify the police about granny, an' Venus can't leave Miss Jewel; she's taking on so."

"O, yer po' granny, Oliver! I jes' cayn't bar up under this. O, where's my mammy! Good Lawd, where's she at?"

XXV

Terrible discovery this morning in Treasury building! Arrest, on suspicion, of Mr. Cuthbert Sumner!"

That was the startling head-line that met Jewel Bowen's eyes on that eventful Monday morning, and sent the blood back to her heart.

She had opened the paper lazily, glanced at the leaders, and with, "There's never anything interesting in the paper," turned to another sheet, and suddenly sat transfixed, her wide eyes seeing nothing but that one startling head-line that danced before her straining gaze, then stood still,—that at first appeared to be printed in great black type and then turned into blood-red letters!

In an instant the reserve and coldness of weeks was swept aside. He was again her lover. His deadly peril gripped her very heart-strings, and filled her whole being anew with all the strength and passion of woman's noblest love, that, at once, without a second's pause, throws aside all but honor itself for the being who is her world.

She had not read the account of the tragedy, but not for one instant did a thought of guilt associate itself in her mind with Cuthbert Sumner. *Guilty of a heinous crime!* She laughed aloud at the bare idea. In that moment she forgot the new duties lately assumed toward another. Promises had been forced upon her she had told herself often of late, with regret, and none could blame her if she swerved in the moment of trial from the exact path of duty. Now, she thanked God it was not yet a crime to think of the man she loved.

She calmed herself presently, and read the brief account given in the morning edition of the "Washington News." With the sheet closely clutched in her hand she sought her mother. Mrs. Bowen's maid was just serving her lady with breakfast as Jewel knocked and then entered the room. Mrs. Bowen was seated comfortably before the fire, opening her morning mail.

"Jewel, what on earth is the matter? What is wrong?" exclaimed her mother, startled at the strange look on her face.

"Cuthbert is arrested, charged with murder!"

Mrs. Bowen turned very white.

"Great heaven! Jewel! No, no, it is too horrible!"

"Read that," said the girl, laying the paper in her mother's lap.

The elder woman read the printed sheet and gazed up at her daughter with incredulous eyes.

"You do not believe him guilty?"

"*Guilty!*" the one word spoke volumes.

"What can we do to help him? It is unfortunate that your father is away."

"I have not thought yet." The determined woman spoke in the next sentence, "I shall visit him first of all."

"Jewel!" exclaimed her mother in a shocked tone. "What will the General think?"

"What he pleases," was the defiant answer.

Before Mrs. Bowen could protest, there was a hurried knock at the door, which, opening, admitted Venus. There were traces of tears on her face.

"Please, Miss, Mr. Sumner's man is in the hall asking if you will see him for a minute."

"Show him right up here, Venus."

John entered the presence of the two ladies with deep distress and alarm in his honest face. He looked years older than he did the day before. There was a strong affection between master and man. He came forward eagerly, his hands holding his cap and twitching nervously.

"Oh, Mrs. Bowen an' young Miss, I beg your pardon, but—but—I don't know what to do. I've telegraphed the ol' gent'man—

"Yes, John—when will he be here?" The ladies spoke together.

"The ol' gent'man's had shock, an' the doctor dassent to tell him, but the family lawyer will be here tomorrow to take charge; but I can't keep still, miss,—ma'am—I had to come an' see you. I've been in the Sumner family, boy an' man, for twenty years, an' they're used me white, ma-am—miss, right straight through. 'Clare, I'd do anyting on yearth for Mr. Cuthbert."

"How does your master bear it, John?"

"Like a lamb, miss—ma'am—I've been there now, jes' cam from there, been taking his orders an' things. All he says is 'John, there's a mistake; it'll be all right in a day or two.' But I don't believe it. I feel oneasy. I thought maybe you all would tell what more I can do."

"That's right, John. We will help you all we can. These are evil days that have come to us lately." But in spite of her brave words, Mrs. Bowen looked about her in a helpless, bewildered way. Then she appealed to her daughter, "Jewel, what do you advise, dear?"

"The first thing to do is to see Cuthbert; I'm going to drive down to the jail and have a long talk with him."

"Jewel!"

"Well, mamma, if we intend to benefit him, there is but one way. Venus, order me a herdic; I won't wait for the carriage," she said, turning to her maid. "Why, what are you crying about, silly child; they can't hang Mr. Sumner without a trial."

"Yes'm; I know that. But it's my granny, too, miss. We can't find her," said the girl with a burst of tears. Again John spoke, trying to explain the matter to the bewildered ladies.

"It's ol' Mis' Sargean'—"

"What did you say?" interrupted Mrs. Bowen sharply, leaning forward in her chair.

"Sergeant, ma'am, Ol' Aunt Henny Sargeant, she's Venus's gran'mother. She's a cleaner up at the department, an' she's disappeared; ain't been seen sense last night, when she went into the building to clean up. Taking that an' putting it with the murder an' other funny things that's been happening about Mr. Sumner lately, it 'pears to me that something underhand is going on," he said with a deferential bow.

"Venus, come with me. John, be good enough to order the herdic. I will look into this matter and see what can be done," and Jewel turned to leave the room.

"Please, miss, do you mind if I take a seat on the box?" asked John.

"Certainly not."

And the trio quitted the room leaving Mrs. Bowen alone.

XXVI

As the day grew older the excitement increased in the city over the murder of Elise Bradford. The circumstances surrounding the victim, as given out in the second editions of the press, the mysterious disappearance of the old scrub-woman and the high social and official position of the accused, gave rise to all sorts of sensational rumors.

"Very queer affair," said one man to another, nodding significantly. "A good deal behind it all, of course. Young men will be young men; you can't put an old head on young shoulders," he added, repeating the trite sayings as if they were original with himself.

"H'm, yes. Ugly facts, though, the wine-glasses especially. I take it the old Negress would be an important witness in the case."

"Yes. What about the wine-glasses? I haven't read the paper very carefully; just sketched it."

"Why, it seems they must have had wine together and he put prussic acid in her glass. But he denies it; says he gave her a glass of wine because she seemed faint, but he took none himself. In short, he cannot explain the presence of the *second* glass. The odd thing about it is his walking out and leaving the body there, if he did it, with no attempt at concealment."

"You don't say so! By Jove, what did he expect? And he claims to be innocent?"

"Yes; but of course, he'd do that. I suppose his lawyers will claim that it was suicide. Fact is, he must have found himself in a mess and took this method of getting clear. These young bloods are as bad as the worst when you corner them."

"It must have been that way. And then, again, what he says may be true, somehow. From what one hears of him, he is incapable of a crime like this. He is called a man of spotless honor."

"Well, perhaps, except where there's a woman in the case. We are men ourselves, and we know."

The other nodded in acquiescence.

Will Badger and Carroll West met in the corridor of the jail, one just coming from a conference with the prisoner, the other seeking an interview.

Kind-hearted Badger was feeling very much cast down over his friend's predicament.

"Think he did it, Badger?" asked West after they had exchanged greetings.

"No more than you or I," was the decisive answer. "I would not believe the blackest evidence against his bare word. I know the man."

"I'm with you, but—well—confound the jade, I say, to get Sumner in this fix. Of course, there's another man. Who is he? Have you an idea?"

Badger shook his head and sighed. "The examination is tomorrow at ten. Try and be there, West."

"I will, sure. The Madisons awfully cut up over this affair; she was almost in hysterics when I stopped in to talk it over. The Major isn't himself either."

"No wonder. Well, we shan't know anything positive until after the hearing. So long."

The friends separated.

Shortly after noon, Jewel arrived at the jail. The interview between her and Cuthbert was long and painful, but both were happier than they had been for many weeks. Sumner told Jewel the facts of his intimacy with Amelia, blaming himself greatly for all the trouble that had followed his first deception. "I should have been frank with you, Jewel, and all would have been well."

Jewel's gentle heart was at last at rest; perfect confidence was established between the re-united lovers. As she rose to go, he said:

"It may go hard with me tomorrow at the examination; indeed, I know it will. There will be difficult work ahead for my attorneys. So many things have happened to separate us, Jewel, that I dread the future."

The tears stood in her eyes. She turned her head to hide them.

"Dare I express my selfish hopes—my wishes?"

For answer she threw herself into his arms again, and as he held her thus he whispered his request with an eager look upon his face.

She blushed violently, hesitated, then drawing herself up proudly said:

"I will do as you wish."

"Tomorrow morning then, at eight, I shall be waiting."

"I will not fail you," was her low reply, as snatching her hand hastily from his detaining clasp, she turned to accompany the officer from the cell.

As she passed through the office she asked the captain for the address of the chief of the secret service.

"You mean Mr. Henson, I take it, Miss?"

"If he is the celebrated detective, he is the very one."

"Well, Miss, it's No.—Pennsylvania Avenue; but he takes no outside cases. His government duties are all that he finds time for."

"Still, I will call on him."

The man bowed, and she passed on. Months ago she remembered hearing her father speak of the great powers of this detective. Why it had lingered in her mind she knew not, but now a hidden force impelled her to seek his aid.

She shrank from nothing that might benefit her lover. Shrink! was that like it, the proud flush on the soft cheek, the warm light in her eyes? Her heart throbbed fast in the excess of happiness it was to know that he was true, that all misunderstandings were buried spectres, and that she—she alone held his heart. Let the world do its worst, she could repay by showing every trust in him. After tomorrow she would have the right to stand beside him, though all the world should frown. Her thoughts did not go beyond the present. He would be proved innocent, she was sure. Money could do anything and there would be no sparing of any moment to clear him.

The herdic seemed to creep over the space between the station and the detective's chambers. Her very heart seemed on fire under intense, suppressed excitement and the emotion that surged beneath her calm, conventional exterior.

No.—Pennsylvania Avenue was a large brick building where lawyers congregated. Jewel alighted from the herdic, leaving Venus in it. Mr. Henson's office was on the second floor. She paused before a door upon the glass panels of which appeared the letters: "J. Henson, Detective." She opened the door and entered. There were a number of clerks in the room busily writing. One elderly man near the door was in charge.

Yes, Mr. Henson was in and would no doubt see the lady if she could wait awhile, he said in reply to Jewel's inquiry. Placing a chair for her he took her card and disappeared behind a door marked "Private." Presently he returned saying that if she would come with him, Mr. Henson would receive her.

The great detective was seated at his desk writing. He did not look up as she entered, but said:

"Be seated, madam; I will give you my attention in one moment."

Jewel saw a well-preserved man of sixty odd years, middle height, and rather broad, but not fleshy. His thick iron-gray hair covered his head fully and curled in masses over a broad forehead. He was well and carefully dressed. Presently he looked up from his work and glanced in her direction; then she saw that he had expressive dark eyes and a pleasant face which might have been handsome in youth, but for a long livid scar that crossed his face diagonally. A sabre might have made that deep, dangerous cut.

The light in the room was faint, and Jewel did not perceive the pallor that spread over the man's face as he gazed at her; the words he was about to utter died away unsaid, his chest heaved an instant in a convulsive movement which he controlled by a violent effort. There was silence as the man and girl gazed at each other, mutually attracted by a hidden affinity. It was but a second that the pause endured.

"You wish to speak with me, Miss?"

Then Jewel aroused herself from the spell which had held her since she encountered the piercing gaze of the quiet elderly man before her. The sound of his voice generated a feeling of relief in her breast, of trust and confidence. She could not analyze the sensation of complete rest that came to her with the few words just spoken.

"I wish to speak with you," she replied tremulously; then, recovering herself: "When I say that I am deeply interested in the murder that has just been committed, and that Mr. Sumner is my dearest friend, you will know what I want."

"I understand, Miss Bowen," he said, glancing at the card in his hand. "I seldom take cases outside of the government; still, I will hear what you have to tell me. I think this may be an exception to my rule."

He motioned her to the chair beside him and then placed a note-book on the desk before him.

"Mr. Sumner is innocent," said the girl in a trembling voice. "He will have able counsel, I know; but I shall feel better if you will take charge. I have heard so much of your skill and wonderful powers of discernment that no one else could satisfy me."

The man looked at the beautiful girl before him with something akin to worship in his eyes. When he spoke again his voice had taken on an added softness, his words seemed to carry a caress hidden beneath their commonplace utterance.

"Thank you; I am greatly interested. Even the newspaper accounts bear evidence that this is a remarkable case, and there is generally a good deal hidden behind what they give out. Now tell me all you know of the matter."

Calmed by his gentle tones, Jewel gave a brief account of the affair as told her by Sumner. When she ceased speaking Mr. Henson, who had listened with down-cast eyes and unmoved countenance, said:

"It is a curious case, very. There seems no clue; but, if I mistake not, you have suspicions of someone." His eyes rested on her face in a peculiarly impressive manner.

"Why do you think so?"

"I trace it in the tones of your voice. Now tell me the name of the person you suspect and why."

The girl hesitated, then said in a low tone:

"General Benson!"

"Ah!" It was but a breath, but it spoke volumes. "And have you mentioned this to anyone?"

"Only to Mr. Sumner, but he will not entertain the thought. He thinks the idea absurd because the General is in New York, and can hardly know more than the bare outlines of the case as yet."

"Just so. But upon what do you base your thought?"

"Oh, Mr. Henson," and she clasped her hands and raised her wonderful, beseeching gray eyes to his face, "I can not tell. There is a feeling of conviction that he knows all about the crime if he is not the assassin. There has been an adverse fate at work since General Benson crossed my path. There has been a train of unfortunate circumstances attending our whole acquaintance. It is absurd to suspect him I know, but I cannot help it." The detective looked at her again with the immovable expression peculiar to him.

"Your woman's intuition warns you; is that it?"

She bowed her head in acquiescence.

"And I have confidence in intuitive deductions," he muttered; then, aloud, "My dear child, gentlemen like General Benson sometimes do queer things under pressure of circumstances. You may be right. I will see Mr. Sumner; he will probably be more explicit with me than he could be with you. I will do my best for you. In fact, I shall put all my powers into my work, for it is an uncommon riddle you have set me to solve."

As she rose to go she asked his terms. He named a fair price. "But if you succeed in clearing him, and I know that you will, Mr. Henson, you shall receive a princely reward." Jewel laid her check for a goodly retainer, upon the desk before him. Henson looked and tapped the desk with his pencil, but did not notice the check. Then he rose, touched a bell, and accompanied his fair client to the door.

BEFORE NINE O'CLOCK ON TUESDAY morning, attended by her maid, with the jail officials for witnesses, Jewel Bowen became the wife of the suspected murderer, Cuthbert Sumner.

XXVII

The evening of the eventful day that made Jewel, Cuthbert Sumner's wife, closed in heavy and sombre. The hearing had the expected ending, and Sumner was held for trial in the following September, before the grand jury for wilful murder. The evidence was circumstantial, but damaging in the extreme. It showed exclusive opportunity for reasons unknown, but it was whispered about town that the girl had been an unwedded mother. Added to this was the knowledge of the broken engagement between the prisoner and Miss Bowen, and the fact that Miss Madison had at one time been affianced to him, and it was expected that she would be called by the prosecution to show the fickle nature of his relations with women.

At seven o'clock in the evening of that same day, robed in black velvet, Jewel paced restlessly up and down the floor of the library, sometimes pausing to listen to sounds from without, sometimes approaching the window and trying to pierce the gloom. The dinner bell rang; for no matter what our griefs, or how dark the tragedies which are enacted about us, meals are still served and eaten, just as if the hearts assembled about the board were never wrenched nor broken.

The points brought out in the evidence were soon making their way about the city, and excitement and interest grew momentarily. Sumner smiled in bitterness of heart. He hardly knew himself in the picture drawn. Jewel sat in an obscure corner of the audience room of the court, heavily veiled, and listened to the testimony with a heart bursting with indignation. Each moment the load at her heart grew heavier. They both realized at last that this was no child's play but a struggle to the death. Sumner clenched his hands and registered a vow to spend his fortune, if necessary, to clear his name, for the sake of the dear incentive, the thought of whom warmed his heart and made him bold to meet impending disaster.

The two ladies took their accustomed places at table, each secretly regretting the absence of the Senator. With him at home, dinner was wont to be a festive meal, where laughter and wit cheered the household or chance visitor. A dismal air hung over the room now; the servants moved to and fro with unaccustomed solemnity. The mother and daughter addressed each other seldom: each was buried in her own thoughts. Presently both rose from the table and passed into the library, where coffee was served.

After the servants had retired and they were safe from intrusion Mrs. Bowen broke the silence that brooded over them. She had watched Jewel closely all through the meal, studying her looks, thinking over her words and striving to arrive at satisfactory conclusions. At length she said quietly:

"Now, my dear, you have told me next to nothing, nor have I asked seeing how pale and tired you are, but I must talk with you about this marriage. I fear you have been very rash. My dear, I positively dread your father's return; dearly as he loves you, he will be very angry." After a pause she continued, clasping and unclasping her fingers nervously. "Oh, the talk there will be when this affair is known! Why didn't you consult me, child? I could have devised some way of helping the poor fellow without requiring you to sacrifice yourself. I am disappointed in Cuthbert Sumner."

"Do not use the word 'sacrifice,' mamma; I am glad to have the right to stand by Cuthbert in this dark hour. And why say anything to you of our intention? No one can blame you now. Beside, we have agreed to say nothing at present, about the marriage."

"But your whole life will be spoilt if he is found guilty."

"Mother," said the girl, sinking on her knees by Mrs. Bowen's side, "don't despair; it will all come right in a little while, I am sure it will. And you have always called yourself his friend, even when I was against him. You *cannot* believe him guilty; you are too just in your judgment, mamma."

Jewel was kneeling in the full light of the glowing fire, the ruddy glare fell on her white face, and the plaits of bright hair wound closely around her small head. Mrs. Bowen sighed as she gazed in admiration at her daughter. The great gray eyes glowed like diamonds, but there was a world of passionate anguish in their depths. The flower-like mouth was compressed with the intensity of the pain which filled her breast.

Again Mrs. Bowen sighed and moved uneasily in her seat.

"Yes; but this is so different—a man accused of murder."

"How so, mamma? Is friendship in sunshine so different from friendship in shade?" There was sarcasm on the delicately chisseled features.

"What a champion you are, Jewel; once, perhaps, I should have acted and felt as you do."

"But now, mamma—?"

"Now, my child, I am of the world—worldly."

"Do you think papa will be very angry?" asked the girl with trembling lips after a short silence.

"We can expect nothing less. He is too fond of you to hold his anger long, however. I shall stand with you, Jewel, if it is any comfort for you to know it. I am glad, glad, glad, that you cannot marry General Benson." Jewel marvelled much at the strange look on her mother's face as she uttered these words.

"My dear mamma!" and the two women embraced each other. Then followed another silence broken by the elder woman.

"What impression did you receive from the evidence—I mean apart from the conclusions drawn by the jury?" A quiver went through the girl as she replied:

"I was confirmed in my belief in his innocence, although everything seemed to point the other way. Aurelia Madison's evidence was against him. She gave the impression that he came and went at her beck and call."

"She is false to the core—a dangerous woman."

"I agree with you, mamma. But her beauty blinds men. I dread her influence on the jury."

"There is no soul there—nothing but sensuality."

"Soul! there is no need for soul in a woman's beauty for it to dazzle most men," was the bitter answer.

"I marvel much over the matter. It seems to me there is something incomplete in the case—something to be explained. That poor girl! I can see no reason for murdering her. She may have been killed by mistake.

"That is scarcely likely."

"Cases of mistaken identity are common enough. It's a mysterious affair; I hope it may be cleared up without any delay."

"I hope so," added Jewel. "Murder will out; there lies my hope for our success in tracing the murderer."

"What does Mr. Henson say?"

"Not much; we have had no time to talk. He has hardly got to work yet; but he told me to keep my courage up, and that he thought he should be able to throw some light on the dark points of the story. He has talked with Cuthbert."

Before Mrs. Bowen had time to reply the lace and satin portière

was pushed aside and Venus advanced toward them with a solemn and awe-stricken face.

"What is it, Venus?" asked Mrs. Bowen, regarding her with surprise.

"Please, Mrs. Bowen," she said hesitatingly, "Senator Bowen—"

"Oh, papa is come," cried Jewel in delight.

"No. Miss—"

At this point General Benson's well-known figure appeared in the entrance.

"Mrs. Bowen—Jewel—" he exclaimed as he hurried toward them. "I am the bearer of evil tidings. Senator Bowen was taken ill in New York, and we have hastened to bring him home as soon as it was possible to move him. Have a room prepared instantly, the ambulance will arrive almost immediately."

Before another hour had elapsed, the great hush—which is the shadow of the grim visitant, whom no earthly power may shut out—had fallen on the Bowen mansion. The servants walked with noiseless tread and spoke in whispers.

Senator Bowen was ill until death. He had been suddenly stricken down by a shock. The Washington delegation had been tendered a banquet at a famous New York club, and a hilarious time had been enjoyed. The New Yorkers had outdone themselves in catering for the amusement of their guests.

Senator Bowen had enjoyed himself hugely. Along in the early morning hours a servant passing the door of his room had caught the sound of some one struggling for breath within. Entering, he beheld the Senator lying on the bed, one hand pressed to his heart, the other hanging inert. His eyes were wild, his pale countenance lined with purple marks.

The man went for help and soon medical aid had rendered all the relief possible. As soon as he could make himself understood the stricken man urged them to take him home.

After the first burst of grief, Mrs. Bowen and Jewel took up their places in the sick room along with the trained nurses. Each looked at the other in awe and consternation over the awful suddenness of this event. Surprising events had followed one another rapidly the past few days. They dared not think of the next cruel blow that Fate might deal them.

The doctors and nurses came and went softly. The hours drew out their long, anxious length. At the close of the third day the sick man fell into a heavy stupor, from which the doctors said he might rally—probably would—and he might linger two or three days longer; but the end was inevitable. Should he rally he must be kept quiet, and on no account excited; his heart was weak.

Mrs. Bowen undertook to see these instructions carried out. Jewel, pale and distressed, shared her mother's watch. She was in agony; her love for her father was strong, deep and tender. She was his idol, and he was hers, and until she met Cuthbert Sumner she had always felt that if he died she should not care to live another hour. She could never remember his having been cross to her in her whole life. In her eyes his very faults were virtues.

At midnight Mrs. Bowen persuaded her daughter to go and lie down.

"Keep your strength, my child, there is much to go through. If your father wakes I will surely call you."

When alone she drew her chair to the fire and sat there in shadow, watching the face of the silent figure on the bed that looked so ghastly in the light of the shaded light. It was very still; the tired nurses in the next room, dozed. Events long passed, returned in full force and pictured themselves vividly before her inner senses. How kind this man had been to her; how much she owed to his love and care. And now the hour had come for her to lose a protector who had never failed her. Wealth she might have, but it would not supply the tender deference and loving solicitude of wedded life that had been hers.

She shuddered at her thoughts. Why did the past haunt her so persistently? Presently she found herself weeping softly.

There are brave natures—women's perhaps, more often than men's—which bear up in a sea of adversity, and present a bold front to the buffeting winds of life's uncertainties. And sometimes these brave natures fine a safe haven for their frail barks. Mrs. Bowen was one of these. She had never known trouble, save by name, since she met Zenas Bowen some twenty years before; and now behold, she is confronted by a very tempest of sorrow. In the midst of her reveries she was startled to hear her own name pronounced:

"Estelle."

It was Senator Bowen who spoke. In an instant his wife was at his side.

"Dear Zenas, you are better?" she said cheerfully.

"Yes, my brain is clear. I have been watching you, Estelle. Where is Jewel?"

     PAULINE E. HOPKINS

"In her room; I made her lie down. Do you want her?"

"Poor child; let her sleep."

His eyes roved restlessly about the familiar room.

"It is good to be at home—so good."

"Yes—but you must not talk. Drink this and sleep." She held a soothing draught to his lips, lifting the powerless head in her arms with all a mother's tenderness. He drank it obediently and then lay back on his pillow and a satisfied look of peaceful rest overspread his pale features. He held his wife's hand in a nerveless grasp.

"We have been happy, Estelle. You have been a perfect wife. I have left you well provided for. Them rascals got some of it, but not the whole of it by a durned sight; Zenas ain't such a fool as he seems," a gleam of his old fun-loving spirit was on the pain-worn face.

"If Jewel marries the General—"

"No, Zenas," she interrupted; then she stopped remembering the doctor's caution. But the sick man did not grasp the significance of her words. His mind wandered.

"No you don't, General; my little girl shan't be forced. I, her father, say it. When, where and who she likes; that's my idea. I tell you, no!"

Then he looked at his wife with fast-glazing eyes, and said:

"The little hair trunk—tell her—no difference—just the same."

Feebly he raised his arm. His wife knew his desire. She placed it about her neck. Then he drew her head nearer. A soft light radiated his features.

"My faithful wife!" he whispered. The cold lips touched her cheek.

"Zenas, Zenas!" exclaimed Estelle with a burst of emotion as she kissed the chill brow.

There was one long-drawn breath. The distracted wife sprang to the bell and rang a peal that brought the nurses hurrying in.

"Senator Bowen is worse!" she cried, wringing her hands helplessly.

The head nurse bent over the bed, then rising, said:

"Senator Bowen is dead, madam."

Again Washington society was stirred by an unexpected calamity among its leading people. Interest was heightened because of the close association which existed between the Bowens and the chief actor in the Bradford tragedy. The ill-starred trip of the delegation that had started so gaily on its Canadian mission was the talk of the capital.

XXVIII

The funeral was over. Senator Bowen was at rest in the handsomest cemetery of the capital after many honors had been paid to the sterling worth of the rugged Westerner. Condolences flooded the widow and orphan. The contents of the will were not yet known, but it was supposed that both ladies were left fabulously rich.

One event had crowded so closely upon another that General Benson was given no opportunity for confidential conversation with the woman he desired to make his wife.

The loss of her father was a terrible shock to Jewel, and she kept to her rooms, weeping passionate tears and refusing to be comforted. A sense of horrible loneliness, of grief, apprehension, and the weight of some unknown calamity weighed her young heart down. Young, beautiful, well-born, and wealthy, surrounded by every luxury money could purchase or a cultivated taste long for, Jewel was supremely wretched. Her father dead, her husband a prisoner, accused of the deadliest of crimes, the girl was a prey to a thousand vague fears and haunting suspicions. She dreaded, too, the coming of the day set apart for reading the will, for General Benson could no longer be avoided. She had written him a letter asking a release from promises made, but as yet had received no reply.

Senator Bowen had been buried two weeks when, at an early hour, the family lawyer appeared at the house and was ushered into the breakfast room where, attired in deep mourning, Mrs. Bowen sat in solitary state making a pretense of eating.

Mr. Cameron was a pale, small, dark-haired man, with sharp eyes and thin lips; a hard, but honest face, and a short temper.

Somewhat alarmed by the troubled look on the solicitor's face, Mrs. Bowen asked anxiously—

"Is anything wrong, Mr. Cameron?"

"Well, madam, I hope not; but I thought I would ask you for a cup of coffee, lay the case before you and talk it over. I heard some surprising news last night," he continued, as he seated himself and swallowed the steaming beverage that Mrs. Bowen poured for him, the discreet servant having left the room at a glance from his mistress. "Did you know that your husband made a will while in New York?" he questioned abruptly, watching her with keen, bright eyes.

"A will in New York? No—surely not!"

"There is such a will in existence; it is held by General Benson, who came to me last night with the astonishing information. He will be here by eleven to have the instrument read. Of course, this later document leaves the one in my possession null and void."

Mrs. Bowen had grown very white as she listened to the lawyer, and a fixed look of intense thought was in her eyes.

"What are the terms of this new will? do you remember?"

"Not all of them; but Major Madison is left sole trustee, and General Benson executor and guardian of Miss Bowen until she is of age. Think of it!" cried the excitable man, "all the immense business of the estate, ready money, etc., *absolutely* in the control of these men!"

A wonderful change came over Mrs. Bowen at these words. She was stung to the quick. She sprung from her chair as if moved by a spring; her lips quivered, her eyes dilated with what seemed like terror.

"General Benson and Major Madison!" she exclaimed in a hoarse voice, "surely you jest."

"Would it were a jest, my dear madam. Think of it! This magnificent estate and fortune to be left in the hands of two such villains as General Benson and his pal, Major Madison. Yes, villains, madam; and I will undertake to prove my position should they bring action against me for slander. What could my old friend, Bowen, have been thinking about! He must have lost his head completely," continued Mr. Cameron, looking with accusing eyes at the black-robed figure across his second cup of coffee. "Madison had done him out of a million in his bogus company already. A child could see that it was a cheat and a sham."

For one instant, at these words, Mrs. Bowen's face wore the look of a lioness bereft of her young; but her alarm seemed to subside as quickly as it arose. The lawyer was too excited himself to notice the expressions of consternation and alarm that flitted across the pale face of the silent woman before him. After a silence, she asked: "Have you examined this will, Mr. Cameron? Are you sure it is genuine?"

The old attorney put his cup down with emphasis and said with a bow: "Madam, it is a pleasure to talk with you. You have expressed my own thoughts in your question. The Bowen millions would be a great temptation to a set of sharpers. I have not examined the document, but I will; and you may trust me to find any flaw that exists."

"Let us be calm. If it is as we suspect, we shall gain nothing by allowing these men to see that we suspect them. Do not oppose them, but use every legal means to retain control of the estate until we prove our suspicions groundless."

The expression of her face was intense, even fierce; her mouth was tightly closed, her eyes strained as though striving to pierce the veil which hides from us the unseen.

Mr. Cameron looked his admiration of the fearless woman before him, and after a few more words they settled themselves to calmly wait developments.

At this same hour General Benson and his honored associate, Major Madison, sat in the former's room talking earnestly of the business in hand.

"Now, Madison, we have started on the last part of our enterprise and it is full of peril: one flaw will destroy the whole structure which we have labored so hard to raise. We must preserve all our trumps. Aurelia has failed in her part: we must not fail."

"Pshaw!" said the Major, "we shall succeed. What is there to fear? the man is dead."

"There will be many questions asked, and, doubtless, that old fox of a lawyer is even now hunting for evidences of fraud. Don't underrate the danger, Madison. Our projects are dangerous, and the slightest mistake will prove fatal. But while there are one hundred chances against us, there are the same number in our favor. We know this, too, Madison,— necessity knows no law; we must go ahead!"

"There's the old woman: she'll kick on the will, and kick hard. What'll you do with her?"

There was a peculiar smile on the General's face as he said:

"She'll struggle a little: the scene today will be a stormy one, so be prepared; but I hold a trump ahead of her."

"The deuce you do!"

"She can't escape from us any more than the girl can."

The Major whistled softly as he murmured "Amen," and then said: "I have faith in your judgment, Benson."

Benson took several turns up and down the long room and finally assumed his favorite attitude before the mantel.

"You do well to feel so, Major. I anticipate no difficulty in assuming full control of the Bowen millions, and how sorely we need them, you and I know, Major."

"But the girl—how will you manage her?"

Benson's face darkened, but he only waved his hand significantly.

"Be calm. I wish the whole business was as easily disposed of as the girl."

"She's the only link in the chain that appears weak to my thinking, and she is the key of the old man's cash-box. Who would ever have thought of her kicking over the traces so completely and marrying Sumner?" and the Major relighted his cigar, which had gone out while he was talking.

"Keep quiet about that, Madison; let them think us surprised by their news today. Pray observe my caution; I will explain later.

"I am glad it is all right. That old attorney worries me, too. Women are deceitful hussies; a man never knows what they are at." General Benson laughed softly at the Major's suggestion.

"What!" he said, "shall the foolishness of a mere girl stop us now, when we are so near the goal? By no means. If she attempts to thwart me, so much the worse for her. Wait for me, Major," and General Benson left the room to speak with Isaac.

Left alone, Major Madison went to the window and stood looking out at the passing throng.

"It is impossible not to admire Benson's nerve and his infernal penetration," he thought half-aloud. "He reasons out a position and plans from the most trivial circumstances. He always falls on his feet. How many close calls we have had since we joined forces: yet, thanks to his luck, we have come out first best every time. Yes, he has wonderful ability and his extraordinary audacity and nerve may be trusted to carry us safely through a difficult undertaking like the present one. What a profession we have adopted and practised for twenty years. Justice never sleeps, the old fogies tell us, but I'll be dog-goned if the old woman ain't in a dead swoon when Benson's on the rampage."

Shortly after this the two friends stepped from their carriage before the Bowen mansion. The Major, in his black clothes, white cravat and spectacles might readily have passed for an eminent divine about to administer consolation to the bereaved widow and orphan.

Jewel stood in the great library waiting for General Benson, who had requested an interview. The reading of the will had shown her how dependent she would be upon this man. The thought of him as a guardian made her sick at heart. What could her father have been thinking about? She was bewildered by the difficulties which had suddenly beset her path. She who had been petted and shielded all her life saw an existence of strife and danger opening dimly in the future.

"How will it all end," she asked herself drearily, "if Cuthbert should be condemned? He shall not be; he must not be," she told herself, shutting her teeth hard and drawing a long breath.

Presently General Benson entered the room closely followed by Mrs. Bowen, who crossed the room to Jewel's side and took her hand tenderly in hers. Together they faced General Benson, and this silent defiance filled the man with rage. He came to a halt immediately in front of the pale girl, who had risen to her feet on his entrance.

"I want to tell you, Jewel, in answer to your letter, that I shall not give you up," he began abruptly. "Nothing is changed since you gave me your promise and I shall hold you to it. Your father expected it, too, when he made me your guardian."

"Sir," said Jewel, in a voice almost unintelligible from agitation, "I know that my conduct is extraordinary, but so are the circumstances surrounding my acts; I do not propose to justify myself. It is a great favor that I ask at your hands, but I entreat you to relinquish a project so fraught with unhappiness for both of us. Your generosity will spare me many sad and sorrowful hours, and surely you could not desire an unwilling bride."

"All is fair in love, Jewel," replied the General, who had listened apparently cold and unmoved, but inwardly a passion of rage and jealousy was gnawing at his heart. Then he continued with a malicious smile, "Why not yield gracefully to the inevitable?"

At these words the girl's every instinct arose in arms. She contrasted this scene with her father's fond indulgence and in hot anger longed to show this usurper how she despised his brief authority. There was a look of utter disgust on her face.

"I would have spared you, General Benson, but you need no leniency from me. There is no hope that I shall ever become your wife. I am already married to—Cuthbert Sumner!"

In a moment the man's manner changed.

"Ah!" he said, and the exclamation burst from his lips in a hiss; the elegant society man disappeared—hideous passion gave glimpses of depths of infamy—one beheld the countenance of a devil. "I have heard something of this before; but it does not concern me; it does not alter my plans. I should be foolish to allow a dead man to mar my future; and a dead man Sumner will be, for the law will remove him from my path. Nothing can save him." Jewel measured the man before her with flaming eyes; she turned from him toward the door with a gesture expressive of loathing; she halted on the threshold.

PAULINE E. HOPKINS

"Hear me, General Benson, I will never become your wife; never, I swear it. Now do your worst."

As the door closed behind the angry girl the man turned to Mrs. Bowen, who stood watching the scene. "And you, madam, are you in league with the misguided girl who undertakes to defy my authority and rights?" The cool sarcasm of his tones was a combination of insolence and impudence.

"You are speaking to Senator Zenas Bowen's widow. You will kindly alter your words and tone when we are conversing, General Benson." Mrs. Bowen spoke in her usual calm, dignified tone. The General's face became purple, then pale; his white teeth gleamed savagely. His elaborate bow was full of mockery as he replied:

"I await your answer, madam, to my question."

"You shall have it," Mrs. Bowen exclaimed in exasperation. "I shall support Jewel in her desires. I am convinced her father would never force her to act against her inclinations."

There ensued a moment of intense silence when she had finished speaking. General Benson was utterly transfigured. There was not the slightest vestige remaining of the elegant chief of a high official bureau; the sweet voice was changed—it was hard and rasping and had a ring in it that reminded one of the slums. He advanced toward Mrs. Bowen and seized her roughly by the arm.

"So you will assist that headstrong girl to defy me, will you? Well, do it at your peril! Do it, and I will tell your story to the world. I know you; I knew you instantly the first night I saw you in this house. This girl is not your child; why should you care. I have no desire to harm you. Just let things take their course and I will never disturb you in any way."

Uncontrollable terror had spread over Mrs. Bowen's features at these words. Her lips moved but gave forth no sound.

"You do not answer, madam!" exclaimed her tormentor. Then with a diabolical smile of evil triumph he added, "I am correct then in my surmise; you do not deny it?"

The white lips moved: this time her words were distinguishable,— "No! I do not understand what you mean." "I mean—," and he bent toward her and whispered in her ear. That whisper seemed to arouse her benumbered faculties. She moved toward him with disheveled hair, foaming lips and one arm outstretched in menace. He sprang back from her with a smothered oath: "It is true: you cannot deny it."

"I admit nothing; I deny nothing. Prove it if you can," she muttered in a strained tone.

"Then it is war, is it? Very well, I give you until May to think it over. If you do not come to your senses by that time, I shall proceed to act. Think of it, madam; think well," and the General turned and abruptly left the room.

Mrs. Bowen stood there panting, crushed; her eyes alone gave signs of animation; they glared horribly. As the door closed behind her enemy she sighed; she sunk on the carpet. She had fainted.

XXIX

Time passed on, bringing in the early summer. It was the close of a beautiful June day and the sunset was still glowing and burning as it reluctantly bade the world good-night. Venus stood by an open window gazing anxiously into the twilight. Jewel had gone to the jail early in the day, leaving her maid at home. Mrs. Bowen had been in the room a number of times asking for her daughter. She was always uneasy now when Jewel was away from her, and her face wore a strained look of expectancy pitiful to see.

General Benson's anger seemed to have spent itself in the dire threats he had made on the day the will was read; he had left the women in peace, being scrupulously polite when they met to transact business.

Mrs. Bowen was anxious to leave the hot city, and it was agreed between her and Jewel to go to Arlington Heights, where the latter could still be in close proximity to the prisoner and continue her visits with ease. She had gone that day to tell him not to be depressed if the time between her calls was longer than usual.

The glow of sunset faded from the sky, and the summer twilight deepened into night, still Jewel did not appear. It was a warm night; the upper windows were all open; the diamond-studded sky was like a sea of glass. Another hour went by. Mrs. Bowen was pacing the floor restlessly. Venus came up from the servants' quarters with soup and wine for her mistress.

"Now do be persuaded to eat something, madam," said the maid. "You're just as white as death, and you've sat here waiting for Miss Jewel, without your dinner and you must be quite faint. Here it's nine o'clock, and you always dine at half-past seven. I reckon my young lady's all right. She'll turn up presently as bright as a dollar, sure's you're born."

So Mrs. Bowen smiled and allowed herself to be cheered by the devoted girl, and took some soup and a little of the wine; but she could not rest, and listened to every sound that came faintly to the great mansion from the outside.

Hour succeeded hour and it was eleven o'clock; nobody thought of going to bed. As she sat listening there came a sharp quick ring at the outer bell. Venus herself, anxious for tidings from her loved mistress, rushed to the door ahead of the butler. It was a note which was handed her by a man well muffled up, who instantly disappeared in the thick shrubbery about the lawn. Venus hastened to Mrs. Bowen. With a smile she opened the envelope. The next moment she uttered a cry and gasped for breath.

"Whatever is the matter?" cried the frightened maid.

"This letter—this letter! Help me—help me! Your lady has been abducted!" Mrs. Bowen fell back unconscious in her chair.

The terror-stricken maid opened the letter with shaking hands and read the following lines:

"I always keep my word. If you value your reputation and your step-daughter's *welfare,* you will not seek to find her. In due time she will reappear."

MEANWHILE WHAT HAD BECOME OF Jewel? She had elected to walk to the jail and back because of the beauty of the day. At the jail she found Mr. Henson, and they had stayed talking over the difficulties of the case until twilight was falling. But that did not disturb her for Mr. Henson would walk back with her, and the Washington streets, famous for their loneliness and seclusion, stretching like immense parks in all directions, would be robbed of their usual terrors for lone female pedestrians.

Mr. Henson accompanied her to the great entrance gates; there he left her, and she started up the carriage path at a rapid gait. Along the edges of the drive the underwood was so thick, and the foliage of the trees arching overhead so full and dense that towards the centre of the drive it was in semi-twilight, and thick shades of darkness enveloped all things. In the half-light Jewel thought she discerned a vehicle—a close carriage, she fancied—standing at one side of the drive.

Surprised, but not startled, because of the close proximity of the house, the girl advanced. The next moment she was startled enough; a chill of fear went through her woman's heart and it stood still for one instant with a thrill of sickening terror, for suddenly out from the gloomy shade of the trees, into the drive, stepped two men, rough-looking ruffians wearing black half-masks.

The one who was evidently the leader said in a hoarse voice, probably disguised:

"Now, Jim."

Instantly both moved toward her.

Jewel was a Western girl. She did not scream. She had been brought up on a ranch; one of her early habits remained fixed, and even in

Washington she was never unarmed when without male escort. The jewelled toy she carried was a present from her father, and he had taught her to use it with deadly effect. Many a day they had hunted together, the young girl bringing down her game in true sportsmanlike style.

Instantly now her hand sought her pocket, in the very instinct of self-defense and desperation; she drew her revolver with intent to fire, but quick as flash the leader flung himself upon her and wrenched the weapon from her hand. He then threw his arm about her slender form, drawing her towards the carriage.

The passion of terror and desperation lent the girl unnatural strength in her frantic struggle for freedom. The man was forced to place his other hand to stifle her screams.

"You come along quietly, missee, an' you'll be all right; but ef yer screams it won't be pleasant."

"You coward!" she gasped, as he bore her to the carriage. "You coward! Name your price, and let me go."

"Thar you are, now, slick as grease." She was in the carriage then. "Yer money won't help you with me, missee. You're a brave gal, but what's your strength to a man's? Drive on like h—, Jim."

The cold drops of agony stood on the girl's brow as the horror of her position grew upon her each moment.

"Where are you taking me?"

"I'm goin' ter take yer jes' a little journey outside o' Washington fer a few days. Don't you be feared; thar's nuthin' goin' hurt ye."

Who was this man holding her, refusing bribe, yet vowing to protect her from harm. She looked into the masked face in an agony of appeal and doubt and fear in the great grey eyes. The man was touched.

"Don't now, *don't*, missee, look that skeered. Nothin' ain't goin' hurt you, I tell you. Ise got a little gal o' my own."

The girl did not answer. Like a light it flashed across her who was the author of this outrage.

"I know your employer!" she said fiercely. "But he shall learn that I fear him not. I defy him still."

XXX

When Jewel came to herself she was lying on an old-fashioned canopied bed with a coverlet thrown over her. The room was evidently, originally designed for a studio, and was lighted by a skylight; even now a flood of sunlight streamed from above, making more dingy and faded by comparison the appearance of the dusty canvases and once luxurious furniture scattered about the apartment. Evidences of decay were everywhere; a broken easel leant against the wall, and on a table odds and ends of tubes, brushes and other artistic paraphernalia were heaped in a disorderly mass. There were also a couch and easy chairs in faded brocade.

The girl looked about with lanquid interest scarcely realizing what had happened to disturb the serenity of her daily life. Presently, however, the power of thought returned and with it a flood of memories concerning the outrage of the night before. She was a prisoner, but where?

What a terrible sensation it was to wake to the conciousness of being a prisoner! A prisoner! she, Jewel Bowen, who until recently had never known a care in her short existence of twenty years. Now all the waves and billows of life were passing over her threatening to engulf her. Could it be that all her bright hopes for the future were to end here in this lonely chamber?

With the thought she arose hastily from the bed and began walking despairingly about, examining the room. After a tour of the apartment she gave it up. Her prison was well-chosen. The doors were bolted, and no window gave a possibility of escape. There was no chance of attracting attention, by her cries, from passers-by, even if scores of persons traversed the streets about this house; no one would know that within its walls a desolate girl suffered the keenest of mental torture.

She paced the room frantically, and shook the doors of her prison violently until she was obliged to sink exhausted upon the couch. "They will hardly let me die of hunger," she told herself, resolving to save her strength for questioning whoever should bring her food.

Crouching upon the couch, she listened. Not a sound broke upon her ear. It seemed to her that desolation engulfed her. Presently, as she sat there, the sound of a football came to her strained ears, then a key grated in the lock, the door swung open, and a tall, pleasant-featured black man entered the room, bearing a tray. He carefully locked the door behind him, removing the key from the lock. He wheeled forward a small table and deftly arranged the contents of the tray upon it.

Jewel launched an avalanche of questions at him, but he returned no answer. He went and returned a number of times, bringing her clothing, books and luxuries of the toilet, all indicating that a long captivity was in prospect. At lunch time an aged Negress brought her food, but all efforts to engage her in conversation were unavailing; a more morose and repulsive specimen of the race Jewel had never met.

After this there was a monotonous interval of time passed in the agony of silence. Her meals were furnished regularly and all other needs lavishly supplied. One day was the record of another.

Four weeks must have passed since she was brought to this place, still she had no knowledge of her captors, nor where her prison was located. One change, however, was made—they gave her the freedom of an adjoining room as the summer heat increased, but the windows were barred and looked out upon extensive gardens filled with the ruins of what must once have been buildings and offices of a large plantation. The once well-kept walks were overgrown with weeds, and a heavy growth of trees obstructed the view in all directions.

One night she sat by the window gazing at the stars and eating her heart out in agony and tears. She could not sleep; insomnia had added its horrors to her other troubles. Suddenly the sky became overcast and the stars disappeared. A storm threatened. Low mutterings of thunder and gusts of rising wind foretold a summer shower. At intervals a lightning flash lit up the inky blackness of the scene. Finally the flashes became so vivid that the girl moved her seat from the window to a less exposed position with a scornful laugh at her own fear of death. "Truly," she thought bitterly, "self-preservation has been called the first law of nature. How we strive to preserve that which is of so little value."

Up and down the sides of the room her eyes wandered aimlessly; sometimes she felt that she was losing her mind. Presently a painting fixed into the wall arrested her attention. It was the portrait of an impossible wood nymph, but so faded that its beauty—if it had once possessed any—was entirely gone.

As she gazed at it indifferently the centre bulged outward, and a small strip of canvas swung to and fro as if from a draught of air.

Jewel sprang to her feet and ran to the picture. She trembled with sudden hope. Where did the draught come from? Carefully she raised the torn strip of canvas and inserted her hand beneath it, feeling along the wall back of the picture. There was a narrow recess behind it. Greatly excited by this discovery, she flew to the table where her dinner-service still remained, seized a knife and cut the canvas close to the frame for a good distance up. Then she trembling raised the cloth.

Oh! Joy! it revealed a passage usually closed by a door which had become unfastened and now swung idly in the breeze made by the raising wind.

Thank heaven, it was an hour when she was free from interruption. No one would disturb her until morning. She took the lamp in her hand. Escape seemed very near. Scarcely waiting to widen the aperture, she crept through, and soon stood, covered with dust, trembling shaken with emotion, in the dark passage which the canvas had hidden.

She paused and strained her ears to listen for sounds in the silent house. None came. Then she crept on very, very cautiously.

The passage was dark. It had evidently lead to the servants' quarters at the back of the house when mirth and gaiety held high revel in the glorious old mansion. She went swiftly on, till she came to a black baize door. She pushed it open with difficulty. Here she paused irresolute, for this door gave admission to the front of the house; there was a passage at right angles with the one just quitted, with stairs leading above and below. She glided toward the latter, seized hold of the banisters, descended into another passage with many doors opening into it. The doors were all closed.

What a rambling old place it was. In the excitement of the instant she had felt no terror, but now an icy chill seized her and her heart throbbed heavily.

She noticed now that one of the doors in the passage was ajar! Dare she pass it? To advance was appalling, but the case was a desperate one. With her heart throbbing wildly she stood motionless one instant, then she ventured past the unclosed door.

She shaded her lamp with one hand and with fascinated gaze took in, in one brief instant, the contents of the room. Her eyes wandered from the bare floor and walls to the table, the two chairs, and then to a bed in one corner. There her gaze lingered, for on the bed lay a woman of dark brown complexion and wrinkled visage; about her head was wound a many-hued bandanna handkerchief. The woman's eyes were open and fixed in terror and amazement upon the girl who had just entered the room. They gazed at each other for one moment, these two so strangely met, then the old woman threw her arms above her head, exclaiming:

"Bless Gawd! I'se ready! Praise the Lor'! He done sen' his Angel Gabriel to tote me home to glory."

The sound of her voice broke the spell that bound Jewel.

"Who are you, Auntie, and what makes you think me an angel?"

"Lor', honey, is you human sho' nuff? Why when I seen yo' face er'shinin' on me dar, an' hearn yer sof' step comin' en de lonely night, I made sho' it was de Lor' come to carry dis' po' sinner to er home in glory. I 'spec' I been shut up her so long I'se gittin' doaty. I'se a po' ol'black'ooman, been dragged 'way from my home an' chillun an' locked up here by a limb o' de debbil 'cause he's 'fraid I tell his wicked actions. But 'deed chile, whar'd you come from? Does you live in dis place?"

Jewel shook her head sadly.

"I'm a prisoner, too, Auntie. I've been shut up here for four weeks now. I happened to find a way out of my room tonight, and I thought I might possibly escape. Can you tell me where I am?"

"Yes, honey, I can. You's down on de ol' Enson plantation in Ma'lan. I was born on de nex' joinin' place myself. But who brung you here? What's your name, chile?"

"I haven't seen my captor yet, but I believe it to be General Benson. My name is Jewel Bowen."

"Mercy, King! My lovely Lor'd, but ain't dis curus?" exclaimed the old woman, greatly excited. "My gran'darter is yo' waiter, Venus Johnson!"

It was not Jewel's turn to become excited.

"Then you are—?"

"Aunt Hennie Sargent; dat's me."

XXXI

Meanwhile there was mourning at the Bowen Mansion, for the joy of the house had fled with Jewel. Mrs. Bowen sent for the family lawyer and then went to bed; trouble was wearing her out, and there was danger of her becoming a confirmed invalid.

Mr. Cameron put the machinery of the law in motion to find the missing girl, but there progress seemed to end.

Now the sorely tried mistress discovered what a treasure she had in the maid Venus. The girl was everywhere attending to the business of the house and waiting on the invalid mistress. She visited the jail with news for the restless unhappy man confined there, never seeming to weary in well-doing. Venus preserved a discreet silence concerning the letter received on the night of the abduction, but the brain of the little brown maid was busy. She had her own ideas about certain things, and was planning for the deliverance of her loved young mistress.

When Jewel had been absent about two weeks, Venus asked leave to pay her mother a visit one evening. Marthy had heard nothing from the police in relation to Aunt Hennie, and she was overjoyed to see her daughter; it gave her an opportunity to pour her sorrows and griefs into sympathetic ears.

She bustled about the neat kitchen setting out the best that her home afforded for supper, and Oliver dropped his books in honor of his sister's visit, making it a festival.

When the meal was on the table, smoking hot,—corn pone, gumbo soup, chicken and rice and coffee of an amber hue,—the children ate with gusto. The mother's eyes shone with happiness as she watched their enjoyment, pressing upon them, at intervals, extra helps.

"Have some mo' this gumbo soup, my baby. I reckon you don' git nothin' like it up yonder with all the fixin's you has there."

"Well, my Lord, ma, I won't be able to walk to the cars if I keep on stuffing myself," replied Venus as her mother filled her plate again with the delicious soup.

"Say, Venus," broke in Oliver, with a grin on his mischievous face, "who's the good-looking buck that came to the end of the street with you the last time you were home?"

"What's that?" cried Marthy, sharply.

Oliver laughed and clapped his hands, "Ma's like a hen with chickens; she's afraid of the fellows, Vennie."

Venus laughed, too, a little shame-facedly. "Oh, now, Ollie, ain't you got no cover to your mouth? That was Mr. Sumner's man, John. I had to see him about a message from Mrs. Bowen to Mr. Sumner, and so he was polite enough to come with me to our street, it being pretty dark."

"That's all right," said Marthy in a relieved tone. "Mr. Williams is a perfec' gent'man. You're only a leetle gal, Venus, if you is out to work, an' there's time 'nuff for you to git into trubble. You don' wan' to fill yo' head up with 'viggotty notions 'about fellars yet. I got married young when I'd daughter been playin' with baby rags; I don' want my gal to take on eny mo' trubble en her haid than she can kick off at her heels. You, Venus, mark my wurds, an' 'member what I tell's you ef I'm moulderin' in the clay to dus' an' ashes tomorrer,—gittin' jined to a man's a turrible 'spons'bility, 'specially the man. You want to think well an' cal'ate the consequences of the prevus ac'. Mymy, mymy!" she continued musingly, "how that carries me back to the las' time ol' Mis' Sargeant whopped me. She says to me, 'Marthy, did you take the money off my dresser table? tell me the troof,' and I dussan' lie, an' so I said: 'Ys'm; Ike Johnson tol' me to do it an' he'd buy me a red ribbin fer my hair.' Ol' miss says 'Marthy, you's 'mitted the *prevus' ac'*, an' I'm gwine whop you,' an' the ol' lady laid it onto me right smart with her slipper. Ike Johnson's been gittin' me inter tubble ever sense that time.

Oliver, when you was born an' I foun' you was a man chile I said to myself, "Lord, how come you let me bring one of them mule critters into the wurl to make trubble for some po' 'ooman? An' ef ever you git jined, an' treat yo' wife as yo' pa's treated me, I hope you'll git yo' match, an' she'll wallop the yearth with you, 'deed I does."

"Daddy been home lately?" asked Venus carelessly after the meal was cleared away.

"No, chile, he ain't," replied her mother. "He was home—le' me see— jes' befo' the fus' of the munf. He brought me the mor'gage money."

"How much was it?"

"Four hundred dollars Venus, chile, you could have knocked me down with a feather, I was so outdone from 'stonishmen' when he throwed it into my lap and said 'dar's you' mo'gage.'"

"Now, ma, where'd he get *all* that money I'd like to know? He never got it honest, that's my belief."

"Yes, I reckon he did, honey, this time. Gin'ral Benson give it to him. Yo' granny asked the Gin'ral about it 'way in the winter."

"Hump!" exclaimed Venus.

"He ain't been home sense. Gin'ral's bo't a plantation out o' Baltimo' a bit, an' yo' pa's holpin' to fix it up. I reckon he'll be thare 'bout all summer. He took a few clo's an' things with him when he was home." Venus looked at her mother intently, but remained silent.

"Dear, dear, Venus," Marthy continued beginning to cry, "ef I only knew where was yo' granny or what had come to her, I'd be a happy 'ooman this night. An' to think of Miss Jewel, too, that dear beautiful girl with a face like an angel out of glory. The ways of the Lord is pas' follerin', an' that's a fac'."

"What's dad say about granny?" asked Venus suddenly.

"*He* ain't worried none, bless yo' soul. He ain't studyin' 'bout the dear ol' so'l. He ain't got no mo' blood in him than a lizard. He's the onerist man! Says to me, 'quit frettin'; the ol' 'ooman 'll turn up safe quicker'n scat', he says. 'She's tuf; nothin' ain't gwine kill the ol' hornet.' Them's yo' pa's words to me."

"What do you expect from dad, ma? You know him. You ought to if anybody does. Granny makes him toe the mark, that's why he dislikes her."

"That's so, sho' 'nuff, baby; an' what we know 'bout Ike Johnson's mean capers would fill a book. It's twenty years come nix Chris'mus sense we jumped the broomstick together. We was the very las' couple jined befo' the s'render, an' ef it hadn't been for yo' granny, we'd all been in the po' house long ago an' fergit."

When it was time to start for home Oliver escorted his sister to the car. On the way she questioned him closely and learned many things concerning her father that her mother had failed to mention.

"It's as sure as preaching," she told herself late that night as she was preparing for bed, "it's as sure as preaching that somebody who knows something must take hold of Miss Jewel's case or that son of Sodom will carry his point. The police are slower 'n death. Dad's up to his capers. He can fool ma, but he can't pull the wool over my eyes; I'm his daughter. Hump! well, we'll see about it. It's a burning shame for dad to go on this way after all Miss Jewel's kindness to us. But I'll balk him. I'll see him out on this case or my name ain't Venus Johnson."

"I'll see if this one little black girl can't get the best of as mean a set of villains as ever was born," was her last thought as her eyes closed in slumber.

PAULINE E. HOPKINS

Mr. Henson sat in his office the next morning thinking deeply. He had just returned from New York, where he had carefully examined the ground, trying to find a flaw in the Bowen will, drawn and signed in that city, but not a particle of encouragement had rewarded his efforts. He was much depressed over his failure to obtain a clue to what he was convinced was clever forgery committed by two dangerous men. His vast experience did not aid him; he was forced to declare that the criminals had covered their tracks well.

Mr. Cameron had just left him after acknowledging *his* inability to fix a point that would legally stay the enforcement of the will.

All was dark; but the man felt that if he could obtain the slightest clue, he could unravel the whole plot without difficulty. But how to gain a clue was the question. He had determined to start the next day for Kentucky in the hope of finding Elise Bradford's aunt and the child of the dead woman, hoping that this might furnish the key to the mystery.

The morning sunshine streamed into the room. The intense heat was enervating. He drew his chair before the large open window on the side where the sun had not reached and directly in the wake of an electric fan. He leaned his head upon his hand and thought over the situation.

All his efforts had been to ascertain if there were any real grounds for the suspicions, which had been aroused in Miss Bowen's mind, and which his interviews with Sumner had confirmed. The news of her abduction had come as a distinct shock to him when it was given him upon his return from New York. The beautiful girl had aroused all the man's innate chivalry; springs of tenderness long dead to any influence had welled up in his soul, and he felt a mad desire, uncontrollable and irresistible, to rescue her, and take dire vengeance on her captors.

Her haunting influence was wrapped about him; he could see her, feel her presence and almost catch the tones of her low voice in the silent room. Ever and anon he glanced about him as if seeking the actual form of the fair spirit that had so suddenly absorbed his heart and soul.

He was satisfied in his own mind that General Benson was the criminal, but to this man who had become a legal machine, tangible evidence was the only convincing argument that he knew.

Presently a clerk entered the room and announced that a woman wished to speak to him.

"Show her in," he replied to the man's query.

A few seconds passed, and then the opening door admitted a young colored girl who had an extremely intelligent, wide-awake expression.

Venus was not at all embarrassed by the novelty of her surroundings, but advanced toward the chief with a businesslike air, after making sure that the retiring clerk had actually vanished.

"I'm Miss Jewel Bowen's maid," she declared abruptly. The detective whirled around in his chair at her words, and in an instant was all attention. His keen eyes ran over the neat little brown figure standing demurely before him, with a rapid mental calculation of her qualities.

"What is your name?"

"Venus Camilla Johnson."

"How long have you been in Miss Bowen's employ?"

"All the winter."

"Who sent you here?"

"Nobody. I keep my business to myself. Things are too curious around Wash'nton these days to be talking too much."

The shadow of a smile lurked about the corners of Mr. Henson's mouth.

"Well, what do you want? Time is precious with me."

"Yes, sir; I won't keep you long, but you see Miss Jewel's been my good angel and I jus' had to come here and unburden my mind to you or burst. You see, sir, it's this way,—the Bowen family is *white* right through; mos' *too* good for this world. They've got piles of money, but mymy, mymy! Since the Senator's gone, and Mr. Cuthbert's done got into trouble from being in tow with Miss Madison, they be the mos' miserablest two lone women you ever saw."

Venus forgot her education in her eartnestness, and fell into the Negro vernacular, talking and crying at the same time.

Mr. Henson waited patiently. He knew that she would grow calmer if he did not notice her agitation.

"It's hard for me to go back on my own daddy," continued the girl, "but it's got to be done. I suspicion him more and more every minute I'm alive, I do. Miss Jewel's stolen away, and the old lady's taken down to her bed, an' my daddy is waltzing through the country looking after General Benson's business down on a plantation in Maryland. I'm no fool, Mr. Henson; he's my daddy, but Isaac Johnson's a bad pill. He's jus' like a bad white man, sir,—he'll do anything for money when he gets hard up."

Mr. Henson sat with pale face regarding the woman before him. His eyes gleamed and were fixed searchingly upon her.

Finally he asked:

"Who are your parents? I take it they were once slaves. Where were they born?"

"Ma's Aunt Henny Sargeant's daughter Marthy, and daddy's Isaac Johnson. They lived on adjoining plantations in Maryland. Dad belonged to Mr. Enson, and Ma to Mrs. Sargeant. Ma says it was a terrible misfortune that she did live next door to the Ensons, leastwise Oliver and me'd never had Ike Johnson for our daddy."

"Any relation to the Aunt Henny who was employed by the government and who has disappeared?" the detective asked.

"Yes, sir; that's her," replied the girl, nodding her head.

"Poor granny; I reckon she's dead all right. Ma takes it terrible hard. Does nothing but cry after granny all day while she's working. I tell her I *cain't* cry till I find Miss Jewel. Ma says I'm unfeeling; but, Lord, you cain't help being just as you're built. Say, Mr. Henson, I've made bold to bring you something. I took it away from the madam the night Miss Jewel was stolen."

Mr. Henson took the envelope that the girl extended to him, and read the note contained therein.

"Who do you think sent this, Venus?"

"No one but old Benson."

Again the chief smiled at the quaint answer. But he looked at her still more searchingly, as he asked:

"Did anything of a particularly suspicious nature occur to make you hold that opinion?"

"Well, yes, sir; there did. Something I overheard General Benson say to the old lady."

"Oh, then, you were listening."

"I reckon I was, and a good job too, or I wouldn't have this to tell you. It was the day the will was read. Mr. Cameron was gone, and the three of 'em—Mrs. Bowen, Miss Jewel and General Benson were in the library. Miss Jewel went out and left the other two together.

He hollered at the madam like he was crazy, and I was standing there outside the door with the old Senator's boot-jack in my hand, expecting that I'd have to go in and hit the General over the head with it to protect the madam. He says to her, 'So, you will assist that headstrong girl to defy me, will you? Well, do it at your peril!' then he went close up to her—so close that their noses almost touched, and I thought it was about time for the boot-jack, sure,—but all he did was to whisper to her, and the old madam gave a screech and keeled over on the floor like she was dead.

I 'clare to you, Mr. Henson, I was skeered enough to drop, but I didn't say a word, no sir; I just went in as soon as the General went out, and I picked the old lady up and got her to her room, and when she came to her self there was nobody to ask her what was the matter because they didn't know what I could have told them. But Madam hasn't been herself since. I believe my soul that he skeered the life out of her. When Miss Jewel didn't come home, and that note came instead, I just made up my mind it was Venus for General Benson, and that I'd got to cook his goose or he'd cook mine."

"You do not like General Benson, I see."

"Like him! who could, the sly old villain. He's mighty shrewd, and—" She paused.

"Well, what?"

"Foxy," she finished. "He tries to be mighty sweet to me, but I like a gentleman to stay where he belongs and not be loving servant girls on the sly. I owe Miss Jewel what money cain't pay, and I'm not ungrateful."

"*I* believe the old rapscallion has got her shut up somewhere down in Maryland, and dad's helping him. Oh, I didn't tell you, did I, that dad's his private waiter?"

"Ah!" exclaimed the chief, for the first time exhibiting a sign of excitement.

"Now we're getting down to business, my girl. I understand your drift now. You have done well to come to me.

Venus smiled in proud satisfaction at his words of praise. The man sat buried in deep thought for a time before he spoke again. Finally he said:

"I need help, Venus; are you brave enough to risk something for the sake of your mistress?"

"Try me and see," was her proud reply.

"It comes to just this: someone must go down to this plantation in Maryland, and hang around to find out if there is truth in our suspicions. Can you wear boys' clothing?" he asked abruptly.

Venus showed her dazzling teeth in a giggle. She ducked her head and writhed her shoulders in suppressed merriment as she replied:

"*Cain't* I? well, I reckon."

"Then you'll do. There's no time to be lost. Disguise yourself as a boy. Be as secret about it as possible. Tell no one what you are about to do, or where you are going, and meet me at the station tonight in time for the ten o'clock train for Baltimore. My agent will be waiting for you on the Avenue, just by the entrance, disguised as your grandfather Uncle Henry, a crippled old Negro, fond of drink. You are to be Billy, and both of you are going home to Baltimore. We will fix the rest of the business after you reach the village.

God grant that this plan may hasten the discovery I have been seeking."

XXXII

Enson Hall reminded one of an ancient ruin. The main body of the stately dwelling was standing, but scarcely a vestige of the once beautiful outbuildings remained; the cabins in the slave quarters stood like skeletons beneath the nodding leaves and beckoning arms of the grand old beeches. War and desolation had done their best to reduce the stately pile to a wreck. It bore, too, an uncanny reputation. The Negroes declared that the beautiful woods and the lonely avenues were haunted after nightfall. It had grown into a tradition that the ghost of Ellis Enson "walked," accompanied by a lady who bore an infant in her arms.

The Hall was in charge of an old Negress, known all over the country as "Auntie Griffin." She was regarded with awe by both whites and blacks, being a reputed "witch woman" used to dealing and trafficking with evil spirits.

Tall and raw-boned, she was a nightmare of horror. Her body was bent and twisted by disease from its original height. Her protruding chin was sharp like a razor, and the sunken jaws told of toothless gums within.

Her ebony skin was seamed by wrinkles; her eyes, yellow with age, like Hamlet's description of old men's eyes, purged "thick amber and plum-tree gum." The deformed hands were horny and toilworn. Her dress was a garment which had the virtue of being clean, although its original texture had long since disappeared beneath a multitude of many-hued patches.

Auntie Griffin only visited the village for supplies; she was uncongenial and taciturn. She made no visits and received none. Lately, however, it was noticed that the old woman had a male companion at the Hall, an elderly, dudish colored man whom she announced, on her weekly visit to the store, as her brother Ike, come to spend a short time with her.

It was well along in August when an old Negro calling himself Uncle William Henry Jackson, accompanied by his grandson Billy, a spritely lad, scarcely more than a boy, wandered into the village and took possession of one of the dilapidated antebellum huts, formerly the homes of slaves, many of which still adorned the outskirts of the little hamlet.

Uncle William Henry claimed to be a former inhabitant who had belonged to a good old Southern family of wealth, made extinct by the civil strife. The oldest resident—a Negress of advanced age who was an authority on the genealogy of the settlement—claimed to remember him distinctly, whereupon he was adopted into their warm hearts as a son of the soil and received the most hospitable treatment, in two weeks he had settled down as a fixture of the place. The old man claimed to be a veteran of the late Civil War, and that he was in receipt of a small pension which provided food for himself and grandchild. Uncle William spent most of his time sitting on a half-barrel at the door of the general store, chewing tobacco, making fishing rods from branches which Billy brought him from the woods and telling stories, of which he had a wonderful stock. The rods he turned out were really pieces of artistic work when they left his hands, and the owner of the store agreed to find a market for the goods.

Thus the old man was happily established, to quote his own words, "fer de res' ob my days," sitting in the sun with a few old cronies of his own cut—white and black harmoniously blended—spinning yarns of life in camp, and, for the truth must be told, drinking bad moonshine rum.

He never tired of describing the battle scenes through which he had passed.

"Do I know anythin' 'bout Wagner? I should say so, bein' I was in it," was his favorite prelude to a description of the famous charge.

"No, honey, I didn' lef' dat missin' leg dar. I lef' dat leg ober to For' Piller. But fer all dat, Wagner was a corker, yes, sah, a corker. From eleven o'clock Friday 'tel four o'clock Saturday we was gittin' on the transpo'ts, we war rained on, had no tents an' nothin' to eat. Thar was no time fo' we war to lead de charge. We came up at quick time an' when we got wifin 'bout one hunde'd yards, de rebs open a rakin' fire. Why, mon, they jes' vomited the shot inter us from de fo't, an' we a-walkin' up thar in dress parade order; they mowed us down lak sheep. De fus' shot camed down rip-zip, an' ploughed a hole inter us big 'nuff to let in a squadron, an' all we did was ter close up, servin' our fire; but I tell you, gent'men, we looked at each other an' felt kin' o' lonesome fer a sight o' home an' fren's.

Colonel Shaw walked ahead as cool as ef he war up to Boston Common, singing out, 'steady, boys, steady!' Bymeby de order come in a clar ringin' voice, 'charge! Foreard, my brave boys!' We started on a double-quick, an' wif a cheer an' a shout we went pell-mell; wif a rush into an' over de ditch them devils had made an' fenced wif wire. But we kep' right on an' up de hill 'tel we war han' to han' wif de inimy. Colonel Shaw was fus' to scale de walls. He stood up thar straight an' tall lak de angel Gabrul, urgin' de boys to press on. I tell you, sah, 'twas a hot time.

Fus' thing I 'member clearly after I got het up, was I seed a officer standin' wavin' his sword, an' I heard him holler, 'Now, give 'em h—, boys, give 'em h—!' an then thar come a shot; it hit him—zee-rip—an' off went his head; but, gent'men, ef you'll b'lieve me, dat head rolled by me, down de hill sayin' as it went, 'Give 'em h—, boys, give 'em h—!' until it landed in de ditch; an' all de time de mon's arms was a wavin' of his sword."

"Come off, Uncle," exclaimed one of the circle of listeners. "Who ever heard of a man's talkin' after his head was cut off?"

"Gent'men," replied Uncle William solemnly, "dat ar am a fac'; I see it wif my own two eyes, an' hyard it wif my own two ears. *It am a fac'*."

"I've heard lies on lies," drawled another on-looker, "from all kinds of liars—white liars and niggers—but that is the mos' *infernal* one I ever listened to."

"I'll leave it to Colonel Morris thar ef sech things ain't possibul. Ain't you seen cur'us capers cut when you was in battle, sah?"

"Don't bring me into it, Uncle William Henry, I'm listening to you," laughed the Colonel, who had just driven up and was about entering the store to make a purchase.

"It am a fac'; I 'clar it am a fac'," insisted the old man. "Thar was the officer talkin', an' then the shot hit him so suddint dat he hadn't time to stop talkin'. Why de water in de ditch mus' have got in his mouf fer *I seen* him *when he spit it out!*" At this there was a roar of laughter from the crowd, and the first speaker slapped Uncle William Henry on the back with a resounding blow.

"That's a tough one for a professor, Uncle. I know you're dry. Come, have a drink."

When they had all returned to their places, the old man resumed his narrative.

"When I looked agin, Colon Shaw was gone. The Johnnies had pulled him over the parapet down onter de stockades, an' dat was de las' seen of as gallan' a gent'man as ever lived. I tell you, mon, when I seen dat, I fel' lak a she wil' cat, an' I jes' outfit a blin' mule. I tore an' I bit lak a dog. I got clinched wif a reb, an' dog my cats, fus' thing I know'd I

PAULINE E. HOPKINS

was chawin' him in de throat an' I never lef' go 'tel he give a groan an I seed he was gone. Jes' then I seen three or fo' Johnnies running 'long de parapet toward me shoutin', 'S'render, you d—nigger.' I looked an' seen dat all 'bout me they was clubbin', stabbin' an' shootin' our boys to death, an' our men was fightin' lak devils themselves.

"Well, sah, when I seen them Mr. Whitemen makin' fer me, I jes' rolled down de hill to de ditch, an' plantin' my gun ba'net down in de water, I lepped acrost to de other side. I was flyin' fer sho, you may b'lieve, an' fus' thing I heard was, 'Halt! who goes thar?' It was de provy guard, a black North Carolina regiment stationed thar to return stragglers to their posts. I sung out, clar an' loud, thinkin' I was suttinly all right then: 'Fifty-fourth Massachusetts!' But I felt de col' chills creep down my back when I heard de order: 'Git-a-back-a-dar, Fifty-fourth!' an' every mon's gun said 'click, clack.' You may b'lieve, gent'men, dat I got back.

"I wandered aroun' fer a spell lak a los' kitten; finally, I stumbled into de lines, an' I crep' unner a gun-carriage an' slep' thar 'tel mornin'."

Now it happened that Isaac Johnson was lonely in his enforced solitude, and being of social disposition, soon made it a habit to wend his way to the corner store and listen to Uncle William Henry's stories. Having plenty of money, he treated freely and was soon counted a "good fellow" by all the frequenters of the place.

At first Isaac drank moderately, mindful of his responsibilities, but soon his old habits re-asserted themselves. Moreover, Uncle William liked the social glass also; and finally the two became so intimate that they would wend their way to the hut in the woods, where the latter had taken up his residence, and there enjoy to the full the contents of a gallon-jug which was concealed under a loose board in the floor. In short, Isaac got drunk, and losing all sense of caution, remained away from the Hall two days and nights, hidden in the hut from prying eyes. The first time this happened, old William Henry recovered control of himself as soon as Isaac was locked in drunken slumber upon Billy's bed, behind the curtains, which divided the one room into sleeping apartments.

He went to the door then and waved a handkerchief three times, nailed it to the side of the hut and retired.

Ten minutes after this act, the lad Billy entered the woods which led to Enson Hall.

The path, though often ill-defined, was never quite obliterated, and he came at last to where the trees grew thinner, and the Hall was visible.

Then he emerged upon the broad stretch of meadow and crossing it was soon on the grounds. There he paused and looked cautiously about. Twilight was falling. The scene was wild and romantic. There was no sight nor sound of human beings.

He passed the rusty gates and sped swiftly across the law to the shelter of bushes near the wide piazzas. He sank down in their shadow and waited.

Nothing occurred to break the heavy silence. Not a human creature crossed the unkept grounds. The soft summer wind lazily stirred the grass growing in rank luxuriance. The scene was desolate and depressing enough. So it continued for over an hour. Darkness finally succeeded the soft twilight. Then the lad re-appeared and skirted the sides and front of the building carefully.

Presently he espied a wild honeysuckle that had climbed to the third story of the house and blended its tendrils gracefully with the branches of a giant sycamore that stretched its arms so near to the house that they tapped gently against the irons that barred a window high above its head.

With the agility of a cat, the boy was quickly finding his way up, up to the window of the room where Jewel was allowed to exercise and breathe the sweet summer air from the woods and fields. A subdued light gleamed in the window behind the iron bars.

Hush! what noise was that? It was the sound of voices in conversation. The lad ceased his climbing and rested, listening intently for a repetition of the sound. Again it came—first a sweet young voice that had a weary, despondent note; then, in answer the tones of an aged Negro voice in the endeavor to comfort and encourage.

The listener waited no longer, but rapidly mounted to the window just above his head, reached the lower end of the rusty iron bar which divided the broken casement into two, and drew himself up to the ledge, and peered in.

Mr. Henson was aroused from slumber at midnight that night to receive an important telegram, which read: "All O.K. Just as we thought. Come on and bag the game."

XXXIII

By the middle of September Washington awoke from the stagnation incident to the summer vacation, and was ready to begin the business of another working year. The departments were re-opened and hundreds of stragglers returned to work in the great government hives, all eager for the excitement of the great murder trial.

Sunday, the day before the opening of the trial, Cuthbert Sumner sat in his cell looking pale and careworn but still preserving his outward composure though racked by inward torture. Jewel's abduction had been a worse blow to him than his own arrest, and uncertainty as to her fate had nearly driven him wild; but today Hope had smiled her April smile from amid the clouds that threatened and he was at peace. His lawyer had just left him, bidding him to be of good cheer for all things pointed to a happy ending of his troubles.

Absorbed in thought he sat dreaming of the future and planning for a period of felicity that should atone for the suffering of the present time. Suddenly the key grated in the lock and the door swung open to admit a visitor. He recoiled as from a blow when he met the gaze of Aurelia Madison who stood staring at him with a glance in which curiosity, fear and love were mingled. She stood in the center of the gloomy, cell like a statue, her dazzling beauty as marvelous as ever, the red-gold hair still shining in sunny radiance, the velvet eyes resting upon the man before her with a hidden caress in their liquid depths. Sumner shuddered as he gazed and remembered the dead girl's story. When alone with this woman, she had always possessed an irresistible attraction for him, and in spite of the past the old sensation returned in full force at this unexpected encounter, mingled with fear and repulsion. She broke the spell which held them silent.

"Bert! my Bert!" She stretched out her hand to him, but he made no move to take it. The blood flushed her cheek.

"Why will you not take my hand?" She moved a step nearer to him; but he rose to his feet and drew back.

With a passionate cry she fell on her knees before him, seized his hand and covered it with kisses.

"Do not repulse me. See me at your feet. Bert! let me save you. Do not spurn me, I beseech you."

"Save me? Miss Madison, you jest," replied Sumner in a voice made quiet by a strong effort.

"I do not jest. I can and *will* save you." Her eyes were fixed upon his face in eager intensity. With a shock of surprise Sumner was convinced that she spoke the truth; but he stood there looking down upon her with all the coolness and sternness of a judge.

"You tell me news," he said at length.

"Great God! do not doubt me now. I can save you. All I ask in return is that you take me to your heart again as your affianced wife, and I shall be content."

"Ah! I thought so. There is a price attached to your generosity."

"Do not be so merciless. If you only knew—"

"I *do* know!" broke from Sumner's lips as he flung her off. She reeled back, gasping for breath. Still upon her knees, she gazed up into his immovable countenance. For a full minute there was dead silence. Then Sumner spoke.

"Do not let us have any more mistakes. If my acquittal depends upon the plan you have mentioned, Miss Madison, I shall never be free."

"Why do you speak thus?" she asked as she rose to her feet.

"For many reasons," he replied, significantly.

The woman looked utterly despondent. There was a pause—an exciting pause.

"Surely," she said at length, "you can have no hope that Jewel will return to you. Even if you were free, General Benson will hold her to her promise."

"Do not speak her name," cried Sumner, fiercely. "It is sacrilege for your perjured lips to name her whom you have so tricked, deceived and abused. A bad promise is better broken than kept, and *my wife*, formerly Miss Jewel Bowen, felt the truth of the old adage when she consented to *marry me in this very cell*." He could not repress the note of triumph in his voice as he uttered the words, but he was not prepared for what followed.

"No!" she cried out, with a passion terrible to see. "You have not dared—you could not dare—"

"Stop!" said Sumner sternly. "I warn you; do not try me too far. You will act wisely if you drop this whole matter and leave Washington and the society where you have queened it so long under false pretenses, for solitude and seclusion where you may escape the scorn of the world."

"What do you mean?" she demanded, her features pale to the very lips. She stood at bay, but in her face it could be seen that she measured his strength struggling with a new and horrible dread.

"God forbid that I should make you a social outcast!" he replied. "Need I speak plainer?"

Aurelia listened to him with the watchfulness of a tiger, who sees the hunter approaching, her strong, active brain was on the alert, but now her savage nature broke forth; she laughed aloud ferociously and then began a tirade of abuse that would have honored the slums.

Weary of the whole proceeding, disgusted with himself and the infatuation that had once enthralled him, he said at last, in desperation:

"Let us end this scene and all relations that have ever existed,—if you were as pure as snow, and I loved you as my other self, *I would never wed with one of colored blood, an octaroon!*"

Wordless, with corpse-like face and gleaming eyes she faced him unflinchingly.

"If I had a knife in my hand, and could stab you to the heart, I would do it!"

"I know you would!"

"But such weapons as I possess I will use. I will not fly—I will brave you to the last! If the world is to condemn me as the descendant of a race that I abhor, it shall never condemn me as a coward!"

Terrible though her sins might be—terrible her nature, she was but another type of the products of the accursed system of slavery—a victim of "man's inhumanity to man" that has made "countless millions mourn." There was something, too, that compelled admiration in this resolute standing to her guns with the determination to face the worst that fate might have in store for her. Something of all this Sumner felt, but beyond a certain point his New England philanthropy could not reach.

He bowed his head at her words and said,—"As you will, I have warned you!"

She stood at the full of her splendid stature, her eyes gleaming, her ashen lips firmly set, then she turned from him and gave the signal that brought the warden to let her out. Silently, without a backward look, she passed from the cell, and the prisoner was once more left in solitude.

At nine o'clock that same night, Chief Henson stood near a gas-lamp on the platform of the Baltimore & Ohio railroad station, glancing through a few lines from his colored agent, placed in his hands by plucky little Venus Johnson that very morning. The latter had gone on to the Bowen mansion to prepare the mistress for an unexpected arrival.

Chief Henson was particularly pleased with the ability shown by his colored detectives. Smith, the male agent, was a civil war veteran who had left a leg at Honey Hill, and on that account a grateful government had detailed him for duty on Chief Henson's staff of the secret service, and he had helped his chief out of many a difficult position, for which Mr. Henson was not slow nor meagre in his acknowledgments.

Five minutes after the train was in, Chief Henson saw Smith advancing toward him, accompanied by two females, closely veiled.

From out the swarming crowd the great detective stepped and motioned the man to follow with one of the females while he himself led the way with the other to the Bowen carriage outside the depot on the Avenue. Having placed the women in the carriage, and given the coachman his directions he and Smith entered a herdic and were driven rapidly to his office where they remained talking until the first hours of the morning.

Meanwhile Venus had resumed her duties as suddenly as she dropped them. The servants wondered among themselves, but not a comment was made. The news that the faithful girl brought seemed to restore Mrs. Bowen's lost vitality; she insisted on rising and being dressed, and received Jewel in her arms at the great entrance doors.

Supper was served in Mrs. Bowen's private parlor. Anyone who had entered the room would have been surprised at the kind solicitude and graciousness shown old Aunt Henny who was an honored guest. Mrs. Bowen's attention was evenly divided between her step-daughter and the old Negress. Venus waited on the company and for the time all thoughts of caste were forgotten while the representatives of two races met on the ground of mutual interest and regard.

Again and again Venus was called upon to repeat the story of her adventures.

"Yes, Mis' Bowen," she said for the twentieth time, "when I peeked in through that window and saw Miss Jewel an' gran sitting there talkin', I was plum crazy for a minute. Then I climb down as fas' as any squirrel an' I made tracks fer Mr. Smith, an' I told him what I'd seen. He says to me, says he, 'now, Venus, how in time 'm I goin' to get you into that house? We can't break the windows an' git in because they're ironed. 'Clar, says he, 'I don't know where I'm at.' Well, you know Mis' Bowen, I ain't a bit slow, no'm, if I do say it, an' I jus' thought hard fer a minute, an' then *it struck me!* Says I to him, 'git a move on dad there. You and me together mus' tote him to the house. When we git there you knock up the ol' woman an' make her let you put dad in; keep up all the fuss you can,' says I, 'an' in the kick-up why I'll sneak in and hide. You be waitin' by the front door, an' I'll have 'm out in a jiffy.' 'Good!' says he, 'two heads is better'n one if t'other is a sheep's head.' 'Much 'bliged for callin' me a fool,' says I. 'Welcome,' says he, 'but I take off my hat to you, young lady, I does, an' I'm goin' to give the chief a pointer to get you on the staff,' says he. 'Here's something to help the cause along,' an' he gave me a big bunch of keys an' a dark lantern. 'Try the keys on the big front door,' he says.

"Well, everything worked preticularly fine, Mis' Bowen. Dad was so drunk he couldn't stand, an' he didn't know whether he was afoot or ridin'. I slipped in all right, got my lady an' gran, an' got away as slick as grease.

"Dad ain't shown his head since; Mr. Henson's lookin' fer him, but I know he'll keep shy. I reckon he don't want to see ol' Ginral Benson fer one right smart spell. He's skeered all right—skeered to pieces."

Aunt Henny said nothing but once in a while she would nod her turbaned head in seeming perplexity, as she furtively watched every movement made by Mrs. Bowen. For her part, Mrs. Bowen seemed uneasy under the old woman's persistent regard.

XXXIV

At last the eagerly looked for day of the Bradford murder trial came. Society had been on the qui vive ever since Sumner's arrest, and in twenty-four hours preceding the opening of the trial, public interest had gone up to almost unparralled intensity of excitement, which the facts already known of the case increased as the time for the crisis approached. Among these facts was the one of the disappearance of the principal witness for the defense. Extraordinary disclosures were anticipated, and the wildest rumors were afloat, some of which contained a few grains of truth.

The police told off for duty at the court had their work cut out for them, for crowds began to gather long before the opening hour, some to get in—some to see the notables in society, and the government swells arrive in quick succession. Before ten the room was crowded in every available place, and further admission was refused except to those engaged in the case.

Will Badger and Carroll West made their way slowly to their places among a nest of their set, including Mrs. Brewer and Mrs. Vanderpool and other friends of Sumner. Badger and West expected to be called by the defense.

The entrance of General Benson and Major Madison caused a flutter as they took their places in the space reserved for witnesses by the prosecution. Aurelia's tall, graceful form in a handsome dark gown followed the men. She received the various salutes which came to her from all parts of the crowded room with her usual polished elegance, but the fashionable world was puzzled; there was that in her appearance which suggested tragedy.

"Good heaven!" thought Carroll West, "I wonder if there can be any truth in the rumor I have just heard! How exquisite she looks, and pale—yes, and anxious too. I wonder if she cares for Sumner. I wonder what it all means anyhow. Heaven help her safely through this ordeal."

And she had need of all the sympathy that his kind heart could bestow, for the close of the trial would see her homeless, friendless, moneyless, under the ban of a terrible caste prejudice, doubly galling to one who, like herself, had no moral training with which to stem the current of adverse circumstances that had effectually wrecked her young life.

But all society missed its queen, Jewel Bowen, about whom the wildest reports were circulated, but no one knew the truth concerning her trip out of town. Jewel had an interview with her husband early in the morning, and it was decided that Mrs. Bowen and she would not enter the court room until the day when Aunt Henny was to give her testimony. Sure now of Cuthbert's acquittal the ladies were content to wait patiently the law's course.

General Benson was ignorant, as yet, of his prisoner's escape. Isaac had disappeared and Ma'am Griffin did not dare send him word. So in ignorance of the true state of affairs, he was his own imperious self.

Presently counsel were in their places. The Attorney General and a distinguished advocate for the government; and for the defence, ex-Governor Lowe, of Massachusetts, brilliant in criminal cases, had associated with him the Bowen family lawyer, Mr. Cameron, and— mightiest of all in interest of the accused, was the guidance and keen incisive intelligence of the sleuth hound E. Henson, Chief of the Secret Service Division.

Just after ten the buzz of talk suddenly ceased, hushed by the indescribable settling of a crowd long in expectancy, as the officials took their seats. The hush became breathless as the spectators waited the appearance of the one man for whom they had all gathered here that day—the prisoner. A buzz of admiration passed through the crowd as the accused passed to his seat. Erect, easy, dignified, Sumner took his place with the same grace that had marked his entrance into the crowded halls of pleasure. He met the steady stare of those thousand eyes cooly, steadily.

"How splendidly he bears himself!" whispered one to another. He had made a distinctly good impression.

Now came the necessary formalities. The jury to be called a mysterious algebraic proceeding to the uninitiated, where the value of the x is evolved to the amazement of the onlooker. The twelve men good and true were selected in this instance with very little trouble for a case so widely known and discussed. They were unchallenged and so, presently, were duly sworn; then the official question was put:

"How say you, prisoner at the bar—guilty or not guilty?"

The answer came in clear tones, low and steadily:

"Not guilty!"

The Attorney-General arose and began the trial with a recapitulation of the circumstances attending the murder of Elise

Bradford, and the evidence adduced at the inquest. "And," said the learned counsel, "there can be little doubt that the secret of the crime lies in the victim's past. Clever detectives are of that opinion, and they argue logically enough that the fear of exposure of a guilty secret has been once more the motive of a terrible tragedy. The prisoner admits that he had been particularly attracted by the murdered girl at one time. It is known that they were alone together all that fatal Sunday afternoon in the deserted Treasury Building. He alone had exclusive opportunity to commit the crime. He admits that he gave her a glass of wine from the store kept for the chief's private use, but tells us that he left the victim in her usual health at eight that night, she refusing his escort home on a plea of wanting to pack up her belongings as she did not intend to return to work the next week having resigned her position. All this story will be proved a tissue of falsehoods unless the prisoner has the power to prove who *did* administer poison to the dead woman—if he did not do it himself—after he left the office on that fatal night.

The learned counsel weighed strongly all these stubborn facts, in an eloquent speech, which told with the audience. The case looked black for the accused. But the brilliant ex-governor smiled serenely as he glanced over the sea of faces. The trial dragged itself along with varying interest through two days. On the third day Aurelia Madison was called to prove the prisoner's gallantry and fickleness.

She did not glance at the prisoner as she passed to the witness box, impassive and lovely, but gave her evidence in a clear, concise manner that carried conviction with it. When she had finished, the tide of public opinion was strengthened against the prisoner. Like a whited sepulchre, full of hatred, she attempted to swear away the life of an innocent man to gratify her wish for revenge. By her testimony society learned for the first time the secret of the broken engagement between the accused and Jewel Bowen. Her story caused a sensation.

"Heavens! It looks strange!" whispered Mrs. Vanderpool to her neighbor Mrs. Brewer. But the end was not yet. As the witness turned to leave the stand, Governor Lowe said blandly:

"One moment, Miss Madison; I wish to ask you a few questions."

The girl paused; a white shade passed over the classic features.

"You are Major Madison's daughter?"

"Yes."

"He is your father?"

"Yes; so I am told," this last haughtily.

"Describe your mother as you remember her."

"I do not remember my mother—I never saw her. I know nothing of her."

"Where were you born?"

"In Jackson, Mississippi, I am told."

"How much money were you to receive the day Mr. Sumner married you and General Benson married Miss Jewel Bowen?"

"I don't understand your meaning."

"Weren't you to have a million given you the day you married Mr. Sumner? Yes or no."

"My dowry was a million dollars, if that is what you mean."

"Call it what you like, young lady; that was your share of the boodle with the man thrown in. That is all."

A buzz of excitement went over the crowded room. The prosecution looked at each other in blank amazement. Major Madison moved about uneasily in his seat. He was the next one called.

He knew very little of the prisoner. He was abroad at the time the engagement was made between the accused and Miss Madison, and could add little to the testimony already given. Knew Mr. Sumner as a visitor at houses where they were mutually acquainted, and had invited him to card parties in his own home.

Again the brilliant advocate asked but few questions.

"Miss Aurelia Madison is your daughter?"

"Yes."

"Born in Mississippi?" The Major nodded.

"Who was her mother?"

"My wife."

"The servant—slave or what might you call her—that stood to you in that relation? Is it not so?" blandly insinuated the questioner.

"We object," interposed the Attorney-General hurriedly to the evident relief of the enraged witness.

"Your objection is sustained," returned the judge.

Not at all disconcerted, Governor Lowe bowed pleasantly to judge, jury, lawyers and witnesses, in token of submission.

"Well, Major, did you ever know a man by the name of Walker? Or, weren't you known by that name once yourself?"

"Yes, I took that name when I was in money difficulties and hiding from my creditors."

"The man I mean was a slave-trader, notorious all over the South, who was one of the band of conspirators that murdered President Lincoln. Did you ever meet him?"

"I never have," replied the witness visibly disturbed.

"Business good, Major? How are the Arrow-Head gold mine securities turning out?"

"As well as I can expect."

"But not so well as you could wish; meantime you run a faro bank with your daughter as the snare and incidentally black mail and bunco a rich family to repair your shattered fortunes. That is all, major."

The excitement increased momentarily among the spectators. It was easy to perceive that Governor Lowe was but reserving his forces. The last witness called by the prosecution was General Benson, and nothing was elicited from him but the fact that the murdered woman had worked in his department for five years, was competent and faithful. He had no knowledge of her family nor connections outside the office. He had noticed that Mr. Sumner was somewhat partial to the good-looking stenographer, but he attached no importance to that fact, he had been young once himself. The audience was captivated by his winning manners and genial smiles. Governor Lowe took all his rights in the cross-examination.

"You gave your name as Charles Benson, General? Ever known to the public by any other name?"

For a moment the General was nonplussed.

"Sir!" with freezing haughtiness, "I do not understand you."

"My question was a plain one; but I will put it in another form— Weren't you originally known as St. Clair Enson? Isn't that the only name you have a right to wear?"

Sensation in the court room.

"We object," from the Attorney-General.

"Your objection is sustained," from the judge.

Governor Lowe was in no wise disconcerted. Again he bowed to the judge, then faced the witness still bland and smiling.

"How old was Miss Bradford when she entered your employ?"

"Eighteen, I believe."

"Awhile back you said you thought nothing of Mr. Sumner's attentions to the good-looking stenographer because you were young once yourself. I hear you are still very partial to the ladies, age has not deadened your sensibilities to their infinite charms. Did you not also offer attention to your good-looking stenographer? Did not your attentions become so warm that for various *pressing* reasons you promised Miss Bradford marriage?"

"Your questions are an outrage sir!"

"Plain yes or no, that is all I want."

"Most emphatically *No!*" thundered the witness, livid with rage. Again Governor Lowe bowed.

"Just one question more. Where were you on the night of the murder, in New York or Washington?"

"I was in New York."

The silence in the room was intense. One sensational question had followed another so rapidly that the vast throng of people found no expression for their wonderment save in silence. What was this man showing?

"Thank you, General, that is all."

That closed the prosecution.

"By Jove! more lies under this than we can see," whispered West to Badger.

Still the testimony of the state was clear on all essential points strengthened by numberless details pointing toward the guilt of the prisoner. So the third day ended, and the public felt repaid for their interest; it bade fair to go down in history as an extraordinary criminal incident.

XXXV

Thursday there was a settling down for a fresh start, an intense expectancy throughout the court. All felt that they were nearing a crisis. There were many new faces seen amid the throng and among them were the well-known features of Mrs. Bowen and Jewel, both closely shrouded in their sombre mourning robes.

Speculation was rife as to the line of the defense. What were they to hear now? What was, what could be the defense that could overpower the weight of evidence already given which seemed to make a fatal verdict a foregone conclusion? And yet, somehow, from the highest to the lowest of that hushed, excited throng, there was a curious, subtle feeling that some such resistless power lay in that reserved defence now about to be launched.

Perhaps the wish was "father to the thought." The calm confidence and lack of anxiety on the part of the defense hinted of powerful resources.

One lawyer remarked to another, "It looks as if he had a reserve force that will absolutely reverse the battle."

The prisoner sat with folded arms, cool, motionless as a statue, outwardly, but within, the man's blood was on fire.

Now Governor Lowe, with courtly manner and in sonorous tones, took up his part in the drama, beginning with the prisoner's alleged reckless youth as brought out in Miss Madison's testimony, mainly. He admitted that his client had been wild but not to the point of profligacy. He spoke tenderly of the absent, aged father—a helpless invalid—and his indulgence of an only child—motherless, too, from birth—proud, passionate, high-spirited, indulged, uncontrolled personally and in the expenditure of money, and that at this most dangerous period of a lad's life, the young man had met Miss Madison and succumbed to her fascinations, whom he intended to show was but a beautiful adventuress.

"The court," he said, "has been prejudiced against my client more by this woman's evidence than by any other testimony introduced for the government, added to that the sympathy of the whole audience has been aroused by the spectacle of a helpless woman's trust betrayed. Bah! Let me briefly unfold to you, gentlemen of the jury, the truth of the garbled tale so skilfully woven by a designing woman."

Governor Lowe then related the story of the past winter and the broken engagement, as known to our readers, with added facts to show that his client had in no way wronged the woman, who knew perfectly well what she was about, having previously become a party in a conspiracy designed to force Cuthbert Sumner into marriage, and at the same time, give control of the wealth of a well-known family into the hands of 'the gang' through the daughter of the house, the bethrothed of the accused.

Counsel then told of Aurelia's proposition of the day before the opening of the trial, and that the warden was a listener to the conversation between the prisoner and the witness; of her offer to give testimony at the trial which should free him, as she *knew the guilty party;* of the prisoner's scornful rejection of the offer, and his final retort when he told her that if she were as pure as snow, he would *never wed with one of colored blood!*

Here the astute counsel paused for his telling point to take effect. Nor was he disappointed in his calculations, for its action was as an electric shock upon the aristocratic gathering. "And now, your honor, and gentlemen of the jury," he resumed with solemn impressiveness, "I am going to prove that my client's version of his connection with this affair is absolutely true; that he was not the perpetrator of the deed, but by the irony of Fate he has been placed in a position where it was next to impossible for him to prove his innocence. After Mr. Sumner left Miss Bradford in the office on that fatal Sunday night, a person who shall be nameless still, for a time, a man high in official life, a leader in society, did enter said office and talk with the murdered woman whom he had promised to marry in a short time. While there they took wine together, he himself pouring it out and placing in her portion the arsenic, grains of which were found in the empty glass, and in the woman's stomach after death, as testified to before you by the coroner, et al."

Again he paused, for he could feel the horror that thrilled the crowd.

"This man, gentlemen of the jury, was aware of the relation formerly existing between Miss Madison and the accused, and scoundrel that he is, used the woman as a tool for the base purpose of blackmail which fortunately a higher power has frustrated; and for other reasons as well, planned to leave Mr. Sumner so surrounded and connected with Miss Bradford as to render it impossible for him to extricate himself from the charge of murder."

The counsel's manner was most effective as he made his charges; the whole scene so dramatic that only a sensational melo-drama could have rivalled its power. A subdued "whew-w!" went from mouth to mouth as a faint glimmer of the truth began to show something of the possibilities of the line taken by the defence.

"Finally, thanks to the astuteness, experience and daring of the very clever detective, who has really had active charge of the whole case, and to whom the highest praise is due, a *witness of the crime will be produced!*"

The audience was astounded; they had hoped for a sensation; their desire was more than realized.

Governor Lowe wound up his brilliant effort with a slight peroration—knowing well its good effect upon a jury—and amidst murmurs of applause, was ready to call his witness.

The first was John Williams, Sumner's valet, who testified to the regularity of his master's habits and his abstemious living. During the cross-examination, John got angry and told the Attorney-General that the Sumners were top-crust, sure; and never one of them had been known to show up as underdone dough no half-and-half's, if it wasn't so he'd eat his own head; he didn't object to meeting any man who disputed the "pint," in a slugging match, the hardest to "fend" off. The judge called him to order and the witness took his seat in a towering rage over the "imperdunce" of Southern white folks, anyhow.

Then West and Badger took the stand to refute the charge of inveterate gambling that had been made against the prisoner by Miss Madison. West was questioned only about Sumner and not of his own connection with the Madisons for which he was devoutly thankful. The fact was brought out that the Madison house was a gambling palace where men were fleeced of money for the sake of the smiles of the beautiful Aurelia, by the young fellow's tale of Sumner's warning to him against allowing himself to be ensnared by the Madison clique.

The watchmen and one or two cleaners were also placed upon the stand to prove that Mr. Sumner *did* leave the Treasury Building at the hour sworn to by him.

After that the motherless and worse than fatherless child—a beautiful fair-haired boy, was led forward and stood upon a chair in the witness-box to give emphasis to the point made by counsel that the dead woman had a pressing claim upon some man who wished to rid himself of her as encumbrance. Some of the women spectators wept, and many men felt uncomfortable about the eyes. Then Gov. Lowe

PAULINE E. HOPKINS

said: "I call Aunt Henny Sargeant." Two officers led the tottering old Negress from the ante-room to the witness chair. Aunt Henny had aged preceptibly since her imprisonment, but her faculties were as keen as ever. As she entered the crowded court-room, there was a cry, quickly suppressed, from the back seats of the room:

"Oliver, that's yer granny! My God, she's livin' yet!"

"Aunt Henny, I believe you have been in the employ of the government at the Treasury Building?"

"Yes, honey, I has."

"Tell the court how you came to be employed."

"Well, honey, I foun' a big pile o' greenbacks—mus' a bin 'bout a million dollars, I reckon,—one night when I was sweepin', an' I jes' froze to 'em all night. I neber turned 'em loose 'til de officers come in de mornin'; money's a mighty onsartin' article, chillun. People won' steal if they don' get a chance, dat's my b'lief. Then de Presidun' an' lots of other gemman made a big furze over me, an' dey done gib me my job fer life."

"Now, Aunt Henny, do you remember where you were on Sunday evening, March 20, between six and ten o'clock?"

"Yas, honey, I does, fer I warn't in bed, nuther was I to home. I was at the Building doin' some dustin' in Gin'ral Benson's 'partmen', that I'd lef over from the afternoon befo'."

"Yes; well tell us what happened that evening at the Building."

"Well, honey, I wen' in pas' the watchman, who arst me wha' I was after, an' I tol' him. Den I wen' up to Gin'ral Benson's 'partmen', which was whar I'd lef' off. I has a skilton key dat let's me git in whar I wants to go. After I'd been in 'bout an hour, I hearn people talkin' in one ob de rooms—the private office—an' I goes 'cross de entry an' peeks roun' de corner ob de po'ter—"

"The what?" interrupted the judge.

"Po'ter, massa jedge; don' yer kno' what a po'ter am?"

"She means, portière, your honor," explained Gov. Lowe, with a smile. "Go on, aunty."

"I peeked 'roun' de corner ob de po'ter, an' I seed Miss Bradford an' de Gin'ral settin' talkin' as budge as two buzzards. He jes was makin' time sparkin' her like eny young fellar, an' fer a mon as ol' as I kno' *he* is, I tell you, gemmen, he was jes' makin' dat po' gal b'lieve de moon was made o' green cheese an' he'd got the fus' slice."

A suppressed laugh rippled through the room.

"What happened then?"

"Honey, my cur'osity was bilin' hot to see what was gwine on, an' I keep peekin' an' peekin'; byme-by I hearn de glasses clickin', an' I took another look, 'cause, tho' I'm a temprunce 'ooman, an' I b'long to de High Co't o' Gethsemne, an' de Daughters ob de Bridal Veil, I neber b'lieve dat good wine is gwine ter harm on' ol' rheumatiz 'ooman like me; no, sah; dar ain't none o' yer stiff-necked temprunce 'bout yer Aunt Henny; I ain't no better than quality. I know'd dat was good stuff dat de chief had in thar 'cause I'd done taste some ob it befo', and' I'd promis' myself to taste it agin dat very night as soon as dat couple was gone. While I was thinkin' bout it, de Gin'ral turned his back to Miss Bradford as he poured de wine from de 'canter, an' dat brung him full facin' me what I was a peekin' at him, an' bless my soul, gemman, I seed dat villyun drap somethin' white inter de glass an' then turn 'roun' an' han' it to Miss Bradford. I was dat skeered I thought I'd drap, an' while I was a makin' up my min' what do so, suddintly she throwed up both arms an' screeched out *"My God, Charles, you've pizened!"*

Great sensation in the court, and the crier restored order.

"What happened then, Aunty?"

"Bless my soul, honey, I don't know what did happen, somethin' dat neber come across me in all my life befo'. I tell you, gemmen, it takes somethin' to make a colored woman faint, but dat's jes' wha' I did, massa jedge; when I seed dat po gal fro up her arms an' hern her screech I los' all purchase ob myself, and I ain't got over it yet."

The old negress rocked herself to and fro in her chair. She made a weird picture, her large eyes peering out from behind the silver-bowed glasses, her turbaned head and large, gold-hoop earrings, and a spotless white handkerchief crossed on her breast over the neat gingham dress.

"And then, Aunty?" gently prompted Gov. Lowe.

"When I come to myself agin, I was in prison, an' my own son-in-law was a keepin' me locked up."

"Was that the reason you did not inform the authorities of what you had seen?" asked the judge.

"Yas, sah; yas, massa jedge."

"Now, Aunt Henny, I want you to tell the court when and where you knew General Benson before you saw him in the employ of the government," said Gov. Lowe.

"We object, your honor," promptly interrupted the Attorney-General.

"The objection is not well taken, Mr. Attorney-General. I think Gov. Lowe has a right to put the answer in evidence. We are not here to defeat the ends of justice. Proceed, Aunt Henny."

"He ain't Gin'ral Benson no more'n I'm a white 'ooman. His name's St. Clair Enson; he was born nex' do' to de Sargeant place on the Enson plantation. Ise one ob de fus' ones what held him when he was born. Ise got a scar on me, jedge, where dat imp ob de debbil hit me wid a block ob wood when he warn't but seven years ol'. Fus' time I seed him in dat 'partmen' I know'd him time I sot my eye on him, an' den I know'd thar'd be rucktions kicked up, fer ef eber der was a born lim' o' de debbil it's dat same St. Clair Enson."

"That will do, aunty. Perhaps my legal brother may wish to cross-examine."

The Attorney-General then took the witness in hand and conducted a skilful cross-examination without shaking the old woman's testimony. Finally he said:

"One last question and I am through; you spoke of your son-in-law—what has he to do with General Benson?"

"He!" snorted Aunt Henny indignantly, "thar ain't no kind ob devilmen' St. Clair Enson was ever mixed up in dat Ike Johnson warn't dar to help him. Ike's my gal's husban'; he's Gin'ral Benson's valley; he was gave to St. Clair Enson when dat debbil was a baby in de cradle."

During the testimony of this last witness, Gen. Benson and Maj. Madison were busily talking to each other, with an occasional word to the Attorney-General.

As Aunt Henny retired to her seat in the ante-room. Gov. Lowe arose, and in an impassioned speech moved the prisoner's release, and the taking into custody of the man really guilty—General Benson.

Scarcely waiting for him to finish, the Attorney-General sprang to his feet and attacked the defense fiercely. Then ensued a scene unparalleled in the history of courts of justice.

"On what would you base such an unheard of precedent? on the evidence of a Negress? Would you impugn the honor of a brilliant soldier, a brave gentleman—courteous, genial, standing flawless before the eyes of the entire country? Such a man as General Benson cannot be condemned and suspicioned by the idiotic ramblings of an ignorant *nigger* brought here by the defense to divert attention from the real criminal, who attempts to shield himself under the influence of the Bowen millions. In the same spirit that has actuated my legal brother, while deprecating violence of any kind as beneath the dignity of our calling, I would feel myself justified in sounding the slogan of the South—lynch-law! if I thought this honorable body could be influenced to so unjust a course as is suggested by Gov. Lowe."

Instantly a chorus of voices took up the refrain—"That's the talk! No nigger's word against a white man! This is a white man's country yet!"

For a brief space, judge, jury and advocates were non-plussed; women shrieked and men flinched, not knowing what the end might be. But above the uproar, which was answered by the crowd outside, rang the voice of the police-sargeant as he formed his men in line at the door ready to charge the would-be violators of the peace. Before the determined front of the police, the crowd quieted down and order was restored.

Then Gov. Lowe arose once more:

"May it please your honor, and gentlemen of the jury, I have still another witness to present, and the last one, I call the chief of the Secret Service Division."

Once again there was silence in the room. Curiosity was on tiptoe. Many men in high places knew the chief well by reputation but had never met him. He had successfully coped with many important cases and had saved the government millions of dollars. He entered the witness-box calmly as if oblivious of the curiosity of the crowd.

"Mr. Henson, I believe that for any years you have been in the secret service."

"Yes, for fifteen years I have served the government in the capacity of a detective. Previous to that time I was a soldier and served three years, on the Federal side, at the front."

"Now, Mr. Henson, we will ask you to tell the court what you know of this case, in your own way."

At the first sound of his voice, Mrs. Bowen, who up till this time had been sitting with lowered veil, suddenly swept it one side and stared at the man in the witness-box with a strained, startled gaze. His eyes, wandering over the audience, rested on her white face. For one instant he wavered and seemed to hesitate, then by an effort he regained his composure and began his story.

"I was first called into this case by Miss Jewel Bowen. I took hold of it because of the interest she aroused in my mind, and out of pity for her distress. After I met and conversed with Mr. Sumner, I was satisfied in my own mind of his innocence, and that he was the victim of a conspiracy."

In a brief, incisive way, which carried weight to many doubting minds, he detailed the substance of the information he had obtained.

"Being brought into the issues growing out of the intimacy between General Benson and the Bowen family because of his engagement to Miss Bowen, I, very naturally, was placed in charge of the business of accumulating the facts in regard to Senator Bowen's death in New York. I have found out that he made no will while there, and that the one offered here for probate by Gen. Benson *is a forgery.*

"After Senator Bowen's death his daughter was abducted, and in the search which I caused to be made for her, we found, concealed in the same house, the Negress, Aunt Henny. So, step by step, we have been able to fix the murder of Miss Bradford, the forged will of Senator Bowen, the abduction of Miss Bowen and of Aunt Henny—the most important witness in this case—upon a band of conspirators numbering three people, all well known in society and having the entrée to the best houses."

"Do we quite understand you, Mr. Henson," asked the judge, "that in your opinion the prisoner at the bar has been the victim?"

"Yes, your honor, but only because he stood in the way of their obtaining the Bowen millions. That was the intention in the start—to obtain that immense fortune. Other than the strong attachment existing between Miss Bowen and Mr. Sumner, he would never have been molested.

"It now becomes my duty to make a statement in regard to the testimony of the last witness."

His face was set and stern. It was evident that he struggled to maintain his composure.

"What she has said concerning Gen. Benson is absolutely true. It is a long story, gentlemen, but I will be as brief as possible."

Then in graphic words that held the vast crowd spellbound, he told the story of Ellis and St. Clair Enson, as our readers already know it up to the discovery of Hagar's African descent. The judge forgot his dignity, a shock waved over the court-room. People seemed not to breathe, the interest was so intense, as they listened to the burning words of the speaker.

"When Ellis Enson returned home after completing his arrangements for taking his wife abroad, he was set upon in Enson woods by his brother and the unprincipled slave driver, Walker, and beaten into unconsciousness. When he came to himself he was in South Carolina enrolled as a member of the Confederate army. Here he remained until a good opportunity offered, when he deserted and returned home to find that his wife, child and slaves (of whom Aunt Henny was a valued house servant), had been driven to the Washington market, where his wife in desperation had thrown herself and infant into the Potomac river.

"Stripped of his fortune, home and family, cursing God and man, he entered the army on the Federal side, seeking death, but determined to carry destruction first to those who had so cruelly wronged him. But death comes not for the asking, and the ways of God are inscrutable."

He paused and passed his hand over his beaded forehead. Gen. Benson sat like a marble statue, and his nails reddened where he gripped the arms of his chair. The sound of voices came in from the street through the open window. Inside there was silence like the grave.

"Ellis Enson always supposed that his brother St. Clair stayed abroad where he had hidden after he was found guilty as one of the conspirators against the life of President Lincoln, but when I was called into this case, I found that he was in this country, serving the government he had basely betrayed, and still steeped in crime, along with his pal, Walker. Gentlemen, General Benson is St. Clair Enson, and his friend, Major Madison, is the notorious trader, Walker.

"As for me, I no longer need to conceal my identity. Gentlemen—" he gasped and faltered, and put his hand to his throat as though the words choked him.

"*General Benson is my brother—I am Ellis Enson!*"

As he finished speaking Mrs. Bowen sprang to her feet with a scream; she made a step towards him—then stopped—while these words thrilled the hearts of the listeners:

"*Ellis! Ellis! I am Hagar!*"

XXXVI

At Mrs. Bowen's impassioned cry, Chief Henson turned an appealing look upon the judge, who bowed his head as if understanding the mute question; he reached the fainting woman's side with one stride, and lifted her tenderly in his strong arms, then he bore her from the crowded room, followed by the maid and weeping step-daughter. The spectators fell back respectfully before the stern man over whose white face great tears, that did not shame his manhood, coursed unheeded.

When the excitement incident to Chief Henson's story (or Ellis Enson, as we must now call him) had somewhat subsided, the trial was resumed.

Governor Lowe called no other witnesses, but at once rose to address the jury for the prisoner, and never, perhaps, had the great politician and leader been more eloquently brilliant than on that occasion. He ranged up the whole mass of evidence with a bold and masterly grasp that could not be outrivalled.

In burning words he laid bare the details of the plot for millions, explaining that when General Benson found himself defeated in all directions, and threatened with exposure by the woman he had ruined, if he persisted in marrying Miss Bowen, he had conceived the idea of a diabolical deed—to murder Miss Bradford and allow the guilt to rest upon Cuthbert Sumner, thus ridding himself of two obstacles at one stroke.

He painted vividly the stealthy return of General Benson from New York to Washington, his arrival at the Treasury Building, his concealment in the great wardrobes, with which his department was supplied, his long wait for the departure of Mr. Sumner, during which he heard the dead woman's confession to the secretary; his meeting with Miss Bradford, down to the last awful move in the tragedy witnessed by the old Negress, Aunt Henny, who fainted with horror at the tragedy of the night. "He returned to New York as secretly as he left the city," continued the Governor, "because his flight had occurred on the Sabbath, when all the members of the committee were bent on individual pleasure, and as he was in his place on Monday morning no one noticed his absence. Then, in his devotion to his employer's interests, the faithful servant and ex-slave, Isaac Johnson, knowing no law save the will of his former owner, faithful to the traditions of slavery still, concealed the only witness of the crime, failing only in one point—that he did not murder the old woman (his mother-in-law) as commanded by General Benson, but kept her in confinement. In attempting to force Miss Bowen to marry him by abducting her and concealing her in an old country house, detectives searching for her found the missing witness, whom we have heard here today.

"The romance of the situation is enhanced by the fact that in just retribution the brother so inhumanly betrayed and abandoned, even as was Joseph of old, by his brethren, was the Nemesis placed upon the criminal's track to put him in the power of outraged justice."

With a splendid peroration, and a tender reference to the unexpected meeting of the cruelly-separated husband and wife, the Governor sat down and the Attorney-General followed him in a speech of great ability; but he knew the verdict was a foregone one, that his own remarks were but a form, that the weight of evidence in "this most extraordinary case" left him but one course. He felt, too, a savage bitterness towards Benson or Enson, that made him pant for the trial which he knew must come. In fact, officers were already stationed near the precious trio ready to take them in charge the moment all preliminary proceedings were over.

The Attorney-General concluded his speech with the words, "Justice is all that we are seeking, gentlemen of the jury, and in your hands I leave the prisoner's interests, knowing that you will return a verdict in accordance with the evidence given, that will give us all the right to welcome Mr. Sumner among us again fully reinstated in the confidence and esteem of the whole country."

The judge's charge followed, with a finely-balanced summing up which displayed all the power and glory of English jurisprudence; even the prisoner followed him with admiring forgetfulness of self. Finally the case was given to the jury; they consulted together a few minutes for the sake of appearances, without leaving their seats, then the foreman rose and announced: "We find the prisoner not guilty."

"Is this your verdict, Mr. Foreman?" asked the clerk.

"It is," he answered.

"So say you all, gentlemen of the jury?"

"We do," in chorus from the box.

If there had been much doubt which way public opinion and sympathy had set during the trial, there was absolutely none when the verdict "not guilty" was given, for the long-repressed excitement found vent in an outburst of applause that for a time defied official control. Like wildfire the news spread to the people outside, and cheer after cheer rent the air, the crowd swaying and pushing in a vain attempt to get a glimpse of the late prisoner; but as soon as he could, Sumner left in a carriage with Badger and West, faithful John Williams on the box, for his apartments, and later the Bowen mansion.

Sumner could never have told very precisely what passed after the verdict had been given, save that as in a dizzy dream he heard applause within and cheers without; then he saw the fetters on the wrists of General Benson and saw him hurried from the room between two officers, followed by Major Madison and Aurelia. The two villains had sat nonplussed and dumbfounded during the stirring events just chronicled, making no effort to escape. Governor Lowe rushed the business of their arrest, and this was ably seconded by the judge and the Attorney-General.

Presently Sumner found himself in a mass of humanity in a room with Governor Lowe and Mr. Cameron, receiving congratulations and invitations. He thanked all in his pleasant way and declined; he could not bear society just yet.

That verdict gave back life to Jewel and to him, but he was unhappy and anxious over her situation with her stepmother; the wonderful revelation of Mrs. Bowen's identity with the slave Hagar was a shock to him. It was a delicate situation, but, of course, he told himself, Mrs. Bowen could see that with all sympathy for her and her sad story, it was impossible for Jewel to be longer associated with her in so close a relationship as that of mother and daughter. He comforted himself with the thought that the unfortunate woman was the second wife of Senator Bowen, and that was a fortunate fact. He would do all that he could for Mrs. Bowen, but the social position of Mrs. Sumner demanded a prompt separation.

Cuthbert Sumner was born with a noble nature; his faults were those caused by environment and tradition. Chivalrous, generous-hearted—a manly man in the fullest meaning of the term—yet born and bred in an atmosphere which approved of freedom and qualified equality for the Negro, he had never considered for one moment the remote contingency of actual social contact with this unfortunate people.

He had heard the Negro question discussed in all its phases during his student life at "Fair Harvard," and had even contributed a paper to a local weekly in which he had warmly championed their cause; but so had he championed the cause of the dumb and helpless creatures in the animal world about him. He gave large sums to Negro colleges and on the same princpal gave liberally to the Society for the Prevention of Cruelty to Animals, and endowed a refuge for homeless cats. Horses, dogs, cats, and Negroes were classed together in his mind as of the brute creation whose sufferings it was his duty to help alleviate.

And Jewel? She, too, felt that straining of the heart's chords as she waited in her private sitting room for her lover-husband. She was alone. Ellis Enson was with her stepmother. After Mrs. Bowen returned to consciousness, Jewel had stolen away unnoticed by the strangely reunited pair, leaving them in sacred seclusion.

She held the evening paper in her hand. It contained a column headed, "Sensational Ending of the Famous Bradford Tragedy."

After detailing the day's events, the editor gave the story of the white slave Hagar (Mrs. Bowen), and her extraordinary recognition of her former husband and master in the person of Chief Henson of the Secret Service Division. The editor went on to say:

"No trace of woman or child was found after her leap over the bridge into the river. She was supposed to have been drowned. The woman, however, was picked up by a Negro oyster-digger and concealed in his hut for days. At the breaking out of the war she drifted to California and in a few years married the wealthy miner, Zenas Bowen. This story, showing, as it does, the ease with which beautiful half-breeds may enter our best society without detection, is a source of anxiety to the white citizens of our country. At this rate the effects of slavery can never be eradicated, and our most distinguished families are not immune from contact with this mongrel race. Mrs. Bowen has our sympathy, but we cannot, even for such a leader as she has been, unlock the gates of caste and bid her enter. Posterity forbids it. We wait the action of Mr. Ellis Enson (Chief Henson) with impatience, praying that sentiment may not overcome the dictates of duty."

Jewel's tender heart was full of pity and love for her stepmother. Now she knew for the first time whence came the fountain of love so freely lavished upon her by this heartbroken mother.

"How she must have suffered," murmured the girl to herself. Then, as she mentally counted up the years that had passed since the events chronicled by the paper, she said aloud in some surprise, "Why, I must be about the age of the poor baby girl. How wonderful!" She was glad to be alone after all these weeks of tempest and today's climax, with its reaction. Mingled with her own joy at Cuthbert's release was a silent, wordless awe of Chief Henson's declaration in the court room and her stepmother's avowal. But, strange to say, the girl felt none of the repugnance that the announcement of Mrs. Bowen's origin had brought to Sumner. Her own happiness was so great that all worldly selfishness was swept away.

Hush! She suddenly rose from the couch where she was sitting, with wide eyes and quivering form, hearing the soft musical voice outside, so yearned for all these dreadful weeks, now fast disappearing like a horrible nightmare before the rosy glow of Hope's enchanting rays. She saw the door open and shut—saw Cuthbert's tall form enter—she sank upon the couch, putting out her hands to him in a trustful, childlike way.

Without a word he flung himself beside her and folded her in his arms with a passion and strength that were resistless.

"Mine at last! My darling! My one love—my wife!" For a second there was a blank—life itself seemed to stand still, and time and space were obliterated. "Husband!" she said at length with smothered passion. He stopped and kissed her in a strange, awed way—silently, solemnly, as a man might who had been so near the grave—heart to heart, soul to soul, conscious only in that supreme moment paradise was touched! So for some minutes they sat in soul communion. Sumner broke the silence after a time. "Heaven only can reward Chief Henson and Venus Johnson for their rescue of you, my treasure. May heaven forget me if I ever forget their devotion to my dear wife. I tell you, Jewel, I was maddened when the news was brought to me of your abduction. I would have been a murderer in truth could I have been free for one moment to meet Benson!"

The wife's lips touched his softly, lovingly—true woman to the core—as a "ministering angel."

"But, dearest, God protected me."

There was another eloquent pause. Then Sumner said abruptly:

"Tomorrow our marriage must be properly advertised. It is Thursday now; on Monday you must come with me to my father. After you have seen him, you shall plan our future."

Jewel laid her head against him. "Your wishes are mine, Cuthbert."

Then they talked a while of the strange revelations made at the trial, of the discovery of Negro blood in Aurelia Madison and Mrs. Bowen.

"With the knowledge that we now possess of her origin, we can no longer wonder at her wicked duplicity," said Sumner.

"That is true in her case," replied Jewel, "but a truer, sweeter, more perfect woman than mamma does not live on the earth; how do you account for it?"

"Depend upon it, those characteristics are but an accident of environment, not the true nature of her parent stock. I have always heard that the Negro race excelled in low cunning."

"True," repeated Jewel, dreamily, "but then there are Venus and Aunt Henny."

"Yes, and my faithful John. I suppose these exceptions prove the rule. Still I am thankful that Mrs. Bowen is only your step-mother."

Then they drifted back into their lovers' talk once more.

> *"Look thro' mine eyes with thine, true wife,*
> *Round my true heart thine arms entwine;*
> *My other dearer life in life,*
> *Look thro' my very soul with thine!"*

It was midnight when the wedded lovers separated. In the hall they met Ellis Enson, as we shall hereafter call him.

The man's face wore a look of solemn joy. He shook Jewel's hand silently. He urged Sumner to go to his room with him and spend the night, for he had much to say to him in regard to the late trial. Sumner felt obliged to accept the invitation, and the two men went away together.

The early morning hours found them still talking over the trial, but their greatest interest was in the story of the elder man—the strange trials in two lives.

"How do you intend to fix it?" questioned Sumner.

"Of course Mrs. Bowen is very much shaken, but we shall be quietly remarried on Sunday, and then I shall take my wife away. When we return I hope to have possession of Enson Hall, where we shall take up our permanent abode. I hand in my resignation today, to take immediate effect."

"I honor you for your resolution, Enson, but indeed I have not your strength of character. I could never solve the social problem in that high-handed manner. Have you no fear of public opinion?"

"My dear boy, I know just where you are. I went all through the old

PAULINE E. HOPKINS

arguments from your point of view twenty years ago. I wavered and wavered, but nature was stronger than prejudice. I have suffered the torments of hell since I lost my wife and child."

He rose from his seat and strode once down the room, then back again, pausing before the young man.

"Sumner," he said, with impressive solemnity, "race prejudice is all right in theory, but when a man tries to practice it against the laws which govern human life and action, there's a weary journey ahead of him, and he's not got to die to realize the tortures of the damned. This idea of race separation is carried to an extreme point and will, in time, kill itself. Amalgamation has taken place; it will continue, and no finite power can stop it."

"But, my dear Enson, you do not countenance such a such a—well—terrible action as a wholesale union between whites and blacks? Think of it, my dear man! Think of our refinement and intelligence linked to such black bestiality as we find in the slums of this or any other great city where Negroes predominate!"

Enson smiled at the other's vehemence.

"Certainly not, Sumner; but, on the other hand, take the case of Aurelia Madison. Did you ever behold a more gorgeously beautiful woman, or one more fastidiously refined? Had her moral development been equal to her other attainments, and you had loved her, how could you endure to have a narrow, beastly prejudice alone separate you from the woman pre-destined for your life-companion? It is in such cases that the law of caste is most cruel in its results."

"I think that the knowledge of her origin would kill all desire in me," replied Sumner. "The mere thought of the grinning, toothless black hag that was her foreparent would forever rise between us. I am willing to allow the Negroes education, to see them acquire business, money, and social status within a certain environment. I am not averse even to their attaining political power. Farther than this, I am not prepared to go."

"And this is the sum total of what Puritan New England philanthropy will allow—every privilege but the vital one of deciding a question of the commonest personal liberty which is the fundamental principle of the holy family tie."

"When one considers the ignorance, poverty and recent degradation of this people, I feel that my position is well taken," persisted Sumner. "Ought we not, as Anglo-Saxons, keep the fountain head of of our racial stream as unpolluted as possible?"

Enson smiled sadly; a holy light for one instant illumined the scarred face of the veteran:

"'A boy's will is the wind's will, And the thoughts of youth are long, long thoughts,'" he quoted softly. "You will learn one day that there is a higher law than that enacted by any earthly tribunal, and I believe that you will then find your nature nobler than you know."

"You make me feel uncanny, Enson, with your visionary ideas. Thank God, I have my wife; there I am safety anchored."

"Amen!" supplemented Enson softly, as they clasped hands in a warm goodnight.

XXXVII

On Friday the court room was again crowded to the doors by spectators eager to view the closing scenes in the celebrated case.

The soi-disant General Benson was arraigned on a charge of wilfully murdering Elise Bradford, and was committed for trial in October. Major Madison, or Walker, the ex-slave driver, and his daughter Aurelia were also in court, Madison for forgery in connection with Senator Bowen's will.

Nothing criminal was charged against Aurelia; in fact, no one desired to inflict more punishment on the unfortunate woman, and when she left the court room that day she vanished forever from public view.

Deadly pale, but proudly self-possessed, Ellis Enson gave his testimony at the hearing, fixing a steadfast, unflinching gaze on the livid, haggard face that glared back with sullen hate and fear in every line. So for a moment of dead silence, of untold pain to one, those two men, sons of one father, but with a bridgeless gulf between them, stood face to face after many years.

The story had to be told again, however deeply it racked one soul to be forced to give deadly testimony against the murderer, who, outcast by his own evil deeds, was still his father's son. The ghastly facts stood out too clearly for hesitation, and St. Clair Enson, alias Gen. Charles Benson, was remanded for trial.

Owing to the unsavory character of the prisoner extra precautions were taken by the warden to prevent a rescue or an escape.

At one o'clock Saturday morning the guard upon the outer wall that surrounded the jail saw a shadow that seemed to move. At first he thought it a stray cat or dog, then as he watched he saw that it stole along the wall suspiciously; obedient to orders, he fired; the shadow fell to earth.

The men who came running at the sound of the shots bore the wounded man back into the jail, where they found that their burden was the body of St. Clair Enson, and that he was dead. The guard's bullet had taken a fatal effect.

In the prisoner's bed crouched Isaac Johnson in a vain endeavor to cover up his former owner's flight. A gaping hole at one side of the cell told where an entrance had been effected. How Isaac had managed to cut his way through the solid masonry always remained a mystery to the authorities.

Thus ended St. Clair Enson's career of vice and crime. Walker, alias Major Madison, died in the state prison.

XXXVIII

Late Saturday afternoon, Hagar, so long known to us as Mrs. Bowen, reclined in semi-invalid fashion on the couch in her boudoir. She had exchanged her deep mourning for a house dress of white cashmere, profusely touched with costly lace. Her dark hair, showing scarcely a touch of silver, was closely coiled at the back of her shapely head. In spite of a shade of sadness her countenance was serene.

She was happy—happier than she had ever hoped to be in this life. True, no callers begged admittance into the grand mansion, no cards overflowed the receivers in the spacious entrance hall, since the sensational items disclosing her identity had appeared in the columns of the daily press; that fact did not disconcert her in the least. One thing alone troubled her,—Sumner's determination to separate her from Jewel.

The tender-hearted woman who had been his champion and friend throughout dark days of suspicion and despair, could not understand his antipathy to her. The two ladies did not worry themselves unduly, however, trusting that time and their united persuasions would win him to a better frame of mind.

The ceremony of the morrow would see her united to the husband of her youth. She thought only of that.

Ellis wished to settle the whole of Senator Bowen's immense fortune upon Jewel, but the latter would not hear of so unjust a proceeding. So the mansion was to be left in the care of Marthy Johnson, Aunt Henny and Oliver, while Mr. and Mrs. Enson were abroad. Venus was to go to Massachusetts with her young mistress, and the plan was that she and John Williams should be married about Christmas. The travellers were to start on their journeys early Monday morning. Suddenly Senator Bowen's last words, "The little hair trunk!" flashed across the lady's mind. It had been his in his first wife's time. He had clung to it through poverty and prosperity. It was in the late Senator's dressing-room which opened into the room where she was lying. Secretly blaming herself for neglecting the shabby object of his love and care, Hagar rose hastily and passed into the adjoining room.

Everything was as he had left it. How lonely it seemed without the jovial, genial presence of the man who had saved her from despair. Tears came to her eyes as she stood gazing upon familiar objects, each bearing the personality of the man who had gathered them about him. Over in a corner stood the little hair trunk. She moved slowly toward it, and presently was on her knees before it with the lid thrown back.

She sat there, prone upon the floor, for a time, gazing in mute sadness upon the contents—shabby, peculiarly made garments of the fashion in vogue before the war, mementoes of that other wife of his young manhood, and, strange mixture, a number of clay pipes, burned black by use, and fishing tackle, all mingled in a motley heap.

She took up the first wife's picture, opened the case and gazed into the eyes of the blowzy girlish face in its hideous cape bonnet, the long spiral curls falling outside the ruche that faced the head covering. Not a pretty face; no, but honesty and kindliness of heart were written there, silently claiming their tribute, turning the contemptuous smile to gentle reverence.

Hagar closed the case softly and placed it beside her on the floor with the other articles which her sense of neatness and order had caused her to fold carefully in regular piles, ready to replace in the shabby receptacle.

She had often wondered who Jewel resembled and where she had obtained the dainty, high-bred elegance of face and figure; surely not from father nor mother. Today her curiosity was again aroused; the desire to know pursued her so persistently that she was amazed.

The small velvet case containing Senator Bowen's daguerrotype, taken in early youth, had a peculiar fascination for her. His face smiled up at her, round, jolly, rubicund, a dimple in his chin and a laugh in his eyes, which the straight hair, combed flatly to the sides of his head, could not render sedate. Hagar felt a film gather to her eyes. What a god he had been to her! How devoted! How gentle! And he was a man of strong intellect and staunch integrity. She had no cause to be ashamed of him. He had saved her from despair. Next to her God she placed this man, whom she knew instinctively would never have forsaken her, never for one instant would he have wavered from his constancy to her, no matter what the cause, were she but true to him.

Ellis had come back to her; yes, but although love forgave, love worshipped at his shrine, love could not blot out the bitter memory of the time when he had failed her.

She closed the case with a nervous click, and went on with her sorting and folding. The very last thing that she found was a brown paper parcel, tied with coarse string. She undid the knot with the feeling of pride which attends the operation of succeeding in untying a string without cutting it. She smoothed out the kinks and curls and laid it carefully at her side ready for use again; then she removed the paper, expecting to see a man's wearing apparel; to her surprise a roll of white cashmere, yellow with age, met her eyes; it was wrapped about other articles. The kneeling woman felt the room spinning round her as she held the packet in her hand. There was something vaguely familiar in that ordinary piece of yellow cashmere; one side being visible showed a deep embroidered design tracing the edge of the deep hem. She could not move. Every muscle was paralyzed, and a flood of memories rushed in turmoil through her brain.

Trembling, breathless with excitement, she began to unroll the bundle. The last fold, as it fell apart, revealed the outer covering to be an infant's cloak of richest material and beautifully embroidered. With quivering fingers the agitated woman continued to shake out the garments that the cloak enfolded—a tiny dress, dainty skirts, a face cap—in short, all the articles necessary to make up the attire of a child of love and wealth.

"Oh, merciful heaven! How came these here?" she whispered with white lips, as she pressed each tiny garment to her lips, and rained tremulous kisses on the exquisite lace cap. "My baby, my baby!"

She threw herself upon the floor and lay there weeping scalding tears. Before her lay the garments that her own hands had fashioned twenty years before, for the little daughter who had come to bless the union of Ellis Enson and herself. Half in terror she gazed upon them as upon the ghost of one long since departed. She made a movement and a metallic sound drew her attention to an object that slipped from among the clothing to the floor. It was a gold chain, from which depended a locket.

"My mother's locket!" she gasped. "Ah! Until this hour I had forgotten it; it was about my darling's neck when last I dressed her. My God! How comes it here? Why do I find it in Zenas Bowen's trunk?"

She touched a spring and the outer lid sprang back, showing a piece of paper pressed in the space usually devoted to pictures. The paper fell upon the floor unheeded. The writing was in Senator Bowen's hand, but she did not notice it; she was pressing her fingers along the margin of filagree work which decorated the edge of the locket; presently the back fell apart; then she pressed again and a third compartment opened and from it the face of Ellis Enson in his first youth smiled up into her own.

How well she remembered all the minute details of the history of the locket in the shadowy past, brought so vividly to her memory by the dramatic events of the last few days. Her mother had given her the locket at the time of her father's death, and had told her that it was a valued heirloom, and had explained to her the intricate working of the triple case. Probably no one had ever discovered the secret spring, and the case was supposed to be empty. After Mrs. Sargeant's death, she had in turn explained to Ellis, and placed his pictured face there, and when, tortured and tormented by persecution, she was driven from her home to the slave market, she had placed the locket about the baby's neck; why, she knew not.

Gazing at it now with sick and whirling brain, there came a step outside in her sitting room. She dragged her leaden limbs to the door and beheld Ellis. The bright smile on his face at sight of her seemed to chase away the years and renew his lost youth.

"My darling," he began, "you see I have managed to return earlier than I expected. I could not support the purgatory of absence from you longer. But what is the matter?"

Hagar could not answer him. Leaning against the doorframe, she looked him in the eyes, then extended her hand, the open locket lying on her palm.

"Ellis," she said, in a husky whisper, "I have just found this—here—in this room—in Senator Bowen's old trunk of relics. What can it mean? For God's sake, try and explain it to me. I cannot grasp the meaning of it at all."

Ellis's face was as white as her own, but he spoke soothingly to the distracted woman. Then his trained eye travelled beyond her to where the folded paper lay forgotten.

Taking her in his arms, he placed her upon the couch in the sitting-room, and then picked up the paper, first tenderly straightening each tiny garment and placing them all together in a pile upon a chair. Closing the door carefully behind him, he drew a chair to the side of the couch where Hagar lay weeping.

"Now, Hagar, my dear," he said, coaxingly, "you will try and be good and command yourself. God grant by these tokens that we may trace our darling's last resting place—a message from heaven!"

"Oh, how selfish I am, Ellis! You need comfort as much as I do," she cried, her love on fire at sight of the tears in his eyes, which he tried in vain to suppress. And then for a little while the childless parents held each other's hands and wept. Presently Ellis opened the paper from the locket. It seemed but a leaf from a memorandum book, but what a change it wrought in the lives of four people!

> March, 1862
> Went up the Potomac on the "Zenas Bowen" for oysters.
> Brought off 100 guns, 300 pounds of ammunition,
> Charleston, S. C. Picked up log floating outside the bay with
> a girl baby less than one year old attached to it by clothing.
> Must have floated many hours, but the sleeping child was
> unhurt. Clothing rich; no clue to parents or relatives.

> November, 1862
> Have adopted child and shall call her "Jewel." I have
> placed this mem. inside locket found on child for future
> reference.
>
> Zenas Bowen
> Mary Jane Bowen

There was a sound of weeping in the quiet room. "The Divine Father hears all prayers, sees all suffering. In His own good time the All-Merciful has had mercy." The solemn words broke from Ellis.

"And I have said in my anguish, there is no God. He does not heed my woes. Blasphemer that I am!" cried Hagar.

"And she is here in this very house! My God, I thank Thee! Ellis, do not fear, I am strong; go, I beseech you, lose not a moment, bring her to me—bring my Jewel, my daughter, to my arms. Ah, did not my heart yearn over her from the first, when, as a tender baby girl, I held her to my aching heart, and soothed my deep despair? Go, go—at once—Ellis! This suspense is more trying than all that has gone before. You do not know a mother's feelings. Shall I live till your return?"

Ellis, alarmed at her state, choked down his own feelings, and left the room in search of Jewel.

WHO CAN PAINT THE MOST sacred of human emotions? Clasped in her mother's arms, and shown the proofs preserved by her adopted father of her rescue from the death designed by her distracted mother, Jewel doubted not that she was Hagar's daughter.

XXXIX

All night the new-found daughter and husband watched beside Hagar's couch. They feared for her reason. But joy never kills, and at length she slept, and Jewel stole away to take her needed rest.

When alone again in her room, after the startling revelation that had come to her, she sat a long time, trying to realize the complete change in her future which this discovery would bring. She did not deceive herself; the cup of happiness was about to be snatched from her lips. Cuthbert, who was the one object of her passionate hero worship, would turn from her with loathing. There were dark circles about her eyes and her cheeks were ghastly. She loved her mother, she was proud of her father but feelings engendered for twenty years were not to be overcome instantly. It was horrible—a living nightmare, that she, the petted darling of society, should be banned because of her origin. She shrank as from a blow as she pictured herself the astonishment, disgust and contempt of her former associates when they learned her story. The present was terrible, the future more awful still. Overcome by her thoughts, moans burst from her overcharged heart; she stretched out her arms in an abandonment of grief and dropped senseless in the middle of her room, and so Venus found her in the early morning hours. Heaven help her, for it must also be written for her as for her ill-fated mother:

> *"Better the heart strings had never known*
> *The chord that sounded its doom."*

Venus knew the whole story. Mr. Enson had called Marthy, Aunt Henny and Venus into the room and told them very solemnly the facts in the case. There was much weeping and rejoicing.

"My soul," cried Venus to her mother when they were alone, "what about Mr. Sumner? If he goes back on Miss Jewel it'll kill her; it will break her heart."

"It's my 'pinion dat it's already broke, honey; a gal brung up like her has been's gwine break her heart to fin' herself nuthin' but common nigger trash. I jes' hope de debbil's give St. Clair Enson a good hot place down thar to pay him for his devilmen' here on yearth, 'deed I does," said Aunt Henny.

PAULINE E. HOPKINS

Jewel sent for her father and they talked the matter over. Mr. Enson could give her little hope. He was forced to acknowledge that Sumner was strongly prejudiced. He promised to see him, however, and tell him the story and hear his reply to Jewel, who sent also a pathetic note bidding him farewell:

"I know your prejudice against amalgamation: I have believed with you. My sin, for it is a sin to hold one set of God's creatures so much inferior to the rest of creation simply because of the color of the skin, has found me out. Like Miriam of old, I have scorned the Ethiopian and the curse has fallen upon me, and I must dwell outside the tents of happiness forever. I know you pity my poor mother; she has been so unhappy. I am proud of my father; he is a noble man. I will write again tomorrow and perhaps see you; but, oh, pray not today!"

Twenty-four hours passed and left Sumner as they found him, in mental torture. Then his good angel triumphed. He swore he would not give her up, and then he learned the power of prayer. He was ready to overlook and forgive all if only Jewel were left him. As his entreaties went up to a compassionate God the words rose ever before him.

"Many waters cannot quench love, neither can the floods drown it. All Thy waves and Thy billows have gone over me, but the heart is not easily closed. Love is strong as death."

Evening found him hastening toward the Bowen mansion. The house looked desolate. He rang the bell at the great entrance doors. Marthy Johnson answered the imperative summons.

"Lor', Mr. Sumner, Lor', sir!"

"Where are they all, Marthy?" he asked abruptly.

"Gone to de continen', Mr. Sumner. Massa Ellis say, you young folks'll git better lef' by your lonesomes; dat's what he tol' me tell you, Sir."

Sumner left her in deep despair. He went home to his father for a brief time and then started for the Continent himself.

At the end of a year, mindful of poor John's devotion, for he vowed not to marry Venus till his master settled down, Sumner returned to America and again sought the Bowen mansion. Again Marthy answered his summons, and told him that the family were at Enson Hall. He did not notice the pity on the woman's face.

He never paused until he reached the pretty little rustic town in Maryland that held his heart, his dove of peace. And then a great fear fell upon him, undefined and foreboding. He sent John on with his luggage to the Hall, and wandered up the country road with beating heart and feverish pulses. In a few minutes he would see her, she would be beside him, loving, forgiving. The tears came into his eyes, and he whispered a prayer. He drew his hat over his face and wandered off across a daisied field until he had overcome his emotion. A little graveyard nestled close beside the road. He was on the broad Enson acres, and in that enclosure dead and gone Ensons had slumbered for centuries. It was cool and shady and restful, and unconsciously he stepped into it.

Suddenly with a great cry he stood still before a fair, slender shaft of polished cream-white marble,

Jewel, aged 21.
"Not my will, but Thine be done!"

He fell down with his face upon her grave. She had died abroad of Roman fever.

CUTHBERT SUMNER QUESTIONED WHEREIN HE had sinned and why he was so severely punished.

Then it was borne in upon him: the sin is the nation's. It must be washed out. The plans of the Father are not changed in the nineteenth century; they are shown us in different forms. The idolatry of the Moloch of Slavery must be purged from the land and his actual sinlessness was but a meet offering to appease the wrath of a righteous God.

Across the lawn of Enson Hall a child—a boy—ran screaming and laughing, chasing a gorgeous butterfly. It was the child of St. Clair Enson and Elise Bradford, the last representative of the Enson family.

Cuthbert watched him with knitted brows. In him was embodied, a different form, a lesson of the degradation of slavery. Cursed be the practices which pollute the soul, and deaden all our moral senses to the reception of the true doctrines of Divinity.

The holy institution of marriage ignored the life of the slave, breed indifference in the masters to the enormity of illicit connections, with the result that the sacred family relation is weakened and finally ignored in many cases. In the light of his recent experiences Cuthbert Sumner views life and eternity with different eyes and thoughts from what he did before he knew that he had wedded Hagar's daughter. Truly had Ellis Enson spoken when he judged him nobler than he knew.

> *"A boy's will is the wind's will,*
> *And the thoughts of youth are long, long thoughts."*

WINONA: A TALE OF NEGRO LIFE

I

Crossing the Niagara river in a direct line, the Canadian shore lies not more than eight miles from Buffalo, New York, and in the early 50's small bands of Indians were still familiar figures on both the American and Canadian borders. Many strange tales of romantic happenings in this mixed community of Anglo-Saxons, Indians and Negroes might be told similar to the one I am about to relate, and the world stand aghast and try in vain to find the dividing line supposed to be a natural barrier between the whites and the dark-skinned race. No; social intercourse may be long in coming, but its advent is sure; the mischief is already done.

From 1842, the aborigines began to scatter. They gave up the last of their great reservations then before the on-sweeping Anglo-Saxon, moving toward the setting sun in the pasture lands surrounding the Black Hills.

Of those who remained many embraced Christianity; their children were sent to the pale-face schools; they themselves became tillers of the soil, adopting with their agricultural pursuits all the arts of civilized life, and cultivating the friendship of the white population about them. They, however, still clung to their tribal dress of buckskin, beads, feathers, blankets and moccasins, thereby adding picturesqueness of detail to the moving crowds that thronged the busy streets of the lively American city. Nor were all who wore the tribal dress Indians. Here and there a blue eye gleamed or a glint of gold in the long hair falling about the shoulders told of other nationalities who had linked their fortunes with the aborigines. Many white men had been adopted into the various tribes because of their superior knowledge, and who, for reasons best known to themselves, sought to conceal their identity in the safe shelter of the wigwam. Thus it was with White Eagle, who had linked his fortunes with the Senaca Indians. He had come among them when cholera was decimating their numbers at a fearful rate. He knew much of medicine. Finally, he saved the life of the powerful chief Red Eagle, was adopted by the tribe, and ever after reverenced as a mighty medicine man.

Yet, through Erie County urged the Indians farther West, and took up their reservations for white settlers, their thirst for power stopped short of the curtailment of human liberty. The free air of the land of the prairies was not polluted by the foul breath of slavery. We find but one account of slaves brought into the country, and they were soon freed. But the free Negro was seen mingling with other settlers upon the streets, by their presence adding still more to the cosmopolitan character of the shifting panorama, for Buffalo was an antislavery stronghold,—the last most convenient station of the underground railroad.

It was late in the afternoon of a June day. It was uncommonly hot, the heat spoke of mid-summer, and was unusual in this country bordering upon the lakes.

On the sandy beach Indian squaws sat in the sun with their gaudy blankets wrapped about them in spite of the heat, watching the steamers upon the lakes, the constant traffic of the canal boats, their beaded wares spread temptingly upon the firm white sand to catch the fancy of the free-handed sailor or visitor. Upon the bosom of Lake Erie floated a canoe. It had been stationary at different points along the shore for more than an hour. The occupants were fishing; presently the canoe headed for an island lying close in the shadow of Grand Island, about a mile from it. The lad who handled the paddle so skilfully might have been mistaken for an Indian at first glance, for his lithe brown body lacked nothing of the suppleness and grace which constant exercise in the open air alone imparts. He wore moccasins and his dress otherwise was that of a young brave, save for feathers and paint. His flashing black eyes were fixed upon the island toward which the canoe was headed; as the sunlight gleamed upon his bare head it revealed the curly, crispy hair of a Negro.

The sunlight played, too, upon the other occupant of the canoe, as she leaned idly over the side trailing a slim brown hand through the blue water. Over her dress of gaily-embroidered dark blue broadcloth hung two long plaits of sunny hair.

Presently the canoe tossed like a chip at the base of wooded heights as it grated on the pebbly beach. The two children leaped ashore, and Judah pulled the canoe in and piled it and the paddles in the usual place, high in a thicket of balsam fir. Winona had removed her moccasins and carried them in her hand while they made the landing; Judah balanced his gun, the fishing-rods and the morning's catch of fish on a rod.

They took their way along the beach, wading pools and walking around rocks, gradually ascending the wooded heights above them round and round, until they stood upon the crest that overlooked the bay and mainland.

The island was the home of White Eagle. When the Indians gave up Buffalo Creek reservation to Ogeten in 1842, and departed from Buffalo, he had taken up his abode on this small island in the lake, with an old woman, a half-breed, for his housekeeper. Hunting, fishing, trapping and trading with the Indians at Green Bay gave him ample means of support. But it was lonely with only a half-deaf woman for a companion, and one day White Eagle brought to the four-room cottage he had erected a handsome well-educated mulattress who had escaped from slavery via the underground railroad. With her was a mite of humanity whose mother had died during the hard struggle to reach the land of Freedom. In the end White Eagle crossed the Canadian shore and married the handsome mulattress according to English law and with the sanction of the Church; the mite of black humanity he adopted and called "Judah."

In a short time after the birth of Winona, the wife sickened and died, and once more the recluse was alone. Yet not alone, for he had something to love and cling to. Winona was queen of the little island, and her faithful subjects were her father, Judah and old Nokomis.

So transparent was the air on this day in June, that one could distinguish strips of meadow and the roofs of the white Canadian houses and the sand on the edges of the water of the mainland. The white clouds chased each other over the deep blue sky. The dazzling sunshine wearied the eye with its gorgeousness, while under its languorous kiss the lake became a sapphire sea breaking into iridescent spray along the shore.

The children were on a high ridge where lay the sun-flecked woods. They were bound for the other side, where lurked the wild turkeys; and partridges and pigeons abounded, and gulls built their nests upon rocky crests.

Singing and whistling, Judah climbed the slopes, closely followed by Winona, who had resumed her moccasins. The squirrel's shrill, clear chirp was heard, the blackbirds winged the air in flight, and from the boughs above their heads the "robin's mellow music gushed." Great blossoms of pink and yellow fungus spotted the ground. Winona stopped to select from among them the luscious mushroom dear to her father's palate. Daisies and bell-shaped flowers of blue lay thick in the grasses, the maples were still unfolding their leaves; the oak was there and the hemlock with its dark-green, cone-like folliage; the graceful birch brushed the rough walnut and the stately towering pine.

The transparent shadows, the sifted light that glimmered through the trees, the deer-paths winding through the woods, the green world still in its primal existence in this forgotten spot brought back the golden period unknown to the world living now in anxiety and toil.

A distant gleam among the grasses caught the girl's quick eye. She ran swiftly over the open and threaded her sinuous way among the bushes to drop upon her knees in silent ecstacy. In an instant Judah was beside her. They pushed the leaves aside together, revealing the faint pink stems of the delicate, gauzy Indian-pipes.

"Look at them," cried Winona. "Oh, Judah, are they not beautiful?"

The Negro had felt a strange sense of pleasure stir his young heart as he involuntarily glanced from the flowers to the childish face before him, aglow with enthusiasm; her wide brow, about which the hair clustered in rich dark rings, the beautifully chiselled features, the olive complexion with a hint of pink like that which suffused the fragile flowers before them, all gave his physical senses pleasure to contemplate. From afar came ever the regular booming of Niagara's stupendous flood.

"But they turn black as soon as you touch them."

"Yes, I know; but we will leave them here where they may go away like spirits; Old Nokomis told me."

"Old Nokomis! She's only a silly old Indian squaw. You mustn't mind her stories."

"But old Nokomis knows; she speaks truly," persisted the girl, while a stubborn look of determination grew about her rounded chin.

"When you go to school at the convent next winter the nuns will teach you better. Then you will learn what you don't know now. You're only a little girl."

There was silence for a time; Judah sank in the tall grass and aimed for a tempting pigeon roosting low in the branches of a tree. Nearer he stole—his aim was perfect—he was sure of his prey, when a girlish voice piped,—

"Did they tell you that at school?"

"There now! You've spoilt it! why did you speak?"

"Well, I wanted to know," this in a grieved tone.

"Wanted to know what?"

"Did they tell you that at school?"

"Tell me what?"

"That Nokomis is silly?"

"Of course not! They didn't know old Nokomis. But in school you learn not to believe all the silly stories that we are told by the Indians."

The boy spoke with the careless freedom of pompous youth.

They moved on through the woods over the delicate tracery of shadowy foliage, and climbed down the steep sides of the hilly ridge that rose above a quiet cove on the other side where they had made what they called a kitchen. Winona led the way in her eagerness to reach the shore. She had been silent for some time, absorbed in thought.

"I tell you, Judah, I will not go to the convent school. I hate nuns."

"Ho ho!" laughed Judah. "But you must; the father has said it."

"Papa cannot make me. I will not."

"Ah, but you will when the time comes, and you will like it. I doubt not you will want to leave us altogether when you meet girls your own age, and learn their tricks."

"Stop it, Judah!" she cried, stamping her small foot like a little whirlwind, "you shall not torment me. I do not want to leave papa and you for a lot of nuns and strange girls who do not care for me."

"What, again!" said Judah, solemnly. "That makes three times since morning that you've been off like a little fury."

"I know it, Judah," replied the girl, with tears in her eyes, "but you are so tantalizing; you'd make a saint lose her temper, you know you would."

"Oh, well; we shall see—Look, Winona!" he broke off abruptly, pointing excitedly out over the bosom of the lake. Three birds floated in the deep blue ether toward the island. "Gulls!"

"No! No! They're eagles, Judah!" cried the girl, as excited as he.

"Sure enough!" exclaimed the boy.

The birds swerved, and two flew away toward the mainland. The third dropped into the branches of a maple. "It's a young eagle, Winona, and I'm going to drop him!" catching up his weapon he leaned forward, preparing to take careful aim. Suddenly there was a puff of smoke that came from behind a bend in the shore just below where they were standing. A dull report followed and the eagle leaped one stroke in the air and dropped like a shot into the waters of the lake. A boat shot out from the beach with two men in it. They picked up the dead bird and then pulled towards the spot where the children stood intently watching them. They came on rapidly, and in a moment the occupants stood on the beach before the surprised children.

They were white men, garbed in hunter's dress. They seemed surprised to see the girl and boy on an apparently uninhabited island,

and one said something in a low tone to the other, and motioned toward the crisp head of the boy. They spoke pleasantly, asking the name of the island.

Winona shrank behind Judah's back, glancing shyly at them from beneath the clustering curls that hung about her face.

"This island has no name," said Judah.

"Oh, then it is not a part of the Canadian shore?"

The questioner eyes the boy curiously. Judah moved his feet uneasily in the pebbles and sand.

"Not that I ever heard. It's just an island."

"Do you live here?"

"Yes, over there," pointing toward the other side.

"We're mighty hungry," joined in the other man, who had pulled the boat to a safe resting place out of the reach of the incoming tide.

"We'll pay you well for your fish," he added.

"You are welcome to as much as you wish," replied Judah politely, at once passing over a number of trout and a huge salmon.

"Show them our fireplace, Judah," said Winona, at length finding her tongue. Judah led the way silently toward the sheltered cove where they had constructed a rude fireplace of rocks, and where the things necessary for their comfort during long tramps over their wooded domain, were securely hidden.

The children busied themselves with hospitable preparations for a meal, and the men flung themselves down on a bed of dry leaves and moss, lighted their pipes, and furtively watched them.

"Likely nigger," commented one.

"Worth five hundred, sure. But the girl puzzles me. What is she?" replied the one who seemed to be the leader.

"She's no puzzle to me. I'll tell you what she is—she's a nigger, too, or I'll eat my hat!" this with a resounding slap upon the thigh to emphasize his speech.

"Possible!" replied the leader, lazily watching Winona through rings of smoke. "By George! Thomson, you don't suppose we've struck it at last!"

"Mum's the word," said Thomson with an expressive wink. Judah brought some wood and Winona piled it on until a good bed of coals lay within the stone fireplace. Then she hung the fish on pieces of leather string, turning them round and round. Soon they lay in platters of birch, a savory incense filling the air, and in no time the hunters were satisfying their hunger with the delicious salmon and trout, washed down by copious draughts of pure spring water from a nearby rill whose gentle gurgle one could distinguish as it mingled with the noise of the dashing surf and the roar of the falls.

The children stood and watched them. Judah fingering lovingly the feathers of the dead eagle which he had taken from the boat.

"You haven't told us who you are," suggested the leader with a smile.

"She's White Eagle's daughter; I'm adopted."

"I see. Then you're Indians?"

Judah nodded. Somehow he felt uneasy with these men. He did not trust them.

"Not by a long sight," muttered Thomson. "Nothin' but nigger blood ever planted the wool on top of that boy's head."

Suddenly, faint and clear came a blast on a horn, winding in and out the secret recesses of the woods. Again and yet again, then all was still.

The men were startled, but the children hastily gathered up their belongings and without a word to the strangers bounded away, and were soon lost in the dark shadows of the woods.

"Well, cap't, this is a rum 'un. Now what do you reckon that means?"

"I have an idea that we've struck it rich, Thomson. Come, unless we want to stay here all night, suppose we push out for civilization?"

II

One sultry evening in July, about a month later than the opening of our story, a young man was travelling through the woods on the outskirts of the city of Buffalo.

The intense electric heat during the day had foretold a storm, and now it was evident that it would be upon him before he could reach shelter. The clouds sweeping over the sky had brought darkness early. The heavens looked of one uniform blackness, until the lightning, quivering behind them, showed through the magnificent masses of storm-wreck, while the artillery of the Almighty rolled threateningly in the distance.

For the sake of his horse, Maxwell would have turned back, but it was many hours since he had left the railroad, travelling by the stage route toward the city. In vain he tried to pierce the gloom; no friendly light betrayed a refuge for weary man and beast. So they went on.

Suddenly the horse swerved to one side, in affright as the electric fluid darted in a quivering, yellow line from the black clouds, lighting up the landscape, and showing the anxious rider that he was near the turnpike road which led to the main street. He spurred his horse onward to reach the road while the lightning showed the way. Scarcely was he there when the thunder crashed down in a prolonged, awful peal. The storm had commenced indeed. The startled horse reared and plunged in a way to unseat an unskilled rider, but Maxwell sat firmly in the saddle; he drew rein a moment, patted the frightened animal and spoke a few kind words to soothe his terror. On every side now the lightning darted incessantly; the thunder never ceased to roll, while the rain descended in a flood. As the lightning blazed he caught glimpses of the turbulent water of the lake, and the thunder of Niagara's falls rivalled the artillery of heaven. It is no pleasant thing to be caught by such a storm in a strange city, without a shelter.

As he rode slowly on, the road developed a smooth hardness beneath the horse's feet, the vivid flashes showed board sidewalks; they showed, too, deep puddles and sluices of water pouring at a tremendous rate through the steep, canal-like gutters which bordered the way. A disk of landscape was photographed out of the night, etching the foliage of huge, dripping trees on either side, and the wide-spreading meadows and farm lands mingled with thickets and woodland. Only a few farm

PAULINE E. HOPKINS

houses broke the monotony of the road between the stage route and the city.

"Heavens, what a country!" muttered the rider.

It was a pleasant voice, nicely modulated, and the fitful gleams of light showed a slender, well-knit figure, a bright, handsome face, blue eyes and a mobile mouth slightly touched with down on the upper lip. A dimple in the chin told of a light and merry heart within his breast.

"What a figure I must be," he laughed gaily, thinking of his mud-bespattered garments.

With the idea of suiting his dress to the country he was about to visit, Warren Maxwell had fitted himself out in Regent street with a suit of duck and corduroy with wide, soft felt hat, the English idea, at that period, of the "proper caper" for society in America.

As he rode along the lonely way his thoughts turned with sick longing toward his English home. What would they say to see him tonight, weary, hungry and disgusted? But he had come with a purpose; he was determined to succeed. There were three others at home older than himself; his own share in the family estate would amount to an annuity scarcely enough to defray his tailor's bill. Sir John Maxwell, baronet, his father, had reluctantly consented that Warren should study law when he found that neither the church nor medicine were congenial to his youngest, favorite son. Anything was better than trade. The old aristocrat metaphorically held up his hands in horror at the bare thought. In family council, therefore, it was decided that law, with money and old family influence might lead to Parliament in the future; and so Warren took up the work determined to do his best.

One day Mr. Pendleton, head of the firm, called him into his private office and told him that some one in their confidence must go to America. It was on a delicate mission relating to the heir of Carlingford of Carlingford. The other members of the firm were too old to undertake so arduous a journey; here was a chance for a young, enterprising man. If he were successful, they would be generous—in fact, he would become a full partner, sharing all the emoluments of the position at once. Of course Maxwell was interested, and asked to be given the details.

"You see," said the lawyer, "We've had the management of the estates for more than fifty years—all the old lord's time. It was a bad business when young Lord George and his brother fell in love with the same woman. It seems that Captain Henry and Miss Venton—that was the lady's name—had settled the matter to their own liking; but the lady's father favored Lord George because he was the heir and so Captain Henry was forced to see himself supplanted by his brother. Soon after a terrible quarrel that took place between the young men, Lord George was found dead, shot in the back through the heart. The Captain was arrested, tried and convicted of the crime. I remember the trial well, and that my sympathy was all with the accused. He was a bonny and gallant gentleman—the captain. Let me see—" and the old man paused a moment to collect his scattered thoughts.

"Let me see—Wait—Yes, he escaped from prison and fled to America. The lady? Why come to think of it she married a nephew of the old lord."

"And was the guilty party never found?"

"No—I think—In fact, a lot of money was spent on detectives by the old lord trying to clear his favorite and lift the stain from the family name; but to no purpose. Lord George cannot live many months longer, he is eighty-five now, but he thinks that Captain Henry may have married in America, and if so, he wants his children to inherit. For some reason he has taken a strong dislike to his nephew, who, by the way, is living in the southern part of the United States. If you go, your mission must remain a profound secret, for if he lives, Captain Henry is yet amenable to the law which condemned him. Here—read these papers; they will throw more light on the subject, and while doing that make up your mind whether or not you will go to America and institute a search for the missing man." So Maxwell started for America.

"Heavens, what a flash!" exclaimed the young man, aroused from the reverie into which he had fallen. "Ah, what is that yonder?" Before him was a large wooden house with outlying buildings standing back from the road.

"Whoever dwells there will not refuse me shelter on such a night. I will try my luck."

Urging his tired horse forward, in a moment he stood before the large rambling piazza which embraced the entire front of the establishment. From the back of the house came the barking of dogs, and as he sprang to the ground the outer door swung open, shedding forth a stream of light and disclosing a large, gray-bearded man with a good-natured face. Around the corner of the house from the direction of the outbuildings, came quickly a powerful negro.

"Well, stranger, you've took a wet night fer a hossback ride," said the man on the piazza.

"I find it so," replied Warren with a smile. "May I have shelter here until the morning?"

"Shelter!" exclaimed the man with brusque frankness, "that's what the Grand Island Hotel hangs out a shingle fer. Western or furrin's welcome here. I take it from your voice you don't belong to these parts. Come in, and 'Tavius will take yer hoss. 'Tavius! Oh, 'Tavius! Hyar! Take the gentleman's hoss. Unstrap them saddle-bags and hand 'em hyar fus'."

'Tavius did as he was bidden, and Warren stepped into a room which served for office, smoking-room and bar. He followed his host through the room into a long corridor and up a flight of stairs into a spacious apartment neatly though primitively furnished. Having deposited the saddle-bags, the host turned to leave the room, pausing a moment to say:

"Well, mister, my name's Ebenezer Maybee, an' I'm proprieter of this hyar hotel. What may yer name be?"

Warren handed him a visiting card which he scanned closely by the light of the tallow candle.

"'Warren Maxwell, England.' Um, um I s'pose you're an 'ristocrat. Where bound? Canidy?"

"No," replied Warren, "just travelling for pleasure."

"Oh, I see. Rich. Well, Mr. Maxwell, yer supper'll be 'bilin on the table inside a half-hour: Fried chicken, johnny cake and coffee."

In less than an hour the smoking repast was served in the hotel parlor, and having discussed this, wearied by the day's travel, Maxwell retired and speedily fell asleep.

It must have been near midnight when he was awakened by a loud rapping. What was it? Mingled with the knocking was a sound of weeping.

Jumping on to the floor, and throwing on some clothing, Maxwell went into the corridor. All was darkness; the rain still beat against the window panes now and again illuminated by sheet-lightning. Listening, he heard voices in the office or bar-room, and in that direction he started. As he drew nearer he recognized the tones of his host.

"What is it? What is the trouble?" he asked as he entered the room.

A strange group met his eye under the flickering light of the tallow candle—a lad in Indian garb and a girl not more than fourteen, but appearing younger, who was weeping bitterly. She had the sweetest and most innocent of faces, Warren thought, that he had ever seen. A pair of large, soft brown eyes gazed up at him piteously.

"It's White Eagle's son and daughter. Something has happened to him and they want me to go with them to the island. You see I'm a sort of justice of the peace and town constable an' I've done the Injuns in these parts some few favors and they think now I can do anything. But no man can be expected to turn out of a dry bed and brave the lake on sech a night as this. I ain't chicken-hearted myself, but I draw the line thar."

In spite of his hard words and apparent reluctance to leave home, Mr. Maybee had lighted two lanterns and was pulling on his boots preparatory for a struggle with the elements.

"Who is White Eagle?" asked Warren.

"He's a white man; a sort of chief of the few Injuns 'roun' hyar, and he lives out on a small island in the lake with a half-breed squaw and these two children. They're poor—very poor."

"What seems to be the trouble with your father?" asked Warren, turning to the stoical lad and weeping girl.

"I believe he's shot himself, sir," returned the boy respectfully, in good English. "O, come, Mr. Maybee. My father—oh, my father!" exclaimed the girl between her sobs, clinging to the landlord's hand.

The anguish of the tone, the sweet girlish presence, as well as the lad's evident anxiety under his calmness, aroused Warren's compassion.

"If you will wait a moment I will go with you. I know something of medicine, and delay may be dangerous."

Uttering a pleased cry the girl turned to him. "Oh, sir! Will you? Will you come? Do not let us lose time then—poor papa!"

"If you go I suppose I must," broke in Mr. Maybee.

"But you don't know what you're about," he continued as they left the room together: "You must remember, mister, that these people are only niggers and Injuns."

"Niggers! Mr. Maybe, what do you mean?"

"It's a fac'. The boy is a fugitive slave picked up by White Eagle in some of his tramps and adopted. The girl is a quadroon. Her mother, the chief's wife, was a fugitive too, whom he befriended and then married out of pity."

"Still they're human beings, and entitled to some consideration," replied Warren, while he muttered to himself, thinking of the tales he had heard of American slavery,—"What a country!"

"'That's so, mister, that's so; but it's precious little consideration niggers and Injuns git around' hyar an' that's a fac'."

For all his hard words, Ebenezer Maybee was a humane man and had done much for the very class he assumed to despise. He did not hesitate to use methods of the Underground railroad when he deemed it necessary.

When Warren returned to the room, the two children stood where he had left them, and as soon as Mr. Maybee joined them they started out.

Through mud and rain they made their way, the rays from the lanterns but serving to intensify the darkness. Very soon a vivid flash threw into bold relief the whiteness of the hissing lake.

"What did you come over in, Judah, canoe or boat?" shouted Mr. Maybee, who headed the party.

"The boat," called back Judah. "I thought you might come back with us."

"Good!" shouted Mr. Maybee.

When they were all seated in the boat, after some difficulty, Judah stood upright in the bow and shoved off. Each of the two men had an oar.

Not even an Indian would ordinarily trust himself to the mercy of the water on such a night, but Judah steered out boldly for the little isle without a sign of fear.

"Judah knows his business," shouted Mr. Maybee to Maxwell. "He'll take us over all right if anybody can."

At first Warren noticed nothing but the safety of the craft, and the small figure crouched in the bottom of the boat. Every swell of angry waters threatened to engulf them. The boat shivered; foam hissed like steam and spent its wrath upon them. The lightning flashed and the thunder rolled. There was no sky—nothing but inky blackness.

Rain streamed over their faces. Warren's hair hung in strings about his neck. The dangers gathered as they lessened the five miles between the mainland and the island. The young Englishman loved aquatic sports and his blood tingled with the excitement of the battle with the storm. The day had brought him adventures, but he did not shrink from death by drowning were it in good cause.

Presently the shore loomed up before them, and after much skilful paddling, they entered the sheltered cove that answered for a bay. The boat grounded and Judah sprang out, holding it fast while the others landed. It was a relief to them to feel the hard, sandy beach beneath their feet and to know that the danger was over for the present.

"Let us go faster," said Winona. "We are close now, sir—close," turning to Warren.

She ran on in front, threw open the door to the little cottage, and entered. The pictured remained with Warren always,—the bare room with unplastered floor and walls of rough boards; the rude fireplace filled with logs spouting flames; the feeble glow of the "grease lamp"; the rude chairs and tables. At one side, on a bed of skins, was extended the figure of a man. The old squaw was rocking to and fro and moaning.

"Ah! my bird!" said old Nokomis, raising her withered hands. "It is no use—it is too late."

"What do you mean. Nokomis?" demanded Winona.

"White Eagle has answered the call of the Great Spirit," replied the old woman, with a sob.

"Dead! My father!"

The girl gave one quick, heart-breaking cry, and would have fallen had not Warren caught her in his arms. Gently he raised her, and followed Judah into another room, and laid her on a bed.

"Ah," said the lad, "how will she bear it if it is true, when she gets back her senses? How shall we both bear it?"

"Come, let us see if nothing can be done for your father. Nokomis may be mistaken."

"Yes, true;" replied the boy in a hopeless tone.

Back in the kitchen where Mr. Maybee was already applying restoratives, Warren began an examination of the inanimate form before them. It was the figure of a fine, handsome man of sixty years, and well-preserved. They stripped back the hunting shirt and Warren deftly felt for the wound. As he leaned over him, he gave a startled exclamation, and rising erect exclaimed:

"This is no accident. *It is murder!*"

III

M urder!"

The gruesome word seemed to ring through the silent room.

"Murder!" exclaimed old Nokomis, aghast. "It is a mistake. Who would kill White Eagle? There lives not an Indian in the whole country round who does not love him. No, No."

There was horror on the face of the young man regarding her so steadfastly. Her withered, wrinkled face was honest enough, her tones genuine.

"No!" exclaimed Mr. Maybee, recovering from the stupor into which Warren's words had thrown him. "Blame my skin! where's the blud?"

Warren regarded him steadily a moment, then said, "Look! Internal hemorrhage."

He half raised the body and pointed to a bullet hole in the back.

"By the Etarn'l!" was Maybee's horrified exclamation. "Must 'a bled to death whilst we was comin'."

Warren nodded.

"God in heaven!" cried Judah, sinking on his knees beside the bed of skins. "It is true! But who has done it? Who could be so cruel? No one lives here but ourselves. Murdered! My father! My master!"

"Hush!" said Mr. Maybee, sternly. "Hush. 'Tain't no time fer cryin' nor makin' a fuss. Tell us all you know about this business."

"He went out after supper to look after the canoes. In a short time we heard a shout and then a cry, 'Help! help!' and we ran to him, Winona and I. He was leaning against a tree, and said nothing but. 'Get me to the house; get a doctor, I am hurt.' We flew to do his bidding. The rest you know."

Maxwell's brain was in a tumult of confusion. Thoughts flew rapidly through it. Suddenly he had been aroused from his solitary life in a strange land to become an actor in a local tragedy. The man lying on the bed of skins had certainly been murdered. Who then was the assassin?"

Again he looked at Nokomis, who was intently watching him. She shook her head mournfully in answer to his unasked question. Mr. Maybee was nonplussed. "What's to be done? Terrible! Murder! Why, it will kill the girl."

Warren Maxwell started. For a moment he had forgotten the delicate child in the next room rendered so suddenly an orphan, and in so fearful a fashion.

"A doctor must be summoned to certify the cause of death, and the police authorities must be notified," Warren said at length. "Right you are, pard," returned Maybee. "I'm hanged ef this business hain't knocked the spots out of yours truly. I'll take the boat and Judah here, and be back by sunrise."

He turned away, but Judah lingered, giving a wistful look into Maxwell's face.

"Yes," said Warren, laying his hand on the lad's shoulder, "I will tell her."

With a gesture of thanks Judah followed Mr. Maybee out into the night.

Pulling himself together, Warren, followed by Nokomis, entered the room where he had left Winona. She lay on the bed where he had placed her, still unconscious, her long hair lank with the rain, streamed about her face; her lips were lightly parted, even younger and more beautiful than he had at first thought; and as he remembered her story and the position that the death of her father placed her in, his soul went out to her in infinite pity.

"Poor child! Poor little thing!" he mused. "Heaven must have sent me here at this awful moment. You shall not be friendless if I can help you."

He questioned Nokomis closely. The old woman shook her head.

"Alone except for old Nokomis and Judah. White Eagle loved her very much. Old Nokomis will take care of her."

Between them the girl was restored to consciousness, and learned the truth of her father's death told by Warren as gently as possible. She heard him with a stunned expression, pale lips and strained eyes; suddenly, as she realized the meaning of his words, she uttered a piercing cry, and sprang up exclaiming:

"My father! Oh, my father! Murdered!"

She would have rushed from the room. She struggled with Warren, trying with her small fingers to unclasp his, which with tenderness held her; she turned almost fiercely upon him for staying her. The paroxysm died as quickly as it came, leaving her weak and exhausted.

Ebenezer Maybee returned at sunrise, bringing men with him. The great storm had cleared the air of the electric heat, and the morning was gloriously beautiful. The dark forest trees were rich in the sunshine, the streams and waters of the lakes laughed and rippled as happily as if no terrible storm had just passed, carrying in its trail the mystery of a foul and deadly crime. Search revealed no trace of the assassin; no clue. There were but two strangers in the city who had visited the island, and they immediately joined the searchers when they learned of the tragedy. The storm had obliterated all traces of the murderer. There was nothing missing in the humble home that held so little to tempt the cupidity of a thief. There was not even a scrap of paper found to tell who White Eagle might have been in earlier, happier days.

Everyone seemed to regard Warren Maxwell as the person in authority. The police consulted him, referred to him; Mr. Maybee confided in him, and Winona clung to him with slender brown fingers like bands of steel. As far as Warren could learn, she had no friend in the world but the hotel keeper. What a different life this poor child's must have been from any he had ever known.

Old Nokomis repeated many times a day: "Surely it was the Great Father must have sent you to us."

Judah walked about all day with a dazed expression on his face, crying silently but bitterly, and a growing look of sullen fury on his dark face that told of bitter thoughts within. Over and over again his lips unconsciously formed the words:

"I'll find him when I'm older if he's on top of the earth, and then it'll be him or me who will lie as my poor master lies in there today."

Then came the funeral. The Indians gathered from all the adjoining cities and towns and from the Canada short, to see the body of the man they had loved and respected committed to the ground. They buried him beneath the giant pine against which he was found leaning, wounded to death. Curiosity attracted many of the white inhabitants, among whom were the two strangers referred to in the first part of this narrative.

Two days after the funeral, Mr. Maybee and Warren sat in the latter's room talking of Winona and Judah.

"It was a fortunit thing for us all, Mr. Maxwell, that you happened to be aroun' during this hyar tryin' time. You've been a friend in need, sir, durn me ef you ain't."

"Yes;" replied Warren, smiling at the other's quaint speech, "it was a time that would have made any one a friend to those two helpless children."

"Maybe, maybe," returned the hotel keeper, dubiously. "But you must remember that every man warn't built with a soul in his carcass; some of 'em's only got a piece of liver whar the heart orter be." Warren smiled again.

"Mr. Maybee, I want to ask you a question—"

"Go ahead, steamboat; what's the question?"

"What is to become of Winona after I leave this place? It is different with the boy—he can manage somehow—but the girl; that is what troubles me."

"Look hyar, young feller;" said Maybee, stretching out a big, brown hand. "I don' guess she'll ever have to say she's got no friend while Ebenezer Maybee's proprietor of the grand Island Hotel. My wife's plum crazy to git that young kidabid. We's only awaitin' till the news of this unfortunit recurrence has blowed over, and she gits a little used to bein' without her pa. As fer Judah, thar's plenty to do roun' the stables ef he likes. But, Lor,' that lnjun-nigger! You can't tame him down to be just an' onery galoot like the most of 'em you see out hyar. White Eagle taught him to speak like a senator, ride bareback like a hull circus; he can shoot a bird on the wing and hunt and fish like all natur. Fac'." he added noting Warren's look of amusement. "Truth is,—neither of them two forlorn critters realizes what 'bein' a nigger' means; they have no idee of thar true position in this unfrien'ly world. God knows I pity 'em." But to Warren Maxwell it seemed almost sacrilege—the thought of that beautiful child maturing into womanhood among such uncouth surroundings. His mind revolted at the bare idea. At length he said with a sigh:

"What a pity it is that we know nothing of White Eagle's antecedents. There may be those living who would be glad to take the child."

"He was a gentleman, as your class counts 'em, Mr. Maxwell. But he never breathed a word what he was, an' he kept away from his equals— meanin' white men."

"And few men do that without a reason," replied Maxwell. "Do you know whether he was English or German?"

Mr. Maybee shook his head. "He warn't Dutch, that's certain; he was a white man all right. I cal'late he mote 'a been English."

"Mr. Maybee, I've been thinking over the matter seriously, and I have determined to write home and see if something can't be done to educate these children and make them useful members of society. In England, neither their color nor race will be against them. They will be happier there than here. Now, if I can satisfy you that my standing and character are all right, would you object to their going with me when I sail in about three months from now?"

PAULINE E. HOPKINS

Mr. Maybee gazed at him in open-mouthed wonder. "Yer jokin'?" he said at length, incredulously.

"No, I mean it."

Still Mr. Maybee gazed in amazement. Could it be possible that the heard aright?

"Je-rusalem! but I don't know what to say. We don' need no satisfyin' 'bout you; that's all right. But the idea of your thinkin' about edjicatin' them two Injin-niggers. You've plum got me. An' too. I cal'lated some on gittin' the gal fer my wife. Still it would be good fer the gal—durn me, but it would."

Then he turned and grasped Warren's hand hard.

"Mr. Maxwell, you're a white man. I jes' froze to you, I did the fus' night you poked yer head in the door."

"And I to you," replied Warren, as he returned the warm hand-pressure.

"Don' you ever be skeery whilst yer in Amerika an' Ebenezer Maybee's on top o' the earth. By the Etarn'l, I'll stick to you like a burr to a cotton bush, durn me ef I don't."

Again the men clasped hands to seal the bond of brotherhood.

"Meantime, Mr. Maybee, I wish you to take charge of them. I am called to Virginia on important business. I will leave a sum of money in your hands to be used for their needs while I am gone. When I return, I shall be able to tell just what I can do, and the day I shall leave for England."

Mr. Maybee promised all he asked, and then retired to the bar-room to astonish his cronies there by a recital of what the English gent proposed to do for two "friendless niggers." Maxwell rowed over to the island to tell Winona of his departure and the arrangements made for her welfare. He laughed softly to himself as he thought of his own twenty-eight years and his cool assumption of the role of Winona's guardian. Yet he was not sorry. Upon the whole, he was glad she had been surrendered to his care, that there would be no one to intrude between them; and he felt that the girl would also be glad; she appeared to rely upon him with childlike innocence and faith. How could he fail to see that the brown eyes clouded when he went away, and brightened when he approached?

He secured the boat and directed his steps to the tall pine where she usually sat now. She was sitting there by the new-made grave, her hands folded listlessly in her lap. Her eyes were fixed upon the sunlit waves and were the very home of sorrow. At that moment, turning she beheld him. A sudden radiance swept over the girl's features. Sorrow had matured her wonderfully.

"Ah! it is you. I have been waiting for you."

"You were sure I would come," he smiled, taking her hand and seating himself beside her.

"Yes. And I know you never break your word—never. You said you wished to speak to me of my future."

"Exactly. I could not go to England and leave you here alone and friendless, Winona," he replied. "I could not bear it."

The girl shivered. "A month ago, she was a happy, careless child; today she had a woman's heart and endurance. Of course he must go sometime, this kind friend; what should she do then?"

"Yet I must stay. I have nowhere else to go."

"Surely you know of some friends—relatives?"

She shook her head.

"Papa never spoke of any. He used to say that we two had only each other to love, poor papa. Oh!" with a piteous burst of grief, "I wanted no one else but papa, and now he is gone."

"As He gave, so He has a right to take, Winona," said Warren, gravely. He saw that she was indeed "cast upon his care;" surely there must have been some dark shadow in White Eagle's past life to cause him to bury himself here in a wilderness among savages. Well, it must be as he had planned. He explained to Winona all that he had told Mr. Maybee.

"And you will take Judah with you?"

"Certainly," replied Warren, "You shall not be separated." The girl heaved a deep sigh of content. "I will go with you to your home gladly."

Judah was as pleased as Winona when told of the plans for the future. Each looked upon Warren Maxwell as a god. Judah went with him to the mainland. Winona saw him depart bravely. She watched the boat until they effected a landing. Once he turned and waved his hat toward the spot where she was standing. When he was no longer visible she threw herself down upon the new-made grave in an abandonment of grief, weeping passionately.

ONE MONTH FROM THAT DAY Warren Maxwell, bright, smiling and filled with pleasurable anticipations drew rein again before the Grand Island Hotel. As before, 'Tavius was there to take his horse; Mr. Maybee met him at the door; but about them both was an air of restraint.

"Well, Mr. Maybee," he said gaily, "How are you, and how are my island protéges? I'll row over after dinner and surprise them."

"Come with me, Mr. Maxwell, I have something to tell you," replies his host gravely.

Surprised at his solemn manner, Warren followed him to the chamber he had occupied on the occasion of his first visit. "It's a sorry tale sir, I must tell you; and in all my life I never befo' felt ashamed of bein' an American citizen. But I can be bought cheap, sir; less than half price'll git me."

"The day after you lef' thar was a claim put in by two men who had been stoppin' roun' hyar fer a month or more lo-catin thar game, the durned skunks. They was the owners of White Eagle's wife an' Judah's mother, sir—nigger traders from Missouri, sir. They puts in a claim fer the two children under the new act for the rendition of fugitive slaves jes' passed by Congress, an' they swep' the deck before we knowed it or had time to say 'scat.' Ef we'd had the least warnin', Mr. Maxwell, we'd a slipped the boy an' gal over to Canidy in no time, but you never know where a sneakin' nigger thief is goin' to hit ye, 'tain't like fightin' a man. Before we knowed it they had 'em as slick as grease an' was gone."

"But how could they take the children? They were both born free. It was an illegal proceeding," cried Warren in amazement.

"The child follows the condition of the mother. That's the law."

"My God, Mr. Maybee," exclaimed Warren as a light broke in upon his mind. "Where is she now—the poor, pretty child?"

"Down on a Missouri plantation, held as a slave!"

"My God!" Warren gazed at him for a time bereft of speech, dazed by a calamity too great for his mind to grasp. "My God! can such things be?"

IV

A few miles out from Kansas City, Missouri State, on a pleasant plain sloping off toward a murmuring stream, a branch of the mighty river, early in the spring of 1856, stood a rambling frame house two stories high, surrounded with piazzas, over which trailed grape-vines, clematis and Virginia creepers. The air was redolent with the scent of flowers nor needed the eye to seek far for them, for the whole front of the dwelling, and even the adjoining range of wooden stables, were rendered picturesque by rich masses of roses and honeysuckle that covered them, and the high, strong fence that enclosed four acres of cleared ground, at the end of which the buildings stood. Mingled with the scent of the roses was the fragrance of the majestic magnolia whose buds and blossoms nodded at one from every nook and unexpected quarter.

This was "Magnolia Farm," the home of Colonel Titus. He was an Englishman by birth and education who had invested his small fortune in a plantation and many slaves in the great Southwest; he had also traded in horses, selling, training, doctoring, taking care of horses, or, indeed, making money by any means that came in his way (or out of it, for the matter of that); all was grist that came to his mill. In time his enterprising spirit met with its reward and he became a leading man in all affairs pertaining to the interest of the section. The death of his wife, whom he tenderly loved, soon after the birth of their only child, had left him solitary. This affliction tendered, therefore, to deepen his interest in politics, and he eventually became one of the most bitter partisans on the side of slavery, contrary to the principles of most of his nationality. In his pro-slavery utterances he outdid the most rabid native-born Southerners. In 1854 his famous speech at St. Joseph, Missouri, at the beginning of the trouble in Kansas, had occasioned the wildest enthusiasm at the South, and the greatest consternation at the North.

"I tell you to mark every scoundrel among you who is the least tainted with abolitionism, or pro-slavery, and exterminate them. Neither giving nor taking quarter from the d—d rascals. To those who have qualms of conscience as to violating laws, state or national, I say, the time has come when such impositions must be disregarded, as your rights and property are in danger. I advise you, one and all, to enter every election district in Kansas, in defiance of Reeder and his myrmidons, and vote at the point of the bowie-knife and revolver. Neither take or give quarter as the cause demands it. It is enough that the slave-holding interests wills it, from which there is no appeal."

With the memory of recent happenings in the beautiful Southland, against the Negro voter, engraved upon our hearts, these words have a too familiar sound. No, there is very little advancement in that section since 1854, viewed in the light of Gov. Davis' recent action. The South would be as great as were her fathers "if like a crab she could go backward." Reversion is the only god worshipped by the South.

Bill Thomson, whose reputation for pure, unadulterated "cussedness" was notorious in this semi-barbarous section, was his overseer and most intimate friend. Thomson's wife was the Colonel's housekeeper, and, with the owner's invalid daughter, these four persons made up the "family" of the "big house."

The summer sun hung evenly over the great fields of cotton; the rambling house cast no shadow, but the broad piazza at the back afforded ample shade from the mid-day rays, sheltered as it was by great pines; within their reach, too, lay the quarters. The porch overlooked the blooming fields where a thousand acres stretched to the very edge of the muddy Missouri. This porch, with its deep, cool shadows, commanded a view of the working force, and made it a favorite resting place for the Colonel and his daughter Lillian. The crippled girl found complete happiness seated in her rolling chair gazing out upon the dusky toilers who tilled the broad acres of foaming cotton.

His daughter's affliction was a great cross to the Colonel. His thoughts were bitter when he saw other young girls swinging along the highway reveling in youthful strength that seemed to mock the helplessness of his own sweet girl.

"Why had this affliction been sent upon her?" he asked himself. If he had sinned why should punishment be sent upon the innocent and helpless? He rebelled against the text wherein it is taught that evil deeds shall be visited upon the progeny of the doer unto the third and fourth generations.

Far off in lovely England, ancestral halls might yet await her coming, if, perchance, Destiny should leave him in Fortune's lap. There was a letter lying snugly in his pocket, from a firm in London, that promised much, if—

It was near the noon siesta, and the Colonel sat on the piazza smoking his pipe and waiting the time to blow the horn for dinner. His daughter sat there, too, with an open book on her lap, and a dreamy look in her deep blue eyes that would wander from the printed page to the beautiful scene before her.

The sound of sharp words in a high-pitched voice and answering sobs broke in upon the quiet scene.

"There's Mrs. Thomson scolding Tennie again," observed Lillian. The words of that lady came to them distinctly from the hallway:

"What's the matter with you today? You leave your work for the other girls. What are you moping about? Is it Luke?"

"Luke been conjured," came in a stifled voice.

"By whom?"

Mrs. Thomson was a woman of considerable education and undoubted piety, but her patience was as short as piecrust. At her question all Tennie's wrath broke forth.

"Dat yaller huzzy, Clorinder; she conjured Luke till he gone plum wil' over her. Ef eber I gits my han's on her, she goin' 'member me de longes' day she lib."

"Hush, I tell you! This stuff must end right here."

"But, Mistis, dat nigger—"

"Hush your mouth! Don't you 'but' me! Do you get the cowhide and follow me to the cellar, and I'll whip you well for aggravating me as you have today. It seems as if I can never sit down to take a little comfort with the Lord, without your crossing me. The devil always puts you up to disturbing me, just when I'm trying to serve the Lord. I've no doubt I'll miss going to heaven on your account. But I'll whip you well before I leave this world, that I will. Get the cowhide and come with me. You ought to be ashamed of yourself to put me in such a passion. It's a deal harder for me than it is for you. I have to exert myself and it puts me all in a fever; while you have only to stand and take it."

The sounds died away, and once more quiet reigned. The Colonel resumed his train of thought, his brow contracted into a frown as he watched the rings of smoke curling up from the bowl of his pipe. He sighed. His daughter, watching him, echoed his sigh, because she thought her father was changing. He was a tall, powerful man with dark hair and beard fast whitening. He had deep-set eyes that carried a shifting light; they had the trick, too, of not looking one squarely in the face.

"His hair is right gray," she said to herself, sadly, "and he is beginning to stoop; he never stooped before. He's studying, always studying about the mortgages and politics. Oh, dear, if I'd only been a boy! Maybe I could have helped him. But I'm only a girl and a cripple at that." She changed the sigh into a smile, as women learn to do, and said aloud, "Here's Winona with your julep."

The girl bore a goblet on a waiter filled with the ruby liquid and a small forest of mint. The Colonel smiled, his annoyances forgotten for a moment; he lifted the glass gallantly, saying: "Your health, my daughter!"

As he sipped and drank, the girl laughed gleefully and proceeded to refill his pipe, he watching her the while with fond eyes. Winona watched the scene with bent brows. So, happy had she been with her dead father, not so long ago.

She had passed from childhood to womanhood in two years of captivity—a womanhood blessed with glorious beauty that lent a melancholy charm to her fairness when one remembered the future before such as she. She had been allowed at lessons with her young mistress and had wonderfully improved her privileges. The Colonel and Thomson encouraged her desire for music, too; "It'll pay ten dollars for every one invested," remarked the latter. It was now two years since the two friends had returned from a mysterious absence, bringing Winona and Judah with them. The time seemed centuries long to the helpless captives, reared in the perfect freedom of Nature's woods and streams.

Winona was given to Lillian for a maid, and under her gentle rule the horrible nightmare of captivity dragged itself away peacefully if not happily.

With Judah it was different; he was made assistant overseer, because of his intelligence and his enormous strength. As graceful as vigorous, he had developed into a lion of a man. But his nature seemed changed; he had lost his sunny disposition and buoyant spirits. He was a stern, silent man, who apparently, had never known boyhood. He was invaluable as a trainer of horses, and scrupulously attentive to his other work, but in performing these duties he had witnessed scenes that rivalled in cruelty the ferocity of the savage tribes among whom he had passed his boyhood, and had experienced such personal abuse that it had driven smiles forever from his face.

Thomson wore the physique of a typical Southerner. People learning of his English ancestry were surprised and somewhat doubtful as they noted his sharp profile, thin lips, curved nose and hollow cheeks. His moustache and hair, coal black in color, increased the doubt.

As we have said, there was no greater scoundrel in Missouri than Bill Thomson. Men declared there was "a heap in him. Other bad ones were jes' onery scamps; but Bill had a head on him."

He it was who was organizing and drilling numbers of companies of men, in case the d—d Yankees proved unruly, to burn and loot the infant territory and carry it into the slave-holding lines by fire and fraud.

Into this man's hands Judah was given body and soul.

V

Judah's first experience of slave discipline happened in this wise: A man in Kansas City had foolishly paid five hundred dollars for a showy horse, not worth half the amount, a perfect demon whom nobody dared venture near. The purchaser was about to shoot the vicious beast, when Bill Thomson happened along, and offered five hundred even odds that he would take the animal to Magnolia Farm and break him to saddle and bridle in ten days, Thomson being of the opinion that no one knew as much about a horse or a mule as he did, and priding himself on his success with animals.

He soon found that the horse was more than he had bargained for. The beast couldn't be cajoled or coaxed—not a man daring to go near him or within reach of his head. In order to get him to the farm he was starved and drugged.

"Well, boys, I reckon it aint' no use; the ugly beast's beat me, and I lose the bet," said Thomson to the little group of men gathered at a gate of the enclosure, the next morning after the animal arrived at the farm. It was a rough group made up of gamblers and sporting men, who had heard of the bet and came to Magnolia Farm to witness the battle between the horse-dealer and horse.

"Yes, I'm licked. He's a reg'lar fiend that hoss is. I'm a done coon this day, an' the hoss will have to be shot. I invite you all to stop to the shootin' party."

"Never know'd you to git beat befo', Bill," remarked one, striking the haft of his bowie knife; "an' to lose five hundred dollars slick off, too; sho!"

"My mettle's up, boys. If I can't break the hoss in, no one can; that's true, ain't it?"

"For startin' sure!" came from the crowd.

"What's the good of lettin' a vicious brute like that live?" and Thomson ended with a volley of oaths.

"Bill's plum wil'," said one of the crowd.

"'Nough to make him, I reckon," returned the first speaker. "Bill allers did swear worse'n a steamboat cap'n. The Foul Fiend himself would be swearin' to be beat by that tearin' four-legged (beast).

The group waited breathlessly for Thomson's next move as he stood gazing toward the refractory beast. Just at this moment Judah came up and touched his hat respectfully to the group of men.

"Don't shoot him yet, sir; I can tame that horse and win your bet for you," he said to Thomson.

It would be difficult to describe the effect produced on the group by those few cool, daring words—a breathless pause, each looking at the other in incredulous amazement; then a murmur of admiration for the speaker went from man to man, Thomson himself, who had recoiled from the boy, staring in open-eyed wonder at his cool assertion.

"You go near the beast! What do you know about breaking hosses? He'd throw you and kill you or trample you to death, an' I'd be just fifteen hundred dollars more out of pocket by the onery brute."

It was a picture for an artist,—the Negro passively waiting the verdict of his master, his massive head uncovered in humility. There was not among them all so noble a figure of a man, as he stood in a somewhat theatrical attitude—a living statue of a mighty Vulcan. Into the group Colonel Titus walked with a commanding gesture.

"Let him try, Thomson, for the honor of the farm. I believe he can do it. I'll stand the loss if there is any."

A murmur of approval broke from the crowd. At the Colonel's words, Judah stepped forward and began giving his orders without a shade of servility, seeming to forget in the excitement of the moment his position as a slave. Once more he moved as a free man amidst his fellows and for the time being forgot all else. Thomson watched him with an evil smile upon his wicked face.

"Get me a saddle and bridle ready, Sam," he called to a stable boy, "and a strong curb, too." He walked toward the stable at the end of the range which had been given up to the horse, followed by the men of the group.

"Take car', Jude," cautioned Sam. "He'll put his head out an' bite. He tried to kick de do' out yes'day!"

Heedless of the warning, Judah kept on, with the remark, "I think he's feeding."

"Take car', thar!" yelled Sam; "He's comin' at yer," as a savage snort came from within. The crowd fell back respectfully, all save Judah.

The horse rushed forwards, butting his chest against the iron bar, as he thrust his head over the top of the half-door. His ears were laid back, his eyes rolling, and his mouth open to bite, showing rows of terrible teeth. Judah did not move or tremble.

"Got grit," observed one to the other.

"Wish I owned a gang o' niggers jes' like him."

"I don't," replied his neighbor. "Them big, knowin' niggers is dang'rous."

Judah stretched out his hand and gave a half-pat to the animal's nose, withdrawing it as he attempted to seize his arm, snapping viciously.

"Stand back, all of you," commanded the boy, as he moved around, facing the animal. Then began an exhibition of mind over instinct. The power of the hypnotic eye was known and practised among all the Indian tribes of the West. It accounted for their wonderfull success in subduing animals. Judah concentrated all the strength of his will in the gaze that he fixed upon the horse. Not a muscle of his powerful face moved for one instant, his glowing eyes never wavered, his eyelids did not quiver, but immovable as a statue he stood pouring the latent force on which he relied upon the vicious brute. And its effect was curious; he stared back at the boy for a few seconds with rolling eyes and grinning teeth, then his eyes wavered, he pawed the ground uneasily, flung up his head with an angry snort, half of fear, and running backwards, reared erect. Still Judah's gaze did not falter; his eyes were immovably fixed upon the uneasy animal; he dropped again, butted his muzzle on the ground, shook his mane and ran about the shed for five or ten minutes, all to no purpose; when he halted opposite the opening, Judah's unflinching gaze was still fixed upon him. A half hour must have passed in this way. At the end of that time the horse came to the opening again, trembling, and his coat foam-flecked. The men watched in breathless silence the battle-royal.

"Sugar, Sam," called Judah, still keeping his eye on the horse, and stroking his muzzle gently. The horse was much subdued, and took the lumps of sugar from his hand without an attempt at biting.

"Wal, I'm blessed!" came from the crowd.

"Hand me the bit and bridle, Sam."

"You ain't going inside, Jude?" said the Colonel.

"In a minute, yes."

With a sleight-of-hand movement a bit of sugar was in the creature's mouth, together with the bit, and the strap slipped over his head. The animal was bitted, the bridle in his conqueror's hand.

"Unbolt the door, Sam; open it wide enough for me to get in," and Judah entered the stable. "Steady, boy, steady. Sh—ho!" talking to, coaxing the half-cowed beast, the boy got the saddle on his back, and tightened the girths. "Now, gentlemen," called Judah, "Sam will fling open the door the minute I seize the bridle. Stand clear for your lives."

He gathered curb and snaffle at the loop into his bridle-hand, slid his right down and gripped it close at the bit. Before the animal could bite, rare or kick, the door was flung wide and man and steed dashed out together, Judah letting go his right hand and flinging himself into the saddle instantly, tightening the curb with both hands, and driving his feet into the stirrups.

A buzz of excitement and admiration broke from the crowd of men now too deeply stirred for words. The battle-royal had begun. The horse plunged forward, reared wildly, pawed the air, and whirled around. Judah struck him a hard blow between the ears with the whip, only to have him kick out behind in a furious attempt to throw the rider over his head. In rapid succession the animal plunged, reared, kicked, ran to and fro, and suddenly made a buckleap into the air. There was an exclamation, followed by a ringing cheer, as the men saw the boy still keeping his seat. The moment the creature's hoofs touched the ground, Judah drove the spurs into his flanks and they dashed away at a mad gallop. Then followed an exhibition of the most daring horsemanship ever witnessed in Kansas City. Rising in his stirrups, Judah, while keeping perfect control of the animal, converted the four acres of enclosure into a circus-arena, round which the horse was forced at a gallop under the sting of the whip, and in the true style of reckless Indian riding on the Western plains.

"Well done!" "Hurrah for the nigger! he's beat the hoss into the middle o' nex' week!" These and similar exclamations broke from the delighted spectators. Beaten completely, trembling in every limb and flecked with foam, the horse followed his conqueror quietly to the stables.

Colonel Titus was throwing his hat wildly up in the air in the enthusiasm of the moment, but Bill Thomson stood quietly by with an evil look distorting his face into a grin of malice and fury.

"Say, Colonel," whispered a man in the crowd, "I wudn't be in that ar nigger's shoes, not fer no money. Bill's mad 'cause he'd beat the hoss."

"Oh, that's all right. Bill's square. Come, all hands, let's go up to the house and liquor. What'll you have?" The Colonel bore the reputation of being the freest gentleman in Kansas City.

For a number of days after this affair, Thomson went about the farm in a brown study. As the men had said, he was "bilin' mad 'cause the nigger had got the dead wood on him." "He's got to be broken in; he knows too much," he might have been heard muttering between his clinched teeth.

Judah had received an ovation from the sporting fraternity and bade fair to become a popular idol. Thomson was offered large sums of money for him from several men, but refused them all with the words, "Money won't buy him till I'm through with him."

Because of his daughter's feelings slaves were never whipped on the plantation, but were sent to the slave prison in the city.

About a week later Judah was ordered to take a note to the prison in Kansas city. Being a new comer on the plantation, he was not yet familiar with its ways, and taking the note, suspecting no evil, delivered it at the "bell gate." The man who received the note after reading it called to a burly Negro: "Pete take this nigger, and strap him down upon the stretcher; get him ready for business."

"What are you going to do to me?" cried the horrified lad, at the man's words.

"You'll know d—d quick! Strip yourself; I don't wan to tear your clothes with my whip. I'm going to tear your black skin."

Finding that pleading would be in vain, the lad fought madly, until overcome by three sturdy blacks who were called in to assist. They felled him to the ground and bound him with cords.

"Take him to the shed," commanded the whipper. "String him up to a cross-beam. He's to have twenty lashes to begin with, then he's to be whipped until we have orders to stop."

Strung up by his thumbs to the cross-beams, gashed, bleeding, every blow of the whip was torturing agony. The boy uttered not a groan. He had learned his lesson of endurance in the schools of the Indian stoic, and he bore his punishment without a murmur. But every stroke of the merciless lash was engraved on his heart in bleeding stripes that called for vengeance. In the midst of the scene Thomson strolled in.

"Very good," he said, after viewing the work a moment. "Let him breathe a minute, boys, then ten more. Now, Judah, this is a taste of wholesome discipline you're getting. You've got to be brung down. I'm going to do it if I have to have you whipped every month for a year. I'm goin' to break your spirit and teach you a nigger's place; an' if your life's wurth anything to you the quicker you learn your lesson the better. No more high-head carryin', gentlemanly airs, and dictionary talk; breaking hosses in ain't wuth a cent to a nigger," he added with a malicious leer. "All right, boys, give him ten more," and while they were being administered the monster stood by calmly smoking his cigar.

"Got grit," said the whipper. "Ain't whimpered."

"Now, boys, ease up again while I finish my little speech to the gentleman."

"You've got to learn to say 'massa.' It don' matter what you can do nor how much you know, nor how handsome you think yourself, you ain't one grain better than any other nigger on the plantation. If you forget this lesson, it'll be the worse for you. Now, once more, boys," he continued, turning to the whippers, "make it a dozen and smart ones to wind up with."

ALL THIS HAD HAPPENED IN the first year of captivity, and since that time Judah had apparently learned his place.

VI

I t was still the pleasant month of May when, as the Colonel sat in his favorite seat on the back piazza, just before noon Bill Thomson rode up to the back of the house followed by a strange horseman.

"I've brought you a visitor, Colonel, a stranger and yet not a stranger, bein' as we've met before. He brings you news," Thomson called out as they prepared to mount the piazza steps. "Mr. Maxwell, Colonel Titus. Mr. Maxwell has come all the way from London to bring you news from the Hall. Now I know he's welcome. Mr. Maxwell sir, in the Colonel you see a Southron of the Southrons, but old England will always hold first place in his hospitable heart. So, Colonel?"

"That's the right sound, William. Mr. Maxwell, do you stop with us over night sir?"

"I fear that I must tax your hospitality to that extent. Your uncle died six months ago. The estate will be yours in one year if the direct heir is not found. Your signature will be needed to certain papers that will prove your identity and residence here, and we shall also want affidavits made out for filing. All this is a mere formality required by law. Of course, Mr. Pendleton has charge of the estates, being the family lawyer, and is only anxious that the rightful heir inherit. You remember Mr. Pendleton, do you not, Colonel Titus?"

"Oh, yes! Old Pen, we boys used to call him. I hope he'll continue to look after my affairs, if the estate comes to me. I remember him as a very reliable man."

Warren bowed in acknowledgement of the compliment paid his chief. "I have no doubt he will be pleased to serve you. There is very little doubt of your succeeding to the baronetcy—practically we have demonstrated that fact, and I think your claims pass unquestioned."

"Be seated, Mr. Maxwell; make yourself comfortable. Jude!" he called, "Jude, I say!"

Maxwell started involuntarily, as Judah came out from the hallway. At last he had found a clew to the lost ones! His pulses beat fast, but his facial muscles told no tale. But his almost imperceptible start was noticed by the two men, who exchanged glances.

"Take the gentleman's horse, and tell Mrs. Thomson we have a guest over night," said the Colonel to the waiting servant. Judah's impassive face gave forth not a gleam of intelligence as he departed to obey his master's orders.

"Now, Mr. Maxwell," said the Colonel as they sat sipping the fragrant mixture sent out to them by Mrs. Thomson by the unfortunate Tennie, "you said something about no dispute over my being next of kin. Kindly explain that remark."

"Certainly," replied Warren, smiling. "This is my second trip to America in two years, hunting up the Carlingford heirs. I thought I had found Lord George's younger son, Henry, on my first trip, but after a fruitless chase, I was forced to give it up. We are convinced that he is dead and without issue."

"Just so! Poor Henry! His was a sad fate. But it was his destiny. Do you believe in destiny, my young friend?"

"I believe that many things we call destiny may be overcome by resolving to conquer difficulties, not allowing them to conquer us."

"True, very true," replied the Colonel, meditatively.

"Mr. Maxwell, you have expressed the position of our people to a dot concerning the little difficulty we are having with Kansas. Now the North thinks they're going to beat in the fight, and the fools are going to try to fight us, but it's the destiny of the South to rule in this glorious country, an' if it ain't our destiny we'll make it so, d—d if we don't when I get the boys fixed. Got a cool two hundred and fifty coming down here from Virginia nex' week; boys who don' care a cuss what they do so long as they beat the Free States out."

"Thomson," broke in the Colonel, "it appears to me that I have seen Mr. Maxwell before. What do you say?"

"I reckon you have. Don' you remember our hunting trip at Erie two years ago? and the murder of White Eagle?"

"Sure enough! Mr. Maxwell was the young Englishman who took such a prominent part in the affair."

Warren bowed gravely.

"Most unfortunate affair! Strange, too, that the man should have been killed just when the children needed him most. If he had lived, Thomson, in all probability, would not have recovered his property." He paused with a keen glance in Warren's quiet face, but it told nothing. His voice, too, was calm and even as he inquired:

"Then Mr. Thomson was the owner of the unfortunate children?"

"Yes," returned Thomson, "I'd been hunting them gals and their mother for nigh fifteen years, an' it was just luck and chance my meeting up with them young ones."

Warren puffed away at his cigar as though it were his only object in life.

"Fine cigar," he observed, at length.

"Particularly fine. The tobacco was raised by my own hands right over there for my private use," said the Colonel.

"What do you think of our institutions, Mr. Maxwell?" asked Thomson, nonchalently. "They've made this country. 'Spose you have some compunctions of conscience over us, eh? Most Englishmen do at first. But, man, look at the advantage it gives, the prosperity it brings, the prestige it gives our fine gentry all over the world. You must confess that we are a grand people."

"Yet you complained of a tea tax, and fought a 'liberty fight' on that pretext," observed Warren drily.

"Jes' so, jes' so! But see what we've done for the Africans, given them the advantages of Christian training, and a chance to mingle, although but servants, in the best circles of the country. The niggers have decidedly the best of it. The masters suffer from their ignorance and incompetency."

"How do you think the excitement over the Kansas-Nebraska matter will end?" questioned Maxwell, avoiding a statement of his own opinions.

"There are warm times ahead. The Yankees have got to be forced to leave the States. We'll make ourselves a living terror to them. The trouble is bein' stirred up by a lot of psalm singing abolitionists and an old lunatic named Brown. Yankees won't fight; they'll scatter like chaff before my Rangers. Now, there's fighting blood for you; every man owns a nigger and loves the South and her institutions, an' they ain't goin' to be beat out o' Kansas for an extension to the institution."

"Well, gentlemen, my opinion is that you are wrong. A government cannot prosper founded on crushed and helpless humanity," replied Maxwell firmly.

"Well, well," interrupted the Colonel, "There are two sides to every question. Some day—soon, perhaps, you will realize that we are a chivalrous, gallant people, worthy of the admiration of the world."

"While the Free Staters think themselves in the right, you also feel that your side is right."

"Precisely. They have inherited their ideas as we have ours. We do not agree. It is our duty to convince them of their error, and with God's help we will do it."

"But surely, you do not defend the atrocities committed against helpless women and children that are perpetrated by your side in Kansas every day?"

"Defend them? No! But I sympathize with the feelings of the perpetrators. You condemn them wholly without comprehending them or their motives, thus injuring them and doing mischief to yourself. Each group of men in this country has its own standard of right and wrong, and we won't give our ideas up for no d—d greasy, Northern mechanic."

"That's the right sort, Colonel," nodded Thomson, in sypmathetic approval.

The announcement that dinner was served cut short further discussion, much to Warren's relief. The Colonel's words impressed the young man greatly. But ever in opposition to specious argument arose thoughts of Winona and Judah and the terrible work done at the sacking of Oswatamie.

The remainder of the day was spent in riding over the plantation, and studying the beauties of the "institution" as propounded by the philosophical Colonel. Once only, Warren's anxious gaze descried Winona wheeling the chair of her crippled mistress up and down the lawn, but when the men returned to the house both were invisible.

He and the Colonel were seated upon the piazza in the soft Southern night talking over the points of law in claiming the Carlingford estate, when Mrs. Thomson called the latter for a moment into the house. Something blacker than the black night passed him as he sat there alone. Warren was startled, and it was some moments after the figure passed, before he realized that a man had spoken to him in passing: "Leave your window unlatched."

Pleading fatigue, the young man retired early, but not to sleep. His pulse beat at fever heat; his excited fancy could detect the sound of drums and the hurrying of marching feet. He sunk into a feverish slumber, from which he was awakened by the weeping of distressed females. He listened—all was still; it was the imagination again. He could not sleep, so he arose and looked carefully after his pistols. Danger seemed all about him, but he unlatched the window and drew it back softly, then stretched himself again upon the bed.

About one o'clock he was awakened from a light slumber by some one shaking him, and sitting up, found Judah beside him,—his dark face distinctly visible by the moon's dim light. Sitting in the darkness,

PAULINE E. HOPKINS

the sweet scent of the magnolia enveloping them in its fragrance, the faint sounds of insect life mingling with the murmur of rustling leaves. Warren Maxwell listened to whispered words that harrowed up his very soul. To emphasize his story, Judah stripped up his shirt and seizing the young white man's hand pressed it gently over the scars and seams stamped upon his back.

"I could bear it all, Mr. Maxwell," he concluded, "but Winona—" here his voice broke. "They've educated her to increase her value in the slave market, and next week Mr. Thomson takes her and me up the river to sell us to the highest bidder. If help does not come I have sworn to kill her before she shall become slavery's victim. It is impossible for me to put in words the fate of a beautiful female slave on these plantations; the torture of hell cannot surpass it."

A great wave of admiration swept over Warren at Judah's words. It was the involuntary tribute of Nature to nobility of would wherever found. The boy had become a man, and his demeanor was well calculated to inspire admiration and trust. Something truly majestic— beyond his years—had developed in his character. Warren thought him a superb man, and watched him, fascinated by his voice, his language, and his expressive gestures. Slavery had not contaminated him. His life with White Eagle had planted refinement inbred. In him was the true expression of the innate nature of the Negro when given an opportunity equal with the white man.

Impulsively, Maxwell laid his arm affectionately about the neck and shoulders of the youth.

"No extremes, Judah, until all else fails. I can buy you both if it comes to that, and my promise to take you to England with me still holds good."

"I doubt that you will be allowed to buy us. There is a stronger reason for our destruction underlying all this than is apparent. Don't let it be known that we have held any communication with you, or that you are at all interested in our fate. Be cautious."

"I will remember. But I shall have to study this matter over. I hardly know how to meet this issue if the use of money is denied us. When do you leave?"

"Monday, on the 'Crescent.'"

"Then I'll plead pressing business and leave tomorrow to meet you on board the steamer when she sails. Trust me, Judah, I will not fail you."

The tears were in Judah's throat as he tried to thank him. "I do trust you Mr. Maxwell, next to God. I knew you would be here soon; I dreamt a year ago that I saw you coming toward me out of a cloud of intense blackness. I have watched for you ever since. I was not at all surprised when I saw you riding up the avenue today; only for my hope in you as our deliverer, I'd have shot myself months ago."

"There is a God, Judah," replied Warren solemnly.

"But He seems far off from my unfortunate race," replied the man bitterly.

"Never doubt Him; His promises are aye and amen. With God's aid, I will save you or sacrifice myself."

They parted as silently as they had met.

VII

The steamer "Crescent" tugged and pulled at her moorings as if impatient of delay. It wanted two hours of sailing time. Down the gang-plank a strange figure sauntered, clad in buckskin breeches suspended by one strap over a flannel shirt open at the throat; high-topped boots confined the breeches at the knee; a battered hat was pushed back from a rubicand face, and about his waist a belt bristled with pistols and bowie knives. Warren smiled at the odd figure, then, with an exclamation of surprise, threw away his cigar and walked up to the newcomer.

"Mr. Maybee, of Erie?" he queried, holding out his hand.

The party addressed turned his round, smiling face in Maxwell's direction, and after one searching glance that swept his countenance in every lineament, grasped the proffered hand in a mighty clasp.

"Dog my cats, ef it ain't Mr. Maxwell! I'm pow'ful glad to meet you ag'in. How long you been here? Whar you bound?"

"I landed in New York just four weeks ago. Still on business for my firm."

"I 'spose it's in order to look out fer adventures when you an' me gits together. Remember the fus' night we met? What a swingin' ol' time we had. Poor old White Eagle! Nary sound have I heard, Mr. Maxwell, since, of them unfortoonit children neither. Might a been swallered like Jonah by the whale for all I know. I'm right chicken-hearted when I wake up at night, an' think about the leetle gal, po' pretty critter!"

"Mr. Maybee, I feel like a miserable cur whenever I think how supinely I have rested while such a horror was perpetrated—and yet I call myself a man! Your government cannot long survive under a system that thrusts free-born people into slavery as were those helpless children. May I have a word with you in private?"

"Hu—sh!" said Mr. Maybee, looking cautiously around, "them are sentimen's breathes pizen in this loorid atmosphere. Ef one of the galoots walkin' about this deck was to hear you, you'd dance on air at the yard arm in about two minutes. Them's dang'rous opinions to hold onto in free Ameriky," replied Mr. Maybee with a sly twinkle in his eye. "See that pile o' lumber out on the wharf? Well, that's the best place I know on to have a leetle private conversation with a friend. The boat won't start fer some time yet, an' I can straddle one end o' the pile an' keep a sharp lookout for listeners."

"There'll be a war in this country in less than two years, I predict," continued Maxwell, as they walked ashore. "No need o' waitin' two years, mister; jes' make it two months. The prelude to the war that's comin' was struck last fall when all Western Missouri poured into Kansas an' took the ballot out of the hands of our citizens, sir. Eli Thayer's teachin' all the North to emigrate into bleedin' Kansas an' fight it out. That's me, mister; I says to Ma' Jane, my wife, 'good-bye, Ma' Jane, ef I don't come back you'll know I've gone in a good cause, but John Brown's calling for volunteers an' I'm boun' to be in the fight.' So, I've left her power of attorney, an' the business all in her name, an' here I am. It beats all natur how fightin' jes' grows on a man once he's had a taste. Mr. Maxwell, do you know anythin' about the transfiguration of souls that some college fellars advocates? Dad gum it, I believe mos' of us must have been brutes once. Yes, sir, dogs an' vicious hosses, an' contrairy mulses an' venomous repertiles. Yes, sir, there's goin' to be a fight, an' I'm spilin' to git in it."

"Is it possible that matters are as critical as you say?"

"Critical! You may call 'em so, my boy. Six months ago I took up a claim outside o' Lawrence. One mornin', a fortnit later, twenty-eight men tied their hosses to the fence and one asked me: 'Whar you from? East?' 'Yes,' says I. 'Then you're a d—d abolitionist,' another says politely. 'Of course,' says I, an' in less than a half-hour the place was cleaned out, my shack burnt to the ground an' my cattle driven off. Me an' two or three of the boys put up a decent fight or I wouldn't be sittin' here talkin' to you today. 'Taint their fault."

"You amaze me, Mr. Maybee."

"Do I?" queried the other with a grim smile. "Well here's another nice leetle caper o' theirs: Bud Wilson's wife writ home to her folks in Massachusetts detailin' some o' the facts concernin' the sackin' o' Oswatamie, an' addin' a few words in her own language in comments, etc., on certain actions o' the Territory militit (Missouri roughs), an' her folks let the newspapers have the whole story. My soul! The Rangers came over from this side under that devil, Bill Thomson, an' one mornin' when Bud was gone they went to the house an' took his ol' woman inter the woods an' pulled her tongue out as far as possible an' tied it to a sapling. Well, I won't pain yer feelin's by recounterin' the rest o' the po' critter's sufferin's, but they was the mos' dreadfulles' that you can imagine, until she mercifully gave up the ghos' and expired. How's that strike you?"

"My God!" exclaimed Warren, shuddering with horror.

"Here's another: These same Kickapoo Rangers, Bill Thomson captaing, marched to Leavenworth an' took Capt. R. P. Brown (no relation to Capt. John Brown) prisoner, he surrenderin' himself and men on certain conditions. Immejuntly the terms of that surrender was violated. One young feller was knocked down, an' a Ranger was goin' to cut him with his hatchet (Thomson has 'em all carry hatchets so as to skulp the foe like Injuns do), and Capt. Brown prevented him. After that they removed the Captaing up to Easton an' put him in a separate buildin' away from his men. Then the devils rushed on him an' beat him to the floor an' cut him in the head with their hatchets, one wound bein' many inches long an' enterin' the brain. The gallant Captaing was at the mercy of his enemies then, an' they jumped on him an' kicked him. Desparately wounded, he still lived; an' as they kicked him, he said, 'Don't abuse me; it is useless; I am dying.' Then one of the wretches—Bill himself—leaned over the posterate man an' squirted tobacco juice in his eyes. Them's our leetle ways o' doin' things in free Ameriky, Mr. Britisher, when other folks talks too free or dares to have opinions o' thar own without askin' our permission to so think contrary agin us. Yes, sir, I'm a John Brown man. I go with Brown because I can do as I please—more independent-like—than as if I was with Jim Lane, 'though I'll 'low Lane's gittin' in some fine work, an' we'll swing Kansas inter line as a free State quicker'n scat when we git down to bisiness. It's these things brings me on this side noysterin' roun' lookin' for employment."

"I'm a pretty good shot, Mr. Maybee, and after I finish this matter for the firm, I should like nothing better than to put myself and my pistols at the disposal of Mr. Brown," said Warren sternly, with flashing eyes.

Mr. Maybee ejected a small stream of tobacco juice from his mouth and smoothed the end of the board he was whittling, to his entire satisfaction, before replying.

"Volunteers is acceptable, certainly, ef they brings weapins and ammunition. This is goin' to be no child's play. The oppersite party is strong in cussedness; on our side, we know we're right, an' we've made up our minds to die right on the spot, but never to yield. Still, we're not advertisin' our idees on the housetops, my friend; diplomacy, says I an' all of us, is an effectooal weapin' in many cases, therefore I advocate that we perceed to di-plomate—kin' o' play 'roun a spell, an' feel the t'other side. I'll consider it an honor to nesheate you any time you feel too sot, into the ranks of the Free Soilers, John Brown, captaing. Now, what's the business you wanted to lay befo' me?"

Thoroughly aroused by Maybee's words and trembling with excitement, Warren briefly related his unexpected meeting with Judah, and the peril of the captives. Mr. Maybee listened in amazement, chewing and spitting tobacco juice like an automaton in his excitement, with many exclamations of surprise: "Sho now!" "Want ter know!" "That ar Thomson, too! Dad gum 'im fer an onery skunk! I've jes' got to kill 'im; can't help it! He hung three of our best men down to Oscaloosa two weeks ago, tortured 'em fus' tho'." "Cu'rous how things does happen in this sinful wurl!"

"They mus' be rescued right off! right off!" he said, when Warren had finished. "We must git 'em on the Underground railroad this night. You go with the boat an' I'll cut across country an' com—moonicate with Parson Steward. We've got a good hour's start of the vessel, an' there'll be sand-bars to cross,—an',—O Lord, ef we'd only git such a thunder storm as we had the night White Eagle was murdered, it'd be the makin' of this expedition. It's been threat'ning all afternoon. Lord, let her come."

Briefly they arranged their plans.

"Tell Judah to git Thomson drunk; put somethin' in the liquor, if necess'ry, then git ashore somehow at Weston. I'll meet you there with hosses an' we'll put fer Steward's shack. Ef once he gits the gal in his clutches, even Bill Thomson won't git her agin."

With hurried good-byes the men separated, Mr. Maybee going up the wharf at a swift gait. Warren went aboard the steamer and seated himself in a secluded corner to watch for Judah and mature his plans.

Just before the last bell rang Thomson came aboard with his slaves. Even the rude passengers were moved by the beauty of the slave girl. Every soft curve of her waist and supple body was followed by the close-fitting cotton gown; her hair, worn short since captivity, clustered in a rich, ravelled plume about her brows and neck; the soft; gazelle-like eyes were large with anxiety, but her step was firm, and she bore herself like a young princess as she crossed the deck to go below. The girlish figure appealed to Warren's tender heart. He was used to the society of famous beauties in the proudest court of the Old World; he had flirted and danced with them in the abandonment of happy youthful hours, and more than one lovely girl had been smitten with his frank, good-looking boyish face and honest, manly bearing, but never before had his heart contracted and thrilled as it did now under the one appealing glance thrown hurriedly and timidly in his direction by the young slave girl.

Scarcely were they under way when the threatening storm was upon them. It began in a dreary drizzle with occasional mutterings of thunder.

Warren noticed that Judah was seated on the deck in the slave-pen next to an airshaft, and he concluded to find the cabin communication with the shaft and reach Judah by it.

The night fell fast. Maxwell hid himself in his stateroom before supper, having made the pleasing discovery that a port-hole in his stateroom opened directly beside Judah's seat on the deck. A note was easily slipped to the slave telling him of Mr. Maybee's plan, and asking what was the best course to pursue, then he sat there in darkness waiting a movement on Judah's part, assured that his fertile brain would find a plan of escape.

In the cabin Thomson was the center of a congenial set of kindred spirits, young Virginians, going back to St. Louis after a campaign against the Free Soilers. They were reciting the glories of the expedition,—singing, shouting and making night hideous. Their favorite song ended in an uproarious chorus:

> *You Yankees tremble, and*
> *Abolitionists fall:*
> *Our motto is, Southern Rights*
> *For all!*

One of their number had been fatally shot in a quarrel at a hotel in Kansas City; they were carrying the body home, and had ordered the coffin brought in and placed in the center of the cabin, where, as they said, the poor fellow might have the comfort of witnessing one more good time even though beyond the possibility of joining in it.

In the gambling and drinking bout that followed, Thomson was the most reckless, and soon he, and the rest of the party, was stretched upon the floor, on tables, and lounges in a drunken stupor from which nothing could arouse them. The few women passengers were fastened in their staterooms.

Warren took his saddle-bags in his hand, and stole out upon the deck, picking his way in disgust among the bestial party blocking his path. Half-way to Weston they had struck upon a sandbar and there they hung, shuddering and groaning in the teeth of the storm.

He seated himself near the railing. The rolling thunder mingled with the hoarse shouting of the officers and the answering cries of the crew. There were flashes of lightning at intervals. Presently a soft touch fell on his arm. He turned and saw Judah crouching in the shadow of a mast.

"They won't be off this bar before morning. I'm going to drop a boat over the side the next heavy crash that comes. Winona is waiting just back of you. It'll take nerve, but it is the only way. We must be silent and careful."

The soft murmur ended, and once more Maxwell was alone. He had noticed the small boats standing along the sides of the vessel as he came aboard in the afternoon, but had not thought of utilizing them for the purpose of rescue. His heart heat to suffocation, his nerves were strung to their utmost tension. A soft hand stole into his; he pressed it convulsively, instinctively knowing that it was Winona, but they exchanged no words.

There came a deafening crash. The bolt struck a capstan, knocking down the first mate and glancing off into the sea. Surely God was with them. Simultaneously with the crash there was a faint plash in the water, but the vivid lightning flash that followed revealed nothing. There came a lull in the storm but confusion reigned on the vessel; no one thought of the slaves. "Now!" came a warning whisper. In an instant Warren grasped the girl about the waist, swung her clear of the railing and held her suspended by the wrists over the black, boiling flood. "All right, let her drop!" came in another whisper. Warren let go his hold and listened with bated breath for the result. There came another faint plash, a grating sound as the foaming waves carried the little craft against the wooden ribs of the steamer. Then silence.

Judah, standing uptight in the boat, caught Winona in his arms as deftly as a ball is caught and tossed from one player to another. His Indian training in managing canoes made him fearless now, and his giant strength served him well.

"All right; come ahead," came to Warren's listening ears. He dropped his saddle-bags, instantly following them; he let himself down hand over hand, then swung clear and landed lightly in the center of the frail craft, steadied by the giant black. Silently the little party rested in the shadow of the great hull until another lightning flash had passed, then each man settled an oar in the row-locks, and Judah pushed off into the night.

VIII

There came a knock at Preacher Sampson Steward's cabin door that same night about midnight. Instantly his mind was on the alert. He had been stretched on the bed at full length for an hour listening intently to sounds outside. The thunder and lightning had ceased, and the rain and the wind beat a monotonous tattoo against the window panes. There was a world of possibilities in that knock. He could not from the sound tell whether it heralded peace or war, and these were troublous times in Kansas. It was in Preacher Steward's nature to speak his convictions fearlessly, and this made him a special object of hatred to many pro-slavery men who would have gladly rid the country of his presence, did not his well known courage and marksmanship afford him some protection against open attack.

A tallow candle sputtered in its place on the stand. Near the stand was the window, protected by a wooden shutter. Beside him on the bed where he lay half-dressed, his wife and two children lay wrapped in slumber. The knock was repeated; Steward sprang to the floor, reached out his hand and grasped his pistols, laying them handy for use on the stand by the sputtering candle, seized his rifle, cocked it, slipped the heavy iron bolt of the door with his free hand, stepped back a pace and drew a bead on the door, then with set face and tightly drawn lips, he said firmly:

"Come in!"

The door swung open, admitting a gust of rain and wind. The tall, stout figure of Ebenezer Maybee was outlined against the blackness of the night, his attire plentifully sprinkled with the mud and rain. One hand held a driving whip, the other grasped the door-latch, while his keen eyes watched the white face behind the rifle whose muzzle almost touched his breast, yet giving no sign of fear.

"What! The parson turned fighter with a vengeance," he said at length, in quiet tones. "This ain't at all 'bligatory on you, Steward. You ought to know my knock by this time. Put up your gun."

Steward instantly complied.

"Is it you, Maybee?" he queried, standing the weapon with its muzzle against the wall. "Come in!"

"Somethin' interestin' you've picked up by the way of makin' your friends welcome, Steward?" Maybee replied, with a grim smile, as he closed the door and advanced to grasp the minister's extended hand.

"God forgive me, Maybee, but it is more than human nature can stand. Sunday week it was only by a special act of Providence that my congregation escaped massacre. Since then I'm a marked man. I am on special guard duty tonight."

"What's up?"

"Had a message from the Rangers."

An exchange of significant glances followed this speech.

"Oh, I see. Perhaps then we'd better bring in our fugitives at once."

"What have you this time?"

"A young man and woman and a young Englishman, who is helping them away. It's a long story. All of 'em's good shots; the gal ain't slow on a pinch."

"Good!" replied the parson, evidently relieved. "We can put her in the loft. The Lord sent you, Maybee; it's inspiration to have some one to help out in an emergency."

"You're really expectin' trouble, then?"

"Yes; but let's get them in as quickly as possible. After that I'll tell you all about it."

The storm had chilled the air, and the parson kindled a fire in the stove, throwing on a plentiful supply of wood.

"I'm ready. Come to the door."

Maybee obeyed; the parson blew out the candle, leaving the room in darkness.

"Now bring them in. I'll stay here till you return. Be careful, and lose no time."

Maybee opened the door and the darkness instantly swallowed him. When he returned with the fugitives, Steward saw dimly, by the firelight shining among the shadows, the beautiful girl and the stalwart black. He regarded Winona with a look of vague wonder and admiration. In all his life he had seen no women to compare with her.

He noted, too, the golden hair and fair complexion of the young Englishman. It was no common party that sought the shelter of his rude cabin on this stormy night. His familiar eye noted the signs of strength, too, in the youthful figures.

"Good!" he told himself. "If we do have a call from the Rangers, we'll die with our boots on; that's some satisfaction."

He beckoned to Maybee, and speaking a few words to his wife who was awake, thrust his pistols into an inner pocket, and directing Warren to bolt the door after them and not to open save at a given signal, the two men went out into the storm to feed and stable the horses. This accomplished, they returned to the house, and after carefully fastening the door, Steward lighted the candle and began preparing supper for his unexpected guests.

"Now, Maybee, where from and where bound? Tell me all about it."

In a few graphic sentences, in his peculiar mixed dialect, Mr. Maybee rehearsed the story with which we are so well acquainted.

The parson listened intently with an occasional shake of the head or a sympathetic glance in the direction of Winona. "I caught up with 'em at the ferry, an' I took the ol' road so's to lessen the chances of pursuit or of meetin' any on-welcome company on the way. I've sent word to Captaing Brown to look out for us. It was a bluff game with odds, but we've won," he concluded.

Steward laughed.

"We have generally proved winners even with the odds against us."

Warren leaned back against the wall of the rude cabin wearied from the long nervous strain, but listening intently to all that passed.

"Judah's a lion, and Winona has the pluck of a man," Maybee went on. "She doesn't whimper, but jes' saws wood an' keeps to her instructions."

Warren spoke now.

"You have as many manœuvres to gain admittance to your house as some of the Indian fighters I used to read about when a boy. What are you expecting tonight, Mr. Steward?"

"Some of the gang," replied the parson, stopping in his occupation of cutting strips of bacon for the frying pan. "They have threatened me with vengeance because I sheltered John Brown and his men on their way north a month or two back. Reynolds brought me word this morning that they had concluded to visit me tonight. Reynolds hasn't the nerve to come out as I do, and avow his principles, but maybe it's better so that the gang don't know it; through him I keep informed of all their movements."

"Don't know thar leetle program, do you?" carelessly questioned Maybee, as he threw back the lid of the coffeepot to keep its contents from boiling over.

"No; Reynolds didn't learn that," replied Steward, as he adjusted the meat in the pan and placed it over the fire, "He thinks their intention is to decorate my anatomy with tar and feathers."

"Mos' cert'n'ly," nodded Maybee, as he took his turn at tending the frying meat while Steward sliced potatoes to brown in the bacon fat after the meat was cooked.

"Mr. Steward, if we had been of their number when we came to the door just now, what would you have done?" asked Warren.

The parson held his knife over a half-peeled potato, and looked the young man in the face, while his eyes glowed with excitement.

"Well, had you been one of Bill Thomson's riders, I would have sent a bullet through you without a word. It is written: 'This day will the Lord deliver thee into my hand; and I will smite thee, and take thy head from thee.'"

"Pardon me for what I am about to say," continued Warren, "but I cannot understand how you can reconcile such a proposed course with your profession. I make no pretention to piety myself, but I have a profound respect for those who conscientiously do."

The preacher faltered.

"Don't misunderstand me," Warren hastened to say, seeing the man of God hesitate. "I am not charging you with anything. I simply cannot reconcile the two ideas, that's all. I don't quite understand your position."

"That's jest what I've wanted to say to Steward here, many a time, but not being gifted with gab, which mos' people calls eddi-kation, I haven't been able to perceed like the prefesser," meaning our English friend, Mr. Maxwell. "Thar was that secret citizens' meetin' down in the timber, and Steward was fer shootin' down at sight without a trial all onery cusses that was even suspected of bein' onfriendly to the principles of the Free-Staters. Dad gum 'em, that's my methods to a T, but it's kin' o' rough jestice fer a parson," chuckled Maybee.

"Well, gentlemen, what would you do in my place? What show have I against a gang of ten or more men unless I meet them promptly with the initiative? What better course could I have pursued with the mob that came to our church during service? When I beheld them round about us and heard their savage cries, when I saw the terror of the women and children and bethought me of their fate if perchance, the men were all slain, I girded up my loins and taking a pistol in each hand, I led forth my elders and members against the Philistines; and I said to them: 'This day I will give the carcasses of your hosts unto the fowls of the air, and the wild beasts of the earth; that all the earth may know that there is a God in Israel.' Verily, not one was spared.

"Tonight I was here single-handed. I have a wife and two children dependent on me for support. Must I be denied the right of defense gainst superior numbers because I hate slavery and have the courage of my convictions?"

The speaker's eyes—his whole face, in fact—glowed and scintillated with holy wrath and conviction in the justice of his case.

"No, let me explain further!" Warren hastened to exclaim, "It is not your defense that I question, but your aggressive spirit. Now, as I understand it, these men are a part of the territorial militia; if so, do not your acts smack somewhat of treason?"

"Treason! the word by which traitors seek to hang those who resist them. I hate the laws that make this country a nursery for slavery, and I resist them by rescuing all who come to me for refuge. Three hundred will not excuse the number that have passed this station on the underground railroad since I have been here. Oppression is oppression, whether it enslaves men and women and makes them beasts of burden, or shuts your mouth and mine if we utter humane protests against cruelty. If this is treason, make the most of it; there's one thing certain, unless I am caught napping, they are going to pay dearly for whatever advantage they secure over me."

"I concur with you," Warren replied, rising from his seat, and pacing back and forth thoughtfully. "You have a perfect right to defend your home from brutal attack, and so long as I am here I am subject to your orders. But let us hope the storm will soon blow over; the South well see its error and the Negroes will be granted freedom by peaceful means."

Steward and Maybee laughed silently and heartily at the young man's earnest words.

"Ef you stayed 'roun' here long nuff and warn't a British subjec', my fren', you might git a taste of this scrimmage that'd convince you that the South is a horned hornet on the nigger question. Time 'n tide nor God A'mighty won't change the onery skunks. Them's my sentimen's."

"The storm," said Judah with wild exultation in his voice, "the storm is but gathering force. These bloody happenings which are convulsing Missouri and Kansas are but the preliminary happenings to a glorious struggle which will end in the breaking of every chain that binds human beings to servitude in this country."

Warren regarded him in astonishment.

"Why do you think so, Judah?"

"I cannot tell. But I feel that the sin will be punished in a great outpouring of blood and treasure until God says it is enough. The day of deliverance of the Negro is at hand."

"Amen! The boy is a true prophet. 'Behold, the Lord's hand is not shortened, that it cannot save; neither his ear heavy, that it cannot hear.'

Bring your chairs up to the table and have some hot coffee and a bit to eat."

The meal over, from which all rose refreshed and strengthened, Steward placed a ladder against the wall and mounting it, threw back a trap door in the ceiling closely concealed by festoons of strings of dried apples and bunches of onions and herbs. He then returned to the room and lit an extra candle, beckoning Winona to follow him up the steep ascent. Speaking a few words of caution to her, he descended the ladder, which he removed and put out of sight. Warren watched his movements with great curiosity. How fast he was gaining a true knowledge of life and living here in these American wilds among a rough but kindly people. These friends of the fugitive slaves lived by but one principle, "Greater love than this hath no man."

His refined sensibilities were satisfied by the melodramatic coloring of his surroundings. The atmosphere of art had affected him enough for him to perceive the beauties of the picture made by the stalwart men, the gigantic black's refined prowess and the noble lines and graceful pose of Winona's neck and shoulders.

Preacher Steward moved out a number of wooden sea chests from beneath the tall, four-posted bed where his wife and children lay wrapped in slumber. He spread at the extreme back of the open space a pair of blankets and then signed Judah to creep under the bed; when he had done so, the parson pushed back the trunks as nearly as possible to their old positions, thus completely concealing the fugitive from view.

"We can't start before five o'clock, and we may as well get all the rest we can," said Maybee.

It was after midnight when Warren, Maybee and their host lay down upon the floor which was spread with a buffalo robe and blankets.

"It's the best the railroad can offer under the circumstances. The railroad isn't wealthy and we have to put up with some discomforts."

"This beats sleeping on the ground without blankets, as we sometimes bivouac out to Captaing Brown's camp, all holler," replied Maybee, sleepily. "Declar', I'm dead beat."

"As I understand it, this isn't a railroad; it is only hiding fugitives as they pass to Canada."

"Exactly. But many people believe in an underground railroad, with regular trains running on time, stopping points, and everything in railroad style?"

"Really?"

PAULINE E. HOPKINS

"You bet," grunted Maybee, half-asleep.

"Yes, sir; some men of fair intelligence, too, have faith in it. They can account for the results we accomplish in no other way. A fugitive is passed along by us, night after night, until he secures his freedom. Our methods are a profound mystery."

"Let 'm stop right thar," returned Maybee. "You fellers'd better git to sleep."

Steward extinguished the light, placed his weapons where they could be reached instantly, and laid down by Warren. The rain still fell gently down in a patter on the roof, the little clock ticked in its place over the wooden stand. Warren could not sleep. An hour passed. There was a footstep. Warren's ear alone caught the sound. He raised himself on his elbow and grasped his pistol. There were more steps. They came nearer. A hand was passed cautiously over the door. Warren touched the form of Steward.

"What is it?" he asked in a whisper.

"Listen!"

The movement at the door continued as softly as before.

"Who's there?" called out Steward.

"Travellers; we want to find the road."

"Where from?"

"Missouri."

"Where yer boun'?" shouted Maybee, jumping to his feet. There was a sound of parleying in subdued voices at Maybee question. Then came the answer, "Nebraska."

"You're right for that. This is the Jim Lane route. Keep the main road and you'll not miss it," again answered Steward. A moment passed. Then came the inquiry: "Can you put us up till mornin'?"

"Cayn't do it," spoke up Maybee again. "Our beds are full. How many of you?"

"Two."

"Sorry, but you'll have to keep on. Can't do anything for you."

"Say, have you seen anything of a nigger man an' gal an' a white man a-pilotin' 'em?"

"Nary one, mister," again spoke up Maybee.

"Reckon we'll push on then."

The sound of horses' feet died in the distance.

After that there was no more sleep in the cabin, though the remainder of the night passed in quiet.

Steward and his guests were early astir. The storm had cleared. The men left the house to prepare for an early start at the first streaks of dawn; when they returned, Mrs. Steward had breakfast ready.

Silence pervaded the little band. Each was pre-occupied with thoughts he did not care to discuss.

IX

I n the early morning light they rode away through the quiet beauty of the woods. The sweetness of the cool air was grateful to them after the feverish anxiety of the night. The dew of the morning sparkled on bud and leaf, and the sunlight sifted dimly through the trees.

Parson Steward rode at the head of the small cavalcade, and Mr. Maybee at the rear; Winona was between Warren and Judah. It was Warren, however, who had helped her to mount and who did the countless trivial things which add to one's comfort, and are so dear to a woman, coming from one man.

Winona was only sixteen, and she was dreaming the first enchanted dream of youth. She did not attempt to analyze the dazzling happiness it was to once more meet and be remembered by the one object of the pure-hearted and passionate hero-worship of her childish soul; but in which, alas! for her lay the very seed of the woman's love, that must now too surely spring up into full life, forcing her presently to know it by its right name.

For two years he had been a cherished, never forgotten memory; but whom in bodily form she was never to see again. Yet so small is the world, within a week he had suddenly walked into her life again, he had offered his frankest, loyalest friendship, and opened his prisondoors with that strong right hand of his which had both power and will.

She rode along the forest lanes in a waking dream; she was too young to look far into the future, the present was enough for her. One thing was certain, she would never, never marry, because, of course, it was quite impossible she should ever marry Warren Maxwell, and a union with another would be horrible to her.

In the life she had led as a slave, this poor child had learned things from which the doting mother guards the tender maidenhood of her treasure with rigid care; so the girl thought of marriage or its form, with the utmost freedom. No, she would try to serve this man in some way, in the course of her life, she knew not how, but sometime she would be his guardian angel—she would save his life at the sacrifice of her own— nothing was too great to render him in service for his noble generosity.

It was a child's dream in which there mingled unconsciously much of the passionate fervor of the woman, the desire to devote herself and to suffer for her hero, to die for him even, if it would serve him.

As for Warren—no man could look quite unmoved on the living picture the girl made as she sat on her horse with ease and held the reins with no uncertain hand. She was so little changed, yet so much; some taller, but the same graceful form, now so rounded, the same exquisite contour of feature, and soft, dark face so full of character, so vivid with the light of the passionate soul within.

He could not dream the wild leap and throb of the young heart as she turned and caught his blue eyes bent earnestly upon her. She had early learned control in a hard school, but the light in her eyes, the joy in her face, was beyond hiding.

That chemistry of the spirit which draws two irresistibly together, through space and against time and obstacles, kept them conscious only of each other. Winona resisted the intimation of happiness so like what had come to her in her beloved Erie's isle while with her father, yet so unlike. This joy was a beam from heaven; blessedness seemed so near.

Judah watched them, himself forgotten, and his features hardened. Was it for this he had suffered and toiled to escape from his bonds? If they had remained together in slavery, she would have been not one whit above him, but the freedom for which he had sighed had already brought its cares, its duties, its self-abnegation. He had hoped to work for her and a home in Canada; it had been the dream that had buoyed his heart with hope for weary days; the dream was shattered now. He saw that the girl would not be satisfied with his humble love.

"So it is," he told himself bitterly. "The white man has the advantage in all things. Is it worth while struggling against such forces?"

A while he mused in this strain as they swept on in silence, save for the subdued tones of the couple beside him. Then came softer thoughts, and his face lost the hard, revengeful look. He would not despair; the end was not yet. Many men had admired pretty faces. Let Maxwell beware and let it end in admiration only; he knew the worth of a white man's love for a woman of mixed blood; how it swept its scorching heat over a white young life, leaving it nothing but charred embers and burnt-out ashes. God! had he not seen. He—Judah—was her natural protector; he would be faithful to White Eagle's trust.

Towards twilight, they swerved from the direct road and entered a wooded slope. For some hours the hills surrounding Lawrence had been the point they were making. The naked woods showed the cup-like shape of the hills there—a basin from which radiated upward wooded ravines edged with ribs of rock where a few men could hold the entrance against great odds. In this basin on the edges of a creek John Brown was encamped. The smoke of a fire was visible in the dim light. As they advanced, a picket's gun echoed a warning from rock to rock. They halted then and dismounted, tying their horses to the branches of trees and stood ready to answer questions. Two men with guns came out from the bushes, with the words: "Stop thar. Free or pro-slavery? Whar you from?" Warren learned afterwards that these were two of Brown's sons.

Receiving satisfactory answers from Maybee and the Parson, our party passed on until they reached the creek where a group of horses stood saddled for a ride for life, or to hunt for Southern invaders. In an open space was a blazing fire, from which the smoke they had seen came; a pot was hung over it; a woman with an honest, sunburned face was superintending the preparations for supper. Three or four armed men were lying on red and blue blankets on the ground, and two fine-looking youths—grandsons of John Brown—stood near, leaning on their arms.

Old John Brown himself stood near the fire with his shirt sleeves rolled up, a large piece of pork in his hands which he had cut from a pig, barely cold, lying near.

In the woods' dark shadows nestled rude shelter-huts made from the branches of trees.

The travellers received a hearty welcome, and a number of women immediately surrounded Winona and hurried her to the largest hut.

Warren saw her once before leaving the next morning. "Good-bye, Winona; I shall return in a few weeks at longest. You are safe now until we can reach Canada."

"Good-bye, Mr. Maxwell. Do not speak so confidently. How can we tell that you will ever return or that I shall ever see Canada? I hate these good-byes," she said, with trembling lips.

Warren took the childish hand in his and kissed it. "Let us add 'God willing.'"

"No more time," called Parson Steward. "We've a good twenty miles and a bit before night," the next moment they had shaken hands with Maybee and Judah, and were riding out of camp.

The condition of Warren's mind was one of bewilderment. He had never in his life imagined anything like his experiences of the past few days. Now and again across the confusion of his mind, images floated vaguely—a white throat tinted by the firelight, a supple figure, a rapt young face, a head held with all a princess' grace, and dark, flashing eyes. The sound of a sweet voice, soft but not monotonous, fascinated his senses, as he recalled the tones repeating commonplace answers to commonplace questions. Somehow, the poor gown accented the girl's beauty.

Toward the close of the next day, the two men rode along in silence, save when Steward broke forth in song. He was singing now in a good baritone voice.

> *"A charge to keep I have,*
> *A god to glorify;*
> *A never-dying soul to save,*
> *And fit it for the skies."*

Warren listened to him dreamily. The voice chimed in harmoniously with the surroundings. The evening shadows were falling rapidly and the soft twilight folded them in its embrace. Maxwell was to stop another night at the cabin, and then riding on some fifteen miles, connect with the next boat on its regular trip to St. Louis.

Presently the singer changed his song to grand old "Coronation," his powerful voice swelling on the air-waves, mingling with the rustling of the leaves stirred by the balmy air, echoing and reechoing through the wooded glen: "Praise God from whom all blessings flow." The young man wondered that he had never before realized the beauties of the noble hymn.

All the while their horses covered the ground in gallant form. Wonderful to relate, they had met with no marauding parties; but here and there, Steward pointed out to him the signs of desolation in the dreary woods where once prosperous farms had smiled; now the winds sighed over barren fields and broken fences, and the ghostly ruins of charred houses lifted their scarred skeletons against the sky in a mute appeal for vengeance.

The horsemen came to the high-road; soon they would be out in the open, clear of the woods. Warren's mind, by one of those sudden transitions which come to us at times, seemed to carry him bodily into his peaceful English home. He could see the beautiful avenues of noble trees, and the rambling, moss-covered manse; he could see the kindly patrician face of his father, and his brothers and sisters smiled at him from every bush. The Parson was ahead.

Suddenly he saw the horse stop.

"Ssh!"

Steward threw the word of caution over his shoulder at Maxwell. They halted, standing motionless in their tracks. A moment of breathless silence passed; then came the second sound of the soft clink of metal against stone, though no one was visible in the ghostly shadows of the twilight. Warren sat motionless as Steward peered about with the stealthy caution of a fox.

Why should the horse tremble? It was a second before he realized. He lurched forward in the saddle; there was a sharp pain in his shoulder; his arm dropped useless. He heard another shot, followed by a wild shout in the "fighting parson's" voice—"Blow ye the trumpet blow!" "Slay and spare not!"

Then another shot came to his benumbed faculties; then silence; he was galloping on in the darkness. On and on his frightened horse whirled him. By this time he was so faint from his wound that he could only dimly discern objects as he was whirled past the trees. Half a mile farther, the animal stumbled as he leaped over an obstacle in the path. Riderless, he sped over the highway; Warren lay motionless under the blossoming stars.

Out from the shadows of the trees came figures and voices.

"Hold the light. He ain't dead, is he?" queried the familiar voice of Bill Thomson.

"Looks like it, but reckon he's only wounded," replied Gideon Holmes, Bill's lieutenant.

Thomson bent over the insensible man, deftly feeling his heart's motion. Then he raised himself and stood looking down thoughtfully on the youth.

It was a motley crowd of Southern desperadoes, men who stopped at nothing in the line of murder and rapine.

"Say, Jim," whispered a slight, thin man to his neighbor, "I wouldn't be in that young feller's shoes fer money—"

"What's he studyin', do ye reckon, Dan?"

"Hell!" was the expressive answer.

"What's agin the boy?" asked Jim.

"Stole two o' his niggers, so he says."

"Well, sir! Nasty mess. He won't git off easy."

"No. Say, what's Bill doin' neow? Looks interestin'."

Thomson had taken the gold from Warren's money-belt and the contents of his saddle-bags and was parcelling money and clothing impartially among his followers. Warren's revolvers were stowed in Thomson's own belt; then his garments followed suit, one man getting his boots, another his coat, still another his hat and so on.

While this was going on the unfortunate man revived and stared up into the devilish face of Bill Thomson. He groaned and closed his eyes.

"Howd'y, Mr. Maxwell? Didn't think I'd meet up with you so soon again, did you? Well, I've got you. Been after you ever since you left the 'Crescent,' and a mighty pretty chase it's been. Now, I want my niggers. I ain't foolin'. Where's they at?"

"I can't tell you," gasped Warren painfully.

"Look here, my friend, you've got to tell me. It's worth your life to you. You answer me true an' straight an' I'll make it all right for you. If you don't—" He paused ominously. "I'll let a Missouri crowd kill you! It won't be nice, easy killin', neither."

"I can't tell you," again Warren answered, looking up resolutely into the sinister face bending above him.

"Got grit," muttered Sam to Dave.

Warren was trembling, and the cold drops in the roots of his hair ran down his forehead. He was not afraid, he was a man who did not know the name of fear or cowardice, but Thomson's evil looks sent a chill to his heart. Ebenezer Maybee's words of a few nights back rang in his ears monotonously: "You might git a taste of this scrimmage that'd convince you that the South is a horned hornet on the nigger question."

"Well," said Bill, "made up yer mind? Spit it out!"

Warren looked him in the eye without flinching; he did not answer.

Bill Thomson was what is called "foxy." He eyed his prisoner a spell and then said in quite another tone:

"Look a-here. I ain't goin' back on old England. You're my countryman, and I'm goin' to give you a square deal. You're what we call to home a high-tined gentleman. If you'll give us all the points possible an' lead the gang by the rout you've jes' come, you needn't say one word. I don't want no man to give his pals away. Will you?"

Their eyes met. The glitter of steel crossed under the lantern's light. Maxwell compressed his lips. Winona stared at him across the shadows of the dim old woods. "Be true," she whispered to the secret ear of his soul. With rapture he read aright the hopeless passion in her eyes when he left her. He knew now that he loved her. With sudden boldness he answered his tormentor.

"You have no right to claim either Winona or Judah as your slave. They are as free as you or I. I will never aid and abet your barbarous system, understanding it as I do now."

There was a cry and a general movement on the part of the crowd.

"Let him free his mind!" said Bill, waving the men back. "What do you mean by 'barbarous system'?"

"I mean a system that makes it right to force a free man or woman into slavery. A system which makes it a crime to utter one's honest convictions."

"Wal, I reckon that'll do fer now," broke in Gideon Holmes.

"I have committed no crime against your laws; if so, why, leave me in the hands of the law."

"We take the law into our own hands these times," replied Gideon.

"Let me labor with him a spell, Gid." Gideon subsided, muttering.

"In the fus' place you are foun' guilty of associatin' with Northern abolitionists; besides that, they have so far corrupted your better judgment as to cause you to become a party to runnin' off slaves.

"Now, Mr. Maxwell, bein' a british subjec', you may not know that in the South sech actions is accountable with murder and becomes a hangin' affair. Because of your ignorance of our laws, and, whereas, you have fallen into evil company, we will give you a show for your life if you will own up and tell all you know, and help us to recover our property; otherwise, sorry as I should be to deal harshly with a gentleman of your cloth, the law mus' take its course."

"I am aware that I can expect no mercy at your hands. I have spoken freely and stated my honest convictions."

"An' free enough you've been, by gosh!" said Gideon, again breaking in.

Just at this point two men rode out of the woods leading a horse that Warren recognized. It was the parson's.

"Where's he at?" queried Bill.

"Dead's a hammer," answered the one in charge, at whose side dangled the pistols of the "fighting parson."

"Sure?"

"Sure."

"Git anything out of him about my niggers?"

"No use, Bill; they're up to Brown's camp. Nex' week they'll be in Canidy."

"Well, this one won't escape," said Bill, with a great oath, and a black, lowering look at the prisoner.

Without more talk, Warren was lifted to the back of the parson's horse and firmly bound. Then began a long, wild ride through the night in darkness and silence, bound, helpless, stabbed by every stumble.

Sometimes they trotted on high ground, sometimes the horses were up to their knees in the bog; and once Warren felt a heave of his horse's flanks, and heard the wash of water as if the animals were swimming. He tried to collect his thoughts; he tried to pray, but his mind would wander, and with the pain from his wound and the loss of blood, he was half-delirious. His thoughts were a jumble of hideous pictures.

Meanwhile, Sam and Dan talked together in whispers.

"Fifteen hundred dollars for the slaves or the slave-stealer, dead or alive, that's what the Colonel had advertised."

"A right smart o' money," replied Dan, "an' only eight o' us to git it."

"Kin' o' sorry 'bout the parson. It'll make again us up North," continued Sam.

"Ya-as, that's so, fur a fac'," acquiesced Dave.

"An' what a hunter he was, shoot the wink off yer eye! O, Lord, warn't he chock full o' grit. Min' the time he says to Bill, 'you ride fas', but Death'll cotch you, an' after death the judgmen'!'" queried Sam.

Dan chuckled at the recollection. "Got the dead wood on Bill then, I reckon."

"You bet!" replied Sam, with emphasis.

"Dear, dear, ain't it turrible fur't have't do a man like that mean!" continued Dan.

"But 'twould be terrible to lost the money. I can't tell which would be turriblest!"

"That's a fac'."

"Who's that fool gabin'?" came in a fierce whisper from the front. Then followed silence.

They had emerged from the swamp and were riding through a high, fertile region of farming lands. The moon was rolling high in the heavens, while far toward the east was a faint lightning, the promise of dawn.

Once after crossing a bridge they pulled up and listened, and then rode off into the bushes and stood quietly in hiding. They were evidently

PAULINE E. HOPKINS

anxious to avoid pursuit. Once pistol shots followed them as they fled through the night.

At Weston a crowd of men awaited them, and crossed over to the other side in company with Bill's party. Warren was thrown into a wagon. Presently they stepped from the boat to Missouri's shore.

W arren looked about him in the light of the flaming torches. Men poured down to the water's edge as fast as they could come. The crowds which surged through the streets day and night were rushing toward the wagon where lay the prisoner, their faces distorted like demons with evil passions.

Bill Thomson mounted the wagonseat and with an oratorical flourish recounted the prisoner's against the "principles of the institootion."

"Gentlemen, take notice!" said Gid Holmes as Bill finished. "This yere man is a abolitionist an' a nigger thief, two crimes we never overlooks, bein' dangerous to our peace and principles. What's your will, gentlemen? Speak out."

"Give him a thrashing first!" "Hang him!" "Burn him!"

And the ruffians dragged the wounded man from the wagon and threw themselves upon him—kicking him in the body—in the face and head—spitting upon him and maltreating him in every way. He defended himself well for a while; his bright head would rise from their buffeting.

"To the cross-roads!" came the hoarse cry from a thousand throats.

Tramp, tramp, on they rushed like a dark river, with cries whose horror was indescribable. It was not the voices of human beings, but more like the cries of wild animals, the screaming of enraged hyenas, the snarling of tigers, the angry, inarticulate cries of thousands of wild beasts in infuriated pursuit of their prey, yet with a something in it more sinister and blood curdling, for they were men, and added a human ferocity.

On they rushed from north, south, east and west, eyes aflame, faces distorted, the brute latent in every human being coming out from his lair to blot out the man, the awful cries, waning, waxing.

Maxwell was in the midst, half-running, half-dragged by a rope knotted about his neck. He fell; the thirsty executioners lifted him up, loosened the rope and gave him time to breath.

The tall young figure looked at the crowd with scorn. The British idea of fair play was in his mind.

"Thousands against one," he seemed to say, "Cowards!"

The crowd moved on a little more slowly, and Warren was able to keep his feet without a tremor.

Some ran on before, and began gathering wood, for it was determined to burn the prisoner as a more fearful example of the death that awaited the men who dared interfere with the "institution." Warren was dragged to the foot of the crossroads sign and securely bound; the wood was piled about him. The circle was not built as high as his knees, for a slow fire steadily increased, would prolong the enjoyment. Thomson himself carried the brand to light the pile. His eyes met Warren's as he knelt with the blazing pine. Not a word passed between them. A horrible and engrossing interest kept every eve on the glowing light. Presently the barrier of flame began to rise. A thousand voiced cry of brutal triumph arose—not to the skies, so vile a thing could never find the heavenly blue; it must have fallen to the regions of the lost.

They who speak or think lightly of a mob have never heard its voice nor seen its horrible work.

XI

From the town came the ringing of bells set in motion when the party landed, still startling the night with their brazen clamor. The wildest excitement prevailed—armed riders dashed recklessly up and down in front of the place of execution, yelling, cursing, threatening.

The most trivial incidents accompany the progress of death. Warren noticed the faint light of the morning chasing away the stars. His keen sight lost not one change in the landscape. Children were in the crowd worming their way among the promiscuous legs and arms in the endeavor to gain a peep at the proceedings; one wee tot had fallen over backwards felled by the unexpected movement of the particular legs that obstructed his view. Warren was conscious of a deep sense of pity for the infants whom ignorance tortured from childhood's simple holiness as cruelly as the mob was about to torture him. There came to him then a realizing sense of all the Immortal Son must have suffered on His way to Golgotha to die a shameful death through the ignorance and cruelty of a heartless world. If the story of the crucifixion had at times presented difficuties to an inquiring, analytical mind, this experience cleared away the shadows and the application of the story of the Redeemer came to him as a live coal from the altar of Infinite Truth.

The crew of the ferry-boat was hurrying forward with the wood stored aboard for the fires under the boilers; sounds of chopping came to his ears above the yells and shouts of the mob, and reverberated along the edges of the sky. Men were chopping fuel, others ran with armloads of it to build around the stake which had the festive air of a Maypole. Another group thought that the spectacle needed illumination at its beginning and were heaping fuel on a camp-fire, and its crackle could be heard almost as far as its light reached.

Men swaggered about the vast bluster and deep curses, howling for the sacrifice, quenching their thirst and fanning their fury anew at a temporary bar in the wagon where an enterprising individual was dispensing drinks to the crowd at a nominal price.

The sky overhead began to assume a roseate tinge. Swarming figures became more and more distinct. The fragrant wind encroaching from the woods, bringing its sweet odors, swept the smoke sidewise like an inverted curtain.

All was ready. There came a deafening cheer when Thomson moved pompously forward and with a theatrical gesture applied the torch; then followed silence deep and breathless as they waited to gloat over the victim's first awful shriek of agony.

The flames rose. Warren ground his teeth, determined to die and make no moan to please and gratify the crowd. The sweat of physical anguish and faintness moved in drops on his forehead. His face was distinctly visible in the fierce glare. His arms were bound down against his sides, the wounded one causing him frightful torture. His shirt was open at the throat, showing the ivory firmness of his chest and the beating pulse in the white brawn. As the flames gathered headway the sky grew brighter and the shadows melted away; the crowing of cocks came faintly, above the horrid din, borne on the young morning air.

Suddenly off to the right came the sound of galloping hoofs. So imperative was the clatter that the attention of the crowd was forced for a moment from the victim at the stake.

On, on swept the riders in mad haste to the scene of torture, now distinctly visible through the cloud of dust that had at first partially concealed them from view; and now they rose in their stirrups shouting and waving their hats as if in warning. The fiends about the funeral pile made way for the cavalcade which was headed by Colonel Titus. All the party wore the uniform of State constables. "Halt!" cried the Colonel as he sprang from his horse at the edge of the crowd and cleared the open space immediately in front of the signpost at one bound, followed by his companions. The crowd fell back respectfully. He and his men kicked the blazing wood from the stake, and scattered it with hands and feet as far as they could throw it. His own clothing smoked, and his face flamed with the exertion The colonel cut Warren's bonds, while his men continued to stamp out the fire. The crowd watched them in sullen silence.

"Fools!" he shouted, when at length the fire's headway was subdued, "what are you doing?"

"Burning a nigger-thief," shouted Gideon Holmes in reply.

"None of your monkeyin', Bill Thomson; speak up. You had charge of this affair," said Titus, not deigning to notice Holmes. Bill answered with a vile oath.

The crowd stood about in curious clusters. As the fire died down, the dawn became more pronounced. The brutal carnival seemed about to die out with the darkness as quickly as it had arisen.

"And you have been allowing your men to do that which will put us in the power of every Northern mudsill of an abolitionist, and eventually turn the tide which is now in our favor, against us!" The Colonel wheeled about and faced Thomson. "Was this the understanding when you started on the expedition?"

Bill still stood sullen-faced and silent before his accuser.

"Have we not jails strong enough to hold prisoners?" Titus asked, significantly.

"Dead men tell no tales," declared Thomson, with a long look into his questioner's eyes.

"True," returned the Colonel with an answering glance. "But let all things be done in decency and order and according to the process of law. This man ain't no army. There warn't no need of your raisin' and chasin' and burnin' him like a parcel of idiots."

"'Pears to me you're d— finicky 'bout law an' all that jes' this particular time," sneered Bill, with an evil leer on his face.

The Colonel eyed him keenly while a look of disgust spread slowly over his speaking face.

"Thomson, I gave you credit for having more sense. This man is a British subject. How are we to impress the world with our fair and impartial dealing with all mankind, and the slavery question in particular, if you and a lot more hotheaded galoots go to work and call us liars by breaking the slate?"

There were murmurs of approval from the crowd.

"Fac' is thar's nothin' fer us to do but to light out, ain't that the idee, Colonel?" asked Jim Murphy.

"That's the idea, Murphy; burn the wind the whole caboodle of you!" The crowd began to disperse slowly.

"All very good," broke in Thomson with a swagger. "I'll take mine without the law. I'd ruther stay right here and carry out the programme, it'd be more satisfactory to the boys in the long run. Law is a delusion, as the poet says, an' a snare. We git plenty o' law an' no jestice. S'pose the law lets the prisoner go free? You'll be a real pop'lar candidate fer Missouri's next gov'ner."

"No fear of that in this State," replied the Colonel with an ugly, brutal look that caused a shudder to creep over Warren who was surrounded by the constables. So full of malice were the tone and look that all signs of the polished elderly gentleman and doting father were lost, and one felt that this man could perpetrate any crime, however foul. In spite of the quiet tones the Colonel's blood was at boiling point because of Thomson's stubborness. Titus turned to the constables: "Gentlemen, secure the prisoner. Thomson, fall in there and lend a hand; be quick about it. We've had too much of your fool talk a'ready. When I give my men an order, I 'low for them to obey me right up to the chalk mark."

Bill gave him a long look and without a word mounted his horse, and rode away—not with the troop.

The constables instantly obeyed the Colonel's order, and in a second Warren was lifted to the floor of the wagon and driven rapidly toward the jail.

XII

In the Brown camp the great family of fugitives dwelt together in guileless and trusting brotherhood under the patriarchal care of Captain Brown, who daily praised the Eternal Sire, and one soul of harmony and love was infused into each individual dweller.

John Brown was a man of deep religious convictions; but mingled with austerity were perfect gentleness and self-renunciation which inspired love in every breast. But amid the self-denying calmness of his deportment, those who looked deeply into his eyes might discern some cast of that quiet and determined courage which faced his enemies in later years before the Virginia tribunal where, threatened with an ignominious death, he made the unmoved reply—"I am about God's work; He will take care of me."

The fugitive slaves who came in fear and trembling were strengthened and improved by contact with the free, strong spirit of their rescuer and his associate helpers of proscribed Free Staters.

Weeks must elapse, perhaps, before a force of sufficient strength could be organized to protect the fugitives on their perilous trip to Canada. In the interval Captain Brown was pastor, guide and counsellor. The instruction of youth he considered one of the most sacred departments of his office, so it happened that in the camp the ex-slave received his first lessons in the true principles of home-building and the responsibility of freedom. There he first heard God's commands in the words of Holy Writ:

"He hath made of one blood all the nations of the earth."

"There is no respect of persons with God."

"Do to another as you would that another should do to you."

"Remember those in bonds as bound with them."

In the field the negro learned for the first time in his life the sweetness of requited toil together with the manliness of self-defence, for the musket was companion of the implements of rural toil, as in the days of Nehemiah the restorers of Jerusalem wrought "every man with one hand upon the wall and with the other held his spear, having his sword girded by his side;" and also that it was better to die than to live a coward and a slave.

Winona was quartered at the Brown domicile. With her story and her beauty she was an object of uncommon interest to all in the camp.

She became Captain Brown's special care and the rugged Puritan unbent to spoil and pet the "pretty squaw," as he delighted to call her.

And to Winona all the land had changed. The red-golden light that rested upon it near the evening hour was now as the light of heaven. The soft breezes that murmured through the trees and touched her cheek so gently, seemed to whisper, "Peace and rest. Peace and rest once again. Be not cast down."

There was the touch of sympathy and comfort in the rugged Captain's hand pressed upon her short-cropped curls. It gave her courage and robbed her heart of its cold desolation. She felt she was no longer alone; heaven, in her dire need, had sent her this good man, upon whom she might rely, in whom she could trust. Though much older, Captain Brown reminded her of her father, and her quiet childhood dependent upon him for constant companionship had given her a liking for elderly people, and she treated Captain Brown with a reverential respect that at once won his confidence and affection.

But there was not a day nor an hour that she did not think of Maxwell. She craved for news of his safety. When the daily routine of work was ended, the girl would steal into the woods which skirted the camp and climb to a seat on the high rocks watching eastward and westward for some sign of the young Englishman's return.

Some impulse of the wild things among whom she had lived drove her to a hole in under the bluff. It was necessary to descend to find it. Presently she was in a tunnel which led into a cavern. She made herself a divan of dried moss and flung herself down at full length to think. Time's divisions were lost on those days when the girl felt that she neglected no duty by hiding herself in her nook. She had come upon the eternal now as she lay in a sweet stupor until forced to arouse herself. She stared across the space that divided Maxwell from her with all the strength of her inner consciousness. That light which falls on the spot where one's loved one stands, leaving the rest of the landscape in twilight, now rested about him. With rapture she saw again the hopeless passion in Warren's eyes when he left her. Her hands and feet were cold, her muscles knotted, her face white with the force of the cry that she projected through space, "Come back to me!"

And this young creature just escaped from cruel bondage gave not a thought to the difficulties of her position. In the primal life she had led there had entered not a thought of racial or social barriers. The woods calmed her, their grays and greens and interlacing density of stems, and their whisper of a secret that has lasted from the foundation of the world, replacing her fever with the calmness of hope. In the midst of her sweet perplexity came another trouble.

Judah's capabilities were discovered very soon by Captain Brown and his sons, and he was appointed special aid and scout to the camp. Nothing could have suited him better. All day he scoured the woods, following the trail of parties of desperadoes or bringing in the fruits of the line or rifle to supply the needs in fish or meat. Twice he saved them from surprise by bands of marauders, and soon his name was heralded with that of Brown as a brave and fearless man bold to recklessness.

Sometimes Winona accompanied him on his trips when not fraught with much danger; once he tried to broach the subject nearest his heart, but a movement on her part—the carriage of the head, a queenly gesture—served to intimidate him and forced back the words.

The next night he passed in the woods, with his rifle, on a bed of leaves, studying over the problem of his life. "Why should I hesitate? We are of the same condition in life in the eyes of the world." But even while the thought was in his mind he knew that what he desired could never be. Unconsciously he was groping for the solution of the great question of social equality.

But is there such a thing as social equality? There is such a thing as the affinity of souls, congenial spirits, and good fellowship; but social equality does not exist because it is an artificial barrier which nature is constantly putting at naught by the most incongruous happenings. Who is my social equal? He whose society affords the greatest pleasure, whose tastes are congenial, and who is my brother in the spirit of the scriptural text, be he white or black, bond or free, rich or poor.

The next morning Judah built a fire in a deep ravine to cook his breakfast, and then scattered the embers that the smoke should give no sign.

All the morning he waited near her favorite haunts determined to speak out the thoughts that filled his mind. He began to fear at last that she was not coming. A little noise down the path reached his ear. In a moment he could hear slow foot-falls, and the figure of the girl parted the bushes, which closed behind her as she passed through them. She passed quite near him, walking slowly; she was very pale; her face bore traces of mental suffering. For a moment she stood there, listless, and Judah watched her with hungry eyes at a loss what to do. The sun lighted her hair, and in the upturned eyes he saw the shimmer of tears. "Winona!" He couldn't help it. The low cry broke from his lips like a groan; the next instant the girl faced him. She looked with quick wonder at the dark face with its mute appeal. Then a sudden spasm caught her throat, and left her body rigid, her hands shut, and her eyes dry and hard—she knew, instinctively, what he suffered.

"Oh, Judah! Hav'n't we been through enough without this?"

The girl trembling at the knees sank to a seat on the rocks, and folding her arms across her knees, laid her forehead against them.

"I'm going away, Winona, as soon as you are safe in Canada," he went on after a little pause. "It'll be pretty hard to leave you, but I want you to know how I've been thinking about you and sorrowing over your sorrow and hoping that you might get over your liking for Maxwell, seeing that you're only a slip of a girl, and think of me as the one who would die for you and ought naturally to care for your wants—" He spoke hesitatingly; there was a question in his last words, but the girl shook her head sadly, her tears falling to the ground. Her sorrow gave way in a great sob now, and he turned in sharp remorse and stood quite near her.

"Don't cry, Winona," he said. "I'm sorry for you and myself and Maxwell. It's this cursed slavery that's to blame. If your father had lived all this would never have happened."

"I am sorry—so very sorry! But you see, Judah, it cannot be; I have no love to give."

Judah stood beside her, his heart bursting with suppressed emotion. The bitter words would break from his lips.

"The white man gets it all—all!"

"Do you forget all that Mr. Maxwell has done for us, Judah, that you condemn him so bitterly? It is not like you—you who are generally so generous and true-hearted. He knows not of my love and will never know. Is he to blame?"

"You are right—you are right! But how is a man to distinguish between right and wrong? What moral responsibility rests upon him from whom all good things are taken? Answer me that."

They were walking now toward the camp; the shadowy trees tossed their arms in the twilight and the stars came out one by one in the sky. Only the silent tears of the girl at his side gave answer to his question.

A month had passed since the fugitives had reached the camp. Captain Brown eagerly awaited the return of Warren with Parson Steward to help them on the trip to Canada.

The wild flowers swayed above their counterfeits in every gurgling stream; the scent of wild grapes was in the air; the cliffs and rocks blossomed with purple and white and pink blooms. The birds sang and the bees droned in the woods on the morning when, wild and dishevelled, Parson Steward's wife and two children found their way into the Brown camp.

"My heavenly marster!" shrieked the widow in incoherent wailing. "The Rangers done caught my husband and shot him; they've carried the young Englishman to jail. What will become of me and my poor children?"

No one slept that night when the fate of the two gallant men was known, and the oaths uttered were not loud but deep.

Captain Brown, like a prophet of old, drew his spare form erect. Lightning flashed from his mild eyes and sword-thrusts fell from his tongue.

Then and there a rescue party was planned to take Warren out of the hands of the Philistines. The only trouble was to spy out the jail where he was confined; but there seemed little hope of success, for it appeared that since his trial Warren had disappeared from public view, and the Pro-Slavery men were very reticent. Ebenezer Maybee volunteered to secure the desired information.

As was the fashion in those days, the women listened but did not intrude their opinions upon the men, being engaged in performing the part of Good Samaritan to the widow and orphans. But long after the meeting had broken up Winona crept into the woods not to weep, but to think. She leaned against a tree and her hopeless eyes gazed down the darkening aisles; she prayed: "Help me to help save him!"

In the morning she sought an interview with Captain Brown.

XIII

Meanwhile the wagon containing Maxwell and surrounded by constables stopped at the door of a frame building in the heart of the city, and with blows and threats Warren was pushed and dragged into a bare room and told that it was his quarters until business hours. The passageway and room were filled with a motley crowd and the vilest epithets were hurled after him. Presently a man came in with a lighted candle, seized his sound arm and looked him over from head to foot in the most insulting manner. Warren shook him off and asked him if he called himself a man to so insult a wounded stranger.

"Don't you dare speak to a white man except to answer questions, you d—d nigger-thief!"

"I shall appeal to the British consul for protection from your vile insults," said Warren in desperation. "It will cost your government dear for tonight's business."

"If you get the chance to complain," laughed the ruffian. "By G—d! you've got to die today, and by this revolver," he continued, drawing his weapon and brandishing it fiercely. He was applauded by the crowd, and it looked as if Warren were doomed when constables arriving saved further trouble. Maxwell felt that he would almost rather have been burned, than to endure the insults of such brutes.

After much entreaty, he succeeded in getting some water, but nothing more, though almost famished. Burning with fever from his wound and his contact with the funeral pile, and fainting for want of nourishment, not having tasted food since the morning before, the young man felt unable to sustain many more shocks to his system.

At length, without medical attendance, the crowd left him to get such sleep as he might upon the bare floor, without bed or covering of any kind. Retreating to a corner of the room, seated upon the floor with his back to the wall, Warren passed the hours silent and motionless.

He meditated upon his position in the heart of a hostile country although supposed to advocate and champion the most advanced ideas of liberty and human rights. What a travesty the American government was on the noblest principles! Bah! it made him heartsick. He had listened to the tales of Maybee and Steward as exaggerations; he had not believed such scenes as he had just passed through, possible in a civilized land. The words of the man who had just taunted him: "If you get the chance to complain," haunted him.

If he were not allowed to communicate with his consul, then, indeed, hope was dead. What would be his fate? The misery in store for him appalled him. And Winona—! He dared not allow his thoughts to dwell upon her. That way madness lay. So the long hours dragged out their weary length.

At eight o'clock breakfast was brought to him, and when he had begun to despair of receiving medical aid, a doctor came in and dressed his wounded arm. After this, he was marched through the streets to a room in the hotel where he was placed before the glass doors—much as is a wild beast caged in a menagerie. His reception was demoniacal. Everybody was out. Again, while en route to the seat of Justice, he endured the ignominy of oaths, yells and missiles; again the air resounded with cries of "Give him hemp!" "The rope is ready!" And so they arrived at the Court House.

The large unfinished room was filled to overflowing with the unwashed Democracy of Missouri—a roof with bare brick walls and open rafters overhead, from which hung down directly above the prisoner three new ropes with the hangman's knot at the end of each. Fierce faces, rough and dirty, with the inevitable pipe, or tobacco saliva marking the corners of the mouth, filled in the picture, while a running accompaniment of the strongest and vilest oaths ears ever heard suggested all the horrors of mob violence. The court proceeded with its farcical mockery of justice. Warren undertook to act as his own counsel, and drew up the following protest:

I, the undersigned, a British subject, do hereby protest against every step taken thus far by the State of Missouri in this case; declaring that my rights as a British subject have been infamously violated and trampled upon.

Warren Maxwell

This he handed to the magistrate, who, without giving it any attention, threw it one side.

Colonel Titus and Bill Thomson were the principal witnesses against him. The Colonel told how basely the young man had betrayed his hospitality by aiding his slaves, Winona and Judah, to escape.

Thomson testified to the fact that the prisoner consorted with abolitionists of the John Brown stripe, being, when captured, in company with "fighting Steward," a red-handed criminal.

The case was given to the jury who returned a verdict of "guilty," without leaving their seats. Then followed the judge's charge and sentence:

"Warren Maxwell—It is my duty to announce to you the decision of this court as a penalty for the crime you have committed. You have been guilty of aiding slaves to run away and depart from their master's service; and now, for it you are to die!

"'Remember now thy Creator in the days of my youth,' is the language of inspired wisdom. This comes home appropriately to you in this trying moment. You are young; quite too young to be where you are. If you had remembered your Creator in your past days, you would not now be in a felon's place, to receive a felon's judgment. Still, it is not too late to remember your Creator.

"The sentence of the law is that you be taken to the State prison for one year; and that there you be closely and securely confined until Friday, the 26th day of May next; on which day, between the hours of ten in the forenoon and two in the afternoon, you will be taken to the place of public execution, and there be hanged by the neck till your body be dead. And may God have mercy on your soul!"

Overwhelmed by the mockery of a trial, Warren heard the words of the judge but they carried no meaning to his overwrought senses. He sat in a stupor until hurried by the constables to the carriage that was to convey him to prison.

Days of pain and unconsciousness followed, and when at last consciousness returned, he founded himself in a room sixteen feet square, with a small grated window at each end, through which he could catch a glimpse of the street.

Under the room in which he was confined was another of the same size, used as a lock-up for slaves who were usually put there for safe-keeping while waiting to be sent South. The room had a hole for the stove-pipe of the under room to pass through, but the stove had been removed to accommodate a larger number of prisoners. This left a hole in the floor through which one might communicate with those below. This hole in the floor afforded diversion for the invalid who could observe the full operation of the slave system. Sometimes, too, he could communicate with the slaves or some white prisoner by means of the stove-hole. When all was quiet a note was sent down through the hole, the signal being to punch with the broom-handle.

Many heart-rending scenes were enacted before his sight in the lower room. Infamous outrages were committed upon free men of color whose employment as cooks and stewards on steamers and sailing vessels had brought them within the jurisdiction of the State. Such men were usually taken ashore and sold to the highest bidder. One man who had his free papers on his person, produced them to prove the truth of his story; the official took the papers from him, burned them, and sold him the next week at public auction. Two Negroes were whipped to death rather than acknowledge the men who claimed them as their owners. One horror followed another in the crowded cage where a frightful number of human beings were herded together. They could not sleep; that is to say, forget their misery for one moment. And how hot it was already! The rays of the fierce summer sun of the South seemed to burn and sear Warren's suffering brain and dry up the healthful juices into consuming fever and ultimate madness.

One day he was aroused to greater indignation than usual by hearing heart-rending cries come from the lower room. Hurrying to the stove-hole he gazed one moment and then fell fainting with terror and nausea upon the floor. He had seen a Negro undergoing the shameful outrage, so denounced in the Scriptures, and which must not be described in the interests of decency and humanity.

That night Maxwell was again ill—delirious—requiring the care of two physicians and a slave who was detailed to nurse him.

Unhappily we tell no tale of fiction. We have long felt that the mere arm of restraint is but a temporary expedient for the remedy, but not the prevention, of cruelty and crime. If Christianity, Mohammedanism, or even Buddhism, did exercise the gentle and humanizing influence that is claimed for them, these horrors would cease now that actual slavery has been banished from our land; because, as religion is the most universal and potent source of influence upon a nation's action, so it must mould to some extent its general characteristics and individual opinions. Until we can find a religion that will give the people individually and practically an impetus to humane and unselfish dealing with each other, look to see outward forms change, but never look to see the spirit which hates and persecutes that which it no longer dare enslave, changed by any other influence than a change of heart and spirit.

The liberties of a people are not to be violated but with the wrath of God. Indeed, we tremble for our country when we reflect that God is just; that His justice cannot sleep forever; that considering natural means only, a revolution of the wheel of Fortune, an exchange of situation is among the possibilities.

All through the long delirium of pain and weariness Warren was conscious of the tender care of his nurse. To the sick man the wearing, jarring sound of voices rising out of a black pit was ever present and unbearable. At times they were to him the cries of the ruffians who pursued him to the stake; the vengeance of the mob seemed to fill the little room and charge the atmosphere with horror. Again it was the sound of the pistol shot that killed Parson Steward, and the patient would shudder at the blood everywhere—on shirts, hands and faces, and splashing the sides of the bare walls; or it was the flames mounting higher and higher, licking his body with hungry tongues, or it was the rushing of whirling waters against the vessel's side as he swung Winona over the side of "Crescent."

Finally, as he lay tossing and tormented with these phantom terrors in his eyes and ears, the sound died away into the soft hush of a tender voice stilling the tumult.

The nurse was a young mulatto known as Allen Pinks. The boy had been cook and head-waiter on board a steamboat on the Missouri river. He had been paid off, according to his story, at St. Joseph. From there he had started for Leavenworth, walking down the Missouri bank of the river with a white man. At the ferry he was stopped on suspicion of being a fugitive slave and lodged in the calaboose; from there he was removed to the State prison until the time of sale. He had made himself very useful about the jail doing chores and nursing the sick, for which he seemed to have a particular vocation. Very soon Allen Pinks was a great favorite and allowed many privileges; hearing of Maxwell's illness he asked to be allowed to nurse him, and the jailer was more than glad to have him do it.

At last there came a day when the prisoner's wild wide eyes were closed, and the boy rose from his long watch by the side of the rude cot bed with hope in his heart. He stood, for a second, looking down upon the calm face of the sleeper with a sorrowful smile on his dark brown face. "Fast asleep at last," he whispered. "I must go see to his broth."

Just then a hideous yell arose from the room below. With a light bound the lad reached the stove-hole.

"Hush your noise!" he called in a low tone of authority. "Haven't I told you he must sleep?"

"Got a black boss dis time," came up from the hole in a gruff voice, followed by a low laugh.

"He's asleep now, and everything depends on his waking up right. But you set up a howl that would wake the dead!"

"Howl? dat's singing," came again from the hole in the floor.

"Well, keep your singing to yourself."

The noise subsided, and the young nurse turned again to his patient.

He stood for some moments gazing down on the Saxon face so pitifully thin and delicate. The brow did not frown nor the lips quiver; no movement of the muscles betrayed the hopeless despair of the sleeper's heart. The cot gave a creak and a rustle. The nurse was leaning one hand on the edge of the miserable pallet bed bending over the sick man. There was a light touch on his hair; a tear fell on his cheek; the nurse had kissed the patient!

When the door had closed behind the lad, Warren opened his eyes in full consciousness; and as he brushed the tear from his face, there came a puzzled look into his eyes.

Presently Allen returned with the soup and found him awake. His features lighted up with intelligence and sympathy on making the discovery, and finding him free from fever.

"Well, how are you getting on, sir?" he asked in the softest of musical voices, and feeling Warren's pulse, as he seated himself on a stool at the bedside.

"Who are you? Haven't I met you somewhere? Your voice has a familiar sound."

"I fancy you don't know me," replied Allen with a smile.

"You've saved my life."

"That's a subject we won't speak of just now, sir; you must be very quiet."

"Oh, to be well and free once more!" broke in a plaintive tone from the invalid.

"If you will only remain quiet and easy in your mind, there's no doubt all may yet be well," replied the boy with significant emphasis as he held Warren's eye a second with a meaning gaze.

Many questions came crowding to Warren's lips; but Allen silenced him firmly and gently.

PAULINE E. HOPKINS

"Bye and bye, sir, I will tell you all I can, but you must drink this broth now and sleep."

Warren drank the soup and with a feeling of peace new to him, turned his face to the wall and slept.

One week longer Warren lay on his rude bed. Allen refused to talk but told him that he had no cause for anxiety.

Maxwell was fascinated by his nurse; he thought him the prettiest specimen of boyhood he had ever met. The delicate brown features were faultless in outline; the closely cropped black hair was like velvet in its smoothness. He could not shake off the idea that somewhere he had known the lad before in his life. At times this familiarity manifested itself in the tones of the voice soft and low as a woman's, then again it was in the carriage of the head or the flash of the beautiful large dark eyes. It was an evasive but haunting memory.

One day Allen said: "Mr. Maxwell, I'm not to tend you any longer after this week. I'm to be sold."

"Sold!" exclaimed Warren in dismay.

Allen nodded. "It's getting too hot for me, and I'm going to run for it."

"What shall I do without you?" said Warren with a sick feeling of despair at his heart.

"Have you no hope of escape? Have you never thought of being rescued?" asked the lad in a whisper with a cautious motion of the hand toward the door.

"Oh, Allen!" faltered Warren in speechless joy.

The lad gave him time to recover himself a bit; then, after glancing around the corridor to see that no one was listening, returned to his patient.

"I am here in the interest of your friends! I leave tonight. Tomorrow you will receive a communication from your friends. We must hasten our plans for Thomson is expected on a visit here any day."

"Go on; go on; tell me what to do."

"There is nothing for you to do but to be ready at a moment's notice. The plans are all well laid, and will be successful, unless Thomson should upset us."

"I fear that man," replied Warren with a shudder.

"You certainly have good reason," said Allen. "But he does not reside in this vicinity and we may be able to avoid him."

"He would be only too happy to wreak his vengeance upon me. Yes, I fear him."

Allen did his best to reassure Warren, and discussed with him the plan of escape as far as he knew it, and concluded by saying:

"I shall not see you again. Keep up your heart. Barring accident, you will soon be free."

At night Allen went as usual to the well to draw the water for supper, and did not return. The alarm was given, but no trace of the boy was found.

XIV

The next morning dawned hot and sultry; all day there were signs of a thunder storm.

Towards dark the door of Warren's cell opened and a young man with a carpet bag, apparently in a great hurry to catch a train, and accompanied by the jailer, came to the grated door and informed Warren that he had been requested by the British consul at New York, who had heard of his case, to see him and to say to him that his case would be investigated and all done that could be done, and that he would hear from the consul in person in a few days.

The visitor was quite curious about the hall, looking around a great deal, and as he stood with his back to the grated door talking to the jailer, whose attention he directed to some means of ventilation outside, Warren saw a small slip of paper in the hand which he held behind him, and took it.

When he was alone again, he unfolded it with trembling fingers. It contained the words: "Be ready at midnight." Scarcely had he recovered from the excitement which the note caused him, when he heard footsteps and voices again approaching his cell and in a few seconds the sallow, uncanny face of Bill Thomson was framed in the doorway.

"It seems to me, you fellows ain't as careful as you might be. Had a visitor sent by the British consul, did he? Well that won't save his neck. I tell you, Bub," he said, directly addressing the prisoner, "saltpetre won't save you. You've got to go, by G—d. D—n these newspaper men I say; a set of ornery skunks; meddling with business that don't consarn 'em. But they don't euchre me this deal."

Warren made no answer, and in a short time the visitor passed on. With senses strained to their utmost tension, he watched the shades of night envelope the landscape. He listened to the striking of the clock in the corridor outside his cell, tolling the lagging hours, with beating heart. Gradually all sound died away and the hush of night fell upon the earth, broken only by the fury of the storm which now broke scattering destruction in its wake. Far off the river sounded a mimic Niagara as it swelled beyond its boundaries. In the midst of his anxiety the young man noted the strange coincidence of the storms which had attended three critical periods in his history while in America. With this thought in his mind he heard the clock toll off twelve strokes. As the last one died slowly away there came a thundering knock at the outer prison door. It came again, and yet again. He heard a door slam and then the voice of the jailer, "What do you want?"

"We are from Andrew County, with a prisoner we want put in jail for safe keeping."

"Who is he?"

"A notorious horse thief."

"Have you a warrant?"

"No; but it's all right."

"I can't take a man without authority."

"If you don't it will be too bad; he's a desperate character, and we've had hard work to catch him. We'll satisfy you in the morning that it's all right."

The jailer went down and let them in. When they were inside where the light fell upon their faces he started back with the cry:

"It's Allen Pinks!"

The men with him were Maybee and old John Brown.

"Yes, Mr. Owens," said Captain Brown grimly, "it's the boy, and it's too late to make a noise. If you resist or give an alarm, you are a dead man. The lower door is guarded, and the jail surrounded by an armed force."

Warren beheld the scene from between the bars of his cell door with anxious heart; even as he looked he saw a dark object pass behind the group and advance along the corridor wall, but his attention was drawn from the shadow as a door opened far down the row and Bill Thomson, fully dressed, faced the group, pistol in hand.

He advanced step by step with his eyes fixed upon the negro lad. The boy involuntarily uttered a cry and covered his face with his hands.

"Well, sir! if it ain't Winona! Looks interestin', Owens, that you couldn't tell a gal dressed up in boys clo's! This strikes me heavy."

Warren standing helpless in his cell saw and heard all, and understood many things that had puzzled him. There are loves and loves; but Warren told himself that the love of the poor forsaken child before him was of the quality which we name celestial. All the beauty and strength of the man, and every endowment of tenderness came upon him there as the power came upon Samson; and he registered a promise before heaven that night.

"Halt!" cried Captain Brown, as Thomson moved a step nearer. "Halt, or you're a dead man!"

"So it is murder you propose to commit?"

"No; we have come in peace, if let alone, to rescue our friend Maxwell. If you interfere with us the worst is your own. Disarm him, Mr. Maybee."

But Thomson aimed his pistol straight at Winona's breast, and cried: "I fire if you come a step nearer."

Warren groaned. "Oh, for a moment's freedom and a good weapon in my hand!"

Suddenly a lurid glare lighted up the hall, and Warren saw a dark shadow creeping in Thomson's rear. Something of an extraordinary nature was about to happen.

"It is Judah! It is Judah!"

It was indeed Judah. He had crept along gradually advancing nearer and nearer, bending almost double in observation; then like a wild beast preparing to pounce upon his prey, he stiffened his powerful muscles, and with a bound sprang upon Thomson, seizing him in an iron grasp, and dragging him backward to the ground with such violence that his pistol from his hand. Placing one foot upon the breast of the prostrate man to prevent him from rising, he picked up the pistol, crying:

"It is between you and me, now. Our roles are reversed. It is you who must die."

He was about to fire, when Captain Brown hastily interfered:

"No, no; it won't do. Spare him!"

"Spare him! For what? To afford him an opportunity to do more mischief? No, No!"

"Let us release Maxwell first and get outside the building then, if you insist upon this thing," said Maybee.

"Quick, then! I will not answer for myself. Your safety is not the only thing to be considered; I must think of myself as well. If I do not kill this man, he will murder me by inches if I fall into his hands, as he has already tried to do. I hate him, I hate him! It is my enemy I would slay, not yours."

XV

With a rapid movement he stooped, placed the barrel of his pistol at Thomson's forehead and—would have pulled the trigger but for the interference of John Brown, who threw himself upon the enraged black and stayed his hand.

"Don't do it; not this time, Judah. I know your feelings, but you'll have another chance, for these fellows will be after us again. There's too much at stake now; we owe Mr. Maxwell something for all he has suffered. Don't do it."

"Yes," chimed in Maybee; "if you let up now, Judah, I'll be tee-totally smashed if I don't lend you a hand and stand by for fair play."

"Why stay my hand? Vengeance is sweet," replied Judah, his dark, glowing eyes fixed in a threatening gaze upon his foe bound and helpless at his feet.

"There is a time for everything, my son. Stay thy hand and fear not; vengeance is mine," said John Brown.

Judah was silent for a moment, but stood as if gathering strength to resist temptation. Finally he said:

"I am the Lord's instrument to kill this man. Promise me that when this villain's life shall lie in the gift of any man in the camp, he shall be given to me as my right, to deal with him as I see fit."

"We promise," broke from Captain Brown and Ebenezer Maybee simultaneously.

Sternly the determined trio, aided by Winona in her boy's attire, secured the officials of the jail and quieted the prisoners. It was hard to resist the entreaties of the slaves confined there, but, after a hurried consultation, it was deemed advisable not to burden themselves with fugitive slaves.

With few words the business of releasing Maxwell was carried forward. When Maybee unlocked the door of Warren's cell with the warden's key, there were tears in his eyes as he beheld the wreck that two months of imprisonment and brutal treatment had made of the stalwart athlete. The burns were not yet healed, and great red scars disfigured his face in spots; he still wore his arm in a sling; starvation, physical weakness and lack of cleanliness had done their worst.

Maybee's heart was too full for words as he folded the emaciated

PAULINE E. HOPKINS

form in his arms, and openly wiped the tears from his eyes; his were the feelings of a father: "This, my son, was dead and is alive again."

"Oh, never m-min' my cryin'! 'Taint nothin'. Some fellers cries easier than others," he muttered as the tears rolled unchecked down his cheeks. Winona was sobbing in company and Judah was feeling strange about the eyes also.

"I never thought to see you again, boys" said Warren solemnly, as he held their warm, friendly hands and felt the clasp of honest friendship. "I understand the slavery question through and through. Experience is a stern teacher."

"Min' my words to you, Maxwell? But God knows I didn't reckon they'd come home to you so awful an' suddint-like. I have never feared for you, my boy, even when things l-looked blackes'; but if you don' fin' Bill Thomson somewhere, some time, an' choke him an' tear his win'pipe to fiddlestrings, you ain't got a drop of British blood in yer whole carcass!"

"Amen!" exclaimed Captain Brown. "Come, boys, time's up."

Judah lifted Maxwell in his strong arms preparatory to carrying him out to the waiting vehicle. He felt all his passionate jealousy die a sudden death as pity and compassion stirred his heart for the sufferings of his rival. "Here is another white man who does not deserve death at a Negro's hands," he told himself.

Winona was silent and constrained in manner. For the first time since she had adopted her strange dress she felt a wave of self-consciousness that rendered her ashamed. She turned mechanically and walked by Judah's side as he bore his almost helpless burden to the wagon, and seated herself beside the driver, still silent.

Warren, reclining on fresh straw in the bottom of the cart, wondered in semi-consciousness at the sweetness of the air dashed in his face with the great gusts of rain, and at his own stupidity in not recognizing Winona; beneath the stain with which she had darkened her own exquisite complexion, he could now plainly trace the linaments that had so charmed him. Then, lulled by the motion of the vehicle and weakened by excitement, he slept the sleep of exhaustion.

Captain Brown had ordered the prisoners placed in Warren's abandoned cell, and, locking the door, took the key with them to clog the movements of pursuers as much as possible; then they passed out, closing and fastening the great outer door and also taking that key with them.

Meanwhile, outside the building, in the most advantageous positions, hidden by the blackness of the night, ten stalwart Free-State men had waited with impatience the return of Captain Brown and his companions.

The storm favored the rescuing party; not a sound disturbed their watch but the awful peals of thunder reverberating over the land in solemn majesty. Torrents of rain drenched them to the skin, but inured to hardships they rejoiced in the favor which the storm bestowed.

As the rescuers issued from beneath the jail's shadow, Judah bearing Warren in his arms, the guard gathered silently about the wagon in silent congratulation that thus far they had been successful; then mounting their waiting horses, the whole party rode as fast as possible toward the river.

As dawn approached the storm cleared, and the first faint streaks of light that appeared in the east were tinged with the sun-god's brilliant hues. By this time our party had reached the riverbanks, and Warren was removed to the boat, the horses and wagon being returned to the friendly settlers who had loaned them, and in the sweet freshness of the dawn, strong arms propelled the boat toward the Kansas shore.

On the Kansas side fresh horses awaited them and another wagon. Friends met them at short intervals along the route, the people turning out en masse in an ovation to the rescuers and rescued, for Maxwell's story was known in every village and town throughout the country. They stopped at a comfortable farmhouse for breakfast, and Warren was allowed the luxury of a bath and given clean though coarse clothing.

They travelled all day and night, seeming not to feel fatigue but bent upon distancing a pursuing party, finding fresh horses at intervals, and food in abundance. Thus the settlers exemplified in kind acts the sympathy that upheld the common cause of human rights for all mankind.

The journey to the Brown camp was not a short one, and burdened with an invalid, it added to the length of time necessary to make the trip. Every step, too, was fraught with danger, but not a murmur came from the men who with stern faces and senses alert cautiously picked their way to safety. It was still twenty miles across country as the crow flies, after three days of swift travelling; the meandering of the road added five more. Then there was a barrier of foothills, and finally the mountains which lifted themselves abruptly out of the flat rolling surface surrounding them.

There might be marauding parties hiding in the brush and thickets, and for aught the horsemen knew, the stacks of hay and fodder that rose like huge monuments on every side, out of the twilight gloom surrounding the lonely farms, might conceal dozens of their foes. The nights were wearing for they never knew quite how the situation was going to develop.

Most of the time Warren was in a semi-conscious state exciting fears of a return of fever and delirium. The sight of guns and the constant talk of the battle yet to come had a depressing effect upon the invalid; they gave a sinister effect to his freedom. Soon the smiling sunlit valley they were entering became to his disordered fancy a return into the dangers and sufferings of a Missouri prison.

Much to Captain Brown's relief, the late afternoon found them in the pleasant hollow two miles distant from the camp, and night gave them safety within the shadow of the great hills.

XVI

The physical shock to Maxwell's system had worked no lasting harm to his constitution. Freedom, cleanliness and nourishing food were magical in their effects, and a week after his rescue found him up and about gradually joining in the duties of the camp.

And what an experience it was to this young, tenderly nurtured aristocrat! It was his function to watch the shifting panorama of defiance to despotism as outlined in the daily lives of the patriotic abolitionists with whom his lot was now cast. He lived in an atmosphere of suspicion, for to be identified with John Brown was a forfeit of one's life; a price was on the head of every individual associated with him. Yet with all the discouraging aspects of the cause these men had espoused, scarcely a day went by that did not bring news of the movement of the enemy, sent by some friendly well-wisher, or a token of good feeling in the form of much needed supplies, and even delicacies for the sick.

The menace of impending danger, however, hung over them constantly. The very ground was honey-combed with intrigue set on foot by resolute and determined Southerners who vowed to crush out all opposition and make the institution of slavery national, and with this determination conspiracies of every kind were abroad to circumvent the North and its agents, of whom the Kansas pro-slavery men were the most belligerent, in the growing desire of that section to make freedom universal within the borders of the United States. He saw plainly that the nation was fast approaching an alarming crisis in its affairs, and, by contrast with the arguments and attitude of the South, that the weight of principle was with the North where the people had been alarmingly docile and conservative. The efforts, in Congress, and in pro-slavery political conventions, were but an aggravation, and not satisfactory to either side, adding fuel to the flame that was making terrible inroads upon the public peace.

The Brown men were restless because of enforced inactivity, for all felt a blow was impending, marvelling that it was so long delayed, and anxious to force an issue—anything was better than uncertainty—for the lengthened time of waiting was a terrible strain upon the nerves.

Captain Brown sought the company of Maxwell frequently, conversing freely of his hopes and fears. The young man was greatly impressed with the clearness and value of his knowledge of military tactics. He was familiar with all the great battles of ancient and modern times; had visited every noted battlefield of old Europe and carefully sketched plans of the operations and positions of the opposing forces. These maps were a source of delight to the old man who went over them with Warren, explaining with great enthusiasm the intricacies of the manœuvres. During this intimacy, Captain Brown revealed to his guest his own great scheme for an insurrection among the slaves—an uprising of such magnitude that it should once and for all time settle the question of slavery.

Maxwell promised money and ammunition and arms, but his heart was heavy as he listened to plans and purposes that had been long in maturing, brooded over silently and secretly, with much earnest thought, and under a solemn sense of religious duty. What would be the fate of the band of hero-martyrs who would dash themselves to bloody death under the inspired influence of their intrepid leader? The prison walls would shake from summit to foundation, and wild alarm would fill every tyrant heart in all the South, of this he had no doubt, but would the effort be crowned with success? It was hardly possible.

Summer was advancing ever deeper in dust. The sky was tarnishing with haze. The sunsets longer in burning out in the west, in tragic colors. Scouts were continually posting back and forth. Warren had promised himself while in prison never to complain of the dispensations of Providence should he live to enjoy freedom again; but at the end of the second week of convalescence he was imploring to be allowed to join the scouting parties of skirmishers. The stir of the camp fired his blood; he was devoured by anxiety to be among the busy people of the world once more, to know what events had transpired in his absence and how the world had wagged along without his help, forgetting that a vacuum is quickly filled and we are soon forgotten.

"The sooner I get out of this the better, Maybee," he exclaimed one day, rousing himself from painful memories of home and his failure to accomplish the mission he had set out so confidently to perform. "I want to get home!"

"Jest so," replied Maybee, with ready sarcasm. "We'll start tomorrow morning on foot."

"No—you know what I mean. I want to—"

"Oh, yes, cert'nly; jest so. We might, ef you're in a great hurry, start this evenin'. The Rangers are all over the place between here an' civilization, but we won't stop for that, for with a strong fightin' man like you fer a companion there'd be nothin' to fear—about gittin' a through ticket to glory this week."

"Cease jesting, Maybee! What I want is to make every hour tell upon the work of getting well—not only on my own account, but—we owe that poor girl something."

"Hem!" grunted Maybee, shooting the young man a keen look under which he colored slightly. "That's right; always keep the weaker vessel in yer mem'ry; trust in the Lord and keep yer powder dry, as our friend Brown'd say. And that remin's me of "Tarius up home. 'Tarius got religion and when the day came roun' fer the baptism' it was a January blizzard, although well along in the month of April. 'Tarius ain't fond of cold weather no how, and he didn't show up along with the other candidates. Next day the minister came up to look after 'Tarius. 'Don' ye trus' in de Lawd, brother?' says the minister. 'Yes, brother,' says Tarius, 'I trust pintedly in de Lawd; but I ain't gwine fool wif God!' That's my advice to you, Maxwell; don't you fool with Providence; jest let well-enough alone."

The next afternoon Mr. Maybee came rushing back to the cabin which was their mutual home.

"Well, young feller, we're in fer it, an' no mistake. You'll git fightin' a-plenty before forty-eight hours."

"What's it?" queried Maxwell languidly, "another false alarm?"

"No, by gosh; it's the real thing this time. The Rangers are at Carlton's. You remember hearin' Parson Steward speak of Reynolds don' you?" Maxwell nodded.

"He's come up to camp an' brought Brown the news."

"How soon will they get here?"

"Cayn't tell; maybe tomorrow an' perhaps not before nex' week; but it's boun' to come. Dog my cats, if I'm sorry. I fairly itch to git my hands on the onery cusses that killed the parson."

"Anything is better than waiting; it takes the life out of a man. I shall not feel safe until I get my feet on British soil once more. God being my helper, Maybee, I'll never set foot on the soil of the 'greatest Republic on earth' again," he finished earnestly.

Mr. Maybee chuckled.

"Convinced are you? They used ter tell me when I was a little shaver that the proof of the puddin' was in swallerin' the bag—that is, pervidin' it was a biled puddin'. I'll 'low them varmints heat you pretty hot, but there's nothin so convincin' as ex-perience. I might a talked to you fer forty days an' nights, wastin' my breath fer nothin', an' you'd a said to yourself 'Maybee's stretchin' it; 'taint quarter so bad as he makes out;' but jest as soon as they git to work on your anatermy yer fin' out that Maybee was mild by comparison. The South's a horned hornet on the 'nigger' question. Time n'r tide, n'r God A'mighty aint goin' to change 'em this week."

"Well, I'm ready for them; I'm feeling decidedly fit," replied Maxwell.

"Good. Reynolds left you a message, a sort of warning. Thomson says the nex' time he gits you he'll fix you, law or no law; he's goin' to flog you first like a nigger, an' then burn you an' send your ashes to your folks in England in a chiny vase. How's that strike you?"

"He will if he's lucky; but I have my doubts."

Maybee gazed at him in silent admiration a moment before he said: "British grit a plenty in you, by thunder; that's the talk."

Preparations immediately went forward in the camp for meeting the enemy. Winona's cave on the mountainside was to be stored with provision, ammunition and all other necessaries. The men worked all night in detachments, watch and watch.

Warren had seen very little of Winona; she kept with the women.

Thinking of the coming conflict, Warren climbed the slope leading to the top of the highest peak, and established himself there as a lookout. It was near the cave in which supplies were being stored, and where the women and children would find a refuge. Presently he saw Winona loitering up the hillside with downcast eyes. As she drew near, the magnetism of his gaze compelled her glance to seek his face. She started, and would have turned back but Warren called out in a kindly voice not in the least alarming:

"Come, see this fine sweep of country. We cannot be surprised."

The sudden blush that had suffused her cheek at sight of him died out, leaving her serious and calm. The last few days she had thawed somewhat out of her coldness, for care could not live with youth and gaicty and the high-tide of summer weather, and the propinquity, morning, noon and night, of the society of the well-beloved one.

More and more Warren felt toward her as to a darling, irresistible child, and sometimes as to a young goddess far beyond him, as he realized how pure and sweet the inner life of this childwoman. The noisome things that creep and crawl about the life of the bond chattel had fallen away from her. She was unique: a surprise every day in that she was innocence personified and yet so deliciously womanly,

"Standing, with reluctant feet,
Where the brook and river meet,
Womanhood and childhood fleet!"

In this last week of returning strength, Winona imagined, when she saw Maxwell sitting among the men of the camp moody and silent, that he was remembering his home with longing and awaiting the moment for safe departure with impatience.

During her weeks of unselfish devotion when she had played the role of the boy nurse so successfully, she had been purely and proudly glad. Now, little by little, a gulf had opened between them which to her unsophisticated mind could not be bridged. There lay the misery of the present time—she was nothing to him. Does any love resign its self-imposed tasks of delightful cares and happy anxieties without a pang? Like any other young untrained creature, she tormented herself with fears that were but shadows and railed at barriers which she herself had raised, even while she argued that Fate had fixed impassable chasms of race and caste between them.

"How a man glories in war," she said, after a silence, from her seat on a jagged rock overhanging the cliff.

"You, with your Indian training, ought to feel with us and not think of fear," said Warren.

"But then, I am not of the blood."

"True."

His reply fell upon her ear like a reproach—a reflection upon her Negro origin. Her suspicion sounded in her voice as she replied:

"Better an Indian than a Negro? I do not blame you for your preference."

"Why speak with that tone—so scornfully? Is it possible that you can think so meanly of me?"

She could not meet his eye, but her answer was humbly given—her answer couched in the language of the tribes.

"Are you not a white brave? Do not all of them hate the black blood?"

"No; not all white men, thank God. In my country we think not of the color of the skin but of the man—the woman—the heart."

"Oh, your country! Do you know, I believe my dear papa was of the same?"

Her head rested against the tree back of her; the lace-work of the pine ashes formed upon her knees and enveloped her as a cloud.

He nodded in reply, and continued, musingly, as his eyes wandered off over the plain at his feet:

"England is a country to die for—rich, grand, humane! You shall see it for yourself."

"Which is my country, I wonder? Judah says that he will not fight for the Stars and Stripes if war comes—the flag that makes the Negro a slave. This country mine? No, no! The fearful things that I have seen—" she broke off abruptly. "My father's country shall be mine."

"Better reserve your decision until you marry."

"I shall never marry."

"But why?" asked Warren, opening his eyes in surprise. "Nonsense; all girls expect to marry, and do—most of them."

"I cannot marry out of the class of my father," she replied, with head proudly erect. "It follows, then, that I shall never marry."

"Nonsense," again returned Warren. "You will not live and grow old alone. Mere birth does not count for more than one's whole training afterward, and you have been bred among another race altogether."

"But the degradation of the two years just passed can never leave me; life will never seem quite the same," she said in a stifled voice full of pain. "I shall be a nun." She ended with a little laugh, but the voice quivered beneath it.

Warren scarcely knew how to answer her; he felt awkward and mere words sounded hollow.

"See here," he began abruptly; "it is no use to dwell on a painful subject; just strive to forget all about it and take the happiness that comes your way. As for the last alternative—you will not be happy."

"That cannot be helped. Perhaps I should not be happy if I married," she went on with a smile upon her lips, but deep gravity in her eyes. "It would depend upon the man who must know all my past. Nokomis used to say 'they are all the same—the men. When you are beautiful they kill each other for you; when you are plain they sneer at you.'"

"Old Nokomis! She spoke of red men, not white men."

"Yes; all the same Nokomis said: men are men. People will never forget that my mother was an American Negress even if I forget. No," concluded the girl with a wise little shake of her cropped head, "I shall go to the convent."

Warren dissembled his intense amusement, but beneath his smile was a tear for the tender, helpless creature trying so bravely to crush out of sight the tender flowers of her maiden heart. At length he said:

"Who can foresee the future? There are men with red blood in their veins; not all are empty caskets. How can you talk of convents—you who will go to England with me; and perhaps, who can tell, you may marry a duke. But believe me, Winona, you think too seriously of your position," he concluded, dropping his jesting air.

> *"You have too much respect upon the world:*
> *They lose it that do buy it with much care."*

Silence fell between them for a time, and the evening shadows gradually shut the eye of day. Clear and shrill upon the air fell the notes of a bugle, once—twice—thrice—it rose in warning cadence. Winona sprang to her feet with the words, "'Tis Judah! There is danger! Let us go at once!"

So violent was her start that she came perilously near falling to the plain below, which on this side the hill was a sheer descent of many feet, to where the Possawatomie rilled along its peaceful course.

"God!" broke from Warren's white lips as he caught her just in time. For a second he held her in a close embrace, she clinging to him in affright. There was extraordinary gravity in both look and tone as he leaned his cheek against the cropped curly head that nestled close to his throat like a frightened child, and said: "Winona, let me say it now before we go to meet we know not what—thank God I have known you—so noble, so patient, so sweet. Despite the dangers of our situation, the hours we have passed together have been the happiest of my life."

Forgetful of time and place, youth yielded to the sway of the love-god, and for one dazzling instant the glory of heaven shone upon them.

"What harm just once?" thought the girl as she rested in his embrace. "Tomorrow it may not matter about race or creed, one or both of us will belong to eternity; pray God that I may be the one to go."

XVII

It was not Judah who had blown the warning blast, but it came from one of his party sent by him to warn them of the approach of the enemy. The messenger was pale as death, the veins standing out on his forehead, and his left arm hanging useless at his side. The horse, panting and covered with foam, stopped, and Maybee caught the rider in his arms.

"What is it, boy?" he asked.

"Rangers," the poor fellow gasped out. "Three hundred around the old farmhouse. Coming down on you. Judah says he can hold them off until daybreak. I got out, but they shot me."

Captain Brown seemed transformed; his eyes burned like coals. Maybee put his hand on his shoulder.

"What'll you do, Captain, start now or later?"

"Two hours after midnight. The boy knows his business," was the laconic reply as, drawing long, deep breaths, John Brown made for the horses.

The evening was spent in preparations for the start. The camp was abandoned, the women hastily fleeing to the refuge on the mountainside. Three men were to be left to guard the cave, but every woman carried a rifle in her hand and was prepared to use it. Winona was in command of the home-guard.

The last words of counsel and instruction were spoken. It was nearly daylight. Faint streaks of light were already visible in the eastern horizon. They left the camp two hours after midnight and the last look that Warren gave toward the mountain showed him the slight figure of Winona with rifle in hand waving him a farewell salute.

To Maxwell the one hundred intrepid riders, with whom he was associated, represented a hopeless cause. How could they hope to conquer a force of three hundred desperadoes? But Warren knew not the valor of his companions nor the terror which the Brown men inspired.

The attacking point was an hour's fast riding from camp. The dawn increased rapidly. Maybee fell back to Warren's side with an air of repressed excitement, and his eyes blazed. He touched the young man's arm as they rode and pointed to the left where they saw, in a cloud of dust, another party of horsemen coming toward them.

"Who are they, friends or enemies?"

"Reinforcements. They are the boys Reynolds has collected to help us. Nothing the matter with him or them, you bet. Reynolds ain't been the same since Steward was killed. His heart's broke 'long with it an' he's wil' fer revenge. Every one of the boys with him is a fighter, too, from 'way back. I know 'em, Maxwell; an' now,—me, if we don't give them hell-hounds the biggest thrashing they've had since the campaign opened, you may call me a squaw. But who's that riding beside Reynolds?" he broke off abruptly. "Dog my cats, may I be teetotally smashed ef it don't look like Parson Steward!"

"No!" cried Warren in a fever of excitement at the words. "Impossible!"

"We'll soon know," replied Maybee.

On they sped over the space that separated the two parties. Then the order came to halt, and Parson Steward rode into the midst of the column while the men broke into wild cheering at sight of him. There was not much time to spend in greeting, but the vice-like grip of friendly hands spoke louder than words. Warren could not speak for a moment as before his mind the picture of the last night spent in Steward's company passed vividly. The parson, too, was visibly affected.

"Praise God from whom all blessings flow," he said solemnly.

"Amen," supplemented Maxwell, then they rode cautiously forward, the Captain keeping his men at the steady pace at which they had started out. Now and then a stray shot from the farmhouse showed them that Judah was holding his own. The firing increased as they neared the house, coming mainly from the shelter of trees and bushes at the side. Finally it became incessant, and the Captain beckoned to Maybee, after he had halted the column, and they rode cautiously ahead. Soon they returned, and coming to Warren drew him to the flank of the company.

"My boy, you are going under fire. Are you prepared for any happening? Are you all right?"

"All right," replied Warren.

"Well," said Captain Brown with a sigh, "shake hands; fire low; look well to the hinder side of your rifle. God bless you!" and he passed forward to the head of the column. The parson went with him.

Maybee was beside himself with excitement over the parson's rescue.

"Now you'll see some fun," said he; and then, all of a sudden the fire of battle caught him and he flew into a sort of frenzy. He rode quickly behind the men, saying in low, concentrated tones: "Give 'em—boys! Remember our friends they've butchered, and our women and little

PAULINE E. HOPKINS

children. Give 'em—, I say!" Then growing calmer he turned to Warren once more, saying: "Maxwell, I reckon you've got as big a score to settle as anyone of us." Then he, too, wrung Warren's hand and rode away to the head of the column.

A man fell dead in the Brown ranks. The Rangers now advanced in solid column to meet them. Then came the order to charge, and with a wild yell the pent-up excitement of the men broke forth and pell-mell they hurled themselves upon the foe.

Then ensued a wild scene; a turmoil of shots, cries, groans and shrieks—pandemonium on earth. Maxwell very soon found himself in the thickest of it, off his horse and doing his part in a fierce hand-to-hand encounter with one who had fired a pistol straight at him. The bullet flew wide of the mark and in an instant he had flung the snarling demon down and had hurled himself upon him. They struggled fiercely back and forth tearing at each other with all their might. Gideon Holmes' long, lithe fingers were sunk deep in his throat in an endeavor to force him to release his hold. With a mighty effort, Maxwell brought the butt of his pistol down on his enemy's face in a smashing blow. At last he had caught the full spirit of the fiercest; the blood mounted to his brain, and with ungovernable rage, thinking only of the sufferings he had endured in the dreadful time of imprisonment, he continued his rain of blows upon his prostrate foe until the very limpness of the inert body beneath him stayed his hand.

Through the smoke he saw Captain Brown and Parson Steward and Ebenezer Maybee fighting like mad, with blazing rifles, and deep curses from Maybee mingling with the hoarse shouting of passages of Scripture by the parson.

"Behold, the uncircumcised Philistine, how he defies the armies of the living God." And again—"Let no man's heart fail because of him; thy servant will go and fight with this Philistine;" "Fear not, neither be thou dismayed."

It was a terrible struggle between the two great forces—Right and Wrong. Drunken with vile passions, the Rangers fought madly but in vain against the almost supernatural prowess of their oponents; like the old Spartans who braided their hair and advanced with songs and dancing to meet the enemy, the anti-slavery men advanced singing hymns and praising God.

The last stand was made. The desperadoes fled in all directions. Some went toward the hills; among them was Thomson. He spurred his horse across the plain, abandoning him at the edge of the rising ground. For hours he skulked among the trees or crawled or crept over stones and through bushes, gradually rising higher and higher above the plain. Brown's forces swarmed over the ground, slaying as they met the flying foe. He saw Col. Titus pursued by Judah, speeding over the plain; he saw them meet and the Colonel fall. A moment—a moment—a convulsive uplifting of arms, and then Judah turned and slowly began climbing the ascent.

Thomson, regardless of consequences, sprang clear of the underbrush and darted up the mountainside. Once he thought he heard a rifle crack—on—on he sped. He climbed upon a ledge and lay there, peeping through a crevice made by the meeting of gigantic rocks, and gaining his breath. He saw no one. Evidently Judah had missed him, and he began to plan a descent from the opposite side. Searching the cliff for a landing place, he saw the Possawatamie gurgling along sixty feet below over pebbles, a torrent in winter but now only a silver thread that trickled lightly along.

He saw a jutting ledge ten feet below which promised an easy footing to the valley; once there he could soon evade pursuit. He bound his rifle securely to him by his belt and crawled out on the shelving rock; then swinging clear by the aid of a tough sapling, he cautiously dropped. He paused to regain his breath, gazing speculatively about him the while. Yes, it was as he had thought. On this side the cliffs broke into a series of giant steps which led easily to the river. "Lucky once more," he chuckled, speaking his thoughts aloud. "That black demon had missed again. Nex' turn is mine, an' I sha'n't miss him."

Thus musing he turned to begin the descent—and faced Judah where he stood in the shadow of a great boulder, with a smile on his face, watching the movements of his enemy the overseer. Thomson turned as if to run down the mountainside.

"Stop where you are!" thundered the giant black.

The man obeyed, but his hand sought his rifle.

"Hands up!" again came the pealing voice. The order was given along the barrel of a gleaming rifle. Thomson's hands went up obediently.

"You are surprised to see me," said Judah grimly. A period of silence ensued. It was a dramatic scene, far from the scene of recent strife. The morning sun had broke in dazzling splendor over the earth; the birds were feeding their young families and flew from tree to tree in neighborly fashion; the murmur of bees humming and of the stream far below mingled harmoniously. All was peace. But within two human hearts surged the wild passions of fierce animals at bay.

Judah looked at his foe with the air of one about entering upon a momentous task. Thomson stood with the narrow ledge for a foothold and the clouds of heaven at his back, facing he knew not what. His head throbbed and in his ears were the drum-beats of an army; his heart was sick with terror for this human torturer, this man-mangler and womanbeater was an arrant coward. When he could bear the silence no longer he spoke:

"I suppose I am your prisoner?"

Judah smiled. It was a terrible smile, and carried in it all the pent-up suffering of two years of bodily torture and a century of lacerated manhood. Thomson feared him, and well he might. Again he spoke. The sound of his own voice gave him courage; anything to break the horrible silence and the chill of that icy smile.

"I am to be treated as a prisoner of war?"

This time Judah answered him.

"Would you have treated me as a prisoner of war if you had captured me?"

"No," broke involuntarily from Thomson's lips.

"Very well!"

"I demand to be taken before Captain Brown. Surely he is human; he will not give me into the hands of a savage to be tortured!" exclaimed the wretch in frantic desperation.

Again Judah smiled his calm, dispassionate smile as he examined his rifle, and then slowly brought it to his shoulder. "You who torture the slave without a thought of mercy, and who could treat a young white man—one of your own race—as you did Mr. Maxwell, fear to be tortured? Why, where is your boasted Southern bravery that has promised so much?"

Bill's teeth glittered in a grin of hate and fear.

"God! It's murder to kill a man with his hands up!" he shrieked.

"It rests with you whether or not I shoot you," replied Judah calmly. "I am going to give you one chance for life. It is a slim one, but more than you would give me."

Bill eyed him with a venomous look of terror and distrust; but his manner had changed to fawning smoothness.

"Judah," he began, "look a-here, I own I done you dirt mean, I do. I ask yer pardon—I couldn't do more'n that ef you was a white man, could I? Well, sir, I know you're a brave nigger, an' I know, too, it's nat'ral for you to lay it up agin me, fer I done yer dirt an' no mistake. But I had to; ef I'd showed you quarter, every nigger on the plantation'd been hard to handle. It was necessary discipline, boy; nothin' particular agin you."

Bill's beady black eyes never left the Negro's face as he watched for a sign of wavering in the calm smile.

"Look a-here, I can tell you a heap of things'd be worth more'n my life to the gal, an' Titus couldn't blame me for givin' the scheme away; what's money to life? It's worth a fortune to you to know what I can tell you this minute; only let me out of this, Jude."

But Judah knew his man. Not for one instant did Thomson deceive him. He judged it a righteous duty to condemn him to death.

"You stole Winona's liberty and mine. I know what your promises are worth. Do you think I would listen to a proposition coming from you, you infernal scoundrel? Get ready. I've sworn to kill you and I intend to keep my oath. When I count three jump backwards or I put a bullet into your miserable carcass. If you are alive when you strike the river, you can swim ashore; it's one chance in ten. Choose."

Bill grew white; his eyes gleamed like those of a trapped rat, but he seemed to realize that it was useless to plead for mercy at the hands of the calm, smiling Negro before him.

"One!" counted Judah, moving toward Thomson a step as he counted. There he paused, desiring that the wretch should suffer all, in anticipation, that he had caused others to suffer.

"Two!" Thomson moved backward involuntarily, but still he did not lose his footing. Again Judah paused.

"Three!"

With a wild curse, Thomson sprang off the ledge. A fearfully quiet moment followed. Judah did not move. There came a crashing of underbrush, a sound of rolling rocks and gravel, a plash of water— silence.

XVIII

A superb, masterful smile played over the ebon visage of the now solitary figure upon the mountainside. In his face shone a glitter of the untamable torrid ferocity of his tribe not pleasing to see. The first act in his bold and sagacious plans was successful; once free, it only remained for him to carry them out with the same inexorable energy.

The upraised hands and straining eyeballs, rigid and stone-like, the gapping, bloodless lips, the muttered curse—all had passed from sight like an unpleasant dream. Judah, intently listening to the ominous thud, thud, thud, of that falling body, the swish of displaced bushes, and the rattle of gravel and stones, was not moved from the stoicism of his manner, save in the fearful smile that still played over his features. Then, as he listened, there came a last awful cry, a scream that startled all nature and awoke echo after echo along the hillside—a scream like no sound in earth or heaven—unhuman and appalling. He made a step forward to the brink and looked over and then drew back.

A while he leaned upon his gun in meditation. He was a morbid soul preying upon its recollection, without the gift of varied experience; it was not strange that vengeance seemed to him earth's only blessing. To him his recent act was one of simple justice. Hate, impotent hate, had consumed his young heart for two years. An eye for an eye was a doctrine that commended itself more and more to him as he viewed the Negro's condition in life, and beheld the horrors of the system under which he lived.

Judged by the ordinary eye Judah's nature was horrible, but it was the natural outcome or growth of the "system" as practiced upon the black race. He felt neither remorse nor commiseration for the deed just committed. To him it was his only chance of redress for the personal wrongs inflicted upon Winona and himself by the strong, aggressive race holding them in unlawful bondage. Time and place were forgotten as he stood there like a statue. He was back in the past. His thoughts ran backwards in an unbroken train until the scene before him changed to the island and the day when the careless happiness of his free youth was broken by the advent of the strangers, Colonel Titus and Bill Thomson. Then had followed the murder of White Eagle.

Yes, once he had a friend, but he was dead—dead by a man's hand. And he—but a moment since went over the cliff. It was well!

As through a mist, queries and propositions and possibilities took shape, there on the cliffside, that had never before presented themselves to him. As he stood in the blazing sunlight, his brain throbbed intolerably and every pulsation was a shooting pain. Why had he been so dull of comprehension? What if a thought just born in his mind should prove true? O, to be free once more!

There was a rustle of leaves, and out from the shadow of the trees filed a number of anti-slavery men headed by Captain Brown and Parson Steward

"Well, Judah," said Captain Brown, "we've been watching your little drama. You promised to kill him and you've done it."

"Boys," returned Judah, "and all of you, I leave it to you if I'm not right in ridding the world of such a beast as Thomson."

The men set up a cheer that echoed and re-echoed among the hills. The women in the cave heard with joyful hearts.

"I'd kill a snake wherever I f'und him," said one; "wudn't you, Parson?"

"Sure," replied the parson. "This is a holy war, and it's only just begun."

"This is a great day. Praise God from whom all blessings flow; we've put to flight the armies of the Philistines," said Captain Brown.

"It is justice! I am satisfied," said Judah, scanning each solemn face before him with his keen eyes.

Parson Steward wore the same calm, unruffled front touched with faint humor that had characterized him when first introduced to our readers. He was a trifle paler, but that was all that reminded one of the fact that only by a miracle, as it were, he had escaped death at the hands of cruel men. Judah grasped his hand in both of his.

"No wonder we have won, Parson; I heard them cry: 'Look at the Parson!' and then they fled in every direction."

"They reckoned he was dead, an' 'lowed he was a ghost. By gum, how they broke! It was easy work to pick them off," broke in one of the men.

"Perhaps you'll be good enough to tell me where you come from, Parson; you've been dead to us for weeks past."

"Yes; we all want to learn how the Parson got here," said Captain Brown.

"Oh, I been pretty near you right along," replied the Parson, not a whit hurried or excited by the interest of his audience. "That night on the road with young Maxwell was a terrible one. They caught me off my guard for the first time in my life. I was filled with shot and left for dead. Next morning Reynolds got wind of the proceedings and went out to

PAULINE E. HOPKINS

find my remains and give me a decent burial. I was breathing when he got me. That settled it. He toted me on his back to his house and hid me in his loft, and there I lay eight long weeks and every one thinking me dead. Boys, it was a close shave, and when I thought of my wife and children it was tough, turrible tough on the old man, but I left them in the hands of that God who has never failed me yet, and here I am right side up with care, and the old woman and kids safe and hearty here in your camp." He ended solemnly, and the men doffed their ragged hats in humble homage.

"Amen!" said Captain Brown. "All's well that ends well," and they continued their tramp up the mountainside to the cave.

Impelled by a morbid fascination, Judah climbed down the mountain path seeking the bed of the stream below where lay the body of his foe.

XIX

All through the long morning Winona patrolled her beat listening with anxious heart to the sounds of distant firing which the breeze brought to her ears from time to time. At noon one of Captain Brown's daughters brought her coffee; it was the only break in her solitary vigil. She scanned the horizon with anxious eyes, but having no field-glass was unable to distinguish friend from foe among the figures scarcely discernible with the naked eye.

In the dim vistas of the woods it was cool and shady, but the sun beat down mercilessly upon the sides of the cliff, and as she watched the shifting rays she wondered how the battle went in sickening dread, and then rebuked her own impatience for news. As the hours wore on, the shadows began to lengthen; their long fingers crossed the hills pointing darkly toward the river. The girl was unhappy and fearful in her mind; yet she tried to comfort herself, but for a time her firm head played her false enough to picture flames leaping from the woods from the low roofs of the huts amid the corn-stalks, and little children under merciless hoofs, and the awful tumult of flight for life. That was no more than they must expect if the Rangers won. "But they won't win!" she thought, with a brave smile on her face and a heavy heart in her bosom.

Overcome at length by the restless fever within, she determined to risk all in an endeavor to obtain news of her friends—of Warren. She started toward the battle line about the time Judah met Thomson on another spur of the mountain. Reaching the stream Winona followed the bed for some distance in the shadow of the cliff.

Suddenly, far above her head, she heard the gunshot, the scream of agony tearing through space, at once an alarum and rallying cry; it meant to the lonely girl all the savagery of battle; it might mean havoc and despair. She covered her face with her hands a moment, removing them the next instant in time to see a falling body drop into the water almost at her feet. Terror rendered her motionless. The soft waves stole up and flung themselves over the quiet body huddled there breast high in the stream. Then a new thought came to her—"if it should be Warren!" Gathering herself up, she stumbled through the grass to the edge of the river, fell on her knees on the bank and surveyed the helpless shape lying there. A groan broke from the white lips. She nerved herself to move nearer. She took the unconscious head in both hands and turned the face toward herself and—looked into the sightless eyes of Thomson.

Her relief was so great that she sobbed aloud; then after giving broken thanks that it was not Warren, she rose from her knees and began to look about her for means to succor the man before her. He was her enemy, but the mother instinct that dwells in all good women, which can look on death, gave her calmness and strength to do, and the heart to forgive.

She turned to seek help and faced Judah coming out from the trees. "Oh, Judah, he is alive!" she exclaimed, pointing to the inanimate figure in the water. Judah gazed at her in surprise, then said:

"What! Not dead yet? I thought I had settled his case for all time. How came you here?"

"I came out to look for the wounded. Help me to carry this man to camp; surely you are satisfied now. You cannot shoot a dying man," she said, sternly catching the ferocious light that still glimmered in his eyes as he lifted his gun to the hollow of his arm.

"I did it for you as much as for myself. Have you forgotten your father?" he added, reproachfully.

"I do not forget. God forbid! But you have done enough."

"Not enough," replied Judah. "He is the hater of my race. He is of those who enslave both body and soul and damn us with ignorance and vice and take our manhood. I made an oath; it was no idle threat."

He poised his gun. Quick as a flash the girl threw herself before the unconscious Thomson. "You shall not! You make yourself as vile as the vilest of them—our enemies. Let the man die in peace. See, he is almost gone."

"Yes, Judah, it is enough; she is right," said Warren Maxwell's voice as he joined the group by the stream. "Surely you must be sick of bloodshed. Have you not had enough?"

With a glad cry Winona was folded in her lover's arms.

"Let it be as you wish," said Judah after a short time, as he silently viewed the happiness of the lovers. Then he prepared to help Warren lift Thomson from the stream. They turned faint and sick at the sight of the man's wounds. "His back is broken," said Warren, in reply to Winona's questioning eyes.

"It were more merciful to shoot him on the spot," said Judah, but even he felt now the sheer human repulsion from such butchery master him, as they moved slowly and carefully up the steep ascent.

The Rangers were completely routed by the desperate valor of the Brown men. Incredible as it seemed, most of the enemy had been killed outright and a number of prisoners taken, who were to be tried by court-martial and shot, according to the rough justice of the times.

The anti-slavery men met with small loss, but among the wounded was Ebenezer Maybee. With the other wounded men he was carried back to camp; at sunrise the next morning he was aroused form his stupor by a volley of musketry. Steward was at his side. He asked what it meant.

"Well, partner, you know we won the fight," said he. "Captain Brown is a shootin'" all the pris'ners; well, now, ain't that tough fer a prefesser?"

"No, not all the prisoners," replied the Parson. "The most of them have been begged off by young Maxwell. He's the most softest hearted young feller I ever met for such a good shot."

"This yer's a good cause to go in, Parson."

The Parson answered grufly, in a choked voice: "You ain't goin' nowhere, partner; we'll pull you through."

Maybee's face worked, and he planted a knowing wink in vacancy. "We've been partners fer a right smart spell, ain't we, Parson?"

The Parson frowned hard to keep back the tears. "You're a man to tie to, Maybee."

"No, now," sputtered Maybee, breaking down at last; "d— ye Parson, don't make a baby er me." Then with a change of voice he asked, "What's come o' Thomson an' the colonel?"

"Devil's got the colonel and he's waiting fer Thomson; we've got him with a broken back next door to this house. Judah did it. My! but that boy's as ferocious as a tiger."

Maybee nodded. "Well, he's a good boy, is Jude; I've knowed him sense he was knee-high to a toad; been through a heap; don' blame him fer bein' ferocious. I ain't sorry I jined the boys, Parson, fer all I got my ticket. It's a good cause, Parson, a good cause, and you'll see a heap o' fun befo' you're through with it; wish't I could he here to see it, too. You found your ol' woman and the kids all safe, Parson?"

"I did," replied the Person, cordially.

"Jes' break it gently to Ma' Jane, partner, that I got my death in an hones' fight, an' tell her she's all right, havin' everything in her name an' power of attorney to boot."

"I will do so," promised the Parson, solemnly.

PAULINE E. HOPKINS

One of the men came in with a message for the Parson. Thomson was conscious and going fast; he wanted the Parson and Winona.

Thomson still lived; none knew why; his stupor had left him conscious. Paralyzed in every limb, he could talk in a strong voice and was perfectly sane, and recognized those about him, but he was going fast.

"How long do you give me, doc?" he asked Warren, jokingly.

"Until it touches the heart," replied Warren solemnly.

"Then it will be soon?" Warren nodded.

Thomson appeared to be thinking. "No," he muttered finally with a sigh, "I got to own up. Colonel's dead, ain't he?" Warren bowed.

"Well then, 'taint no use holdin' out. Bring in the gal and Judah, an' take down every word I say if you want the gal to have her own. You're a lawyer, ain't you? Sent out here on the Carlingford case, warn't you? Never struck you that me and the Colonel knew where to find the man you was huntin', did it?" His voice was spent, and Warren, his mind in a tumult, held a glass of liquor to the dying man's lips, and then sent for Winona and Judah and Parson Steward. They came instantly, and with the transient vigor imparted by the liquor Thomson opened his eyes again and said, in a clear tone: "I'm here yet, Judah; I almost got the one chance you offered me, but it ain't for long I'll hender you; I'm goin' fast."

No one answered the wretch, baffled alike in base passion and violent deeds, but Parson Steward began a fervent prayer for the dying. Something of his awful need for such a petition must have filtered through the darkness of the sin-cursed heart and he presently comprehended dimly the great change before him. He whispered at the close:

"That's all right, Parson. I know I deviled you an' tried to kill you; I did the same to the nigger—an' to Maxwell—but I done the girl worse'n dirt. That's me you described in your prayer—a devilish wicked cuss, but I warn't always so, an' d— me ef I ain't sorry! I'm goin' to try to make the damage I've done, good—to the girl, anyhow."

"Miserable sinners, miserable sinners, all of us. Madness is in our hearts while we live, and after that we go to the dead. God forgive us," muttered the Parson, not noting the dying man's profanity.

"Take down every word I say, Mr. Maxwell, an' let me kiss the Book that it's all true."

The scene was intensely dramatic. Winona sat with clasped hands folded on her breast; she knew not what new turn of Fortune's wheel awaited her. Judah's dark, handsome face and stalwart form were in the background where he stood in a group formed by Captain Brown and his sons, who had been called to witness the confession.

As for Warren Maxwell, he felt the most intense excitement he had ever experienced in his life. His hands shook; he could scarcely hold the pen. Most of us creatures of flesh and blood know what that terrible feeling of suspense, of dread, with which we approach a crisis in our fate. It is indefinable, but comes alike strong and weak, bold and timid. Such a crisis Maxwell felt was approaching in the fate of Winona and himself. There in we recognize the mesmeric force which holds mankind in an eternal brotherhood. Stronger than all in life, perhaps, is this mysterious force when a man feels that he has

> "Set his life upon a cast,
> And must abide the hazard of the die."

"Mr. Maxwell, you came to America to find the lost Captain Henry Carlingford, heir to the great Carlingford estates. You thought you were on a hopeless quest, did you not?" Warren nodded. It was noticeable that the man spoke in well-bred phrases, and had dropped his Southwestern accent. "You found the captain all right, but you never knew it. White Eagle was the man you wanted!"

There was a cry of astonishment from the listeners. Winona was in tears. Into Judah's eyes there crept the old ferocious glitter as he said:

"And so you murdered him! I have suspected as much for two years."

"No, no, Judah; I wasn't in that. Titus did the killing."

Now Warren lost sight of all personal interest in the case, seeing nothing but its legal aspect. He wrote rapidly questioning the man closely.

"Why did Col. Titus commit this murder? How came you to know this?"

With great effort Thomson replied:

"Titus hated him because he stood between him and a vast fortune, and he was also jealous of his wife's love for Henry Carlingford; he was her lover from childhood, and she loved him until death."

"Then if you know this, I want you to tell me who killed young Lord George. Miss Venton was affianced to him. You can tell if you will, for Miss Venton married Colonel Titus." Warren spoke sternly and solemnly.

Thomson muttered to himself and then was silent; all waited breathlessly in painful silence. Would he solve the riddle, and tell the story of the crime for which a guiltless man had been condemned by a jury of his peers years before?

"No, it won't neither," they heard him say, and then he spoke aloud: "Everything must be made clear?"

"Yes," said Warren, "if you wish to help this poor girl whom you have wronged so cruelly."

"It won't be against you when you get on the other side, Thomson. Free your mind, my friend; it'll do you good. Terrible, verily, sir, is the Lord our God, but full of mercy," said Parson Steward.

"I'll take your word for it, Parson, but I never was much on religion; perhaps I'd fared better if I had been. Well, then, I killed Lord George. I swore to bring disgrace upon the entire Carlingford family. And I have done it; I have had a rich revenge. I was Lord George's valet; my sister, Miss Venton's maid. Lord George could never resist a pretty face, and my sister was more than that. Miss Venton loved Captain Henry, and Lord George found her an indifferent woman. She but obeyed her father's orders, and so Lord George made love to the maid, deceived her, and when he tired of his toy abandoned her to the usual fate of such women—the street. I found her when it was too late, and I swore revenge so long as one lived with a drop of the blood in his veins.

"One day the brothers quarrelled bitterly over Miss Venton; then was my chance. I shot Lord George in the back, and fled, knowing that suspicion would fall on Capt. Henry. It did; and two of my enemies were out of my way, for the Captain was tried and convicted and lived an outcast among savages for years; that was my little scheme for getting even. For the sake of his daughter Lillian, Colonel Titus killed White Eagle and held Winona as a slave, thus cutting off the last direct heir to Carlingford."

The faint voice ceased. The narrative was finished with great difficulty; the man failed rapidly. With a great effort he added: "Will you call it square, young fellow?—you and Winona—and Judah? I've done you bad, but I've told the truth at last. Mr. Maxwell—you know the rest—I reckon you'll marry the heiress—I'm glad.—Land in Canidy soon, boys; they'll be after you inside a week—big Government force—." Warren preserved his impassiveness by a struggle; the others followed the faint voice of the dying man with breathless attention; they felt that every word of this important confession was true.

Maxwell was filled with a hope that agitated him almost beyond control.

"Why, surely," he said, at length, in a voice that trembled in spite of himself, as he rose and joined Winona and Judah at the bedside, "I'm awfully grateful to you for telling me this; it makes my work easy."

"I sort o' hated to tell, fer a fac'," he said, falling back into his usual vernacular, "but I'm glad I done it." His voice failed; a gray shadow crept over the white face; all was still.

"Let us pray," and Parson Steward broke the silence. As they knelt about the bed, the crack of rifles broke in upon the fervent petition for mercy sent upwards by the man of God. It was the volley that carried death to the last of the captured Rangers. Guilty soul joined guilty soul in their flight to Eternity.

Ebenezer Maybee expressed no surprise when told of Thomson's confession.

"These happenings 'min' me o' the words o' the Psalmist that I've heard Parson quote so often: 'Thy right hand shall teach thee terrible things.'"

"Amen," said Steward. "But full of mercy, also, since they will deliver this poor girl from the hand of the spoiler."

Many tears were shed over Maybee's precarious condition, for he was dear to every soul in the camp. Winona and Judah established themselves as nurses at his bedside, bringing all their Indian knowledge of medicine to bear upon his case, and declaring that they would pull him through.

"My children," he said, after musing a while on the exciting tale just told him, "I believe I can match that story o' Thomson's. I have a surprisin' secret to unfol' to you. It will make the whole business clear. White Eagle must a perceived his end, an' he says to me, says he, jes' about a month before his disease, he says, 'Maybee, keep this here package if anything comes across me, 'tell my girl's a responsible age.' After he was dead I said to myself—in the words of Scripter, 'a charge to keep I have' an't ain't safe to keep it; so I give the package to Ma' Jane an' she has it unto this day."

PAULINE E. HOPKINS

XX

A week later our fugitives started for Canada via Buffalo, N. Y., by a circuitous path well known to Captain Brown. Mr. Maybee went along in an improvised ambulance, much improved in health and bearing well the fatigue of travel.

The Brown camp was deserted, and the Government troops, when they arrive, found only the blackened remains of the once busy settlement. Where the Rangers had paid the penalty of their crimes against the farmers of Kansas, the grass covered the sod as if it had never been disfigured or stained. The last gun had been fired in Kansas by Brown's forces, and he was next heard of in the Virginia insurrection which ended so fatally for the intrepid leader.

After many startling adventures and narrow escapes from capture, a group of bronzed and bearded men and one woman rode up one morning to the entrance of the Grand Island Hotel. It was our friends and the Brown family. The other refugees had passed in safety over the border into Canada, and the fugitive slaves were, at last, rejoicing on free soil.

The front of the hotel was deserted, the women being busy in the rear with their morning duties, and the usual hangers-on not being about.

Mr. Maybee, who was lying on a bed in the bottom of the wagon, sat up as the cavalcade paused, and cried:

"Ma' Jane! Ma'—Jane!"

"Ya'as," screamed a female voice from the rear, not "like a song from afar;" or, if so, it was set in four sharps. "What's up neow?"

To which Maybee, probably reckoning on the magnetic attraction of female curiosity, made no reply, which diplomatic course instantly drew his worthy better half—a big one, too—and far better than her vocal organ. She came followed by the cook, Aunt Vinnie, and 'Tavius. "Law sakes!" she cried, sticking her plump arms akimbo and staring in amazement at the company before her, "if it ain't Ebenezer—an' the Englishman—an' Jude!—an' 'Nona!!" Her astonishment could go no farther. The next instant she had folded the girlish form in her arms in an agony of joy.

"My precious child! Thank heaven we've got you back safe! It's been an awful time fer you."

"Wall, darn my skin!" cried Maybee, wiping his own eyes in sympathy with the weeping woman, "here's me, wounded an' dyin', been a stranger an' a pilgrim in hostile parts fer months, an' when I git home the wife of my bosom ain't no eyes fer me nor tears nuther—everybody else is fus'. I call all you boys to witness my treatment; I enter a suit for devorce at once. Ma' Jane, I'm goin' ter leave your bed an' board."

"You ain't no call to be jealous, Maybee, as you well know. Ef you're sick, I'll nuss you; ef you're hungry, I'll feed you."

Then these pilgrims of the dusty roads received a royal welcome from the bewildered woman. Their brown hands were shaken, their torn clothes embraced, their sunburnt faces kissed with a rapture that was amazing.

"Come in, everybody. 'Tavius, git a move on with them hosses and things! Vinnie, stop your grinnin' an' hustle with the dinner."

Mrs. Maybee expanded, metaphorically,—literal expansion would have jammed her in the doorway,—on hospitable cares intent.

'Tavius marched away grinning, while Mrs. Maybee ushered her guests into the house. How long seemed the time to Winona and Judah since they had been torn from that kindly shelter by the slave-hunters; terrible, indeed, had been the times that followed so swiftly.

After the travelers were somewhat rested and refreshed, the story of their adventures was rehearsed, and the stranger one of the wrongs and sorrows of White Eagle and his true name and position in the world was told to an interested crowd of listeners, for the news of Maybee's arrival with Winona and Judah had been industriously circulated by 'Tavius as soon as he could steal away from his duties, and a crowd of leading citizens filled the office, hall and piazza, anxious to see the wanderers and hear the miraculous story of their escape.

"Now, Ma' Jane, you remember the papers I gave you—White Eagle's paper's?"

"Of course."

"I want you to fetch 'em out and give 'em to the child before us all. Then Mr. Lawyer Maxwell will see ef they is all correc'."

Mrs. Maybee brought a long tin box and placed it in her husband's hand. He opened it. "Let's see. Three legal dockymen's and a few pieces of jewelry. Them's 'em, I reckon. There you are, my girl," he said, tenderly, as he handed the package to Winona. Her attitude was at once tragic and pathetic as she drew back, for one instant, and stood in silent self-repression. A dizziness swept over her. What would the papers reveal? Their contents meant life or death to her hopes. She took the papers without speaking and passed them on to Warren almost mechanically.

"Read them—I cannot."

"Right, child," said Maybee.

There was breathless silence in the room as Warren unfolded the paper lying on top of the packet like a thick letter. All—honor for dead and living, ancient lands and name, home for the fondly loved child—lay sealed in the certificate of marriage and birth lying in Maxwell's right hand. The other papers related to his own story—a record of happenings after the fugitive from justice had arrived in America. The jewelry was jeweled family portraits, including one of Captain Henry when a young man; also a ring bearing the family crest. Nothing was missing—the chain of evidence was complete, even to the trained eye of the legal critic.

Then followed congratulations and good wishes from the friends who had done so much to make the present joy possible.

"I for one," said the representative to Congress, "from this day out condemn this cursed 'system' of ours. We're a laughing stock for the whole world, to say nothing of the wickedness of the thing."

"Right you are, Jameson; put them sentiments down for every man of us," cried a voice in the crowd.

Judah could say nothing, but he wrung Warren's hand hard.

"You go with us to England, Judah, and share prosperity as you have shared adversity. You shall choose your own path in life and be a man among men."

"I ain't any words to say, my girl!!" Maybee said huskily to Winona; "but you know what's in my ol' heart, I reckon, by what's in your own. I know you won't forget us when you're a great lady. Poor White Eagle, he had a rocky time of it, sure."

MANY VISITS WERE MADE TO the island by our three friends before the day when they embarked from Canada for old England. Oh the rare delight they felt in the movement of the light canoe as they glided over the blue waters of the lake, and the thunders of Niagara sounded in their ears like a mighty orchestra rejoicing in their joy.

Again they stood on the high ridge where lay the sun-flecked woods, climbed the slopes and listened to the squirrel's shrill, clear chirp; watched the blackbirds winging the air in flight and heard the robin's mellow music gushing from the boughs above their heads. The Indian-pipes with their faint pink stems lay concealed among the bushes as of old.

Beneath the great pine that shaded White Eagle's grave they rested reverent, tempered sadness in their hearts. Winona buried her face in her lover's bosom with smothered, passionate sobs. Warren folded her close to him.

"My heart's dearest, you must not grieve; your time of mourning is past. He is happy now as he sees your future assured. Through you he has conquered death and the grave; justice and honor are his after many years of shame." And she was comforted.

They made no plans for the future. What necessity was there of making plans for the future? They knew what the future would be. They loved each other; they would marry sooner or later, after they reached England, with the sanction of her grandfather, old Lord George; that was certain. American caste prejudice could not touch them in their home beyond the sea.

A long story full of deep interest might be written concerning the subsequent fortunes of John Brown and his sons and their trusty followers—a story of hardships, ruined homes and persecutions, and retribution to their persecutors, after all, through the happenings of the Civil War. But with these events we are all familiar. Judah never returned to America. After the news of John Brown's death had aroused the sympathies of all christendom for the slaves, he gave up all thoughts of returning to the land of his birth and entered the service of the Queen. His daring bravery and matchless courage brought its own reward; he was knighted; had honors and wealth heaped upon him, and finally married into one of the best families of the realm.

Winona celebrated in her letters to Mr. Maybee the wonders of her life in England, where all worshipped the last beautiful representative of an ancient family. The premature, crushing experiences of her young girlhood, its shocks and shameful surprises were not without good fruit. She is a noble woman. She is fortified against misfortune now by her deep knowledge of life and its inevitable sorrows, by love. Greater joy than hers, no woman, she believes, has ever known.

At intervals Aunt Vinnie found herself the center of groups of curious neighbors, white and black, who never tired of hearing her tell the story of Winona's strange fortunes. She invariably ended the tale with a short sermon on the fate of her race.

"Glory to God, we's boun' to be free. Dar's dat gal, she's got black blood nuff in her to put her on de block in this fersaken country, but over dar she's a lady with de top crus' of de crus'. Somethin's gwine happen."

An elderly white woman among the visitors drew a long breath, and declared that she had been lifted out of her bed three times the previous night.

"To be course," said Aunt Vinnie. "That's de angelic hos' hoverin' roun' you. Somethin's gwine drap. White folks been ridin' a turrible hoss in this country, an' dat hoss gwine to fro 'em' you hyar me."

"De mule kicked me three times dis morning' an' he never did dat afore in his life," said a colored brother; "dat means good luck."

"Jestice been settin' on de sprangles ob de sun a long time watchin' dese people how dey cuts der shines; um, um!" continued Vinnie.

"A rabbit run across my path twice comin' through de graveyard las' Sunday. I believe in my soul you're right, Aunt Vinnie," said 'Tavius.

"Course I'm right. Watch de sun an' see how he run; gwine to hear a mighty rumblin' 'mongst de dry bones 'cause jestice gwine plum' de line, an' set de chillun free," and as she retired to the kitchen her voice came back to them, in song:

> *"Ole Satan's mad, an' I am glad,*
> *Send de angels down.*
> *He missed the soul he thought he had,*
> *O, send dem angels down.*
> *Dis is de year of Jubilee,*
> *Send dem angels down.*
> *De Lord has come to set us free,*
> *O, send dem angels down."*

OF ONE BLOOD OR, THE HIDDEN SELF

I

The recitations were over for the day. It was the first week in November and it had rained about every day the entire week; now freezing temperature added to the discomforture of the dismal season. The lingering equinoctial whirled the last clinging yellow leaves from the trees on the campus and strewed them over the deserted paths, while from the leaden sky fluttering snow-white flakes gave an unexpected touch of winter to the scene.

The east wind for which Boston and vicinity is celebrated, drove the sleet against the window panes of the room in which Reuel Briggs sat among his books and the apparatus for experiments. The room served for both living and sleeping. Briggs could have told you that the bareness and desolateness of the apartment were like his life, but he was a reticent man who knew how to suffer in silence. The dreary wet afternoon, the cheerless walk over West Boston bridge through the soaking streets had but served to emphasize the loneliness of his position, and morbid thoughts had haunted him all day: To what use all this persistent hard work for a place in the world—clothes, food, a roof? Is suicide wrong? he asked himself with tormenting persistency. From out the storm, voices and hands seemed beckoning him all day to cut the Gordian knot and solve the riddle of whence and whither for all time.

His place in the world would soon be filled; no vacuum remained empty; the eternal movement of all things onward closed up the gaps, and the wail of the newly-born augmented the great army of mortals pressing the vitals of mother Earth with hurrying tread. So he had tormented himself for months, but the courage was yet wanting for strength to rend the veil. It had grown dark early. Reuel had not stirred from his room since coming from the hospital—had not eaten nor drank, and was in full possession of the solitude he craved. It was now five o'clock. He sat sideways by the bare table, one leg crossed over the other. His fingers kept the book open at the page where he was reading, but his attention wandered beyond the leaden sky, the dripping panes, and the sounds of the driving storm outside.

He was thinking deeply of the words he had just read, and which the darkness had shut from his gaze. The book was called "The Unclassified Residuum," just published and eagerly sought by students of *mysticism*, and dealing with the great field of new discoveries in psychology. Briggs was a close student of what might be termed "absurdities" of supernatural phenomena or mysticism, best known to the every-day world as "effects of the imagination," a phrase of mere dismissal, and which it is impossible to make precise; the book suited the man's mood. These were the words of haunting significance:

"All the while, however, the phenomena are there, lying broadcast over the surface of history. No matter where you open its pages, you find things recorded under the name of divinations, inspirations, demoniacal possessions, apparitions, trances, ecstasies, miraculous healing and productions of disease, and occult powers possessed by peculiar individuals over persons and things in their neighborhood."

"The mind-curers and Christian scientists, who are beginning to lift up their heads in our communities, unquestionably get remarkable results in certain cases. The ordinary medical man dismisses them from his attention with the cut-and-dried remark that they are 'only the effects of the imagination.' But there is a meaning in this vaguest of phrases."

"We know a non-hysterical woman who in her trances knows facts which altogether transcend her *possible* normal consciousness, facts about the lives of people whom she never saw or heard of before. I am well aware of all the liabilities to which this statement exposes me, and I make it deliberately, having practically no doubt whatever of its truth."

Presently Briggs threw the book down, and, rising from his chair, began pacing up and down the bare room.

"That is it," at length he said aloud. "I have the power, I know the truth of every word—of all M. Binet asserts, and could I but complete the necessary experiments, I would astonish the world. O Poverty, Ostracism! have I not drained the bitter cup to the dregs!" he apostrophized, with a harsh, ironical laugh.

MOTHER NATURE HAD BLESSED REUEL Briggs with superior physical endowments, but as yet he had never had reason to count them blessings. No one could fail to notice the vast breadth of shoulder, the strong throat that upheld a plain face, the long limbs, the sinewy hands. His head was that of an athlete, with close-set ears, and covered with an abundance of black hair, straight and closely cut, thick and smooth; the nose was the aristocratic feature, although nearly spoiled by broad nostrils, of this remarkable young man; his skin was white, but of a tint suggesting olive, an almost sallow color which is a mark of strong, melancholic temperaments. His large mouth concealed powerful long white teeth which gleamed through lips even and narrow, parting generally in a smile at once grave, genial and singularly sweet; indeed Briggs' smile changed the plain face at once into one that interested and fascinated men and women. True there were lines about the mouth which betrayed a passionate, nervous temperament, but they accorded well with the rest of his strong personality. His eyes were a very bright and piercing gray, courageous, keen and shrewd. Briggs was not a man to be despised—physically or mentally.

None of the students associated together in the hive of men under the fostering care of the "benign mother" knew aught of Reuel Briggs's origin. It was rumored at first that he was of Italian birth, then they "guessed" he was a Japanese, but whatever land claimed him as a son, all voted him a genius in his scientific studies, and much was expected of him at graduation. He had no money, for he was unsocial and shabby to the point of seediness, and apparently no relatives, for his correspondence was limited to the letters of editors of well known local papers and magazines. Somehow he lived and paid his way in a third-rate lodging-house near Harvard square, at the expense of the dull intellects or the idle rich, with which a great university always teems, to whom Briggs acted as "coach," and by contributing scientific articles to magazines on the absorbing subject of spiritualistic phenomena. A few of his articles had produced a profound impression. The monotonous pacing continued for a time, finally ending at the mantel, from whence he abstracted a disreputable looking pipe and filled it.

"Well," he soliloquized, as he reseated himself in his chair, "Fate has done her Worst, but she mockingly beckons me on and I accept her challenge. I shall not yet attempt the bourne. If I conquer, it will be by strength of brain and willpower. I shall conquer; I must and will."

The storm had increased in violence; the early dusk came swiftly down, and at this point in his revery the rattling window panes, as well as the whistle and shriek of gusts of moaning wind, caught his attention. "Phew! a beastly night." With a shiver, he drew his chair closer to the cylinder stove, whose glowing body was the only cheerful object in the bare room.

As he sat with his back half-turned to catch the grateful warmth, he looked out into the dim twilight across the square and into the broad paths of the campus, watching the skeleton arms of giant trees tossing in the wind, and the dancing snow-flakes that fluttered to earth in their fairy gowns to be quickly transformed into running streams that fairly overflowed the gutters. He fell into a dreamy state as he gazed, for which he could not account. As he sent his earnest, penetrating gaze into the night, gradually the darkness and storm faded into tints of cream and rose and soft moist lips. Silhouetted against the background of lowering sky and waving branches, he saw distinctly outlined a fair face framed in golden hair, with soft brown eyes, deep and earnest—terribly earnest they seemed just then—rose-tinged baby lips, and an expression of wistful entreaty. O how real, how very real did the passing shadow appear to the gazer!

He tried to move, uneasily conscious that this strange experience was but "the effect of the imagination," but he was powerless. The unknown countenance grew dimmer and farther off, floating gradually out of sight, while a sense of sadness and foreboding wrapped him about as with a pall.

A wilder gust of wind shook the window sashes. Reuel stared about him in a bewildered way like a man awakening from a heavy sleep. He listened to the wail of the blast and glanced at the fire and rubbed his eyes. The vision was gone; he was alone in the room; all was silence and darkness. The ticking of the cheap clock on the mantel kept time with his heart-beats. The light of his own life seemed suddenly eclipsed with the passing of the lovely vision of Venus. Conscious of an odd murmur in his head, which seemed to control his movements, he rose and went toward the window to open it; there came a loud knock at the door.

Briggs did not answer at once. He wanted no company. Perhaps the knocker would go away. But he was persistent. Again came the knock ending in a double rat-tat accompanied by the words:

"I know you are there; open, open, you son of Erebus! You inhospitable Turk!"

Thus admonished Briggs turned the key and threw wide open the door.

"It's you, is it? Confound you, you're always here when you're not wanted," he growled.

THE VISITOR ENTERED AND CLOSED the door behind him. With a laugh he stood his dripping umbrella back of the stove against the chimney-piece, and immediately a small stream began trickling over the uncarpeted floor; he then relieved himself of his damp outer garments.

"Son of Erebus, indeed, you ungrateful man. It's as black as Hades in this room; a light, a light! Why did you keep me waiting out there like a drowned rat?"

The voice was soft and musical. Briggs lighted the student lamp. The light revealed a tall man with the beautiful face of a Greek God; but the sculptured features did not inspire confidence. There was that in the countenance of Aubrey Livingston that engendered doubt. But he had been kind to Briggs, was, in fact, his only friend in the college, or, indeed, in the world for that matter.

By an act of generosity he had helped the forlorn youth, then in his freshman year, over obstacles which bade fair to end his college days. Although the pecuniary obligation was long since paid, the affection and worship Reuel had conceived for his deliverer was dog-like in its devotion.

"Beastly night," he continued, as he stretched his full length luxuriously in the only easy chair the room afforded. "What are you mooning about all alone in the darkness?"

"Same old thing," replied Briggs briefly.

"No wonder the men say that you have a twist, Reuel."

"Ah, man! but the problem of whence and whither! To solve it is my life; I live for that alone; let'm talk."

"You ought to be re-named the 'Science of Trance-States,' Reuel. How a man can grind day and night beats me." Livingston handed him a cigar and for a time they smoked in silence.

At length Reuel said:

"Shake hands with Poverty once, Aubrey, and you will solve the secret of many a student's success in life."

"Doubtless it would do me good," replied Livingston with a laugh, "but just at present, it's the ladies, bless their sweet faces who disturb me, and not delving in books nor weeping over ways and means. Shades of my fathers, forbid that I should ever have to work!

"Lucky dog!" growled Reuel, enviously, as he gazed admiringly at the handsome face turned up to the ceiling and gazing with soft caressing eyes at the ugly whitewashed wall through rings of curling smoke. "Yet you have a greater gift of duality than I," he added dreamily. "Say what you will; ridicule me, torment me, but you know as well as I that the wonders of a material world cannot approach those of the undiscovered country within ourselves—the hidden self lying quiescent in every human soul."

"True, Reuel, and I often wonder what becomes of the mind and morals, distinctive entities grouped in the republic known as man, when death comes. Good and evil in me contend; which will gain the mastery? Which will accompany me into the silent land?"

"Good and evil, God and the devil," suggested Reuel. "Yes, sinner or saint, body or soul, which wins in the life struggle? I am not sure that it matters which," he concluded with a shrug of his handsome shoulders. "I should know if I never saw you again until the struggle was over. Your face will tell its own tale in another five years. Now listen to this:" He caught up the book he had been reading and rapidly turning the leaves read over the various passages that had impressed him.

"A curious accumulation of data; the writer evidently takes himself seriously," Livingston commented.

"And why not?" demanded Reuel.

"You and I know enough to credit the author."

"Yes; but are we prepared to go so far?"

"This man is himself a mystic. He gives his evidence clearly enough."

"And do you credit it?"

"Every word! Could I but get the necessary subject, I would convince you; I would go farther than M. Binet in unveiling the vast scheme of compensation and retribution carried about in the vast recesses of the human soul."

"Find the subject and I will find the money," laughed Aubrey.

"Do you mean it, Aubrey? Will you join me in carrying forward a search for more light on the mysteries of existence?"

"I mean it. And now, Reuel, come down from the clouds, and come with me to a concert."

"Tonight?"

"Yes, 'tonight'" mimicked the other. "The blacker the night, the greater the need of amusement. You go out too little."

"Who gives the concert?"

"Well, it's a new departure in the musical world; something Northerners know nothing of; but I who am a Southerner, born and bred, or as the vulgar have it, 'dyed in the wool,' know and understand Negro music. It is a jubilee concert given by a party of Southern colored people at Tremont Temple. I have the tickets. Redpath has them in charge."

"Well, if you say so, I suppose I must." Briggs did not seem greatly impresses.

PAULINE E. HOPKINS

"Coming down to the practical, Reuel, what do you think of the Negro problem? Come to think of it, I have never heard you express an opinion about it. I believe it is the only burning question in the whole category of live issues and ologies about which you are silent."

"I have a horror of discussing the woes of unfortunates, tramps, stray dogs and cats and Negroes—probably because I am an unfortunate myself."

They smoked in silence.

II

The passing of slavery from the land marked a new era in the life of the nation. The war, too, had passed like a dream of horrors, and over the resumption of normal conditions in business and living, the whole country, as one man, rejoiced and heaved a deep sigh of absolute content.

Under the spur of the excitement occasioned by the Proclamation of Freedom, and the great need of schools for the blacks, thousands of dollars were contributed at the North, and agents were sent to Great Britain, where generosity towards the Negroes was boundless. Money came from all directions, pouring into the hands of philanthropists, who were anxious to prove that the country was able, not only to free the slave, but to pay the great debt it owed him,—protection as he embraced freedom, and a share in the great Government he had aided to found by sweat and toil and blood. It was soon discovered that the Negro possessed a phenomenal gift of music, and it was determined to utilize this gift in helping to support educational institutions of color in the Southland.

A band of students from Fisk University were touring the country, and those who had been fortunate enough to listen once to their matchless untrained voices singing their heartbreaking minor music with its grand and impossible intervals and sound combinations, were eager to listen again and yet again.

Wealthy and exclusive society women everywhere vied in showering benefits and patronage upon the new prodigies who had suddenly become the pets of the musical world. The Temple was a blaze of light, and crowded from pit to dome. It was the first appearance of the troupe in New England; therefore it was a gala night, and Boston culture was out in force.

The two friends easily found their seats in the first balcony, and from that position idly scanned the vast audience to beguile the tedious waiting. Reuel's thoughts were disturbed; he read over the program, but it carried no meaning to his pre-occupied mind; he was uneasy; the face he had seen outlined in the twilight haunted him. A great nervous dread of he knew not what possessed him, and he actually suffered as he sat there answering at random the running fire of comments made by Livingston on the audience, and replying none too cordially to the greetings of fellow-students, drawn to the affair, like himself, by curiosity.

"Great crowd for such a night," observed one. "The weather matches your face, Briggs; why didn't you leave it outside? Why do you look so down?"

Reuel shrugged his shoulders.

"They say there are some pretty girls in the troupe; one or two as white as we," continued the speaker unabashed by Reuel's surliness.

"They range at home from alabaster to ebony," replied Livingston. "The results of amalgamation are worthy the careful attention of all medical experts."

"Don't talk shop, Livingston," said Briggs peevishly.

"You are really more disagreeable than usual," replied Livingston, pleasantly. "Do try to be like the other fellows, for once, Reuel."

Silence ensued for a time, and then the irrepressible one of the party remarked: "The soprano soloist is great; heard her in New York." At this there was a general laugh among the men. Good natured Charlie Vance was generally "stuck" once a month with the "loveliest girl, by jove, you know."

"That explains your presence here, Vance; what's her name?"

"Dianthe Lusk."

"Great name. I hope she comes up to it,—the flower of Jove."

"Flower of Jove, indeed! You'll say so when you see her," cried Charlie with his usual enthusiasm.

"What! again, my son? 'Like Dian's kiss, unmasked, unsought, Love gives itself'" quoted Livingston, with a smile on his handsome face.

"Oh, stow it! Aubrey, even your cold blood will be stirred at sight of her exquisite face; of her voice I will not speak; I cannot do it justice."

"If this is to be the result of emancipation, I for one vote that we ask Congress to annul the Proclamation," said Reuel, drily.

Now conversation ceased; a famous local organist began a concert on the organ to occupy the moments of waiting. The music soothed Reuel's restlessness. He noticed that the platform usually occupied by the speaker's desk, now held a number of chairs and a piano. Certainly, the assiduous advertising had brought large patronage for the new venture, he thought as he idly calculated the financial result from the number in the audience.

Soon the hot air, the glare of lights, the mingling of choice perfumes emanating from the dainty forms of elegantly attired women, acted upon him as an intoxicant. He began to feel the pervading excitement—the flutter of expectation, and presently the haunting face left him.

The prelude drew to a close; the last chord fell from the fingers of the artist; a line of figures—men and women—dark in hue. and neatly dressed in quiet evening clothes, filed noiselessly from the anterooms and filled the chairs upon the platform. The silence in the house was painful. These were representatives of the people for whom God had sent the terrible scourge of blood upon the land to free from bondage. The old abolitionists in the vast audience felt the blood leave their faces beneath the stress of emotion.

The opening number was "The Lord's Prayer." Stealing, rising, swelling, gathering, as it thrilled the ear, all the delights of harmony in a grand minor cadence that told of deliverance from bondage and homage to God for his wonderful aid, sweeping the awed heart with an ecstasy that was almost pain; breathing, hovering, soaring, they held the vast multitude in speechless wonder.

Thunders of applause greeted the close of the hymn. Scarcely waiting for a silence, a female figure rose and came slowly to the edge of the platform and stood in the blaze of lights with hands modestly clasped before her. She was not in any way the preconceived idea of a Negro. Fair as the fairest woman in the hall, with wavy bands of chestnut hair, and great, melting eyes of brown, soft as those of childhood; a willowy figure of exquisite mold, clad in a sombre gown of black. There fell a voice upon the listening ear, in celestial showers of silver that passed all conceptions, all comparisons, all dreams; a voice beyond belief—a great soprano of unimaginable beauty, soaring heavenward in mighty intervals.

"Go down, Moses, way down in Egypt's land, Tell ol' Pharaoh, let my people go." sang the woman in tones that awakened ringing harmonies in the heart of every listener.

"By Jove!" Reuel heard Livingston exclaim. For himself he was dazed, thrilled; never save among the great artists of the earth, was such a voice heard alive with the divine fire.

Some of the women in the audience wept; there was the distinct echo of a sob in the deathly quiet which gave tribute to the power of genius. Spellbound they sat beneath the outpoured anguish of a suffering soul. All the horror, the degredation from which a race had been delivered were in the pleading strains of the singer's voice. It strained the senses almost beyond endurance. It pictured to that self-possessed, highly-cultured

New England assemblage as nothing else ever had, the awfulness of the hell from which a people had been happily plucked.

Reuel was carried out of himself; he leaned forward in eager contemplation of the artist; he grew cold with terror and fear. Surely it could not be—he must be dreaming! It was incredible! Even as he whispered the words to himself the hall seemed to grow dim and shadowy; the sea of faces melted away; there before him in the blaze of light—like a lovely phantom—stood a woman wearing the face of his vision of the afternoon!

III

I t was Hallow-eve.

The north wind blew a cutting blast over the stately Charles, and broke the waves into a miniature flood; it swept the streets of the University city, and danced on into the outlying suburbs tossing the last leaves about in gay disorder, not even sparing the quiet precincts of Mount Auburn cemetery. A deep, clear, moonless sky stretched overhead, from which hung myriads of sparkling stars.

It Mount Auburn, where the residences of the rich lay far apart, darkness and quietness had early settled down. The main street seemed given over to die duskiness of the evening, and with one exception, there seemed no light on earth or in heaven save the cold gleam of the stars.

THE ONE EXCEPTION WAS IN the home of Charlie Vance, or "Adonis," as he was called by his familiars. The Vance estate was a spacious house with rambling ells, tortuous chimney-stacks, and corners, eaves and iedges; the grounds were extensive and well kept telling silently of the opulence of its owner. Its windows sent forth a cheering light. Dinner was just over.

Within, on an old-fashioned hearth, blazed a glorious wood fire, which gave a rich coloring to the oak-paneled walls, and fell warmly on a group of young people seated and standing, chatting about the fire. At one side of it, in a chair of the Elizabethan period, sat the hostess, Molly Vance, only daughter of James Vance, Esq., and sister of "Adonis," a beautiful girl of eighteen.

At the opposite side, leaning with folded arms against the high carved mantel, stood Aubrey Livingston; the beauty of his fair hair and blue eyes was never more marked as he stood there in the gleam of the fire and the soft candlelight. He was talking vivaciously, his eyes turning from speaker to speaker, as he ran on, but resting chiefly with pride on his beautiful betrothed, Molly Vance.

The group was completed by two or three other men, among them Reuel Briggs, and three pretty girls. Suddenly a clock struck the hour.

"Only nine," exclaimed Molly. "Good people, what shall we do to wile the tedium of waiting for the witching hour? Have any one of you enough wisdom to make a suggestion?"

"Music," said Livingston.

"We don't want anything so commonplace."

"Blind Man's Buff," suggested "Adonis."

"Oh! please not that, the men are so rough!"

"Let us," broke in Cora Scott, "tell ghost stories."

"Good, Cora! yes, yes, yes."

"No, no!" exclaimed a chorus of voices.

"Yes, yes," laughed Molly, gaily, clapping her hands. "It is the very thing. Cora, you are the wise woman of the party. It is the very time, tonight is the new moon, and we can try our projects in the Hyde house."

"The moon should be full to account for such madness," said Livingston.

"Don't be disagreeable, Aubrey," replied Molly. "The 'ayes' have it. You're with me, Mr. Briggs?"

"Of course, Miss Vance," answered Reuel, "to go to the North Pole or Hades—only please tell us where is 'Hyde house.'"

"Have you never heard? Why it's the adjoining estate. It is reputed to be haunted, and a lady in white haunts the avenue in the most approved ghostly style."

"Bosh!" said Livingston.

"Possibly," remarked the laughing Molly, "but it is the 'bosh' of a century."

"Go on, Miss Vance; don't mind Aubrey. Who has seen the lady?"

"She is not easily seen," proceeded Molly, "she only appears on Hallow-eve, when the moon is new, as it will be tonight. I had forgotten that fact when I invited you here. If anyone stands, tonight, in the avenue leading to the house, he will surely see the tall veiled figure gliding among the old hemlock trees."

One or two shivered.

" If, however, the watcher remain, the lady will pause, and utter some sentence of prophecy of his future."

"Has anyone done this?" queried Reuel.

"My old nurse says she remembers that the lady was seen once."

"Then, we'll test it again tonight!" exclaimed Reuel, greatly excited over the chance to prove his pet theories.

"Well, Molly, you've started Reuel off on his greatest hobby; I wash my hands of both of you."

"Let us go any way!" chorused the venturesome party.

"But there are conditions," exclaimed Molly. "Only one person must go at a time."

Aubrey laughed as he noticed the consternation in one or two faces.

"So," continued Molly, "as we cannot go together, I propose that each shall stay a quarter of an hour, then whether successful or not, return and let another take his or her place. I will go first."

"No—" it was Charlie who spoke—"I put my veto on that, Molly. If you are mad enough to risk colds in this mad freak, it shall be done fairly. We will draw lots."

"And I add to that, not a girl leave the house; we men will try the charm for the sake of your curiosity, but not a girl goes. You can try the ordinary Hallow-eve projects while we are away."

With many protests, but concealed relief, this plan was reluctantly adopted by the female element. The lots were prepared and placed in a hat, and amid much merriment, drawn.

"You are third, Mr. Briggs," exclaimed Molly who held the hat and watched the checks.

"I'm first," said Livingston, "and Charlie second."

"While we wait for twelve, tell us the story of the house, Molly," cried Cora.

Thus adjured, Molly settled herself comfortably in her chair and began: "Hyde House is nearly opposite the cemetery, and its land joins that of this house; it is indebted for its ill repute to one of its owners, John Hyde. It has been known for years as a haunted house, and avoided as such by the superstitious. It is low-roofed, rambling, and almost entirely concealed by hemlocks, having an air of desolation and decay in keeping with its ill-repute. In its dozen rooms were enacted the dark deeds which gave the place the name of the 'haunted house.'

"The story is told of an unfaithful husband, a wronged wife and a beautiful governess forming a combination which led to the murder of a guest for his money. The master of the house died from remorse, under peculiar circumstances. These materials give us the plot for a thrilling ghost story."

"Well, where does the lady come in?" interrupted "Adonis."

There was a general laugh.

"This world is all a blank without the ladies for Charlie," remarked Aubrey. "Molly, go on with your story, my child."

"You may all laugh as much as you please, but what I am telling you is believed in this section by every one. A local magazine speaks of it as follows, as near as I can remember:

"'A most interesting story is told by a woman who occupied the house for a short time. She relates that she had no sooner crossed the threshold than she was met by a beautiful woman in flowing robes of black, who begged permission to speak through her to her friends. The friends were thereupon bidden to be present at a certain time. When all were assembled they were directed by invisible powers to kneel. Then the spirit told the tale of the tragedy through the woman. The spirit was the niece of the murderer, and she was in the house when the crime was committed. She discovered blood stains on the door of the woodshed, and told her uncle that she suspected him of murdering the guest, who had mysteriously disappeared. He secured her promise not to betray him. She had always kept the secret. Although both had been dead for many years, they were chained to the scene of the crime, as was the governess, who was the man's partner in guilt. The final release of the niece from the place was conditional on her making a public confession. This done she would never be heard from again. And she never was, except on Hallow-eve, when the moon is new.'"

"Bring your science and philosophy to bear on this, Reuel. Come, come, man, give us your opinion," exclaimed Aubrey.

"Reuel doesn't believe such stuff; he's too sensible," added Charlie.

"If these are facts, they are only for those who have a mental affinity with them. I believe that if we could but strengthen our mental sight, we could discover the broad highway between this and the other world on which both good and evil travel to earth," replied Reuel.

"And that first highway was beaten out of chaos by Satan, as Milton has it, eh, Briggs?"

"Have it as you like, Smith. No matter. For my own part, I have never believed that the whole mental world is governed by the faculties we understand, and can reduce to reason or definite feeling. But I will keep my ideas to myself; one does not care to be laughed at."

The conversation was kept up for another hour about indifferent subjects, but all felt the excitement underlying the frivolous chatter. At quarter before twelve, Aubrey put on his ulster with the words: "Well, here goes for my lady." The great doors were thrown open, and the company grouped about him to see him depart.

"Mind, honor bright, you go," laughed Charlie.

"Honor bright," he called back.

Then he went on beyond the flood of light into the gloom of the night. Muffled in wraps and ulsters they lingered on the piazzas waiting his return.

"Would he see anything?"

"Of course not!" laughed Charlie and Bert Smith. "Still, we bet he'll be sharp to his time."

They were right. Aubrey returned at five minutes past twelve, a failure.

Charlie ran down the steps briskly, but in ten minutes came hastening back.

"Well," was the chorus, "did you see it?"

"I saw something—a figure in the trees!"

"And you did not wait?" said Molly, scornfully.

"No, I dared not; I own it."

"It's my turn; I'm third," said Reuel.

"Luck to you, old man," they called as he disappeared in the darkness.

Reuel Briggs was a brave man. He knew his own great physical strength and felt no fear as he traversed the patch of woods lying between the two estates. As he reached the avenue of hemlocks he was not thinking of his mission, but of the bright home scene he had just left—of love and home and rest—such a life as was unfolding before Aubrey Livingston and sweet Molly Vance.

"I suppose there are plenty of men in the world as lonely as I am," he mused; "but I suppose it is my own fault. A man though plain and poor can generally manage to marry; and I am both. But I don't regard a wife as one regards bread—better sour bread than starvation; better an uncongenial life-companion than none! What a frightful mistake! No! The woman I marry must be to me a necessity, because I love her; because so loving her, 'all the current of my being flows to her,' and I feel she is my supreme need."

Just now he felt strangely happy as he moved in the gloom of the hemlocks, and lie wondered many times after that whether the spirit is sometimes mysteriously conscious of the nearness of its kindred spirit; and feels, in anticipation, the "sweet unrest" of the master-passion that rules the world.

The mental restlessness of three weeks before seemed to have possession of him again. Suddenly the "restless, unsatisfied longing," rose again in his heart. He turned his head and saw a female figure just ahead of him in the path, coming toward him. He could not see her features distinctly, only the eyes—large, bright and dark. But their expression! Sorrowful, wistful—almost imploring—gazing straightforward, as if they saw nothing—like the eyes of a person entirely absorbed and not distinguishing one object from another.

She was close to him now, and there was a perceptible pause in her step. Suddenly she covered her face with her clasped hands, as if in uncontrollable grief. Moved by a mighty emotion, Briggs addressed the lonely figure:

"You are in trouble, madam; may I help you?"

Briggs never knew how he survived the next shock. Slowly the hands were removed from the face and the moon gave a distinct view of the lovely features of the jubilee singer—Dianthe Lusk.

She did not seem to look at Briggs, but straight before her, as she said in a low, clear, passionless voice:

"You can help me, but not now; tomorrow."

Reuel's most prominent feeling was one of delight. The way was open to become fully acquainted with the woman who had haunted him sleeping and waking, for weeks past.

"Not now! Yet you are suffering. Shall I see you soon? Forgive me—but oh! tell me—"

He was interrupted. The lady moved or floated away from him, with her face toward him and gazing steadily at him.

He felt that his whole heart was in his eyes, yet hers did not drop, nor did her cheek color.

"The time is not yet," she said in the same, clear, calm, measured tones, in which she had spoken before. Reuel made a quick movement toward her, but she raised her hand, and the gesture forbade him to follow her. He paused involuntarily, and she turned away, and disappeared among the gloomy hemlock trees.

He parried the questions of the merry crowd when he returned to the house, with indifferent replies. How they would have laughed at him—slave of a passion as sudden and romantic as that of Romeo for Juliet; with no more foundation than the "presentments" in books which treat of the "occult." He dropped asleep at last, in the early morning hours, and lived over his experience in his dreams.

IV

*Although not yet a practitioner, Reuel Briggs was a
recognized power in the medical profession. In brain
diseases he was an authority.*

Early the next morning he was aroused from sleep by imperative
knocking at his door. It was a messenger from the hospital. There
had been a train accident on the Old Colony road, would he come
immediately?

Scarcely giving himself time for a cup of coffee, he arrived at the
hospital almost as soon as the messenger.

The usual silence of the hospital was broken; all was bustle and
movement, without confusion. It was a great call upon the resources of
the officials, but they were equal to it. The doctors passed from sufferer
to sufferer, dressing their injuries; then they were borne to beds from
which some would never rise again.

"Come with me to the women's ward, Doctor Briggs," said a nurse.
"There is a woman there who was taken from the wreck. She shows
no sign of injury, but the doctors cannot restore her to consciousness.
Doctor Livingston pronounces her dead, but it doesn't seem possible.
So young, so beautiful. Do something for her, Doctor."

The men about a cot made way for Reuel, as he entered the ward.
"It's no use Briggs," said Livingston to him in reply to his question.
"Your science won't save her. The poor girl is already cold and stiff."

He moved aside disclosing to Reuel's gaze the lovely face of Dianthe
Lusk!

The most marvelous thing to watch is the death of a person. At
that moment the opposite takes place to that which took place when
life entered the first unit, after nature had prepared it for the inception
of life. I low the vigorous life watches the passage of the liberated life
out of its earthly environment! What a change is this! How important
the knowledge of whither life tends! Here is shown the setting free of a
disciplined spirit giving up its mortality for immortality,—the condition
necessary to know God. Death! There is no death. Life is everlasting,
and from its reality can have no end. Life is real and never changes, but
preserves its identity eternally as the angels, and the immortal spirit of
man, which are the only realities and continuities in the universe, God

being over all, Supreme Ruler and Divine Essence from whom comes all life. Somewhat in this train ran Reuel's thoughts as he stood beside the seeming dead girl, the cynosure of all the medical faculty there assembled.

To the majority of those men, the case was an ordinary death, and that was all there was to it. What did this young upstart expect to make of it? Of his skill and wonderful theories they had heard strange tales, but they viewed him coldly as we are apt to view those who dare to leave the beaten track of conventionality.

Outwardly cool and stolid, showing no sign of recognition, he stood for some seconds gazing down on Dianthe: every nerve quivered, every pulse of his body throbbed. Her face held for him a wonderful charm, an extraordinary fascination. As he gazed he knew that once more he beheld what he had vaguely sought and yearned for all his forlorn life. His whole heart went out to her; destiny, not chance, had brought him to her. He saw, too, that no one knew her, none had a clue to her identity; he determined to remain silent for the present, and immediately he sought to impress Livingston to do likewise.

His keen glance swept the faces of the surrounding physicians. "No, not one," he told himself, "holds the key to unlock this seeming sleep of death." He alone could do it. Advancing far afield in the mysterious regions of science, he had stumbled upon the solution of one of life's problems: the *reanimation of the body after seeming death*.

He had hesitated to tell of his discovery to any one; not even to Livingston had he hinted of the daring possibility, fearing ridicule in case of a miscarriage in his calculations. But for the sake of this girl he would make what he felt to be a premature disclosure of the results of his experiments. Meantime, Livingston, from his place at the foot of the cot, watched his friend with fascinated eyes. He. too. had resolved, contrary to his first intention, not to speak of his knowledge of the beautiful patient's identity. Curiosity was on tiptoe; expectancy was in the air. All felt that something unusual was about to happen.

Now Reuel, with gentle fingers, touched rapidly the clammy brow, the icy, livid hands, the region of the pulseless heart. No breath came from between the parted lips; the life-giving organ was motionless. As he concluded his examination, he turned to the assembled doctors:

"As I diagnose this case, it is one of suspended animation. This woman has been long and persistently subjected to mesmeric influences, and the nervous shock induced by the excitement of the accident has thrown her into a cataleptic sleep."

"But, man!" broke from the head physician in tones of exasperation, "rigor mortis in unmistakable form is here. The woman is dead!"

At these words there was a perceptible smile on the faces of some of the students—associates who resented" his genius as a personal affront, and who considered these words as good as a reprimand for the daring student, and a settler of his pretensions. Malice and envy, from Adam's time until today, have loved a shining mark.

But the reproof was unheeded. Reuel was not listening. Absorbed in thoughts of the combat before him, he was oblivious to all else as he bent over the lifeless figure on the cot. He was full of an earnest purpose. He was strung up to a high tension of force and energy. As he looked down upon the unconscious girl whom none but he could save from the awful fate of a death by post-mortem, and who by some mysterious mesmeric affinity existing between them, had drawn him to her rescue, he felt no fear that he should fail.

Suddenly he bent down and took both cold hands into his left and passed his right hand firmly over her arms from shoulder to wrist. He repeated the movements several times; there was no response to the passes. He straightened up, and again stood silently gazing upon the patient. Then, like a man just aroused from sleep, he looked across the bed at Livingston and said abruptly:

"Dr. Livingston, will you go over to my room and bring me the case of vials in my medicine cabinet? I cannot leave the patient at this point."

Livingston started in surprise as he replied: "Certainly, Briggs, if it will help you any."

"The patient does not respond to any of the ordinary methods of awakening. She would probably lie in this sleep for months, and death ensue from exhaustion, if stronger remedies are not used to restore the vital force to a normal condition."

Livingston left the hospital; he could not return under an hour; Reuel took up his station by the bed whereon was stretched an apparently lifeless body, and the other doctors went the rounds of the wards attending to their regular routine of duty. The nurses gazed at him curiously; the head doctor, upon whom the young student's earnestness and sincerity had evidently made an impression, came a number of times to the bare little room to gaze upon its silent occupants, but there was nothing new. When Livingston returned, the group again gathered about the iron cot where lay the patient.

"Gentlemen," said Reuel, with quiet dignity, when they were once more assembled, "will you individually examine the patient once more and give your verdicts?"

Once more doctors and students carefully examined the inanimate figure in which the characteristics of death were still more pronounced. On the outskirts of the group hovered the house-surgeon's assistants ready to transport the body to the operating room for the post-mortem. Again the head physician spoke, this time impatiently.

"We are wasting our time, Dr. Briggs; I pronounce the woman dead. She was past medical aid when brought here."

"There is no physical damage, apparent or hidden, that you can see, Doctor?" questioned Reuel, respectfully.

"No; it is a perfectly healthful organism, though delicate. I agree entirely with your assertion that death was induced by the shock."

"Not *death*, Doctor," protested Briggs.

"Well, well, call it what you like—call it what you like, it amounts to the same in the end," replied the doctor testily.

"Do you all concur in Doctor Hamilton's diagnosis?" Briggs included all the physicians in his sweeping glance. There was a general assent.

"I am prepared to show you that in some cases of seeming death— or even death in reality—consciousness may be restored or the dead brought back to life. I have numberless times in the past six months restored consciousness to dogs and cats after rigor mortis had set in," he declared calmly.

"Bosh!" broke from a leading surgeon.

In this manner the astounding statement, made in all seriousness, was received by the group of scientists mingled with an astonishment that resembled stupidity. But in spite of their scoffs, the young student's confident manner made a decided impression upon his listeners, unwilling as they were to be convinced.

Reuel went on rapidly; his eyes kindled; his whole person took on the majesty of conscious power, and pride in the knowledge he possessed. "I have found by research that life is not dependent upon organic function as a principle. It may be infused into organized bodies even after the organs have ceased to perform their legitimate offices. Where death has been due to causes which have not impaired or injured or destroyed tissue formation or torn down the structure of vital organs, life may be recalled when it has become entirely extinct, which is not so in the present case. This I have discovered by my experiments in animal magnetism."

The medical staff was fairly bewildered. Again Dr. Hamilton spoke:

"You make the assertion that the dead can be brought to life, if I understand your drift, Dr. Briggs, and you expect us to believe such utter nonsense." He added significantly, "My colleagues and I are here to be convinced."

"If you will be patient for a short time longer, Doctor, I will support my assertion by action. The secret of life lies in what we call volatile magnetism—it exists in the free atmosphere. You, Dr. Livingston, understand my meaning; do you see the possibility in my words?" he questioned, appealing to Aubrey for the first time.

"I have a faint conception of your meaning, certainly," replied his friend.

"This subtile magnetic agent is constantly drawn into the body through the lungs, absorbed and held in bounds until chemical combination has occurred through the medium of mineral agents always present in normal animal tissue When respiration ceases this magnetism cannot be drawn into the lungs. It must be artificially supplied. This, gentlemen, is my discovery. I supply this magnetism. I have it here in the case Dr. Livingston has kindly brought me." He held up to their gaze a small phial wherein reposed a powder. Physicians and students, now eager listeners, gazed spell-bound upon him, straining their ears to catch every tone of the low voice and every change of the luminous eyes; they pressed forward to examine the contents of the bottle. It passed from eager hand to eager hand, then back to the owner.

"This compound, gentlemen, is an exact reproduction of the conditions existing in the human body. It has common salt for its basis. This salt is saturated with oleo resin and then exposed for several hours in an atmosphere of free ammonia. The product becomes a powder, and *that* brings back the seeming dead to life."

"Establish your theory by practical demonstration, Dr. Briggs, and the dreams of many eminent practitioners will be realized," said Dr. Hamilton, greatly agitated by his words.

"Your theory smacks of the supernatural, Dr. Briggs, charlatanism, or dreams of lunacy," said the surgeon. "We leave such assertions to quacks, generally, for the time of miracles is past."

"The supernatural presides over man's formation always," returned Reuel, quietly. "Life is that evidence of supernatural endowment which originally entered nature during the formation of the units for the evolution of man. Perhaps the superstitious masses came nearer to solving the mysteries of creation than the favored elect will ever come. Be that as it may, I will not contend. I will proceed with the demonstration."

There radiated from the speaker the potent presence of a truthful mind, a pure, unselfish nature, and that inborn dignity which repels the shafts of lower minds as ocean's waves absorb the drops of rain. Something like respect mingled with awe hushed the sneers, changing them into admiration as he calmly proceeded to administer the so-called life-giving powder. Each man's watch was in his hand; one minute passed—another—and still another. The body remained inanimate.

A cold smile of triumph began to dawn on the faces of the older members of the profession, but it vanished in its incipiency, for a tremor plainly passed over the rigid form before them. Another second—another convulsive movement of the chest!

"She moves!" cried Aubrey at last, carried out of himself by the strain on his nerves. "Look, gentlemen, she breathes! *She is alive*; Briggs is right! Wonderful! Wonderful!"

"We said there could not be another miracle, and here it is!" exclaimed Dr. Hamilton with strong emotion.

Five minutes more and the startled doctors fell back from the bedside at a motion of Reuel's hand. A wondering nurse, with dilated eyes, unfolded a screen, placed it in position and came and stood beside the bed opposite Reuel. Holding Dianthe's hands, he said in a low voice: "Are you awake?" Her eyes unclosed in a cold, indifferent stare which gradually changed to one of recognition. She looked at him— she smiled, and said in a weak voice, "Oh, it is you; I dreamed of you while I slept."

She was like a child—so trusting that it went straight to the young man's heart, and for an instant a great lump seemed to rise in his throat and choke him. He held her hands and chafed them, but spoke with his eyes only. The nurse said in a low voice: "Dr. Briggs, a few spoonfuls of broth will help her?"

"Yes, thank you, nurse; that will be just right." He drew a chair close beside the bed, bathed her face with water and pushed back the tangle of bright hair. He felt a great relief and quiet joy that his experiment had been successful.

"Have I been ill? Where am I?" she asked after a pause, as her face grew troubled and puzzled.

"No, but you have been asleep a long time; we grew anxious about you. You must not talk until you are stronger."

The muse returned with the broth; Dianthe drank it eagerly and called for water, then with her hand still clasped in Reuel's she sank into a deep sleep, breathing softly like a tired child. It was plain to the man of science that hope for the complete restoration of her faculties would depend upon time, nature and constitution. Her effort to collect her thoughts was unmistakable. In her sleep, presently, from her lips fell incoherent words and phrases; but through it all she clung to Reuel's hand, seeming to recognize in him a friend.

A little later the doctors filed in noiselessly and stood about the bed gazing down upon the sleeper with awe, listening to her breathing, feeling lightly the fluttering pulse. Then they left the quiet house of suffering, marveling at the miracle just accomplished in their presence. Livingston lingered with Briggs after the other physicians were gone.

"This is a great day for you, Reuel," he said, as he laid a light caressing hand upon the other's shoulder.

Reuel seized the hand in a quick convulsive clasp. "True and tried friend, do not credit me more than I deserve. No praise is due me. I am an instrument—how I know not—a child of circumstances. Do you not percieve something strange in this case? Can you not deduce conclusions from your own intimate knowledge of this science?"

"What can you mean, Reuel?"

"I mean—it is a *dual* mesmeric trance! The girl is only partly normal now. Binet speaks at length of this possibility in his treatise. We have stumbled upon an extraordinary case. It will take a year to restore her to perfect health."

"In the meantime we ought to search out her friends."

"Is there any hurry, Aubrey?" pleaded Reuel, anxiously.

"Why not wait until her memory returns; it will not be long, I believe, although she may still be liable to the trances."

"We'll put off the evil day to any date you may name, Briggs; for my part, I would preserve her incognito indefinitely."

Reuel made no reply. Livingston was not sure that he heard him.

V

The world scarcely estimates the service rendered by those who have unlocked the gates of sensation by the revelations of science; and yet it is to the clear perception of things which we obtain by the study of nature's laws that we are enabled to appreciate her varied gifts. The scientific journals of the next month contained wonderful and *wondering* accounts of the now celebrated case,—re-animation after seeming death. Reuel's lucky star was in the ascendant; fame and fortune awaited him; he had but to grasp them. Classmates who had once ignored him now sought familiar association, or else gazed upon him with awe and reverence. "How did he do it?" was the query in each man's mind, and then came a stampede for all scientific matter bearing upon animal magnetism.

How often do we look in wonder at the course of other men's lives, whose paths have diverged so widely from the beaten track of our own, that, unable to comprehend the one spring upon which, perhaps, the whole secret of the diversity hinged, we have been fain to content ourselves with summing up our judgment in the common phrase. "Well, it's very strange; what odd people there are in the world to be sure!"

Many times this trite sentence was uttered during the next few months, generally terminating every debate among medical students in various colleges.

Unmindful of his growing popularity. Reuel devoted every moment of his spare time to close study of his patient. Although but a youth, the scientist might have passed for any age under fifty, and life for him seemed to have taken on a purely mechanical aspect since he had become first in this great cause. Under pretended indifference to public criticism, throbbed a heart of gold, sensitive to a fault; desiring above all else the well-being of all humanity; his faithfulness to those who suffered amounted to complete self-sacrifice. Absolutely free from the vices which beset most young men of his age and profession, his daily life was a white, unsullied page to the friend admitted to unrestricted intercourse, and gave an irresistible impetus to that friendship, for Livingston could not but admire the newly developed depths of nobility which he now saw unfolding day by day in Reuel's character. Nor was Livingston far behind the latter in his interest in all that affected Dianthe. Enthused by its scientific aspect, he vied with Reuel in close attention to the medical side of the case, and being more worldly did not neglect the material side.

He secretly sought out and obtained the address of the manager of the jubilee singers and to his surprise received the information that Miss Lusk had left the troupe to enter the service of a traveling magnetic physician—a woman—for a large salary. They (the troupe) were now in Europe and had heard nothing of Miss Lusk since.

After receiving this information by cable, Livingston sat a long time smoking and thinking: people often disappeared in a great city, and the police would undoubtedly find the magnetic physician if he applied to them. Of course that was the sensible thing to do, but then the publicity, and he hated that for the girl's sake. Finally he decided to compromise the matter by employing a detective. With him to decide that it was expedient to do a certain thing was the same as to act; before night the case was in the hands of an expert detective who received a goodly retainer. Two weeks from that day—it was December twenty-fourth—before he left his boarding place, the detective was announced. He had found the woman in a small town near Chicago. She said that she had no knowledge of Miss Lusk's whereabouts. Dianthe had remained with her three weeks, and at the end of that time had mysteriously disappeared; she had not heard of her since.

Livingston secured the woman's name and address, gave the man a second check together with an admonition to keep silence concerning Miss Lusk. That closed the episode. But of his observations and discoveries, Aubrey said nothing, noting every phase of this strange happening in silence.

Strangely enough, none of the men that had admired the colored artist who had enthralled their senses by her wonderful singing a few weeks before, recognized her in the hospital waif consecrated to the service of science. Her incognito was complete.

The patient was now allowed the freedom of the corridors for exercise, and was about her room during the day. The returns of the trance-state were growing less regular, although she frequently fell into convulsions, thereby enduring much suffering, sometimes lying for hours in a torpid state. Livingston had never happened to be present on these occasions, but he had heard of them from eye-witnesses. One day he entered the room while one was occurring. His entrance was unnoticed as he approached lightly over the uncarpeted floor, and stood transfixed by the scene before him.

Dianthe stood upright, with closed eyes, in the middle of the room. Only the movement of her bosom betrayed breath. The other occupants of the room preserved a solemn silence. She addressed Reuel, whose outstretched arms were extended as if in blessing over her head.

"Oh! Dearest friend! hasten to cure me of my sufferings. Did you not promise at that last meeting? You said to me, 'You are in trouble and I can help you.' And I answered, 'The time is not yet.' Is it not so?"

"Yes," replied Reuel. "Patience a while longer; all will be well with you."

"Give me the benefit of your powerful will," she continued. "I know much but as yet have not the power to express it: I see much clearly, much dimly, of the powers and influences behind the Veil, and yet I cannot name them. Sometime the full power will be mine; and mine shall be thine. In seven months the sick will be restored—she will awake to worldly cares once more." Her voice ceased; she sank upon the cot in a recumbent position. Her face was pale; she appeared to sleep. Fifteen minutes passed in death-like stillness, then she extended her arms, stretched, yawned, rubbed her eyes—awoke.

Livingston listened and looked in a trance of delight, his keen artistic sense fully aroused and appreciative, feeling the glamour of her presence and ethereal beauty like a man poring over a poem that he has unexpectedly stumbled upon, losing himself in it, until it becomes, as it were, a part of himself. He felt as he watched her that he was doing a foolish thing in thus exposing himself to temptation while his honor and faith were pledged to another. But then, foolishness is so much better than wisdom, particularly to a man in certain stages of life. And then he fell to questioning if there could be temptation for him through this girl—he laughed at the thought and the next instant dismay covered him with confusion, for like a flash he realized that the mischief was already done.

As we have already hinted, Aubrey was no saint; he knew that fickleness was in his blood; he had never denied himself anything that he wanted very much in his whole life. Would he grow to want this beautiful woman very much? Time would tell.

VI

It was Christmas-time—a good, sensible seasonable day before Christmas, with frost and ice in abundance, and a clear, bright, wintry sky above. Boston was very full of people—mostly suburban visitors—who were rushing here and there bent on emptying their purses on the least provocation. Good-nature prevailed among the pedestrians; one poor wretch stood shivering, with blue, wan face, on the edge of the sidewalk, his sightless eyes staring straight before him, trying to draw a tune from a consumptive violin—the embodiment of despair. He was, after all, in the minority, to judge by the hundreds of comfortably-clad forms that hurried past him, breathing an atmosphere of peace and prosperity. Tomorrow the church bells would ring out tidings that another Christmas was born, bidding all rejoice.

This evening, at six o'clock, the two friends went to dine in a hotel in a fashionable quarter. They were due to spend the night and Christmas day at the Vance house. As they walked swiftly along with the elastic tread of youth, they simultaneously halted before the blind musician and pressed into his trembling hand a bountiful gift; then they hurried away to escape his thanks.

At the hotel Livingston called for a private dining room, and after the coffee was served, he said:

"Tell me, Briggs, what is the link between you and your patient. There is a link, I am sure. Her words while in the trance made a great impression upon me.

There was a pause before Reuel replied in a low tone, as he rested his arm on the opposite side of the table and propped his head up on his hand:

"Forgive me, Aubrey!"

"For what?"

"This playing with your confidence. I have not been entirely frank with you."

"Oh, well! you are not bound to tell me everything you know. You surely have the right to silence about your affairs, if you think best."

"Listen, Aubrey. I should like to tell you all about it. I would feel better. What you say is true; there is a link; but I never saw her in the flesh before that night at the Temple. With all our knowledge, Aubrey, we are but barbarians in our ideas of the beginning, interim and end

PAULINE E. HOPKINS

of our creation. Why were we created? for whose benefit? can anyone answer that satisfactorily?

"'Few things are hidden from the man who devotes himself earnestly and seriously to the solution of a mystery.' Hawthorne tells us," replied Aubrey. "Have not you proved this, Reuel?"

"Well, yes— or, we prove rather, that our solution but deepens the mystery or mysteries. I have surely proved the last. Aubrey, I look natural, don't I? There is nothing about me that seems wrong?"

"Wrong! No."

"Well, if I tell you the truth you will call me a lunatic. You have heard of people being haunted by hallucinations?"

AUBREY NODDED. "I AM ONE of those persons. Seven weeks ago I saw Dianthe first, but not in the flesh. Hallow-eve I spoke to her in the garden of the haunted house, but not in the flesh. I thought: t strange to be sure, that this face should lurk in my mind so much of the time; but I never dreamed what a crisis it was leading up to. The French and German schools of philosophy have taught us that going to places and familiar passages in books, of which we have had no previous knowledge, is but a proof of Plato's doctrine— the soul's transmigration, and reflections from the invisible world surrounding us."

"Finally a mad desire seized me to find that face a living reality that I might love and worship it. Then I saw her at the Temple—I found her at the hospital—*in the flesh*! My desire was realized."

"And having found her, what then?" He waited breathlessly for the reply.

"I am mightily pleased and satisfied. I will cure her. She is charming; and if it is insanity to be in love with her, I don't care to be sane."

Livingston did not reply at once. His face was like marble in its impassiveness. The other's soft tremulous tones, fearless yet moist eyes and broken sentences, appeared to awaken no response in his breast. Instead, a far-off gleam came into his blue eyes. At last he broke the silence with the words:

"You name it well; it is insanity indeed, for you to love this woman."

"Why?" asked his friend, constrainedly.

"Because it is not for the best."

"For her or me?"

"Oh, for *her*!" he finished the sentence with an expressive gesture.

"I understand you, Aubrey. I should not have believed it of you. If it were one of the other fellows; but you are generally so charitable."

"You forget your own words: 'Tramps, stray dogs and Negroes,'" he quoted significantly. "Then there is your professional career to be considered,—you mean honorable, do you not? How can you succeed if it be hinted abroad that you are married to a Negress?"

"I have thought of all that. I am determined. I will marry her in spite of hell itself! Marry her before she awakens to consciousness of her identity. I'm not unselfish; I don't pretend to be. There is no sin in taking her out of the sphere where she was born. God and science helping me, I will give her life and love and wifehood and maternity and perfect health. God, Aubrey! you, with all you have had of life's sweetness, petted idol of a beautiful world, you who will soon feel the heart-beats of your wife against your breast when lovely Molly is eternally bound to you, what do you know of a lonely, darkened life like mine? I have not the manner nor the charm which wins women. Men like me get love from them which is half akin to pity, when they get anything at all. It is but the shadow. This is my opportunity for happiness; I seize it. Fate has linked us together and no man and no man's laws shall part us."

Livingston sipped his wine quietly, intently watching Reuel's face. Now he leaned across the table and stretched out his hand to Briggs; his eyes looked full into his. As their hands met in a close clasp, he whispered a sentence across the board. Reuel started, uttered an exclamation and flushed slowly a dark, dull red.

"How—where—how did you know it?" he stammered.

"I have known it since first we met; but the secret is safe with me."

VII

The scene which met the gaze when an hour later the young men were ushered into the long drawing-room of the Vance house was one well-calculated to remove all gloomy, pessimistic reasoning.

Warmth, gaiety, pretty women, luxury,—all sent the blood leaping through the veins in delightful anticipation.

Their entrance was greeted by a shout of welcome.

"Oh, Aubrey! I am so glad you are come," cried Molly from the far end of the room. "Fancy tomorrow being Christmas! Shall we be ready for all that company tomorrow night and the ballroom, dining room and hall yet to be trimmed? Is it possible to be ready?"

"Not if we stand dwadling in idle talk."

This from "Adonis," who was far as stretched full length on the sitting-room sofa, with a cigarette between his lips, his hands under his handsome head, surrounded by a bevy of pretty, chattering girls, prominent among whom was Cora Scott, who aided and abbetted Charlie in every piece of mischief.

Molly curled her lip but deigned no reply.

Bert Smith, from a corner of the room where he was about ascending a step-ladder, flung a book heavily at Adonis's lazy figure.

"Don't confuse your verbs," exclaimed Aubrey. "How can you stand when you are lying clown, and were you ever known to do anything else but dwadle, Adonis—eh?"

"I give it up," said Charlie, sleepily, kicking the book off the sofa.

"Is this an amateur grocery shop, may I ask, Miss Vance?" continued Aubrey as he and Briggs made their way to their hostess through an avalanche of parcels and baskets strewn on the tables and the floor.

Molly laughed as she greeted them.

"No wonder you are surprised. I am superintending the arrangement of my poor people's gifts," she explained. "They must all be sent out tonight. I don't know what I should have done without all these good people to help me. But there are *piles* to be done yet. There is the tree, the charades, etc., etc.," she continued, in a plaintive little voice.

"More particularly cetra, cetra," said Aubrey from Bert's corner where he had gone to help along the good works of placing holly wreaths.

"Oh, you, Aubey—stop being a maq pie." Aubrey and Molly were very matter of fact lovers.

"Molly," again broke in Charlie, "suppose the box from Pierson's has never come, won't you be up a tree?" and the speaker opened his handsome eyes wide, and shook off his cigarette-ash.

Molly maintained a dignified silence toward her brother. The firelight danced and dwelt upon her lovingly. She was so pretty, so fair, so slender, so graceful. Now in her gray plush tea-gown, with her hair piled picturesquely on the top of her small head, and fixed there with a big tortoise-shell pin, it would have been difficult to find a more delightful object for the gaze to rest upon.

"We shall have to fall back upon the wardrobes," she said at length. "You are a horrid wet-blanket, Charlie! I am sure I——"

Her remarks were cut short as the door opened, and with laughter and shouting a bevy of young people who had been at work in another part of the house rushed in. "It is come; it's all right; don't worry, Molly!" they sang in chorus.

"Do be quiet all of you; one can hardly hear oneself speak!"

The box from the costumer's had arrived; the great costume party was saved; in short, excitement and bustle were in full swing at Vance Hall as it had been at Christmas-time since the young people could remember.

Adonis lifted himself from the sofa and proposed to open the box of dresses at once, and try them on.

"Charlie, you are a brick!—the very thing!"

"Oh! yes, yes; let us try them on!"

Molly broke through the eager voices:

"And we have not done the ballroom yet!" she said reproachfully.

"Oh! bother the ballroom!" declared Adonis, now thoroughly aroused. "We have all night. We can't do better than to don our finery."

Molly sat down with an air of resigned patience. "I promised Mr. Pierson," she observed quietly, "that the box should not be touched until he was here to superintend matters."

"Oh, Pierson be blowed" elegantly observed her brother. But Reuel Briggs suddenly dropped his work, walked over, and sided with Molly.

"You are quite right, Miss Molly; and you Charlie and Aubrey and the rest of you men, if you want to open the box tonight you must first decorate the ballroom, business before pleasure."

"Saved!—saved! Sec my brave, true knight defends his lady fair." Molly danced, practicing the step she was about to astonish the company with on Christmas-night. "I think I am what the Scotch call 'fev'" she laughed. "I don't know why I feel so awfully jolly tonight. I could positively fly from sheer excitement and delight."

"Don't you know why?" observed Cora. "I will tell you. It is because this is you last Christmas as Molly Vance; next year—"

"Ah, do not!" interrupted Molly, quickly. "Who knows what a year may bring forth. Is it not so. Dr. Briggs?" she turned appealingly to Reuel. "Grief follows joy as clouds the sunlight. 'Woe! Woe! Each heart must bleed, must break.'" was his secret thought as he bowed gravely. But on his face was a look of startled perplexity, for suddenly as she spoke to him it appeared that a dark veil settled like a pall over the laughing face at his side. He shivered.

"What's the matter, Briggs?" called out Adonis. They had all reached the ballroom and were standing over the piles of holly and evergreen, ready for an onslaught on the walls.

"Don't be surprised if Briggs acts strangely," continued Charlie. "It is in order for him to whoop it up in the spirit line."

"Why, Charlie! What do you mean?" questioned Molly with an anxious glance at Reuel.

"Anything interesting, Charlie?" called out a jolly girl across the room.

"Briggs is our 'show' man. Haven't you heard, girls, what a celebrity is with you tonight? Briggs is a philosopher—mesmerism is his specialty. Say, old man, give the company a specimen of your infernal art, can't you? He goes the whole hog, girls; can even raise the dead."

"Let up, Charlie," said Aubrey in a low tone. "It's no joking matter."

There were screams and exclamations from the girls. With reckless gaiety Adonis continued, "What is to be the outcome of the great furor you have created, Briggs?"

"Nothing of moment, I hope," smiled Reuel, good-naturedly. "I have been simply an instrument; I leave results to the good angels who direct events. What does Longfellow say about the arrow and the song?

'Long: lone: afterwards, in an oak
I found the arrow still unbroke;
And the song, from beginning to end,
I found in the heart of a friend.'

May it be so with my feeble efforts."

"But circumstances alter cases. In this rase, the 'arrow' is a girl and a devilish handsome one, too; and the 'air' is the whole scientific world.

Your philosophy and mysticism gave way before Beauty. Argument is a stubborn man's castle, but the heart is still unconvinced."

"'I mixed those children up, and not a creature knew it,'" hummed Pert Smith. "Your ideas are mixed, Don: stick to the ladies, you understand girls and horseflesh; philosophy isn't in your line."

"Oh, sure!" said Adonis unruffled by his friend's words.

"Charlie Vance," said Molly severely, "if we have any more swearing from you tonight, you leave the room until you learn to practice good manners. I'm surprised at your language!"

"Just the same, Briggs is a fraud. I shall keep my eye on him. It's a case of beauty and the beast. Oh," he continued in malicious glee, "wouldn't you girls turn green with envy, every man jack of you, if you could see the beauty!"

Thereupon the girls fell to pelting him with holly wreaths and evergreen festoons, much to the enjoyment of Mr. Vance, who had entered unperceived in the general melee.

"What is it all about, Dr. Briggs?" asked Molly in a low voice.

"It is the case of a patient who was in a mesmeric sleep and I was fortunate enough to awaken her. She is a waif; and it will be months before she will be well and strong, poor girl."

"Do you make a study of mesmerism, Doctor?" asked Mr. Vance from his armchair by the glowing fire.

"Yes sir; and a wonderful science it is."

Before Mr. Vance could continue, Livingston said: "If you folks will be still for about ten minutes, I'll tell you what happened in my father's house when I was a very small boy; I can just remember it."

"If it's a ghost story, make it strong, Aubrey, so that not a girl will sleep tonight. Won't the dears look pretty blinking and yawning tomorrow night? We'll hear 'em, fellows, in the small hours of the morning, 'Molly, Molly! I'm so frightened. I do believe someone is in my room; may I come in with you, dear?'"

"Charlie, stop your nonsense," laughed his father, and Adonis obediently subsided.

"My father was Dr. Aubrey Livingston too," began Aubrey, "and he owned a large plantation of slaves. My father was deeply interested in the science of medicine, and I believe made some valuable discoveries along the line of mesmeric phenomena, for some two or three of his books are referred to even at this advanced stage of discovery, as marvelous in some of their data."

"Among the slaves was a girl who was my mother's waiting maid, and I have seen my father throw her into a trance-state many times when I was so small that I had no conception of what he was doing."

"Many a time I have known him to call her into the parlor to perform tricks of mind-reading for the amusement of visitors, and many wonderful things were done by her as the record given in his books shows.

"One day there was a great dinner party given at our place, and the elite of the county were bidden. It was about two years before the civil war, and our people were not expecting war; thinking that all unpleasantness must end in their favor, they gave little heed to the ominous rumble of public opinion that was arising at the North, but went on their way in all their pride of position and wealth without a care for the future."

"Child as I was I was impressed by the beauty and wit of the women and the chivalric bearing of the men gathered about my father's hospitable board on that memorable day. When the feasting and mirth began to lag, someone called for Mira—the maid—and my father sent for her to come and amuse the guests."

"My father made the necessary passes and from a serious, rather sad Negress, very mild with everyone, Mira changed to a gay, noisy, restless woman, full of irony and sharp jesting. In this case this peculiar metamorphosis always occurred. Nothing could be more curious than to see her and hear her. 'Tell the company what you see, Mira,' commanded my father.

"You will not like it, captain; but if I must, I must. All the women will be widows and the men shall sleep in early graves. They come from the north, from the east, from the west, they sweep to the gulf through a trail of blood. Your houses shall burn, your fields be laid waste, and a down-trodden race shall rule in your land. For you, captain, a prison cell and a pauper's grave."

"The dinner-party broke up in a panic, and from that time my father could not abide the girl. He finally sold her just a few months before the secession of the Confederate States, and that was the last we ever knew of her."

"And did the prophecy come true about your father?" asked Mr. Vance.

"Too true, sir; my father died while held as a prisoner of war, in Boston Harbor. And every woman at the table was left a widow. There is only too much truth in science of mesmeric phenomena. The world is a wonderful place."

"Wonderful!" declared his hearers.

"I am thinking of that poor, pretty creature lying ill in that gloomy hospital without a friend. Men are selfish! I tell you what, folks, tomorrow after lunch we'll make a Christmas visit to the patients, and carry them fruit and flowers. As for your beautiful patient, Dr. Briggs, she shall not be friendless any longer, she shall come to us at Vance Hall."

"Molly!" broke simultaneously from Aubrey and Charlie.

"Oh, I mean it. There is plenty of room in this great house, and here she shall remain until she is restored to health."

Expostulation was in vain. The petted heiress was determined, and when Mr. Vance was appealed to, he laughed and said, as he patted her hand:

"The queen must have her own."

At length the costumer's box was opened amidst jest, song and laughter. The characters were distributed by the willful Molly. Thus attired, to the music of Tannhauser's march, played by one of the girls on the piano, the gay crowd marched and counter-marched about the spacious room.

In the early morning hours, Aubrey Livingston slept and dreamed of Dianthe Lusk, and these words haunted his sleep and lingered with him when he woke:

"She had the glory of heaven in her voice, and in her face the fatal beauty of man's terrible sins."

Aubrey Livingston knew that he was as hopelessly lost as was Adam when he sold his heavenly birthright for a woman's smile.

VIII

Through days and days, and again through days and days, over and over again, Reuel Briggs fought to restore his patient to a normal condition of health. Physically, he succeeded; but mentally his treatment was a failure. Memory remained a blank to the unhappy girl. Her life virtually began with her awakening at the hospital. A look of wonder and a faint smile were the only replies that questions as to the past elicited from her. Old and tried specialists in brain diseases and hypnotic states came from every part of the Union on bootless errands. It was decided that nothing could be done; rest, freedom from every care and time might eventually restore the poor, violated mind to its original strength. Thus it was that Dianthe became the dear adopted daughter of the medical profession. Strange to say, Molly Vance secured her desire, and wearing the name of Felice Adams. Dianthe was domiciled under the roof of palatial Vance hall, and the small annuity provided by the generous contributions of the physicians of the country was placed in the hands of Mr. Vance, Sr., to be expended for their protege.

The astonishing nature of the startling problems he had unearthed, the agitation and indignation aroused in him by the heartless usage to which his patient must have been exposed, haunted Briggs day and night. He believed that he had been drawn into active service for Dianthe by a series of strange coincidences, and the subtle forces of immortality; what future acts this service might require he knew not, he cared not; he registered a solemn promise to perform all tasks allotted him by Infinity, to the fullest extent of his power.

The brilliant winter days merged themselves into spring. After one look into Dianthe's eyes, so deep, clear and true, Molly Vance had surrendered unconditionally to the charm of the beautiful stranger, drawn by an irresistible bond of sympathy. "Who would believe," she observed to Livingston, "that at this stage of the world's progress one's identity could be so easily lost and one still be living. It is like a page from an exciting novel."

With the impulsiveness of youth, a wonderful friendship sprang up between the two; they rode, walked and shopped together; in short, became inseparable companions. The stranger received every attention in the family that could be given an honored guest. Livingston and Briggs watched her with some anxiety; would she be able to sustain the position of intimate friendship to which Molly had elected her? But both breathed more freely when they noted her perfect manners, the ease and good-breeding displayed in all her intercourse with those socially above the level to which they knew this girl was born. She accepted the luxury of her new surroundings as one to the manner born.

"We need not have feared for her; by Jove, she's a thorough-bred!" exclaimed Aubrey one day to Reuel. The latter nodded as he looked up from his hook.

"And why not? Probably the best blood of the country flows in the poor girl's veins. Who can tell? Why should she not be a thorough-bred."

"True," replied Aubrey, as a slight frown passed over his face,

"I am haunted by a possibility, Aubrey," continued Reuel. "What if memory suddenly returns? Is it safe to risk the unpleasantness of a public reawakening of her sleeping faculties? I have read of such things."

Aubrey shrugged his handsome shoulders. "We must risk something for the sake of science; where no one is injured by deception there is no harm done."

"Now that question has presented itself to me repeatedly lately: Is deception justifiable for any reason? Somehow it haunts me that trouble may come from this. I wish we had told the exact truth about her identity."

"If 'twere done when 'tis done, then 'twere well it were done quickly" murmured Aubrey with a sarcastic smile on his face. "How you balk at nothing, Reuel," he drawled mockingly.

"Oh, call me a fool and done with it, Aubrey: I suppose I am; but one didn't make one's self."

Drives about the snow-clad suburbs of Cambridge with Briggs and Molly, at first helped to brighten the invalid; then came quiet social diversions at which Dianthe was the great attraction.

It was at an afternoon function that Reuel took courage to speak of his love. A dozen men buzzed about "Miss Adams" in the great bay window where Molly had placed Dianthe, her superb beauty set off by a simple toilet. People came and went constantly. Musical girls, generally with gold eyeglasses on aesthetic noses, played grim classical preparations, which have as cheerful an effect on a gay crowd as the perfect, irreproachable skeleton of a by-gone beauty might have; or articulate, with cultivation and no voices to speak of, arias which would sap the life of a true child of song to render as the maestro intended.

The grand, majestic voice that had charmed the hearts from thousands of bosoms, was pinioned in the girl's throat like an imprisoned song-bird. Dianthe's voice was completely gone along with her memory. But music affected her strangely, and Reuel watched her anxiously.

Her face was a study in its delicate, quickly changing tints, its sparkle of smiles running from the sweet, pure tremor of the lovely mouth to the swift laughter of eyes and voice.

Mindful of her infirmity, Reuel led her to the conservatory to escape the music. She lifted her eyes to his with a curious and angelic light in them. She was conscious that he loved her with his whole most loving heart. She winced under the knowledge, for while she believed in him, depended upon him and gathered strength from his love, what she gave in return was but a slight, cold affection compared with his adoration.

He brought her refreshments in the conservatory, and then told his love and asked his fate. She did not answer at once, but looked at his plain face, at the stalwart elegance of his figure, and again gazed into the dark, true, clever eyes, and with the sigh of a tired child crept into his arms, and into his heart for all time and eternity. Thus Aubrey Livingston found them when the company had departed. So it was decided to have the wedding in June. What need for these two children of misfortune to wait?

Briggs, with his new interest in life, felt that it was good just to be alive. The winter passed rapidly, and as he threaded the streets coming and going to his hospital duties, his heart sang. No work was now too arduous; he delighted in the duty most exacting in its nature. As the spring came in it brought with it thoughts of the future. He was almost penniless, and he saw no way of obtaining the money he needed. He had not been improvident, but his lonely life had lived a reckless disregard of the future, and the value of money. He often lived a day on bread and water, at the same time sitting without a fire in the coldest weather because his pockets were empty and he was too proud to ask a loan, or solicit credit from storekeepers. He now found himself in great difficulty. His literary work and the extra cases which his recent triumph had brought him, barely sufficed for his own present needs. Alone in his bachelor existence he would call this luxury, but it was not enough to furnish a suitable establishment for Dianthe. As the weeks rolled by and nothing presented itself, he grew anxious, and finally resolved to consult Livingston.

All things had become new to him, and in the light of his great happiness the very face of old Cambridge was changed. Fate had always been against him and had played him the shabbiest of tricks, but now he felt that she might do her worst, he held a talisman against misfortune while his love remained to him. Thinking thus he walked along briskly, and the sharp wind brought a faint color into his sallow face. He tried to think and plan, but his ideas were whirled away befort they had taken form, and he felt a giant's power to overcome with each inspiring breath of the crisp, cool March air. Aubrey should plan for him, but he would accomplish.

Livingston had apartments on Dana Hill, the most aristocratic portion of Cambridge. There he would remain till the autumn, when he would marry Molly Vance, and remove to Virginia and renew the ancient splendor of his ancestral home. He was just dressing for an evening at the theatre when Briggs entered his rooms. He greeted him with his usual genial warmth.

"What!" he said gaily, "the great scientist here, at this hour?"

Then noticing his visitor's anxious countenance he added:

"What's the matter?"

"I am in difficulties and come to you for help," replied Reuel.

"How so? What is it? I am always anxious to serve you, Briggs."

"I certainly think so or I would not be here now," said Reuel. "But you are just going out, an engagement perhaps with Miss Molly. My business will take some time—"

Aubrey interrupted him, shaking his head negatively. "I was only going out to wile away the time at the theatre. Sit down and free your mind, old man."

Thus admonished, Reuel flung himself among the cushions of the divan, and began to state his reasons for desiring assistance: when he finished, Livingston asked:

"Has nothing presented itself?"

"O yes; two or three really desirable offers which I wrote to accept, but to my surprise, in each case I received polite regrets that circumstances had arisen to prevent the acceptance of my valuable services. That is what puzzles me. What the dickens did it mean?"

Aubrey said nothing but continued a drum solo on the arm of his chair. Finally he asked abruptly: "Briggs, do you think anyone knows or suspects your origin?"

PAULINE E. HOPKINS

Not a muscle of Reuel's face moved as he replied, calmly: "I have been wondering if such can be the case."

"This infernal prejudice is something horrible. It closes the door of hope and opportunity in many a good man's face. I am a Southerner, but I am ashamed of my section," he added warmly.

Briggs said nothing, but a dark, dull red spread slowly to the very roots of his hair. Presently Aubrey broke the painful silence.

"Briggs, I think I can help you."

"How?"

"There's an expedition just about starting from England for Africa; its final destination is, I believe, the site of ancient Ethiopian cities; its object to unearth buried cities and treasure which the shifting sands of Sahara have buried for centuries. This expedition lacks just such a medical man as you; the salary is large, but you must sign for two years; that is my reason for not mentioning it before. It bids fair to be a wonderful venture and there will be plenty of glory for those who return, beside the good it will do to the Negro race if it proves the success in discovery that scholars predict. I don't advise you to even consider this opportunity, but you asked for my help and this is all I can offer at present."

"But Dianthe!" exclaimed Reuel faintly.

"Yes," smiled Aubrey. "Don't I know how I would feel if it were Molly and I was in your place? You are like all other men, Reuel. Passion does not calculate, and therein lies its strength. As long as common sense lasts we are not in love. Now the answer to the question of ways and means is with you; it is in your hands. You will choose love and poverty I suppose; I should. There are people fools enough to tell a man in love to keep cool. Bah! It is an impossible thing."

"Does true love destroy our reasoning faculties?" Reuel asked himself as he sat there in silence after his friend ceased speaking. He felt then that he could not accept this offer. Finally he got upon his feet, still preserving his silence, and made ready to leave his friend. When he reached the door, he turned and said: "I will see you in the morning."

For a long time after Briggs had gone, Aubrey sat smoking and gazing into the glowing coals that filled the open grate.

All that night Reuel remained seated in his chair or pacing the cheerless room, conning ways and means to extricate himself from his dilemma without having recourse to the last extremity proposed by Aubrey. It was a brilliant opening; there was no doubt of that; a year—six months ago—he would have hailed it with delight, but if he accepted it, it would raise a barrier between his love and him which could not be overcome—the ocean and thousands of miles.

"Oh, no!" he cried, "a thousand times no! Rather give up my ambitions."

Then growing more rational he gazed mournfully around the poor room and asked himself if he could remain and see his wife amid such surroundings? That would be impossible. The question then, resolved itself into two parts: If he remained at home, they could not marry, therefore separation; if he went abroad, marriage and separation. He caught at the last thought eagerly. If then they were doomed to separate, of two evils why not choose the least? The African position would at least bind them irrevocably together. Instantly hope resumed its sway in Reuel's breast so fertile is the human mind in expedients to calm the ruffled spirit; he began to estimate the advantages he would gain by accepting the position: He could marry Dianthe, settle a large portion of his salary upon her thus rendering her independent of charity, leave her in the care of the Vance family, and return in two years a wealthy man no longer fearing poverty. He had never before builded golden castles, but now he speculated upon the possibility of unearthing gems and gold from the mines of ancient Meroe and the pyramids of Ethiopia. In the midst of his fancies he fell asleep. In the morning he felt a wonderful relief as he contemplated his decision. Peace had returned to his mind. He determined to see Aubrey at once and learn all the particulars concerning the expedition. Providentially, Aubrey was just sitting down to breakfast and over a cup of steaming coffee Reuel told his decision, ending with these words: "Now, my dear Aubrey, it may be the last request I may ever ask of you, for who can tell what strange adventures may await me in that dark and unknown country to which Fate has doomed me?"

Livingston tried to remonstrate with him.

"I know what I am saying. The climate is murderous, to begin with, and there are many other dangers. It is better to be prepared. I have no friend but you."

"Between us, Reuel, oaths are useless; you may count upon my loyalty to all your interests," said Aubrey with impressiveness.

"I shall ask you to watch over Dianthe. I intrust her to you as I would intrust her to my brother, had I one. This is all I ask of you when I am in that far country."

With open brow, clear eyes and grove face, Aubrey Livingston replied in solemn tones:

"Reuel, you may sail without a fear. Molly and I will have her with us always like a dear sister."

Hand clasped in hand they stood a moment as if imploring heaven's blessing on the solemn compact. Then they turned the conversation on the business of securing the position at once.

IX

Reuel was greatly touched during the next three months by the devotion of his friend Livingston, whose unselfishness in his behalf he had before had cause to notice. Nor was this all; he seemed capable of any personal sacrifice that the welfare of Briggs demanded.

Before many days had passed he had placed the young man in direct communication with the English officials in charge of the African expedition. The salary was most generous; in fact, all the arrangements were highly satisfactory. Whatever difficulties really existed melted, as it were, before Aubrey's influence, and Reuel would have approached the time of departure over a bed of roses but for the pain of parting with Dianthe.

At length the bustle of graduation was over. The last article of the traveler's outfit was bought. The morning of the day of departure was to see the ceremony performed that would unite the young people for life. It was a great comfort to Reuel that Charlie Vance had decided to join the party as a tourist for the sake of the advantages of such a trip.

The night before their departure Aubrey Livingston entertained the young men at dinner in his rooms along with a number of college professors and other learned savans. The most complimentary things were said of Reuel in the after-dinner toasts, the best of wishes were uttered together with congratulations on the marriage of the morrow for they all admired the young enthusiast. His superiority was so evident that none disputed it; they envied him, but were not jealous. The object of their felicitations smiled seldom.

"Come, for heaven sake shake off your sadness; he the happy groom upon whom Fortune, fickle jade, has at last consented to smile," cried Adonis. So, amid laughter and jest, the night passed and the morrow came.

After his guests had departed, Aubrey Livingston went to the telegraph office and sent a message:

"To Jim Titus,
"Laurel Hill, Virginia:—
    "Be on hand at the New York dock, Trans-Atlantic
Steamship Co., on the first. I will be there to make things

right for you. Ten thousand if you succeed the first six
months.

A. L.

It was noon the next day and the newly wedded stood with clasped
hands uttering their good-byes.

"You must not be unhappy, dear. The time will run by before you
know it, and I shall be with you again. Meanwhile there is plenty to
occupy you. You have Molly and Aubrey to take you about. But pray
remember my advice,—don't attempt too much; you're not strong by
any means."

"No, I am not strong!" she interrupted with a wild burst of tears.
"Reuel, if you knew how weak I am you would not leave me."

Her husband drew the fair head to his bosom, pressing back the
thick locks with a lingering lover's touch.

"I wish to God I could take you with me," he said tenderly after a
silence. "Dear girl, you know this grief of yours would break my heart,
only that it shows how well you love me. I am proud of every tear."
She looked at him with an expression he could not read; it was full of
unutterable emotion—love, anguish, compassion.

"Oh," she said passionately, "nothing remains long with us but
sorrow and regret Every good thing may be gone tomorrow—lost! Do
you know, I sometimes dream or have waking visions of a past time in
my life? But when I try to grasp the fleeting memories they leave me
groping in darkness. Can't you help me, Reuel?"

With a laugh he kissed away her anxieties, although he was dismayed
to know that at most any time full memory might return. He must
speak to Aubrey. Then he closed her lips with warm lingering kisses.

"Be a good girl and pray for your husband's safety, that God may let
us meet again and be happy! Don't get excited. That you *must* guard
against."

And Reuel Briggs, though his eyes were clouded with tears, was a
happy man at heart that day. Just that once he tasted to the full all that
there is of happiness in human life. Happy is he who is blessed with even
one perfect day in a lifetime of sorrow. His last memory of her was a mute
kiss and a low "God bless you," broken by a sob. And so they parted.

In the hall below Molly Vance met him with a sisterly kiss for good-
bye; outside in the carriage sat Mr. Vance, Sr. Charlie and Aubrey
waiting to drive to depot.

Reuel Briggs, Charlie Vance and their servant, Jim Titus, sailed from New York for Liverpool, England, on the first day of July.

The departure of the young men made a perceptible break in the social circle at Vance Hall. Mr. Vance buried himself in the details of business and the two girls wandered disconsolately about the house and grounds attended by Livingston, who was at the Hall constantly and pursued them with delicate attentions.

By common consent it was determined that no summer exodus could be thought of until after the travelers had reached August, all being well, they would seek the limit of civilized intercourse in Africa. While waiting, to raise the spirits of the family, it was decided to invite a house party for the remainder of July, and in the beauties of Bar Harbor. Soon gaiety and laughter filled the grand old rooms; the days went merrily by.

Two men were sitting in the billiard loom lounging over iced punch. Light, perfumed and golden, poured from the rooms below upon the summer night, and the music of a waltz made its way into the darkness.

"What an odd fish Livingston has grown to be," said one, relighting a thin, delicate-looking cigar. "I watched him out of curiosity a while ago and was struck at the change in him."

"Ah!" drawled the other sipping the cooling beverage. "Quite a Priuli on the whole, eh?"

"Y-e-s! Precisely. And I have fancied that the beautiful Mrs. Briggs is his Clarisse. What do you think? She shudders every time he draw s near, and sinks to the ground under the steady gaze of his eye. Odd, isn't it?"

"Deucedly odd! About to marry Miss Vance, isn't he?"

"That don't count. Love is not always legitimate. If there's anything in it, it is only a flirtation probably; that's the style."

"What you say is true, Skelton. Let's drink the rest of this stuff and go down again. I know we're missed already."

When they had swallowed the punch and descended, the first person they saw was Livingston leaning against the door of the salon. His face was abstracted and in dead repose, there lurked about the corners of his full lips implacable resolution. The waltz was ended.

Some interminable argument was going on, generally, about the room. Conversation progressed in sharp, brisk sentences, which fell from the lips like the dropping shots of sharpshooters. There was a call for music. Molly mentally calculated her available talent and was about to give up the idea and propose something else, when she was amazed to see Dianthe rise hurriedly from her seat on an ottoman, go to the piano unattended and sit down. Unable to move with astonishment she watched in fascination the slender white fingers flash over the keys. There was a strange rigid appearance about the girl that was unearthly. Never once did she raise her eyes. At the first sharp treble note the buzz in the room was hushed at stillness. Livingston moved forward and rested his arm upon the piano fastening his gaze upon the singer's quivering lips.

Slowly, tremulously at first, pealed forth the notes:

"Go down, Moses, way down in Egypt's land, Tell or Pharaoh, let my people go."

Scarcely was the verse begun when every person in the room started suddenly and listened with eager interest. As the air proceeded, some grew visibly pale, and not daring to breathe a syllable, looked horrified into each other's faces. "Great heaven!" whispered Mr. Vance to his daughter, "do you not hear another voice beside Mrs. Briggs?"

It was true, indeed. A weird contralto, veiled as it were, rising and falling upon every wave of the great soprano, and reaching the ear as from some strange distance. The singer sang on, her voice dropping sweet and low, the echo following it, and at the closing word, she fell back in a dead faint. Mr. Vance caught her in his arms.

"Mrs. Briggs has the soul of an artiste. She would make a perfect prima donna for the Grand Opera," remarked one man to Molly.

"We are as surprised as anyone," replied the young girl; "we never knew that Mrs. Briggs was musical until this evening. It is a delightful surprise."

They carried her to the quiet, cool library away from the glaring lights and the excitement, and at her request left her there alone. Her thoughts were painful. Memory had returned in full save as to her name. She knit her brow in painful thought, finally leaning back among her cushions wearily, too puzzled for further thought. Presently a step paused beside her chair. She looked up into Livingston's face.

"Are you feeling better?" he asked, gently taking in his slender wrist and counting the pulse-beats.

Instead of answering his question, she began Abruptly: "Mr. Livingston, Reuel told me to trust you implicitly. Can you and will you tell me what has happened to me since last I sang the song I have sung here tonight? I try to recall the past, but all is confusion and mystery. It makes my head ache so to think."

Livingston suddenly drew closer to her.

"Yes, Felice, there *is* a story in your life! I can save you."

"Save me!" exclaimed the girl.

"Yes, and will! Listen to me." In gentle accents he recounted to her there in the stillness, with the pulsing music of the viols beating and throbbing in her ears like muffled drums, the story of Dianthe Lusk as we have told it here. At the close of the tale the white-faced girl turned to him in despair the more eloquent because of her quietness.

"Did Reuel know that I was a Negress?"

"No; no one recognized you but myself."

She hid her face in her hands.

"Whoever suffered such torture as mine?" she cried, bitterly. "And there is no rest out of the grave!" she continued.

"Yes, there is rest and security in my love! Felice, Dianthe, I have learned to love you!"

She sprang from his touch as if stung.

He continued: "I love you better than all in the world. To possess you I am prepared to prove false to my friend—I am prepared to save you from the fate that must be yours if ever Reuel learns your origin."

"You would have me give up all for you?" she asked with a shudder.

"Ay, from your husband—from the world! We will go where none can ever find us. If you refuse, I cannot aid you."

"Pity me!"

She sank upon her knees at his feet.

"I give you a week to think it over. I can love, but cannot pity."

In vain the girl sought to throw off the numbing influence of the man's presence. In desperation she tried to defy him, but she knew that she had lost her will-power and was but a puppet in the hands of this false friend.

X

The Doctor is so good to you about letters; so different from poor Charlie. I can't imagine what he finds to write about."

It was the first of August, and the last guest had left the mansion; tomorrow they started for Bar Harbor. Molly, Dianthe and Livingston sat together in the morning room.

"He tells me the incidents of the journey. This is the last letter for three months," said Dianthe, with a sigh.

"Of course, there is no love-making," said Aubrey, lazily letting fall his newspaper, and pushing his hands through his bright hair. He was a sight for gods and men. His handsome figure outlined against the sky, as he stood by the window in an attitude of listless grace, his finely-cut face, so rich in color and the charm of varying expression, turned indolently toward the two women to whom the morning mail had brought its offering.

"Have you ever read one of Reuel's letters?" Dianthe said, quietly. "You may see this if you like." A tap sounded on the door.

"Miss Molly, if you please, the dressmaker has sent the things."

"Oh, thank you, Jennie, I'll come at once!" and gathering up her letters, Molly ran off with a smile and a nod of apology.

Aubrey stood by the window reading Reuel's letter. His face was deadly white, and his breath came quick and short. He read half the page; then crushed it in his hand and crossed the room to Dianthe. She, too, was pale and there was something akin to fear in the gaze that she lifted to his face.

"How dare you?" he asked breathlessly; "but you are a woman! Not one of you has any delicacy in her heart! Not one!"

He tore the letter across and flung it from him.

"I do not suffer enough," he said in a suffocated voice. "You taunt me with this view of conjugal happiness—with his *right* to love and care for you."

"I DID NOT DO IT to hurt you," she answered. "Do you have no thought for Molly's sufferings if I succumb to your threats of exposure and weakly allow myself to be frightened into committing the great wrong you contemplate toward two true-hearted people? I thought you could realize if you could know how Reuel loves and trusts me, and how true and noble is his nature."

"Do you think I have room to pity Reuel—Molly—while my own pain is more than I can bear? Without you my ambition is destroyed, my hope for the future—my life is ruined."

He turned from her and going to a distant part of the room, threw himself into a chair and covered his face with his hands. Against her will, better promptings and desires, the unfortunate girl is drawn by invisible influences across the room to the man's side. Presently he holds her in his eager, strong embrace, his face and tears hidden against her shoulder. She does not struggle in his clasp, only looks into the future with the hopeless agony of dumb despair.

At length he broke the silence. "There is nothing you can feel, or say to me that I do not realize—the sin, the shame, the lasting disgrace. I know it all. I told you once I loved you; I tell you now that I cannot *live* without you!"

An hour later Dianthe sat alone in the pleasant room. She did not realize the beauty of the lanquid mid-summer day. She thought of nothing but the wickedness of betraying her friends. Her perfect features were like marble. The dark eyes had deep, black circles round them and gazed wistfully into the far, far distance, a land where spirit only could compass the wide space. As she sat there in full possession of all her waking faculties, suddenly there rose from out the very floor, as it were, a pale and lovely woman. She neither looked at Dianthe nor did she speak; but walked to the table and opened a book lying upon it and wrote; then coming back, stood for a moment fixed; then sank, just as she rose, and disappeared. Her dress was that of a servant. Her head was bare; her hair fell loosely around her in long black curls. Her complexion was the olive of mulattoes or foreigners. As the woman passed from her view, Dianthe rose and went to the table to examine the book. She did not feel at all frightened, recognizing instantly the hand of mysticism in this strange occurrence. There on the open page, she perceived heavy marks in ink, under-scoring the following quotation from the 12th chapter of Luke: "For there is nothing covered that shall not be revealed." On the margin, at the end of this passage was written in a fine female hand, the single word, "Mira."

After luncheon Aubrey proposed that they go canoeing on the river. The idea was eagerly embraced and by five o'clock the large and luxurious canoe floated out from the boat-house upon the calm bosom of the lovely Charles rocking softly to the little waves that lapped her sides.

The day had been oppressive, but upon the river a refreshing breeze was blowing now that the sun had gone down. For the time all Dianthe's cares left her and her tortured mind was at peace. Molly was full of life and jested and sang and laughed. She had brought her mandolin with her and gave them soft strains of delicious waltzes.

On, on they glided under the impetus of the paddle-strokes in Aubrey's skillful hands, now past the verdure-clad pine hills, now through beds of fragrant waterlilies getting gradually farther and farther from the companionship of other pleasure-seekers. On, into the uninhabited portion where silent woods and long green stretches of pasture-land added a wild loneliness to the scene.

How lovely was the evening sky with its white clouds dotting the azure and the pink tinting of the sunset casting over all its enlivening glow; how deep, and dark was the green of the water beneath the shadowing trees. From the land came the lowing of cows and the sweet scent of freshly spread hay.

Suddenly Aubrey's paddle was caught and held in the meshes of the water-lily stems that floated all about them. He leaned far over to extricate it and in a moment the frail craft was bottom up, its living freight struggling in the river. Once, twice, thrice a thrilling call for help echoed over the darkening land; then all was still.

XI

The expedition with which Reuel Briggs found himself connected was made up of artists, savans and several men—capitalists—who represented the business interests of the venture. Before the white cliffs of the English coast were entirely lost to view, Reuel's natural propensities for leadership were being fully recognized by the students about him. There was an immediate demand for his professional services and he was kept busy for many days. And it was the best panacea for a nature like his—deep and silent and self-suppressing. He had abandoned happiness for duty; he had stifled all those ominous voices which rose from the depth of his heart, and said to him: "Will you ever return? and if you return will you find your dear one? and, if you find her, will she not have changed? will she have preserved your memory as faithfully as you will preserve hers?

A thousand times a day while he performed his duties mechanically, his fate haunted him—the renunciation which called on him to give up happiness, to open to mishap the fatal door absence. All the men of the party were more or less silent and distrait, even Charlie Vance was subdued and thoughtful. But Briggs suffered more than any of them, although he succeeded in affecting a certain air of indifference. As he gradually calmed down and peace returned to his mind, he was surprised to feel the resignation that possessed him. Some unseen presence spoke to his inner being words of consolation and hope. He was shown very clearly his own inability to control events, and that his fate was no longer in his own hands but ordered by a being of infinite pity and love. After hours spent in soul-communion with the spirit of Dianthe, he would sink into refreshing slumber and away in peace. Her letters were bright spots, very entertaining and describing minutely her life and daily occupation since his departure. He lived upon them during the voyage to Tripoli, sustained by the hope of finding one upon arriving at that city.

One fine evening when the sun was setting, they arrived at Tripoli. Their course lay toward the southward, and standing on deck, Reuel watched the scene—a landscape strange in form, which would have delighted him and filled him with transports of joy; now he felt something akin to indifference.

The ripples that flit the burnished surface of the long undulating billows tinkled continually on the sides of the vessel. He was aware of a low-lying spectral-pale band of shore. That portion of Africa whose nudity is only covered by the fallow mantle of the desert gave a most sad impression to the gazer. The Moors call it "Bled el Ateusch," the Country of Thirst; and, as there is an intimate relation between the character of a country and that of its people, Reuel realized vividly that the race who dwelt here must be different from those of the rest of the world.

"Ah! that is our first glimpse of Africa, is it?" said Adonis's voice, full of delight, beside him.

He turned to see his friend offering him a telescope. "At last we are here. In the morning we shall set our feet on the enchanted ground."

In the distance one could indeed make out upon the deep blue of the sky the profile of Djema el Gomgi, the great mosque on the shores of the Mediterranean. At a few cable lengths away the city smiles at them with all the fascination of a modern Cleopatra, circled with an oasis of palms studded with hundreds of domes and minarets. Against a sky of amethyst the city stands forth with a penetrating charm. It is the eternal enchantment of the cities of the Orient seen at a distance; but, alas! set foot within them, the illusion vanishes and disgust seizes you. Like beautiful bodies they have the appearance of life, but within the worm of decay and death eats ceaselessly.

At twilight in this atmosphere the city outlines itself faintly, then disappears in dusky haze. One by one the stars came into the sky until the heavens were a twinkling blaze; the sea murmured even her soft refrain and slept with the transparency of a mirror, flecked here and there with fugitive traces of phosphorescence.

The two young men stood a long time on the deck gazing toward the shore.

"Great night!" exclaimed Adonis at length with a long-drawn sigh of satisfaction. "It promises to be better than anything Barnum has ever given us even at a dollar extra reserved seat."

Reuel smiled in spite of himself; after all, Charlie was a home-line warranted to ward off homesickness. On board there was the sound of hurrying feet and a murmur of suppressed excitement, but it had subsided shortly; an hour later "sleep and oblivion reigned over all."

In the morning, amid the bustle of departure the mail came on board. There were two letters for Reuel. He seated himself in the seclusion of the cabin safe from prying eyes. Travelling across the space that separated him from America, his thoughts were under the trees in the garden of Vance Hall. In the fresh morning light he thought he could discern the dress of his beloved as she came toward him between the trees.

Again he was interrupted by Charlie's jolly countenance. He held an open letter in his hand. "There, Doc, there's Molly's letter. Read it, read it; don't have any qualms of conscience about it. There's a good bit in it concerning the Madam, see? I thought you'd like to read it." Then he sauntered away to talk with Jim Titus about the supplies for the trip across the desert.

Jim was proving himself a necessary part of the expedition. He was a Negro of the old regime who felt that the Anglo-Saxon was appointed by God to rule over the African. He showed his thoughts in his obsequious manner, his subservient "massa," and his daily conversation with those about him. Jim superintended the arrangement of the table of the exploring party, haggled over prices with the hucksters, quarreled with the galley cooks and ended by doing all the cooking for his party in addition to keeping his eye on "Massa Briggs." All of this was very pleasant, but sometimes Reuel caught a gleam in Jim's furtive black eye which set him thinking and wondering at the latter's great interest in himself; but he accounted for this because of Livingston's admonitions to Jim to "take care of Dr. Briggs."

Willing or not, the company of travelers were made to take part in the noisy scene on deck when a horde of dirty rascals waylaid them, and after many uses and combination of all sorts over a few cents, they and their luggage were transported to the Custom House. "Ye gods!" exclaimed Charlie in deep disgust, "what a jostling, and what a noise."

All the little world about them was in an uproar, everyone signaling, gesticulating, speaking at once. Such a fray bewilders a civilized man, but those familiar with Southern exuberance regard it tranquilly, well knowing the disorder is more apparent than real. Those of the party who were familiar with the scene, looked on highly amused at the bewilderment of the novices.

Most of them had acquired the necessary art of not hurrying, and under their direction the examination of the baggage proceeded rapidly. Presently, following a robust porter, they had traversed an open place filled with the benches and chairs of a "cafe," and soon the travelers were surprised and amused to find themselves objects of general curiosity. Coffee and nargiles were there merely as a prelext, in reality the gathering was in their honor. The names of the members of the expedition were known, together with its object of visiting Meroe of ancient fame, the arrival of such respectable visitors is a great event. Then, too, Tripoli is the natural road by which Africa has been attacked by many illustrious explorers because of the facility of communication with the country of the Black's. Nowhere in northern Africa does the Great Desert advance so near the sea. The Atlas range rises from the Atlantic coast, extending far eastward.. This range loses itself in the gulf of Little Syrta, and the vast, long-pent-up element, knowing no more barrier, spreads its yellow, sandy waves as far as the Nile. enveloping the last half-submerged summits which form a rosary of oases.

Under the Sultan's rule Tripoli has remained the capital of a truly barbaric state, virgin of improvements, with just enough dilapidated abandon, dirt and picturequeness to make the delight of the artist. Arabs were everywhere; veiled women looked at the Christians with melting eyes above their wrappings. Mohammedanism, already twelve centuries old, has, after a period of inactivity, awakened anew in Africa, and is rapidly spreading. Very unlike the Christians, the faithful of today are the same fervid Faithful of Omar and Mohammed. Incredulity, indifference, so widely spread among other sects are unknown to them.

Supper-time found the entire party seated on the floor around a well-spread tray, set on a small box. They had taken posses-ion of the one living-room of a mud house. It was primitive but clean. A post or two supported the thatched ceiling. There were no windows. The furniture consisted of a few rugs and cushions. But the one idea of the party being sleep, they were soon sunk in a profound and dreamless slumber.

The next day and the next were spent in trying to gain an audience with the Sheik Mohammed Abdallah, and the days lengthened into weeks and a month finally rolled into oblivion. Meantime there were no letters for Dr. Briggs and Charlie Vance. Every one else in the part had been blessed with many letters, even Jim was not forgotten.

Reuel had learned to be patient in the dolce far niente of the East but not so Charlie. He fumed and fretted continually after the first weeks had passed. But promptly at two, one hot afternoon, the Sheik knocked at the door of their hut. He was a handsome man of forty years—tall, straight, with clear brown eyes, good features, a well-shaped moustache and well-trimmed black beard. Authority surrounded him like an atmosphere. He greeted the party in French and Arabic and invited them to his house where a feast was spread for them. Presents were given and received and then they were introduced to Ababdis, an owner of camels who was used to leading parties into the wilderness. After much haggling over prices, it was decided to take lit teen camels and their drivers. Supplies were to consist of biscuit, rice, tea, sugar, coffee, wax candles, charcoal and a copious supply of water bags. It was decided not to start until Monday, after the coming of the mail, which was again due. After leaving Tripoli, it was doubtful when they would receive news from America again. The mail came. Again Jim was the only one who received a letter from the United States. Reuel handed it to him with a feeling of homesickness and a sinking of the heart.

Monday morning found them mounted and ready for the long journey across the desert to the first oasis. From the back of a camel Charlie Vance kept the party in good humor with his quaint remarks. "Say, Doc, it's worth the price. How I wish the pater, your wife and Molly could see us now, Livingston wouldn't do a thing to these chocolate colored gentry of Arabia."

"And Miss Scott? where does she come in?" questioned Reuel with an assumption of gaiety he was far from feeling.

"Oh," replied Charlie, not at all non-plussed. "Cora isn't in the picture; I'm thinking of a houri."

"Same old thing, Charlie—the ladies?"

"No," said Charlie, solemnly. "It's business this time. Say, Briggs, the sight of a camel always makes me a child again. The long-necked beast is inevitably associated in my mind with Barnum's circus and playing hookey. Pop wants me to put out my sign and go in for business, but the show business suits me better. For instance," he continued with a wave of his hand including the entire caravan, "Arabs, camels, stray lions, panthers, scorpions, serpents, explorers, etc., with a few remarks by yours truly, to the accompaniment of the band—always the band you know, would make an interesting show—a sort of combination of Barnuna and Kiralfy. The houris would do Kiralfy's act, you know. There's money in it."

"Were you ever serious in your life, Charlie?"

"What the deuce is the need of playing funeral all the time, tell me that, Briggs, will you?"

The great desert had the sea's monotony. They rode on and on hour after hour. The elements of the view were simple. Narrow valleys and plains bounded by picturesque hills lay all about them. The nearer hills to the right had shoulders and hollows at almost regular intervals,

PAULINE E. HOPKINS

and a sky-line of an almost regular curve. Under foot the short grass always seemed sparse, and the low sage-shrubs rather dingy, but as they looked over the plain stretching away in every direction, it had a distinctly green tint. They saw occasionally a red poppy and a purple iris. Not a tree was to be seen, nor a rock. Sometimes the land lay absolutely level and smooth, with hardly a stone larger than a bean. The soft blue sky was cloudless, the caravan seemed to be the only living creature larger than a gazelle in the great solitude. Even Reuel was aroused to enthusiasm by the sight of a herd of these graceful creatures skimming the plain. High in the air the larks soared and sang.

As they went southward the hot sun poured its level rays upon them, and the song of the drivers was a relief to their thoughts. The singing reminded travelers of Venetian gondoliers, possessing as it did the plaintive sweetness of the most exquisite European airs. There was generally a leading voice answered by a full chorus. Reuel thought he had never heard music more fascinating. Ababdis would assume the leading part. "Ah, when shall I see my family again; the rain has fallen and made a canal between me and my home. Oh, shall I never see it more?" Then would follow the chorus of drivers: "Oh, what pleasure, what delight, to see my family again; when I see my father, mother, brothers, sisters, I will hoist a flag on the head of my camel fur joy!" About the middle of the week they were making their way over the Great Desert where it becomes an elevated plateau crossed by rocky ridges, with in veiling sandy plains mostly barren, but with here and there a solitary tree, and sometimes a few clumps of grass. The caravan was skirting the base of one of these ridges, which culminated in a cliff looking, in the distance, like a half-ruined castle, which the Arabs believed to be enchanted. Reuel determined to visit this cliff, and saving nothing to any one, and accompanied only by Jim and followed by the warnings of the Arabs to beware of lions, they started for the piles of masonry, which they reached in a couple of hours. The moon rose in unclouded splendor, and Moore's lines came to his heart:

> "O, such a blessed night as this,
> I often think if friends were near,
> How we should feel, and gaze with bliss
> Upon the moonlight scenery here."

He strolled into the royal ruin, stumbling over broken carvings, and into hollows concealed by luminous plants, beneath whose shades dwelt noisome things that wriggled away in the marvelous white light. Climbing through what was once a door, he stepped out on a ledge of masonry, that hung sheer seven hundred feet over the plain. Reuel got out his pipe and it was soon in full blast, while the smoker set to building castles in the curls of blue smoke, that floated lightly into space. Jim with the guns waited for him at the foot of the hill.

Under the influence of the soothing narcotic and the spell of the silver moon, Reuel dreamed of fame and fortune he would carry home to lay at a little woman's feet. Presently his castle-building was interrupted by a low vail—not exactly the mew of a cat, nor yet the sound of a lute.

Again the sound.

What could it be?

"Ah, I have it!" muttered Reuel; "it's the Arabs singing in the camp."

Little did he imagine that within ten paces of him crouched an enormous leopard.

Little did he imagine that he was creeping, creeping toward him, as a cat squirms at a bird.

He sat on the ruined ledge of the parapet, within two feet of the edge; seven hundred feet below the desert sand glittered like molten silver in the gorgeous moonlight.

He was unarmed, having given Jim his revolver to hold.

Reuel sat there entirely unconscious of danger; presently a vague feeling struck him, not of fear, not of dread, but a feeling that if he turned his head he would see an enemy, and without knowing why, he slowly turned his head.

Great heavens! what did he see? A trill of horror passed through him as his eyes rested upon those of an enormous brute, glaring like hot coals set in blood-red circles.

Its mouth was wide open, its whiskers moving like the antennal of a lobster. It by on its belly, its hindquarters raised, its forepaws planted in the tawny sand ready to spring.

The moon played on the spots of its body. The dark spots became silvered, and relapsed into darkness as the animal breathed, while its tail lashed about, occasionally whipping the sand with a peculiar whish.

How was he to withstand its spring?

The weight of its body would send him over the precipice like a shot.

PAULINE E. HOPKINS

Strange to say a grim satisfaction came to him at the thought that the brute must go down with him. Where could he hold? Could he clutch at anything? he asked himself.

He dared not remove his eyes from those of the leopard. He could not in fact. But in a sort of introverted glance he saw that nothing stood between him and space but a bare, polished wall, that shone white beneath the moonbeams.

"Was there a loose stone—a stone that would crush in the skull of the blood-thirsty animal?" Not so much as a pebble to cast into the depths, for he had already searched for one to fling over, as people do when perched on imminences. He cried for help, "Jim! Jim! O-o-o-h, Jim!"

There came no reply; not the slightest sound broke the stillness as the sound of his cries died away.

Reuel was now cool—cool as a cucumber—so cool that he deliberately placed himself in position to receive the rush of the terrific brute. He felt himself moving gently back his right foot, shuffling it back until his heel came again an unevenness in the rock, which gave him a sort of purchase—something to back it.

He gathered himself together for a supreme effort, every nerve being at the highest condition of tension.

It is extraordinary all the thoughts that pass like lightning in a second of time, through the mind, while face to face with death. Volumes of ideas flashed through his brain as he stood on the stone ledge, with eternity awaiting him, knowing that this would be the end of all his hopes and fears and pleasant plans for future happiness, that he would go down to death in the embrace of the infuriated animal before him, its steel-like claws buried in his flesh, its fetid breath filling his nostrils. He thought of his darling love, and of how the light would go out of her existence with his death. He thought of Livingston, of the fellows who had gathered to bid him God speed, of the paragraphs in the papers. All these things came as harrowing pictures as he stood at bay in the liquid pearl of the silent moon.

The leopard began to move its hindquarters from side to side. A spring was at hand.

Reuel yelled then—yelled till the walls of the ruined castle echoed again—yelled as if he had 10,000 voices in his throat—yelled, as a man only yells when on his being heard depends his chance for dear life.

The beast turned its head sharply, and prepared to spring. For a second Briggs thought that a pantomime trick might give him a chance.

What if he were to wait until the animal actually leaped, and then turn aside?

Carried forward by its own weight and momentum it would go over the ledge and be dashed to pieces on the rocks below.

It was worth trying. A drowning man catches at a straw. Instinctively Reuel measured his distance. He could step aside and let the brute pass but that was all. The ledge was narrow. He was, unhappily, in very good addition. The sea-voyage had fattened torn, and it was just a chance that he could escape being carried over by the brute.

He accepted the chance.

Then came the fearful moment.

The leopard swayed a little backward!

Then, to his intense delight, he heard a shout of encouragement in Vance's well-known voice, "Coming, Briggs, coming!"

The next moment a hand was laid on his shoulder from a window above; it was Charlie, who trembling with anxiety had crept through the ruin, and, oh, blessed sight! Handed Reuel his revolver.

Briggs made short work of the leopard: he let him have three barrels—all in the head.

Vance had become alarmed for the safety of his friend, and had gone to the ruin to meet him. When very nearly there, he had heard the first cry for help, and had urged his camel forward. Arrived at the castle he had found Tim apparently dead with sleep, coiled up on the warm sand. How he could sleep within sound of the piercing cries uttered by Briggs was long a mystery to the two friends.

XII

The caravan had halted for the night. Professor Stone, the leader of the expedition, sat in Reliefs tent enjoying a pipe and a talk over the promising features of the enterprise. The nearer they approached the goal of their hopes—the ancient Ethiopian capital Meroe—the greater was the excitement among the leaders of the party. Charlie from his bed of rugs listened with ever-increasing curiosity to the conversation between the two men.

"It is undoubtedly true that from its position as the capital of Ethiopia and the interpret of trade between the North and South, between the East and West, Meroe must have held vast treasures. African caravans poured ivory, frankincense and gold into the city. My theory is that somewhere under those pyramids we shall find invaluable records and immense treasure."

"Your theories may be true, Professor, but if so, your discoveries will establish the primal existence of the Negro as the most ancient source of all that you value in modern life, even antedating Egypt. Plow can the Anglo-Saxon world bear the establishment of such a theory?" There was a hidden note of sarcasm in his voice which the others did not notice.

The learned savan settled his glasses and threw back his head.

"You and I, Briggs, know that the theories of prejudice are swept away by the great tide of facts. It is a fact that Egypt drew from Ethiopia all the arts, sciences and knowledge of which she was mistress. The very soil of Egypt was pilfered by the Nile from the foundations of Meroe. I have even thought," he continued meditatively, "that black was the original color of man in prehistoric times. You remember that Adam was made from the earth; what more natural than that he should have retained the color of the earth? What puzzles me is not the origin of the Blacks, but of the whites. Miriam was made a leper outside the tents for punishment; Naaman was a leper until cleansed. It is a question fraught with big possibilities which Cod alone can solve. But of this we are sure—all records of history, sacred and profane,, unite in placing the Ethiopian as the primal race."

"Gee whiz!" exclaimed Charlie from his bed on the floor "Count me out!"

"Don't touch upon the origin of the Negro: you will find yourself in a labyrinth, Professor. That question has provoked more discussion than any other concerning the different races of man on the globe. Speculation has exhausted itself, yet the mystery appears to remain unsolved."

"Nevertheless the Biblical facts are very explicit, and so simple as to force the very difficulties upon mankind that Divinity evidently designed to avoid."

"The relationship existing between the Negro and other people of the world is a quest inn of absorbing interest. For my part, I shall be glad to add to my ethnological knowledge by anything we may learn at Meroe." Thus speaking Reuel seemed desirous of dismissing the subject. More conversation followed on indifferent subjects, and presently the Professor bade them good night and retired to his own tent.

Reuel employed himself in making entries in his journal, Charlie continued to smoke, at times evincing by a musical snore that he was in the land of dreams. Jim sat at some distance reading a letter that he held in his hand.

The night was sultry, the curtains of the tent undrawn; from out the silent solitude came the booming call of a lion to his mate.

Suddenly a rush of balmy air seemed to pass over the brow of the scribe, and a dim shadow fell across the tent door. It was the form of the handsome Negress who had appeared to Dianthe, and signed herself "Mira."

There was no fear in Reuel's gaze, no surprise; it was as if a familiar and welcome visitor had called upon him. For a moment an impulse to spring away into the wide, wide realms of air, seemed to possess him; the next, the still, dreamy ecstasy of a past time; and then he saw Jim—who sat directly behind him—placed like a picture on his very table. He saw him knit his brow, contract his lip, and then, with a face all seamed with discontent, draw from his vest a letter, seemingly hidden in a private pocket, reading thus:—

> "Use your discretion about the final act, but be sure the letters are destroyed. I have advised the letters sent in your care as you will probably be detailed for the mail. But to avoid mishap call for the mail for both parties. Address me at Laurel Hill—Thomas Johnson."
>
> A. L.

Twice did the visionary scene, passing behind the seer, recross his entranced eyes; and twice did the shadowy finger of the shining apparition in the tent door point, letter by letter, to the pictured page of the billet, which Jim was at that very moment perusing with his natural, and Reuel Briggs with his spiritual eyes. When both had concluded the reading, Jim put up his letter. The curtains of the tent slightly waved; a low, long sigh, like the night's wind wail, passed over the cold, damp brow of the seer. A shudder, a blank. He looked out into the desert beyond. All was still. The stars were out for him, but the vision was gone.

Thus was explained to Reuel, by mesmeric forces, the fact that his letters had been withheld.

He had not once suspected Jim of perfidy. What did it mean? he asked himself. The letter was in Livingston's handwriting! His head swam; he could not think. Over and over again he turned the problem and then, wishing that something more definite had been given him, retired, but not to sleep.

Try as he would to throw it off, the most minute act of Jim since entering his service persisted in coming before his inner vision. The night when he was attacked by the leopard and Jim's tardiness in offering help, returned with great significance. What could he do but conclude that he was the victim of a conspiracy.

"There is no doubt about it," was his last thought as he dropped into a light doze. How long he slept he could not tell, but he woke with a wild, shrill cry in his ears: "Reuel, Reuel, save me!"

Three times it was repeated, clear, distinct, and close beside his ear, a pause between the repetitions.

He roused his sleeping friend. "Charlie, Charlie! wake up and listen!"

Charlie, still half asleep, looked with blinking eyes at the candle with dazzled sight.

"Charlie, for the love of God wake up!"

At this, so full of mortal fear were his words, Adonis shook off his drowsiness and sat up in bed, wide awake and staring at him in wonder.

"What the deuce!" he began, and then stopped, gazing in surprise at the white face and trembling hands of his friend.

"Charlie," he cried, "some terrible event has befallen Dianthe, or like a sword hangs over our heads. Lister, listen!"

Charlie did listen but heard nothing but the lion's boom which now broke the stillness.

"I hear nothing, Reuel."

"O Charlie, are you sure?"

"Nothing but the lion. But that 'll be enough if he should take it into his mind to come into camp for his supper."

"I suppose you are right, for you can hear nothing, and I can hear nothing now. But, oh Charlie! it was so terrible, and I heard it so plainly; though I daresay it was only my—Oh God! there it is again! listen! listen!"

This time Charlie heard—heard clearly and unmistakably, and hearing, felt the blood in his veins turn to ice.

Shrill and clear above the lion's call rose a prolonged wail, or rather shriek, as of a human voice rising to heaven in passionate appeal for mercy, and dying away in sobbing and shuddering despair. Then came the words:

"Charlie, brother, save me!"

Adonis sprang to his feet, threw back the curtain of the tent and looked out. All was calm and silent, not even a cloud flecked the sky where the moon's light cast a steady radiance.

Long he looked and listened; but nothing could be seen or heard. But the cry still rang in his ears and clamored at his heart; while his mind said it was the effect of imagination.

Reuel's agitation had swallowed up his usual foresight. He had forgotten his ability to resort to that far-seeing faculty which he had often employed for Charlie's and Aubrey's amusement when at home.

Charlie was very calm, however, and soothed his friend's fears, and after several ineffectual attempts to concentrate his powers for the exercise of the clairvoyant sight of the hypnotice trance, was finally able to exercise the power.

In low, murmuring cadence, sitting statuesque and rigid beneath the magnetic spell, Reuel rehearsed the terrible scene which had taken place two months before in the United States in the ears of his deeply-moved friend.

"Ah, there is Molly, poor Molly; and see your father weeps, and the friends are there and they too weep, but where is my own sweet girl, Dianthe, love, wife! No, I cannot see her, I do not find the poor maimed body of my love. And Aubrey! What! Traitor, false friend! I shall return for vengeance.

"Wake me, Charlie," was his concluding sentence.

A few upward passes of his friend's hands, and the released spirit became lord of its casket once more. Consciousness returned, and with it memory. In short whispered sentences Reuel told Vance of his suspicions, of the letter he read while it lay in Jim's hand, of his deliberate intention to leave him to his fate in the leopard's claws.

The friends laid their plans,—they would go on to Meroe, and then return instantly to civilization as fast as steam could carry them, if satisfactory letters were not waiting them from America.

XIII

L ate one afternoon two weeks later, the caravan halted at the edge of the dirty Arab town which forms the outposts to the island of Meroe.

Charlie Vance stood in the door of his tent and let his eyes wander over the landscape in curiosity. Clouds of dust swept over the sandy plains; when they disappeared the heated air began its dance again, and he was glad to re-enter the tent and stretch himself at full length in his hammock. The mail was not yet in from Cairo, consequently there were no letters; his eyes ached from straining them for a glimpse of the Ethiopian ruins across the glassy waters of the tributaries of the Nile which encircled the island.

It was not a simple thing to come all these thousands of miles to look at a pile of old ruins that promised nothing of interest to him after all. This was what he had come for—the desolation of an African desert, and the companionship of human fossils and savage beasts of prey. The loneliness made him shiver. It was a desolation that doubled desolateness, because his healthy American organization missed the march of progress attested by the sound of hammers on unfinished buildings that told of a busy future and cosy modern homeliness. Here there was no future. No railroads, no churches, no saloons, no schoolhouses to echo the voices of merry children, no promise or the life that produces within the range of his vision. Nothing but the monotony of past centuries dead and forgotten save by a few learned savans.

As he rolled over in his hammock, Charlie told himself that next to seeing the pater and Molly, he'd give ten dollars to be able to thrust his nose into twelve inches of whiskey and soda, and remain there until there was no more. Then a flicker of memory made Charlie smile as he remembered the jollities of the past few months that he had shared with Cora Scott.

"Jolly little beggar," he mentally termed her. "I wonder what sort of a fool she'd call me if she could see me now whistling around the ragged edge of this solid block of loneliness called a desert."

Then he fell asleep and dreamed he was boating on the Charles, and that Molly was a mermaid sporting in a bed of water-lilies.

Ancient writers, among them Strabo, say that the Astabora unites its stream with the Nile, and forms the island of Meroe. The most famous historical city of Ethiopia is commonly called Carthage, but Meroe was the queenly city of this ancient people. Into it poured the traffic of the world in gold, frankincense and ivory. Diodorus states the island to be three hundred and seventy-five miles long and one hundred and twenty-five miles wide. The idea was borne in upon our travelers in crossing the Great Desert that formerly wells must have been established at different stations for the convenience of man and beast. Professor Stone and Reuel had discovered traces of a highway and the remains of cisterns which must have been marvelous in skill and prodigious in formation.

All was bustle and commotion in the camp that night. Permission had been obtained to visit and explore the ruins from the Arab governor of the Province. It had cost money, but Professor Stone counted nothing as lost that would aid in the solution of his pet theories.

The leaders of the enterprise sat together late that night, listening to the marvelous tales told by the Professor of the city's ancient splendor, and examining closely the chart which had remained hidden for years before it fell into his hands. For twenty-five years this apostle of learning had held the key to immense wealth, he believed, in his hands. For years he had tried in vain to interest the wealthy and powerful in his scheme for finding the city described in his chart, wherein he believed lay the gold mines from which had come the streams of precious metal which made the ancient Ethiopians famous.

The paper was in a large envelope sealed with a black seal formed to resemble a lotus flower. It was addressed:

To The Student Who, Having Counted the Cost, Is Resolute to Once More Reveal to the Sceptical, The Ancient Glory of Hoary Meroe.

Within the envelope was a faded parchment which the Professor drew forth with trembling hands. The little company drew more closely about the improvised table and its flickering candle which revealed the faded writing to be in Arabic. There was no comment, but each one listened intently to the reader, who translated very fully as he went along.

"Be it known to you, my brother, that the great and surpassing wealth mentioned in this parchment is not to be won without braving many dangers of a deadly nature. You who may read this message, then, I entreat to consider well the perils of your course. Within the mines of Meroe, four days' journey from the city toward Arabia, are to be found gold in bars and gold in flakes, and diamonds, and rubies whose beauty excels all the jewels of the earth. For some of them were hidden by the priests of Osiris that had adorned the crown of the great Semiramis, and the royal line of Queen Candace, even from ancient Babylon's pillage these jewels came, a spectacle glorious beyond compare. There, too, is the black diamond of Senechus's crown (Senechus who suffered the captivity of Israel by the Assyrians), which exceeds all imagination for beauty and color.

"All these jewels with much treasure beside you will gain by following my plain directions.

"Four days journey from Meroe toward Arabia is a city founded by men from the Upper Nile; the site is near one of its upper sources, which still has one uniform existence. This city is situated on a forked tributary, which takes its rise from a range of high, rocky mountains, almost perpendicular on their face, from which descend two streams like cataracts, about two miles apart, and form a triangle, which holds the inner city. The outer city occupies the opposite banks on either side of the streams, which after joining, form a river of considerable size, and running some five miles, loses itself in the surrounding swamps. The cities are enclosed within two great walls, running parallel with the streams. There are also two bridges with gates, connecting the inner and outer cities; two great gates also are near the mountain ranges, connecting the outer city with the agricultural lands outside the walls. The whole area is surrounded by extensive swamps, through which a passage, known only to the initiated runs, and forms an impassible barrier to the ingress or egress of strangers.

"But there is another passage known to the priests and used by them, and this is the passage which the chart outlines beneath the third great pyramid, leading directly into the mines and giving access to the city."

"When Egypt rose in power and sent her hosts against the mother country, then did the priests close with skill and cunning this approach to the hidden city of refuge, where they finally retired, carrying with them the ancient records of Ethiopia's greatness, and closing forever, as they thought, the riches of her marvelous mines, to the world."

"Beneath the Sphinx' head lies the secret of the entrance, and yet not all, for the rest is graven on the sides of the cavern which will be seen when the mouth shall gape. But beware the tank to the right where dwells the sacred crocodile, still living, although centuries have rolled by and men have been gathered to the shades who once tended on his wants. And beware the fifth gallery to the right where abide the sacred serpents with jeweled crowns, for of a truth are they terrible."

"This the writer had from an aged priest whose bones lie embalmed in the third pyramid above the Sphinx."

With this extraordinary document a chart was attached, which, while an enigma to the others, seemed to be perfectly clear to Professor Stone.

The letter ended abruptly, and the chart was a hopeless puzzle to the various eyes that gazed curiously at the straggling outlines.

"What do you make of it, Professor?" asked Reuel, who with all his knowledge, was at sea with the chart. "We have been looking for mystery, and we seem to have found it."

"What do I make of it? Why, that we shall find the treasure and all return home rich," replied the scholar testily.

"Rubbish!" snorted Charlie with fine scorn.

"How about the sacred crocodile and the serpents? My word, gentlemen, if you find the back door key of the Sphinx' head, there's a chance that a warm welcome is awaiting us."

Charlie's words met with approval from the others, but the Professor and Reuel said nothing. There was silence for a time, each man drawing at his pipe in silent meditation.

"Well, I'm only travelling for pleasure, so it matters not to me how the rest of you elect to shuffle off this mortal coil, I intend to get some fun out of this thing," continued Charlie.

There was a shout of laughter from his companions.

"Pleasure!" cried one. "O Lord! You've come to the wrong place. This is business, solid business. If we get out with our skins it will be something to be thankful for."

"Well," said Reuel, rousing himself from a fit of abstraction, "I come out to do business and I have determined to see the matter through if all is well at home. We'll prove whether there's a hidden city or not before we leave Africa."

The Professor grasped his hand in gratitude, and then silence fell upon the group. The curtains of the tent were thrown back. Bright fell the moonlight on the sandy plain, the Nile, the indistinct ruins of Meroe, hiding all imperfections by its magic fingers. It was a wonderful sight to see the full moon looking down on the ruins of centuries. The weird light increased, the shadows lengthened and silence fell on the group, broken only by the low tones of Professor Stone as he told in broken sentences the story of ancient Ethiopia.

"For three thousand years the world has been mainly indebted for its advancement to the Romans, Greeks, Hebrews, Germans and Anglo-Saxons; but it was otherwise in the first years. Babylon and Egypt—Nimrod and Mizraim—both descendants of Ham—led the way, and acted as the pioneers of mankind in the untrodden fields of knowledge. The Ethiopians, therefore, manifested great superiority over all the nations among whom they dwelt, and their name became illustrious throughout Europe, Asia and Africa.

"The father of this distinguished race was Cush, the grandson of Noah, an Ethiopian."

"Old Chaldea, between the Euphrates and Tigris rivers, was the first home of the Cushites. Nimrod, Ham's grandson, founded Babylon. The Babylonians early developed the energy of mind which made their country the first abode of civilization. Canals covered the land, serving the purposes of traffic, defense and irrigation. Lakes were dug and stored with water, dykes built along the banks of rivers to fertilize the land, and it is not surprising to learn that from the earliest times Babylonia was crowded with populous cities. This grandeur was brought about by Nimrod the Ethiopian."

"Great Scott!" cried Charlie, "you don't mean to tell me that all this was done by *niggers*?"

The Professor smiled. Being English, he could not appreciate Charlie's horror at its full value.

"Undoubtedly your Afro-Americans are a branch of the wonderful and mysterious Ethiopians who had a prehistoric existence of magnificence, the full record of which is lost in obscurity."

"We associate with the name 'Chaldea' the sciences of astronomy and philosophy and chronology. It was to the Wise Men of the East to whom the birth of Christ was revealed; they were Chaldeans—of the Ethiopians. Eighty-eight years before the birth of Abraham, these people, known in history as 'Shepherd Kings,' subjugated the whole of Upper Egypt, which they held in bondage more than three hundred years."

"It is said that Egyptian civilization antedates that of Ethiopia," broke in Reuel. "How do you say, Professor?"

"Nothing of the sort, nothing of the sort. I know that in connecting Egypt with Ethiopia, one meets with most bitter denunciation from most modern scholars. Science has done its best to separate the race from Northern Africa, but the evidence is with the Ethiopians. If I mistake not, the ruins of Meroe will prove my words. Traditions with respect to Memnon connect Egypt and Ethiopia with the country at the head of the Nile. Memnon personifies the ethnic identity of the two races. Ancient Greeks believed it. All the traditions of Armenia, where lies Mt. Ararat, are in accordance with this fact. The Armenian geography applies the name of Cush to four great regions—Media, Persia, Susiana, Asia, or the whole territory between the Indus and the Tigris. Moses of Chorene identifies Belus, king of Babylon with Nimrod."

"But the Biblical tradition is paramount to all. In it lies the greatest authority that we have for the affiliation of nations, and it is delivered to us very simply and plainly: 'The sons of Ham were Cush and Mizraim and Phut and Canaan. . . and Cush begot Nimrod. . . and the beginning of his kingdom was Babel and Erech and Accad and Calneh, in the land of Shinar.' It is the best interpretation of this passage to understand it as asserting that the four races—Egyptians, Ethiopians, Libyans and Canaanites—were ethnically connected, being all descended from Ham; and that the primitive people of Babylon were a subdivision of one of these races; namely, of the Cushite or Ethiopian."

"These conclusions have lately received important and unexpected confirmation from the results of linguistic research. After the most remarkable of Mesopotamian mounds had yielded their treasures, and supplied the historical student with numerous and copious documents, bearing upon the history of the great Assyrian and Babylonian empires, it was determined to explore Chaldea proper, where mounds of considerable height marked the site of several ancient cities. Among unexpected results was the discovery of a new form of speech, differing greatly from the later Babylonian language. In grammatical structure this ancient tongue resembles dialects of the Turanian family, but its vocabulary has been pronounced to be decidedly Cushite or Ethiopian; and the modern languages to which it approaches nearest are thought to be the Mahen of Southern Arabia and the Galla of Abyssinia. Thus comparative philology appears to confirm old traditions. An Eastern Ethiopia instead of being the invention of bewildered ignorance, is rather a reality which it will require a good deal of scepticism to doubt, and the primitive race that bore sway in Chaldea proper belongs to this ethnic type. Meroe was the queenly city of this great people."

"It is hard to believe your story. From what a height must this people have fallen to reach the abjectness of the American Negro," exclaimed a listener.

"True," replied the Professor. "But from what a depth does history show that the Anglo-Saxon has climbed to the position of the first people of the earth today."

Charlie Vance said nothing. He had suffered so many shocks from the shattering of cherished idols since entering the country of mysteries that the power of expression had left him.

"Twenty-five years ago, when I was still a young man, the camel-driver who accompanied me to Thebes sustained a fatal accident. I helped him in his distress, and to show his gratitude he gave me the paper and chart I have shown you tonight. He was a singular man, black hair and eyes, middle height, dark-skinned, face and figure almost perfect, he was proficient in the dialects of the region, besides being master of the purest and most ancient Greek and Arabic. I believe be was a native of the city he described."

"He believed that Ethiopia antedated Egypt, and helped me materially in fixing certain data which time has proved to be correct. He added a fact which the manuscript withholds,—that from lands beyond unknown seas, to which many descendants of Ethiopia had been borne as slaves, should a king of ancient line—an offspring of that Ergamenes who lived in the reign of the second Ptolemy—return and restore the former glory of the race. The preservation of this hidden city is for his reception. This Arab also declared that Cush was his progenitor."

"That's bosh. How would they know their future king after centuries of obscurity passed in strange lands, and amalgamation with other races?" remarked the former speaker.

"I asked him that question; he told me that every descendant of the royal line bore a lotus-lily in the form of a birthmark upon his breast."

It might have been the unstable shadows of the moon that threw a tremulous light upon the group, but Charlie Vance was sure that Reuel Briggs started violently at the Professor's words.

One by one the men retired to rest, each one under the spell of the mysterious forces of a past life that brooded like a mist over the sandy plain, the dark Nile rolling sluggishly along within a short distance of their camp, and the ruined city now a magnificent Necropolis. The long shadows grew longer, painting the scene into beauty and grandeur. The majesty of death surrounded the spot and its desolation spoke in trumpet tones of the splendor which the grave must cover, when even the memory of our times shall be forgotten.

XIV

Next morning the camp was early astir before the dawn; and before the sun was up, breakfast was over and the first boat-load of the explorers was standing on the site of the ruins watching the unlfading of the apparatus for opening solid masonry and excavating within the pyramids.

The feelings of every man in the party were ardently excited by the approach to the city once the light of the world's civilization. The great French writer, Volney, exclaimed when first his eyes beheld the sight, "How are we astonished when we reflect that to the race of Negroes, the object of our extreme contempt, we owe our arts, sciences and even the use of speech!"

From every point of view rose magnificent groups of pyramids rising above pyramids. About eighty of them remaining in a state of partial preservation. The principal one was situated on a hill two and a half miles from the river, commanding an extensive view of the plain. The explorers found by a hasty examination that most of them could be ascended although their surfaces were worn quite smooth. That the pyramids were places of sepulture they could not doubt. From every point of view the sepulchres were imposing; and they were lost in admiration and wonder with the first superficial view of the imposing scene.

One of the approaches or porticoes was most interesting, the roof being arched in regular masonic style, with what may be called a keystone. Belonging without doubt to the remotest ages, their ruined and defaced condition was attributed by the scientists to their great antiquity. The hieroglyphics which covered the monuments were greatly defaced. A knowledge of these characters in Egypt was confined to the priests, but in Ethiopia they were understood by all showing that even in that remote time and place learning and the arts had reached so high a state as to be diffused among the common people.

For a time the explorers wandered from ruin to ruin, demoralized as to routine work, gazing in open astonishment at the wonders before them. Many had visited Thebes and Memphis and the Egyptian monuments, but none had hoped to find in this neglected corner, so much of wonder and grandeur. Within the pyramids that had been opened to the curious eye, they found the walls covered with the

pictures of scenes from what must have been the daily life,—death, burial, marriage, birth, triumphal processions, including the spoils of war.

Reuel noticed particularly the figure of a queen attired in long robe, tight at neck and ankles, with closely fitted legs. The Professor called their attention to the fact that the entire figure was dissimilar to those represented in Egyptian sculpture. The figure was strongly marked by corpulency, a mark of beauty in Eastern women. This rotundity is the distinguishing feature of Ethiopian sculpture, more bulky and clumsy than Egypt, but pleasing to the eye.

The queen held in one hand the lash of Osiris, and in the other a lotus flower. She was seated on a lion, wearing sandals resembling those specimens seen in the ban figures. Other figures grouped about poured libations to the queen, or carried the standards graced and ornamented by the figures of the jackal, ibis and hawk. At the extremity of each portico was the representation of a monolithic temple, above which were the traces of a funeral boat filled with figures.

Professor Stone told them that Diodorus mentions that some of the Ethiopians preserved the bodies of their relatives in glass cases (probably alabaster), in order to have them always before their eyes. These porticoes, he thought, might have been used for that purpose. The hair of the women was dressed in curls above the forehead and in ringlets hanging on their shoulders.

One who had visited the chief galleries of Europe holding the treasures accumulated from every land, could not be unmoved at finding himself on the site of the very metropolis where science and art had their origin. If he had admired the architecture of Rome and the magnificent use they had made of the arch in their baths, palaces and temples, he would be, naturally, doubly interested at finding in desolate Meroe the origin of that discovery. The beautiful sepulchres of Meroe would give to him evidence of the correctness of the historical records. And then it was borne in upon him that where the taste for the arts had reached such perfection, one might rest assured that other intellectual pursuits were not neglected nor the sciences unknown. Now, however, her schools are closed forever; not a vestige remaining. Of the houses of her philosophers, not a stone rests upon another; and where civilization and learning once reigned, ignorance and barbarism have reassumed their sway.

This is the people whose posterity has been denied a rank among the human race, and has been degraded into a species of talking baboons!

"Land of the mighty Dead!
There science once displayed
And art, their charms;
There awful Pharaohs swayed
Great nations who obeyed;
There distant monarchs laid
Their vanquished arms.
"They hold us in survey—
They cheer us on our way—
They loud proclaim,
From pyramidal hall—
Prom Carnac's sculptured wall—
Prom Thebes they loudly call—
Retake your fame"

"Arise and now prevail
O'er all your foes:
In truth and righteousness—
In all the arts of peace—
Advance and still increase,
Though hosts oppose."

Under the inspiration of the moment, Charlie, the irrepressible, mounted to the top of the first pyramid, and from its peak proceeded to harangue his companions, lugging in the famous Napoleon's: "From the heights of yonder Pyramids forty centuries are contemplating you," etc. This was admirably done, and the glances and grimaces of the eloquent young American must have outvied in ugliness the once gracious-countenanced Egyptian Sphinx.

We may say here that before the excavations of the explorers were ended, they found in two of the pyramids, concealed treasures,— golden plates and tables that must have been used by the priests in their worship. Before one enormous image was a golden table, also of enormous proportions. The seats and steps were also of gold, confirming the ancient Chaldean records which tell of 800 talents of metal used in constructing this statue.

There was also a statue of Candace, seated in a golden chariot. On her knees crouched two enormous silver serpents, each weighing thirty talents. Another queen (Professor Stone said it must be Dido from certain peculiar figures) carried in her right hand a serpent by the head, in her left hand a sceptre garnished with precious stones.

All of this treasure was collected finally, after indemnifying the government. carefully exported to England, where it rests today in the care of the Society of Geographical Research.

They never forgot that sunset over the ancient capital of Ethiopia at the close of the first day spent on the city's site, in the Desert. The awe-inspiring Pyramids throwing shadows that reminded one of the geometrical problems of his student days; the backsheesh-loving Arabs, in the most picturesque habiliments and attitudes; the patient camels, the tawny sands, and the burnished coppery sunlight! They had brought tents with them, leaving the most of the outfit on the opposite bank under the care of Jim Titus, whom Reuel had desired the professor to detail for that duty. Somehow since his adventure in the ruins with the leopard, and the mysterious letter-reading, he had felt a deep-seated mistrust of the docile servant. He concluded not to keep him any nearer his person than circumstances demanded. In this resolve Charlie Vance concurred; the two friends resolved to keep an eye on Titus, and Ababdis was sent for the mail.

Reuel Briggs had changed much. Harassed by anxieties which arose from his wife's silence, at the end of two months he was fast becoming a misanthrope. Charlie felt anxious as he looked at him walking restlessly up and down in the pale moonlight, with fiery eyes fixed on space. Charlie suppressed his own feelings over the silence of his father and sister to comfort Reuel.

"You ought not, my dear Briggs," he would say. "Come, for heaven's sake shake off that sadness which may make an end of you before you are aware." Then he would add, jestingly, "Decidedly, you regret the leopard's claws!"

On this night the excitement of new scenes had distracted the thoughts of both men from their homes, and they lay smoking in their hammocks before the parted curtains of the tent lazily watching Ababdis advancing with a bundle in his hand. It was the long expected mail!

XV

It was some three weeks after this before Briggs was able to assume his duties. The sudden shock of the news of his wife's death overweighted a brain already strained to the utmost. More than once they despaired of his life—Professor Stone and Vance, who had put aside his own grief to care for his friend. Slowly the strong man had returned to life once more. He did not rave or protest; Fate had no power to move him more; the point of anguish was passed, and in its place succeeded a dumb stupidity more terrible by far, though far more blessed.

His love was dead. He himself was dead for any sensibility of suffering that he possessed. So for many days longer he lay in his hammock seemingly without a thought of responsibility.

They had carried him back to the camp across the river, and there he spent the long days of convalescence. What did he think of all day as he moved like a shadow among the men or swung listlessly in the hammock? Many of the men asked themselves that question as they gazed at Briggs. One thought repeated itself over and over in his brain, "Many waters cannot quench love, neither can the floods drown it." "Many waters"—"many waters"—the words whispered and sung appealingly, invitingly, in his ears all day and all night. "Many waters, many waters."

One day he heard them tell of the removal of the door in the pyramid two and one-half miles on the hill. They had found the Snhinx' head as described in the manuscript, but had been unable to move it with any instrument in their possession. Much to his regret, Professor Stone felt obliged to give the matter up and content himself with the valuable relics he had found. The gold mines, if such there were, were successfully hidden from searchers, and would remain a mystery.

The white orb of the moon was high in the heavens; the echoless sand gave back no sound; that night Reuel rose, took his revolver and ammunition, and leaving a note for Vance telling him he had gone to the third pyramid and not to worry, he rowed himself over to Meroe. He had no purpose, no sensation. Once he halted and tried to think. His love was dead:—that was the one fact that filled his thoughts at first. Then another took its place. Why should he live? Of course not; better rejoin her where parting was no more. He would lose himself in the pyramid. The manuscript had spoken or dangers—he would seek them.

As he went on the moon rose in full splendor behind him. Some beast of the night plunged through a thicket along the path.

The road ascended steadily for a mile or more, crossing what must have once been carriage drives. Under the light of the setting moon the gradually increasing fertility of the ground shone silver-white. Arrived at the top of the hill, he paused to rest and wipe the perspiration from his face. After a few minutes' halt, he plunged on and soon stood before the entrance of the gloomy chamber; as he stumbled along he heard a low, distinct hiss almost beneath his feet. Reuel jumped and stood still. He who had been desirous of death but an hour before obeyed the first law of nature. Who can wonder? It was but the re-awakening of life within him, and that care for what has been entrusted to us by Omnipotence, will remain until death has numbed our senses. The dawn wind blew all about him. He would do no more until the dawn. Presently the loom of the night lifted and he could see the outlines of the building a few yards away. From his position he commanded the plain at his feet as level as a sea. The shadows grew more distinct, then without warning, the red dawn shot up behind him. The sepulchre before him flushed the color of blood, and the light revealed the horror of its emptiness.

Fragments of marble lay about him. It seemed to the lonely watcher that he could hear the sound of the centuries marching by in the moaning wind and purposeless dust.

The silence and sadness lay on him like a pall and seemed to answer to the desolation of his own life.

For a while he rambled aimlessly from wall to wall examining the gigantic resting place of the dead with scrupulous care. Here were ranger great numbers of the dead in glass cases; up and up they mounted to the vaulted ceiling. His taper flickered in the sombreness, giving but a feeble light. The air grew cold and damp as he went on. Once upon a time there had been steps cut in the granite and leading down to a well-like depression near the center of the great chamber. Down he went holding the candle high above his head as he carefully watched for the Sphinx' head. He reached a ledge which ran about what was evidently once a tank. The ledge ran only on one side. He looked about for the Sphinx; unless it was here he must retrace his steps, for the ledge ran only a little way about one side of the chamber.

He was cold and damp, and turned suddenly to retrace his steps, when just in front of him to the left the candle's light fell full on the devilish countenance of the Ethiopian Sphinx.

He moved quickly toward it; and then began an examination of the figure. As he stepped backward his foot crushed through a skull; he retreated with a shudder. He saw now that he stood in a space of unknown dimensions. He fancied he saw rows of pillars flickering drunkenly in the gloom. The American man is familiar with many things because of the range of his experience, and Reuel Briggs was devoid of fear, but in that moment he tasted the agony of pure, physical terror.

For the first time since he received his letters from home, he was himself again filled with pure, human nature. He turned to retrace his steps; something came out of the darkness like a hand, passed before his face emitting a subtle odor as it moved; he sank upon the ground and consciousness left him.

XVI

From profound unconsciousness, deep, merciful, oblivious to pain and the flight of time, from the gulf of the mysterious shadows wherein earth and heaven are alike forgotten, Reuel awoke at the close of the fourth day after his entrance into the Great Pyramid. That Lethean calm induced by narcotic odors, saved his reason. Great pain, whether physical or mental, cannot last long, and human anguish must find relief or take it.

A soft murmur of voices was in his ears as he languidly unclosed his eyes and gazed into the faces of a number of men grouped about the couch on which he lay, who surveyed him with looks of respectful admiration and curiosity mingled with awe. One of the group appeared to be in authority, for the others listened to him with profound respect as they conversed in low tones, and were careful not to obtrude their opinions.

Gradually his senses returned to him, and Reuel could distinguish his surroundings. He gazed about him in amazement Gone were all evidences of ruin and decay, and in their place was bewildering beauty that filled him with dazzling awe. He reclined on a couch composed of silken cushions, in a room of vast dimensions, formed of fluted columns of pure white marble upholding a domed ceiling where the light poured in through rose-colored glass in soft prismatic shades which gave a touch of fairyland to the scene.

The men beside him were strangers, and more unreal than the vast chamber. Dark-visaged, he noticed that they ranged in complexion from a creamy tint to purest ebony; the long hair which fell upon their shoulders, varied in texture from soft, waving curls to the crispness of the most pronounced African type. But the faces into which he gazed were perfect in the cut and outline of every feature; the forms hidden by soft white drapery, Grecian in effect, were athletic and beautifully molded. Sandals covered their feet.

The eyes of the leader followed Reuel's every movement

"Where am I?" cried Briggs impetuously, after a hurried survey of the situation.

Immediately the leader spoke to his companions in a rich voice, commanding, but with all the benevolence of a father.

"Leave us" he said. "I would be alone with the stranger."

He spoke in ancient Arabic known only to the most profound students of philology. Instantly the room was cleared, each figure vanished behind the silken curtains hanging between the columns at one side of the room.

"How came I here?" cried Reuel again.

"Peace," replied the leader, extending his arms as if in benediction above the young man's head. "You have nothing to fear. You have been brought hither for a certain purpose which will shortly be made clear to you; you shall return to your friends if you desire so to do, after the council has investigated your case. But why, my son, did you wander at night about the dangerous passages of the pyramid? Are you, too, one of those who seek for hidden treasure?"

In years the speaker was still young, not being over forty despite his patriarchal bearing. The white robe was infinitely becoming, emphasizing breadth of shoulder and chest above the silver-clasped arm's-eye like nothing he had seen save in the sculptured figures of the ruined cities lately explored. But the most striking thing about the man was his kingly countenance, combining force, sweetness and dignity in every feature. The grace of a perfect life invested him like a royal robe. The musical language flowed from his lips in sonorous' accents that charmed the scholar in his listener, who, to his own great surprise and delight, found that conversation between them could be carried on with ease. Reuel could not repress a smile as he thought of the astonishment of Professor Stone if he could hear them rolling out the ancient Arabic tongue as a common carrier of thought. It seemed sacrilegious.

"But where am I?" he persisted, determined to locate his whereabouts.

"You are in the hidden city Telassar. In my people you will behold the direct descendants of the inhabitants of Meroe. We are but a remnant, and here we wait behind the protection of our mountains and swamps, secure from the intrusion of a world that has forgotten, for the coming of our king who shall restore to the Ethiopian race its ancient glory. I am Ai, his faithful prime minister."

Hopelessly perplexed by the words of the speaker, Reuel tried to convince himself that he was laboring under a wild hallucination; but his senses all gave evidence of the reality of his situation. Somewhere in Milton he had read lines that now came faintly across his memory:

PAULINE E. HOPKINS

Eden stretched her lines
From Auran eastward to the royal tow'rs
Of great Seleucia, built by Grecian kings,
Or where the sons of Eden long before
Dwelt in Telassar.

Something of his perplexity Ai must have read in his eyes, for he smiled as he said, "Not Telassar of Eden, but so like to Eden's beauties did our ancestors find the city that thus did they call it."

"Can it be that you are an Ethiopian of those early days, now lost in obscurity? Is it possible that a remnant of that once magnificent race yet dwells upon old mother Earth? You talk of having lived at Meroe; surely, you cannot mean it. Were it true, what you have just uttered, the modern world would stand aghast."

Ai bowed his head gravely. "It is even so, incredible though it may seem to you, stranger. Destroyed and abased because of her idolatries, Ethiopia's arrogance and pride have been humbled in the dust. Utter destruction has come upon Meroe the glorious, as was predicted. But there was a hope held out to the faithful worshippers of the true God that Ethiopia should stretch forth her hand unto Eternal Goodness, and that then her glory should again dazzle the world. I am of the priestly caste, and the office I hold descends from father to son, and has so done for more than six thousand years before the birth of Christ. But enough of this now; when you are fully rested and recovered from the effect of the narcotics we were forced to give you, I will talk with you, and I will also show you the wonders of our hidden city. Come with me."

Without more speech he lifted one of the curtains at the side of the room, revealing another apartment where running water in marble basins invited one to the refreshing bath. Attendants stood waiting, tall, handsome, dark-visaged, kindly, and into their hands he resigned Reuel.

Used as he was to the improvements and luxuries of life in the modern Athens, he could but acknowledge them as poor beside the combination of Oriental and ancient luxury that he now enjoyed. Was ever man more gorgeously housed than this? Overhead was the tinted glass through which the daylight fell in softened glow. In the air was the perfume and lustre of precious incense, the flash of azure and gold, the mingling of deep and delicate hues, the gorgeousness of waving plants in blossom and tall trees—palms, dates, orange, mingled with the gleaming statues that shone forth in brilliant contrast to the dark green foliage. The floor was paved with varied mosaic and dotted here and there with the skins of wild animals.

After the bath came a repast of fruit, game and wine, served him on curious golden dishes that resembled the specimens taken from ruined Pompeii. By the time he had eaten night had fallen, and he laid himself down on the silken cushions of his couch, with a feeling of delicious languor and a desire for repose. His nerves were in a quiver of excitement and he doubted his ability to sleep, but in a few moments, even while he doubted, he fell into a deep sleep of utter exhaustion.

XVII

When he arose in the morning he found that his own clothing had been replaced by silken garments fashioned as were Ai's with the addition of golden clasps and belts. In place oi his revolver was a jeweled dagger literally encrusted with gems.

After the bath and breakfast, Ai entered the room with his noiseless tread, and when the greetings had been said, invited him to go with him to visit the public buildings and works of Telassar. With a swift, phantomlike movement, Ai escorted his guest to the farther end of the great hall. Throwing aside a curtain of rich topaz silk which draped the large entrance doors he ushered him into another apartment opening out on a terrace with a garden at its foot—a garden where a marvelous profusion of flowers and foliage ran riot amid sparkling fountains and gleaming statuary.

Through a broad alley, lined with majestic palms, they passed to the extreme end of the terrace, and turning faced the building from which they had just issued. A smile quivered for a moment on Ars face as he noted Reuel's ill-concealed amazement He stood for a moment stock-still, overcome with astonishment at the size and splendor of the palace that had sheltered him over night. The building was dome-shaped and of white marble, surrounded by fluted columns, end fronted by courts where fountains dashed their spray up to the blue sky, and flowers blushed in myriad colors and birds in gorgeous plumage flitted from bough to bough.

It appeared to Reuel that they were on the highest point of what might be best described as a horse-shoe curve whose rounded end rested on the side of a gigantic mountain. At their feet stretched a city beautiful, built with an outer and inner wall. They were in the outer city. Two streams descended like cataracts to the plain below, at some distance from each other, forming a triangle which held another city. Far in the distance like a silver thread, he could dimly discern where the rivers joined, losing themselves in union. As he gazed he recalled the description of the treasure city that Professor Stone had read to the explorers.

As far as the eye could reach stretched fertile fields; vineyards climbed the mountain side. Again Reuel quoted Milton in his thoughts, for here was the very embodiment of his words:

> *"Flowers of all hue, and without thorn the rose,*
> *Another side, umbrageous grots and caves*
> *Of cool recess, o'er which the mantling vine*
> *Lays forth her purple grape, and gently creeps*
> *Luxuriant; meanwhile murmuring waters fall*
> *Down the slope hills, dispersed, or in a lake,*
> *That to the fringed bank with myrtle crown'd*
> *Her crystal mirror holds, unite their streams.*
> *The birds their choir apply; airs, vernal airs,*
> *Breathing the smell of field and grove, attune*
> *The trembling leaves, while universal Pan,*
> *Knit with the Graces and the Hours in dance,*
> *Led on th' eternal spring.*

Far below he could dimly discern moving crowds; great buildings reared their stately heads towards a sky so blue and bewildering beneath the sun's bright rays that the gazer was rendered speechless with amazement. Shadowy images of past scenes and happenings flitted across his brain like transient reflection of a past perfectly familiar to him.

"Do you find the prospect fair?" asked Ai at length, breaking the settled silence.

"Fairer than I can find words to express; and yet I am surprised to find that it all seems familiar to me, as if somewhere in the past I had known just such a city as this."

Ai smiled a smile of singular sweetness and content; Reuel could have sworn that there was a degree of satisfaction in his pleasure.

"Come, we will go down into the city. You who know the wonders of modern life at its zenith, tell me what lesson you learn from the wonders of a civilization which had its zenith six thousand years before Christ's birth."

"Six thousand years before Christ!" murmured Reuel in blank stupidity.

"Aye; here in Telassar are preserved specimens of the highest attainments the world knew in ancient days. They tell me that in many things your modern world is yet in its infancy."

"How!" cried Reuel, "do you then hold communion with the world outside your city?"

"Certain members of our Council are permitted to visit outside the gates. Do you not remember Ababdis?"

"Our camel-driver?"

Ai bowed. "He is the member who brought us news of your arrival, and the intention of the expedition to find our city for the sake of its treasure."

More and more mystified by the words and manner of his guide, Reuel made no reply. Presently they entered a waiting palanquin and were borne swiftly toward the city. The silken curtains were drawn one side, and he could drink in the curious sights. They soon left the country behind them and entered a splendid square, where stately homes were outlined against the dense blue of the sky. A statue of an immense sphinx crouched in the center of the square, its giant head reaching far into the ethereal blue. Fountains played on either side, dashing their silvery spray beyond the extreme height of the head. Under umbrageous trees were resting-places, and on the sphinx was engraved the words: "That which hath been, is now; and that which is to be, hath already been; and God requireth that which is past."

Suddenly a crowd of men surged into the square, and a deep-toned bell sounded from a distance. Swiftly sped the bearers, urged forward by the general rush. The booming of the bell continued. They reached the end of the avenue and entered a side street, through a court composed of statues. They paused before a stately pile, towering in magnificence high in the heavens, a pile of marvelously delicate architecture worked in stone. The entrance was of incomparable magnificence. Reuel judged that the four colossal statues before it represented Rameses the Great. They were each sculptured of a single block of Syene granite of mingled red and black. They were seated on cubical stones. The four Colosses sitting there before that glittering pile produced a most imposing effect

The steps of the temple were strewn with flowers; the doors stood open, and music from stringed instruments vibrated upon the air. The bearers stopped at a side entrance, and at a sign from Ai, Reuel followed him into the edifice.

All was silence, save for the distant hum of voices, and the faint sound of music. They halted before a curtain which parted silently for their entrance. It was a small room, but filled with a light of soft colors; when Reuel could command his gaze, he beheld about twenty men prostrated before him. Presently they arose and each filed past him, reverently touching the hem of his white robe. Among them was Ababdis, so transformed by his gorgeous robes of office as to be almost unrecognizable.

Ai now assumed an azure robe embroidered in silver stars and crescents that formed a sunburst in shape of a Grecian cross. He then advanced towards Reuel bearing on a silken cushion a magnificent crown, where the principal aigrette was shaped as a cross set with gems priceless in value. Astounded at the sight, the young man stood motionless while it was adjusted by golden chains about his head. The gems blazed with the red of the ruby, the green of the emerald, the blue of the sapphire, the yellow of the topaz, the cold white of priceless diamonds. But dulling all the glories of precious stones, peerless in their own class, lay the center ornament—the black diamond of Senechus's crown, spoken of in Professor Stone's record. A white robe of silken stuff was added to his costume, and again his companions filed past him in deepest reverence. Reuel was puzzled to understand why so great homage was paid to him. While he turned the thought in his mind, a bugle sounded somewhere in the distance, sweet and high. Instantly, he felt a gliding motion as if the solid earth were slipping from beneath his feet, the curtains before him parted silently, and he found himself alone on a raised platform in the center of a vast auditorium, crowded with humanity. Lights twinkled everywhere; there was the fragrance of flowers, there were columns of marble draped in amber, azure and green, and glittering lamps encrusted with gems and swung by golden chains from the sides of the building. A blazing arch formed of brilliant lamps raised like a gigantic bow in the heavens and having in its center the words

"Hail! Ergamenes!"

in letters of sparkling fire, met his startled gaze. Then came a ringing shout from the throats of the assembled multitude, "Ergamenes! Ergamenes!" Again and again the throng lifted up the joyous cry. Presently as Reuel stood there undecided what to do—not knowing what was expected of him, as silently as lie had come, he felt the motion of the platform where he stood. The crowd faded from sight, the curtains fell; once more he stood within the little room, surrounded by his companions.

"Ababdis, Ai," he demanded, sternly, "What is the meaning of this strange happening, more like a scene from the Arabian Nights? Who is Ergamenes?"

"Thou art Ergamenes—the long-looked-for king of Ethiopia, for whose reception this city was built! But we will return to the palace, now that the people have satisfied somewhat their curiosity. At supper you shall know more."

Once more the bearers carried them swiftly beyond the confines of the city, and soon the palace walls rose before them. Reuel had hardly collected his scattered wits before he found himself seated at table and on either side of the board the Council reclined on silken cushions. His own seat was raised and placed at the head of the table. There was no talking done while what seemed to be a solemn feast was in progress. Servants passed noiselessly to and fro attending to their wants, while from an alcove the music of stringed instruments and sweetest vocal numbers was borne to their ears.

After supper, they still reclined on the couches. Then from the hidden recesses the musicians came forth, and kneeling before Reuel, one began a song in blank verse, telling the story of Ergamenes and his kingdom.

> *"Hail! oh, hail, Ergamenes!*
> *The dimmest sea-cave below thee,*
> *The farthest sky-arch above,*
> *In their innermost stillness know thee,*
> *And heave with the birth of Love.*
> *"All hail!*
> *We are thine, all thine, forevermore;*
> *Not a leaf on the laughing shore,*
> *Not a wave on the heaving sea,*
> *Nor a single sigh*
> *In the boundless sky,*
> *But is vowed evermore to thee!"*

"Son of a fallen dynasty, outcast of a sunken people, upon your breast is a lotus lily, God's mark to prove your race and descent. You, Ergamenes, shall begin the restoration of Ethiopia. Blessed be the name of God for ever and ever, for wisdom and might are His, and He changeth the times and seasons; He removeth kings and countries, and setteth them up again; He giveth wisdom unto the wise, and knowledge to them that know understanding! He revealeth the deep and secret things; He knoweth what is in the darkness, and the light dwelleth with Him!

"Great were the sins of our fathers, and the white stranger was to Ethiopia but a scourge in the hands of an offended God. The beautiful temples of Babylon, filled with vessels of silver and gold, swelled the treasures of the false god Bel. Babylon, where our monarchs dwelt in splendor, once the grandest city to be found in the world. Sixty miles round were its walls, of prodigious height, and so broad that seven chariots could be driven abreast on the summit! One hundred gates of solid brass gave entrance into the city, guarded by lofty towers. Beautiful buildings rose within, richly adorned and surrounded by gardens. One magnificent royal palace was girdled by three walls, the outermost of which was seven miles and a half in compass. In its grounds rose the far-famed hanging gardens, terraces built one above another to the height of three hundred and fifty feet, each terrace covered with thick mold, and planted with flowers and shrubs, so that the skill of man created a verdant hill on a plain. Nearly in the center rose the lofty temple of Belus, the tower of Babel, whose builders had hoped to make its summit touch the very skies. Millions of dollars in gold were gathered in the chambers of the temple. The wealth, power and glory of the world were centered in the mighty city of Babylon."

"On the throne of this powerful city sat your forefathers, O Ergamenes!"

Part of the story had been given in recitative, one rich voice carrying grandly the monotonous notes to the accompaniment of the cornet, flute, sackbut, dulcimer and harp. Reuel had listened to the finest trained voices attempting the recitative in boasted musical circles, but never in so stately and impressive a manner as was now his privilege to hear. They continued the story.

"And Meroe, the greatest city of them all, pure-blooded Ethiopian. Once the light of the world's civilization, now a magnificent Necropolis."

"Standing at the edge of the Desert, fertile in soil, rich in the luxuries of foreign shores; into her lap caravans poured their treasures gathered from the North, South, East and West. All Africa poured into this queenly city ivory, frankincense and gold. Her colossal monuments were old before Egypt was; her wise men monopolized the learning of the ages, and in the persons of the Chaldeans have figured conspicuously the wisdom of ages since Meroe has fallen."

"Mother of ancient warfare, her horsemen and chariots were the wonder and terror of her age; from the bows of her warriors, the arrows sped like a flight of birds, carrying destruction to her foes,—a lamb in peace, a lion in time of war."

Once more the measure changed, and another voice took up the story in verse.

"Who will assume the bays
That the hero wore?
Wreaths on the Tomb of Days

Gone evermore!
Who shall disturb the brave
Or one leaf of their holy grave?
The laurel is vow'd to them,
Leave the bay on its sacred stem!
But hope, the rose, the unfading rose,
Alike for slave and freeman grows!

On the summit, worn and hoary,
Of Lybia's solemn hills,
The tramp of the brave is still!
And still is the poisoned dart,
In the pulse of the mighty hearts,
Whose very blood was glory!

Who will assume the bays
That the hero wore?
Wreaths on the Tomb of Days
Gone evermore!"

Upon Reuel a strange force seemed working. If what he heard were true, how great a destiny was his! He had carefully hidden his Ethiopian extraction from the knowledge of the world. It was a tradition among those who had known him in childhood that he was descended from a race of African kings. He remembered his mother well. From her he had inherited his mysticism and his occult powers. The nature of the mystic within him was, then, but a dreamlike devotion to the spirit that had swayed his ancestors; it was the shadow of Ethiopia's power. The lotus upon his breast he knew to be a birthmark. Many a night he had been aroused from childhood's slumbers, to find his mother bending above him, candle in hand, muttering broken sentences of prayer to Almighty God as she examined his bosom by the candle's rays. He had wondered much; now he guessed the rest. Once more the clanging strings of the instruments chained his attention. The recitative was resumed.

"The Most High ruleth in the kingdom of men, and giveth it to whomsoever He will. He delivereth and rescueth, and He worketh signs and wonders in heaven and in earth. Preeminent in peace, invincible in war—once the masters of mankind, how have we fallen from our high estate!"

"Stiff-necked, haughty, no conscience but that of intellect, awed not by God's laws, worshipping Mammon, sensual, unbelieving, God has punished us as he promised in the beginning. Gone are our ancient glories, our humbled pride cries aloud to God in the travail of our soul. Our sphinx, with passionless features, portrays the dumb suffering of our souls."

Their look, with the reach of past ages, was wise, And the soul of eternity thought in their eyes.

"By divine revelation David beheld the present time, when, after Christ's travail for the sins of humanity, the time of Ethiopia's atonement being past, purged of idolatry, accepting the One Only God through His Son Jesus, suddenly should come a new birth to the descendants of Ham, and Ethiopia should return to her ancient glory! Ergamenes, all hail!"

> *"You come from afar*
> *From the land of the stranger,*
> *The dreadful in war,*
> *The daring in danger;*
> *Before him our plain*
> *Like Eden is lying;*
> *Behind him remain*
> *But the wasted and dying.*
>
> *The weak finds not ruth,*
> *Nor the patriot glory;*
> *No hope for the youth,*
> *And no rest for the hoary;*
> *O'er Ethiop's lost plains*
> *The victor's sword flashes,*
> *Her sons are in chains,*
> *And her temples in ashes!*

> *Who will assume the bays*
> *That the hero wore?*
> *Wreaths on the Tomb of Days*
> *Gone evermore!"*

Upon his companions the song of the past of Ethiopia had a strange effect. Soothing at times, at times exciting, with the last notes from the instruments the company sprang to their feet; with flashing dark eyes, faces reflecting inward passions, they drew their short, sabrelike arms and circled about Reuel's throne with the shout "Ergamenes! Ergamenes!"

XVIII

Once more Reuel found himself alone with Ai. It was far into the night, but he felt sleepless and restless. At last Ai broke a long silence:

"Tell me of the country from which you come, Ergamenes. Is it true that the Ethiopian there is counted less than other mortals?"

"It is true, Ai," replied Reuel. "There, the dark hue of your skin, your waving hair with its trace of crispness, would degrade you below the estate of any man of fair hue and straight locks, belonging to any race outside the Ethiopian, for it is a deep disgrace to have within the veins even one drop of the blood you seem so proud of possessing."

"That explains your isolation from our race, then?"

Reuel bowed his head in assent, while over his face passed a flush of shame. He felt keenly now the fact that he had played the coward's part in hiding his origin. What though obstacles were many, some way would have been shown him to surmount the difficulties of caste prejudice.

"And yet, from Ethiopia came all the arts and cunning inventions that make your modern glory. At our feet the mightiest nations have worshipped, paying homage to our kings, and all nations have sought the honor of alliance with our royal families because of our strength, grandeur, riches and wisdom. Tell me of all the degradation that has befallen the unfortunate sons of Ham."

Then in the deep, mysterious silence of the night, Reuel gave in minutest detail the story of the Negro, reciting with dramatic effect the history of the wrongs endured by the modern Ethiopian.

To his queries as to the history of these mountain-dwelling Ethiopians, Ai gave the following reply:

"We are a singular people, governed by a female monarch, all having the same name, Candace, and a Council of twenty-five Sages, who are educated for periodical visits to the outer world. Queen Candace is a virgin queen who waits the coming of Ergamenes to inaugurate a dynasty of kings. Our virgins live within the inner city, and from among them Candace chooses her successor at intervals of fifteen years."

"To become a Sage, a man must be married and have at least two children; a knowledge of two out-world languages, and to pass a severe examination by the court as to education, fitness and ability. After an arduous preparation they are initiated into the secrets of this kingdom. They are chosen for life. The inner city is the virgins' court, and it is adorned with beautiful gardens, baths, schools and hospitals. When a woman marries she leaves this city for the outer one."

"We have a great temple, the one you entered, dedicated to the Supreme or Trinity. It is a masterpiece of beauty and art. The population assembles there twice a year for especial service. It seats about 12,000 persons. The Sages have seen nothing equal to it in the outer world. Octagonal in shape, with four wings or galleries, on opposite sides; the intervening spaces are filled with great prism columns, twenty-five feet high, made of a substance like glass, malleable, elastic and pure. The effect is gorgeous. The decorations of the hall are prepared natural flowers; that is, floral garlands are subjected to the fumes of the crystal material covering them like a film and preserving their natural appearance. This is a process handed down from the earliest days of Ethiopian greatness. I am told that the modern world has not yet solved this simple process," he said, with a gentle smile of ridicule.

"We preserve the bodies of our most beautiful women in this way. We suspend reflecting plates of the crystal material arranged in circles, pendant from the ceiling of the central hall, and thus the music of the instruments is repeated many times in sweetest harmony."

"We have services at noon every seventh day, chiefly choral, in praise of the attributes of the Supreme. Our religion is a belief in One Supreme Being, the center of action in all nature. He distributed a portion of Himself at an early age to the care of man who has attained the highest development of any of His terrestrial creatures. We call this everliving faculty or soul Ego.

"After its transition Ego has the power of expressing itself to other bodies, with like gift and form, its innate feeling; and by law of affinity, is ever striving to regain its original position near the great Unity; but the physical attractions of this beautiful world have such a fascination on the organism of man that there is ever a contention against the greater object being attained; and unless the Ego can wean the body from gross desires and raise it to the highest condition of human existence, it cannot be united to its Creator. The Ego preserves its individuality after the dissolution of the body. We believe in re-incarnation by natural laws regulating material on earth. The Ego can never be destroyed. For instance, when the body of a good man or woman dies, and the Ego is not sufficiently fitted for the higher condition of another world, it is re-associated with another body to complete the necessary fitness for heaven."

"What of the Son of man? Do you not know the necessity of belief in the Holy Trinity? Have not your Sages brought you the need of belief in God's Son?" Ai looked somewhat puzzled.

"We have heard of such a God, but have not paid much attention to it. How believe you, Ergamenes?"

"In Jesus Christ, the Son of God," replied Reuel solemnly.

"O Ergamenes, your belief shall be ours; we have no will but yours. Deign to teach your subjects."

When at last Reuel closed his eyes in slumber, it was with a feeling of greater responsibility and humility than he had ever experienced. Who was he that so high a destiny as lay before him should be thrust upon his shoulders?

XIX

After these happenings, which we have just recorded, every day Reuel received callers in state. It seemed to him that the entire populace of that great hidden city turned out to do him homage. The Sages, clad in silver armor, attended him as a body-guard, while soldiers and officials high in the councils of the State, were ranged on both sides of the immense hall. The throne on which he sat was a massive one of silver, a bronze Sphinx couched on either side. The steps of the throne were banked with blossoms, offerings from the procession of children that filed slowly by, clad in white, wearing garlands of roses, and laying branches of palm, oleander flowers, lilies and olive sprays before their king.

Offerings of gold, silver and gems, silken cloths, priceless articles molded into unique and exquisite designs, sword of tempered steel, beside which a Damascus blade was coarse and unfinished, filled his artist soul with delight and wonder. Later, Ai escorted him to the underground workshops where brawny smiths plied their trades; and there the secrets of centuries dead and gone were laid bare to his curious gaze.

How was it possible, he asked himself again and again, that a nation so advanced in literature, science and the arts, in the customs of peace and war, could fall as low as had the Ethiopian? Even while he held the thought, the answer came: As Daniel interpreted Nebuchadnezzar's dream, so has it been and is with Ethiopia. "They shall drive thee from men, and thy dwelling shall be with the beasts of the field, and they shall make thee to eat grass as oxen, and they shall wet thee with the dew of heaven, and seven times shall pass over thee, till thou knowest that the Most High ruleth in the kingdom of men, and giveth it to whomsoever He will. Thy kingdom shall be sure unto thee; after that thou shalt have known that the heavens do rule."

But the excitement and changes through which he had passed began to tell upon a constitution already weakened by mental troubles. Ai observed with much concern, the apathy which foretold a serious illness. Hoping to arouse him from painful thoughts which now engrossed his mind, Ai proposed that the visit to the inner city, postponed by the pressure of other duties, be made the next day.

That morning a company, of which the Sages formed a part, started for the inner city. They were to spend the night in travel, resting by day. The progress of the party was very slow, and in a direction Reuel had not yet explored. A deep yellow glow suffused the sky. This soon gave way to the powerful but mellow light of the African moon, casting long shadows over the silvery green of the herbage and foliage. They encountered a perfect network of streams, pursuing their way through virgin forests, brilliant by daylight with beautiful flowers. The woods were inhabited by various kinds of birds of exquisite note and plumage. There were also a goodly number of baboons, who descended from the trees and ranged themselves on the ground to obtain a nearer view of the travelers. They grinned and chattered at the caravan, seeming to regard them as trespassers in their domains.

The character of the country improved as they neared the interior. Reuel noticed that this was at variance with the European idea respecting Central Africa, which brands these regions as howling wildernesses or an uninhabitable country. He found the landscape most beautiful, the imaginary desert "blossomed like the rose," and the "waste sandy valleys" and "thirsty wilds," which had been assigned to this location, became, on close inspection, a gorgeous scene, decorated with Nature's most cheering garniture, teeming with choice specimens of vegetable and animal life, and refreshed by innumerable streams, branches of the rivers, not a few of which were of sufficient magnitude for navigation and commerce. But Reuel remembered the loathsome desert that stood in grim determination guarding the entrance to this paradise against all intrusion, and with an American's practical common sense, bewailed this waste of material.

Proceeding along a mountain gorge, our travelers found the path straitened between the impending mountain on one side and a rapid and sparkling stream on the other. On the opposite side of the ravine the precipices rose abruptly from the very edge of the water. The whole appearance of this mountain pass was singularly grand, romantically wild and picturesquely beautiful. They were often obliged to clamber over huge masses of granite, fallen from the cliffs above; and, on this account, progress was slow and toilsome. On turning an angle of the rock, about the center of the gorge, the party were suddenly confronted by a huge, tawny lion, which stood directly in the path, with not a wall and scarce a space between. The path was so narrow in this place that it would have been impossible to pass the brute without touching him. Used to the king of the African jungle, the company did not shrink, but faced the animal boldly, although not without some natural physical

PAULINE E. HOPKINS

fear. The lion, too, seemed to be taken by surprise. Thus the opponents stood at a distance of five yards, each staring at the other for several minutes. Had the travelers shown the least signs of fear, or had they attempted to escape, the fate of one, at least, would have been sealed. Now appeared an exhibition of the power of magnetism. Reuel stepped in advance of the foremost bearer, fixed his wonderful and powerful eyes upon the beast, literally transfixing him with a glance, poured the full force of his personal magnetism upon the animal, which almost instantly responded by low growls and an uneasy twisting of the head; finally, the terrible glance remaining inflexible and unwavering, the beast turned himself about and slowly withdrew with a stately and majestic tread, occasionally looking back and uttering a low growl, as if admonishing the travelers to keep their distance.

Murmurs of wonder and admiration broke from Reuel's companions, who were aware of the danger attending the meeting of a hungry lion at close quarters. His admirable intrepidity, and the remarkable powers which were his birthright, had preserved him and his companions.

"Truly, he is the King!" they murmured among themselves. And more than ever Ai watched him with increasing love and the fondness of a father.

Without further adventure they reached the portals of the inner city. Their arrival was evidently anticipated, for they were received by a band of young females under the guardianship of a matron. By this escort they were shown to the palace and into the rooms set apart for their reception. Having rested for an hour, bathed and dined, they were ready for the ceremony of introduction. Another guard of women took them in charge, and the procession started down one passage, crossed a great, aisle-like hall, and came to a corresponding passage on the other side. On through seemingly endless colonnades they passed, till they came to a huge door formed of great winged creatures. Reuel had thought that nothing could surpass the palace in the outer city for beauty and luxury, but words failed him as his eyes drank in the glories of the lofty apartment into which they stepped, as an Amazon in silver mail threw wide the glittering doors, disclosing the splendor of the royal Presence-chamber. It was a lofty saloon lined with gilded columns, the sunlight falling from the open roof upon the mosaic floor beneath. The tapestries which lined the walls bore exquisite paintings of love and warfare.

As the door opened, a voice called. The company halted before a curtained recess, guarded by a group of beautiful girls. Never had Reuel beheld such subtle grace of form and feature, such masses of coal-black hair, such melting eyes of midnight hue. Each girl might have posed for a statue of Venus.

The heavy curtains were lifted now, and discovered the Queen reclining upon a pile of silken cushions—a statue of Venus worked in bronze.

"The Queen is here!" exclaimed a voice. In an instant all present prostrated themselves upon the floor. Reuel alone stood erect, his piercing eyes fixed upon the woman before him.

Grave, tranquil and majestic, surrounded by her virgin guard, she advanced gracefully, bending her haughty head; then, gradually her sinuous body bent and swayed down, down, until she, too, had prostrated herself, and half-knelt, half-lay, upon the marble floor at Reuel's feet.

"O Ergamenes, hast thou indeed returned to thine inheritance?" murmured a voice like unto silver chimes. Reuel started, for it seemed to him that Dianthe's own voice was breathing in his ears.

Knowing now what was expected of him, he raised the Queen with one hand, addressed her courteously in Arabic, led her to her silken couch, seated himself, and would have placed her beside him, but she, with a gesture of dissent, sank upon the cushions at his feet that had served her for footstools.

By this time the Sages had risen and now reclined on the silken couches with which the apartment was well supplied. Ai advanced and addressed the Queen; during this exchange of courtesies, Reuel gazed upon her curiously.

She reminded him strongly of his beautiful Dianthe; in fact, the resemblance was so striking that it was painful, and tears, which were no disgrace to his manhood, struggled to his eyes. She was the same height as Dianthe, had the same well-developed shoulders and the same admirable bust What suppleness in all her movements! What grace, and, at the same time, what strength! Yes; she was a Venus, a superb statue of bronze, molded by a great sculptor; but an animated statue, in which one saw the blood circulate, and from which life flowed. And what an expressive face, full of character! Long, jet-black hair and totally free, covered her shoulders like a silken mantle; a broad, square forehead, a warm bronze complexion; thick black eyebrows, great black eyes, now soft and languishing—eyes which could weep in sorrow or shoot forth lightning in their anger; a delicate nose with quivering nostrils, teeth of dazzling whiteness behind lips as red as a rose; in her smile of grace and sweetness lurked a sense of power. He was astonished and lost in admiration in spite of himself. Her loveliness was absolutely and ideally perfect. Her attitude of unstudied grace accorded well with the seriousness of her face; she seemed the embodiment of all chastity.

The maidens of her household waited near her—some of them with baskets of flowers upheld in perfect arms. Some brought fruit in glittering dishes and wine in golden goblets of fairy-like fretwork, which were served from stands of ivory and gold. One maiden knelt at her lyre, prepared to strike its chords at pauses in the conversation.

The attendants now retired modestly into the background, while Ai and the other Sages conversed with the Queen. She listened with downcast eyes, occasionally casting a curious, though deferential glance at the muscular figure beside her.

"And dost thou agree, and art thou willing to accept the destiny planned by the Almighty Trinity for thee and me from the beginning of all things, my lord?" she questioned at length in her flute-like voice.

"Queen Candace, thy beauty and graciousness dazzle me. I feel that I can love thee with all my heart; I will fulfill my destiny gladly, and I will cleave to thee until the end."

"Now," answered the Queen with sweet humility, "now, when thou, my lord, doth speak so royally, it doth not become me to lag in generosity." She paused.

Reuel, gazing into her beautiful face, was deeply moved by strong emotions. Again she spoke:

"Behold! in token of submission I bow to my lord, King Ergamenes." She bent herself slowly to the ground, and pressed her knees for one instant upon the mosaic floor. "Behold," and she touched his forehead lightly with her lips, "in earnest of connubial bliss, I kiss thee, King Ergamenes. Behold," and she placed her hand upon his heart, "I swear to thee eternal fealty by the Spirit—the never-changing Trinity." This ceremony ended she seated herself once more beside him. Reuel felt himself yielding readily to her infinite attractiveness. In the azure light and regal splendor of the fragrant apartment, there was rest and satisfaction. All the dreams of wealth and ambition that had haunted the feverish existence by the winding Charles, that had haunted his days of obscure poverty in the halls of Harvard, were about to be realized. Only once had he known joy in his checkered life, and that was when he basked in the society of Dianthe, whom he now designated his spirit-bride. The delirium of that joy had ended in lamentation. Doubts and misgivings had assailed him in the silence of the night when Ai had left him and his influence was withdrawn. Then he had but a faint-hearted belief in the wonderful tale told to him, but here, under Queen Candace's magic influence, all doubts disappeared, and it seemed the most natural thing in the world to be sitting here among these descendants of the ancient Ethiopians, acknowledged as their King, planning a union with a lovely woman, that should give to the world a dynasty of dark-skinned rulers, whose destiny should be to restore the prestige of an ancient people.

Verily, if the wonders he had already seen and heard could be possible in the nineteenth century of progress and enlightenment, nothing was impossible. Dianthe was gone. The world outside held nothing dear to one who had always lived much within himself. The Queen was loving, beautiful—why not accept this pleasant destiny which held its alluring arms so seductively towards him? A sudden moisture filled his eyes; a curious vague softness and tenderness stole over him. Turning abruptly toward his hostess, he held out his own swimming goblet:

"Drink we a loving cup together, oh Queen Candace!" he said in a voice that trembled with earnestness. "I pledge my faith in return for thine!"

The Queen returned his ardent gaze with one of bright surprise and joyous happiness, and bending her head, drank a deep draught of the proffered wine.

"Almost thou lovest me, Ergamenes. May the Eternal Trinity hold fast our bonds!" With a graceful salute she returned the goblet. Reuel drank off in haste what remained within it.

"Behold! I have prepared against this happy hour," continued the Queen, and going to an inlaid cabinet at one side of the room, she took from it a curious ring of dull gold, bearing one priceless gem cut in the form of a lotus lily. "Hold forth thy hand," she said, and on his finger placed the ring.

"Thus do I claim thee for all eternity."

The Sages had watched the actors in this life-drama with jealous eyes that noted every detail with open satisfaction. At Queen Candace's last words, Ai extended his arms with the solemn words:

"And now it is done and never can be undone or altered. Let us hence, that the union may be speedily accomplished."

PAULINE E. HOPKINS

XX

In a month the marriage was to be celebrated with great pomp and rejoicing. Preparations began as soon as the interview between the Queen and the prospective King was over.

After his return from this betrothal, the power of second sight which seemed to have left Reuel for a time, returned in full force. Restlessness was upon him; Dianthe's voice seemed ever calling to him through space. Finally, when his feelings became insupportable, he broached the subject to Ai.

The latter regarded his questioner gravely. "Of a truth thou art a legitimate son of Ethiopia. Thou growest the fruits of wisdom. Descendant of the wise Chaldeans, still powerful to a degree undreamed of by the pigmies of this puny age, you look incredulous, but what I tell you is the solemn truth."

"The Chaldeans disappeared from this world centuries ago," declared Reuel.

"Not all—in me you behold their present head; within this city and the outer world, we still number thousands."

Reuel uttered an exclamation of incredulous amazement. "Not possible!"

Silently Ai went to his cabinet and took down a small, square volume which he placed in Reuel's hand. "It is a record of the wisdom and science of your ancestors."

Reuel turned it over carefully,—the ivory pages were covered with characters sharply defined and finely engraved.

"What language is this? It is not Hebrew, Greek nor Sanskrit, nor any form of hieroglyphic writing."

"It is the language once commonly spoken by your ancestors long before Babylon was builded. It is known to us now as the language of prophecy."

Reuel glanced at the speaker's regal form with admiration and reverence.

"Teach me what thou knowest, Ai," he said humbly, "for, indeed, thou art a wonderful man."

"Gladly," replied Ai, placing his hand in loving tenderness upon the bowed head of the younger man. "Our destiny was foreordained from the beginning to work together for the upbuilding of humanity and the restoration of the race of our fathers. This little book shall teach your soul all that you long to know, and now grasp but vaguely. You believe in the Soul?"

"Most assuredly!"

"As a Personality that continues to live after the body perishes?"

"Certainly."

"And that Personality begins to exert its power over our lives as soon as we begin its cultivation. Death is not necessary to its manifestation upon our lives. There are always angels near! To us who are so blessed and singled out by the Trinity there is a sense of the supernatural always near us—others whom we cannot see, but whose influence is strong upon us in all the affairs of life. Man only proves his ignorance if he denies this fact. Some in the country from which you come contend that the foundations of Christianity are absurd and preposterous, but all the prophecies of the Trinity shall in time be fulfilled. They are working out today by the forces of air, light, wind, the common things of daily life that pass unnoticed. Ethiopia, too, is stretching forth her hand unto God, and He will fulfill her destiny. The tide of immigration shall set in the early days of the twentieth century, toward Afric's shores, so long bound in the chains of barbarism and idolatry."

Reuel listened entranced, scarce breathing.

"I was warned of your coming long before the knowledge was yours. The day you left your home for New York. I sat within my secret chamber, and all was revealed to me."

"Av, Ai," Reuel answered, feeble. "But "how?""

"You believe that we can hold communion with the living though seas divide and distance is infinite, and our friends who have passed to the future life of light are allowed to comfort us here?"

"I believe."

"'Tis so," continued Ai. "Half by chance and half by learning, I long ago solved one of the great secrets of Nature. Life is wonderful, but eternity is more wonderful." He paused, regarding affectionately Reuel's troubled face.

"I will answer thy question presently. But can I do aught for thee? Dost memories of that world from which thou hast recently come disturb thee, Ergamenes? I have some feeble powers; if thou wilt, command them." Ai fell into the use of "thee" and "thou" always when greatly moved, and Reuel had become very dear to him.

"I would know some happenings in the world I have left; could my desire be granted, I might, perchance, lose this restlessness which now oppresses me."

Ai regarded him intently. "How far hast thou progressed in knowledge of Infinity?" he asked at length.

"You shall be the judge," replied Reuel. And then ensued a technical conversation on the abstract science of occultism and the future state.

"I see thou are well versed," said Ai finally, evidently well pleased with the young man's versatility. "Come with me. Truly we have not mistaken thee, Ergamenes. Wonderfully hast thou been preserved and fitted for the work before thee."

Reuel had the freedom of the palace, but he knew that there were rooms from which he was excluded. One room especially seemed to be the sanctum sanctorum of the Sages. It was to this room that Ai now conducted him.

Reuel was nearly overpowered with the anticipation of being initiated into the mysteries of this apartment. He found nothing terrifying, however, in the plain, underground room into which he was ushered. A rough table and wooden stools constituted the furniture. The only objects of mystery were a carved table at one end of the apartment, with a silken cloth thrown over its top, and a vessel like a baptismal font, cut in stone, full of water. Air and light came from an outside source, for there were no windows in the room. After closing the door securely, Ai advanced and removed the cloth from the table. "Sit," he commanded. "You ask me how I knew of your coming to my land. Lo, I have followed your career from babyhood. Behold, Ergamenes! What would you see upon the mirror's face? Friend or foe?"

Reuel advanced and looked upon the surface of a disk of which the top of the table was composed. The material of which the polished surface was composed was unknown to Reuel; it was not glass, though quite transparent; it was not metal, though bright as polished steel.

Reuel made no wish, but thought of the spot where the accident had occurred upon the River Charles weeks before. He was startled to observe a familiar scene where he had often rowed for pleasure on pleasant summer evenings. Every minute particular of the scenery was distinctly visible. Presently the water seemed to darken, and he saw distinctly the canoe containing Aubrey, Molly and Dianthe gliding over the water. He started back aghast, crying out, "It is magical!"

"No, no, Ergamenes, this is a secret of Nature. In this disk I can show thee what thou wilt of the past. In the water of the font we see the future. Think of a face, a scene—I will reflect it for thee on this disk. This is an old secret, known to Ethiopia, Egypt and Arabia centuries ago. I can reflect the past and the faces of those passed away, but the living and the future are cast by the water."

Reuel was awed into silence. He could say nothing, and listened to Ai's learned remarks with a reverence that approached almost to worship before this proof of his supernatural powers. What would tec professors of Harvard have said to this, he asked himself. In the heart of Africa was a knowledge of science that all the wealth and learning of modern times could not emulate. For some time the images came and went upon the mirror, in obedience to his desires. He saw the scenes of his boyhood, the friends of his youth, and experienced anew the delights of life's morning. Then he idly desired to see the face of his loved Dianthe, as she last appeared on earth. The surface of the disk reflected nothing!

"You have not reached perfection then, in this reflector?"

"Why think you so?" asked Ai gravely.

"I have asked to see the face of a friend who is dead. The mirror did not reflect it."

"The disk cannot err," said Ai "Let us try the water in the font."

"But that reflects the living, you say; she is dead."

"The disk cannot err," persisted Ai. He turned to the font, gazed in its surface, and then beckoned Reuel to approach. From the glassy surface Dianthe's face gazed back at him, worn and lined with grief.

"'Tis she!" he cried, "her very self."

"Then your friend still lives," said Ai, calmly.

"Impossible!"

"Why do you doubt my word, Ergamenes?"

Then with great suppressed excitement and much agitation, Reuel repeated the story of Dianthe's death as brought to him by the last mail he had received from America.

"You say that 'Molly' as you call her, was also drowned?"

"Yes."

"Let us try the disk."

They returned to the mirror and instantly the face of Molly Vance gazed at them from the river's bed, surrounded by seaweed and grasses.

"Can a man believe in his own sanity!" exclaimed Reuel in an agony of perplexity.

PAULINE E. HOPKINS

Ai made no reply, but returned to the font. "I think it best to call up the face of your enemy. I am sure you have one." Immediately the water reflected the debonair face of Aubrey Livingston, which was almost instantly blotted out by the face of Jim Titus.

"Two!" murmured Ai. "I thought so."

"If she then lives, as your science seems to insist, show me her present situation," cried Reuel, beside himself with fears.

"I must have a special preparation for the present," said Ai, calmly. He set about preparing a liquid mixture. When this was accomplished he washed the face of the disk with a small sponge dipped in the mixture. A film of sediment instantly formed upon it.

"When this has dried, I will scrape it off and polish the mirror, then we shall be ready for the demonstration. One picture only will come— this will remain for a number of days, after that the disk will return to its normal condition. But, see! the sediment is caked. Now to remove it and finish our test." At last it was done, and the disk repolished. Then standing before it, Ai cried, in an earnest voice:

"Let the present appear upon the disk, if it be for the benefit of Thy human subjects!"

Ai appeared perfectly calm, but his hands shook. Reuel remained a short remove from him, awaiting his summons.

"Come, Ergamenes."

For a few moments Reuel gazed upon the plate, his eyes brilliant with expectation, his cheeks aglow with excitement. Then he involuntarily shuddered, a half suppressed groan escaped him, and he grew ashy pale. In a trice he became entirely unnerved, and staggered back and forth like a drunken man. Greatly alarmed, and seeing he was about to fall, Ai sprang to his side and caught him. Too late. He fell to the floor in a swoon. The picture reflected by the disk was that of the ancestral home of the Livingstons. It showed the parlor of a fine old mansion; two figures stood at an open window, their faces turned to the interior. About the woman's waist the man's arm was twined in a loving embrace. The faces were those of Aubrey and Dianthe.

Late that night Reuel tossed upon his silken couch in distress of mind. If the disk were true, then Dianthe and Aubrey both lived and were together. He was torn by doubts, haunted by dreadful fears of he knew not what. If the story of the disk were true, never was man so deceived and duped as he had been. Then in the midst of his anger and despair came an irresistible impulse to rise from his bed. He did so, and distinctly felt the pressure of a soft hand upon his brow, and a yielding body at his side. The next instant he could have sworn that he heard the well-known tones of Dianthe in his ears, saying:

"Reuel, it is I."

Unable to answer, but entirely conscious of a presence near him, he had presence of mind enough to reiterate a mental question. His voiceless question was fully understood, for again the familiar voice spoke:

"I am not dead, my husband; but I am lost to you. Not of my own seeking has this treachery been to thee, O beloved. The friend into whose care you gave me has acquired the power over me that you alone possessed, that power sacred to our first meeting and our happy love. Why did you leave me in the power of a fiend in human shape, to search for gold? There are worse things in life than poverty."

Calming the frenzy of his thoughts by a strong effort, Reuel continued his mental questions until the whole pitiful story was his. He knew not how long he continued in this communion. Over and over he turned the story he had learned in the past few hours. Ungovernable rage against his false friend possessed him. "Blind, fool, dupe, dotard!" he called himself, not to have seen the treachery beneath the mask of friendship. And then to leave her helpless in the hands of this monster, who had not even spared his own betrothed to compass his love for another.

But at least revenge was left him. He would return to America and confront Aubrey Livingston with his guilt. But how to get away from the hidden city. He knew r that virtually he was a prisoner.

Still turning over ways and means, he fell into an uneasy slumber, from which he was aroused by a dreadful shriek.

XXI

It was now two months since Reuel's strange disappearance from the camp of the explorers. Day after day they had searched even-inch of the ground within and about the pyramids, with no success. Charlie Vance was inconsolable, and declared his intention of making his home at Meroe until Reuel was found. He scouted the idea of his death by falling a prey to wild beasts, and hung about the vicinity of the Great Pyramid with stubborn persistence. He was no longer the spoiled darling of wealth and fashion, but a serious-minded man of a taciturn disposition.

He spent money like water in his endeavor to find the secret passage, believing that it existed, and that in it Reuel was lost.

One morning he and Jim Titus laid bare a beautifully worked marble wall, built of fine masonry, with even blocks, each a meter and a half long, and below the exquisitely worked molding two further layers of well-worked calcareous stone. The whole formed a foundation for a structure which had fallen into ruins about two and a half meters high. But this wall continued for thirteen meters only, and then returned at right angles at each end. On the inner side this marble structure was backed by large blocks of calcareous stone, and in the inner angles, they had with much labor to break up and remove two layers of blocks superimposed at right angles, one upon another. The entire party was much puzzled to learn what this structure could have been.

Sculptures and paintings lined the walls. As usual, there was a queen, attired in a long robe. The queen had in one hand the lash of Osiris and in the other a lotus flower.

At the extremity of each portico was the representation of a monolithic temple, above which were the traces of a funeral boat filled with figures.

After two days' work, the skilled diggers assured the explorers that they could do nothing with the debris but to leave it, as it was impossible to open the structure. But in the night, Charlie was kept awake by the thought that this curious structure might hold the expedition's secret; and remembering that perseverance was never beaten, set to work there the next morning, digging into the interior and breaking up the huge blocks which impeded his progress. The next day another impediment was reached, and it was decided to give it up. Again Charlie was awake all night, puzzling over the difficulties encountered, and again he made up his mind not to give it up. Charlie was learning many needed lessons in bitterness of spirit out in these African wilds. Sorrow had come to him here in the loss of his sister, and the disappearance of his friend. As Reuel had done in the night weeks before, so he did now, rising and dressing and securing his weapons, but taking the precaution to awaken Jim, and ask him to accompany him for a last visit to the Pyramid.

Jim Titus seemed strangely subdued and quiet since Reuel's disappearance. Charlie decided that their suspicions were wrong, and that Jim was a good fellow, after all.

As they trudged along over the sandy paths in the light of the great African moon, Charlie was glad of Jim's lively conversation. Anecdotes of Southern life flowed glibly from his tongue, illustrated by songs descriptive of life there. It really seemed to Vance that a portion of the United States had been transported to Africa.

They entered the great Pyramid, as Reuel had done before them, lit their torches, and began slowly and carefully to go over the work of excavation already done.

They passed down a side passage opening out of the outer passage, down a number of steps and along an underground shaft made by the workmen. Suddenly the passage ended. They halted, held up the lamps and saw such a scene as they were not likely to see again. They stood on the edge of an enormous pit, hedged in by a wall of rock. There was an opening in the wall, made by a hinged block of stone. This solid door had opened noiselessly, (lark figures had stolen forth, and had surrounded the two men. As they discovered their strange companions, weapons of burnished steel flashed and seemed to fill the vault. Not a sound was heard but the deep breathing of men in grim determination and on serious business bent. Instantly the two travelers were bound and gagged.

XXII

Instantly, after the seizure, the eyes of the prisoners were blindfolded; then they were half led, half dragged along by their captors. As he felt the grip of steel which impelled a forward movement, Charlie bitterly cursed his own folly in undertaking so mad a venture. "Poor Reuel," he lamented, "was this the explanation of his disappearance?" Reuel had been the life of the party; next to Professor Stone, he was looked up to as leader and guide, and with his loss, all interest seemed to have dropped from the members of the expedition.

For half an hour they were hurried along what must have been deep underground passages. Charlie could feel the path drop beneath his feet on solid rock which seemed to curve over like the edges of a waterfall. He stumbled, and would have fallen if strong arms had not upheld him. He could feel the rock worn into deep gutters smoother than ice. For the first time he heard the sound of his captors' voices. One in command gave an order in an unknown tongue. Charlie wished then that he had spent more time in study and less in sport.

"Oh," he groaned in spirit, "what a predicament for a free-born American citizen, and one who has had on the gloves with many a famous ring champion!" He wondered how Jim was faring, for since the first frightened yell from his lips, all had been silence.

There came another brief command in the unknown tongue, and the party halted. Then Charlie felt himself lifted into what he finally determined was a litter. He settled himself comfortably, and the bearers started. Charlie was of a philosophical nature; if he had been born poor and forced to work for a living, he might have become a learned philosopher. So he lay and reflected, and wondered where this experience would end, until, lulled by the yielding motion and the gentle swaying, he fell asleep.

He must have slept many hours, for when he awoke he felt a strong sensation of hunger. They were still journeying at a leisurely pace. Charlie could feel the sweet, fresh air in his face, could hear the song of birds, and smell the scented air, heavy with the fragrance of flowers and fruits. Mentally thanking God that he still lived, he anxiously awaited the end of this strange journey. Presently he felt that they entered a building, for the current of air ceased, and the soft footsteps of the bearers gave forth a metallic sound. There came another command in the unknown tongue, and the bearers stopped; he was told to descend, in unmistakable English, by a familiar voice. He obeyed the voice, and instantly he was relieved of his bandage; before his sight became accustomed to the semi-darkness of the room, he heard the retreating steps of a number of men. As his sight returned in full, he saw before him Ai and Abdallah and Jim.

Abdallah regarded him with a gaze that was stolid and unrecognizing. The room in which he stood was large and circular. Floors and walls were of the whitest marble, and from the roof light and air were supplied. There were two couches in the room, and a divan ran about one of its sides. There was no door or entrance visible—nothing but the unvarying white walls and flooring.

"Stranger," said Ai, in his mellow voice, speaking English in fluent tones, "Why hast thou dared to uncover the mysteries of centuries? Art thou weary of life that thou hast dared to trifle with Nature's secrets? Scarce an alien foot has traversed this land since six thousand years have passed. Art weary of living?" As he asked the last question, Charlie felt a chill of apprehension. This man, with his strange garb, his dark complexion, his deep eyes and mystic smile, was to be feared and reverenced. Summoning up all his sang froid and determination not to give in to his fears, he replied,—

"We came to find old things, that we may impart our knowledge to the people of our land, who are eager to know the beginning of all things. I come of a race bold and venturesome, who know not fear if we can get a few more dollars and fresh information."

"I have heard of your people," replied Ai, with a mysterious sparkle in his eyes. "They are the people who count it a disgrace to bear my color; is it not so?"

"Great Scott!" thought Charlie, turning mental somersaults to find an answer that would placate the dignitary before him. "Is it possible that the ubiquitous race question has got ahead of the expedition! By mighty, ifs time something was done to stop this business. Talk of Banquo's ghost! Banquo ain't in it if this is the race question I'm up against." Aloud he said, "My venerable and esteemed friend, you could get there all right with your complexion in my country. We would simply label you 'Arab, Turk, Malay or Filipino,' and in that costume you'd slide along all right; not the slightest trouble when you showed your ticket at the door. Savee?" He finished with a profound bow.

Ai eyed him sadly for a moment, and then said,—

"O, flippant-tongued offspring of an ungenerous people, how is it with my brother?" and he took Jim's unresisting hand and led him up to Charlie. "Crisp of hair," and he passed his hand softly over Jim's curly pate. "Black of skin! How do you treat such as this one in your country?"

Charlie felt embarrassed in spite of his assurance. "Well, of course, it has been the custom to count Africans as our servants, and they have fared as servants."

"And yet, ye are all of one blood; descended from one common father. Is there ever a flock or herd without its black member? What more beautiful than the satin gloss of the raven's wing, the soft glitter of eyes of blackest tint or the rich black fur of your own native animals? Fair-haired worshippers of Mammon, do you not know that you have been weighed in the balance and found wanting? that your course is done? that Ethoapia's bondage is about over, her travail passed?"

Charlie smiled in inward mirth at what he called the "fossilized piece of antiquity" "Touched in the forehead; crank," was his mental comment. "I'd better put on the brakes, and not aggravate this lunatic. He's probably some kind of a king, and might make it hot for me." Aloud he said, "Pardon, Mr. King, but what has this to do with making me a prisoner? Why have I been brought here?"

"You will know soon enough," replied Ai, as he clapped his hands. Abdallah moved to the side of the room, and instantly a marble block slid from its position, through which Ai and he departed, leaving the prisoners alone.

For a while the two men sat and looked at each other in helpless silence. Then Jim broke the silence with lamentations.

"Oh, Lord! Mr. Vance, there's a hoo-doo on this business, and I'm the hoo-doo!"

"Nonsense!" exclaimed Vance. "Be a man, Jim, and help me find a way out of this infernal business."

But Jim sat on the divan, lamenting and refusing to be comforted. Presently food was brought to them, and then after many and useless conjectures, they lay down and tried to sleep.

The night passed very comfortably on the whole, although the profound silence was suggestive of being buried alive. Another day and night passed without incident. Food was supplied them at regular intervals. Charlie's thoughts were varied. He—fastidious and refined— who had known no hardship and no sorrow,—why had he left his country to wander among untutored savages?

None were there to comfort him of all his friends. These walls would open but to admit the savage executioner. He ground his teeth. He thought of Cora Scott; doubtless she thought him dead. Dead! No; nor would he die. He'd find a way out of this or perish; he'd go home and marry Cora. Now this was a most surprising conclusion, for Charlie had been heard to say many times that "he'd be drawn and quartered before he'd tie up to a girl of the period," which Cora undoubtedly was. As if aroused from a dream, he jumped up and going over to Jim, shook him. The Negro turned uneasily in his sleep and groaned. Again he shook him.

"Get up, Jim. Come, I'm going to try to get out of this."

"I'm afraid, Mr. Vance; it's no use."

"Come on, Jim; be a man."

"I'm ready for anything, only show me the way," replied Jim in desperation. Their pistols had been taken from them, but their knives remained. They stored what food remained about their persons and began a thorough examination of the room.

"They certainly find an exit here somewhere, Jim, and we must find it too."

"Easier said than done, I fear, sir."

An hour—two hours, passed in fruitless search; the marble walls showed not a sign of exit or entrance. They rested then, sitting on the sides of the divans and gazing at each other in utter helplessness. The full moonlight showered the apartment with a soft radiance from the domed roof. Suddenly, Jim sprang forward and inserted his knife in a crevice in the floor. Instantly Charlie was beside him, working like mad on the other side. The slab began to waver to and fro, as though shaken by a strong force—the crack widened—they saw a round, flat metal button— Jim seized it with one hand and pried with the knife in the other—a strong breeze of subterranean air struck through the narrow opening— and with a dull reverberation half the flooring slid back, revealing what seemed to be a vast hole.

The men recoiled, and lay panting from their labors on the edges of the subway. Charlie blessed his lucky stars that hidden in his clothes was a bundle of tapers used by the explorers for just such emergencies. By great good fortune, his captors had not discovered them.

"What's to be done now, Jim?"

"Git down there and explore, but hanged if I want the job, Mr. Vance."

"We'll go together, Jim. Let's see," he mused, "What did Prof. Stone's parchment say? 'Beware the tank to the right where dwells the sacred crocodile, still living, although centuries have rolled by, and men have been gathered to the shades who once tended on his wants. And beware the fifth gallery to the right where abide the sacred serpents with jeweled crowns, for of a truth are they terrible,'" quoted Charlie, dreamily.

"You don't suppose this is the place you were hunting for, do you?" queried Jim, with eyes big with excitement.

"Jim, my boy, that's a question no man can answer at this distance from the object of our search. But if it is, as I suspect, the way to the treasure will lead us to liberty, for the other end must be within the pyramid. I'm for searching this passage. Come on if you are with me."

He lighted his taper and swung it into the abyss, disclosing steps of granite leading off in the darkness. As his head disappeared from view, Jim, with a shudder, followed. The steps led to a passage or passages, for the whole of the underground room was formed of vaulted passages, sliding off in every direction. The stairs ended in another passage; the men went down it; it was situated, as nearly as they could judge, directly beneath the room where they had been confined. Silently the two figures crept on, literally feeling their way. Shortly they came to another passage running at right angles; slowly they crept along the tunnel, for it was nothing more, narrowing until it suddenly ended in a sort of cave, running at right angles; they crossed this, halting at the further side to rest and think. Charlie looked anxiously about him for signs, but saw nothing alarming in the smooth sandy floor, and irregular contorted sides. The floor was strewn with bowlders like the bed of a torrent. As they went on, the cavern widened into an amphitheatre with huge supporting columns. To the right and left of the cave there were immense bare spaces stretching away into immense galleries. Here they paused to rest, eating sparingly of the food they had brought. "Let us rest here," said Charlie, "I am dead beat."

"Is it not safer to go on? We cannot be very far from the room where we were confined."

"I'll sit here a few moments, anyhow," replied Charlie. Jim wandered aimlessly about the great vault, turning over stones and peering into crevices.

"What do you expect to find, Jim, the buried treasure?" laughed Charlie, as he noted the earnestness of the other's search.

Jim was bending over something—wrenching off a great iron cover. Suddenly he cried out, "Mr. Vance, here it is!"

Charlie reached his side with a bound. There sat Jim, and in front of him lay, imbedded in the sand of the cavern's floor, a huge box, long and wide and deep, whose rusted hinges could not withstand the stalwart Negro's frantic efforts.

With a shuddering sigh the lid was thrust back, falling to one side with a great groan of almost mortal anguish as it gave up the trust committed to its care ages before. They both gazed, and as they gazed were well-nigh blinded. For this is what they saw:—

At first, a blaze of darting rays that sparkled and shot out myriad scintillations of color—red, violet, orange, green, and deepest crimson. Then by degrees, they saw that these hues came from a jumbled heap of gems—some large, some small, but together in value beyond all dreams of wealth.

Diamonds, rubies, sapphires, amethysts, opals, emeralds, turquoises—lay roughly heaped together, some polished, some uncut, some as necklaces and chains, others gleaming in rings and bracelets—wealth beyond the dreams of princes.

Near to the first box lay another, and in it lay gold in bars and gold in flakes, hidden by the priests of Osiris, that had adorned the crowns of queens Candace and Semiramis—a spectacle glorious beyond compare.

"The Professor's parchment told the truth," cried Charlie, after a few moments, when he had regained his breath. "But what shall we do with it, now we have it?" asked Jim in disconsolate tones. "We can't carry it with us."

"True for you, Jim," replied Vance, sadly. "This wealth is a mockery now we have it. Jim, we're left, badly left. Here we've been romping around for almost six months after this very treasure, and now we've got it we can't hold it. This whole expedition has been like monkeying with a saw mill, Jim, my boy, and I for one, give in beaten. Left, I should say so; 'badly left, when I counted Africa a played-out hole in the ground. And, Jim, when we get home, if ever we do, the drinks are on me. Now, old man, stow some of these glittering baubles in your clothing, as I am going to do, and then we'll renew our travels." He spoke in jest, but the tears were in his eyes, and as he clasped Jim's toil-hardened black hand, he told himself that Ai's words were true. Where was the color line now? Jim was a brother; the nearness of their desolation in this uncanny land, left nothing but a feeling of brotherhood. He felt then the truth of the words, "Of one blood have I made all races of men."

PAULINE E. HOPKINS

As they stooped to replace the cover, Jim's foot knocked against an iron ring set in the sandy flooring. "I believe it's another box, Mr. Vance," he called out, and dropping his work, he pulled with all his might.

"Careful, Jim," called Charlie's warning voice. Too late! The ring disappeared at the second tug, revealing a black pit from which came the odor of musk. From out the darkness came the sweeping sound of a great body moving in wavelets over a vast space. Fascinated into perfect stillness, Vance became aware of pale emerald eyes watching him, and the sound of deep breathing other than their own. There was a wild rattle and rush in the darkness, as Jim, moving forward, flung down his taper and turned to flee.

"The serpents! The serpents! Fly for your life, Jim!" shouted Charlie, as he dashed away from the opening. Too late! There came a terrible cry, repeated again and again. Charlie Vance sunk upon the ground, overcome with horror.

XXIII

It must have been about one o'clock in the morning when Reuel started out of a fitful slumber by the sound of that terrible scream. He sprang to his feet and listened. He heard not a sound; all was silence within the palace. But his experience was so vivid that reason could not control his feelings; he threw wide the dividing curtains, and fled out upon the balcony. All was silence. The moonlight flooded the landscape with the strength of daylight. As he stood trying to calm himself, a shadow fell across his path, and raising his eyes, he beheld the form of Mira; she beckoned him on, and he, turning, followed the shadowy figure, full of confidence that she would show him the way to that fearful scream.

On they glided like two shadows, until the phantom paused before what seemed a solid wall, and with warning gaze and uplifted finger, bade him enter. It was a portion of the palace unfamiliar to him; the walls presented no hope of entrance. What could it mean? Mira faded from his gaze, and as he stood there puzzling over this happening, suddenly the solid wall began to glide away, leaving a yawning space, in which appeared Ai's startled and disturbed face.

"Back!" he cried, as he beheld his King. "Back, Ergamenes! how come you here?"

"What was the cry I heard, Ai? I cannot rest. I have been led hither," he continued, significantly. Then, noticing the other's disturbed vision, he continued, "Tell me. I command you."

With a murmured protest, Ai stepped aside, saying, "Perhaps it is best."

Reuel advanced into the room. The hole in the floor was securely closed, and on the divans lay Charlie Vance, white and unconscious, and Jim Titus, crushed almost to a jelly but still alive. Abdallah and a group of natives were working over Vance, trying to restore consciousness. Reuel gave one startled, terrified glance at the two figures, and staggered backward to the wall.

Upon hearing that cry, Jim Titus stirred uneasily, and muttered, "It's him!"

"He wishes to speak with you," said Ai, gravely.

"How came they here, and thus?" demanded Reuel in threatening anger.

PAULINE E. HOPKINS

"They were searching for you, and we found them, too, in the pyramid. We confined them here, debating what was best to do, fearing you would become dissatisfied. They tried to escape and found the treasure and the snakes. The black man will die."

"Are you there, Mr. Reuel?" came in a muffled voice from the dying man.

Reuel stood beside him and took his hand,—"Yes, Jim, it is I; how came you thus?"

"The way of the transgressor is hard," groaned the man. "I would not have been here had I not consented to take your life. I am sure you must have suspected me; I was but a bungler, and often my heart failed me."

"Unhappy man! how could you plot to hurt one who has never harmed you?" exclaimed Reuel.

"Aubrey Livingston was my foster brother, and I could deny him nothing."

"Aubrey Livingston! Was he the instigator?"

"Yes," sighed the dying man. "Return home as soon as possible and rescue your wife—your wife, and yet not your wife—for a man may not marry his sister."

"What!" almost shrieked Reuel. "What!"

"I have said it. Dianthe Lusk is your own sister, the half-sister of Aubrey Livingston, who is your half-brother."

Reuel stood for a moment, apparently struggling for words to answer the dying man's assertion, then fell on his knees in a passion of sobs agonizing to witness. "You know then, Jim, that I am Mira's son?" he said at length.

"I do. Aubrey planned to have Miss Dianthe from the first night he saw her; he got you this chance with the expedition; he kept you from getting anything else to force you to a separation from the girl. He bribed me to accidentally put you out of the way. He killed Miss Molly to have a free road to Dianthe. Go home, Reuel Briggs, and at least rescue the girl from misery. Watch, watch, or he will outwit you yet." Reuel started in a frenzy of rage to seize the man, but Ai's hand was on his arm.

"Peace, Ergamenes; he belongs to the ages now."

One more convulsive gasp, and Jim Titus had gone to atone for the deeds done in the flesh.

With pallid lips and trembling frame, Reuel turned from the dead to the living. As he sat beside his friend, his mind was far away in America looking with brooding eyes into the past and gazing hopelessly into the future. Truly hath the poet said,—

"The evil that men do lives after them."

And Reuel cursed with a mighty curse the bond that bound him to the white race of his native land.

XXIV

One month after the events narrated in the previous chapter, a strange party stood on the deck of the out-going steamer at Alexandria, Egypt—Reuel and Charlie Vance, accompanied by Ai and Abdallah in the guise of servants. Ai had with great difficulty obtained permission of the Council to allow King Ergamenes to return to America. This was finally accomplished by Ai's being surety for Reuel's safe return, and so the journey was begun which was to end in the apprehension and punishment of Aubrey Livingston.

Through the long journey homeward two men thought only of vengeance, but with very different degrees of feeling. Charlie Vance held to the old Bible punishment for the pure crime of manslaughter, but in Reuel's wrongs lay something beyond the reach of punishment by the law's arm; in it was the accumulation of years of foulest wrongs heaped upon the innocent and defenceless women of a race, added to this last great outrage. At night he said, as he paced the narrow confines of the deck, "Thank God, it is night;" and when the faint streaks of dawn glowed in the distance, gradually creeping across the expanse of waters, "Thank God, it is morning." Another hour, and he would say, "Would God it were night!" By day or night some phantom in his ears holloes in ocean's roar or booms in thunder, howls in the winds or murmurs in the breeze, chants in the voice of the sea-fowl—"Too late, too late. 'Tis done, and worse than murder."

Westward the vessel sped—westward while the sun showed only as a crimson bull in its Arabian setting, or gleamed through a veil of smoke off the English coast, ending in the grey, angry, white-capped waves of the Atlantic in winter.

XXV

It was believed by the general public and Mr. Vance that Molly and Dianthe had perished beneath the waters of the Charles River, although only Molly's body was recovered. Aubrey was picked up on the bank of the river in an unconscious state, where he was supposed to have made his way after vainly striving to rescue the two girls.

When he had somewhat recovered from the shock of the accident, it was rumored that he had gone to Canada with a hunting party, and so he disappeared from public view.

But Dianthe had not perished. As the three struggled in the water, Molly, with all the confidence of requited love, threw her arms about her lover. With a muttered oath, Aubrey tried to shake her off, but her clinging arms refused to release him. From the encircling arms he saw a sight that maddened him—Dianthe's head was disappearing beneath the waters where the lily-stems floated in their fatal beauty, holding in their tenacious grasp the girl he loved. An appalling sound had broken through the air as she went down—a heart-stirring cry of agony—the tone of a voice pleading with God for life! the precious boon of life! That cry drove away the man, and the brute instinct so rife within us all, ready always to leap to the front in times of excitement or danger, took full possession of the body. He forgot honor, humanity, God.

With a savage kick he freed himself and swam swiftly toward the spot where Dianthe's golden head had last appeared. He was just in time. Grasping the flowing locks with one hand and holding her head above the treacherous water, he swam with her to the bank.

Pretty, innocent, tender-hearted Molly sank never to rise again. Without a word, but with a look of anguished horror, her despairing face was covered b. the glistening, greedy waters that lapped so hungrily about the water-lily beds.

As Aubrey bore Dianthe up the bank his fascinated gaze went backward to the spot where he had seen Molly sink. To his surprise and horror, as he gazed the body rose to the surface and floated as did poor Elaine:

> *"In her right hand the lily,*
> *—All her bright hair streaming down—*

> *—And she herself in white,*
> *All but her face, and that clear-featured face*
> *Was lovely, for she did not seem as dead,*
> *But fast asleep, and lay as tho' she smiled."*

Staggering like a drunken man, he made his way to a small cottage up the bank, where a woman, evidently expecting him, opened the door without waiting for his knock.

"Quick! here she is. Not a word. I will return tonight." With these words Livingston sped back to the river bank, where he was found by the rescuing party, in a seemingly exhausted condition.

For weeks after these happenings Dianthe lived in another world, unconscious of her own identity. It was early fall before her full faculties were once more with her. The influence which Livingston had acquired rendered her quiescent in his hands, and not too curious as to circumstances of time and place. One day he brought her a letter, stating that Reuel was dead.

Sick at heart, bending beneath the blight that thus unexpectedly fell upon her, the girl gave herself up to grief, and weary of the buffets of Fate, yielded to Aubrey's persuasions and became his wife. On the night which witnessed Jim Titus's awful death, they had just returned to Livingston's ancestral home in Maryland.

It would be desecration to call the passion which Aubrey entertained for Dianthe, love. Yet passion it was—the greatest he had ever known—with its shadow, jealousy. Indifference on the part of his idol could not touch him; she was his other self, and he hated all things that stood between him and his love.

It was a blustering night in the first part of November. It was twilight Within the house profound stillness reigned. The heavens were shut out of sight by masses of sullen, inky clouds, and a piercing north wind was howling. Within the room where Dianthe lay, a glorious fire burnt in a wide, low grate. A table, a couch and some chairs were drawn near to it for warmth. Dianthe lay alone. Presently there came a knock at the door. "Enter," said the pale woman on the couch, never once removing her gaze from the whirling flakes and sombre sky.

Aubrey entered and stood for some moments gazing in silence at the beautiful picture presented to his view. She was gowned in spotless white, her bright hair flowed about her unconstrained by comb or pin. Her features were like marble, the deep grey eyes gazed wistfully into the far distance. The man looked at her with hungry, devouring eyes. Something, he knew not what, had come between them. His coveted happiness, sin-bought and crime-stained, had turned to ashes—Dead-Sea fruit indeed. The cold gaze she turned on him half froze him, and changed his feelings into a corresponding channel with her own.

"You are ill, Dianthe. What seems to be your trouble? I am told that you see spirits. May I ask if they wear the dress of African explorers?"

It had come to this unhappy state between them.

"Aubrey," replied the girl in a calm, dispassionate tone, "Aubrey, at this very hour in this room, as I lay here, not sleeping, nor disposed to sleep, there where you stand, stood a lovely woman; I have seen her thus once before. She neither looked at me nor spoke, but walked to the table, opened the Bible, stooped over it a while, seeming to write, then seemed to sink, just as she rose, and disappeared. Examine the book, and tell me, is that fancy?"

Crossing the room, Aubrey gazed steadfastly at the open book. It was the old family Bible, and the heavy clasps had grown stiff and rusty. It was familiar to him, and intimately associated with his life-history. There on the open page were ink lines underscoring the twelfth chapter of Luke: "For there is nothing covered that shall not be revealed, neither hid that shall not be known." At the end of this passage was written the one word "Nina."

Without a comment, but with anxious brows, Aubrey returned to his wife's couch, stooped and impressed several kisses on her impassive face. Then he left the room.

Dianthe lay in long and silent meditation. Servants came and went noiselessly. She would have no candles. The storm ceased; the moon came forth and flooding the landscape, shone through the windows upon the lonely watcher. Dianthe's restlessness was soothed, and she began tracing the shadows on the carpet and weaving them into fantastic images of imagination. What breaks her reverie? The moonlight gleams on something white and square; it is a letter. She left the couch and picked it up. Just then a maid entered with a light, and she glanced at the envelope. It bore the African postmark! She paused. Then as the girl left the room, she slipped the letter from the envelope and read:

"Master Aubrey,
I write to inform you that I have not been able to comply with your wishes. Twice I have trapped Dr. Briggs, but he

has escaped miraculously from my hands. I shall not fail the third time. The expedition will leave for Meroe next week, and then something will surely happen. I have suppressed all letters, according to your orders, and both men are feeling exceedingly blue. Kindly put that first payment on the five thousand dollars to my sister's credit in a Baltimore bank, and let her have the bank book. Next mail you may expect something definite."

Yours faithfully,
Jim Titus

Aubrey Livingston had gone to an adjoining city on business, and would be absent three or four days.

That night Dianthe spent in his library behind locked doors, and all about her lay open letters—letters addressed to her, and full of love and tenderness, detailing Reuel's travels and minutely describing every part of his work.

Still daylight found her at her work. Then she quitted it, closed up the desk, tied up the letters, replaced them, left the room, and returned to her boudoir to think. Her brain was in a giddy whirl, and but one thought stood out clearly in her burning brain. Her thoughts took shape in the one word "Reuel," and by her side stood again the form of the pale, lovely mulattress, her long black curls enveloping her like a veil. One moment—the next the room was vacant save for herself.

Reuel was living, and she a bigamist—another's wife! made so by fraud and deceit. The poor overwrought brain was working like a machine now—throbbing, throbbing, throbbing. To see him, hear his voice—this would be enough. Then came the thought—lost to her, or rather she to him—and how? By the plans of his would-be murderer. O, horrible, inhuman wretch! He had stolen her by false tales, and then had polluted her existence by the breath of murder. Murder! What was murder? She paused and gasped for breath; then come the trembling thought, "Would he were dead!"

He would return and discover the opening of the letters. "O, that he were dead!"

She wandered about the grounds in the cold sunshine, burning with fever, and wild with a brain distraught She wished the trees were living creatures and would fall and crush him. The winds in their fury, would they but kill him! O, would not something aid her? At last she sat down, out of breath with her wanderings and wearied by the tumult within her breast. So it went all day; the very heavens beckoned her to commit a deed of horror. She slept and dreamed of shapeless, nameless things that lurked and skulked in hidden chambers, waiting the signal to come forth. She woke and slept no more. She turned and turned the remainder of the night; her poor warped faculties recalled the stories she had read of Cenci, the Borgias, and even the Hebrew Judith. And then she thought of Reuel, and the things he had told her on many an idle day, of the properties of medicine, and how in curiosity she had fingered his retorts used in experiments. And he had told her she was apt, and he would teach her many things of his mysterious profession. And as she thought and speculated, suddenly something whispered, as it were, a name—heard but once—in her ear. It was the name of a poison so subtle in its action as to defy detection save by one versed in its use. With a shudder she threw the thought from her, and rose from her couch.

We know we're tempted. The world is full of precedents, the air with impulses, society with men and spirit tempters. But what invites sin? Is it not a something within ourselves? Are we not placed here with a sinful nature which the plan of salvation commands us to overcome? If we offer the excuse that we were tempted, where is the merit of victory if we do not resist the tempter? God does not abandon us to evil prompters without a white-robed angel, stretching out a warning hand and pointing out the better way as strongly as the other. When we conquer sin, we say we are virtuous, triumphant, and when we fall, we excuse our sins by saying, "It is fate."

The days sped on. To the on-looker life jogged along as monotonously at Livingston Hall as in any other quiet home. The couple dined and rode, and received friends in the conventional way. Many festivities were planned in honor of the beautiful bride. But, alas! these days but goaded her to madness. The uncertainty of Reuel's fate, her own wrongs as a wife yet not a wife, her husband's agency in all this woe, the frailness of her health, weighed more and more upon a mind weakened by hypnotic experiments. Her better angel whispered still, and she listened until one day there was a happening that turned the scale, and she pronounced her own dreadful doom—"For me there's no retreat."

XXVI

It was past midday about two weeks later that Dianthe wandered about the silent woods, flitting through the mazes of unfamiliar forest paths. Buried in sad thoughts she was at length conscious that her surroundings were strange, and that she had lost her way. Every now and then the air was thick and misty with powdery flakes of snow which fell, or swept down, rather, upon the brown leaf-beds and withered grass. The buffeting winds which kissed her glowing hair into waving tendrils brought no color to her white cheeks and no light to her eyes. For days she had been like this, thinking only of getting away from the busy house with its trained servants and its loathsome luxury which stifled her. How to escape the chains which bound her to this man was now her only thought. If Reuel lived, each day that found her still beneath the roof of this man whose wife she was in the eyes of the world, was a crime. Away, away, looking forward to she knew not what, only to get away from the sight of his hated face.

Presently she paused and looked about her. Where was she? The spot was wild and unfamiliar. There was no sight or sound of human being to question as to the right direction to take, not that it mattered much, she told herself in bitterness of spirit. She walked on more slowly now, scanning the woods for signs of a human habitation. An opening in the trees gave a glimpse of cultivated ground in a small clearing, and a few steps farther revealed a typical Southern Negro cabin, from which a woman stepped out and faced her as if expecting her coming. She was very aged, but still erect and noble in form. The patched figure was neat to scrupulousness, the eye still keen and searching.

As the woman advanced slowly toward her, Dianthe was conscious of a thrill of fear, which quickly passed as she dimly remembered having heard the servants jesting over old Aunt Hannah, the most noted "voodoo" doctor or witch in the country.

"Come in, honey, and res'," were her first words after her keen eyes had traveled over the woman before her. Dianthe obeyed without a murmur; in truth, she seemed again to have lost her own will in another's.

The one-roomed cabin was faultlessly neat, and the tired girl was grateful for the warmth of the glowing brands upon the wide hearth. Very soon a cup of stimulating coffee warmed her tired frame and brought more animation to her tired face.

"What may your name be, Auntie?" she asked at length, uneasy at the furtive glances cast by the eyes of the silent figure seated in the distant shadow of the chimney-corner. The eyes never wavered, but no answer was vouchsafed her by the woman in the corner. Somewhere she had read a description of an African princess which fitted the woman before her.

> "I knew a princess; she was old,
> Crisp-haired, flat-featured, with a look
> Such as no dainty pen of gold
> Would write of in a fairy book.
> Her face was like a Sphinx's face, to me,
> Touched with vast patience, desert grace,
> And lonesome, brooding mystery."

Suddenly a low sound, growing gradually louder, fell upon Dianthe's ear; it was the voice of the old woman crooning a mournful minor cadence, but for an instant it sent a chill about the girl's heart. It was a funeral chant commonly sung by the Negroes over the dead. It chimed in with her gloomy, despairing mood and startled her. She arose hastily to her feet to leave the place.

"How can I reach the road to Livingston Place?" she asked with a shudder of apprehension as she glanced at her entertainer.

"Don't be 'feared, child; Aunt Hannah won't hurt a ha'r of that purty head. Hain't it these arms done missed ev'ry Livingston? I knowed your mother, child; for all you're married to Marse Aubrey, you isn't a white 'ooman."

"I do not deny what you say, Auntie; I have no desire so to do," replied Dianthe gently.

With a cry of anguish the floodgates of feeling were unloosed, and the old Negress flung her arms about the delicate form. "Gawd-a-mercy! My Mira's gal! My Mira's gal!" Then followed a harrowing scene.

Dianthe listened to the old story of sowing the wind and reaping the whirlwind. A horrible, paralyzing dread was upon her. Was she never to cease from suffering and be at rest? Rocking herself to and fro, and moaning as though in physical pain, the old woman told her story.

"I was born on de Livingston place, an' bein' a purty likely gal, was taken to de big house when I was a tot. I was trained by ol' Miss'. As soon as I was growed up, my mistress changed in her treatment of me,

PAULINE E. HOPKINS

for she soon knowed of my relations with massa, an' she was hurt to de heart, po' 'ooman. Mira was de onlies' child of ten that my massa lef' me for my comfort; all de res' were sold away to raise de mor'gage off de prop'rty."

"Ol marse had only one chil', a son; he was eddicated for a doctor, and of all the limb o' de devil, he was de worst. After ol' marse an' ol' miss' was dead he took a shine to Mira, and for years he stuck to her in great shape. Her fust child was Reuel—"

"What!" shrieked Dianthe. "Tell me—quick, for God's sake! Is he alive, and by what name is he known?" She was deathly white, and spread out her hands as if seeking support.

"Yes, he's living, or was a year ago. He's called Dr. Reuel Briggs, an' many a dollar he has sent his ol' granny, may the good Marster bless him!"

"Tell me all—tell me the rest," came from the lips of the trembling girl.

"Her second child was a girl,—a beautiful, delicate child, an' de Doctor fairly worshipped her. Dat leetle gal was yourself, an' Im your granny."

"Then Reuel Briggs is my brother!"

"Certain; but let me tell you de res', honey. Dese things jes' got to happen in slavery, but I isn't gwine to wink at de debbil's wurk wif both eyes open. An' I doesn't want you to keep on livin' with Marse Aubrey Livingston. It's too wicked; it's flyin' in de face ob Almighty God. I'se wanted to tell you eber sense I knowed who he'd married. After a while de Doctor got to thinkin' 'bout keepin' up de family name, an' de fus' thing we knows he up an' marries a white lady down to Charleston, an' brings her home. Well! when she found out all de family secrets she made de house too hot to hol' Mira, and it was ordered that she mus' be sold away. I got on my knees to Marse an' I prayed to him not to do it, but to give Mira a house on de place where she could be alone an' bring up de childrun, an' he would a done it but for his wife."

The old woman paused to moan and rock and weep over the sad memories of the past. Dianthe sat like a stone woman.

"Den I believe de debbil took possession of me body and soul. A week before my po' gal was to be sol', Misses' child was born, and died in about an hour; at about de same time Mira gave birth to a son, too. In de 'citemen' de idea come to me to change de babies, fer no one would know it, I being alone when de chil' died, an' de house wil' fer fear misses would die. So I changed de babies, an' tol' Marse Livingston dat Mira's boy was de dead one. So, honey, Aubrey is your own blood brother an' you got to quit dat house mejuntly."

"My brother!"

Dianthe stood over the old woman and shook her by the arm, with a look of utter horror that froze her blood. "My brothers! both those men!"

The old woman mumbled and groaned, then started up.

Aunt Hannah breathed hard once or twice. Minute after minute passed. From time to time she glanced at Dianthe, her hard, toil-worn hands strained at the arms of her chair as if to break them. Her mind seemed wavering as she crooned:

"My Mira's children; by de lotus-lily on each leetle breast I claim them for de great Osiris, mighty god. Honey, hain't you a flower on your breast?"

Dianthe bowed her head in assent, for speech had deserted her. Then old Aunt Hannah undid her snowy kerchief and her dress, and displayed to the terrified girl the perfect semblance of a lily cut, as it were, in shining ebony.

"Did each of Mira's children have this mark?"

"Yes, honey; all of one blood!"

Dianthe staggered as though buffeted in the face. Blindly, as if in some hideous trance, reeling and stumbling, she fell. Cold and white as marble, she lay in the old woman's arms, who thought her dead. "Better so," she cried, and then laughed aloud, then kissed the poor, drawn face. But she was not dead.

Time passed; the girl could not speak. The sacrilege of what had been done was too horrible. Such havoc is wrought by evil deeds. The first downward step of an individual or a nation, who can tell where it will end, through what dark and doleful shades of hell the soul must pass in travail?

> "The laws of changeless justice bind
> Oppressor and oppressed;
> And close as sin and suffering joined,
> We march to Fate abreast."

The slogan of the hour is "Keep the Negro down!" but who is clear enough in vision to decide who hath black blood and who hath it not?

PAULINE E. HOPKINS

Can any one tell? No, not one; for in His own mysterious way He has united the white race and the black race in this new continent By the transgression of the law He proves His own infallibility: "Of one blood have I made all nations of men to dwell upon the whole face of the earth," is as true today as when given to the inspired writers to be recorded. No man can draw the dividing line between the two races, for they are both of one blood!

Bending a little, as though very weak, and leaning heavily upon her old grandmothers arm, Dianthe at length set out for the Hall. Her face was lined and old with suffering. All hope was gone; despair was heavy on her young shoulders whose life was blasted in its bloom by the passions of others.

As she looked upward at the grey, leaden sky, tears slowly trickled down her cheeks. "God have mercy!" she whispered.

XXVII

For two days Mrs. Livingston brooded in her chamber. Fifty times a day Aubrey asked for her. The maid told him she was ill, but not alarmingly so; no physician was called. She was simply indisposed, could not be seen.

Gazing in Dianthe's face, the maid whispered, "She sleeps. I will not disturb her."

Alone, she springs from her couch with all the energy of life and health. She paced the room. For two long hours she never ceased her dreary walk. Memories crowded around her, wreathing themselves in shapes which floated mistily through her brain. Her humble school days at Fisk; her little heart leaping at the well-won prize; the merry play with her joyous mates; in later years, the first triumphant throb when wondering critics praised the melting voice, and world-admiring crowds applauded. And, O, the glorious days of travel in Rome and Florence! the classic scenes of study; intimate companionship with Beethoven, Mozart and Hayden; the floods of inspiration poured in strains of self-made melody upon her soul. Then had followed the reaction, the fall into unscrupulous hands, and the ruin that had come upon her innocent head.

The third day Mrs. Livingston arose, dressed, and declaring herself quite well, went to walk. She returned late in the afternoon, dined with her husband, conversed and even laughed. After dinner they walked a while upon the broad piazzas, beneath the silent stars and gracious moon, inhaling the cold, bracing air. Then Aubrey begged her for a song. Once again she sang "Go down, Moses," and all the house was hushed to drink in the melody of that exquisite voice.

To mortal eyes, this young pair and their surroundings marked them as darlings of the gods enjoying the world's heaped-up felicity. Could these same eyes have looked deeper into their hearts, not the loathsome cell of the wretch condemned to death could have shown a sight more hideous. 'Twas late. Pausing at her chamber door, Aubrey raised her hand to his lips with courtly grace, and bade her goodnight.

It was the first hours of the morning. From the deepest and most dreamless slumber that had ever sealed his eyes, Aubrey awoke just as the clock was striking two. 'Twas quite dark, and at first he felt that the striking clock had awakened him; yet sleep on the instant was as effectually banished from his eyes as if it were broad daylight. He could not distinguish the actual contact of any substance, and yet he could not rid himself of the feeling that a strong arm was holding him forcibly down, and a heavy hand was on his lips. He saw nothing, though the moon's rays shone full into the room. He felt nothing sensuously, but everything sensationally; and thus it was that with eyes half-closed, and seemingly fixed as by an iron vice, he beheld the door of his dressing-room—the private means of communication with Dianthe's rooms—very cautiously opened, and Dianthe herself, in a loose robe, crept into the room, and stealthily as a spirit glide to the side of his bed.

Arrested by the same trance-like yet conscious power that bound his form but left perception free, Aubrey neither spoke nor moved. And yet he felt, and partially beheld her stoop over him, listen to his breathing, pass her hand before his eyes to try if they would open; then he, with sidelong glance, beheld her, rapidly as thought, take up the night glass standing on his table, and for the glass containing clear cold water, which it was his custom to swallow every morning upon first awakening, substitute one which, he had seen from the first, she carried in her hand. This done, the stealthy figure moved away, gently drew back the door, and would have passed; but no—the spell was broken. A hand was on her shoulder—a hand of iron. Back it dragged her—into the room just left, shut the door and locked it, held her in its sinewy strength till other doors were locked, then bore her to the bed, placed her upon it, and then released her. And there she sat, white and silent as the grave, whilst before her stood Aubrey, pale as herself, but no longer silent.

Taking the glass which she had substituted, he held it to her lips, and pronounced the one word—"Drink!" But one word; but O, what a world of destiny, despair, and agony hung on that word; again and again repeated. Her wild and haggard eyes, her white, speechless lips, all, alas! bore testimony to her guilt—to a mind unbalanced, but only added determination to Aubrey's deep, unflinching purpose.

"Drink! deeper yet! Pledge me to the last drop; drink deep; drink all!"

"Aubrey, Aubrey! mercy, as you look for it! let me explain—" The shrinking woman was on her knees, the half-drained glass in her hand.

"To Reuel!" gasped Dianthe, and set

"Drink!" shouted Aubrey. "Drain the glass to Reuel!" the glass down empty. Once more Aubrey led his bride of three months back to the door of her room. Once more before her chamber door he paused; and once again, but now in mockery, he stooped and kissed her hand.

"Farewell, my love," he said. "When we meet, 'twill be—"

"In judgment, Aubrey; and may God have mercy on our guilty souls!"

XXVIII

'Twas a cold gray morning; the dawn of such a day as seems to wrap itself within the shroud of night, hiding the warm sun in its stony bosom, and to creep through time arrayed in mourning garments for the departed stars. Aubrey was up by the earliest glimpse of dawn. Uncertain what to do or where to go, he made a pretence of eating, sitting in solemn state in the lonely breakfast room, where the servants glided about in ghostly silence, which was too suggestive for the overwrought nerves of the master of all that magnificence. Fifty times he asked the maid for Mrs. Livingston. The woman told him she was ill,—not alarmingly so; no physician's services were needed, neither his own nor another's. He did not ask to see her, yet with a strange and morbid curiosity, he kept on questioning how she was, and why she kept her chamber, until the knowing laugh and sly joke about the anxiety of bridegrooms over the welfare of brides made the servants' quarters ring with hilarity. At length, tired of his aimless wandering, he said he'd go. His valet asked him where. He could not tell. 'Pack up some things."

"For how long a time, sir?"

"I cannot tell, James."

"Shall I order the carriage?"

"Anything, something! A horse; yes. I'll have the swiftest one in the stable. A valise—no more; no, you need not come. I must be alone."

In Dianthe's room the attendants tread noiselessly, and finally leave her to enjoy her feigned slumber. She waits but the closing of the door, to spring from her couch with all the seeming energy of life and health. First she went to the window and flung wide the hangings, letting in a flood of light upon the pale, worn face reflected in the mirror. What a wondrous change was there! The long white drapery of her morning robe fell about her like a shroud, yet, white as it was, contrasted painfully with the livid ash-hue of her skin. Her arms were thin and blue, her hands transparent; her sunny hair hung in long disheveled, waving masses, the picture of neglect; the sunken, wan brow, and livid lips, the heavy eyes with deep, black halos round them—all these made up a mined temple.

"When he comes he will not know me," she murmured to herself; then sighing deeply, turned and paced the room. What she thought of, none could say. She spoke not; never raised her eyes from off the ground, nor ceased her dreary walk for two long hours. She sometimes sobbed, but never shed a tear.

Here we drop the veil. Let no human eye behold the writhings of that suffering face, the torture of that soul unmoored, and cast upon the sea of wildest passion, without the pilot, principle, or captain of all salvation, God, to trust in,—passion, adoration of a human idol, hereditary traits entirely unbalanced, generous, but fervid impulses, her only guides. She knew that her spiritual person must survive the grave, but what that world was where her spirit was fast tending, only the dread tales of fear and superstition shadowed truth; and now, when her footsteps were pressing to it, horror and dread dogged every footprint.

Hour after hour elapsed alone. O, 'twas agony to be alone! She could not bear it. She would call her maid; but no, her cold, unimpassioned face would bring no comfort to her aching heart, aching for pity, for some cheering bosom, where she might sob her ebbing life away. The door opens,—and O joy! old Aunt Hannah's arms enfold her. For hours the two sat in solemn conference, while the servants wondered and speculated over the presence of the old witch.

At last night fell and she murmured softly raising her head from off her damp pillow, "In every golden cloud is printed with the fleecy words of glory. 'I will return.'" She pointed to the golden clouds banking the western sky. "O, will our spirits come, like setting suns, on each tomorrow of eternity?"

For answer, the old woman raised her hand in warning gesture. There sounded distinct and clear—three loud, yet muffled knocks on the panel directly above the couch where Dianthe lay.

"'Tis nothing, mother; I'm used to it now," said the girl with indifference.

"You say 'tis nuffin, honey; but yer limbs are quiverin' wif pain, and the drops ob agony is on yer po' white face. You can't 'ceive me, chile; yer granny knows de whole circumstance. I seed it all las' night in my dreams. Vengeance is mine; I will repay. One comes who is de instrumen' ob de Lord." And the old woman muttered and rocked and whispered.

Whatever was the cause of Mrs. Livingston's illness, its character was unusual and alarming. The maid, who was really attached to the beautiful bride, pleaded to be allowed to send for medical aid in vain. The causes for her suffering, as stated by Dianthe, were plausible; but her resolve to have no aid, inflexible. As evening advanced, her restlessness,

PAULINE E. HOPKINS

and the hideous action of spasmodic pains across her livid face, became distressing. To all the urgent appeals of her servants, she simply replied she was waiting for some one. He was coming soon—very soon and then she would be quite well.

And yet he came not. From couch to door, from door to window, with eager, listening ear and wistful eyes the poor watcher traversed her chamber in unavailing expectancy. At length a sudden calm seemed to steal over her; the incessant restlessness of her wearied frame yielded to a tranquil, passive air. She lay upon cushions piled high upon the couch commanding a view of the broad hallways leading to her apartments. The beams of the newly risen moon bathed every object in the dim halls. Clear as the vesper bell, sounding across a far distant lake, strains of delicious music, rising and falling in alternate cadence of strong martial measure, came floating in waves of sound down the corridor.

Dianthe and Aunt Hannah and the maid heard the glorious echoes; whilst in the town the villagers heard the music as of a mighty host Louder it grew, first in low and wailing notes, then swelling, pealing through arch and corridor in mighty diapason, until the very notes of different instruments rang out as from a vast orchestra. There was the thunder of the organ, the wild harp's peal, the aeolian's sigh, the trumpet's peal, and the mournful horn. A thousand soft melodious flutes, like trickling streams upheld a bird-like treble; whilst ever and anon the muffled drum with awful beat precise, the rolling kettle and the crashing cymbals, kept time to sounds like tramping of a vast but viewless army. Nearer they came. The dull, deep beat of falling feet—in the hall—up the stairs. Louder it came and louder. Louder and yet more loud the music swelled to thunder! The unseen mass must have been the disembodied souls of every age since Time began, so vast the rush and strong the footfalls. And then the chant of thousands of voices swelling in rich, majestic choral tones, joined in the thundering crash. It was the welcome of ancient Ethiopia to her dying daughter of the royal line.

Upspringing from her couch, as through the air the mighty hallelujah sounded, Dianthe with frantic gestures and wild distended eyes, cried: "I see them now! the glorious band! Welcome, great masters of the world's first birth! All hail, my royal ancestors—Candace, Semiramis, Dido, Solomon, David and the great kings of early days, and the great masters of the world of song. O, what long array of souls divine, lit with immortal fire from heaven itself! O, let me kneel to thee! And to thee, too, Beethoven, Mozart, thou sons of song! Divine ones, art thou come to take me home? Me, thy poor worshipper on earth? O, let me be thy child in paradise!

The pageant passed, or seemed to pass, from her whose eyes alone of all the awe-struck listeners, with mortal gaze beheld them. When, at length, the last vibrating echoes of the music seemed to die away in utter vacant silence to the terrified attendants, Dianthe still seemed to listen. Either her ear still drank in the music, or another sound had caught her attention.

"Hark, hark! 'Tis carriage wheels. Do you not hear them? Now they pass the railroad at the crossing. Hasten, O hasten! Still they have a long mile to traverse. O, hasten! They call me home."

For many minutes she sat rigid and cold as marble. The trembling maid wept in silent terror and grief, for the gentle bride was a kind mistress. Old Aunt Hannah, with a fortitude born of despair, ministered in every possible way to the dying girl. To the great relief of all, at last, there came to their ears the very distant rumbling of wheels. Nearer it came—it sounded in the avenue—it paused at the great entrance, some one alighted—a stir—the sound of voices—then footsteps—the ascent of footsteps on the stairs. Nearer, nearer yet; hastily they come, like messengers of speed. They're upon the threshold—enter. Then, and not till then, the rigid lady moved. With one wild scream of joy she rushed forward, and Reuel Briggs clasped her in his arms.

For a few brief moments, the wretched girl lived an age in heaven. The presence of that one beloved—this drop of joy sweetened all the bitter draught and made for her an eternity of compensation. With fond wild tenderness she gazed upon him, gazed in his anxious eyes until her own looked in his very soul, and stamped there all the story of her guilt and remorse. Then winding her cold arms around his neck, she laid her weary head upon his shoulder and silently as the night passed through the portals of the land of souls.

XXIX

'Twas midnight. The landscape was still as death. Hills, rocks, rivers, even the babbling brooks, seemed locked in sleep. The moonbeams dreamt upon the hillside; stars slept in the glittering sky; the silent vales were full of dreaming flowers whose parti-colored cups closed in sleep. In all that solemn hush of silence one watcher broke the charmed spell. 'Twas Aubrey Livingston. Now he moves swiftly over the plain as if some sudden purpose drove him on; then he turns back in the self-same track and with the same impulsive speed. What is he doing in the lonely night? All day, hour after hour, mile on mile, the scorching midday sun had blazed upon his head, and still he wandered on. The tranquil sunset purpled round his way and still the wanderer hastened on. In his haggard eyes one question seems to linger—"I wonder if she lives!"

Many, many dreary times he said this question over! He has a secret and 'tis a mighty one; he fears if human eye but look upon him, it must be revealed. Hark! suddenly there falls upon his ear the sound of voices, surely some one called! Again! His straining ear caught a familiar sound.

"Aubrey! Aubrey Livingston!"

"By heaven, it is her voice!" he told himself. And as if to assure him still more of who addressed him, close before his very eyes moved two figures. Hand in hand they passed from out a clump of sheltering trees, and slowly crossed his path. One face was turned toward him, the other from him. The moon revealed the same white robe in which he had last beheld her, the long, streaming hair, her slippered feet—all were there. Upon his wondering eyes her own were fixed in mute appeal and deepest anguish; then both figures passed away, he knew not where.

"'Twas she, and in full life. God of heaven, she lives!"

Pausing not to think he was deceived, enough for him, she lived. He turned his steps toward his home, with flying feet he neared the hall. Just as he reached the great entrance gates, he saw the two figures slightly in advance of him. This time Dianthe's face was turned away, but the silver moonbeams threw into bold relief the accusing face of Molly Vance!

With a sudden chill foreboding, he entered the hall and passed up the stairs to his wife's apartments. He opened wide the door and stood within the chamber of the dead.

There lay the peaceful form—spread with a drapery of soft, white gauze around her, and only the sad and livid, poisoned face was visible above it; and kneeling by the side of her, his first love and his last—was Reuel Briggs.

Rising from the shadows as Aubrey entered, Charlie Vance, flanked on either side by Ai and Abdadis, moved to meet him, the stern brow and sterner words of an outraged brother and friend greeted him:

"Welcome, murderer!"

DIANTHE WAS DEAD, POISONED; THAT was clear. Molly Vance was unduly done to death by the foul treachery of the same hand. All this was now clear to the thinking public, for so secluded had Aubrey Livingston lived since his return to the United States, that many of his intimate associates still believed that he had perished in the accident on the Charles. It was quite evident to these friends that his infatuation for the beautiful Dianthe had led to the commission of a crime. But the old adage that, "the dead tell no tales," was not to be set aside for visionary ravings unsupported by lawful testimony.

Livingston's wealth purchased shrewd and active lawyers to defend him against the charges brought by the Vances—father and son,—and Reuel Briggs.

One interview which was never revealed to public comment, took place between Ai, Abdadis, Aunt Hannah, Reuel Briggs and Aubrey Livingston.

Aubrey sat alone in his sumptuous study. An open book was on his knees, but his eyes were fixed on vacancy. He was changed and his auburn locks were prematurely grey. His eyes revealed an impenetrable mystery within into whose secret depths no mortal eye might look. Thus he sat when the group we have named above silently surrounded him. "Peace, O son of Osiris, to thy parting hour!"

Thus Ai greeted him. There was no mistaking these words, and gazing into the stern faces of the silent group Aubrey knew that something of import was about to happen.

Aubrey did not change countenance, although he glanced at Reuel as if seeking mercy. The latter did not change countenance; only his eyes, those strange deep eyes before whose fixed gaze none could stand unflinching, took on a more sombre glow. Again Ai spoke:

"God has willed it! Great is the God of Ergamenes, we are but worms beneath His feet. His will be done." Then began a strange, weird scene. Round and round the chair where Aubrey was seated walked the kingly Ai chanting in a low, monotone in his native tongue, finally advancing with measured steps to a position directly opposite and facing Livingston, and stood there erect and immovable, with arms raised as if in invocation. His eyes glittered with strange, fascinating lights in the shaded room. To the man seated there it seemed that an eternity was passing. Why did not these two men he had injured take human vengeance in meting out punishment to him? And why, oh! why did those eyes, piercing his own like poinards, hold him so subtly in their spell?

Gradually he yielded to the mysterious beatitude that insensibly enwrapped his being. Detached from terrestrial bonds, his spirit soared in regions of pure ethereal blue. A delicious torpor held him in its embrace. His head sank upon his breast. His eyes closed in a trancelike slumber.

Ai quitted his position, and approaching Aubrey, lifted one of the shut eyelids. "He sleeps!" he exclaimed.

Then standing by the side of the unconscious man he poured into his ear—speaking loudly and distinctly,—a few terse sentences. Not a muscle moved in the faces of those standing about the sleeper. Then Ai passed his hands lightly over his face, made a few upward passes, and turning to his companions, beckoned them to follow him from the room. Silently as they had come the group left the house and grounds, gained a waiting carriage and were driven rapidly away. In the shelter of the vehicle Charlie Vance spoke, "Is justice done?" he sternly queried.

"Justice will be done," replied Ai's soothing tones.

"Then I am satisfied."

But Reuel spoke not one word.

One day note very long after this happening, the body of Aubrey Livingston was found floating in the Charles river at the very point where poor Molly Vance had floated in the tangled lily-bed. The mysterious command of Ai, "death by thine own hand," whispered in his ear while under hypnotic influence, had been followed to the last letter.

Thus Aubrey had become his own executioner according to the ancient laws of the inhabitants of Telassar. Members of the royal family in direct line to the throne became their own executioners when guilty of the crime of murder.

Reuel Briggs returned to the Hidden City with his faithful subjects, and old Aunt Hannah. There he spends his days in teaching his people all that he has learned in years of contact with modern culture. United to Candace, his days glide peacefully by in good works; but the shadows of great sins darken his life, and the memory of past joys is ever with him. He views, too, with serious apprehension, the advance of mighty nations penetrating the dark, mysterious forests of his native land.

"Where will it stop?" he sadly questions. "What will the end be?"

But none save Omnipotence can solve the problem.

To our human intelligence these truths depicted in this feeble work may seem terrible,—even horrible. But who shall judge the handiwork of God, the Great Craftsman! Caste prejudice, race pride, boundless wealth, scintillating intellects refined by all the arts of the intellectual world, are but puppets in His hand, for His promises stand, and He will prove His words, "Of one blood have I made all races of men."

A Note About the Author

Pauline Elizabeth Hopkins (1859–1930) was an African American novelist, playwright, and historian. Born in Portland, Maine, Hopkins was raised in Boston by her mother and adopted father. Supported in her academic pursuits from a young age, Hopkins excelled at Girls High School, where she won a local competition for her essay on the raising of children. In 1877, she began her career as a dramatist with a production in Saratoga, which encouraged her to write a musical entitled *Slaves' Escape; or, The Underground Railroad* (1880). In 1900, she published "Talma Gordon," now considered the first mystery story written by an African American author. Having established herself as a professional writer, she published three serial novels in the periodical *The Colored American Magazine*, including *Hagar's Daughter: A Story of Southern Caste Prejudice* (1901–1902) and *Winona: A Tale of Negro Life in the South and Southwest* (1902–1903). Often compared to her contemporaries Charles Chestnutt and Paul Laurence Dunbar, Hopkins made a name for herself as a successful and ambitious author who advocated for the rights of African Americans at a time of intense violence and widespread oppression.

A Note from the Publisher

Spanning many genres, from non-fiction essays to literature classics to children's books and lyric poetry, Mint Edition books showcase the master works of our time in a modern new package. The text is freshly typeset, is clean and easy to read, and features a new note about the author in each volume. Many books also include exclusive new introductory material. Every book boasts a striking new cover, which makes it as appropriate for collecting as it is for gift giving. Mint Edition books are only printed when a reader orders them, so natural resources are not wasted. We're proud that our books are never manufactured in excess and exist only in the exact quantity they need to be read and enjoyed.

bookfinity™

Discover more of your favorite classics with Bookfinity™.

- Track your reading with custom book lists.
- Get great book recommendations for your personalized Reader Type.
- Add reviews for your favorite books.
- AND MUCH MORE!

Visit **bookfinity.com** and take the fun Reader Type quiz to get started.

Enjoy our classic and modern companion pairings!